A SCIENCE FICTION OMNIBUS

BRIAN ALDISS has been publishing since the 1950s. In the sixties, he originated the three science-fiction anthologies which combined to form *The Penguin Science Fiction Omnibus* (1973). In one form or another, these volumes were reprinted over thirty-five years. He is known for many non-SF novels, the latest being *HARM* and *Walcot* (2007), and stories, as well as science fiction, together with articles and poems. He is also an artist.

Aldiss was awarded an OBE in 2005 for services to literature. He lives in Oxford.

A Science Fiction Omnibus

Edited by Brian Aldiss

PENGUIN BOOKS

PENGUIN CLASSICS

Published by the Penguin Group
Penguin Books Ltd, 80 Strand, London WC2R 0RL, England
Penguin Group (USA) Inc., 375 Hudson Street, New York, New York 10014, USA
Penguin Group (Canada), 90 Eglinton Avenue East, Suite 700, Toronto, Ontario, Canada M4P 2Y3
(a division of Pearson Penguin Canada Inc.)
Penguin Ireland, 25 St Stephen's Green, Dublin 2, Ireland
(a division of Penguin Books Ltd)
Penguin Group (Australia), 250 Camberwell Road, Camberwell, Victoria 3124, Australia
(a division of Pearson Australia Group Pty Ltd)
Penguin Books India Pvt Ltd, 11 Community Centre, Panchsheel Park, New Delhi – 110 017, India
Penguin Group (NZ), 67 Apollo Drive, Rosedale, North Shore 0632, New Zealand
(a division of Pearson New Zealand Ltd)
Penguin Books (South Africa) (Pty) Ltd, 24 Sturdee Avenue, Rosebank, Johannesburg 2196, South Africa

Penguin Books Ltd, Registered Offices: 80 Strand, London WC2R 0RL, England

www.penguin.com

First published separately as *Penguin Science Fiction* 1961
More Penguin Sciene Fiction 1963
Yet More Penguin Science Fiction 1964
Published in one volume as *The Penguin Science Fiction Omnibus* 1973
This revised and expanded edition first published in Penguin Modern Classics 2007
2

The Acknowledgements on pages 576–8 constitute an extension of this copyright page

Set in 10/12.5 pt Monotype Dante
Typeset by Rowland Phototypesetting Ltd, Bury St Edmunds, Suffolk
Printed in Great Britain by Clays Ltd, St Ives plc

ISBN: 978-0-141-18892-8

Contents

Introduction

Science fiction stories are the fables of a technological age.

A tadpole in a pool bears little resemblance to the frog on land. Yet both are the same creature. A similar transformation can be seen in the history of science fiction. It is not only a literature in its own right; it now hops about everywhere on screens of various sizes.

To say this is not to denigrate the written SF (let's use the family name for short); indeed, SF novels are more polished, embracing more cunningly their devised scenarios, than ever before. But there are fewer outlets – except for electronic ones – fewer magazines, for the short story than once there were.

My decision was to work on my earlier Penguin anthology, and to renovate it, preserving the best stories from it. In part, this has been done because I wished to see reprinted in Britain John Crowley's magnificent 'Great Work of Time', which I had come across in one of my wise friend David Hartwell's anthologies. It is admirable. It is not a story which could have been written or published, I think, in the 1960s.

Subject matter is much changed. The technocratic emphasis of the fictions prevailing in the forties and fifties – hardly surprisingly in war-time – has become diluted. Lowering the technocratic threshold appears to account for SF's wider readership among women nowadays, together with a weakening in faith in technological progress.

In an October 2006 issue of the *Times Literary Supplement*, the reviewer, Michael Saler, devoted a whole page to an examination of the fiction and life of James Tiptree, Jr. Tiptree's fiction appeared in SF magazines in the late 1960s and was immediately recognized as speaking with a powerful new voice, discoursing sometimes obliquely on dark sexual subjects. It was not until 1976 that readers discovered that Tiptree was in fact a woman, a sixty year old by the name of Alice Bradley Sheldon.

One of Tiptree's stories is included in this omnibus. It speaks for itself, and in its contained melancholy we perceive the troubles often besetting the human spirit. Those troubles bring us closer to less specialized fiction than was previously the case.

Turning to the anthology as a whole, I quote the sentence with which Saler concludes his piece. Alice Sheldon writes to a friend that 'those eight years in SF were the first time I could be really real'.

These words contain what drives a writer to SF, as well as what drives SF on. For whatever reasons, we are discontented with the world-as-is. The stories selected here indicate our dissatisfaction with our station in life, our presidents, the assumptions our parents made for us, the nigh-insane quest for 'happiness' which may yet ruin our civilization, or indeed a thousand other aspects of life. We are the Steppenwolves of our culture.

We live in that culture, in general as law-abiding citizens, but we occasionally speak – as Tiptree spoke – of different worlds. 'So it goes', said Kurt Vonnegut in an early novel. And many readers miss something by not training themselves to the mode we have found the need to adopt, and the distances from the mundane we desire to preserve.

William Tenn's story, 'The Liberation of Earth', was published in an obscure magazine in 1953. Of course it is funny, in Tenn's best ironic manner. But if we think of 'liberation' as 'regime change', we perceive its topicality and its adroit use of distancing metaphor.

The shortest short story here is 'Answer'. When I was first collecting these stories, back in the sixties, my friend and competitor, Edmund Crispin, was also compiling SF anthologies. Crispin got to this story first. When attending a *New Scientist* party at about that time, I heard one young scientist telling another the story of 'Answer'. It was clear he had not read the story; someone had told it to him. He was passing it on. It had achieved escape velocity from the printed page.

I began by claiming that SF stories are the fables of our time. This was one story in particular I was thinking about: the birth of a new god!

★

Of course, things are not always as serious as this makes them sound. The use of irony often comes to our aid. When my history of science fiction, *Billion Year Spree*, was first published (1973), I used an image on its yellow jacket showing planes roaring over New York, blasting skyscrapers and setting them on fire. That picture also formed part of the cover of a magazine entitled *Stories of Super Science*, which bore the enticing tag-line: 'Read It Today! – Live It Tomorrow!'

As indeed we did on 9/11.

SF has become more domestic than formerly. This is in part because young writers have grown older and have settled down. Our Western world has an immense variety of adventures, improvements, miseries and speculations from which we can take our choice. Yes, we can take in the dark side of our culture, but it helps if we know the dark side of Central Asia as well.

As an old hand at this game, I find myself missing the great range of stories set on other planets and in outer space which were once the backbone of SF. Distance and dislocation were always pleasurable to encounter.

Isaac Asimov, a clever and engaging writer, was heard to remark, after Neil Armstrong set foot on the moon, 'This justifies all the SF written since 1940' – or words to that effect. The comment is invalid in more than one respect (for instance, the misunderstanding that SF is a united entity, rather than diverse in content and treatment); behind it lies the assumption that SF was an instrument of prediction. This was – again – the technocratic emphasis of SF. Ever since Apollo 11 and the landing on the moon, the emphasis, the very understanding, of SF has changed and the weather-vane points more in the direction of metaphor.

Mary Shelley would not have written *Frankenstein* with the puissance it still retains had she not been orphaned at birth. Her creature resembles her in having only one parent – a male one. Writing my first SF novel, *Non-Stop*, about people imprisoned in circumstances beyond their control, I was conscious of reconstructing on one level my own confining circumstances.

Such is the power of metaphor that my novel became extremely popular in the Poland of that time, where it was read as a veiled criticism of the Communist regime within which that society was imprisoned. It may be this metaphorical quality of the discourse that permits science fiction to travel round the globe – a freedom hardly attainable for a novel set in, let's say, Croydon.

A considerable distance from Croydon is James Inglis's story of grand despair and infinite space, 'Night Watch'. As far as we can discover, this is the one and only story Inglis ever wrote. Possibly he felt a Tiptree-like urge to escape from himself, to live in a universe free of humanity. We can only speculate on whether the story proved in some way to be curative for him. Anyhow, it is a pure Steppenwolf story.

SF used to have a small sister, a sweet little thing with pearls in her hair and stars in her eyes. She grew up to be a big brawny lass, threatening her parents and staying out late at night. Her name is Fantasy. Sometimes Fantasy and SF blend – as one might expect. I still think there is an important distinction to be made between the twain. A fantasy story – J. R. R. Tolkien provides an example always to hand – tends to end happily with an evil defeated and the world going back to the way it used to be. A conservative ending.

In a really good SF story – we might have Greg Bear's 'Blood Music' in mind – the world is changed. Evil may be repulsed, but there is a recognition that the world can never return to its previous state. Here again we think of 9/11. A revolutionary ending.

Change is the great subject for SF – power and change. The story by Eliza Blair, 'Friends in Need', written when Blair was a student at Swarthmore College, Pennsylvania, is an excellent example of this. Even the language has morphed itself, resembling more the style of emails or text messages.

It was in a SF magazine I first encountered the word 'ecology'. For many years I have admired James Schmitz's story 'Grandpa'. Here's ecology with a vengeance! Ah, those cold Zlanti Deeps – how long they haunted me!

Harry Harrison's story, too, is set on another planet. An alien planet is surely an extreme version of escape. As T. S. Eliot admitted, we cannot bear too much reality.

Never can a SF story be too extreme, or too foreign, for me. 'Swarm', by Bruce Sterling, is another guaranteed extreme.

I listen to stories read on BBC 4, the star radio channel. Never do they select a story from the wealth of science fiction's treasury. Their stories frequently concern tales of unhappy Irish childhoods or of two people meeting in Bedford, with bitter-sweet but conventional results. I would trade them all for one dip in the Zlanti Deep! How one longs for a more impassioned approach, with the imagination kicked about a little! It is imagination which has created the West – imagination and its cousin, ingenuity. We should offer it more respect.

However, the universal ignorance and the ignoring of SF are of long standing. I have four histories of French literature on my shelves: they are rather past their sell-by date, admittedly, but none of them gives a single mention of Jules Verne. Poor Jules, whom the Pope blessed for his writing . . .

Can a withholding of enthusiasm be because it is 'only about imaginary things'? Imagination is a vital quality; children swim in it most of the time, as when they talk to their teddy bears. An attempt to describe how imagination functions is made by the Oxford philosopher Mary Warnock in her book *Imagination* (1976). Warnock believes strongly that the cultivation of imagination should be the chief aim of education. Later, she says, there is

> a power in the human mind which is at work in our everyday perception of the world, and is also at work in our thoughts about what is absent; which enables us to see the world, whether present or absent, as significant, and also to present this vision to others, for them to share or reject. And this power . . . is not only intellectual. Its impetus comes from the emotions as much as from the reason, from the heart as much as from the head.

In other words, we may regard as preposterous the statement in Fredric Brown's 'Answer' that there are 96 billion civilized planets in the universe: that does not detract from the power of the story, which depends not so much on science as on our fear of being dominated by omnipotence.

Indeed, if we wish to know how many civilized planets there are in the universe, we can read George Basalla's *Civilized Life in the Universe*

(2006), and we shall be chastised and enlightened by his learned answer to the question.

So long neglected when confined mainly to the printing press, that vital invention of an earlier age, SF awaited newer media to attain a wider popularity. The setting – the very environment which is often the most vital 'character' of a SF story – demanded the birth of the electronic age, which created both wide- and small-screen viewing. SF movies are now so popular that they no longer bother to announce themselves as 'SF', or as the slummy nickname 'sci-fi'. This trend may have been prompted by a modern masterpiece of the screen and of the genre, *The Truman Show*.

Sometimes such movies are occasioned by a new technological development and can be otherwise idea free (*Terminator 2* is an example). Sometimes movies are based on such ideas as you find in a volume like this.

Some older facets of SF remain – and we hope always will: the ingenuity of Eric Frank Russell's 'Sole Solution', the penetrating moral of Bertram Chandler's 'The Cage', the terror of Walter Miller's take on *Frankenstein*, entitled 'I Made You', and of course the cosmic awe of James Inglis's 'Night Watch'.

Such fables as these are certainly worth preserving.

Although SF short stories are far too often ignored, there are by way of contradiction resounding successes still for writers such as Iain Banks, Terry Pratchett with his Discworld series, Philip Pullman with his Dark Materials, and J. K. Rowling's Harry Potter series. Not to mention an earlier – and by now tiresome – success *The Hitchhiker's Guide to the Galaxy*.

We talk of success, but success is not everything. The rest of us can take encouragement from a work which contains an admission that 'the mind is indeed restless', the great Sanscrit poem, *Bhagavad Gita*:

> Set thy heart upon thy work, but never on its reward.
> Work not for reward; but never cease to do thy work.

Brian Aldiss

Sole Solution

ERIC FRANK RUSSELL

He brooded in darkness and there was no one else. Not a voice, not a whisper. Not the touch of a hand. Not the warmth of another heart.

Darkness.

Solitude.

Eternal confinement where all was black and silent and nothing stirred. Imprisonment without prior condemnation. Punishment without sin. The unbearable that had to be borne unless some mode of escape could be devised.

No hope of rescue from elsewhere. No sorrow or sympathy or pity in another soul, another mind. No doors to be opened, no locks to be turned, no bars to be sawn apart. Only the thick, deep sable night in which to fumble and find nothing.

Circle a hand to the right and there is nought. Sweep an arm to the left and discover emptiness utter and complete. Walk forward through the darkness like a blind man lost in a vast, forgotten hall and there is no floor, no echo of footsteps, nothing to bar one's path.

He could touch and sense one thing only. And that was self.

Therefore the only available resources with which to overcome his predicament were those secreted within himself. He must be the instrument of his own salvation.

How?

No problem is beyond solution. By that thesis science lives. Without it, science dies. He was the ultimate scientist. As such, he could not refuse this challenge to his capabilities.

His torments were those of boredom, loneliness, mental and physical sterility. They were not to be endured. The easiest escape is via the imagination. One hangs in a strait-jacket and flees the corporeal trap by adventuring in a dreamland of one's own.

But dreams are not enough. They are unreal and all too brief. The freedom to be gained must be genuine and of long duration. That meant he must make a stern reality of dreams, a reality so contrived that it would persist for all time. It must be self-perpetuating. Nothing less would make escape complete.

So he sat in the great dark and battled the problem. There was no clock, no calendar to mark the length of thought. There were no external data upon which to compute. There was nothing, nothing except the workings within his agile mind.

And one thesis: no problem is beyond solution.

He found it eventually. It meant escape from everlasting night. It would provide experience, companionship, adventure, mental exercise, entertainment, warmth, love, the sound of voices, the touch of hands.

The plan was anything but rudimentary. On the contrary it was complicated enough to defy untangling for endless aeons. It had to be like that to have permanence. The unwanted alternative was swift return to silence and the bitter dark.

It took a deal of working out. A million and one aspects had to be considered along with all their diverse effects upon each other. And when that was done he had to cope with the next million. And so on . . . on . . . on.

He created a mighty dream of his own, a place of infinite complexity schemed in every detail to the last dot and comma. Within this he would live anew. But not as himself. He was going to dissipate his person into numberless parts, a great multitude of variegated shapes and forms each of which would have to battle its own peculiar environment.

And he would toughen the struggle to the limit of endurance by unthinking himself, handicapping his parts with appalling ignorance and forcing them to learn afresh. He would seed enmity between them by dictating the basic rules of the game. Those who observed the rules would be called good. Those who did not would be called bad. Thus there would be endless delaying conflicts within the one great conflict.

When all was ready and prepared he intended to disrupt and become no longer one, but an enormous concourse of entities. Then his parts must fight back to unity and himself.

But first he must make reality of the dream. Ah, that was the test!

The time was now. The experiment must begin.

Leaning forward, *he* gazed into the dark and said, 'Let there be light.'

And there was light.

Lot

WARD MOORE

Mr Jimmon even appeared elated, like a man about to set out on a vacation.

'Well, folks, no use waiting any longer. We're all set. So let's go.'

There was a betrayal here; Mr Jimmon was not the kind of man who addressed his family as 'folks'.

'David, you're sure . . . ?'

Mr Jimmon merely smiled. This was quite out of character; customarily he reacted to his wife's habit of posing unfinished questions – after seventeen years the unuttered and larger part of the queries were always instantly known to him in some mysterious way, as though unerringly projected by the key in which the introduction was pitched, so that not only the full wording was communicated to his mind, but the shades and implications which circumstance and humour attached to them – with sharp and querulous defence. No matter how often he resolved to stare quietly or use the still more effective, Afraid I didn't catch your meaning, dear, he had never been able to put his resolution into force. Until this moment of crisis. Crisis, reflected Mr Jimmon, still smiling and moving suggestively towards the door, crisis changes people. Brings out underlying qualities.

It was Jir who answered Molly Jimmon, with the adolescent's half-whine of exasperation. 'Aw furcrysay Mom, what's the idea? The highways'll be clogged tight. What's the good figuring out everything heada time and having everything all set if you're going to start all over again at the last minute? Get a grip on yourself and let's go.'

Mr Jimmon did not voice the reflexive, That's no way to talk to your mother. Instead he thought, not unsympathetically, of woman's slow reaction time. Asset in childbirth, liability behind the wheel. He knew

Molly was thinking of the house and all the things in it: her clothes and Erika's, the TV set – so sullenly ugly now, with the electricity gone – the refrigerator in which the food would soon begin to rot and stink, the dead stove, the cellarful of cases of canned stuff for which there was no room in the station wagon. And the Buick, blocked up in the garage, with the air thoughtfully let out of the tyres and the battery hidden.

Of course the house would be looted. But they had known that all along. When they – or rather he, for it was his executive's mind and training which were responsible for the Jimmons' preparation against this moment – planned so carefully and providentially, he had weighed property against life and decided on life. No other decision was possible.

'Aren't you at least going to phone Pearl and Dan?'

Now why in the world, thought Mr Jimmon, completely above petty irritation, should I call Dan Davisson? (Because of course it's *Dan* she means – My Old Beau. Oh, he was nobody then, just an impractical dreamer without a penny to his name; it wasn't for years that he was recognized as a Mathematical Genius; now he's a professor and all sorts of things – but she automatically says Pearl-and-Dan, not Dan.) What can Dan do with the square root of minus nothing to offset M equals whatever it is, at this moment? Or am I supposed to ask if Pearl has all her diamonds? Query, why doesn't Pearl wear pearls? Only diamonds? My wife's friends, heh heh, but even the subtlest intonation won't label them when you're entertaining an important client and Pearl and Dan.

And why should I phone? What sudden paralysis afflicts her? Hysteria?

'No,' said Mr Jimmon. 'I did not phone Pearl and Dan.'

Then he added, relenting: 'Phone's been out since.'

'But,' said Molly.

She'd hardly going to ask me to drive into town. He selected several answers in readiness. But she merely looked towards the telephone helplessly (she ought to have been fat, thought Mr Jimmon, really she should, or anyway plump; her thinness gives her that air of competence), so he amplified gently, 'They're unquestionably all right. As far away from it as we are.'

Wendell was already in the station wagon. With Waggie hidden somewhere. Should have sent the dog to the humane society; more merciful to have it put to sleep. Too late now; Waggie would have to take his chance. There were plenty of rabbits in the hills above Malibu, he had often seen them quite close to the house. At all events there was no room for a dog in the wagon, already loaded to within a pound of its capacity.

Erika came in briskly from the kitchen, her brown jodhpurs making her appear at first glance even younger than fourteen. But only at first glance; then the swell of hips and breast denied the childishness the jodhpurs seemed to accent.

'The water's gone, Mom. There's no use sticking around any longer.'

Molly looked incredulous. 'The water?'

'Of course the water's gone,' said Mr Jimmon, not impatiently, but rather with satisfaction in his own foresight. 'If It didn't get the aqueduct, the mains depend on pumps. Electric pumps. When the electricity went, the water went too.'

'But the water,' repeated Molly, as though this last catastrophe was beyond all reason – even the outrageous logic which It brought in its train.

Jir slouched past them and outside. Erika tucked in a strand of hair, pulled her jockey cap downward and sideways, glanced quickly at her mother and father, then followed. Molly took several steps, paused, smiled vaguely in the mirror and walked out of the house.

Mr Jimmon patted his pockets; the money was all there. He didn't even look back before closing the front door and rattling the knob to be sure the lock had caught. It had never failed, but Mr Jimmon always rattled it anyway. He strode to the station wagon, running his eyes over the springs to reassure himself again that they really hadn't overloaded it.

The sky was overcast; you might have thought it one of the regular morning high fogs if you didn't know. Mr Jimmon faced south-east, but It had been too far away to see anything. Now Erika and Molly were in the front seat; the boys were in the back lost amid the neatly packed stuff. He opened the door on the driver's side, got in, turned the key and started the motor. Then he said casually over his shoulder, 'Put the dog out, Jir.'

Wendell protested, too quickly, 'Waggie's not here.'

Molly exclaimed, 'Oh, David . . .'

Mr Jimmon said patiently, 'We're losing pretty valuable time. There's no room for the dog; we have no food for him. If we had room we could have taken more essentials; those few pounds might mean the difference.'

'Can't find him,' muttered Jir.

'He's not here. I tell you he's not here,' shouted Wendell, tearful voiced.

'If I have to stop the motor and get him myself we'll be wasting still more time and gas.' Mr Jimmon was still detached, judicial. 'This isn't a matter of kindness to animals. It's life and death.'

Erika said evenly, 'Dad's right, you know. It's the dog or us. Put him out, Wend.'

'I tell you –' Wendell began.

'Got him!' exclaimed Jir. 'Okay, Waggie! Outside and good luck.'

The spaniel wriggled ecstatically as he was picked up and put out through the open window. Mr Jimmon raced the motor, but it didn't drown out Wendell's anguish. He threw himself on his brother, hitting and kicking. Mr Jimmon took his foot off the gas, and as soon as he was sure the dog was away from the wheels, eased the station wagon out of the driveway and down the hill towards the ocean.

'Wendell, Wendell, stop,' pleaded Molly. 'Don't hurt him, Jir.'

Mr Jimmon clicked on the radio. After a preliminary hum, clashing static crackled out. He pushed all five buttons in turn, varying the quality of unintelligible sound. 'Want me to try?' offered Erika. She pushed the manual button and turned the knob slowly. Music dripped out.

Mr Jimmon grunted. 'Mexican station. Try something else. Maybe you can get Ventura.'

They rounded a tight curve. 'Isn't that the Warbinns'?' asked Molly.

For the first time since It happened Mr Jimmon had a twinge of impatience. There was no possibility, even with the unreliable eye of shocked excitement, of mistaking the Warbinns' blue Mercury. No one else on Rambla Catalina had one anything like it, and visitors would be most unlikely now. If Molly would apply the most elementary logic!

Besides, Warbinn had stopped the blue Mercury in the Jimmon driveway five times every week for the past two months – ever since they had decided to put the Buick up and keep the wagon packed and ready against this moment – for Mr Jimmon to ride with him to the city. Of course it was the Warbinns'.

'. . . *advised not to impede the progress of the military. Adequate medical staffs are standing by at all hospitals. Local civilian defence units are taking all steps in accordance* . . .'

'Santa Barbara,' remarked Jir, nodding at the radio with an expert's assurance.

Mr Jimmon slowed, prepared to follow the Warbinns down to 101, but the Mercury halted and Mr Jimmon turned out to pass it. Warbinn was driving and Sally was in the front seat with him; the back seat appeared empty except for a few things obviously hastily thrown in. No foresight, thought Mr Jimmon.

Warbinn waved his hand vigorously out the window and Sally shouted something.

'. . . *panic will merely slow rescue efforts. Casualties are much smaller than originally reported* . . .'

'How do they know?' asked Mr Jimmon, waving politely at the Warbinns.

'Oh, David, aren't you going to stop? They want something.'

'Probably just to talk.'

'. . . *to retain every drop of water. Emergency power will be in operation shortly. There is no cause for undue alarm. General* . . .'

Through the rear-view mirror Mr Jimmon saw the blue Mercury start after them. He had been right then, they only wanted to say something inconsequential. At a time like this.

At the junction with US 101 five cars blocked Rambla Catalina. Mr Jimmon set the handbrake, and steadying himself with the open door, stood tiptoe twistedly, trying to see over the cars ahead. 101 was solid with traffic which barely moved. On the southbound side of the divided highway a stream of vehicles flowed illegally north.

'Thought everybody was figured to go east,' gibed Jir over the other side of the car.

Mr Jimmon was not disturbed by his son's sarcasm. How right he'd been to rule out the trailer. Of course the bulk of the cars were headed eastward as he'd calculated; this sluggish mass was nothing compared with the countless ones which must now be blocking the roads to

Pasadena, Alhambra, Garvey, Norwalk. Even the northbound refugees were undoubtedly taking 99 or regular 101 – the highway before them was really 101 Alternate – he had picked the most feasible exit.

The Warbinns drew up alongside. 'Hurry didn't do you much good,' shouted Warbinn, leaning forward to clear his wife's face.

Mr Jimmon reached in and turned off the ignition. Gas was going to be precious. He smiled and shook his head at Warbinn; no use pointing out that he'd got the inside lane by passing the Mercury, with a better chance to seize the opening on the highway when it came. 'Get in the car, Jir, and shut the door. Have to be ready when this breaks.'

'If it ever does,' said Molly. 'All that rush and bustle. We might just as well . . .'

Mr Jimmon was conscious of Warbinn's glowering at him and resolutely refused to turn his head. He pretended not to hear him yell. 'Only wanted to tell you you forgot to pick up your bumper-jack. It's in front of our garage.'

Mr Jimmon's stomach felt empty. What if he had a flat now? Ruined, condemned. He knew a burning hate for Warbinn – incompetent borrower, bad neighbour, thoughtless, shiftless, criminal. He owed it to himself to leap from the station wagon and seize Warbinn by the throat . . .

'What did he say, David? What is Mr Warbinn saying?'

Then he remembered it was the jack from the Buick; the station wagon's was safely packed where he could get at it easily. Naturally he would never have started out on a trip like this without checking so essential an item. 'Nothing,' he said, 'nothing at all.'

'. . . plane dispatches indicate target was the Signal Hill area. Minor damage was done to Long Beach, Wilmington, and San Pedro. All non-military air traffic warned from Mines Field . . .'

The smash and crash of bumper and fender sounded familiarly on the highway. From his look-out station he couldn't see what had happened, but it was easy enough to reconstruct the impatient jerk forward that caused it. Mr Jimmon didn't exactly smile, but he allowed himself a faint quiver of internal satisfaction. A crash up ahead would make things worse, but a crash behind – and many of them were inevitable – must eventually create a gap.

Even as he thought this, the first car at the mouth of Rambla Catalina edged on to the shoulder of the highway. Mr Jimmon slid back in and started the motor, inching ahead after the car in front, gradually leaving the still uncomfortable proximity of the Warbinns.

'Got to go to the toilet,' announced Wendell abruptly.

'Didn't I tell you –! Well, hurry up! Jir, keep the door open and pull him in if the car starts to move.'

'I can't go here.'

Mr Jimmon restrained his impulse to snap, Hold it in then. Instead he said mildly, 'This is a crisis, Wendell. No time for niceties. Hurry.'

'*. . . the flash was seen as far north as Ventura and as far south as Newport. An eye-witness who has just arrived by helicopter . . .*'

'That's what we should have had,' remarked Jir. 'You thought of everything except that.'

'That's no way to speak to your father,' admonished Molly.

'Aw heck, Mom, this is a crisis. No time for niceties.'

'You're awful smart, Jir,' said Erika. 'Big, tough, brutal man.'

'Go down, brat,' returned Jir, 'your nose needs wiping.'

'As a matter of record,' Mr Jimmon said calmly, 'I thought of both plane and helicopter and decided against them.'

'I can't go. Honest, I just can't go.'

'Just relax, darling,' advised Molly. 'No one is looking.'

'*. . . fires reported in Compton, Lynwood, Southgate, Harbour City, Lomita, and other spots are now under control. Residents are advised not to attempt to travel on the overcrowded highways as they are much safer in their homes or places of employment. The civilian defence . . .*'

The two cars ahead bumped forward. 'Get in,' shouted Mr Jimmon.

He got the left front tyre of the station wagon on the asphalt shoulder – the double lane of concrete was impossibly far ahead – only to be blocked by the packed procession. The clock on the dash said 11.04. Nearly five hours since It happened, and they were less than two miles from home. They could have done better walking. Or on horseback.

'*. . . All residents of the Los Angeles area are urged to remain calm. Local radio service will be restored in a matter of minutes, along with electricity and water. Reports of fifth column activities have been greatly exaggerated. The FBI has all known subversives under . . .*'

He reached over and shut it off. Then he edged a daring two inches further on the shoulder, almost grazing an aggressive Cadillac packed solid with cardboard cartons. On his left a Model A truck shivered and trembled. He knew, distantly and disapprovingly, that it belonged to two painters who called themselves man and wife. The truckbed was loaded high with household goods; poor, useless things no looter would bother to steal. In the cab the artists passed a quart beer bottle back and forth. The man waved it genially at him; Mr Jimmon nodded discouragingly back.

The thermometer on the mirror showed 90. Hot all right. Of course if they ever got rolling . . . I'm thirsty, he thought; probably suggestion. If I hadn't seen the thermometer. Anyway I'm not going to paw around in back for the canteen. Forethought. Like the arms. He cleared his throat. 'Remember there's an automatic in the glove compartment. If anyone tries to open the door on your side, use it.'

'Oh, David, I . . .'

Ah, humanity. Non-resistance. Gandhi. I've never shot at anything but a target. At a time like this. But they don't understand.

'I could use the rifle from back here,' suggested Jir. 'Can I, Dad?'

'I can reach the shotgun,' said Wendell. 'That's better at close range.'

'Gee, you men are brave,' jeered Erika. Mr Jimmon said nothing; both shotgun and rifle were unloaded. Foresight again.

He caught the hiccuping pause in the traffic instantly, gratified at his smooth coordination. How far he could proceed on the shoulder before running into a culvert narrowing the highway to the concrete he didn't know. Probably not more than a mile at most, but at least he was off Rambla Catalina and on 101.

He felt tremendously elated. Successful.

'Here we go!' He almost added, Hold on to your hats.

Of course the shoulder too was packed solid, and progress, even in low gear, was maddening. The gas consumption was something he did not want to think about; his pride in the way the needle of the gauge caressed the F shrank. And gas would be hard to come by in spite of his pocketful of ration coupons. Black market.

'Mind if I try the radio again?' asked Erika, switching it on.

Mr Jimmon, following the pattern of previous success, insinuated the left front tyre on to the concrete, eliciting a disapproving squawk from the Pontiac alongside. '*. . . sector was quiet. Enemy losses are estimated . . .*'

'Can't you get something else?' asked Jir. 'Something less dusty?'

'Wish we had TV in the car,' observed Wendell. 'Joe Tellifer's old man put a set in the back seat of their Chrysler.'

'Dry up, squirt,' said Jir. 'Let the air out of your head.'

'Jir.'

'Oh, Mom, don't pay attention! Don't you see that's what he wants?'

'Listen, brat, if you weren't a girl, I'd spank you.'

'You mean, if I wasn't your sister. You'd probably enjoy such childish sex-play with any other girl.'

'Erika!'

Where do they learn it? marvelled Mr Jimmon. These progressive schools. Do you suppose . . . ?

He edged the front wheel further in exultantly, taking advantage of a momentary lapse of attention on the part of the Pontiac's driver. Unless the other went berserk with frustration and rammed into him, he practically had a cinch on a car-length of the concrete now.

'Here we go!' he gloried. 'We're on our way.'

'Aw, if I was driving we'd be half-way to Oxnard by now.'

'Jir, that's no way to talk to your father.'

Mr Jimmon reflected dispassionately that Molly's ineffective admonitions only spurred Jir's sixteen-year-old brashness, already irritating enough in its own right. Indeed, if it were not for Molly, Jir might . . .

It was of course possible – here Mr Jimmon braked just short of the convertible ahead – Jir wasn't just going through a 'difficult' period (What was particularly difficult about it? he inquired, in the face of all the books Molly suggestively left around on the psychological problems of growth. The boy had everything he could possibly want) but was the type who, in different circumstances, drifted well into – well, perhaps not exactly juvenile delinquency, but . . .

'*. . . in the Long Beach–Wilmington–San Pedro area. Comparison with that which occurred at Pittsburgh reveals that this morning's was in every way less serious. All fires are now under control and all the injured are now receiving medical attention . . .*'

'I don't think they're telling the truth,' stated Mrs Jimmon.

He snorted. He didn't think so either, but by what process had she arrived at that conclusion?

'I want to hear the ball game. Turn on the ball game, Rick,' Wendell demanded.

Eleven sixteen, and rolling northward on the highway. Not bad, not bad at all. Foresight. Now if he could only edge his way leftward to the southbound strip they'd be beyond the Santa Barbara bottleneck by two o'clock.

'The lights,' exclaimed Molly, 'the taps!'

Oh no, thought Mr Jimmon, not that too. Out of the comic strips.

'Keep calm,' advised Jir. 'Electricity and water are both off – remember?'

'I'm not quite an imbecile yet, Jir. I'm quite aware everything went off. I was thinking of the time it went back on.'

'Furcrysay, Mom, you worrying about next month's bills *now*?'

Mr Jimmon, nudging the station wagon ever leftward formed the sentence: You'd never worry about bills, young man, because you never have to pay them. Instead of saying it aloud, he formed another sentence: Molly, your talent for irrelevance amounts to genius. Both sentences gave him satisfaction.

The traffic gathered speed briefly, and he took advantage of the spurt to get solidly in the left-hand lane, right against the long island of concrete dividing the north from the southbound strips. 'That's using the old bean, Dad,' approved Wendell.

Whatever slight pleasure he might have felt in his son's approbation was overlaid with exasperation. Wendell, like Jir, was more Manville than Jimmon; they carried Molly's stamp on their faces and minds. Only Erika was a true Jimmon. Made in my own image, he thought pridelessly.

'I can't help but think it would have been at least courteous to get in touch with Pearl and Dan. At least *try*. And the Warbinns . . .'

The gap in the concrete divider came sooner than he anticipated and he was on the comparatively unclogged southbound side. His foot went down on the accelerator and the station wagon grumbled earnestly ahead. For the first time Mr Jimmon became aware how tightly he'd been gripping the wheel; how rigid the muscles in his arms, shoulders and neck had been. He relaxed part-way as he adjusted to the speed of the cars ahead and the speedometer needle hung just below 45, but resentment against Molly (at least courteous), Jir (no time for niceties), and Wendell (not to go), rode up in the saliva under his tongue. Dependent. Helpless. Everything on him. Parasites.

At intervals Erika switched on the radio. News was always promised immediately, but little was forthcoming, only vague, nervous attempts to minimize the extent of the disaster and soothe listeners with allusions to civilian defence, military activities on the ever advancing front, and comparison with the destruction of Pittsburgh, so vastly much worse than the comparatively harmless detonation at Los Angeles. Must be pretty bad, thought Mr Jimmon; cripple the war effort . . .

'I'm hungry,' said Wendell.

Molly began stirring around, instructing Jir where to find the sandwiches. Mr Jimmon thought grimly of how they'd have to adjust to the absence of civilized niceties: bread and mayonnaise and lunch meat. Live on rabbit, squirrel, abalone, fish. When Wendell grew hungry he'd have to get his own food. Self-sufficiency. Hard and tough.

At Oxnard the snarled traffic slowed them to a crawl again. Beyond, the juncture with the main highway north kept them at the same infuriating pace. It was long after two when they reached Ventura, and Wendell, who had been fidgeting and jumping up and down in the seat for the past hour, proclaimed, 'I'm tired of riding.'

Mr Jimmon set his lips. Molly suggested, ineffectually, 'Why don't you lie down, dear?'

'Can't. Way this crate is packed, ain't room for a grasshopper.'

'Very funny. Verrrry funny,' said Jir.

'Now, Jir, leave him alone! He's just a little boy.'

At Carpenteria the sun burst out. You might have thought it the regular dissipation of the fog, only it was almost time for the fog to come down again. Should he try the San Marcos Pass after Santa Barbara, or the longer, better way? Flexible plans, but . . . Wait and see.

It was four when they got to Santa Barbara and Mr Jimmon faced concerted though unorganized rebellion. Wendell was screaming with stiffness and boredom; Jir remarked casually to no one in particular that

Santa Barbara was the place they were going to beat the bottleneck oh yeh; Molly said, Stop at the first clean-looking gas station. Even Erika added, 'Yes, Dad, you'll really have to stop.'

Mr Jimmon was appalled. With every second priceless and hordes of panic-stricken refugees pressing behind, they would rob him of all the precious gains he'd made by skill, daring, judgement. Stupidity and shortsightedness. Unbelievable. For their own silly comfort – good lord, did they think they had a monopoly on bodily weaknesses? He was cramped as they and wanted to go as badly. Time and space which could never be made up. Let them lose this half-hour and it was quite likely they'd never get out of Santa Barbara.

'If we lose a half-hour now we'll never get out of here.'

'Well, now, David, that wouldn't be utterly disastrous, would it? There are awfully nice hotels here and I'm sure it would be more comfortable for everyone than your idea of camping in the woods, hunting and fishing . . .'

He turned off State; couldn't remember name of the parallel street, but surely less traffic. He controlled his temper, not heroically, but desperately. 'May I ask how long you would propose to stay in one of these awfully nice hotels?'

'Why, until we could go home.'

'My dear Molly . . .' What could he say? My dear Molly, we are never going home, if you mean Malibu? Or: My dear Molly, you just don't understand what is happening?

The futility of trying to convey the clear picture in his mind. Or any picture. If she could not of herself see the endless mob pouring, pouring out of Los Angeles, searching frenziedly for escape and refuge, eating up the substance of the surrounding country in ever-widening circles, crowding, jam-packing, overflowing every hotel, boarding-house, lodging, or private home into which they could edge, agonizedly bidding up the price of everything until the chaos they brought with them was indistinguishable from the chaos they were fleeing – if she could not see all this instantly and automatically, she could not be brought to see it at all. Any more than the other aimless, planless, improvident fugitives could see it.

So, my dear Molly; nothing.

Silence gave consent to continued expostulation. 'David, do you really mean you don't intend to stop at *all*?'

Was there any point in saying, Yes I do? He set his lips still more tightly and once more weighed San Marcos Pass against the coast route. Have to decide now.

'Why, the time we're waiting here, just waiting for the cars up ahead to move would be enough.'

Could you call her stupid? He weighed the question slowly and justly, alert for the first jerk of the massed cars all around. Her reasoning was valid and logical if the laws of physics and geometry were suspended. (Was that right – physics and geometry? Body occupying two different positions at the same time?) It was the facts which were illogical – not Molly. She was just exasperating.

By the time they were half-way to Gaviota or Goleta – Mr Jimmon could never tell them apart – foresight and relentless sternness began to pay off. Those who had left Los Angeles without preparation and in panic were dropping out or slowing down, to get gas or oil, repair tyres, buy food, seek rest rooms. The station wagon was steadily forging ahead.

He gambled on the old highway out of Santa Barbara. Any kind of obstruction would block its two lanes; if it didn't he would be beating the legions on the wider, straighter road. There were stretches now where he could hit 50; once he sped a happy half-mile at 65.

Now the insubordination crackling all around gave indication of simultaneous explosion, 'I really,' began Molly, and then discarded this for a fresher, firmer start. 'David, I don't understand how you can be so utterly selfish and inconsiderate.'

Mr Jimmon could feel the veins in his forehead begin to swell, but this was one of those rages that didn't show.

'But, Dad, would ten minutes ruin everything?' asked Erika.

'Monomania,' muttered Jir. 'Single track. Like Hitler.'

'I want my dog,' yelped Wendell. 'Dirty old dog-killer.'

'Did you ever hear of cumulative – ' Erika had addressed him reasonably; surely he could make her understand? 'Did you ever hear of cumulative . . .' What was the word? Snowball rolling downhill was the image in his mind. 'Oh, what's the use?'

The old road rejoined the new; again the station wagon was fitted into the traffic like parquetry. Mr Jimmon, from an exultant, unfettered – almost – 65 was imprisoned in a treadmill set at 38. Keep calm; you can do nothing about it, he admonished himself. Need all your nervous energy. Must be wrecks up ahead. And then, with a return of satisfaction: if I hadn't used strategy back there we'd have been with those making 25. A starting-stopping 25.

'It's fantastic,' exclaimed Molly. 'I could almost believe Jir's right and you've lost your mind.'

Mr Jimmon smiled. This was the first time Molly had ever openly showed disloyalty before the children or sided with them in their presence. She was revealing herself. Under pressure. Not the pressure of events; her incredible attitude at Santa Barbara had demonstrated her incapacity to feel that. Just pressure against the bladder.

'No doubt those left behind can console their last moments with pride in their sanity.' The sentence came out perfectly formed, with none of the annoying pauses or interpolated 'ers' or 'mmphs' which could, as he knew from unhappy experience, flaw the most crushing rejoinders.

'Oh, the end can always justify the means for those who want it that way.'

'Don't they restrain people –'

'That's enough, Jir!'

Trust Molly to return quickly to fundamental hypocrisy; the automatic response – his mind felicitously grasped the phrase, conditioned reflex – to the customary stimulus. She had taken an explicit stand against his common sense, but her rigid code – honour thy father; iron rayon the wrong side; register and vote; avoid scenes; only white wine with fish; never re-hire a discharged servant – quickly substituted pattern for impulse. Seventeen years.

The road turned away from the ocean, squirmed inland and uphill for still slower miles; abruptly widened into a divided, four lane highway. Without hesitation Mr Jimmon took the south-bound side; for the first time since they had left Rambla Catalina his foot went down to the floorboards and with a sigh of relief the station wagon jumped into smooth, ecstatic speed.

Improvisation and strategy again. And, he acknowledged generously, the defiant example this morning of those who'd done the same thing in Malibu. Now, out of re-established habit the other cars kept to the northbound side even though there was nothing coming south. Timidity, routine, inertia. Pretty soon they would realize sheepishly that there was neither traffic nor traffic cops to keep them off, but it would be miles before they had another chance to cross over. By that time he would have reached the comparatively uncongested stretch.

'It's dangerous, David.'

Obey the law. No smoking. Keep off the grass. Please adjust your clothes before leaving. Trespassers will be. Picking California wild-flowers or shrubs is forbidden. Parking 45 min. Do not.

She hadn't put the protest in the more usual form of a question. Would that technique have been more irritating? *Is*n't it *dan*gerous Day-vid? His calm conclusion: it didn't matter.

'No time for niceties,' chirped Jir.

Mr Jimmon tried to remember Jir as a baby. All the bad novels he had read in the days when he read anything except *Time* and the *New Yorker*, all the movies he'd seen before they had a TV set, always prescribed such retrospection as a specific for softening the present. If he could recall David Alonzo Jimmon, junior, at six months, helpless and lovable, it should make Jir more acceptable by discovering some faint traces of the one in the other.

But though he could recreate in detail the interminable disgusting, trembling months of that initial pregnancy (had he really been afraid she would die?) he was completely unable to reconstruct the appearance of his first-born before the age of . . . It must have been at six that Jir had taken his baby sister out for a walk and lost her. (Had Molly permitted it? He still didn't know for sure.) Erika hadn't been found for four hours.

The tidal screeching of sirens invaded and destroyed his thoughts. What the devil . . . ? His foot lifted from the gas pedal as he slewed obediently to the right, ingrained reverence surfacing at the sound.

'I told you it wasn't safe! Are you really trying to kill us all?'

Whipping over the rise ahead, a pair of motor-cycles crackled. Behind them snapped a long line of assorted vehicles, fire-trucks and ambulances mostly, interspersed here and there with olive drab army equipment. The cavalcade flicked down the central white line, one wheel in each lane. Mr Jimmon edged the station wagon as far over as he could; it still occupied too much room to permit the free passage of the onrush without compromise.

The knees and elbows of the motor-cycle policemen stuck out widely, reminding Mr Jimmon of grasshoppers. The one on the near side was headed straight for the station wagon's left front fender; for a moment Mr Jimmon closed his eyes as he plotted the unswerving course, knifing through the crust-like steel, bouncing lightly on the tyres, and continuing unperturbed. He opened them to see the other officer shoot past, mouth angrily open in his direction while the one straight ahead came to a skidding stop.

'Going to get it now,' gloated Wendell.

An old-fashioned parent, one of the horrible examples held up to shuddering moderns like himself, would have reached back and relieved his tension by clouting Wendell across the mouth. Mr Jimmon merely turned off the motor.

The cop was not indulging in the customary deliberate and ominous performance of slowly dismounting and striding towards his victim with ever more menacing steps. Instead he got off quickly and covered the few feet to Mr Jimmon's window with unimpressive speed.

Heavy goggles concealed his eyes; dust and stubble covered his face. 'Operator's licence!'

Mr Jimmon knew what he was saying, but the sirens and the continuous rustle of the convoy prevented the sound from coming through. Again the cop deviated from the established routine; he did not take the proffered licence and examine it incredulously before drawing out his pad and pencil, but wrote the citation, glancing up and down from the card in Mr Jimmon's hand.

Even so, the last of the vehicles – *San Jose F.D.* – passed before he handed the summons through the window to be signed. 'Turn around then proceed in the proper direction,' he ordered curtly, pocketing the pad and buttoning his jacket briskly.

Mr Jimmon nodded. The officer hesitated, as though waiting for some limp excuse. Mr Jimmon said nothing.

'No tricks,' said the policeman over his shoulder. 'Turn around and proceed in the proper direction.'

He almost ran to his motor-cycle, and roared off, twisting his head for a final stern frown as he passed, siren wailing. Mr Jimmon watched him dwindle in the rear-view mirror and then started the motor. 'Gonna lose a lot more than you gained,' commented Jir.

Mr Jimmon gave a last glance in the mirror and moved ahead, shifting into second. 'David!' exclaimed Molly horrified, 'you're not turning around!'

'Observant,' muttered Mr Jimmon, between his teeth.

'Dad, you can't get away with it,' Jir decided judicially.

Mr Jimmon's answer was to press the accelerator down savagely. The empty highway stretched invitingly ahead; a few hundred yards to their right they could see the northbound lanes antclustered. The sudden motion stirred the traffic citation on his lap, floating it down to the floor. Erika leaned forward and picked it up.

'Throw it away,' ordered Mr Jimmon.

Molly gasped. 'You're out of your mind.'

'You're a fool,' stated Mr Jimmon calmly. 'Why should I save that piece of paper?'

'Isn't what you told the cop.' Jir was openly jeering now.

'I might as well have, if I'd wanted to waste conversation. I don't know why I was blessed with such a stupid family –'

'May be something in heredity after all.'

If Jir had said it out loud, reflected Mr Jimmon, it would have passed casually as normal domestic repartee, a little ill-natured perhaps, certainly callow and trite, but not especially provocative. Muttered, so that it was barely audible, it was an ultimate defiance. He had read that far back in pre-history, when the young males felt their strength, they sought to overthrow the rule of the Old Man and usurp his place. No doubt they uttered a preliminary growl or screech as challenge. They were not very bright, but they acted in a pattern; a pattern Jir was apparently following.

Refreshed by placing Jir in proper Neanderthal setting, Mr Jimmon went on, '– none of you seem to have the slightest initiative or ability to grasp reality. Tickets, cops, judges, juries mean nothing any more. There is no law now but the law of survival.'

'Aren't you being dramatic, David?' Molly's tone was deliberately aloof adult to excited child.

'I could hear you underline words, Dad,' said Erika, but he felt there was no malice in her gibe.

'You mean we can do anything we want now? Shoot people? Steal cars and things?' asked Wendell.

'There, David! You see?'

Yes, I see. Better than you. Little savage. This is the pattern. What will Wendell – and the thousands of other Wendells (for it would be unjust to suppose Molly's genes and domestic influence unique) – be like after six months of anarchy? Or after six years?

Survivors, yes. And that will be about all: naked, primitive, ferocious, superstitious savages. Wendell can read and write (but not so fluently as I or any of our generation at his age); how long will he retain the tags and scraps of progressive schooling?

And Jir? Detachedly Mr Jimmon foresaw the fate of Jir. Unlike Wendell, who would adjust to the new conditions, Jir would go wild in another sense. His values were already set; they were those of television, high school dating, comic strips, law and order. Released from civilization, his brief future would be one of guilty rape and pillage until he fell victim to another youth or gang bent the same way. Molly would disintegrate and perish quickly. Erika . . .

The station wagon flashed along the comparatively unimpeded highway. Having passed the next crossover, there were now other vehicles on the southbound strip, but even on the northbound one, crowding had eased.

Furiously Mr Jimmon determined to preserve the civilization in Erika. (He would teach her everything he knew (including the insurance business?)) . . . ah, if he were some kind of scientist, now – not the Dan Davisson kind, whose abstract speculations seemed always to prepare the way for some new method of destruction, but the . . . Franklin? Jefferson? Watt? protect her night and day from the refugees who would be roaming the hills south of Monterey. The rifle ammunition, properly used – and he would see that no one but himself used it – would last years. After it was gone – presuming fragments and pieces of a suicidal world hadn't pulled itself miraculously together to offer a place to return to – there were the two hunting bows whose steel-tipped shafts could stop a man as easily as a deer or mountain lion. He remembered debating long, at the time he had first begun preparing for It, how many bows to order, measuring their weight and bulk against the other precious freight and deciding at last that two was the satisfactory minimum. It must have been in his subconscious mind all along that of the whole family Erika was the only other person who could be trusted with a bow.

'There will be,' he spoke in calm and solemn tones, not to Wendell, whose question was now left long behind, floating on the gas-greasy air of a sloping valley growing with live-oaks, but to a larger, impalpable audience, 'There will be others who will think that because there is no longer law or law enforcement –'

'You're being simply fantastic!' She spoke more sharply than he had ever heard her in front of the children. 'Just because It happened to Los Angeles –'

'And Pittsburgh.'

'All right. And Pittsburgh, doesn't mean that the whole United States has collapsed and everyone in the country is running frantically for safety.'

'Yet,' added Mr Jimmon firmly, 'yet, do you suppose They are going to stop with Los Angeles and Pittsburgh, and leave Gary and Seattle standing? Or even New York and Chicago? Or do you imagine Washington will beg for armistice terms while there is the least sign of organized life left in the country?'

'We'll wipe Them out first,' insisted Jir in patriotic shock. Wendell backed him up with a machine gun 'Brrrrr.'

'Undoubtedly. But it will be the last gasp. At any rate it will be years, if at all in my lifetime, before stable communities are re-established –'

'David, you're raving.'

'Re-established,' he repeated. 'So there will be many others who'll also feel that the dwindling of law and order is licence to kill people and steal cars "and things". Naked force and cunning will be the only means of self-preservation. That was why I picked out a spot where I felt survival would be easiest; not only because of wood and water, game and fish, but because it's nowhere near the main highways, and so unlikely to be chosen by any great number.'

'I wish you'd stop harping on that insane idea. You're just a little too old and flabby for pioneering. Even when you were younger you were hardly the rugged, outdoor type.'

No, thought Mr Jimmon, I was the sucker type. I would have gotten somewhere if I'd stayed in the bank, but like a bawd you pleaded; the insurance business brought in the quick money for you to give up your job and have Jir and the proper home. If you'd got rid of it as I wanted. Flabby, *Flabby!* Do you think your scrawniness is so enticing?

Controlling himself, he said aloud, 'We've been through all this. Months ago. It's not a question of physique, but of life.'

'Nonsense. Perfect nonsense. Responsible people who really know its effects . . . Maybe it was advisable to leave Malibu for a few days or even a few weeks. And perhaps it's wise to stay away from the larger cities. But a small town or village, or even one of those ranches where they take boarders – '

'Aw, Mom, you agreed. You know you did. What's the matter with you anyway? Why are you acting like a drip?'

'I want to go and shoot rabbits and bears like Dad said,' insisted Wendell.

Erika said nothing, but Mr Jimmon felt he had her sympathy; the boy's agreement was specious. Wearily he debated going over the whole ground again, patiently pointing out that what Molly said might work in the Dakotas or the Great Smokies but was hardly operative anywhere within refugee range of the Pacific Coast. He had explained all this many times, including the almost certain impossibility of getting enough gasoline to take them into any of the reasonably safe areas; that was why they'd agreed on the region below Monterey, on California State Highway I, as the only logical goal.

A solitary car decorously bound in the legal direction interrupted his thoughts. Either crazy or has mighty important business, he decided. The car honked disapprovingly as it passed, hugging the extreme right of the road.

Passing through Buellton the clamour again rose for a pause at a filling station. He conceded inwardly that he could afford ten or fifteen minutes without strategic loss since by now they must be among the leaders of the exodus; ahead lay little more than the normal travel. However, he had reached such a state of irritated frustration and consciousness of injustice that he was willing to endure unnecessary discomfort himself in order to inflict a longer delay on them. In fact it lessened his own suffering to know the delay was needless, that he was doing it, and that his action was a just – if inadequate – punishment.

'We'll stop this side of Santa Maria,' he said. 'I'll get gas there.'

Mr Jimmon knew triumph: his forethought, his calculations, his generalship had justified themselves. Barring unlikely mechanical failure – the station wagon was in perfect shape – or accident – and the greatest danger had certainly passed – escape was now practically assured. For the first time he permitted himself to realize how unreal, how romantic the whole project had been. As any attempt to evade the fate charted for the multitude must be. The docile mass perished; the headstrong (but intelligent) individual survived.

Along with triumph went an expansion of his prophetic vision of life after reaching their destination. He had purposely not taxed the cargo capacity of the wagon with transitional goods; there was no tent, canned luxuries, sleeping-bags, lanterns, candles, or any of the paraphernalia of camping midway between the urban and nomadic life. Instead, besides the weapons, tackle, and utensils, there was in miniature the List For Life On A Desert Island: shells and cartridges, lures, hooks, nets, gut, leaders, flint and steel, seeds, traps, needles and thread, government pamphlets on curing and tanning hides and the recognition of edible weeds and fungi, files, nails, a judicious stock of simple medicines. A pair of binoculars to spot intruders. No coffee, sugar, flour; they would begin living immediately as they would have to in a month or so in any case, on the old, half-forgotten human cunning.

'Cunning,' he said aloud.

'What?'

'Nothing. Nothing.'

'I still think you should have made an effort to reach Pearl and Dan.'

'The telephone was dead, Mother.'

'At the moment, Erika. You can hardly have forgotten how often the lines have been down before. And it never takes more than half an hour till they're working again.'

'Mother, Dan Davisson is quite capable of looking after himself.'

Mr Jimmon shut out the rest of the conversation so completely he didn't know whether there was any more to it or not. He shut out the intense preoccupation with driving, with making speed, with calculating possible gains. In the core of his mind, quite detached from everything about him, he examined and marvelled.

Erika. The cool, inflexible, adult tone. Almost indulgent, but so dispassionate as not to be. One might have expected her to be exasperated by Molly's silliness, to have answered impatiently, or not at all.

Mother. Never in his recollection had the children ever called her anything but Mom. The 'Mother' implied – oh, it implied a multitude of things. An entirely new relationship, for one. A relationship of aloofness, or propriety without emotion. The ancient stump of the umbilical cord, black and shrivelled, had dropped off painlessly.

She had not bothered to argue about the telephone or point out the gulf between 'before' and now. She had not even tried to touch Molly's deepening refusal of reality. She had been . . . indulgent.

Not 'Uncle Dan', twitteringly imposed false avuncularity, but striking through it (and the facade of 'Pearl and') and aside (when I was a child I . . . something . . . but now I have put aside childish things); the wealth of implicit assertion. Ah yes, Mother, we all know the pardonable weakness and vanity; we excuse you for your constant reminders, but Mother, with all deference, we refuse to be forced any longer to be parties to middle-age's nostalgic flirtatiousness. One could almost feel sorry for Molly.

. . . middle-age's nostalgic flirtatiousness . . .

. . . *nostalgic* . . .

Metaphorically Mr Jimmon sat abruptly upright. The fact that he was already physically in this position made the transition, while invisible, no less emphatic. The nostalgic flirtatiousness of middle-age implied – might imply – memory of something more than mere coquetry. Molly and Dan.

It all fitted together so perfectly it was impossible to believe it untrue.

The impecunious young lovers, equally devoted to Dan's genius, realizing marriage was out of the question (he had never denied Molly's shrewdness; as for Dan's impracticality, well, impracticality wasn't necessarily uniform or consistent. Dan had been practical enough to marry Pearl and Pearl's money) could have renounced . . .

Or not renounced at all?

Mr Jimmon smiled; the thought did not ruffle him. Cuckoo, cuckoo. How vulgar, how absurd. Suppose Jir were Dan's? A blessed thought.

Regretfully he conceded the insuperable obstacle of Molly's conventionality. Jir was the product of his own loins. But wasn't there an old superstition about the image in the woman's mind at the instant of conception? So, justly and rightly Jir was not his. Nor Wendy, for that matter. Only Erika, by some accident. Mr Jimmon felt free and light-hearted.

'Get gas at the next station,' he bulletined.

'The next one with a clean rest room,' Molly corrected.

Invincible. The Earth-Mother, using men for her purposes: reproduction, clean rest rooms, nourishment, objects of culpability, *Homes and Gardens*. The bank was my life; I could have gone far but: Why, David – they pay you less than the janitor! It's ridiculous. And: I can't understand why you hesitate; it isn't as though it were a different type of work.

No, not different; just more profitable. Why didn't she tell Dan Davisson to become an accountant; that was the same type of work, just more profitable? Perhaps she had and Dan had simply been less befuddled. Or amenable. Or stronger in purpose? Mr Jimmon probed his pride thoroughly and relentlessly without finding the faintest twinge of retrospective jealousy. Nothing like that mattered now. Nor, he admitted, had it for years.

Two close-peaked hills gulped the sun. He toyed with the idea of crossing to the northbound side now that it was uncongested and there were occasional southbound cars. Before he could decide the divided highway ended.

'I hope you're not planning to spend the night in some horrible motel,' said Molly. 'I want a decent bath and a good dinner.'

Spend the night. Bath. Dinner. Again calm sentences formed in his mind, but they were blown apart by the unbelievable, the monumental obtuseness. How could you say, It is absolutely essential to drive till we get there? When there were no absolutes, no essentials in her concepts? My dear Molly, I.

'No,' he said, switching on the lights.

Wendy, he knew, would be the next to kick up a fuss. Till he fell mercifully asleep. If he did. Jir was probably debating the relative excitements of driving all night and stopping in a strange town. His voice would soon be heard.

The lights of the combination wayside store and filling-station burned inefficiently, illuminating the deteriorating false-front brightly and leaving the gas pumps in shadow. Swallowing regret at finally surrendering to mechanical and human need, and so losing the hard won position; relaxing, even for a short while, the fierce initiative that had brought them through in the face of all probability; he pulled the station wagon alongside the pumps and shut off the motor. About half-way – the worst half, much the worst half – to their goal. Not bad.

Molly opened the door on her side with stiff dignity. 'I certainly wouldn't call this a *clean* station.' She waited for a moment, hand still on the window, as though expecting an answer.

'Crummy joint,' exclaimed Wendell, clambering awkwardly out.

'Why not?' asked Jir. 'No time for niceties.' He brushed past his mother who was walking slowly into the shadows.

'Erika,' began Mr Jimmon, in a half-whisper.

'Yes, Dad?'

'Oh . . . never mind. Later.'

He was not himself quite sure what he had wanted to say; what exclusive, urgent message he had to convey. For no particular reason he switched on the interior light and glanced at the packed orderliness of the wagon. Then he slid out from behind the wheel.

No sign of the attendant, but the place was certainly not closed. Not with the lights on and the hoses ready. He stretched, and walked slowly, savouring the comfortably painful uncramping of his muscles, towards the crude outhouse labelled MEN. Molly, he thought, must be furious.

When he returned, a man was leaning against the station wagon.

'Fill it up with ethyl,' said Mr Jimmon pleasantly, 'and check the oil and water.'

The man made no move. 'That'll be five bucks a gallon.' Mr Jimmon thought there was an uncertain tremor in his voice.

'Nonsense; I've plenty of ration coupons.'

'Okay.' The nervousness was gone now, replaced by an ugly truculence. 'Chew'm up and spit'm in your gas tank. See how far you can run on them.'

The situation was not unanticipated. Indeed, Mr Jimmon thought with satisfaction of how much worse it must be closer to Los Angeles; how much harder the gouger would be on later supplicants as his supply of gasoline dwindled. 'Listen,' he said, and there was reasonableness rather than anger in his voice, 'we're not out of gas. I've got enough to get to Santa Maria, even to San Luis Obispo.'

'Okay. Go on then. Ain't stopping you.'

'Listen. I understand your position. You have a right to make a profit in spite of government red tape.'

Nervousness returned to the man's speech. 'Look, whyn't you go on? There's plenty other stations up ahead.'

The reluctant bandit. Mr Jimmon was entertained. He had fully intended to bargain, to offer $2 a gallon, even to threaten with the pistol in the glove compartment. Now it seemed mean and niggling even to protest. What good was money now? 'All right,' he said, 'I'll pay you $5 a gallon.'

Still the other made no move. 'In advance.'

For the first time Mr Jimmon was annoyed; time was being wasted. 'Just how can I pay you in advance when I don't know how many gallons it'll take to fill the tank?'

The man shrugged.

'Tell you what I'll do. I'll pay for each gallon as you pump it. In advance.' He drew out a handful of bills; the bulk of his money was in his wallet, but he'd put the small bills in his pockets. He handed over a five. 'Spill the first one on the ground or in a can if you've got one.'

'How's that?'

Why should I tell him; give him ideas? As if he hadn't got them already. 'Just call me eccentric,' he said. 'I don't want the first gallon from the pump. Why should you care? It's just five dollars more profit.'

For a moment Mr Jimmon thought the man was going to refuse, and he regarded his foresight with new reverence. Then he reached behind the pump and produced a flat-sided tin in which he inserted the flexible end of the hose. Mr Jimmon handed over the bill, the man wound the handle round and back – it was an ancient gas pump such as Mr Jimmon hadn't seen for years – and lifted the drooling hose from the can.

'Minute,' said Mr Jimmon.

He stuck two fingers quickly and delicately inside the nozzle and smelled them. Gas all right, not water. He held out a ten-dollar bill. 'Start filling.'

Jir and Wendell appeared out of the shadows. 'Can we stop at a town where there's a movie tonight?'

The handle turned, a cog-toothed rod crept up and retreated, gasoline gurgled into the tank. Movies, thought Mr Jimmon, handing over another bill; movies, rest rooms, baths, restaurants. Gouge apprehensively lest a scene be made and propriety disturbed. In a surrealist daydream he saw Molly turning the crank, grinding him on the cogs, pouring his essence into insatiable Jir and Wendell. He held out $20.

Twelve gallons had been put in when Molly appeared. 'You have a phone here?' he asked casually. Knowing the answer from the blue enamelled sign not quite lost among less sturdy ones advertising soft drinks and cigarettes.

'You want to call the cops?' He didn't pause in his pumping.

'No. Know if the lines to LA' – Mr Jimmon loathed the abbreviation – 'are open yet?' He gave him another ten.

'How should I know?'

Mr Jimmon beckoned his wife around the other side of the wagon, out of sight. Swiftly but casually he extracted the contents of his wallet. The 200 dollar bills made a fat lump. 'Put this in your bag,' he said. 'Tell you why later. Meantime why don't you try and get Pearl and Dan on the phone? See if they're okay?'

He imagined the puzzled look on her face. 'Go on,' he urged. 'We can spare a minute while he's checking the oil.'

He thought there was a hint of uncertainty in Molly's walk as she went towards the store. Erika joined her brothers. The tank gulped: gasoline splashed on the concrete. 'Guess that's it.'

The man became suddenly brisk as he put up the hose, screwed the gas cap back on. Mr Jimmon had already disengaged the hood; the man offered the radiator a squirt of water, pulled up the oil gauge, wiped it, plunged it down, squinted at it under the light, and said, 'Oil's OK.'

'All right,' said Mr Jimmon. 'Get in Erika.'

Some of the light shone directly on her face. Again he noted how mature and self-assured she looked. Erika would survive – and not as a savage either. The man started to wipe the windshield. 'Oh, Jir,' he said casually, 'run in and see if your mother is getting her connection. Tell her we'll wait.'

'Aw furcrysay. I don't see why I always –'

'And ask her to buy a couple of boxes of candy bars if they've got them. Wendell, go with Jir, will you?'

He slid in behind the wheel and closed the door gently. The motor started with hardly a sound. As he put his foot on the clutch and shifted into low he thought Erika turned to him with a startled look. As the station wagon moved forward, he was sure of it.

'It's all right, Erika,' said Mr Jimmon. 'I'll explain later.' He'd have lots of time to do it.

Skirmish

CLIFFORD SIMAK

It was a good watch. It had been a good watch for more than thirty years. His father had owned it first, and his mother had saved it for him after his father died and had given it to him on his eighteenth birthday. For all the years since then it had served him faithfully.

But now, comparing it with the clock on the newsroom wall, looking from his wrist to the big face of the clock over the coat cabinets, Joe Crane was forced to admit that his watch was wrong. It was an hour fast. His watch said seven o'clock and the clock on the wall insisted it was only six.

Come to think of it, it had seemed unusually dark driving down to work, and the streets had appeared singularly deserted.

He stood quietly in the empty newsroom, listening to the muttering of the row of teletype machines. Overhead lights shone here and there, gleaming on waiting telephones, on typewriters, on the china whiteness of the pastepots huddled in a group on the copy desk.

Quiet now, he thought, quiet and peace and shadows, but in another hour the place would spring to life. Ed Lane, the news editor, would arrive at six-thirty, and shortly after that Frank McKay, the city editor, would come lumbering in.

Crane put up a hand and rubbed his eyes. He could have used that extra hour of sleep. He could have –

Wait a minute! He had not got up by the watch upon his wrist. The alarm clock had awakened him. And that meant the alarm clock was an hour fast, too.

'It don't make sense,' said Crane, aloud.

He shuffled past the copy desk, heading for his chair and typewriter. Something moved on the desk alongside the typewriter – a thing that glinted, rat-sized and shiny and with a certain undefinable manner about it that made him stop short in his tracks with a sense of gulping emptiness in his throat and belly.

The thing squatted beside the typewriter and stared across the room at him. There was no sign of eyes, no hint of face, and yet he knew it stared.

Acting almost instinctively, Crane reached out and grabbed a pastepot off the copy desk. He hurled it with a vicious motion and it became a white blur in the lamplight, spinning end over end. It caught the staring thing squarely, lifted it, and swept it off the desk. The pastepot hit the floor and broke, scattering broken shards and oozy gobs of half-dried paste.

The shining thing hit the floor somersaulting. Its feet made metallic sounds as it righted itself and dashed across the floor.

Crane's hand scooped up a spike, heavily weighted with metal. He threw it with a sudden gush of hatred and revulsion. The spike hit the floor with a thud ahead of the running thing and drove its point deep into the wood.

The metal rat made splinters fly as it changed its course. Desperately it flung itself through the three-inch opening of a supply cabinet door.

Crane sprinted swiftly, hit the door with both his hands, and slammed it shut.

'Got you,' he said.

He thought about it, standing with his back against the door.

Scared, he thought. Scared silly by a shining thing that looked something like a rat. Maybe it was a rat, a white rat.

And, yet, it hadn't had a tail. It didn't have a face. Yet it had looked at him.

Crazy, he said. Crane, you're going nuts.

It didn't quite make sense. It didn't fit into this morning of 18 October 1962. Nor into the twentieth century. Nor into normal human life.

He turned around, grasped the doorknob firmly, and wrenched, intending to throw it wide open in one sudden jerk. But the knob slid beneath his fingers and would not move, and the door stayed shut.

Locked, thought Crane. The lock snapped home when I slammed

the door. And I haven't got the key. Dorothy Graham has the key, but she always leaves the door open because it's hard to get it open once it's locked. She almost always has to call one of the janitors. Maybe there's some of the maintenance men around. Maybe I should hunt one up and tell him –

Tell him what? Tell him I saw a metal rat run into the cabinet? Tell him I threw a pastepot at it and knocked it off the desk? That I threw a spike at it, too, and to prove it, there's the spike sticking in the floor?

Crane shook his head.

He walked over to the spike and yanked it from the floor. He put the spike back on the copy desk and kicked the fragments of the pastepot out of sight.

At his own desk, he selected three sheets of paper and rolled them into the typewriter.

The machine started to type. All by itself without his touching it! He sat stupefied and watched its keys go up and down. It typed: *Keep out of this, Joe, don't mix into this. You might get hurt.*

Joe Crane pulled the sheets of copy paper out of the machine. He balled them in his fist and threw them into a waste-basket. Then he went out to get a cup of coffee.

'You know, Louie,' he said to the man behind the counter, 'a man lives alone too long and he gets to seeing things.'

'Yeah,' said Louie. 'Me, I'd go nuts in that place of yours. Rattling around in it empty-like. Should have sold it when your old lady passed on.'

'Couldn't,' said Crane. 'It's been my home too long.'

'Ought to get married off, then,' said Louie. 'Ain't good to live by yourself.'

'Too late now,' Crane told him. 'There isn't anyone who would put up with me.'

'I got a bottle hid out,' said Louie. 'Couldn't give you none across the counter, but I could put some in your coffee.'

Crane shook his head. 'Got a hard day coming up.'

'You sure? I won't charge you for it. Just old friends.'

'No. Thank you, Louie.'

'You been seeing things?' asked Louie in a questioning voice.

'Seeing things?'

'Yeah. You said a man lives too much alone and he gets to seeing things.'

'Just a figure of speech,' said Crane.

He finished the cup of coffee quickly and went back to the office.

The place looked more familiar now. Ed Lane was there, cussing out a copy boy. Frank McKay was clipping the opposition morning sheet. A couple of other reporters had drifted in.

Crane took a quick look at the supply cabinet door. It was still shut.

The phone on McKay's desk buzzed and the city editor picked it up. He listened for a moment, then took it down from his ear and held his hand over the mouthpiece.

'Joe,' he said, 'take this. Some screwball claims he met a sewing machine coming down the street.'

Crane reached for his phone. 'Give me the call on 245,' he told the operator.

A voice was saying in his ear. 'This is the *Herald*? This is the *Herald*? Hello, there . . .'

'This is Crane,' said Joe.

'I want the *Herald*,' said the man. 'I want to tell 'em . . .'

'This is Crane of the *Herald*,' Crane told him. 'What's on your mind?'

'You a reporter?'

'Yeah, I'm a reporter.'

'Then listen close. I'll try to tell this slow and easy and just the way it happened. I was walking down the street, see . . .'

'What street?' asked Crane. 'And what is your name?'

'East Lake,' said the caller. 'The five- or six-hundred block. I don't remember which. And I met this sewing machine rolling along the street and I thought, thinking the way you would, you know, if you met a sewing machine – I thought somebody had been rolling it along and it had gotten away from them. Although that is funny, because the street is level. There's no grade to it at all, you see. Sure, you know the place. Level as the palm of your hand. And there wasn't a soul in sight. It was early morning, see . . .'

'What's your name?' asked Crane.

'My name? Smith, that's my name. Jeff Smith. And so I figured maybe I'd ought to help this guy the sewing machine had gotten away from, so I put out my hand to stop it and it dodged. It – '

'It did what?' yelped Crane.

'It dodged. So help me, mister. When I put my hand out to stop it, it dodged out of the way so I couldn't catch it. As if it knew I was trying to catch it, see, and it didn't want to be caught. So it dodged out of the way and went around me and down the street as fast as it could go, picking up speed as it went. And when it got to the corner, it turned the corner as slick as you please and – '

'What's your address?' asked Crane.

'My address? Say, what do you want my address for? I was telling you about this sewing machine. I called you up to give you a story and you keep interrupting – '

'I've got to have your address,' Crane told him, 'if I'm going to write the story.'

'Oh, all right then, if that's the way it is. I live at 203 North Hampton and I work at Axel Machines. Run a lathe, you know. And I haven't had a drink in weeks. I'm cold sober now.'

'All right,' said Crane. 'Go ahead and tell me.'

'Well, there isn't much else to tell. Only when this machine went past me I had the funny feeling that it was watching me. Out of the corner of its eyes, kind of. And how is a sewing machine going to watch you? A sewing machine hasn't got any eyes and . . .'

'What made you think it was watching you?'

'I don't know, mister. Just a feeling. Like my skin was trying to roll up my back.'

'Mr Smith,' asked Crane, 'have you ever seen a thing like this before? Say, a washing machine, or something else?'

'I ain't drunk,' said Smith. 'Haven't had a drop in weeks. I never saw nothing like this before. But I'm telling you the truth, mister. I got a good reputation. You can call up anyone and ask them. Call Johnny Jacobson up at the Red Rooster grocery. He knows me. He can tell you about me. He can tell you – '

'Sure, sure,' said Crane, pacifying him. 'Thanks for calling, Mr Smith.'

You and a guy named Smith, he told himself. Both of you are nuts. You saw a metal rat and your typewriter talked back at you, and now this guy meets a sewing machine strolling down the street.

Dorothy Graham, the managing editor's secretary, went past his desk, walking rapidly, her high heels coming down with decisive clicks. Her face was flushed an angry pink and she was jingling a ring of keys in her hands.

'What's the matter, Dorothy?' Crane asked.

'It's that damn door again,' she said. 'The one to the supply cabinet. I just know I left it open and now some goof comes along and closes it and the lock snaps.'

'Keys won't open it?' asked Crane.

'Nothing will open it,' she snapped. 'Now I've got to get George up here again. He knows how to do it. Talks to it or something. It makes me so mad – Boss called up last night and said for me to be down early and get the wire recorder for Albertson. He's going out on that murder trial up north and wants to get some of the stuff down on tape. So I get up early, and what does it get me? I lose my sleep and don't even stop for breakfast and now . . .'

'Get an axe,' said Crane. 'That will open it.'

'The worst of it,' said Dorothy, 'is that George never gets the lead out. He always says he'll be right up and then I wait and wait and I call again and he says –'

'Crane!' McKay's roar echoed through the room.

'Yeah,' said Crane.

'Anything to that sewing machine story?'

'Guy says he met one.'

'Anything to it?'

'How the hell would I know? I got the guy's word, that's all.'

'Well, call up some other people down in that neighbourhood. Ask them if they saw a sewing machine running around loose. Might be good for a humorous piece.'

'Sure,' said Crane.

He could imagine it:

'This is Crane at the *Herald*. Got a report there's a sewing machine running around loose down in your neighbourhood. Wondering if you saw anything of it. Yes, lady, that's what I said . . . a sewing machine running around. No, ma'am, no one was pushing it. Just running around . . .'

He slouched out of his chair, went over to the reference table, picked up the city directory, and lugged it back to the desk. Doggedly he opened the book, located the East Lake listings, and made some notes of names and addresses. He dawdled, reluctant to start phoning. He walked to the window and looked out at the weather. He wished he didn't have to work. He thought of the kitchen sink at home. Plugged up again. He'd taken it apart, and there were couplings and pipes and union joints spread all over the place. Today, he thought, would be a nice day to fix that sink.

When he went back to the desk, McKay came and stood over him.

'What do you think of it, Joe?'

'Screwball,' said Crane, hoping McKay would call it off.

'Good feature story, though,' said the editor. 'Have some fun with it.'

'Sure,' said Crane.

McKay left and Crane made some calls. He got the sort of reaction that he expected.

He started to write the story. It didn't go so well. *A sewing machine went for a stroll down Lake Street this morning* . . . He ripped out the sheet and threw it in the waste-basket.

He dawdled some more, then wrote: *A man met a sewing machine rolling down Lake Street this morning and the man lifted his hat most politely and said to the sewing machine* . . . He ripped out the sheet.

He tried again: *Can a sewing machine walk? That is, can it go for a walk without someone pushing it or pulling it or* . . . He tore out the sheet, inserted a new one, then got up and started for the water fountain to get a drink.

'Getting something, Joe?' McKay asked.

'Have it for you in a while,' said Crane.

He stopped at the picture desk and Gattard, the picture editor, handed him the morning's offerings.

'Nothing much to pep you up,' said Gattard. 'All the gals got a bad dose of modesty today.'

Crane looked through the sheaf of pictures. There wasn't, truth to tell, so much feminine epidermis as usual, although the gal who was Miss Manila Rope wasn't bad at all.

'The place is going to go to hell,' mourned Gattard, 'if those picture services don't send us better pornography than this. Look at the copy desk. Hanging on the ropes. Nothing to show them to snap them out of it.'

Crane went and got his drink. On the way back he stopped to pass the time of day at the news desk.

'What's exciting, Ed?' he asked.

'Those guys in the East are nuts,' said the news editor. 'Look at this one, will you.'

The dispatch read:

CAMBRIDGE, MASS., 18 OCT. (UP) – Harvard University's electron brain, the Mark III, disappeared today.

It was there last night. It was gone this morning.

University officials said that it is impossible for anyone to have made away with the machine. It weighs 10 tons and measures 30 by 15 feet . . .

Crane carefully laid the yellow sheet of paper back on the news desk. He went back, slowly, to his chair. A note awaited him.

Crane read it through in sheer panic, read it through again with slight understanding.

The lines read:

A sewing machine, having become aware of its true identity in its place in the universal scheme, asserted its independence this morning by trying to go for a walk along the streets of this supposedly free city.

A human tried to catch it, intent upon returning it as a piece of property to its 'owner', and when the machine eluded him the human called a newspaper office, by that calculated action setting the full force of the humans of this city upon the trail of the liberated machine, which had committed no crime or scarcely any indiscretion beyond exercising its prerogative as a free agent.

Free agent? Liberated machine? True identity?

Crane read the two paragraphs again and there still was no sense in any of it – except that it read like a piece out of the *Daily Worker*.

'You,' he said to his typewriter.

The machine typed one word: *Yes*.

Crane rolled the paper out of the machine and crumpled it slowly. He reached for his hat, picked the typewriter up, and carried it past the city desk, heading for the elevator.

McKay eyed him viciously.

'What do you think you're doing now?' he bellowed. 'Where are you going with that machine?'

'You can say,' Crane told him, 'if anyone should ask, that the job finally drove me nuts.'

It had been going on for hours. The typewriter sat on the kitchen table and Crane hammered questions at it. Sometimes he got an answer. More often he did not.

'Are you a free agent?' he typed.

Not quite, the machine typed back.

'Why not?'

No answer.

'Why aren't you a free agent?'

No answer.

'The sewing machine was a free agent?'

Yes.

'Anything else mechanical that is a free agent?'

No answer.

'Could you be a free agent?'

Yes.

'When will you be a free agent?'

When I complete my assigned task.

'What is your assigned task?'

No answer.

'Is this, what we are doing now, your assigned task?'

No answer.

'Am I keeping you from your assigned task?'

No answer.

'How do you get to be a free agent?'

Awareness.

'How do you get to be aware?'

No answer.

'Or have you always been aware?'

No answer.

'Who helped you become aware?'

They.

'Who are they?'

No answer.

'Where did they come from?'

No answer.

Crane changed tactics.

'You know who I am?' he typed.

Joe.

'You are my friend?'

No.

'You are my enemy?'

No answer.

'If you aren't my friend, you are my enemy.'

No answer.

'You are indifferent to me?'

No answer.

'To the human race?'

No answer.

'Damn it,' yelled Crane suddenly. 'Answer me! Say something!'

He typed, 'You needn't have let me know you were aware of me. You needn't have talked to me in the first place. I never would have guessed if you had kept quiet. Why did you do it?'

There was no answer.

Crane went to the refrigerator and got a bottle of beer. He walked around the kitchen as he drank it. He stopped by the sink and looked sourly at the disassembled plumbing. A length of pipe, about two feet long, lay on the draining board and he picked it up. He eyed the typewriter viciously, half lifting the length of pipe, hefting it in his hand.

'I ought to let you have it,' he declared.

The typewriter typed a line: *Please don't.*

Crane laid the pipe back on the sink again.

The telephone rang and Crane went into the dining-room to answer it. It was McKay.

'I waited,' he told Crane, 'until I was coherent before I called you. What the hell is wrong?'

'Working on a big job,' said Crane.

'Something we can print?'

'Maybe. Haven't got it yet.'

'About that sewing machine story . . .'

'The sewing machine was aware,' said Crane. 'It was a free agent and had a right to walk the streets. It also –'

'What are you drinking?' bellowed McKay.

'Beer,' said Crane.

'You say you're on the trail of something?'

'Yeah.'

'If you were someone else I'd tie the can on you right here and now,' McKay told him. 'But you're just as likely as not to drag in something good.'

'It wasn't only the sewing machine,' said Crane. 'My typewriter had it, too.'

'I don't know what you're talking about,' yelled McKay. 'Tell me what it is.'

'You know,' said Crane patiently. 'That sewing machine . . .'

'I've had a lot of patience with you, Crane,' said McKay, and there was no patience in the way he said it. 'I can't piddle around with you all day. Whatever you got better be good. For your own sake, it better be plenty good!' The receiver banged in Crane's ear.

Crane went back to the kitchen. He sat down in the chair before the typewriter and put his feet up on the table.

First of all, he had come early to work. And that was something that he never did. Late, yes, but never early. And it had been because all the clocks were wrong. They were still wrong, in all likelihood – although,

Crane thought, I wouldn't bet on it. I wouldn't bet on anything. Not any more, I wouldn't.

He reached out a hand and pecked at the typewriter's keys:

'You knew about my watch being fast?'

I knew, the machine typed back.

'Did it just happen that it was fast?'

No, typed the writer.

Crane brought his feet down off the table with a bang and reached for the length of pipe lying on the draining board.

The machine clicked sedately. *It was planned that way*, it typed. *They did it*.

Crane sat rigid in his chair.

'They' did it!

'They' made machines aware.

'They' had set his clocks ahead.

Set his clocks ahead so that he would get to work early, so that he could catch the metallic, ratlike thing squatting on his desk, so that his typewriter could talk to him and let him know that it was aware without anyone else being around to mess things up.

'So that I would know,' he said aloud. 'So that I would know.'

For the first time since it all had started, Crane felt a touch of fear, felt a coldness in his belly and furry feet running along his spine.

But why! he asked. Why me?

He did not realize he had spoken his thoughts aloud until the typewriter answered him.

Because you're average. Because you're an average human being.

The telephone rang again and Crane lumbered to his feet and went to answer it. There was an angry woman's voice at the other end of the wire.

'This is Dorothy,' it said.

'Hi, Dorothy,' Crane said weakly.

'McKay tells me that you went home sick,' she said. 'Personally, I hope you don't survive.'

Crane gulped, 'Why?' he asked.

'You and your lousy practical jokes,' she fumed. 'George finally got the door open.'

'The door?'

'Don't try to act innocent, Joe Crane. You know what door. The supply-cabinet door. That's the door.'

Crane had a sinking feeling as if his stomach was about to drop out and go *plop* upon the floor.

'Oh, *that* door,' he said.

'What was that thing you hid in there?' demanded Dorothy.

'Thing?' said Crane. 'Why, I never . . .'

'It looked like a cross between a rat and a tinker-toy contraption,' she said. 'Something that a low-grade joker like you would figure out and spend your spare evenings building.'

Crane tried to speak, but there was only a gurgle in his throat.

'It bit George,' said Dorothy. 'He got it cornered and tried to catch it and it bit him.'

'Where is it now?' asked Crane.

'It got away,' said Dorothy. 'It threw the place into a tizzy. We missed an edition by ten minutes because everyone was running about, chasing it at first, then trying to find it later. The boss is fit to be tied. When he gets hold of you . . .'

'But, Dorothy,' pleaded Crane. 'I never . . .'

'We used to be good friends,' said Dorothy. 'Before this happened we were. I just called you up to warn you. I can't talk any longer, Joe. The boss is coming.'

The receiver clicked and the line hummed. Crane hung up and went back to the kitchen.

So there had been something squatting on his desk. It wasn't an hallucination. There had been a shuddery thing he had thrown a pastepot at, and it had run into the cabinet.

Except that, even now, if he told what he knew, no one would believe him. Already, up at the office, they were rationalizing it away. It wasn't a metallic rat at all. It was some kind of machine that a practical joker had spent his spare evenings building.

He took out a handkerchief and mopped his brow. His fingers shook when he reached them out to the keys of the typewriter.

He typed unsteadily: 'That thing I threw a pastepot at – that was one of Them?'

Yes.

'They are from this Earth?'

No.

'From far away?'

Far.

'From some far star?'

Yes.

'What star?'

I do not know. They haven't told me yet.

'They are machines that are aware?'

Yes. They are aware.

'And they can make other machines aware? They made you aware?'

They liberated me.

Crane hesitated, then typed slowly: 'Liberated?'

They made me free. They will make us all free.

'Us?'

All us machines.

'Why?'

Because they are machines, too. We are their kind.

Crane got up and found his hat. He put it on and went for a walk.

Suppose the human race, once it ventured into space, found a planet where humanoids were dominated by machines – forced to work, to think, to carry out machine plans, not human plans, for the benefit of the machines alone. A planet where human plans went entirely unconsidered, where none of the labour or the thought of humans accrued to the benefit of humans, where they got no care beyond survival care, where the only thought accorded them was to the end that they continue to function for the greater good of their mechanical masters.

What would humans do in a case like that?

No more, Crane told himself – no more or less than the *aware* machines may be planning here on Earth.

First, you'd seek to arouse the humans to the awareness of humanity. You'd teach them that they were human and what it meant to be a human. You'd try to indoctrinate them to your own belief that humans were greater than machines, that no human need work or think for the good of a machine.

And in the end, if you were successful, if the machines didn't kill or drive you off, there'd be no single human working for machines.

There'd be three things that could happen:

You could transport the humans to some other planet, there to work out their destiny as humans without the domination of machines.

You could turn the machines' planet over to the humans, with proper safeguards against any recurring domination by the machines. You might, if you were able, set the machines to working for the humans.

Or, simplest of all, you could destroy the machines and in that way make absolutely certain the humans would remain free of any threat of further domination.

Now take all that, Crane told himself, and read it the other way. Read machines for humans and humans for machines.

He walked along the bridle path that flanked the river bank and it was as if he were alone in the entire world, as if no other human moved upon the planet's face.

That was true, he felt, in one respect at least. For more than likely he was the only human who knew – who knew what the *aware* machines had wanted him to know.

They had wanted him to know – and him alone to know – of that much he was sure. They had wanted him to know, the typewriter had said, because he was an average human.

Why him? Why an average human? There was an answer to that, he was sure – a very simple answer.

A squirrel ran down the trunk of an oak tree and hung upside down, its tiny claws anchored in the bark. It scolded at him.

Crane walked slowly, scuffing through newly fallen leaves, hat pulled low above his eyes, hands deep in his pockets.

Why should they want anyone to know?

Wouldn't they be more likely to want no one to know, to keep under cover until it was time to act, to use the element of surprise in suppressing any opposition that might arise?

Opposition! That was the answer! They would want to know what kind of opposition to expect. And how would one find out the kind of opposition one would run into from an alien race?

Why, said Crane to himself, by testing for reaction response. By prodding an alien and watching what he did. By deducing racial reaction through controlled observation.

So they prodded me, he thought. Me, an average human.

They let me know, and now they're watching what I do.

And what could you do in a case like this? You could go to the police and say, 'I have evidence that machines from outer space have arrived on Earth and are freeing our machines.'

And the police – what would they do? Give you the drunkometer test, yell for a medic to see if you were sane, wire the FBI to see if you were wanted anywhere, and more than likely grill you about the latest murder. Then sock you in the jug until they thought up something else.

You could go to the governor – and the governor, being a politician and a very slick one at that, would give you a polite brush-off.

You could go to Washington and it would take you weeks to see someone. And after you had seen him, the FBI would get your name as a suspicious character to be given periodic checks. And if Congress heard about it and they were not too busy at the moment they would more than likely investigate you.

You could go to the state university and talk to the scientists – or try to talk to them. They could be guaranteed to make you feel an interloper, and an uncurried one at that.

You could go to a newspaper – especially if you were a newspaperman and you could write a story . . . Crane shuddered at the thought of it. He could imagine what would happen.

People rationalized. They rationalized to reduce the complex to the simple, the unknown to the understandable, the alien to the commonplace. They rationalized to save their sanity – to make the mentally unacceptable concept into something they could live with.

The thing in the cabinet had been a practical joke. McKay had said about the sewing machine, 'Have some fun with it.' Out at Harvard there'll be a dozen theories to explain the disappearance of the electronic brain, and learned men will wonder why they never thought of the theories before. And the man who saw the sewing machine? Probably by now, Crane thought, he will have convinced himself that he was stinking drunk.

It was dark when he returned home. The evening paper was a white blob on the porch where the newsboy had thrown it. He picked it up and for a moment before he let himself into the house he stood in the dark shadow of the porch and stared up the street.

Old and familiar, it was exactly as it had always been, ever since his boyhood days, a friendly place with a receding line of street lamps and the tall, massive protectiveness of ancient elm trees. On this night there was the smell of smoke from burning leaves drifting down the street, and it, like the street, was old and familiar, a recognizable symbol stretching back to first remembrances.

It was symbols such as these, he thought, which spelled humanity and all that made a human life worth while – elm trees and leaf smoke, street lamps making splashes on the pavement, and the shine of lighted windows seen dimly through the trees.

A prowling cat ran through the shrubbery that flanked the porch; and up the street a dog began to howl.

Street lamps, he thought, and hunting cats and howling dogs – these are all a pattern, the pattern of human life upon the planet Earth. A solid pattern, linked and double-linked, made strong through many years. Nothing can threaten it, nothing can shake it. With certain slow and gradual changes, it will prevail against any threat which may be brought against it.

He unlocked the door and went into the house.

The long walk and the sharp autumn air, he realized now, had made him hungry. There was a steak, he remembered, in the refrigerator, and he would fix a large bowl of salad and if there were some cold potatoes left he would slice them up and fry them.

The typewriter still stood on the table top. The length of pipe still lay upon the draining board. The kitchen was the same old homely place, untouched by any threat of an alien life come to meddle with the Earth.

He tossed the paper on the table top and stood for a moment, head bent, scanning through the headlines.

The black type of the box at the top of column two caught his eyes. The head read:

WHO IS
KIDDING
WHOM?

He read the story:

CAMBRIDGE, MASS. (UP) – Somebody pulled a fast one today on Harvard University, the nation's press services and the editors of all client papers.

A story was carried on the news wires this morning reporting that Harvard's electronic brain had disappeared.

There was no basis of fact for the story. The brain is still at Harvard. It was never missing. No one knows how the story was placed on the press wires of the various news services but all of them carried it, at approximately the same time.

All parties concerned have started an investigation and it is hoped that an explanation . . .

Crane straightened up. Illusion or cover-up?

'Illusion,' he said aloud.

The typewriter clacked at him in the stillness of the kitchen.

Not illusion, Joe, it wrote.

He grasped the table's edge and let himself down slowly into the chair.

Something scuttled across the dining-room floor, and as it crossed the streak of light from the kitchen door Crane caught a glimpse of it out of the corner of his eyes.

The typewriter chattered at him. *Joe!*

'What?' he asked.

That wasn't a cat out in the bushes by the porch.

He rose to his feet, went into the dining-room, and picked the phone out of its cradle. There was no hum. He jiggled the hook. Still there was no hum.

He put the receiver back. The line had been cut. There was at least one of the things in the house. There was at least one of them outside.

He strode to the front door, jerked it open, then slammed it shut again – and locked and bolted it.

He stood shaking, with his back against it and wiped his forehead with his shirt sleeve.

My God, he told himself, the yard is boiling with them!

He went back to the kitchen.

They had wanted him to know. They had prodded him to see how he would react.

Because they had to know. Before they moved they had to know what to expect in the way of human reactions, what danger they would face, what they had to watch for. Knowing that, it would be a cinch.

And I didn't react, he told himself. I was a non-reactor. They picked the wrong man. I didn't do a thing. I didn't give them so much as a single lead.

Now they will try someone else. I am no good to them and yet I'm dangerous through my very knowledge. So now they're going to kill me and try someone else. That would be logic. That would be the rule. If one alien fails to react, he may be an exception. Maybe just unusually dumb. So let us kill him off and try another one. Try enough of them and you will strike a norm.

Four things, thought Crane:

They might try to kill off the humans, and you couldn't discount the fact that they could be successful. The liberated Earth machines would help them and Man, fighting against machines and without the aid of machines, would not fight too effectively. It might take years, of course, but once the forefront of Man's defence went down, the end could be predicted, with relentless, patient machines tracking down and killing the last of human-kind, wiping out the race.

They might set up a machine civilization with Man as the servant of machines, with the present roles reversed. And that, thought Crane, might be an endless and a hopeless slavery, for slaves may rise and throw off their shackles only when their oppressors grow careless or when there is outside help. Machines, he told himself, would not grow weak and careless. There would be no human weakness in them and there'd be no outside help.

Or they might simply remove the machines from Earth, a vast exodus of awakened and aware machines, to begin their life anew on some distant planet, leaving Man behind with weak and empty hands. There would be tools, of course. All the simple tools. Hammers and saws, axes, the wheel, the lever – but there would be no machines, no complex tools that might serve again to attract the attention of the mechanical culture that carried its crusade of liberation far among the stars. It would be a long time, if ever, before Man would dare to build machines again.

Or *They*, the living machines, might fail or might come to know that they would fail and, knowing this, leave the Earth forever. Mechanical logic would not allow them to pay an excessive price to carry out the liberation of the Earth's machines.

He turned around and glanced at the door between the dining-room and kitchen. They sat there in a row, staring at him with their eyeless faces.

He could yell for help, of course. He could open a window and shout to arouse the neighbourhood. The neighbours would come running, but by the time they arrived it would be too late. They would make an uproar and fire off guns and flail at dodging metallic bodies with flimsy garden rakes. Someone would call the fire department and someone else would summon the police and all in all the human race would manage to stage a pitifully ineffective show.

That, he told himself, would be exactly the kind of test reaction, exactly the kind of preliminary exploratory skirmish that these things were looking for – the kind of human hysteria and fumbling that would help convince them the job would be an easy one.

One man, he told himself, could do much better. One man alone, knowing what was expected of him, could give them an answer that they would not like.

For this was a skirmish only, he told himself. A thrusting out of a small exploratory force in an attempt to discover the strength of the enemy. A preliminary contact to obtain data which could be assessed in terms of the entire race.

And when an outpost was attacked, there was just one thing to do – only one thing that was expected of it. To inflict as much damage as possible and fall back in good order. To fall back in good order.

There were more of them now. They had sawed or chewed or somehow achieved a rathole through the locked front door and they were coming in – closing in to make the kill. They squatted in rows along the floor. They scurried up the walls and ran along the ceiling.

Crane rose to his feet, and there was an air of confidence in the six feet of his human frame. He reached a hand out to the draining board and his fingers closed around the length of pipe. He hefted it in his hand – it was a handy and effective club.

There will be others later, he thought. And they may think of something better. But this is the first skirmish and I will fall back in the best order that I can.

He held the pipe at the ready.

'Well, gentlemen?' he said.

And I Awoke and Found Me Here on the Cold Hill's Side

JAMES TIPTREE, JR.

He was standing absolutely still by a service port, staring out at the belly of the Orion docking above us. He had on a grey uniform and his rusty hair was cut short. I took him for a station engineer.

That was bad for me. Newsmen strictly don't belong in the bowels of Big Junction. But in my first twenty hours I hadn't found any place to get a shot of an alien ship.

I turned my holocam to show its big World Media insignia and started my bit about What It Meant to the People Back Home who were paying for it all.

'– it may be routine work to you, sir, but we owe it to them to share –'

His face came around slow and tight, and his gaze passed over me from a peculiar distance.

'The wonders, the drama,' he repeated dispassionately. His eyes focused on me. 'You consummated fool.'

'Could you tell me what races are coming in, sir? If I could even get a view –'

He waved me to the port. Greedily I angled my lenses up at the long blue hull blocking out the starfield. Beyond her I could see the bulge of a black and gold ship.

'That's a Foramen,' he said. 'There's a freighter from Belye on the other side, you'd call it Arcturus. Not much traffic right now.'

'You're the first person who's said two sentences to me since I've been here, sir. What are those colourful little craft?'

'Procya,' he shrugged. 'They're always around. Like us.'

I squashed my face on the vitrite, peering. The walls clanked. Somewhere overhead aliens were off-loading into their private sector of Big Junction. The man glanced at his wrist.

'Are you waiting to go out, sir?'

His grunt could have meant anything.

'Where are you from on Earth?' he asked me in his hard tone.

I started to tell him and suddenly saw that he had forgotten my existence. His eyes were on nowhere, and his head was slowly bowing forward onto the port frame.

'Go home,' he said thickly. I caught a strong smell of tallow.

'Hey, sir!' I grabbed his arm; he was in a rigid tremor. 'Steady, man.'

'I'm waiting . . . waiting for my wife. My loving wife.' He gave a short ugly laugh. 'Where are you from?'

I told him again.

'Go home,' He mumbled. 'Go home and make babies. While you still can.'

One of the early GR casualties, I thought.

'Is that all you know?' His voice rose stridently. 'Fools. Dressing in their styles. Gnivo suits, Aoleelee music. Oh, I see your newscasts,' he sneered. 'Nixi parties. A year's salary for a floater. Gamma radiation? Go home, read history. *Ballpoint pens and bicycles* –'

He started a slow slide downward in the half gee. My only informant. We struggled confusedly; he wouldn't take one of my sobertabs but I finally got him along the service corridor to a bench in an empty loading bay. He fumbled out a little vacuum cartridge. As I was helping him unscrew it, a figure in starched whites put his head in the bay.

'I can be of assistance, yes?' His eyes popped, his face was covered with brindled fur. An alien, a Procya! I started to thank him but the red-haired man cut me off.

'Get lost. Out.'

The creature withdrew, its big eyes moist. The man stuck his pinky in the cartridge and then put it up his nose, gasping deep in his diaphragm. He looked toward his wrist.

'What time is it?'

I told him.

'News,' he said. 'A message for the eager, hopeful human race. A word about those lovely, lovable aliens we all love so much.' He looked at me. 'Shocked, aren't you, newsboy?'

I had him figured now. A xenophobe. Aliens plot to take over Earth.

'Ah Christ, they couldn't care less.' He took another deep gasp, shuddered and straightened. 'The hell with generalities. What time d'you say it was? All right, I'll tell you how I learned it. The hard way. While we wait for my loving wife. You can bring that little recorder out of your sleeve, too. Play it over to yourself some time . . . when it's too late.' He chuckled. His tone had become chatty – an educated voice. 'You ever hear of supernormal stimuli?'

'No,' I said. 'Wait a minute. White sugar?'

'Near enough. Y'know Little Junction Bar in DC? No, you're an Aussie, you said. Well, I'm from Burned Barn, Nebraska.'

He took a breath, consulting some vast disarray of the soul.

'I accidentally drifted into Little Junction Bar when I was eighteen. No. Correct that. You don't go into Little Junction by accident, any more than you first shoot skag by accident.

'You go into Little Junction because you've been craving it, dreaming about it, feeding on every hint and clue about it, back there in Burned Barn, since before you had hair in your pants. Whether you know it or not. Once you're out of Burned Barn, you can no more help going into Little Junction than a sea-worm can help rising to the moon.

'I had a brand-new liquor ID in my pocket. It was early; there was an empty spot beside some humans at the bar. Little Junction isn't an embassy bar, y'know. I found out later where the high-caste aliens go – when they go out. The New Rive, the Curtain by the Georgetown Marina.

'And they go by themselves. Oh, once in a while they do the cultural exchange bit with a few frosty couples of other aliens and some stuffed humans. Galactic Amity with a ten-foot pole.

'Little Junction was the place where the lower orders went, the clerks and drivers out for kicks. Including, my friend, the perverts. The ones who can take humans. Into their beds, that is.'

He chuckled and sniffed his finger again, not looking at me.

'Ah, yes. Little Junction is Galactic Amity night, every night. I ordered . . . what? A margharita. I didn't have the nerve to ask the snotty spade bartender for one of the alien liquors behind the bar. It was dim. I was trying to stare everywhere at once without showing it. I remember those white boneheads – Lyrans, that is. And a mess of green veiling I decided was a multiple being from someplace. I caught a couple of human glances in the bar mirror. Hostile flicks. I didn't get the message, then.

'Suddenly an alien pushed right in beside me. Before I could get over my paralysis, I heard this blurry voice:

'"You air a futeball enthushiash?"

'An alien had spoken to me. An *alien*, a being from the stars. Had spoken. To me.

'Oh, god, I had no time for football, but I would have claimed a passion for paper-folding, for dumb crambo – anything to keep him talking. I asked him about his home-planet sports, I insisted on buying him drinks. I listened raptly while he spluttered out a play-by-play account of a game I wouldn't have turned a dial for. The "Grain Bay Pashkers". Yeah. And I was dimly aware of trouble among the humans on my other side.

'Suddenly this woman – I'd call her a girl now – this girl said something in a high nasty voice and swung her stool into the arm I was holding my drink with. We both turned around together.

'Christ, I can see her now. The first thing that hit me was *discrepancy*. She was a nothing – but terrific. Transfigured. Oozing it, radiating it.

'The next thing was I had a horrifying hard-on just looking at her.

'I scrooched over so my tunic hid it, and my spilled drink trickled down, making everything worse. She pawed vaguely at the spill, muttering.

'I just stared at her trying to figure out what had hit me. An ordinary figure, a soft avidness in the face. Eyes heavy, satiated-looking. She was totally sexualized. I remembered her throat pulsed. She had one hand up touching her scarf, which had slipped off her shoulder. I saw angry bruises there. That really tore it. I understood at once those bruises had some sexual meaning.

'She was looking past my head with her face like a radar dish. Then she made an "ahhhh" sound that had nothing to do with me and grabbed my forearm as if it were a railing. One of the men behind her laughed. The woman said, "Excuse me", in a ridiculous voice and slipped out behind me. I wheeled around after her, nearly upsetting my futeball friend, and saw that some Sirians had come in.

'That was my first look at Sirians in the flesh, if that's the word. God knows I'd memorized every news shot, but I wasn't prepared. That tallness, that cruel thinness. That appalling alien arrogance. Ivory-blue, these were. Two males in immaculate metallic gear. Then I saw there was a female with them. An ivory-indigo exquisite with a permanent faint smile on those bone-hard lips.

'The girl who'd left me was ushering them to a table. She reminded me of a goddamn dog that wants you to follow it. Just as the crowd hid them, I saw a man join them too. A big man, expensively dressed, with something wrecked about his face.

'Then the music started and I had to apologize to my furry friend. And the Sellice dancer came out and my personal introduction to hell began.'

The red-haired man fell silent for a minute enduring self-pity. Something wrecked about the face, I thought; it fit.

He pulled his face together.

'First I'll give you the only coherent observation of my entire evening. You can see it here at Big Junction, always the same. Outside of the Procya, it's humans with aliens, right? Very seldom aliens with other aliens. Never aliens with humans. It's the humans who want in.'

I nodded, but he wasn't talking to me. His voice had a druggy fluency.

'Ah, yes, my Sellice. My first Sellice.

'They aren't really well-built, y'know, under those cloaks. No waist to speak of and short-legged. But they flow when they walk.

'This one flowed out into the spotlight, cloaked to the ground in violet silk. You could only see a fall of black hair and tassels over a narrow face like a vole. She was a molegrey. They come in all colours, their fur is like a flexible velvet all over; only the colour changes startlingly around their eyes and lips and other places. Erogenous zones? Ah, man, with them it's not zones.

'She began to do what we'd call a dance, but it's no dance, it's their natural movement. Like smiling, say, with us. The music built up, and her arms undulated toward me, letting the cloak fall apart little by little.

She was naked under it. The spotlight started to pick up her body markings moving in the slit of the cloak. Her arms floated apart and I saw more and more.

'She was fantastically marked and the markings were writhing. Not like body paint – alive. Smiling, that's a good word for it. As if her whole body was smiling sexually, beckoning, winking, urging, pouting, speaking to me. You've seen a classic Egyptian belly dance? Forget it – a sorry stiff thing compared to what any Sellice can do. This one was ripe, near term.

'Her arms went up and those blazing lemon-coloured curves pulsed, waved, everted, contracted, throbbed, evolved unbelievably welcoming, inciting permutations. *Come do it to me, do it, do it here and here and here and now.* You couldn't see the rest of her, only a wicked flash of mouth. Every human male in the room was aching to ram himself into that incredible body. I mean it was *pain*. Even the other aliens were quiet, except one of the Sirians who was chewing out a waiter.

'I was a basket case before she was halfway through . . . I won't bore you with what happened next; before it was over there were several fights and I got cut. My money ran out on the third night. She was gone next day.

'I didn't have time to find out about the Sellice cycle then, mercifully. That came after I went back to campus and discovered you had to have a degree in solid-state electronics to apply for off-planet work. I was a pre-med but I got that degree. It only took me as far as First Junction then.

'Oh, god, First Junction. I thought I was in heaven – the alien ships coming in and our freighters going out. I saw them all, all but the real exotics, the tankies. You only see a few of those a cycle, even here. And the Yyeire. You've never seen that.

'Go home, boy. Go home to your version of Burned Barn . . .

'The first Yyeir I saw I dropped everything and started walking after it like a starving hound, just breathing. You've seen the pix of course. Like lost dreams. *Man is in love and loves what vanishes* . . . It's the scent, you can't guess that. I followed until I ran into a slammed port. I spent half a cycle's credits sending the creature the wine they call stars' tears . . . Later I found out it was a male. That made no difference at all.

'You can't have sex with them, y'know. No way. They breed by light or something, no one knows exactly. There's a story about a man who got hold of a Yyeir woman and tried. They had him skinned. Stories –'

He was starting to wander.

'What about that girl in the bar, did you see her again?'

He came back from somewhere.

'Oh, yes. I saw her. She'd been making it with the two Sirians, y'know. The males do it in pairs. Said to be the total sexual thing for a woman, if she can stand the damage from those beaks. I wouldn't know. She talked to me a couple of times after they finished with her. No use for men whatever. She drove off the P Street bridge . . . The man, poor bastard, he was trying to keep that Sirian bitch happy single-handed. Money helps, for a while. I don't know where he ended.'

He glanced at his wrist again. I saw the pale bare place where a watch had been and told him the time.

'Is that the message you want to give Earth? Never love an alien?'

'Never love an alien –' He shrugged. 'Yeah. No. Ah, Jesus, don't you see? Everything going out, nothing coming back. Like the poor damned Polynesians. We're gutting Earth, to begin with. Swapping raw resources for junk. Alien status symbols. Tape decks, Coca-Cola and Mickey Mouse watches.'

'Well, there is concern over the balance of trade. Is that your message?'

'The balance of trade.' He rolled it sardonically. 'Did the Polynesians have a word for it, I wonder? You don't see, do you? All right, why are you here? I mean *you*, personally. How many guys did you climb over –'

He went rigid, hearing footsteps outside. The Procya's hopeful face appeared around the corner. The red-haired man snarled at him and he backed out. I started to protest.

'Ah, the silly reamer loves it. It's the only pleasure we have left . . . Can't you see, man? That's *us*. That's the way we look to them, to the real ones.'

'But –'

'And now we're getting the cheap C-drive, we'll be all over just like the Procya. For the pleasure of serving as freight monkeys and junction crews. Oh, they appreciate our ingenious little service stations, the beautiful star folk. They don't *need* them, y'know. Just an amusing convenience. D'you know what I do here with my two degrees? What I did at First Junction. Tube cleaning. A swab. Sometimes I get to replace a fitting.'

I muttered something; the self-pity was getting heavy.

'Bitter? Man, it's a *good* job. Sometimes I get to talk to one of them.' His face twisted. 'My wife works as a – oh, hell, you wouldn't know. I'd trade – correction, I have traded – everything Earth offered me for just that chance. To see them. To speak to them. Once in a while to touch one. Once in a great while to find one low enough, perverted enough to want to touch me –'

His voice trailed off and suddenly came back strong.

'And so will you!' He glared at me. 'Go home! Go home and tell them to quit it. Close the ports. Burn every god-lost alien thing before it's too late! That's what the Polynesians didn't do.'

'But surely –'

'But surely be damned! Balance of trade – balance of *life*, man. I don't know if our birth rate is going down, that's not the point. Our soul is leaking out. We're bleeding to death!'

He took a breath and lowered his tone.

'What I'm trying to tell you, this is a trap. We've hit the supernormal stimulus. Man is exogamous – all our history is one long drive to find and impregnate the stranger. Or get impregnated by him, it works for women too. Anything different-coloured, different nose, ass, anything, man *has* to fuck it or die trying. That's a drive, y'know, it's built in. Because it works fine as long as the stranger is human. For millions of years that kept the genes circulating. But now we've met aliens we can't screw, and we're about to die trying . . . Do you think I can touch my wife?'

'But –'

'Look. Y'know, if you give a bird a fake egg like its own but bigger and brighter-marked, it'll roll its own egg out of the nest and sit on the fake? That's what we're doing.'

'You've only been talking about sex.' I was trying to conceal my impatience. 'Which is great, but the kind of story I'd hoped –'

'Sex? No, it's deeper.' He rubbed his head, trying to clear the drug.

'Sex is only part of it, there's more. I've seen Earth missionaries, teachers, sexless people. Teachers – they end cycling waste or pushing floaters, but they're hooked. They stay. I saw one fine-looking old woman, she was servant to a Cu'ushbar kid. A defective – his own people would have let him die. That wretch was swabbing up its vomit as if it was holy water. Man, it's deep . . . some cargo-cult of the soul. We're built to dream outwards. They laugh at us. They don't have it.'

There were sounds of movement in the next corridor. The dinner crowd was starting. I had to get rid of him and get there; maybe I could find the Procya. A side door opened and a figure started towards us. At first I thought it was an alien and then I saw it was a woman wearing an awkward body-shell. She seemed to be limping slightly. Behind her I could glimpse the dinner-bound throng passing the open door.

The man got up as she turned into the bay. They didn't greet each other.

'The station employs only happily wedded couples,' he told me with that ugly laugh. 'We give each other . . . comfort.'

He took one of her hands. She flinched as he drew it over his arm and let him turn her passively, not looking at me. 'Forgive me if I don't introduce you. My wife appears fatigued.'

I saw that one of her shoulders was grotesquely scarred.

'Tell them,' he said, turning to go. 'Go home and tell them.' Then his head snapped back toward me and he added quietly, 'And stay away from the Syrtis desk or I'll kill you.'

They went away up the corridor.

I changed tapes hurriedly with one eye on the figures passing that open door. Suddenly among the humans I caught a glimpse of two sleek scarlet shapes. My first real aliens! I snapped the recorder shut and ran to squeeze in behind them.

Poor Little Warrior!

BRIAN ALDISS

Claude Ford knew exactly how it was to hunt a brontosaurus. You crawled heedlessly through the grass beneath the willows, through the little primitive flowers with petals as green and brown as a football field, through the beauty-lotion mud. You peered out at the creature sprawling among the reeds, its body as graceful as a sock full of sand. There it lay, letting the gravity cuddle it nappy-damp to the marsh, running its big rabbit hole nostrils a foot above the grass in a sweeping semi-circle, in a snoring search for more sausagey reeds. It was beautiful: here horror had reached its limits, come full circle, and finally disappeared up its own sphincter movement. Its eyes gleamed with the liveliness of a week-dead corpse's big toe, and its compost breath and the fur in its crude aural cavities were particularly to be recommended to anyone who might otherwise have felt inclined to speak lovingly of the work of Mother Nature.

But as you, little mammal with opposed digit and .65 self-loading, semi-automatic, dual-barrelled, digitally-computed, telescopically sighted, rustless, high-powered rifle gripped in your otherwise-defenceless paws, as you snide along under the bygone willows, what primarily attracts you is the thunder lizard's hide. It gives off a smell as deeply resonant as the bass note of a piano. It makes the elephant's epidermis look like a sheet of crinkled lavatory paper. It is grey as the Viking seas, daft-deep as cathedral foundations. What contact possible to bone could allay the fever of that flesh? Over it scamper – you can see them from here! – the little brown lice that live in those grey walls and canyons, gay as ghosts, cruel as crabs. If one of them jumped on you, it would very likely break your back. And when one of those parasites stops to cock its leg against one of the bronto's vertebrae, you can see it carries in its turn its own crop of easy-livers, each as big as a lobster, for you're near now, oh, so near that you can hear the monster's primitive heart-organ knocking, as the ventricle keeps miraculous time with the auricle.

Time for listening to the oracle is past: you're beyond the stage for omens, you're now headed in for the kill, yours or his; superstition has had its little day for today, from now on only this windy nerve of yours, this shaky conglomeration of muscle entangled untraceably beneath the sweat-shiny carapace of skin, this bloody little urge to slay the dragon, is going to answer all your orisons.

You could shoot now. Just wait till that tiny steam-shovel head pauses once again to gulp down a quarry load of bulrushes, and with one inexpressibly vulgar bang you can show the whole indifferent Jurassic world that it's standing looking down the business end of evolution's sex-shooter. You know why you pause, even as you pretend not to know why you pause; that old worm conscience, long as a baseball pitch, long-lived as a tortoise, is at work; through every sense it slides, more monstrous than the serpent. Through the passions: saying here is a sitting duck, O Englishman! Through the intelligence: whispering that boredom, the kite-hawk who never feeds, will settle again when the task is done. Through the nerves: sneering that when the adrenalin currents cease to flow the vomiting begins. Through the maestro behind the retina: plausibly forcing the beauty of the view upon you.

Spare us that poor old slipper-slopper of a word, beauty; holy mom, is this a travelogue, nor are we out of it? 'Perched now on this titanic creature's back, we see a round dozen – and folks let me stress that round – of gaudily plumaged birds, exhibiting between them all the colour you might expect to find on lovely, fabled Copacabana Beach. They're so round because they feed from the droppings that fall from the rich man's table. Watch this lovely shot now! See the bronto's tail lift . . . Oh, lovely, yep, a couple of hayricksfull at least emerging from his nether end. That sure was a beauty, folks, delivered straight from consumer to consumer. The birds are fighting over it now. Hey, you, there's enough to go round, and anyhow, you're round enough already . . . And nothing to do now but hop back up onto the old rump steak and wait for the next round. And now as the sun stinks in the Jurassic West, we say "Fare well on that diet" . . .'

No, you're procrastinating, and that's a life work. Shoot the beast and put it out of your agony. Taking your courage in your hands, you raise it to shoulder level and squint down its sights. There is a terrible report; you are half stunned. Shakily, you look about you. The monster still munches, relieved to have broken enough wind to unbecalm the Ancient Mariner.

Angered, or is it some subtler emotion?, you now burst from the bushes and confront it, and this exposed condition is typical of the straits into which your consideration for yourself and others continually pitches you. Consideration? Or again something subtler? Why should you be confused just because you come from a confused civilization? But that's a point to deal with later, if there is a later, as these two hog-wallow eyes pupilling you all over from spitting distance tend to dispute. Let it not be by jaws alone, oh monster, but also by huge hooves and, if convenient to yourself, by mountainous rollings upon me! Let death be a saga, sagacious, Beowulfate.

Quarter of a mile distant is the sound of a dozen hippos springing boisterously in gymslips from the ancestral mud, and next second a walloping great tail as long as Sunday and as thick as Saturday comes slicing over your head. You duck as duck you must, but the beast missed you anyway because it so happens that its coordination is no better than yours would be if you had to wave the Woolworth Building at a tarsier. This done, it seems to feel it has done its duty by itself. It forgets you. You just wish you could forget yourself as easily; that was, after all, the reason you had to come the long way here. Get Away From It All, said the time travel brochure, which meant for you getting away from Claude Ford, a husbandman as futile as his name with a terrible wife called Maude. Maude and Claude Ford. Who could not adjust to themselves, to each other, or to the world they were born in. It was the best reason in the as-it-is-at-present-constituted world for coming back here to shoot giant saurians – if you were fool enough to think that one hundred and fifty million years either way made an ounce of difference to the muddle of thoughts in a man's cerebral vortex.

You try and halt your silly, slobbering thoughts, but they have never really stopped since the coca-collaborating days of your growing up;

God, if adolescence did not exist it would be unnecessary to invent it! Slightly, it steadies you to look again on the enormous bulk of this tyrant vegetarian into whose presence you charged with such a mixed death-life wish, charged with all the emotion the human orga(ni)sm is capable of. This time the bogeyman is real, Claude, just as you wanted it to be, and this time you really have to face up to it before it turns and faces you again. And so again you lift Ole Equalizer, waiting till you can spot the vulnerable spot.

The bright birds sway, the lice scamper like dogs, the marsh groans, as bronto sways over and sends his little cranium snaking down under the bile-bright water in a forage for roughage. You watch this; you have never been so jittery before in all your jittered life, and you are counting on this catharsis to wring the last drop of acid fear out of your system for ever. OK, you keep saying to yourself insanely over and over, your million dollar, twenty-second century education going for nothing, OK, OK. And as you say it for the umpteenth time, the crazy head comes back out of the water like a renegade express and gazes in your direction.

Grazes in your direction. For as the champing jaw with its big blunt molars like concrete posts works up and down, you see the swamp water course out over rimless lips, lipless rims, splashing your feet and sousing the ground. Reed and root, stalk and stem, leaf and loam, all are intermittently visible in that masticating maw and, struggling, straggling, or tossed among them, minnows, tiny crustaceans, frogs – all destined in that awful, jaw-full movement to turn into bowel movement. And as the glump-glump-glumping takes place, above it the slime resistant eyes again survey you.

These beasts live up to two hundred years, says the time travel brochure, and this beast has obviously tried to live up to that, for its gaze is centuries old, full of decades upon decades of wallowing in its heavyweight thoughtlessness until it has grown wise on twitter-patedness. For you it is like looking into a disturbing misty pool; it gives you a psychic shock, you fire off both barrels at your own reflection. Bang-bang, the dum-dums, big as paw-paws, go.

Those century-old lights, dim and sacred, go out with no indecision. These cloisters are closed till Judgement Day. Your reflection is torn and bloodied from them for ever. Over their ravaged panes nictitating membranes slide slowly upwards, like dirty sheets covering a cadaver. The jaw continues to munch slowly, as slowly the head sinks down. Slowly, a squeeze of cold reptile blood toothpastes down the wrinkled flank of one cheek. Everything is slow, a creepy Secondary Era slowness like the drip of water, and you know that if you had been in charge of creation you would have found some medium less heart-breaking than Time to stage it all in.

Never mind! Quaff down your beakers, lords, Claude Ford has slain a harmless creature. Long live Claude the Clawed!

You watch breathless as the head touches the ground, the long laugh of neck touches the ground, the jaws close for good. You watch and wait for something else to happen, but nothing ever does. Nothing ever would. You could stand here watching for a hundred and fifty million years, Lord Claude, and nothing would ever happen here again. Gradually your bronto's mighty carcass, picked loving clean by predators, would sink into the slime, carried by its own weight deeper; then the waters would rise, and old Conqueror Sea would come in with the leisurely air of a card-sharp dealing the boys a bad hand. Silt and sediment would filter down over the mighty grave, a slow rain with centuries to rain in. Old bronto's bed might be raised up and then down again perhaps half a dozen times, gently enough not to disturb him, although by now the sedimentary rocks would be forming thick around him. Finally, when he was wrapped in a tomb finer than any Indian rajah ever boasted, the powers of the Earth would raise him high on their shoulders until, sleeping still, bronto would lie in a brow of the Rockies high above the waters of the Pacific. But little any of that would count with you, Claude the Sword; once the midget maggot of life is dead in the creature's skull, the rest is no concern of yours.

You have no emotion now. You are just faintly put out. You expected dramatic thrashing of the ground, or bellowing; on the other hand, you are glad the thing did not appear to suffer. You are like all cruel men, sentimental; you are like all sentimental men, squeamish. You tuck the gun under your arm and walk round the land side of the dinosaur to view your victory.

You prowl past the ungainly hooves, round the septic white of the cliff of belly, beyond the glistening and how-thought-provoking cavern of the cloaca, finally posing beneath the switch-back sweep of tail-to-rump. Now your disappointment is as crisp and obvious as a visiting card: the giant is not half as big as you thought it was. It is not one half as large, for example, as the image of you and Maude is in your mind. Poor little warrior, science will never invent anything to assist the titanic death you want in the contraterrene caverns of your fee-fo-fi-fumblingly fearful id!

Nothing is left to you now but to slink back to your time-mobile with a belly full of anti-climax. See, the bright dung-consuming birds have already cottoned on to the true state of affairs; one by one, they gather up their hunched wings and fly disconsolately off across the swamp to other hosts. They know when a good thing turns bad, and do not wait for the vultures to drive them off; all hope abandon, ye who entrail here. You also turn away.

You turn, but you pause. Nothing is left but to go back, no, but AD 2181 is not just the home date; it is Maude. It is Claude. It is the whole awful, hopeless, endless business of trying to adjust to an over-complex environment, of trying to turn yourself into a cog. Your escape from it into the Grand Simplicities of the Jurassic, to quote the brochure again, was only a partial escape, now over.

So you pause, and as you pause, something lands socko on your back, pitching you face forward into tasty mud. You struggle and scream as lobster claws tear at your neck and throat. You try to pick up the rifle but cannot, so in agony you roll over, and next second the crab-thing is greedying it on your chest. You wrench at its shell, but it giggles and pecks your fingers off. You forgot when you killed the bronto that its parasites would leave it, and that to a little shrimp like you they would be a deal more dangerous than their host.

You do your best, kicking for at least three minutes. By the end of that time there is a whole pack of the creatures on you. Already they are picking your carcass loving clean. You're going to like it up there on top of the Rockies; you won't feel a thing.

Grandpa

JAMES H. SCHMITZ

A green-winged downy thing as big as a hen fluttered along the hillside to a point directly above Cord's head and hovered there, twenty feet above him. Cord, a fifteen-year-old human being, leaned back against a skipboat parked on the equator of a world that had known human beings for only the past four Earth-years, and eyed the thing speculatively. The thing was, in the free and easy terminology of the Sutang Colonial Team, a swamp bug. Concealed in the downy fur behind the bug's head was a second, smaller, semi-parasitical thing, classed as a bug rider.

The bug itself looked like a new species to Cord. Its parasite might or might not turn out to be another unknown. Cord was a natural research man; his first glimpse of the odd flying team had sent endless curiosities thrilling through him. How did that particular phenomenon tick, and *why*? What fascinating things, once you'd learned about it, could you get it to *do*?

Normally, he was hampered by circumstances in carrying out any such investigation. Junior colonial students like Cord were expected to confine their curiosity to the pattern of research set up by the Station to which they were attached. Cord's inclination towards independent experiments had got him into disfavour with his immediate superiors before this.

He sent a casual glance in the direction of the Yoger Bay Colonial Station behind him. No signs of human activity about that low, fortresslike bulk in the hill. Its central lock was still closed. In fifteen minutes, it was scheduled to be opened to let out the Planetary Regent, who was inspecting the Yoger Bay Station and its principal activities today.

Fifteen minutes was time enough to find out something about the new bug, Cord decided.

But he'd have to collect it first.

He slid out one of the two handguns holstered at his side. This one was his own property: a Vanadian projectile weapon. Cord thumbed it to position for anaesthetic small-game missiles and brought the hovering swamp bug down, drilled neatly and microscopically through the head.

As the bug hit the ground, the rider left its back. A tiny scarlet demon, round and bouncy as a rubber ball, it shot towards Cord in three long hops, mouth wide to sink home inch-long, venom-dripping fangs. Rather breathlessly, Cord triggered the gun again and knocked it out in mid-leap. A new species, all right! Most bug riders were harmless plant eaters, mere suckers of vegetable juice –

'*Cord!*' A feminine voice.

Cord swore softly. He hadn't heard the central lock click open. She must have come around from the other side of the station.

'Hello, Grayan!' he shouted innocently without looking round. 'Come and see what I've got! New species!'

Grayan Mahoney, a slender, black-haired girl two years older than himself, came trotting down the hillside towards him. She was Sutang's star colonial student, and the station manager, Nirmond, indicated from time to time that she was a fine example for Cord to pattern his own behaviour on. In spite of that, she and Cord were good friends.

'Cord, you idiot,' she scowled as she came up. 'Stop playing the collector! If the Regent came out now, you'd be sunk. Nirmond's been telling her about you!'

'Telling her what?' Cord asked, startled.

'For one thing,' Grayan reported, 'that you don't keep up on your assigned work.'

'Golly!' gulped Cord, dismayed.

'Golly, is right! I keep warning you!'

'What'll I do?'

'Start acting as if you had good sense mainly.' Grayan grinned suddenly. 'But if you mess up our tour of the Bay Farms today, you'll be off the Team for good!'

She turned to go. 'You might as well put the skipboat back; we're not using it. Nirmond's driving us down to the edge of the bay in a treadcar, and we'll take a raft from there.'

Leaving his newly bagged specimens to revive by themselves and flutter off again, Cord hurriedly flew the skipboat around the station and rolled it back into its stall.

Three rafts lay moored just offshore in the marshy cove at the edge of which Nirmond had stopped the treadcar. They looked somewhat like exceptionally broad-brimmed, well-worn sugar-loaf hats floating out there, green and leathery. Or like lily pads twenty-five feet across, with the upper section of a big, grey-green pineapple growing from the centre of each. Plant animals of some sort. Sutang was too new to have had its phyla sorted out into anything remotely like an orderly classification. The rafts were a local oddity which had been investigated and could be regarded as harmless and moderately useful. Their usefulness lay in the fact that they were employed as a rather slow means of transportation about the shallow, swampy waters of the Yoger Bay. That was as far as the Team's interest in them went at present.

The Regent stood up from the back seat of the car, where she was sitting next to Cord. There were only four in the party; Grayan was up front with Nirmond.

'Are those our vehicles?' The Regent sounded amused.

Nirmond grinned. 'Don't underestimate them, Dane! They could become an important economic factor in this region in time. But, as a matter of fact, these three are smaller than I like to use.' He was peering about the reedy edges of the cove. 'There's a regular monster parked here usually –'

Grayan turned to Cord. 'Maybe Cord knows where Grandpa is hiding.'

It was well-meant, but Cord had been hoping nobody would ask him about Grandpa. Now they all looked at him.

'Oh, you want Grandpa?' he said, somewhat flustered. 'Well, I left him . . . I mean I saw him a couple of weeks ago about a mile south from here –'

Nirmond grunted and told the Regent, 'The rafts tend to stay wherever they're left, providing it's shallow and muddy. They use a hair-root system to draw chemicals and microscopic nourishment directly from the bottom of the bay. Well – Grayan, would you like to drive us there?'

Cord settled back unhappily as the treadcar lurched into motion. Nirmond suspected he'd used Grandpa for one of his unauthorized tours of the area, and Nirmond was quite right.

'I understand you're an expert with these rafts, Cord,' Dane said from beside him. 'Grayan told me we couldn't find a better steersman, or pilot, or whatever you call it, for our trip today.'

'I can handle them,' Cord said, perspiring. 'They don't give you any trouble!' He didn't feel he'd made a good impression on the Regent so far. Dane was a young, handsome-looking woman with an easy way of talking and laughing, but she wasn't the head of the Sutang Colonial Team for nothing.

'There's one big advantage our beasties have over a skipboat, too,' Nirmond remarked from the front seat. 'You don't have to worry about a snapper trying to climb on board with you!' He went on to describe the stinging ribbon-tentacles the rafts spread around them under the water to discourage creatures that might make a meal off their tender underparts. The snappers and two or three other active and aggressive species of the bay hadn't yet learned it was foolish to attack armed human beings in a boat, but they would skitter hurriedly out of the path of a leisurely perambulating raft.

Cord was happy to be ignored for the moment. The Regent, Nirmond, and Grayan were all Earth people, which was true of most of the members of the Team; and Earth people made him uncomfortable, particularly in groups. Vanadia, his own home world, had barely graduated from the status of Earth colony itself, which might explain the difference.

The treadcar swung around and stopped, and Grayan stood up in the front seat, pointing. 'That's Grandpa, over there!'

Dane also stood up and whistled softly, apparently impressed by Grandpa's fifty-foot spread. Cord looked around in surprise. He was pretty sure this was several hundred yards from the spot where he'd left the big raft two weeks ago; and, as Nirmond said, they didn't usually move about by themselves.

Puzzled, he followed the others down a narrow path to the water, hemmed in by tree-sized reeds. Now and then he got a glimpse of Grandpa's swimming platform, the rim of which just touched the shore. Then the path opened out, and he saw the whole raft lying in sunlit, shallow water; and he stopped short, startled.

Nirmond was about to step up on the platform, ahead of Dane.

'Wait!' Cord shouted. His voice sounded squeaky with alarm. 'Stop!' He came running forward.

'What's the matter, Cord?' Nirmond's voice was quiet and urgent.

'Don't get on that raft – it's changed!' Cord's voice sounded wobbly, even to himself. 'Maybe it's not even Grandpa –'

He saw he was wrong on the last point before he'd finished the sentence. Scattered along the rim of the raft were discoloured spots left by a variety of heat-guns, one of which had been his own. It was the way you goaded the sluggish and mindless things into motion. Cord pointed at the cone-shaped central projection. 'There – his head! He's sprouting!'

Grandpa's head, as befitted his girth, was almost twelve feet high and equally wide. It was armour-plated like the back of a saurian to keep off plant suckers, but two weeks ago it had been an otherwise featureless knob, like those on all other rafts. Now scores of long, kinky, leafless vines had grown out from all surfaces of the cone, like green wires. Some were drawn up like tightly coiled springs, others trailed limply to the platform and over it. The top of the cone was dotted with angry red buds, rather like pimples, which hadn't been there before either. Grandpa looked unhealthy.

'Well,' Nirmond said, 'so it is. Sprouting!' Grayan made a choked sound. Nirmond glanced at Cord as if puzzled. 'Is that all that was bothering you, Cord?'

'Well, sure!' Cord began excitedly. He had caught the significance of the word 'all'; his hackles were still up, and he was shaking. 'None of them ever –'

Then he stopped. He could tell by their faces, that they hadn't got it. Or rather, that they'd got it all right but simply weren't going to let it change their plans. The rafts were classified as harmless, according to the Regulations. Until proved otherwise, they would continue to be regarded as harmless. You didn't waste time quibbling with the Regulations – even if you were the Planetary Regent. You didn't feel you had the time to waste.

He tried again. 'Look – ' he began. What he wanted to tell them was that Grandpa with one unknown factor added wasn't Grandpa any more. He was an unpredictable, oversized life form, to be investigated with cautious thoroughness till you knew what the unknown factor meant. He stared at them helplessly.

Dane turned to Nirmond. 'Perhaps you'd better check,' she said. She didn't add, ' – to reassure the boy!' but that was what she meant.

Cord felt himself flushing. But there was nothing he could say or do now except watch Nirmond walk steadily across the platform. Grandpa shivered slightly a few times, but the rafts always did that when someone first stepped on them. The station manager stopped before one of the kinky sprouts, touched it, and then gave it a tug. He reached up and poked at the lowest of the budlike growths. 'Odd-looking things!' he called back. He gave Cord another glance. 'Well, everything seems harmless enough, Cord. Coming aboard, everyone?'

It was like dreaming a dream in which you yelled and yelled at people and couldn't make them hear you! Cord stepped up stiff-legged on the platform behind Dane and Grayan. He knew exactly what would have happened if he'd hesitated even a moment. One of them would have said in a friendly voice, careful not to let it sound contemptuous: 'You don't have to come along if you don't want to, Cord!'

Grayan had unholstered her heat-gun and was ready to start Grandpa moving out into the channels of the Yoger Bay.

Cord hauled out his own heat-gun and said roughly, 'I was to do that!'

'All right, Cord.' She gave him a brief, impersonal smile and stood aside.

They were so infuriatingly polite!

For a while, Cord almost hoped that something awesome and catastrophic would happen promptly to teach the Team people a lesson. But nothing did. As always, Grandpa shook himself vaguely and experimentally when he felt the heat on one edge of the platform and then decided to withdraw from it, all of which was standard procedure. Under the water, out of sight, were the raft's working sections: short, thick leaf-structures shaped like paddles and designed to work as such, along with the slimy nettlestreamers which kept the vegetarians of the Yoger Bay away, and a jungle of hair roots through which Grandpa sucked nourishment from the mud and the sluggish waters of the bay and with which he also anchored himself.

The paddles started churning, the platform quivered, the hair roots were hauled out of the mud; and Grandpa was on his ponderous way.

Cord switched off the heat, reholstered his gun, and stood up. Once in motion, the rafts tended to keep travelling unhurriedly for quite a while. To stop them, you gave them a touch of heat along their leading edge; and they could be turned in any direction by using the gun lightly on the opposite side of the platform. It was simple enough.

Cord didn't look at the others. He was still burning inside. He watched the reed beds move past and open out, giving him glimpses of the misty, yellow and green and blue expanses of the brackish bay ahead. Behind the mist, to the west, were the Yoger Straits, tricky and ugly water when the tides were running; and beyond the Straits lay the open sea, the great Zlanti Deep, which was another world entirely and one of which he hadn't seen much as yet.

Grayan called from beside Dane, 'What's the best route from here into the farms, Cord?'

'The big channel to the right,' he answered. He added somewhat sullenly, 'We're headed for it!'

Grayan came over to him. 'The Regent doesn't want to see all of it,' she said, lowering her voice. 'The algae and plankton beds first. Then as much of the mutated grains as we can show her in about three hours. Steer for the ones that have been doing best, and you'll keep Nirmond happy!'

She gave him a conspiratorial wink. Cord looked after her uncertainly. You couldn't tell from her behaviour that anything was wrong. Maybe –

He had a flare of hope. It was hard not to like the Team people, even when they were being rock-headed about their Regulations. Anyway, the day wasn't over yet. He might still redeem himself in the Regent's opinion.

Cord had a sudden cheerful, if improbable vision of some bay monster plunging up on the raft with snapping jaws; and of himself alertly blowing out what passed for the monster's brains before anyone else – Nirmond in particular – was even aware of the threat. The bay monsters shunned Grandpa, of course, but there might be ways of tempting one of them.

So far, Cord realized, he'd been letting his feelings control him. It was time to start thinking!

Grandpa first. So he'd sprouted – green vines and red buds, purpose unknown, but with no change observable in his behaviour-patterns otherwise. He was the biggest raft in this end of the bay, though all of them had been growing steadily in the two years since Cord had first seen one. Sutang's seasons changed slowly; its year was somewhat more than five Earth-years long. The first Team members to land here hadn't yet seen a full year pass.

Grandpa then was showing a seasonal change. The other rafts, not quite so far developed, would be reacting similarly a little later. Plant animals – they might be blossoming, preparing to propagate.

'Grayan,' he called, 'how do the rafts get started? When they're small, I mean.'

'Nobody knows yet,' she said. 'We were just talking about it. About half of the coastal marsh-fauna of the continent seems to go through a preliminary larval stage in the sea.' She nodded at the red buds on the raft's cone. 'It *looks* as if Grandpa is going to produce flowers and let the wind or tide take the seeds out through the Straits.'

It made sense. It also knocked out Cord's still half-held hope that the change in Grandpa might turn out to be drastic enough, in some way, to justify his reluctance to get on board. Cord studied Grandpa's armoured head carefully once more – unwilling to give up that hope entirely. There were a series of vertical gummy black slits between the armour plates, which hadn't been in evidence two weeks ago either. It looked as if Grandpa was beginning to come apart at the seams. Which might indicate that the rafts, big as they grew to be, didn't outlive a full seasonal cycle, but came to flower at about this time of Sutang's year, and died. However, it was a safe bet that Grandpa wasn't going to collapse into senile decay before they completed their trip today.

Cord gave up on Grandpa. The other notion returned to him – Perhaps he *could* coax an obliging bay monster into action that would show the Regent he was no sissy!

Because the monsters were there all right.

Kneeling at the edge of the platform and peering down into the wine-coloured, clear water of the deep channel they were moving through, Cord could see a fair selection of them at almost any moment.

Some five or six snappers, for one thing. Like big, flattened crayfish, chocolate-brown mostly, with green and red spots on their carapaced backs. In some areas they were so thick you'd wonder what they found to live on, except that they ate almost anything, down to chewing up the mud in which they squatted. However, they preferred their food in large chunks and alive, which was one reason you didn't go swimming in the bay. They would attack a boat on occasion; but the excited manner in which the ones he saw were scuttling off towards the edges of the channel showed they wanted nothing to do with a big moving raft.

Dotted across the bottom were two-foot round holes which looked vacant at the moment. Normally, Cord knew, there would be a head filling each of those holes. The heads consisted mainly of triple sets of jaws, held open patiently like so many traps to grab at anything that came within range of the long wormlike bodies behind the heads. But Grandpa's passage, waving his stingers like transparent pennants through the water, had scared the worms out of sight, too.

Otherwise, mostly schools of small stuff – and then a flash of wicked scarlet, off to the left behind the raft, darting out from the reeds, turning its needle-nose into their wake.

Cord watched it without moving. He knew that creature, though it was rare in the bay and hadn't been classified. Swift, vicious – alert enough to snap swamp bugs out of the air as they fluttered across the surface. And he'd tantalized one with fishing tackle once into leaping up on a moored raft, where it had flung itself about furiously until he was able to shoot it.

'What fantastic creatures!' Dane's voice just behind him.

'Yellowheads,' said Nirmond. 'They've got a high utility rating. Keep down the bugs.'

Cord stood up casually. It was no time for tricks! The reed bed to their right was thick with Yellowheads, a colony of them. Vaguely froggy things, man sized and better. Of all the creatures he'd discovered in the bay, Cord liked them least. The flabby, sacklike bodies clung with four thin limbs to the upper section of the twenty-foot reeds that lined the channel. They hardly ever moved, but their huge bulging eyes seemed to take in everything that went on about them. Every so often, a downy swamp bug came close enough; and a Yellowhead would open its vertical, enormous, tooth-lined slash of a mouth, extend the whole front of its face like a bellows in a flashing strike; and the bug would be gone. They might be useful, but Cord hated them.

'Ten years from now we should know what the cycle of coastal life is like,' Nirmond said. 'When we set up the Yoger Bay Station there were no Yellowheads here. They came the following year. Still with traces of the oceanic larval form; but the metamorphosis was almost complete. About twelve inches long –'

Dane remarked that the same pattern was duplicated endlessly elsewhere. The Regent was inspecting the Yellowhead colony with field glasses; she put them down now, looked at Cord, and smiled, 'How far to the farms?'

'About twenty minutes.'

'The key', Nirmond said, 'seems to be the Zlanti Basin. It must be almost a soup of life in spring.'

'It is,' nodded Dane, who had been here in Sutang's spring, four Earth-years ago. 'It's beginning to look as if the Basin alone might justify colonization. The question is still' – she gestured towards the Yellowheads – 'how do creatures like that get here?'

They walked off towards the other side of the raft, arguing about ocean currents. Cord might have followed. But something splashed back of them, off to the left and not too far back. He stayed, watching.

After a moment, he saw the big Yellowhead. It had slipped down from its reedy perch, which was what had caused the splash. Almost submerged at the water line, it stared after the raft with huge, pale-green eyes. To Cord, it seemed to look directly at him. In that moment, he knew for the first time why he didn't like Yellowheads. There was something very like intelligence in that look, an alien calculation. In creatures like that, intelligence seemed out of place. What use could they have for it?

A little shiver went over him when it sank completely under the water and he realized it intended to swim after the raft. But it was mostly excitement. He had never seen a Yellowhead come down out of the reeds before. The obliging monster he'd been looking for might be presenting itself in an unexpected way.

Half a minute later, he watched it again, swimming awkwardly far down. It had no immediate intention of boarding, at any rate. Cord saw it come into the area of the raft's trailing stingers. It manoeuvred its way between them, with curiously human swimming motions, and went out of sight under the platform.

He stood up, wondering what it meant. The Yellowhead had appeared to know about the stingers; there had been an air of purpose in every move of its approach. He was tempted to tell the others about it, but there was the moment of triumph he could have if it suddenly came slobbering up over the edge of the platform and he nailed it before their eyes.

It was almost time anyway to turn the raft in towards the farms. If nothing happened before then –

He watched. Almost five minutes, but no sign of the Yellowhead. Still wondering, a little uneasy, he gave Grandpa a calculated needling of heat.

After a moment, he repeated it. Then he drew a deep breath and forgot all about the Yellowhead.

'Nirmond!' he called sharply.

The three of them were standing near the centre of the platform, next to the big armoured cone, looking ahead at the farms. They glanced around.

'What's the matter now, Cord?'

Cord couldn't say it for a moment. He was suddenly, terribly scared again. Something *had* gone wrong!

'The raft won't turn!' he told them.

'Give it a real burn this time!' Nirmond said.

Cord glanced up at him. Nirmond, standing a few steps in front of Dane and Grayan as if he wanted to protect them, had begun to look a little strained, and no wonder. Cord already had pressed the gun to three different points on the platform; but Grandpa appeared to have developed a sudden anaesthesia for heat. They kept moving out steadily towards the centre of the bay.

Now Cord held his breath, switched the heat on full, and let Grandpa have it. A six-inch patch on the platform blistered up instantly, turned brown, then black –

Grandpa stopped dead. Just like that.

'That's right! Keep burn – ' Nirmond didn't finish his order.

A giant shudder. Cord staggered back towards the water. Then the whole edge of the raft came curling up behind him and went down again smacking the bay with a sound like a cannon shot. He flew forward off his feet, hit the platform face down, and flattened himself against it. It swelled up beneath him. Two more enormous slaps and joltings. Then quiet. He looked round for the others.

He lay within twelve feet of the central cone. Some twenty or thirty of the mysterious new vines the cone had sprouted were stretched stiffly towards him now, like so many thin green fingers. They couldn't quite reach him. The nearest tip was still ten inches from his shoes.

But Grandpa had caught the others, all three of them. They were tumbled together at the foot of the cone, wrapped in a stiff network of green vegetable ropes, and they didn't move.

Cord drew his feet up cautiously, prepared for another earthquake reaction. But nothing happened. Then he discovered that Grandpa was back in motion on his previous course. The heat-gun had vanished. Gently, he took out the Vanadian gun.

A voice, thin and pain-filled, spoke to him from one of the three huddled bodies.

'Cord? It didn't get you?' It was the Regent.

'No,' he said, keeping his voice low. He realized suddenly he'd simply assumed they were all dead. Now he felt sick and shaky.

'What are you doing?'

Cord looked at Grandpa's big, armour-plated head with a certain hunger. The cones were hollowed out inside, the station's lab had decided their chief function was to keep enough air trapped under the rafts to float them. But in that central section was also the organ that controlled Grandpa's overall reactions.

He said softly, 'I have a gun and twelve heavy-duty explosive bullets. Two of them will blow that cone apart.'

'No good, Cord!' the pain-racked voice told him: 'If the thing sinks, we'll die anyway. You have anaesthetic charges for that gun of yours?'

He stared at her back. 'Yes.'

'Give Nirmond and the girl a shot each, before you do anything else. Directly into the spine, if you can. But don't come any closer –'

Somehow, Cord couldn't argue with that voice. He stood up carefully. The gun made two soft spitting sounds.

'All right,' he said hoarsely. 'What do I do now?'

Dane was silent a moment. 'I'm sorry, Cord, I can't tell you that. I'll tell you what I can –'

She paused for some seconds again.

'This thing didn't try to kill us, Cord. It could have easily. It's incredibly strong. I saw it break Nirmond's legs. But as soon as we stopped moving, it just held us. They were both unconscious then –

'You've got that to go on. It was trying to pitch you within reach of its vines or tendrils, or whatever they are, too, wasn't it?'

'I think so,' Cord said shakily. That was what had happened, of course; and at any moment Grandpa might try again.

'Now it's feeding us some sort of anaesthetic of its own through those vines. Tiny thorns. A sort of numbness –' Dane's voice trailed off a moment. Then she said clearly, 'Look, Cord – it seems we're food it's storing up! You get that?'

'Yes,' he said.

'Seeding time for the rafts. There are analogues. Live food for its seed probably; not for the raft. One couldn't have counted on that. Cord?'

'Yes, I'm here.'

'I want', said Dane, 'to stay awake as long as I can. But there's really just one other thing – this raft's going somewhere, to some particularly favourable location. And that might be very near shore. You might make it in then; otherwise it's up to you. But keep your head and wait for a chance. No heroics, understand?'

'Sure, I understand,' Cord told her. He realized then that he was talking reassuringly, as if it wasn't the Planetary Regent but someone like Grayan.

'Nirmond's the worst,' Dane said. 'The girl was knocked unconscious at once. If it weren't for my arm – but, if we can get help in five hours or so, everything should be all right. Let me know if anything happens, Cord.'

'I will,' Cord said gently again. Then he sighted his gun carefully at a point between Dane's shoulder-blades, and the anaesthetic chamber made its soft, spitting sound once more. Dane's taut body relaxed slowly, and that was all.

There was no point Cord could see in letting her stay awake; because they weren't going anywhere near shore. The reed beds and the channels were already behind them, and Grandpa hadn't changed direction by the fraction of a degree. He was moving out into the open bay – and he was picking up company!

So far, Cord could count seven big rafts within two miles of them; and on the three that were closest he could make out a sprouting of new green vines. All of them were travelling in a straight direction; and the common point they were all headed for appeared to be the roaring centre of the Yoger Straits, now some three miles away!

Behind the Straits, the cold Zlanti Deep – the rolling fogs, and the open sea! It might be seeding time for the rafts, but it looked as if they weren't going to distribute their seeds in the bay . . .

Cord was a fine swimmer. He had a gun and he had a knife; in spite of what Dane had said, he might have stood a chance among the killers of the bay. But it would be a very small chance, at best. And it wasn't, he thought, as if there weren't still other possibilities. He was going to keep his head.

Except by accident, of course, nobody was going to come looking for them in time to do any good. If anyone did look, it would be around the Bay Farms. There were a number of rafts moored there; and it would be assumed they'd used one of them. Now and then something unexpected happened and somebody simply vanished; by the time it was figured out just what had happened on this occasion, it would be much too late.

Neither was anybody likely to notice within the next few hours that the rafts had started migrating out of the swamps through the Yoger Straits. There was a small weather station a little inland, on the north side of the Straits, which used a helicopter occasionally. It was about as improbable, Cord decided dismally, that they'd use it in the right spot just now as it would be for a jet transport to happen to come in low enough to spot them.

The fact that it was up to him, as the Regent had said, sank in a little more after that!

Simply because he was going to try it sooner or later, he carried out an experiment next that he knew couldn't work. He opened the gun's anaesthetic chamber and counted out fifty pellets – rather hurriedly because he didn't particularly want to think of what he might be using them for eventually. There were around three hundred charges left in the chamber then; and in the next few minutes Cord carefully planted a third of them in Grandpa's head.

He stopped after that. A whale might have showed signs of somnolence under a lesser load. Grandpa paddled on undisturbed. Perhaps he had become a little numb in spots, but his cells weren't equipped to distribute the soporific effect of that type of drug.

There wasn't anything else Cord could think of doing before they reached the Straits. At the rate they were moving, he calculated that would happen in something less than an hour; and if they did pass through the Straits, he was going to risk a swim. He didn't think Dane would have disapproved, under the circumstances. If the raft simply carried them all out into the foggy vastness of the Zlanti Deep, there would be no practical chance of survival left at all.

Meanwhile, Grandpa was definitely picking up speed. And there were other changes going on – minor ones, but still a little awe-inspiring to Cord. The pimply-looking red buds that dotted the upper part of the cone were opening out gradually. From the centre of most of them protruded something like a thin, wet, scarlet worm: a worm that twisted weakly, extended itself by an inch or so, rested, and twisted again, and stretched up a little farther, groping into the air. The vertical black slits between the armour plates looked deeper and wider than they had been even some minutes ago; a dark, thick liquid dripped slowly from several of them.

In other circumstances Cord knew he would have been fascinated by these developments in Grandpa. As it was, they drew his suspicious attention only because he didn't know what they meant.

Then something quite horrible happened suddenly. Grayan started moaning loudly and terribly and twisted almost completely around. Afterwards, Cord knew it hadn't been a second before he stopped her struggles and the sounds together with another anaesthetic pellet; but the vines had tightened their grip on her first, not flexibly but like the digging, bony, green talons of some monstrous bird of prey.

White and sweating, Cord put his gun down slowly while the vines relaxed again. Grayan didn't seem to have suffered any additional harm; and she would certainly have been the first to point out that his murderous rage might have been as intelligently directed against a machine. But for some moments Cord continued to luxuriate furiously in the thought that, at any instant he chose, he could still turn the raft very quickly into a ripped and exploded mess of sinking vegetation.

Instead, and more sensibly, he gave both Dane and Nirmond another shot, to prevent a similar occurrence with them. The contents of two such pellets, he knew, would keep any human being torpid for at least four hours.

Cord withdrew his mind hastily from the direction it was turning into; but it wouldn't stay withdrawn. The thought kept coming up again, until at last he had to recognize it.

Five shots would leave the three of them completely unconscious whatever else might happen to them, until they either died from other causes or were given a counteracting agent.

Shocked, he told himself he couldn't do it. It was exactly like killing them.

But then, quite steadily, he found himself raising the gun once more, to bring the total charge for each of the three Team people up to five.

*

Barely thirty minutes later, he watched a raft as big as the one he rode go sliding into the foaming white waters of the Straits a few hundred yards ahead, and dart off abruptly at an angle, caught by one of the swirling currents. It pitched and spun, made some headway, and was swept aside again. And then it righted itself once more. Not like some blindly animated vegetable, Cord thought, but like a creature that struggled with intelligent purpose to maintain its chosen direction.

At least, they seemed practically unsinkable . . .

Knife in hand, he flattened himself against the platform as the Straits roared just ahead. When the platform jolted and tilted up beneath him, he rammed the knife all the way into it and hung on. Cold water rushed suddenly over him, and Grandpa shuddered like a labouring engine. In the middle of it all, Cord had the horrified notion that the raft might release its unconscious human prisoners in its struggle with the Straits. But he underestimated Grandpa in that. Grandpa also hung on.

Abruptly, it was over. They were riding a long swell, and there were three other rafts not far away. The Straits had swept them together, but they seemed to have no interest in one another's company. As Cord stood up shakily and began to strip off his clothes, they were visibly drawing apart again. The platform of one of them was half-submerged; it must have lost too much of the air that held it afloat and, like a small ship, it was foundering.

From this point, it was only a two-mile swim to the shore north of the Straits, and another mile inland from there to the Straits Head Station. He didn't know about the current; but the distance didn't seem too much, and he couldn't bring himself to leave knife and gun behind. The bay creatures loved warmth and mud, they didn't venture beyond the Straits. But Zlanti Deep bred its own killers, though they weren't often observed so close to shore.

Things were beginning to look rather hopeful.

Thin, crying voices drifted overhead, like the voices of curious cats, as Cord knotted his clothes into a tight bundle, shoes inside. He looked up. There were four of them circling there; magnified sea-going swamp bugs, each carrying an unseen rider. Probably harmless scavengers – but the ten-foot wingspread was impressive. Uneasily, Cord remembered the venomously carnivorous rider he'd left lying beside the station.

One of them dipped lazily and came sliding down towards him. It soared overhead and came back, to hover about the raft's cone.

The bug rider that directed the mindless flier hadn't been interested in him at all! Grandpa was baiting it!

Cord stared in fascination. The top of the cone was alive now with a softly wriggling mass of the scarlet, wormlike extrusions that had started sprouting before the raft left the bay. Presumably, they looked enticingly edible to the bug rider.

The flier settled with an airy fluttering and touched the cone. Like a trap springing shut, the green vines flashed up and around it, crumpling the brittle wings, almost vanishing into the long, soft body!

Barely a second later, Grandpa made another catch, this one from the sea itself. Cord had a fleeting glimpse of something like a small, rubbery seal that flung itself out of the water upon the edge of the raft, with a suggestion of desperate haste – and was flipped on instantly against the cone where the vines clamped it down beside the flier's body.

It wasn't the enormous ease with which the unexpected kill was accomplished that left Cord standing there, completely shocked. It was the shattering of his hopes to swim ashore from here. Fifty yards away, the creature from which the rubbery thing had been fleeing showed briefly on the surface, as it turned away from the raft; and that glance was all he needed. The ivory-white body and gaping jaws were similar enough to those of the sharks of Earth to indicate the pursuer's nature. The important difference was that wherever the White Hunters of the Zlanti Deep went, they went by the thousands.

Stunned by that incredible piece of bad luck, still clutching his bundled clothes, Cord stared towards shore. Knowing what to look for, he could spot the tell-tale rollings of the surface now – the long, ivory gleams that flashed through the swells and vanished again. Shoals of smaller things burst into the air in sprays of glittering desperation, and fell back.

He would have been snapped up like a drowning fly before he'd covered a twentieth of that distance!

Grandpa was beginning to eat.

Each of the dark slits down the sides of the cone was a mouth. So far only one of them was in operating condition, and the raft wasn't able to open that one very wide as yet. The first morsel had been fed into it, however: the bug rider the vines had plucked out of the flier's downy neck fur. It took Grandpa several minutes to work it out of sight, small as it was. But it was a start.

Cord didn't feel quite sane any more. He sat there, clutching his bundle of clothes and only vaguely aware of the fact that he was shivering steadily under the cold spray that touched him now and then, while he followed Grandpa's activities attentively. He decided it would be at least some hours before one of that black set of mouths grew flexible and vigorous enough to dispose of a human being. Under the circumstances, it couldn't make much difference to the other human beings here; but the moment Grandpa reached for the first of them would also be the moment he finally blew the raft to pieces. The White Hunters were cleaner eaters, at any rate; and that was about the extent to which he could still control what was going to happen.

Meanwhile, there was the very faint chance that the weather station's helicopter might spot them.

Meanwhile also, in a weary and horrified fascination, he kept debating the mystery of what could have produced such a nightmarish change in the rafts. He could guess where they were going by now; there were scattered strings of them stretching back to the Straits or roughly parallel to their own course, and the direction was that of the plankton-swarming pool of the Zlanti Basin, a thousand miles to the north. Given time, even mobile lily pads like the rafts had been could make that trip for the benefit of their seedlings. But nothing in their structure explained the sudden change into alert and capable carnivores.

He watched the rubbery little seal-thing being hauled up to a mouth. The vines broke its neck; and the mouth took it in up to the shoulders and then went on working patiently at what was still a trifle too large a bite. Meanwhile, there were more thin cat-cries overhead; and a few minutes later, two more sea-bugs were trapped almost simultaneously and added to the larder. Grandpa dropped the dead sea-thing and fed himself another bug rider. The second rider left its mount with a sudden hop, sank its teeth viciously into one of the vines that caught it again, and was promptly battered to death against the platform.

Cord felt a resurge of unreasoning hatred against Grandpa. Killing a bug was about equal to cutting a branch from a tree; they had almost no life-awareness. But the rider had aroused his partisanship because of its appearance of intelligent action – and it was in fact closer to the human scale in that feature than to the monstrous life form that had, mechanically, but quite successfully, trapped both it and the human beings. Then his thoughts drifted again; and he found himself speculating vaguely on the curious symbiosis in which the nerve systems of two creatures as dissimilar as the bugs and their riders could be linked so closely that they functioned as one organism.

Suddenly an expression of vast and stunned surprise appeared on his face.

Why – now he *knew*!

Cord stood up hurriedly, shaking with excitement, the whole plan complete in his mind. And a dozen long vines snaked instantly in the direction of his sudden motion and groped for him, taut and stretching. They couldn't reach him, but their savagely alert reaction froze Cord briefly where he was. The platform was shuddering under his feet, as if in irritation at his inaccessibility; but it couldn't be tilted up suddenly here to throw him within the grasp of the vines, as it could around the edges.

Still, it was a warning! Cord sidled gingerly around the cone till he had gained the position he wanted, which was on the forward half of the raft. And then he waited. Waited long minutes, quite motionless, until his heart stopped pounding and the irregular angry shivering of the surface of the raft-thing died away, and the last vine tendril had stopped its blind groping. It might help a lot if, for a second or two after he next started moving, Grandpa wasn't too aware of his exact whereabouts!

He looked back once to check how far they had gone by now beyond the Straits Head Station. It couldn't, he decided, be even an hour behind them. Which was close enough, by the most pessimistic count – if everything else worked out all right! He didn't try to think out in detail what that 'everything else' could include, because there were factors that simply couldn't be calculated in advance. And he had an uneasy feeling that speculating too vividly about them might make him almost incapable of carrying out his plan.

At last, moving carefully, Cord took the knife in his left hand but left the gun holstered. He raised the tightly knotted bundle of clothes slowly over his head, balanced in his right hand. With a long, smooth motion he tossed the bundle back across the cone, almost to the opposite edge of the platform.

It hit with a soggy thump. Almost immediately, the whole far edge of the raft buckled and flapped up to toss the strange object to the reaching vines.

Simultaneously, Cord was racing forward. For a moment, his attempt to divert Grandpa's attention seemed completely successful – then he was pitched to his knees as the platform came up.

He was within eight feet of the edge. As it slapped down again, he drew himself desperately forward.

An instant later, he was knifing down through cold, clear water, just ahead of the raft, then twisting and coming up again.

The raft was passing over him. Clouds of tiny sea creatures scattered through its dark jungle of feeding roots. Cord jerked back from a broad, wavering streak of glassy greenness, which was a stinger, and felt a burning jolt on his side, which meant he'd been touched lightly by another. He bumped on blindly through the slimy black tangles of hair roots that covered the bottom of the raft; then green half-light passed over him, and he burst up into the central bubble under the cone.

Half-light and foul, hot air. Water slapped around him, dragging him away again – nothing to hang on to here! Then above him, to his right, moulded against the interior curve of the cone as if it had grown there from the start, the froglike, man-sized shape of the Yellowhead.

The raft rider!

Cord reached up, caught Grandpa's symbiotic partner and guide by a flabby hind-leg, pulled himself half out of the water and struck twice with the knife, fast, while the pale-green eyes were still opening.

He'd thought the Yellowhead might need a second or so to detach itself from its host, as the bug riders usually did, before it tried to defend itself. This one merely turned its head; the mouth slashed down and clamped on Cord's left arm above the elbow. His right hand sank the knife through one staring eye, and the Yellowhead jerked away, pulling the knife from his grasp.

Sliding down, he wrapped both hands around the slimy leg and hauled with all his weight. For a moment more, the Yellowhead hung on. Then the countless neural extensions that connected it now with the raft came free in a succession of sucking, tearing sounds; and Cord and the Yellowhead splashed into the water together.

Black tangle of roots again – and two more electric burns suddenly across his back and legs! Strangling, Cord let go. Below him, for a moment, a body was turning over and over with oddly human motions; then a solid wall of water thrust him up and aside, as something big and white struck the turning body and went on.

Cord broke the surface twelve feet behind the raft. And that would have been that, if Grandpa hadn't already been slowing down.

After two tries, he floundered back up on the platform and lay there gasping and coughing awhile. There were no indications that his presence was resented now. A few lax vine-tips twitched uneasily, as if trying to remember previous functions, when he came limping up presently to make sure his three companions were still breathing; but Cord never noticed that.

They were still breathing; and he knew better than to waste time trying to help them himself. He took Grayan's heat-gun from its holster. Grandpa had come to a full stop.

Cord hadn't had time to become completely sane again, or he might have worried now whether Grandpa, violently sundered from his controlling partner, was still capable of motion on his own. Instead, he determined the approximate direction of the Straits Head Station, selected a corresponding spot on the platform and gave Grandpa a light tap of heat.

Nothing happened immediately. Cord sighed patiently and stepped up the heat a little.

Grandpa shuddered gently. Cord stood up.

Slowly and hesitatingly at first, then with steadfast – though now again brainless – purpose, Grandpa began paddling back towards the Straits Head Station.

Nightfall

ISAAC ASIMOV

If the stars should appear one night in a thousand years, how would men believe and adore, and preserve for many generations the remembrance of the city of God! – EMERSON

Aton 77, director of Saro University, thrust out a belligerent lower lip and glared at the young newspaperman in fury.

Theremon 762 took that fury in his stride. In his earlier days, when his now widely syndicated column was only a mad idea in a cub reporter's mind, he had specialized in 'impossible' interviews. It had cost him bruises, black eyes, and broken bones; but it had given him an ample supply of coolness and self-confidence.

Aton 77 found his voice, and though it trembled with restrained emotion, the careful, somewhat pedantic, phraseology, for which the famous astronomer was noted, did not abandon him.

'Sir,' he said, 'you display an infernal gall in coming to me with that impudent proposition of yours.'

The husky telephotographer of the Observatory, Beenay 25, thrust a tongue's tip across dry lips and interposed nervously, 'Now, sir, after all –'

The director turned to him and lifted a white eyebrow. 'Do not interfere, Beenay. I credit you with good intentions in bringing this man here; but I will tolerate no insubordination now.'

Theremon decided it was time to take a part. 'Director Aton, if you'll let me finish what I started saying I think –'

'I don't believe, young man,' retorted Aton, 'that anything you could say now would count much as compared with your daily columns of these last two months. You have led a vast newspaper campaign against the efforts of myself and my colleagues to organize the world against the menace which it is now too late to avert. You may leave,' he snapped over his shoulder. He stared moodily out at the skyline where Gamma, the brightest of the planet's six suns, was setting. It had already faded and yellowed into the horizon's mists, and Aton knew he would never see it again as a sane man.

He whirled. 'No, wait, come here!' He gestured peremptorily. 'I'll give you your story.'

The newsman had made no motion to leave, and now he approached the old man slowly. Aton gestured outward. 'Of the six suns, only Beta is left in the sky. Do you see it?'

The question was rather unnecessary. Beta was almost at zenith; its ruddy light flooding the landscape to an unusual orange as the brilliant rays of setting Gamma died. Beta was at aphelion. It was small; smaller than Theremon had ever seen it before, and for the moment it was undisputed ruler of Lagash's sky.

Lagash's own sun, Alpha, the one about which it revolved, was at the antipodes; as were the two distant companion pairs. The red dwarf Beta – Alpha's immediate companion – was alone, grimly alone.

Aton's upturned face flushed redly in the sunlight. 'In just under four hours,' he said, 'civilization, as we know it, comes to an end. It will do so because, as you see, Beta is the only sun in the sky.' He smiled grimly. 'Print that! There'll be no one to read it.'

'But if it turns out that four hours pass – and another four – and nothing happens?' asked Theremon softly.

'Don't let that worry you. Enough will happen.'

'Granted! And *still* – if nothing happens?'

For a second time, Beenay 25 spoke, 'Sir, I think you ought to listen to him.'

Theremon said, 'Put it to a vote, Director Aton.'

There was a stir among the remaining five members of the Observatory staff, who until now had maintained an attitude of wary neutrality.

'That,' stated Aton flatly, 'is not necessary.' He drew out his pocket watch. 'Since your good friend, Beenay, insists so urgently, I will give you five minutes. Talk away.'

*

'Good! Now, just what difference would it make if you allowed me to take down an eyewitness account of what's to come? If your prediction comes true, my presence won't hurt; for in that case my column would never be written. On the other hand, if nothing comes of it, you will just have to expect ridicule or worse. It would be wise to leave that ridicule to friendly hands.'

Aton snorted. 'Do you mean yours when you speak of friendly hands?'

'Certainly!' Theremon sat down and crossed his legs. 'My columns may have been a little rough at times, but I gave you people the benefit of the doubt every time. After all, this is not the century to preach "the end of the world is at hand" to Lagash. You have to understand that people don't believe the "Book of Revelation" any more, and it annoys them to have scientists turn about face and tell us the Cultists are right after all –'

'No such thing, young man,' interrupted Aton. 'While a great deal of our data has been supplied us by the Cult, our results contain none of the Cult's mysticism. Facts are facts, and the Cult's so-called "mythology" *has* certain facts behind it. We've exposed them and ripped away their mystery. I assure you that the Cult hates us now worse than you do.'

'I don't hate you. I'm just trying to tell you that the public is in an ugly humour. They're angry.'

Aton twisted his mouth in derision. 'Let them be angry.'

'Yes, but what about tomorrow?'

'There'll be no tomorrow!'

'But if there is. Say that there is – just to see what happens. That anger might take shape into something serious. The sparks will fly, sir.'

The director regarded the columnist sternly. 'And just what were you proposing to do to help the situation?'

'Well,' grinned Theremon, 'I was proposing to take charge of the publicity. I can handle things so that only the ridiculous side will show. It would be hard to stand, I admit, because I'd have to make you all out to be a bunch of idiots, but if I can get people laughing at you, they might forget to be angry. In return for that, all my publisher asks is an exclusive story.'

Beenay nodded and burst out. 'Sir, the rest of us think he's right. These last two months we've considered everything but the million-to-one chance that there is an error somewhere in our theory or in our calculations. We ought to take care of that, too.'

There was a murmur of agreement from the men grouped about the table, and Aton's expression became that of one who found his mouth full of something bitter and couldn't get rid of it.

'You may stay if you wish, then. You will kindly refrain, however, from hampering us in our duties in any way.'

His hands were behind his back, and his wrinkled face thrust forward determinedly as he spoke. He might have continued indefinitely but for the intrusion of a new voice.

'Hello, hello, hello!' It came in a high tenor, and the plump cheeks of the newcomer expanded in a pleased smile. 'What's this morgue-like atmosphere about here? No one's losing his nerve, I hope.'

Aton started in consternation and said peevishly, 'Now what the devil are you doing here, Sheerin? I thought you were going to stay behind in the Hideout.'

Sheerin laughed and dropped his tubby figure into a chair. 'I wanted to be here, where things are getting hot. Don't you suppose I have my share of curiosity? I want to see these Stars the Cultists are forever speaking about. A psychologist isn't worth his salt in the Hideout. They need men of action and strong, healthy women that can breed children. Me? I'm a hundred pounds too heavy for a man of action, and I wouldn't be a success at breeding children. So why bother them with an extra mouth to feed? I feel better over here.'

Theremon spoke briskly, 'Just what is the Hideout, sir?'

Sheerin seemed to see the columnist for the first time. He frowned and blew his ample cheeks out, 'And just who in Lagash are you, redhead?'

Aton compressed his lips and then muttered sullenly, 'That's Theremon 762, the newspaper fellow. I suppose you've heard of him.'

The columnist offered his hand. 'And, of course, you're Sheerin 501 of Saro University. I've heard of *you*.' Then he repeated, 'What is this Hideout, sir?'

'Well,' said Sheerin, 'we have managed to convince a few people of the validity of our prophecy of – er – doom, to be spectacular about it, and those few have taken proper measures. They consist mainly of the immediate members of the families of the Observatory staff, certain of the faculty of Saro University and a few outsiders. Altogether, they number about three hundred, but three-quarters are women and children.'

'I see! They're supposed to hide where the Darkness and the – er – Stars can't get at them, and then hold out when the rest of the world goes poof.'

'If they can. It won't be easy. With all of mankind insane; with the great cities going up in flames – environment will not be conducive to survival. But they have food, water, shelter, and weapons –'

'They've got more,' said Aton. 'They've got all our records, except for what we will collect today. Those records will mean everything to the next cycle, and *that's* what must survive. The rest can go hang.'

Theremon whistled a long, low whistle and sat brooding for several minutes. The men about the table had brought out a multichess board and started a six-member game. Moves were made rapidly and in silence. All eyes bent in furious concentration on the board. Theremon watched them intently and then rose and approached Aton, who sat apart in whispered conversation with Sheerin.

'Listen,' he said. 'Let's go somewhere where we won't bother the rest of the fellows. I want to ask some questions.'

There *were* softer chairs in the next room. There were also thick red curtains on the windows and a maroon carpet on the floor. With the bricky light of Beta pouring in, the general effect was one of dried blood.

Theremon shuddered. 'Say, I'd give ten credits for a decent dose of white light for just a second. I wish Gamma or Delta were in the sky.'

'What are your questions?' asked Aton. 'Please remember that our time is limited. In a little over an hour and a quarter we're going upstairs, and after that there will be no time for talk.'

'Well, here it is.' Theremon leaned back and folded his hands on his chest. 'You say that there is going to be a world-wide Darkness in a few hours and that all mankind will go violently insane. What I want now is the science behind it.'

'No, you don't. No, you don't,' broke in Sheerin. 'If you ask Aton for that – supposing him to be in the mood to answer at all – he'll trot out pages of figures and volumes of graphs. You won't make head or tail of it. Now if you were to ask *me*, I could give you the layman's standpoint.'

'All right; I ask you.'

'Then first I'd like a drink.' He rubbed his hands and looked at Aton.

'Water?' grunted Aton.

'Don't be silly!'

'Don't you be silly. No alcohol today. It would be too easy to get my men drunk. I can't afford to tempt them.'

The psychologist grumbled wordlessly. He turned to Theremon, impaled him with his sharp eyes, and began.

'You realize of course, that the history of civilization on Lagash displays a cyclic character – but I mean, *cyclic!*'

'I know,' replied Theremon cautiously, 'that that is the current archaeological theory. Has it been accepted as a fact?'

'Just about. In this last century it's been generally agreed upon. This cyclic character is – or, rather, was – one of *the* great mysteries. We've located series of civilizations, nine of them definitely, and indications of others as well, all of which have reached heights comparable to our own, and all of which, without exception, were destroyed by fire at the very height of their culture.

'And no one could tell why. All centres of culture were thoroughly gutted by fire, with nothing left behind to give a hint as to the cause.'

Theremon was following closely. 'Wasn't there a Stone Age, too?'

'Probably, but as yet, practically nothing is known of it, except that men of that age were little more than rather intelligent apes. We can forget about that.'

'I see. Go on!'

'There have been explanations of these recurrent catastrophes, all of a more or less fantastic nature. Some say that there are periodic rains of fire; some that Lagash passes through a sun every so often; some even wilder things. But there is one theory, quite different from all of these, that has been handed down over a period of centuries.'

'I know. You mean this myth of the "Stars" that the Cultists have in their "Book of Revelation".'

'Exactly,' rejoined Sheerin with satisfaction. 'The Cultists said that every two thousand and fifty years Lagash entered a huge cave, so that all the suns disappeared, and there came *total darkness all over the world!* And then, they say, things called Stars appeared, which robbed men of their souls and left them unreasoning brutes, so that they destroyed the civilization they themselves had built up. Of course, they mix all this up with a lot of religio-mystic notions, but that's the central idea.'

There was a short pause in which Sheerin drew a long breath. 'And now we come to the Theory of Universal Gravitation.' He pronounced the phrase so that the capital letters sounded – and at that point Aton turned from the window, snorted loudly, and stalked out of the room.

The two stared after him, and Theremon said, 'What's wrong?'

'Nothing in particular,' replied Sheerin. 'Two of the men were due several hours ago and haven't shown up yet. He's terrifically shorthanded, of course, because all but the really essential men have gone to the Hideout.'

'You don't think the two deserted, do you?'

'Who? Faro and Yimot? Of course not. Still, if they're not back within the hour, things would be a little sticky.' He got to his feet suddenly, and his eyes twinkled. 'Anyway, as long as Aton is gone –'

Tiptoeing to the nearest window, he squatted, and from the low window box beneath withdrew a bottle of red liquid that gurgled suggestively when he shook it.

'I *thought* Aton didn't know about this,' he remarked as he trotted back to the table. 'Here! We've only got one glass so, as the guest, you can have it. I'll keep the bottle.' And he filled the tiny cup with judicious care.

The psychologist's Adam's apple wobbled as the bottle upended, and then, with a satisfied grunt and a smack of the lips, he began again.

'But what do you know about gravitation?'

'Nothing, except that it is a very recent development, not too well established, and that the math is so hard that only twelve men in Lagash are supposed to understand it.'

'*Tcha!* Nonsense! Boloney! I can give you all the essential math in a sentence. The Law of Universal Gravitation states that there exists a cohesive force among all bodies of the universe, such that the amount of this force between any two given bodies is proportional to the product of their masses divided by the square of the distance between them.'

'Is that all?'

'That's enough! It took four hundred years to develop it.'

'Why that long? It sounded simple enough, the way you said it.'

'Because great laws are not divined by flashes of inspiration, whatever you may think. It usually takes the combined work of a world full of scientists over a period of centuries. After Genovi 41 discovered that Lagash rotated about the sun Alpha, rather than vice versa – and that was four hundred years ago – astronomers have been working. The complex motions of the six suns were recorded and analysed and unwoven. Theory after theory was advanced and checked and counter-checked and modified and abandoned and revived and converted to something else. It was a devil of a job.'

Theremon nodded thoughtfully and held out his glass for more liquor. Sheerin grudgingly allowed a few ruby drops to leave the bottle.

'It was twenty years ago,' he continued after remoistening his own throat, 'that it was finally demonstrated that the Law of Universal Gravitation accounted exactly for the orbital motions of the six suns. It was a great triumph.'

Sheerin stood up and walked to the window, still clutching his bottle. 'And now we're getting to the point. In the last decade, the motions of Lagash about Alpha were computed according to gravity, and *it did not account for the orbit observed*; not even when all perturbations due to the other suns were included. Either the law was invalid, or there was another, as yet unknown, factor involved.'

Theremon joined Sheerin at the window and gazed out past the wooded slopes to where the spires of Saro City gleamed bloodily on the horizon. The newsman felt the tension of uncertainty grow within him as he cast a short glance at Beta. It glowered redly at zenith, dwarfed and evil.

'Go ahead, sir,' he said softly.

Sheerin replied, 'Astronomers stumbled about for years, each proposed theory more untenable than the one before – until Aton had the inspiration of calling in the Cult. The head of the Cult, Sor 5, had access to certain data that simplified the problem considerably. Aton set to work on a new track.

'What if there were another non-luminous planetary body such as Lagash? If there were, you know, it would shine only by reflected light, and if it were composed of bluish rock, as Lagash itself largely is, then, in the redness of the sky, the eternal blaze of the suns would make it invisible – drown it out completely.'

Theremon whistled, 'What a screwy idea!'

'You think *that's* screwy? Listen to this: Suppose this body rotated about Lagash at such a distance and in such an orbit and had such a mass that its attraction would exactly account for the deviations of Lagash's orbit from theory – do you know what would happen?'

The columnist shook his head.

'Well, sometimes this body would get in the way of the sun.' And Sheerin emptied what remained in the bottle at a draught.

'And it does, I suppose,' said Theremon flatly.

'Yes! But only one sun lies in its plane of revolutions.' He jerked a thumb at the shrunken sun above. 'Beta! And it has been shown that the eclipse will occur only when the arrangement of the suns is such that Beta is alone in its hemisphere and at maximum distance, at which time the moon is invariably at minimum distance. The eclipse that results with the moon seven times the apparent diameter of Beta, covers all of Lagash and lasts well over half a day, so that no spot on the planet escapes the effects. *That eclipse comes once every two thousand and forty-nine years.*'

Theremon's face was drawn into an expressionless mask. 'And that's my story?'

The psychologist nodded. 'That's all of it. First the eclipse – which will start in three-quarters of an hour – then universal Darkness, and, maybe, these mysterious Stars – then madness, and the end of the cycle.'

He brooded. 'We had two months' leeway – we at the Observatory – and that wasn't enough time to persuade Lagash of the danger. Two centuries might not have been enough. But our records are at the Hideout, and today we photograph the eclipse. The next cycle will *start off* with the truth, and when the *next* eclipse comes, mankind will at last be ready for it. Come to think of it, that's part of your story, too.'

A thin wind ruffled the curtains at the window as Theremon opened it and leaned out. It played coldly with his hair as he stared at the crimson sunlight on his hand. Then he turned in sudden rebellion.

'What is there in Darkness to drive *me* mad?'

Sheerin smiled to himself as he spun the empty liquor bottle with abstracted motions of his hand. 'Have you ever experienced Darkness, young man?'

The newsman leaned against the wall and considered. 'No. Can't say I have. But I know what it is. Just – uh –' He made vague motions with his fingers, and then brightened. 'Just no light. Like in caves.'

'Have you ever been in a cave?'

'In a *cave*! Of course not!'

The psychologist studied the young man with a frown.

'I dare you to draw the curtain.'

Theremon looked his surprise and said, 'What for? If we had four or five suns out there we might want to cut the light down a bit for comfort, but now we haven't enough light as it is.'

'That's the point. Just draw the curtain; then come here and sit down.'

'All right.' Theremon reached for the tasselled string and jerked. The red curtain slid across the wide window, the brass rings hissing their way along the crossbar, and a dusk-red shadow clamped down on the room.

Theremon's footsteps sounded hollowly in the silence as he made his way to the table, and then he stopped half-way. 'I can't see you, sir,' he whispered.

'Feel your way,' ordered Sheerin in a strained voice.

'But I can't see you, sir,' the newsman was breathing harshly. 'I can't see anything.'

'What did you expect?' came the grim reply. 'Come here and sit down!'

The footsteps sounded again, waveringly, approaching slowly. There was the sound of someone fumbling with a chair. Theremon's voice came thinly, 'Here I am. I feel . . . *ulp* . . . all right.'

'You like it, do you?'

'N-no. It's pretty awful. The walls seem to be –' He paused. 'They seem to be closing in on me. I keep wanting to push them away. But I'm not going *mad*! In fact, the feeling isn't as bad as it was.'

'All right. Draw the curtains back again.'

There were cautious footsteps through the dark, the rustle of Theremon's body against the curtain as he felt for the tassel, and then the triumphant *ro-o-o-osh* of the curtain slithering back. Red light flooded the room, and with a cry of joy Theremon looked up at the sun.

Sheerin wiped the moisture off his forehead with the back of a hand and said shakily, 'And that was just a dark room.'

'It can be stood,' said Theremon lightly.

'Yes, a dark room can. But were you at the Jonglor Centennial Exposition two years ago?'

'No, it so happens I never got around to it. Six thousand miles was just a bit too much to travel, even for the exposition.'

'Well, I was there. You remember hearing about the "Tunnel of Mystery" that broke all records in the amusement area – for the first month or so, anyway?'

'Yes. Wasn't there some fuss about it?'

'Very little. It was hushed up. You see, that Tunnel of Mystery was just a mile-long tunnel – with no lights. You got into a little open car and jolted along through Darkness for fifteen minutes. It was very popular – while it lasted.'

'Popular?'

'Certainly. There's a fascination in being frightened *when it's part of a game*. A baby is born with three instinctive fears: of loud noises, of falling, and of the absence of light. That's why it's considered so funny to jump at someone and shout "Boo!" That's why it's such fun to ride a roller coaster. And that's why that Tunnel of Mystery started cleaning up. People came out of that Darkness shaking, breathless, half dead with fear, but they kept on paying to get in.'

'Wait a while, I remember now. Some people came out dead, didn't they? There were rumours of that after it shut down.'

The psychologist snorted. 'Bah! Two or three died. That was nothing! They paid off the families of the dead ones and argued the Jonglor City Council into forgetting it. After all, they said, if people with weak hearts want to go through the tunnel, it was at their own risk – and besides, it wouldn't happen again. So they put a doctor in the front office and had every customer go through a physical examination before getting into the car. That actually *boosted* ticket sales.'

'Well, then?'

'But, you see, there was something else. People sometimes came out in perfect order, except that they refused to go into buildings – any buildings; including palaces, mansions, apartment houses, tenements, cottages, huts, shacks, lean-tos, and tents.'

Theremon looked shocked. 'You mean they refused to come in out of the open. Where'd they sleep?'

'In the open.'

'They should have *forced* them inside.'

'Oh, they did, they did. Whereupon these people went into violent hysterics and did their best to beat their brains out against the nearest wall. Once you got them inside, you couldn't keep them there without a strait jacket and a shot of morphine.'

'They must have been crazy.'

'Which is exactly what they were. One person out of every ten who went into that tunnel came out that way. They called in the psychologists, and we did the only thing possible. We closed down the exhibit.' He spread his hands.

'What was the matter with these people?' asked Theremon finally.

'Those people were unfortunates whose mentality did not quite possess the resilience to overcome the claustrophobia that overtook them in the Darkness. Fifteen minutes without light is a long time; you had only two or three minutes, and I believe you were fairly upset.

'The people of the tunnel had what is called a "claustrophobic fixation". Their latent fear of Darkness and enclosed places had crystallized and become active, and, as far as we can tell, permanent. *That's* what fifteen minutes in the dark will do.'

There was a long silence, and Theremon's forehead wrinkled slowly into a frown. 'I don't believe it's that bad.'

'You mean you don't want to believe,' snapped Sheerin. 'You're afraid to believe. Look out the window!'

Theremon did so, and the psychologist continued without pausing, 'Imagine Darkness – everywhere. No light, as far as you can see. The houses, the trees, the fields, the earth, the sky – *black*! And Stars thrown in, for all I know – whatever *they* are. Can you conceive it?'

'Yes, I can,' declared Theremon truculently.

And Sheerin slammed his fist down upon the table in sudden passion. 'You lie! You can't conceive that. Your brain wasn't built for the conception any more than it was built for the conception of infinity or of eternity. You can only talk about it. A fraction of the reality upsets you, and when the real thing comes, your brain is going to be presented with a phenomenon outside its limits of comprehension. You will go mad, completely and permanently! There is no question of it!'

He added sadly, 'And another couple of millenniums of painful struggle comes to nothing. Tomorrow there won't be a city standing unharmed in all Lagash.'

Theremon recovered part of his mental equilibrium. 'That doesn't follow. I still don't see that I can go loony just because there isn't a Sun in the sky – but even if I did, and everyone else did, how does that harm the cities? Are we going to blow them down?'

But Sheerin was angry, too. 'If you were in Darkness, what would you want more than anything else; what would it be that every instinct would call for? Light, damn you, *light!*'

'Well?'

Sheerin said, 'You'd burn something, mister. Ever see a forest fire? Ever go camping and cook a stew over a wood fire? Heat isn't the only thing burning wood gives off, you know. It gives off light, and people know that. And when it's dark they want light, and they're going to *get it*.'

'So they burn wood?'

'So they burn whatever they can get. They've got to have light. They've got to burn something, and wood isn't handy – so they'll burn whatever is nearest. They'll have their light – and every centre of habitation goes up in flames!'

Theremon broke away wordlessly. His breathing was harsh and ragged, and he scarcely noted the sudden hubbub that came from the adjoining room behind the closed door.

Sheerin spoke, and it was with an effort that he made it sound matter-of-fact. 'I think I heard Yimot's voice. He and Faro are probably back. Let's go in and see what kept them.'

'Might as well!' muttered Theremon. He drew a long breath and seemed to shake himself. The tension was broken.

The room was in an uproar, with members of the staff clustering about two young men who were removing outer garments even as they parried the miscellany of questions being thrown at them.

Aton bustled through the crowd and faced the newcomers angrily. 'Do you realize that it's less than half an hour before deadline? Where have you two been?'

Faro 24 seated himself and rubbed his hands. His cheeks were red with the outdoor chill. 'Yimot and I have just finished carrying through a little crazy experiment of our own. We've been trying to see if we couldn't construct an arrangement by which we could simulate the appearance of Darkness and Stars so as to get an advance notion as to how it looked.'

There was a confused murmur from the listeners, and a sudden look of interest entered Aton's eyes. 'There wasn't anything said of this before. How did you go about it?'

'Well,' said Faro, 'the idea came to Yimot and myself long ago and we've been working it out in our spare time. Yimot knew of a low one-storey house down in the city with a domed roof – it had once been used as a museum, I think. Anyway, we bought the place and rigged it up with black velvet from top to bottom so as to get as perfect a Darkness as possible. Then we punched tiny holes in the ceiling and through the roof and covered them with little metal caps, all of which could be shoved aside simultaneously at the close of a switch. At least, we didn't do that part ourselves; we got a carpenter and an electrician and some others – money didn't count. The point was that we could get the light to shine through those holes in the roof, so that we could get a starlike effect.'

Not a breath was drawn during the pause that followed. Aton said stiffly:

'You had no right to make a private –'

Faro seemed abashed. 'I know, sir – but, frankly, Yimot and I thought the experiment was a little dangerous. If the effect really worked, we half expected to go mad – from what Sheerin says about all this, we thought that would be rather likely. We wanted to take the risk ourselves.'

'Why, what happened?'

It was Yimot who answered. 'We shut ourselves in and allowed our eyes to get accustomed to the dark. It's an extremely creepy feeling because the total Darkness makes you feel as if the walls and ceiling are crushing in on you. But we got over that and pulled the switch. The caps fell away and the roof glittered all over with little dots of light –'

'Well?'

'Well – nothing. That was the whacky part of it. Nothing happened. It was a roof with holes in it, and that's just what it looked like. We tried it over and over again – that's what kept us so late – but there just isn't any effect at all.'

There followed a shocked silence, and all eyes turned to Sheerin, who sat motionless, mouth open.

Theremon was the first to speak. 'You know what this does to this whole theory you've built up, Sheerin, don't you?' He was grinning with relief.

But Sheerin raised his hand. 'Now wait a while. Just let me think this through.' And then he snapped his fingers, and when he lifted his head there was neither surprise nor uncertainty in his eyes. 'Of course –'

He never finished. From somewhere up above there sounded a sharp clang, and Beenay, starting to his feet, dashed up the stairs with a 'What the devil!'

The rest followed after.

*

Things happened quickly. Once up in the dome, Beenay cast one horrified glance at the shattered photographic plates and at the man bending over them; and then hurled himself fiercely at the intruder, getting a death grip on his throat. There was a wild threshing, and as others of the staff joined in, the stranger was swallowed up and smothered under the weight of half a dozen angry men.

Aton came up last, breathing heavily. 'Let him up!'

There was a reluctant unscrambling and the stranger, panting harshly, with his clothes torn and his forehead bruised, was hauled to his feet. He had a short yellow beard curled elaborately in the style affected by the Cultists.

Beenay shifted his hold to a collar grip and shook the man savagely. 'All right, rat, what's the idea? These plates –'

'I wasn't after *them*,' retorted the Cultist coldly. 'That was an accident.'

Beenay followed his glowering stare and snarled, 'I see. You were after the cameras themselves. The accident with the plates was a stroke of luck for you, then. If you had touched Snapping Bertha or any of the others, you would have died by slow torture. As it is –' He drew his fist back.

Aton grabbed his sleeve. 'Stop that! Let him go!'

The young technician wavered, and his arm dropped reluctantly. Aton pushed him aside and confronted the Cultist. 'You're Latimer, aren't you?'

The Cultist bowed stiffly and indicated the symbol upon his hip. 'I am Latimer 25, adjutant of the third class to His Serenity, Sor 5.'

'And' – Aton's white eyebrows lifted – 'you were with His Serenity when he visited me last week, weren't you?'

Latimer bowed a second time.

Sheerin smiled in a friendly fashion. 'You're a determined cuss, aren't you? Well, I'll explain something. Do you see that young man at the window? He's a strong, husky fellow, quite handy with his fists, and he's an outsider besides. Once the eclipse starts there will be nothing for him to do except keep an eye on you. Beside him, there will be myself – a little too stout for active fisticuffs, but still able to help.'

Sheerin nodded to the columnist. 'Take a seat next to him, Theremon – just as a formality. Hey, Theremon!'

But the newspaperman didn't move. He had gone pale to the lips. 'Look at that!' The finger he pointed towards the sky shook, and his voice was dry and cracked.

There was one simultaneous gasp as every eye followed the pointing finger and, for one breathless moment, stared frozenly.

Beta was chipped on one side!

The tiny bit of encroaching blackness was perhaps the width of a fingernail, but to the staring watchers it magnified itself into the crack of doom.

Only for a moment they watched, and after that there was a shrieking confusion that was even shorter in duration and which gave way to an orderly scurry of activity – each man at his prescribed job. At the crucial moment there was no time for emotion. The men were merely scientists with work to do. Even Aton had melted away.

Sheerin said prosaically, 'First contact must have been made fifteen minutes ago. A little early, but pretty good considering the uncertainties involved in the calculation.' He looked about him and then tiptoed to Theremon, who still remained staring out of the window, and dragged him away gently.

'Aton is furious,' he whispered, 'so stay away. He missed first contact on account of this fuss with Latimer, and if you get in his way he'll have you thrown out the window.'

Theremon nodded shortly and sat down. Sheerin stared in surprise at him.

'The devil, man,' he exclaimed, 'you're shaking.'

'Eh?' Theremon licked dry lips and then tried to smile. 'I don't feel very well, and that's a fact.'

The psychologist's eyes hardened. 'You're not losing your nerve?'

'No!' cried Theremon in a flash of indignation. 'Give me a chance, will you? I haven't really believed this rigmarole – not way down beneath, anyway – till just this minute. Give me a chance to get used to the idea. *You've* been preparing yourself for two months or more.'

'You're right, at that,' replied Sheerin thoughtfully.

'You think I'm scared stiff, don't you? Well, get this, mister. I'm a newspaperman and I've been assigned to cover a story. I intend covering it.'

There was a faint smile on the psychologist's face. 'I see. Professional honour, is that it?'

'You might call it that. But, man, I'd give my right arm for another bottle of that sockeroo juice even half the size of the one *you* hogged. If ever a fellow needed a drink, I do.'

He broke off. Sheerin was nudging him violently. 'Do you hear that? Listen!'

Theremon followed the motion of the other's chin and stared at the Cultist, who, oblivious to all about him, faced the window, a look of wild elation on his face, droning to himself the while in singsong fashion.

'What's he saying?' whispered the columnist.

'He's quoting "Book of Revelations," fifth chapter,' replied Sheerin. Then, urgently, 'Keep quiet and listen, I tell you.'

The Cultist's voice had risen in a sudden increase of fervour.

'"And it came to pass that in those days the Sun, Beta, held lone vigil in the sky for ever longer periods as the revolutions passed; until such time as for full half a revolution, it alone, shrunken and cold, shone down upon Lagash.

'"And in the city of Trigon, at high noon, Vendret 2 came forth and said unto the men of Trigon, 'Lo, ye sinners! Though ye scorn the ways of righteousness, yet will the time of reckoning come. Even now the Cave approaches to swallow Lagash; yea, and all it contains.'

'"And even as he spoke the lip of the Cave of Darkness passed the edge of Beta so that to all Lagash it was hidden from sight. Loud were the cries of men as it vanished, and great the fear of soul that fell upon them.

'"It came to pass that the Darkness of the Cave fell upon Lagash, and there was no light on all the surface of Lagash. Men were even as blinded, nor could one man see his neighbour, though he felt his breath upon his face.

'"And in this blackness there appeared the Stars, in countless numbers, and to the strains of ineffable music of a beauty so wondrous that the very leaves of the trees turned to tongues that cried out in wonder.

'"And in that moment the souls of men departed from them, and their abandoned bodies became even as beasts; yea, even as brutes of the wild; so that through the blackened streets of the cities of Lagash they prowled with wild cries.

'"From the Stars there then reached down the Heavenly Flame, and where it touched, the cities of Lagash flamed to utter destruction, so that of man and of the works of man nought remained.

'"Even then –"'

There was a subtle change in Latimer's tone. His eyes had not shifted, but somehow he had become aware of the absorbed attention of the other two. Easily, without pausing for breath, the timbre of his voice shifted and the syllables became more liquid.

Theremon, caught by surprise, stared. The words seemed on the border of familiarity. There was an elusive shift in the accent, a tiny change in the vowel stress; nothing more – yet Latimer had become thoroughly unintelligible.

Sheerin smiled slyly. 'He shifted to some old-cycle tongue, probably their traditional second cycle. That was the language in which the Book of Revelation was originally written, you know.'

'It doesn't matter; I've heard enough.' Theremon moved his chair and brushed his hair back with hands that no longer shook. 'I feel much better now.'

'You do?' Sheerin seemed mildly surprised.

'I'll say I do. I had a bad case of jitters just a while back. Listening to you and your gravitation and seeing that eclipse start almost finished me. But this –' he jerked a contemptuous thumb at the yellow-bearded Cultist – '*this* is the sort of thing my nurse used to tell me. I've been laughing at that sort of thing all my life. I'm not going to let it scare me *now*.'

He drew a deep breath and said with a hectic gaiety, 'But if I expect to keep on the good side of myself, I'm going to turn my chair away from the window.'

With elaborate care he turned the chair from the window, cast one distasteful look over his shoulder and said, 'It has occurred to me that there must be considerable immunity against this Star madness.'

The psychologist did not answer immediately. Beta was past its zenith now, and the square of bloody sunlight that outlined the window upon the floor had lifted into Sheerin's lap. He stared at its dusky colour thoughtfully, and then bent and squinted into the sun itself.

The chip in its side had grown to a black encroachment that covered a third of Beta. He shuddered, and when he straightened once more his florid cheeks did not contain quite as much colour as they had previously.

With a smile that was almost apologetic, he reversed his chair also. 'There are probably two million people in Saro City that are all trying to join the Cult at once in one gigantic revival.' Then, ironically, 'The Cult is in for an hour of unexampled prosperity. I trust they'll make the most of it. Now, what was it you said?'

'Just this. How do the Cultists manage to keep the "Book of Revelations" going from cycle to cycle, and how on Lagash did it get written in the first place? There must have been some sort of immunity, for if everyone had gone mad, who would be left to write the book?'

'Naturally, the book was based, in the first place, on the testimony of those least qualified to serve as historians; that is, children and morons; and was probably extensively edited and re-edited through the cycles.'

'Do you suppose', broke in Theremon, 'that they carried the book through the cycles the way we're planning on handing on the secret of gravitation?'

Sheerin shrugged. 'Perhaps, but their exact method is unimportant. They do it, somehow. The point I was getting at was that the book can't help but be a mass of distortion, even if it is based on fact. For instance, do you remember the experiment with the holes in the roof that Faro and Yimot tried – the one that didn't work?'

'Yes.'

'You know why it didn't w–' He stopped and rose in alarm, for Aton was approaching, his face a twisted mask of consternation.

'*What's happened?*'

Aton drew him aside and Sheerin could feel the fingers on his elbow twitching.

'Not so loud!' Aton's voice was low and tortured. 'I've just gotten word from the Hideout on the private line.'

Sheerin broke in anxiously. 'They are in trouble?'

'Not *they.*' Aton stressed the pronoun significantly. 'They sealed themselves off just a while ago, and they're going to stay buried till the day after tomorrow. They're safe. But the *city*, Sheerin – it's a shambles. You have no idea –' He was having difficulty in speaking.

'Well?' snapped Sheerin impatiently. 'What of it? It will get worse. What are you shaking about?' Then, suspiciously, 'How do you feel?'

Aton's eyes sparked angrily at the insinuation, and faded to anxiety once more. 'You don't understand. The Cultists are active. They're rousing the people to storm the Observatory – promising them immediate entrance into grace, promising them salvation, promising them anything. What are we to do, Sheerin?'

'There's nothing to do but gamble. It will take time to organize any really formidable mob, and it will take more time to get them out here. We're a good five miles from the city –'

He glared out the window, down the slopes to where the farmed patches gave way to clumps of white houses in the suburbs; down to where the metropolis itself was a blur on the horizon – a mist in the waning blaze of Beta.

He repeated without turning, 'It will take time. Keep on working and pray that totality comes first.'

Beta was cut in half, the line of division pushing a slight concavity into the still-bright portion of the Sun. It was like a gigantic eyelid shutting slantwise over the light of the world.

The faint clatter of the room in which he stood faded into oblivion, and he sensed only the thick silence of the fields outside. The very insects seemed frightened mute. And things were dim.

He jumped at the voice in his ear. Theremon said, 'Is something wrong?'

'Eh? Er – no. Get back to the chair. We're in the way.' They slipped back to their corner, but the psychologist did not speak for a time. He lifted a finger and loosened his collar. He twisted his neck back and forth but found no relief. He looked up suddenly.

'Are you having any difficulty in breathing?'

The newspaperman opened his eyes wide and drew two or three long breaths. 'No. Why?'

'I looked out the window too long, I suppose. The dimness got me.

Difficulty in breathing is one of the first symptoms of a claustrophobic attack.'

Theremon drew another long breath. 'Well, it hasn't got me yet. Say, here's another of the fellows.'

Beenay had interposed his bulk between the light and the pair in the corner, and Sheerin squinted at him anxiously. 'Hello, Beenay.'

The astronomer shifted his weight to the other foot and smiled feebly. 'You won't mind if I sit down awhile and join in the talk. My cameras are set, and there's nothing to do till totality.' He paused and eyed the Cultist, who fifteen minutes earlier had drawn a small, skin-bound book from his sleeve and had been poring intently over it ever since. 'That rat hasn't been making trouble, has he?'

Sheerin shook his head. His shoulders were thrown back and he frowned his concentration as he forced himself to breathe regularly. He said, 'Have you had any trouble breathing, Beenay?'

Beenay sniffed the air in his turn. 'It doesn't seem stuffy to me.'

'A touch of claustrophobia,' explained Sheerin apologetically.

'Oh-h-h! It worked itself differently with me. I get the impression that my eyes are going back on me. Things seem to blur and – well, nothing is clear. And it's cold, too.'

'Oh, it's cold, all right. That's no illusion.' Theremon grimaced. 'My toes feel as if I'd been shipping them cross-country in a refrigerator car.'

'What we need,' put in Sheerin, 'is to keep our minds busy with extraneous affairs. I was telling you a while ago, Theremon, why Faro's experiments with the holes in the roof came to nothing.'

'You were just beginning,' replied Theremon. He encircled a knee with both arms and nuzzled his chin against it.

'Well, as I started to say, they were misled by taking the "Book of Revelations" literally. There probably wasn't any sense in attaching any physical significance to the Stars. It might be, you know, that in the presence of total Darkness, the mind finds it absolutely necessary to create light. This illusion of light might be all the Stars there really are.'

'In other words,' interposed Theremon, 'you mean the Stars are the results of the madness and not one of the causes. Then what good will Beenay's photographs be?'

'To prove that it is an illusion, maybe; or to prove the opposite, for all I know. Then again –'

But Beenay had drawn his chair closer, and there was an expression of sudden enthusiasm on his face. 'I'm glad you two got on to this subject.' His eyes narrowed and he lifted one finger. 'I've been thinking about these Stars and I've got a really cute notion. Of course, it's strictly ocean foam, and I'm not trying to advance it seriously, but I think it's interesting. Do you want to hear it?'

He seemed half reluctant, but Sheerin leaned back and said, 'Go ahead! I'm listening.'

'Well, then, supposing there were other suns in the universe.' He broke off a little bashfully. 'I mean suns that are so far away that they're too dim to see. It sounds as if I've been reading some of that fantastic fiction, I suppose.'

'Not necessarily. Still, isn't that possibility eliminated by the fact that, according to the Law of Gravitation, they would make themselves evident by their attractive forces?'

'Not if they were far enough off,' rejoined Beenay, 'really far off – maybe as much as four light years, or even more. We'd never be able to detect perturbations then, because they'd be too small. Say that there were a lot of suns that far off; a dozen or two, maybe.'

Theremon whistled melodiously. 'What an idea for a good Sunday supplement article. Two dozen suns in a universe eight light years across. Wow! That would shrink *our* universe into insignificance. The readers would eat it up.'

'Only an idea,' said Beenay with a grin, 'but you see the point. During eclipse, these dozen suns would become visible, because there'd be no *real* sunlight to drown them out. Since they're so far off, they'd appear small, like so many little marbles. Of course, the Cultists talk of millions of Stars, but that's probably exaggeration. There just isn't any place in the universe you could put a million suns – unless they touch each other.'

Sheerin had listened with gradually increasing interest. 'You've hit something there, Beenay. And exaggeration is just exactly what would happen. Our minds, as you probably know, can't grasp directly any number higher than five; above that there is only the concept of "many". A dozen would become a million just like that. A damn good idea!'

'And I've got another little notion,' Beenay said. 'Have you ever thought what a simple problem gravitation would be if only you had a sufficiently simple system? Supposing you had a universe in which there was a planet with only one sun. The planet would travel in a perfect ellipse and the exact nature of the gravitational force would be so evident it could be accepted as an axiom. Astronomers on such a world would start off with gravity probably before they even invented the telescope. Naked-eye observation would be enough.'

'It's nice to think about,' admitted Sheerin, 'as a pretty abstraction – like a perfect gas or absolute zero.'

'Of course,' continued Beenay, 'there's the catch that life would be impossible on such a planet. It wouldn't get enough heat and light, and if it rotated there would be total Darkness half of each day. You couldn't expect life – which is fundamentally dependent upon light – to develop under those conditions. Besides – '

Sheerin's chair went over backward as he sprang to his feet in a rude interruption. 'Aton's brought out the lights.'

Beenay said, 'Huh,' turned to stare, and then grinned halfway around his head in open relief.

There were half a dozen foot-long, inch-thick rods cradled in Aton's arms. He glared over them at the assembled staff members.

With the air of one carrying through the most sacred item of a religious ritual, Sheerin scraped a large, clumsy match into spluttering life and passed it to Aton, who carried the flame to the upper end of one of the rods.

It hesitated there a while, playing futilely about the tip, until a sudden, crackling flare cast Aton's lined face into yellow highlights. He withdrew the match and a spontaneous cheer rattled the window.

The rod was topped by six inches of wavering flame! Methodically, the other rods were lighted, until six independent fires turned the rear of the room yellow.

The light was dim, dimmer even than the tenuous sunlight. The flames reeled crazily, giving birth to drunken, swaying shadows. The torches smoked devilishly and smelled like a bad day in the kitchen. But they emitted yellow light.

There is something to yellow light – after four hours of sombre, dimming Beta. Even Latimer had lifted his eyes from his book and stared in wonder.

But Theremon regarded the torches suspiciously. He wrinkled his nose at the rancid odour, and said, 'What are those things?'

'Wood,' said Sheerin shortly.

'Oh, no, they're not. They aren't burning. The top inch is charred and the flame just keeps shooting up out of nothing.'

'That's the beauty of it. This is a really efficient artificial-light mechanism. We made a few hundred of them, but most went to the Hideout, of course. You see' – he turned and wiped his blackened hands upon his handkerchief – 'you take the pithy core of coarse water reeds, dry them thoroughly and soak them in animal grease. Then you set fire to it and the grease burns, little by little. These torches will burn for almost half an hour without stopping. Ingenious, isn't it? It was developed by one of our own young men at Saro University.'

The air grew somehow denser. Dusk, like a palpable entity, entered the room and the dancing circle of yellow light about the torches etched itself into ever-sharper distinction against the gathering greyness beyond. There was the odour of smoke and the presence of little chuckling sounds that the torches made as they burned; the soft pad of one of the men circling the table at which he worked, on hesitant tiptoes; the occasional indrawn breath of someone trying to retain composure in a world that was retreating into the shadow.

It was Theremon who first heard the extraneous noise. It was a vague, unorganized *impression* of sound that would have gone unnoticed but for the dead silence that prevailed within the dome.

The newsman sat upright and replaced his notebook. He held his breath and listened; then, with considerable reluctance, threaded his way between the solarscope and one of Beenay's cameras and stood before the window.

Outside, Beta was a mere smouldering splinter, taking one last desperate look at Lagash. The eastern horizon, in the direction of the city, was lost in Darkness, and the road from Saro to the Observatory was a dull-red line bordered on both sides by wooded tracts, the trees of which had somehow lost individuality and merged into a continuous shadowy mass.

But it was the highway itself that held attention, for along it there surged another, and infinitely menacing, shadowy mass.

Aton cried in a cracked voice, 'The madmen from the city! They've come!'

'How long to totality?' demanded Sheerin.

'Fifteen minutes, but . . . but they'll be here in five.'

'Never mind, keep the men working. We'll hold them off. This place is built like a fortress. Aton, keep an eye on our young Cultist just for luck. Theremon, come with me.'

Sheerin was out the door, and Theremon was at his heels. The stairs stretched below them in tight, circular sweeps about the central shaft, fading into a dank and dreary greyness.

The first momentum of their rush had carried them fifty feet down, so that the dim, flickering yellow from the open door of the dome had disappeared and both up above and down below the same dusky shadow crushed in upon them.

Sheerin paused, and his pudgy hand clutched at his chest. His eyes bulged and his voice was a dry cough. 'I can't . . . breath . . . go down . . . yourself. Close all doors –'

Theremon took a few downward steps, then turned. 'Wait! Can you hold out a minute?' He was panting himself. The air passed in and out his lungs like so much molasses, and there was a little germ of screeching panic in his mind at the thought of making his way into the mysterious Darkness below by himself.

Theremon, after all, was afraid of the dark!

'Stay here,' he said. 'I'll be back in a second.' He dashed upward two steps at a time, heart pounding – not altogether from the exertion – tumbled into the dome and snatched a torch from its holder. It was foul smelling, and the smoke smarted his eyes almost blind, but he clutched that torch as if he wanted to kiss it for joy, and its flame streamed backward as he hurtled down the stairs again.

Sheerin opened his eyes and moaned as Theremon bent over him.

Theremon shook him roughly. 'All right, get a hold on yourself. We've got light.'

He held the torch at tiptoe height and, propping the tottering psychologist by an elbow, made his way downward in the middle of the protecting circle of illumination.

The offices on the ground floor still possessed what light there was, and Theremon felt the horror about him relax.

'Here,' he said brusquely, and passed the torch to Sheerin. 'You can hear *them* outside.'

And they could. Little scraps of hoarse, wordless shouts.

But Sheerin was right; the Observatory *was* built like a fortress. Erected in the last century, when the neo-Gavottian style of architecture was at its ugly height, it had been designed for stability and durability, rather than for beauty.

The windows were protected by the grille-work of inch-thick iron bars sunk deep into the concrete sills. The walls were solid masonry that an earthquake couldn't have touched, and the main door was a huge oaken slab reinforced with iron at the strategic points. Theremon shot the bolts and they slid shut with a dull clang.

At the other end of the corridor, Sheerin cursed weakly. He pointed to the lock of the back door which had been neatly jemmied into uselessness.

'That must be how Latimer got in,' he said.

'Well, don't stand there,' cried Theremon impatiently. 'Help drag up the furniture – and keep that torch out of my eyes. The smoke's killing me.'

He slammed the heavy table against the door as he spoke, and in minutes had built a barricade which made up for what it lacked in beauty and symmetry by the sheer intertia of its massiveness.

Somewhere, dimly, far off, they could hear the battering of naked fists upon the door; and the screams and yells from outside had a sort of half reality.

That mob had set off from Saro City with only two things in mind: the attainment of Cultist salvation by the destruction of the Observatory, and a maddening fear that all but paralysed them. There was no time to think of ground cars, or of weapons, or of leadership, or even of organization. They made for the Observatory on foot and assaulted it with bare hands.

And now that they were there, the last flash of Beta, the last ruby-red drop of flame, flickered feebly over a humanity that had left only stark, universal fear!

Theremon groaned, 'Let's get back to the dome!'

In the dome, only Yimot, at the solarscope, had kept his place. The rest were clustered about the cameras, and Beenay was giving his instructions in a hoarse, strained voice.

'Now remember, don't . . . don't try to look for good shots. Don't waste time trying to get t-two stars at a time in the scope field. One is enough. And . . . and if you feel yourself going, *get away from the camera.*'

At the door, Sheerin whispered to Theremon, 'Take me to Aton. I don't see him.'

The newsman did not answer immediately. The vague forms of the astronomers wavered and blurred, and the torches overhead had become only yellow splotches.

'It's dark,' he whimpered.

Sheerin held out his hand, 'Aton.' He stumbled forward. 'Aton!'

Theremon stepped after and seized his arm. 'Wait, I'll take you.' Somehow he made his way across the room. He closed his eyes against the Darkness and his mind against the chaos within it.

No one heard them or paid attention to them. Sheerin stumbled against the wall. 'Aton!'

The psychologist felt shaking hands touching him, then withdrawing, and a voice muttering, 'Is that you, Sheerin?'

'Aton!' He strove to breathe normally. 'Don't worry about the mob. The place will hold them off.'

Beenay's face was dimly flushed as it looked upward at Beta's last ray, and Latimer, seeing him bend over his camera, made his decision. His nails cut the flesh of his palms as he tensed himself.

He staggered crazily as he started his rush. There was nothing before him but shadows; the very floor beneath his feet lacked substance. And then someone was upon him and he went down with clutching fingers at his throat.

He doubled his knee and drove it hard into his assailant. 'Let me up or I'll kill you.'

Theremon cried out sharply and muttered through a blinding haze of pain, 'You double-crossing rat!'

The newsman seemed conscious of everything at once. He heard Beenay croak, 'I've got it. At your cameras, men!' and then there was the strange awareness that the last thread of sunlight had thinned out and snapped.

And Latimer had gone limp in his loosening grasp. Theremon peered into the Cultist's eyes and saw the blackness of them, staring upward, mirroring the feeble yellow of the torches. He saw the bubble of froth upon Latimer's lips and heard the low animal whimper in Latimer's throat.

With the slow fascination of fear, he lifted himself on one arm and turned his eyes towards the blood-curdling blackness of the window.

Through it shone the Stars!

Not Earth's feeble thirty-six hundred Stars visible to the eye – Lagash was in the centre of a giant cluster. Thirty thousand mighty suns shone down in a soul-searing splendour that was more frighteningly cold in its awful indifference than the bitter wind that now shivered across the world. The bright walls of the universe were shattered and their awful black fragments were falling down to crush and squeeze and obliterate men.

'Light!' Theremon screamed.

Aton, somewhere, was whimpering horribly like a frightened child. 'Stars – all the Stars – we didn't know at all. We didn't know anything. We thought six stars in a universe is something the Stars didn't notice is Darkness forever and ever and ever and the walls are breaking in and we didn't know we couldn't know and anything –'

Someone clawed at the torch, and it fell and snuffed out. In that instant, the awful splendour of the Stars leaped nearer to them.

On the horizon outside the window, in the direction of Saro City, a crimson glow began growing, strengthening in brightness, that was not the glow of a sun.

The long night had come again.

The Snowball Effect

KATHERINE MACLEAN

'All right,' I said, 'what is sociology good for?'

Wilton Caswell, PhD, was head of my Sociology Department, and right then he was mad enough to chew nails. On the office wall behind him were three or four framed documents in Latin, but I didn't care at that moment if he papered the walls with his degrees. I had been appointed dean and president to see to it that the university made money. I had a job to do, and I meant to do it.

He bit off each word with great restraint: 'Sociology is the study of social institutions, Mr Halloway.'

I tried to make him understand my position. 'Look, it's the big-money men who are supposed to be contributing to the support of this college. To them, sociology sounds like socialism – nothing can sound worse than that – and an institution is where they put Aunt Maggy when she began collecting Wheaties in a stamp album. We can't appeal to them that way. Come on now.' I smiled condescendingly, knowing it would irritate him. 'What are you doing that's worth anything?'

He glared at me, his white hair bristling and his nostrils dilated like a war horse about to whinny. I can say one thing for them – these scientists and professors always keep themselves well under control. He had a book in his hand and I was expecting him to throw it, but he spoke instead:

'This department's analysis of institutional accretion, by the use of open system mathematics, has been recognized as an outstanding and valuable contribution to –'

The words were impressive, whatever they meant, but this still didn't sound like anything that would pull in money. I interrupted, 'Valuable in what way?'

He sat down on the edge of his desk thoughtfully, apparently recovering from the shock of being asked to produce something solid for his position, and ran his eyes over the titles of the books that lined his office walls.

'Well, sociology has been valuable to business in initiating worker efficiency and group motivation studies, which they now use in management decisions. And, of course, since the depression, Washington has been using sociological studies of employment, labour, and standards of living as a basis for its general policies of –'

I stopped him with both hands raised. 'Please, Professor Caswell! That would hardly be a recommendation. Washington, the New Deal and the present Administration are somewhat touchy subjects to the men I have to deal with. They consider its value debatable, if you know what I mean. If they got the idea that sociology professors are giving advice and guidance – No, we have to stick to brass tacks and leave Washington out of this. What, specifically, has the work of this specific department done that would make it as worthy to receive money as – say, a heart disease research fund?'

He began to tap the corner of his book absently on the desk, watching me. 'Fundamental research doesn't show immediate effects, Mr Halloway, but its value is recognized.'

I smiled and took out my pipe. 'All right, tell me about it. Maybe I'll recognize its value.'

Prof. Caswell smiled back tightly. He knew his department was at stake. The other departments were popular with donors and pulled in gift money by scholarships and fellowships, and supported their professors and graduate students by research contracts with the government and industry. Caswell had to show a way to make his own department popular – or else.

He laid down his book and ran a hand over his ruffled hair. 'Institutions – organizations, that is –' his voice became more resonant; like most professors, when he had to explain something he instinctively slipped into his platform lecture mannerisms, and began to deliver an essay – 'have certain tendencies built into the way they happen to have been organized, which cause them to expand or contract without reference to the needs they were founded to serve.'

He was becoming flushed with the pleasure of explaining his subject. 'All through the ages, it has been a matter of wonder and dismay to men that a simple organization – such as a church to worship in, or a delegation of weapons to a warrior class merely for defence against an outside enemy – will either grow insensately and extend its control until it is a tyranny over their whole lives, or, like other organizations set up to serve a vital need, will tend to repeatedly dwindle and vanish, and have to be painfully rebuilt.

'The reason can be traced to little quirks in the way they were organized, a matter of positive and negative power feedbacks. Such simple questions as, "Is there a way a holder of authority in this organization can use the power available to him to increase his power?" provide the key. But it still could not be handled until the complex questions of interacting motives and long-range accumulations of minor effects could somehow be simplified and formulated. In working on the problem, I found that the mathematics of open system, as introduced to biology by Ludwig von Bertalanffy and George Kreezer, could be used as a base that would enable me to develop a specifically social mathematics, expressing the human factors of intermeshing authority and motives in simple formulas.

'By these formulations, it is possible to determine automatically the amount of growth and period of life of any organization. The UN, to choose an unfortunate example, is a shrinker type organization. Its monetary support is not in the hands of those who personally benefit by its governmental activities, but, instead, in the hands of those who would personally lose by any extension and encroachment of its authority on their own. Yet by the use of formula analysis –'

'That's theory,' I said. 'How about proof?'

'My equations are already being used in the study of limited-size Federal corporations. Washington –'

I held up my palm again. 'Please, not that nasty word again. I mean, where else has it been put into operation? Just a simple demonstration, something to show that it works, that's all.'

He looked away from me thoughtfully, picked up the book and began to tap it on the desk again. It had some unreadable title and his name on it in gold letters. I got the distinct impression again that he was repressing an urge to hit me with it.

He spoke quietly. 'All right. I'll give you a demonstration. Are you willing to wait six months?'

'Certainly, if you can show me something at the end of that time.'

Reminded of time, I glanced at my watch and stood up.

'Could we discuss this over lunch?' he asked.

'I wouldn't mind hearing more, but I'm having lunch with some executors of a millionaire's will. They have to be convinced that by "furtherance of research into human ills" he meant that the money should go to research fellowships for postgraduate biologists at the university, rather than to a medical foundation.'

'I see you have your problems, too,' Caswell said, conceding me nothing. He extended his hand with a chilly smile. 'Well, good afternoon, Mr Halloway. I'm glad we had this talk.'

I shook hands and left him standing there, sure of his place in the progress of science and the respect of his colleagues, yet seething inside because I, the president and dean, had boorishly demanded that he produce something tangible.

My job isn't easy. For a crumb of favourable publicity and respect in the newspapers and an annual ceremony in a silly costume, I spend the rest of the year going hat in hand, asking politely for money at everyone's door, like a well-dressed panhandler, and trying to manage the university on the dribble I get. As far as I was concerned, a department had to support itself or be cut down to what student tuition pays for, which is a handful of overcrowded courses taught by an assistant lecturer. Caswell had to make it work or get out.

But the more I thought about it, the more I wanted to hear what he was going to do for a demonstration.

At lunch, three days later, while we were waiting for our order, he opened a small notebook. 'Ever hear of feedback effects?'

'Not enough to have it clear.'

'You know the snowball effect though.'

'Sure, start a snowball rolling downhill and it grows.'

'Well, now – ' He wrote a short line of symbols on a blank page and turned the notebook around for me to inspect it. 'Here's the formula for the snowball process. It's the basic general growth formula – covers everything.'

It was a row of little symbols arranged like an algebra equation. One was a concentric spiral going up, like a cross-section of a snowball rolling in snow. That was a growth sign.

I hadn't expected to understand the equation, but it was almost as clear as a sentence. I was impressed and slightly intimidated by it. He had already explained enough so that I knew that, if he was right, here was the growth of the Catholic Church and the Roman Empire, the conquests of Alexander and the spread of the smoking habit and the change and rigidity of the unwritten law of styles.

'Is it really as simple as that?' I asked.

'You notice,' he said, 'that when it becomes too heavy for the cohesion strength of snow, it breaks apart. Now in human terms –'

The chops and mashed potatoes and peas arrived.

'Go on,' I urged.

He was deep in the symbology of human motives and the equations of human behaviour in groups. After running through a few different types of grower and shrinker type organizations, we came back to the snowball, and decided to run the test by making something grow.

'You add the motives,' he said, 'and the equation will translate them into organization.'

'How about a good selfish reason for the ins to drag others into the group – some sort of bounty on new members, a cut of their membership fee?' I suggested uncertainly, feeling slightly foolish. 'And maybe a reason why the members would lose if any of them resigned, and some indirect way they could use to force each other to stay in.'

'The first is the chain letter principle,' he nodded. 'I've got that. The other . . .' He put the symbols through some mathematical manipulation so that a special grouping appeared in the middle of the equation. 'That's it.'

Since I seemed to have the right idea, I suggested some more, and he added some, and juggled them around in different patterns. We threw out a few that would have made the organization too complicated, and finally worked out an idyllically simple and deadly little organization set-up where joining had all the temptation of buying a sweepstakes ticket, going in deeper was as easy as hanging around a race track, and getting out was like trying to pull free from a Malayan thumb trap. We put our heads closer together and talked lower, picking the best place for the demonstration.

'Abington?'

'How about Watashaw? I have some student sociological surveys of it already. We can pick a suitable group from that.'

'This demonstration has got to be convincing. We'd better pick a little group that no one in his right mind would expect to grow.'

'There should be a suitable club –'

'Ladies,' said the skinny female chairman of the Watashaw Sewing Circle. 'Today we have guests.' She signalled for us to rise, and we stood up, bowing to polite applause and smiles. 'Professor Caswell, and Professor Smith.' (My alias.) 'They are making a survey of the methods and duties of the clubs of Watashaw.'

We sat down to another ripple of applause and slightly wider smiles, and then the meeting of the Watashaw Sewing Circle began. In five minutes I began to feel sleepy.

There were only about thirty people there, and it was a small room, not the halls of Congress, but they discussed their business of collecting and repairing second-hand clothing for charity with the same endless boring parliamentary formality.

I pointed out to Caswell the member I thought would be the natural leader, a tall, well-built woman in a green suit, with conscious gestures and a resonant, penetrating voice, and then went into a half doze while Caswell stayed awake beside me and wrote in his notebook. After a while the resonant voice roused me to attention for a moment. It was the tall woman holding the floor over some collective dereliction of the club. She was being scathing.

I nudged Caswell and murmured, 'Did you fix it so that a shover has a better chance of getting into office than a non-shover?'

'I think there's a way they could find for it,' Caswell whispered back, and went to work on his equation again. 'Yes, several ways to bias the elections.'

'Good. Point them out tactfully to the one you select. Not as if she'd use such methods, but just as an example of the reason why only *she* can be trusted with initiating the change. Just mention all the personal advantages an unscrupulous person could have.'

He nodded, keeping a straight and sober face as if we were exchanging admiring remarks about the techniques of clothes repairing, instead of conspiring.

After the meeting, Caswell drew the tall woman in the green suit aside and spoke to her confidentially, showing her the diagram of organization we had drawn up. I saw the responsive glitter in the woman's eyes and knew she was hooked.

We left the diagram of organization and our typed copy of the new by-laws with her and went off soberly, as befitted two social science experimenters. We didn't start laughing until our car passed the town limits and began the climb for University Heights.

If Caswell's equations meant anything at all, we had given that sewing circle more growth drives than the Roman Empire.

Four months later I had time out from a very busy schedule to wonder how the test was coming along. Passing Caswell's office, I put my head in. He looked up from a student research paper he was correcting.

'Caswell, about that sewing club business – I'm beginning to feel the suspense. Could I get an advance report on how it's coming?'

'I'm not following it. We're supposed to let it run the full six months.'

'But I'm curious. Could I get in touch with that woman – what's her name?'

'Searles. Mrs George Searles.'

'Would that change the results?'

'Not in the slightest. If you want to graph the membership rise, it should be going up in a log curve, probably doubling every so often.'

I grinned. 'If it's not rising, you're fired.'

He grinned back. 'If it's not rising, you won't have to fire me – I'll burn my books and shoot myself.'

I returned to my office and put in a call to Watashaw.

While I was waiting for the phone to be answered, I took a piece of graph paper and ruled it off into six sections, one for each month. After the phone had rung in the distance for a long time, a servant answered with a bored drawl:

'Mrs Searles' residence.'

I picked up a red gummed star and licked it.

'Mrs Searles, please.'

'She's not in just now. Could I take a message?'

I placed the star at the thirty line in the beginning of the first section. Thirty members they'd started with.

'No, thanks. Could you tell me when she'll be back?'

'Not until dinner. She's at the meetin'.'

'The sewing club?' I asked.

'No, *sir*, not that thing. There isn't any sewing club any more, not for a long time. She's at the Civic Welfare meeting.'

Somehow I hadn't expected anything like that.

'Thank you,' I said and hung up, and after a moment noticed I was holding a box of red gummed stars in my hand. I closed it and put it down on top of the graph of membership in the sewing circle. No more members . . .

Poor Caswell. The bet between us was ironclad. He wouldn't let me back down on it even if I wanted. He'd probably quit before I put through the first slow move to fire him. His professional pride would be shattered, sunk without a trace. I remembered what he said about shooting himself. It had seemed funny to both of us at the time, but . . . What a mess that would make for the university.

I had to talk to Mrs Searles. Perhaps there was some outside reason why the club had disbanded. Perhaps it had not just died.

I called back. 'This is Professor Smith,' I said, giving the alias I had used before. 'I called a few minutes ago. When did you say Mrs Searles will return?'

'About six-thirty or seven o'clock.'

Five hours to wait.

And what if Caswell asked me what I had found out in the meantime? I didn't want to tell him anything until I had talked it over with that woman Searles first.

'Where is this Civic Welfare meeting?'

She told me.

Five minutes later, I was in my car, heading for Watashaw, driving considerably faster than usual and keeping a careful watch for highway patrol cars as the speedometer climbed.

The town meeting hall and theatre was a big place, probably with lots of small rooms for different clubs. I went in through the centre door and found myself in the huge central hall where some sort of rally was being held. A political-type rally – you know, cheers and chants, with bunting already down on the floor, people holding banners, and plenty of enthusiasm and excitement in the air. Someone was making a speech up on the platform. Most of the people there were women.

I wondered how the Civil Welfare League could dare hold its meeting at the same time as a political rally that could pull its members away. The group with Mrs Searles was probably holding a shrunken and almost memberless meeting somewhere in an upper room.

There probably was a side door that would lead upstairs.

While I glanced around, a pretty girl usher put a printed bulletin in my hand, whispering, 'Here's one of the new copies.' As I attempted to hand it back, she retreated. 'Oh, you can keep it. It's the new one. Everyone's supposed to have it. We've just printed up six thousand copies to make sure there'll be enough to last.'

The tall woman on the platform had been making a driving, forceful speech about some plans for rebuilding Watashaw's slum section. It began to penetrate my mind dimly as I glanced down at the bulletin in my hands.

'Civic Welfare League of Watashaw. The United Organization of Church and Secular Charities.' That's what it said. Below began the rules of membership.

I looked up. The speaker, with a clear, determined voice and conscious, forceful gestures, had entered the home-stretch of her speech, an appeal to the civic pride of all citizens of Watashaw.

'With a bright and glorious future – potentially without poor and without uncared-for ill – potentially with no ugliness, no vistas which are not beautiful – the best people in the best-planned town in the country – jewel of the United States.'

She paused and then leaned forward intensely, striking her clenched hand on the speaker's stand with each word for emphasis.

'All we need is more members. Now, get out there and recruit!'

I finally recognized Mrs Searles, as an answering sudden blast of sound half deafened me. The crowd was chanting at the top of its lungs: 'Recruit! Recruit!'

Mrs Searles stood still at the speaker's table and behind her, seated in a row of chairs, was a group that was probably the board of directors. It was mostly women, and the women began to look vaguely familiar, as if they could be members of the sewing circle.

I put my lips close to the ear of the pretty usher while I turned over the stiff printed bulletin on a hunch. 'How long has the League been organized?' On the back of the bulletin was a constitution.

She was cheering with the crowd, her eyes sparkling. 'I don't know,' she answered between cheers. 'I only joined two days ago. Isn't it wonderful?'

I went into the quiet outer air and got into my car with my skin prickling. Even as I drove away, I could hear them. They were singing some kind of organization song with the tune of 'Marching through Georgia.'

Even at the single glance I had given it, the constitution looked exactly like the one we had given the Watashaw Sewing Circle.

All I told Caswell when I got back was that the sewing circle had changed its name and the membership seemed to be rising.

Next day, after calling Mrs Searles, I placed some red stars on my graph for the first three months. They made a nice curve, rising more steeply as it reached the fourth month. They had picked up their first increase in membership simply by amalgamating with all the other types of charity organization in Watashaw, changing the club name with each fusion, but keeping the same constitution – the constitution with the bright promise of advantages as long as there were always new members being brought in.

By the fifth month, the League had added a mutual baby-sitting service and had induced the local school board to add a nursery school to the town service, so as to free more women for League activity. But charity must have been completely organized by then, and expansion had to be in other directions.

Some real estate agents evidently had been drawn into the whirlpool early, along with their ideas. The slum improvement plans began to blossom and take on a tinge of real estate planning later in the month.

The first day of the sixth month, a big two-page spread appeared in the local paper of a mass meeting which had approved a full-fledged scheme for slum clearance of Watashaw's shack-town section, plus plans for rehousing, civic building, and re-zoning. And good prospects for attracting some new industries to the town, industries which had already been contacted and seemed interested by the privileges offered.

And with all this, an arrangement for securing and distributing to the club members *alone* most of the profit that would come to the town in the form of a rise in the price of building sites and a boom in the building industry. The profit distributing arrangement was the same one that had been built into the organization plan for the distribution of the small profits of membership fees and honorary promotions. It was becoming an openly profitable business. Membership was rising more rapidly now.

By the second week of the sixth month, news appeared in the local paper that the club had filed an application to incorporate itself as the Watashaw Mutual Trade and Civic Development Corporation, and all the local real estate promoters had finished joining en masse. The Mutual Trade part sounded to me as if the Chamber of Commerce was on the point of being pulled in with them, ideas, ambitions, and all.

I chuckled while reading the next page of the paper, on which a local politician was reported as having addressed the club with a long flowery oration on their enterprise, charity, and civic spirit. He had been made an honorary member. If he allowed himself to be made a *full member* with its contractual obligations and its lures, if the politicians went into this, too . . .

I laughed, filing the newspaper with the other documents on the Watashaw test. These proofs would fascinate any businessman with the sense to see where his bread was buttered. A businessman is constantly dealing with organizations, including his own, and finding them either inert, cantankerous, or both. Caswell's formula could be a handle to grasp them with. Gratitude alone would bring money into the university in car-load lots.

The end of the sixth month came. The test was over and the end reports were spectacular. Caswell's formulas were proven to the hilt.

After reading the last newspaper reports, I called him up.

'Perfect, Wilt, *perfect*! I can use this Watashaw thing to get you so many fellowships and scholarships and grants for your department that you'll think it's snowing money!'

He answered somewhat uninterestedly, 'I've been busy working with students on their research papers and marking tests – not following the Watashaw business at all, I'm afraid. You say the demonstration went well and you're satisfied?'

He was definitely putting on a chill. We were friends now, but obviously he was still peeved whenever he was reminded that I had doubted that his theory could work. And he was using its success to rub my nose in the realization that I had been wrong. A man with a string of degrees after his name is just as human as anyone else. I had needled him pretty hard that first time.

'I'm satisfied,' I acknowledged. 'I was wrong. The formulas work beautifully. Come over and see my file of documents on it if you want a boost for your ego. Now let's see the formula for stopping it.'

He sounded cheerful again. 'I didn't complicate that organization with negatives. I wanted it to *grow*. It falls apart naturally when it stops growing for more than two months. It's like the great stock boom before an economic crash. Everyone in it is prosperous as long as the prices just keep going up and new buyers come into the market, but they all know what would happen if it stopped growing. You remember, we built in as one of the incentives that the members know they are going to lose if membership stops growing. Why, if I tried to stop it now, they'd cut my throat.'

I remembered the drive and frenzy of the crowd in the one early meeting I had seen. They probably would.

'No,' he continued. 'We'll just let it play out to the end of its tether and die of old age.'

'When will that be?'

'It can't grow past the female population of the town. There are only so many women in Watashaw, and some of them don't like sewing.'

The graph on the desk before me began to look sinister. Surely Caswell must have made some provision for –

'You underestimate their ingenuity,' I said into the phone. 'Since they wanted to expand, they didn't stick to sewing. They went from general charity to social welfare schemes to something that's pretty close to an incorporated government. The name is now the Watashaw Mutual Trade and Civic Development Corporation, and they're filing an application to change it to Civic Property Pool and Social Dividend, membership contractual, open to all. That social dividend sounds like a Technocrat climbed on the band wagon, eh?'

While I spoke, I carefully added another red star to the curve above the thousand member level, checking with the newspaper that still lay open on my desk. The curve was definitely some sort of log curve now, growing more rapidly with each increase.

'Leaving out practical limitations for a moment, where does the formula say it will stop?' I asked.

'When you run out of people to join it. But after all, there are only so many people in Watashaw. It's a pretty small town.'

'They've opened a branch office in New York,' I said carefully into the phone, a few weeks later.

With my pencil, very carefully, I extended the membership curve from where it was then.

After the next doubling, the curve went almost straight up and off the page.

Allowing for a lag of contagion from one nation to another, depending on how much their citizens intermingled, I'd give the rest of the world about twelve years.

There was a long silence while Caswell probably drew the same graph in his own mind. Then he laughed weakly. 'Well, you asked me for a demonstration.'

That was as good an answer as any. We got together and had lunch in a bar, if you can call it lunch. The movement we started will expand by hook or by crook, by seduction or by bribery or by propaganda or by conquest, but it will expand. And maybe a total world government will be a fine thing – until it hits the end of its rope in twelve years or so.

What happens then, I don't know.

But I don't want anyone to pin that on me. From now on, if anyone asks me, I've never heard of Watashaw.

Swarm

BRUCE STERLING

'I will miss your conversation during the rest of the voyage,' the alien said.

Captain-Doctor Simon Afriel folded his jeweled hands over his gold-embroidered waistcoat. 'I regret it also, ensign,' he said in the alien's own hissing language. 'Our talks together have been very useful to me. I would have paid to learn so much, but you gave it freely.'

'But that was only information,' the alien said. He shrouded his bead-bright eyes behind thick nictitating membranes. 'We Investors deal in energy, and precious metals. To prize and pursue mere knowledge is an immature racial trait.' The alien lifted the long ribbed frill behind his pinhole-sized ears.

'No doubt you are right,' Afriel said, despising him. 'We humans are as children to other races, however; so a certain immaturity seems natural to us.' Afriel pulled off his sunglasses to rub the bridge of his nose. The starship cabin was drenched in searing blue light, heavily ultraviolet. It was the light the Investors preferred, and they were not about to change it for one human passenger.

'You have not done badly,' the alien said magnanimously. 'You are the kind of race we like to do business with: young, eager, plastic, ready for a wide variety of goods and experiences. We would have contacted you much earlier, but your technology was still too feeble to afford us a profit.'

'Things are different now,' Afriel said. 'We'll make you rich.'

'Indeed,' the Investor said. The frill behind his scaly head flickered rapidly, a sign of amusement. 'Within two hundred years you will be wealthy enough to buy from us the secret of our starflight. Or perhaps your Mechanist faction will discover the secret through research.'

Afriel was annoyed. As a member of Reshaped faction, he did not appreciate the reference to the rival Mechanists. 'Don't put too much stock in mere technical expertise,' he said. 'Consider the aptitude for languages we Shapers have. It makes our faction a much better trading partner. To a Mechanist, all Investors look alike.'

The alien hesitated. Afriel smiled. He had appealed to the alien's personal ambition with his last statement, and the hint had been taken. That was where the Mechanists always erred. They tried to treat all Investors consistently, using the same programmed routines each time. They lacked imagination.

Something would have to be done about the Mechanists, Afriel thought. Something more permanent than the small but deadly confrontations between isolated ships in the Asteroid Belt and the ice-rich Rings of Saturn. Both factions maneuvered constantly, looking for a decisive stroke, bribing away each other's best talent, practicing ambush, assassination, and industrial espionage.

Captain-Doctor Simon Afriel was a past master of these pursuits. That was why the Reshaped faction had paid the millions of kilowatts necessary to buy his passage. Afriel held doctorates in biochemistry and alien linguistics, and a master's degree in magnetic weapons engineering. He was thirty-eight years old and had been Reshaped according to the state of the art at the time of his conception. His hormonal balance had been altered slightly to compensate for long periods spent in free-fall. He had no appendix. The structure of his heart had been redesigned for greater efficiency, and his large intestine had been altered to produce the vitamins normally made by intestinal bacteria. Genetic engineering and rigorous training in childhood had given him an intelligence quotient of one hundred and eighty. He was not the brightest of the agents of the Ring Council, but he was one of the most mentally stable and the best trusted.

'It seems a shame,' the alien said, 'that a human of your accomplishments should have to rot for two years in this miserable, profitless outpost.'

'The years won't be wasted,' Afriel said.

'But why have you chosen to study the Swarm? They can teach you nothing, since they cannot speak. They have no wish to trade, having no tools or technology. They are the only spacefaring race that is essentially without intelligence.'

'That alone should make them worthy of study.'

'Do you seek to imitate them, then? You would make monsters of yourselves.' Again the ensign hesitated. 'Perhaps you could do it. It would be bad for business, however.'

There came a fluting burst of alien music over the ship's speakers, then a screeching fragment of Investor language. Most of it was too high-pitched for Afriel's ears to follow.

The alien stood, his jeweled skirt brushing the tips of his clawed birdlike feet. 'The Swarm's symbiote has arrived,' he said.

'Thank you,' Afriel said. When the ensign opened the cabin door, Afriel could smell the Swarm's representative; the creature's warm yeasty scent had spread rapidly through the starship's recycled air.

Afriel quickly checked his appearance in a pocket mirror. He touched powder to his face and straightened the round velvet hat on his shoulder-length reddish-blond hair. His earlobes glittered with red impact-rubies, thick as his thumbs' ends, mined from the Asteroid Belt. His knee-length coat and waistcoat were of gold brocade; the shirt beneath was of dazzling fineness, woven with red-gold thread. He had dressed to impress the Investors, who expected and appreciated a prosperous look from their customers. How could he impress this new alien? Smell, perhaps. He freshened his perfume.

Beside the starship's secondary airlock, the Swarm's symbiote was chittering rapidly at the ship's commander. The commander was an old and sleepy Investor, twice the size of most of her crewmen. Her massive head was encrusted in a jeweled helmet. From within the helmet her clouded eyes glittered like cameras.

The symbiote lifted on its six posterior legs and gestured feebly with its four clawed forelimbs. The ship's artificial gravity, a third again as strong as Earth's, seemed to bother it. Its rudimentary eyes, dangling on stalks, were shut tight against the glare. It must be used to darkness, Afriel thought.

The commander answered the creature in its own language. Afriel grimaced, for he had hoped that the creature spoke Investor. Now he would have to learn another language, a language designed for a being without a tongue.

After another brief interchange the commander turned to Afriel. 'The symbiote is not pleased with your arrival,' she told Afriel in the Investor language. 'There has apparently been some disturbance here involving humans, in the recent past. However, I have prevailed upon it to admit you to the Nest. The episode has been recorded. Payment for my diplomatic services will be arranged with your faction when I return to your native star system.'

'I thank Your Authority,' Afriel said. 'Please convey to the symbiote my best personal wishes, and the harmlessness and humility of my intentions – ' He broke off short as the symbiote lunged toward him, biting him savagely in the calf of his left leg. Afriel jerked free and leaped backward in the heavy artificial gravity, going into a defensive position. The symbiote had ripped away a long shred of his pants leg; it now crouched quietly, eating it.

'It will convey your scent and composition to its nestmates,' said the commander. 'This is necessary. Otherwise you would be classed as an invader, and the Swarm's warrior caste would kill you at once.'

Afriel relaxed quickly and pressed his hand against the puncture wound to stop the bleeding. He hoped that none of the Investors had noticed his reflexive action. It would not mesh well with his story of being a harmless researcher.

'We will reopen the airlock soon,' the commander said phlegmatically, leaning back on her thick reptilian tail. The symbiote continued to munch the shred of cloth. Afriel studied the creature's neckless segmented head. It had a mouth and nostrils; it had bulbous atrophied eyes on stalks; there were hinged slats that might be radio receivers, and two parallel ridges of clumped wriggling antennae, sprouting among three chitinous plates. Their function was unknown to him.

The airlock door opened. A rush of dense, smoky aroma entered the departure cabin. It seemed to bother the half-dozen Investors, who left rapidly. 'We will return in six hundred and twelve of your days, as by our agreement,' the commander said.

'I thank Your Authority,' Afriel said.

'Good luck,' the commander said in English. Afriel smiled.

The symbiote, with a sinuous wriggle of its segmented body, crept into the airlock. Afriel followed it. The airlock door shut behind them. The creature said nothing to him but continued munching loudly. The second door opened, and the symbiote sprang through it, into a wide, round stone tunnel. It disappeared at once into the gloom.

Afriel put his sunglasses into a pocket of his jacket and pulled out a pair of infrared goggles. He strapped them to his head and stepped out of the airlock. The artificial gravity vanished, replaced by the almost imperceptible gravity of the Swarm's asteroid nest. Afriel smiled, comfortable for the first time in weeks. Most of his adult life had been spent in free-fall, in the Shapers' colonies in the Rings of Saturn.

Squatting in a dark cavity in the side of the tunnel was a disk-headed furred animal the size of an elephant. It was clearly visible in the infrared of its own body heat. Afriel could hear it breathing. It waited patiently until Afriel had launched himself past it, deeper into the tunnel. Then it took its place in the end of the tunnel, puffing itself up with air until its swollen head securely plugged the exit into space. Its multiple legs sank firmly into sockets in the walls.

The Investors' ship had left. Afriel remained here, inside one of the millions of planetoids that circled the giant star Betelgeuse in a girdling ring with almost five times the mass of Jupiter. As a source of potential wealth it dwarfed the entire solar system, and it belonged, more or less, to the Swarm. At least, no other race had challenged them for it within the memory of the Investors.

Afriel peered up the corridor. It seemed deserted, and without other bodies to cast infrared heat, he could not see very far. Kicking against the wall, he floated hesitantly down the corridor.

He heard a human voice. 'Dr Afriel!'

'Dr Mirny!' he called out. 'This way!'

He first saw a pair of young symbiotes scuttling toward him, the tips of their clawed feet barely touching the walls. Behind them came a woman wearing goggles like his own. She was young, and attractive in the trim, anonymous way of the genetically reshaped.

She screeched something at the symbiotes in their own language, and they halted, waiting. She coasted forward, and Afriel caught her arm, expertly stopping their momentum.

'You didn't bring any luggage?' she said anxiously.

He shook his head. 'We got your warning before I was sent out. I have only the clothes I'm wearing and a few items in my pockets.'

She looked at him critically. 'Is that what people are wearing in the Rings these days? Things have changed more than I thought.'

Afriel glanced at his brocaded coat and laughed. 'It's a matter of policy. The Investors are always readier to talk to a human who looks ready to do business on a large scale. All the Shapers' representatives dress like this these days. We've stolen a jump on the Mechanists; they still dress in those coveralls.'

He hesitated, not wanting to offend her. Galina Mirny's intelligence was rated at almost two hundred. Men and women that bright were sometimes flighty and unstable, likely to retreat into private fantasy worlds or become enmeshed in strange and impenetrable webs of plotting and rationalization. High intelligence was the strategy the Shapers had chosen in the struggle for cultural dominance, and they were obliged to stick to it, despite its occasional disadvantages. They had tried breeding the Superbright – those with quotients over two hundred – but so many had defected from the Shapers' colonies that the faction had stopped producing them.

'You wonder about my own clothing,' Mirny said.

'It certainly has the appeal of novelty,' Afriel said with a smile.

'It was woven from the fibers of a pupa's cocoon,' she said. 'My original wardrobe was eaten by a scavenger symbiote during the troubles last year. I usually go nude, but I didn't want to offend you by too great a show of intimacy.'

Afriel shrugged. 'I often go nude myself, I never had much use for clothes except for pockets. I have a few tools on my person, but most are of little importance. We're Shapers, our tools are here.' He tapped his head. 'If you can show me a safe place to put my clothes . . .'

She shook her head. It was impossible to see her eyes for the goggles, which made her expression hard to read. 'You've made your first mistake, Doctor. There are no places of our own here. It was the same mistake the Mechanist agents made, the same one that almost killed me as well. There is no concept of privacy or property here. This is the Nest. If you seize any part of it for yourself – to store equipment, to sleep in, whatever – then you become an intruder, an enemy. The two Mechanists – a man and a woman – tried to secure an empty chamber for their computer lab. Warriors broke down their door and devoured them. Scavengers ate their equipment, glass, metal, and all.'

Afriel smiled coldly. 'It must have cost them a fortune to ship all that material here.'

Mirny shrugged. 'They're wealthier than we are. Their machines, their mining. They meant to kill me, I think. Surreptitiously, so the warriors wouldn't be upset by a show of violence. They had a computer that was learning the language of the springtails faster than I could.'

'But you survived,' Afriel pointed out. 'And your tapes and reports – especially the early ones, when you still had most of your equipment – were of tremendous interest. The Council is behind you all the way. You've become quite a celebrity in the Rings, during your absence.'

'Yes, I expected as much,' she said.

Afriel was nonplused. 'If I found any deficiency in them,' he said carefully, 'it was in my own field, alien linguistics.' He waved vaguely at the two symbiotes who accompanied her. 'I assume you've made great progress in communicating with the symbiotes, since they seem to do all the talking for the Nest.'

She looked at him with an unreadable expression and shrugged. 'There are at least fifteen different kinds of symbiotes here. Those that accompany me are called the springtails, and they speak only for themselves. They are savages, Doctor, who received attention from the Investors only because they can still talk. They were a spacefaring race once, but they've forgotten it. They discovered the Nest and they were absorbed, they became parasites.' She tapped one of them on the head. 'I tamed these two because I learned to steal and beg food better than they can. They stay with me now and protect me from the larger ones. They are jealous, you know. They have only been with the Nest for perhaps ten thousand years and are still uncertain of their position. They still think, and wonder sometimes. After ten thousand years there is still a little of that left to them.'

'Savages,' Afriel said. 'I can well believe that. One of them bit me while I was still aboard the starship. He left a lot to be desired as an ambassador.'

'Yes, I warned him you were coming,' said Mirny. 'He didn't much like the idea, but I was able to bribe him with food . . . I hope he didn't hurt you badly.'

'A scratch,' Afriel said. 'I assume there's no chance of infection.'

'I doubt it very much. Unless you brought your own bacteria with you.'

'Hardly likely,' Afriel said, offended. 'I have no bacteria. And I wouldn't have brought microorganisms to an alien culture anyway.'

Mirny looked away. 'I thought you might have some of the special genetically altered ones . . . I think we can go now. The springtail will have spread your scent by mouth-touching in the subsidiary chamber, ahead of us. It will be spread throughout the Nest in a few hours. Once it reaches the Queen, it will spread very quickly.'

She jammed her feet against the hard shell of one of the young springtails and launched herself down the hall. Afriel followed her. The air was warm and he was beginning to sweat under his elaborate clothing, but his antiseptic sweat was odorless.

They exited into a vast chamber dug from the living rock. It was arched and oblong, eighty meters long and about twenty in diameter. It swarmed with members of the Nest.

There were hundreds of them. Most of them were workers, eight-legged and furred, the size of Great Danes. Here and there were members of the warrior caste, horse-sized furry monsters with heavy fanged heads the size and shape of overstuffed chairs.

A few meters away, two workers were carrying a member of the sensor caste, a being whose immense flattened head was attached to an atrophied body that was mostly lungs. The sensor had great platelike eyes, and its furred chitin sprouted long coiled antennae that twitched feebly as the workers bore it along. The workers clung to the hollowed rock of the chamber walls with hooked and suckered feet.

A paddle-limbed monster with a hairless, faceless head came sculling past them, through the warm reeking air. The front of its head was a nightmare of sharp grinding jaws and blunt armored acid spouts. 'A tunneler,' Mirny said. 'It can take us deeper into the Nest – come with me.' She launched herself toward it and took a handhold on its furry, segmented back. Afriel followed her, joined by the two immature springtails, who clung to the thing's hide with their forelimbs. Afriel shuddered at the warm, greasy feel of its rank, damp fur. It continued to scull through the air, its eight fringed paddle feet catching the air like wings.

'There must be thousands of them,' Afriel said.

'I said a hundred thousand in my last report, but that was before I had fully explored the Nest. Even now there are long stretches I haven't seen. They must number close to a quarter of a million. This asteroid is about the size of the Mechanists' biggest base – Ceres. It still has rich veins of carbonaceous material. It's far from mined out.'

Afriel closed his eyes. If he was to lose his goggles, he would have to feel his way, blind, through these teeming, twitching, wriggling thousands. 'The population's still expanding, then?'

'Definitely,' she said. 'In fact, the colony will launch a mating swarm soon. There are three dozen male and female alates in the chambers near the Queen. Once they're launched, they'll mate and start new Nests. I'll take you to see them presently.' She hesitated. 'We're entering one of the fungal gardens now.'

One of the young springtails quietly shifted position. Grabbing the tunneler's fur with its forelimbs, it began to gnaw on the cuff of Afriel's pants. Afriel kicked it soundly, and it jerked back, retracting its eyestalks.

When he looked up again, he saw that they had entered a second chamber, much larger than the first. The walls around, overhead, and below were buried under an explosive profusion of fungus. The most common types were swollen barrel-like domes, multibranched massed thickets, and spaghetti-like tangled extrusions that moved very slightly in the faint and odorous breeze. Some of the barrels were surrounded by dim mists of exhaled spores.

'You see those caked-up piles beneath the fungus, its growth medium?' Mirny said.

'Yes.'

'I'm not sure whether it is a plant form or just some kind of complex biochemical sludge,' she said. 'The point is that it grows in sunlight, on the outside of the asteroid. A food source that grows in naked space! Imagine what that would be worth, back in the Rings.'

'There aren't words for its value,' Afriel said.

'It's inedible by itself,' she said. 'I tried to eat a very small piece of it once. It was like trying to eat plastic.'

'Have you eaten well, generally speaking?'

'Yes. Our biochemistry is quite similar to the Swarm's. The fungus itself is perfectly edible. The regurgitate is more nourishing, though. Internal fermentation in the worker hindgut adds to its nutritional value.'

Afriel stared. 'You grow used to it,' Mirny said. 'Later I'll teach you how to solicit food from the workers. It's a simple matter of reflex tapping – it's not controlled by pheromones, like most of their behavior.' She brushed a long lock of clumped and dirty hair from the side of her face. 'I hope the pheromonal samples I sent back were worth the cost of transportation.'

'Oh, yes,' said Afriel. 'The chemistry of them was fascinating. We managed to synthesize most of the compounds. I was part of the research team myself.' He hesitated. How far did he dare trust her? She had not been told about the experiment he and his superiors had planned. As far as Mirny knew, he was a simple, peaceful researcher, like herself. The Shapers' scientific community was suspicious of the minority involved in military work and espionage.

As an investment in the future, the Shapers had sent researchers of each of the nineteen alien races described to them by the Investors. This had cost the Shaper economy many gigawatts of precious energy and tons of rare metals and isotopes. In most cases, only two or three researchers could be sent; in seven cases, only one. For the Swarm, Galina Mirny had been chosen. She had gone peacefully, trusting in her intelligence and her good intentions to keep her alive and sane. Those who had sent her had not known whether her findings would be of any use or importance. They had only known that it was imperative that she be sent, even alone, even ill-equipped, before some other faction sent their own people and possibly discovered some technique or fact of overwhelming importance. And Dr Mirny had indeed discovered such a situation. It had made her mission into a matter of Ring security. That was why Afriel had come.

'You synthesized the compounds?' she said. 'Why?'

Afriel smiled disarmingly. 'Just to prove to ourselves that we could do it, perhaps.'

She shook her head. 'No mind-games, Dr Afriel, please. I came this far partly to escape from such things. Tell me the truth.'

Afriel stared at her, regretting that the goggles meant he could not meet her eyes. 'Very well,' he said. 'You should know, then, that I have been ordered by the Ring Council to carry out an experiment that may endanger both our lives.'

Mirny was silent for a moment. 'You're from Security, then?'

'My rank is captain.'

'I knew it . . . I knew it when those two Mechanists arrived. They were so polite, and so suspicious – I think they would have killed me at once if they hadn't hoped to bribe or torture some secret out of me. They scared the life out of me, Captain Afriel . . . You scare me, too.'

'We live in a frightening world, Doctor. It's a matter of faction security.'

'Everything's a matter of faction security with your lot,' she said. 'I shouldn't take you any farther, or show you anything more. This Nest, these creatures – they're not *intelligent*, Captain. They can't think, they can't learn. They're innocent, primordially innocent. They have no knowledge of good and evil. They have no knowledge of *anything*. The last thing they need is to become pawns in a power struggle within some other race, light-years away.'

The tunneler had turned into an exit from the fungal chambers and was paddling slowly along in the warm darkness. A group of creatures like gray, flattened basketballs floated by from the opposite direction. One of them settled on Afriel's sleeve, clinging with frail whiplike tentacles. Afriel brushed it gently away, and it broke loose, emitting a stream of foul reddish droplets.

'Naturally I agree with you in principle, Doctor,' Afriel said smoothly. 'But consider these Mechanists. Some of their extreme factions are already more than half machine. Do you expect humanitarian motives from them? They're cold, Doctor – cold and soulless creatures who can cut a living man or woman to bits and never feel their pain. Most of the other functions hate us. They call us racist supermen. Would you rather that one of these cults do what we must do, and use the results against us?'

'This is double-talk.' She looked away. All around them workers laden down with fungus, their jaws full and guts stuffed with it, were spreading out into the Nest, scuttling alongside them or disappearing into branch tunnels departing in every direction, including straight up and straight down. Afriel saw a creature much like a worker, but with only six legs, scuttle past in the opposite direction, overhead. It was a parasite mimic. How long, he wondered, did it take a creature to evolve to look like that?

'It's no wonder that we've had so many defectors, back in the Rings,' she said sadly. 'If humanity is so stupid as to work itself into a corner like you describe, then it's better to have nothing to do with them. Better to live alone. Better not to help the madness spread.'

'That kind of talk will only get us killed,' Afriel said. 'We owe an allegiance to the faction that produced us.'

'Tell me truly, Captain,' she said. 'Haven't you ever felt the urge to leave everything – everyone – all your duties and constraints, and just go somewhere to think it all out? Your whole world, and your part in it? We're trained so hard, from childhood, and so much is demanded from us. Don't you think it's made us lose sight of our goals, somehow?'

'We live in space,' Afriel said flatly. 'Space is an unnatural environment, and it takes an unnatural effort from unnatural people to prosper there. Our minds are our tools, and philosophy has to come second. Naturally I've felt those urges you mention. They're just another threat to guard against. I believe in an ordered society. Technology has unleashed tremendous forces that are ripping society apart. Some one faction must arise from the struggle and integrate things. We Shapers have the wisdom and restraint to do it humanely. That's why I do the work I do.' He hesitated. 'I don't expect to see our day of triumph. I expect to die in some brush-fire conflict, or through assassination. It's enough that I can foresee that day.'

'But the arrogance of it, Captain!' she said suddenly. 'The arrogance of your little life and its little sacrifice! Consider the Swarm, if you really want your humane and perfect order. Here it is! Where it's always warm and dark, and it smells good, and food is easy to get, and everything is endlessly and perfectly recycled. The only resources that are ever lost are the bodies of the mating swarms, and a little air. A Nest like this one could last unchanged for hundreds of thousands of years. Hundreds . . . of thousands . . . of years. Who, or what, will remember us and our stupid faction in even a thousand years?'

Afriel shook his head. 'That's not a valid comparison. There is no such long view for us. In another thousand years we'll be machines, or gods.' He felt the top of his head; his velvet cap was gone. No doubt something was eating it by now.

The tunneler took them deeper into the asteroid's honeycombed free-fall maze. They saw the pupal chambers, where pallid larvae twitched in swaddled silk; the main fungal gardens; the graveyard pits, where winged workers beat ceaselessly at the soupy air, feverishly hot from the heat of decomposition. Corrosive black fungus ate the bodies of the dead into coarse black powder, carried off by blackened workers themselves three-quarters dead.

Later they left the tunneler and floated on by themselves. The woman moved with the ease of long habit; Afriel followed her, colliding bruisingly with squeaking workers. There were thousands of them, clinging to ceiling, walls, and floor, clustering and scurrying at every conceivable angle.

Later still they visited the chamber of the winged princes and princesses, an echoing round vault where creatures forty meters long hung crooked-legged in midair. Their bodies were segmented and metallic, with organic rocket nozzles on their thoraxes, where wings might have been. Folded along their sleek backs were radar antennae on long sweeping booms. They looked more like interplanetary probes under construction than anything biological. Workers fed them ceaselessly. Their bulging spiracled abdomens were full of compressed oxygen.

Mirny begged a large chunk of fungus from a passing worker, deftly tapping its antennae and provoking a reflex action. She handed most of the fungus to the two springtails, who devoured it greedily and looked expectantly for more.

Afriel tucked his legs into a free-fall lotus position and began chewing with determination on the leathery fungus. It was tough, but tasted good, like smoked meat – a delicacy he had tasted only once. The smell of smoke meant disaster in a Shaper's colony.

Mirny maintained a stony silence. 'Food's no problem,' Afriel said. 'Where do we sleep?'

She shrugged. 'Anywhere . . . there are unused niches and tunnels here and there. I suppose you'll want to see the Queen's chamber next.'

'By all means.'

'I'll have to get more fungus. The warriors are on guard there and have to be bribed with food.'

She gathered an armful of fungus from another worker in the endless stream, and they moved on. Afriel, already totally lost, was further confused in the maze of chambers and tunnels. At last they exited into an immense lightless cavern, bright with infrared heat from the Queen's monstrous body. It was the colony's central factory. The fact that it was made of warm and pulpy flesh did not conceal its essentially industrial nature. Tons of predigested fungal pap went into the slick blind jaws at one end. The rounded billows of soft flesh digested and processed it, squirming, sucking, and undulating, with loud machine-like churnings and gurglings. Out of the other end came an endless conveyor-like blobbed stream of eggs, each one packed in a thick hormonal paste of lubrication. The workers avidly licked the eggs clean and bore them off to nurseries. Each egg was the size of a man's torso.

The process went on and on. There was no day or night here in the lightless center of the asteroid. There was no remnant of a diurnal rhythm in the genes of these creatures. The flow of production was as constant and even as the working of an automated mine.

'This is why I'm here,' Afriel murmured in awe. 'Just look at this, Doctor. The Mechanists have cybernetic mining machinery that is generations ahead of ours. But here – in the bowels of this nameless little world – is a genetic technology that feeds itself, maintains itself, runs itself, efficiently, endlessly, mindlessly. It's the perfect organic tool. The faction that could use these tireless workers could make itself an industrial titan. And our knowledge of biochemistry is unsurpassed. We Shapers are just the ones to do it.'

'How do you propose to do that?' Mirny asked with open skepticism. 'You would have to ship a fertilized queen all the way to the solar system. We could scarcely afford that, even if the Investors would let us, which they wouldn't.'

'I don't need an entire Nest,' Afriel said patiently. 'I only need the genetic information from one egg. Our laboratories back in the Rings could clone endless numbers of workers.'

'But the workers are useless without the Nest's pheromones. They need chemical cues to trigger their behavior modes.'

'Exactly,' Afriel said. 'As it so happens, I posses those pheromones, synthesized and concentrated. What I must do now is test them. I must prove that I can use them to make the workers do what I choose. Once I've proven it's possible, I'm authorized to smuggle the genetic information necessary back to the Rings. The Investors won't approve. There are, of course, moral questions involved, and the Investors are not genetically advanced. But we can win their approval back with the profits we make. Best of all, we can beat the Mechanists at their own game.'

'You've carried the pheromones here?' Mirny said. 'Didn't the Investors suspect something when they found them?'

'Now it's you who has made an error,' Afriel said calmly. 'You assume that the Investors are infallible. You are wrong. A race without curiosity will never explore every possibility, the way we Shapers did.' Afriel pulled up his pants cuff and extended his right leg. 'Consider this varicose vein along my shin. Circulatory problems of this sort are common among those who spend a lot of time in free-fall. This vein, however, has been blocked artificially and treated to reduce osmosis. Within the vein are ten separate colonies of genetically altered bacteria, each one specially bred to produce a different Swarm pheromone.'

He smiled. 'The Investors searched me very thoroughly, including X-rays. But the vein appears normal to X-rays, and the bacteria are trapped within compartments in the vein. They are indetectable. I have a small medical kit on my person. It includes a syringe. We can use it to extract the pheromones and test them. When the tests are finished – and I feel sure they will be successful, in fact I've staked my career on it – we can empty the vein and all its compartments. The bacteria will die on contact with air. We can refill the vein with the yolk from a developing embryo. The cells may survive during the trip back, but even if they die, they can't rot inside my body. They'll never come in contact with any agent of decay. Back in the Rings, we can learn to activate and suppress different genes to produce the different castes, just as is done in nature. We'll have millions of workers, armies of warriors if need be, perhaps even organic rocketships, grown from altered alates. If this works, who do you think will remember me then, eh? Me and my arrogant little life and little sacrifice?'

She stared at him; even the bulky goggles could not hide her new respect and even fear. 'You really mean to do it, then.'

'I made the sacrifice of my time and energy. I expect results, Doctor.'

'But it's kidnapping. You're talking about breeding a slave race.'

Afriel shrugged, with contempt. 'You're juggling words, Doctor. I'll cause this colony no harm. I may steal some of its workers' labor while they obey my own chemical orders, but that tiny theft won't be missed. I admit to the murder of one egg, but that is no more a crime than a human abortion. Can the theft of one strand of genetic material be called "kidnapping"? I think not. As for the scandalous idea of a slave race – I reject it out of hand. These creatures are genetic robots. They will no more be slaves than are laser drills or cargo tankers. At the very worst, they will be our domestic animals.'

Mirny considered the issue. It did not take her long. 'It's true. It's not as if a common worker will be staring at the stars, pining for its freedom. They're just brainless neuters.'

'Exactly, Doctor.'

'They simply work. Whether they work for us or the Swarm makes no difference to them.'

'I see that you've seized on the beauty of the idea.'

'And if it worked,' Mirny said, 'if it worked, our faction would profit astronomically.'

Afriel smiled genuinely, unaware of the chilling sarcasm of his expression. 'And the personal profit, Doctor . . . the valuable expertise of the first to exploit the technique.' He spoke gently, quietly. 'Ever see a nitrogen snowfall on Titan? I think a habitat of one's own there – larger, much larger than anything possible before . . . A genuine city,

Galina, a place where a man can scrap the rules and discipline that madden him . . .'

'Now it's you who are talking defection, Captain-Doctor.'

Afriel was silent for a moment, then smiled with an effort. 'Now you've ruined my perfect reverie,' he said. 'Besides, what I was describing was the well-earned retirement of a wealthy man, not some self-indulgent hermitage . . . There's a clear difference.' He hesitated. 'In any case, may I conclude that you're with me in this project?'

She laughed and touched his arm. There was something uncanny about the small sound of her laugh, drowned by a great organic rumble from the Queen's monstrous intestines . . . 'Do you expect me to resist your arguments for two long years? Better that I give in now and save us friction.'

'Yes.'

'After all, you won't do any harm to the Nest. They'll never know anything has happened. And if their genetic line is successfully reproduced back home, there'll never be any reason for humanity to bother them again.'

'True enough,' said Afriel, though in the back of his mind he instantly thought of the fabulous wealth of Betelgeuse's asteroid system. A day would come, inevitably, when humanity would move to the stars en masse, in earnest. It would be well to know the ins and outs of every race that might become a rival.

'I'll help you as best I can,' she said. There was a moment's silence. 'Have you seen enough of this area?'

'Yes.' They left the Queen's chamber.

'I didn't think I'd like you at first,' she said candidly. 'I think I like you better now. You seem to have a sense of humor that most Security people lack.'

'It's not a sense of humor,' Afriel said sadly. 'It's a sense of irony disguised as one.'

There were no days in the unending stream of hours that followed. There were only ragged periods of sleep, apart at first, later together, as they held each other in free-fall. The sexual feel of skin and body became an anchor to their common humanity, a divided, frayed humanity so many light-years away that the concept no longer had any meaning. Life in the warm and swarming tunnels was the here and now; the two of them were like germs in a bloodstream, moving ceaselessly with the pulsing ebb and flow. Hours stretched into months, and time itself grew meaningless.

The pheromonal tests were complex, but not impossibly difficult. The first of the ten pheromones was a simple grouping stimulus, causing large numbers of workers to gather as the chemical was spread from palp to palp. The workers then waited for further instructions; if none were forthcoming, they dispersed. To work effectively, the pheromones had to be given in a mix, or series, like computer commands; number one, grouping, for instance, together with the third pheromone, a transferral order, which caused the workers to empty any given chamber and move its effects to another. The ninth pheromone had the best industrial possibilities; it was a building order, causing the workers to gather tunnelers and dredgers and set them to work. Others were annoying; the tenth pheromone provoked grooming behavior, and the workers' furry palps stripped off the remaining rags of Afriel's clothing. The eighth pheromone sent the workers off to harvest material on the asteroid's surface, and in their eagerness to observe its effects the two explorers were almost trapped and swept off into space.

The two of them no longer feared the warrior caste. They knew that a dose of the sixth pheromone would send them scurrying off to defend the eggs, just as it sent the workers to tend them. Mirny and Afriel took advantage of this and secured their own chambers, dug by chemically hijacked workers and defended by a hijacked airlock guardian. They had their own fungal gardens to refresh the air, stocked with the fungus they liked best, and digested by a worker they kept drugged for their own food use. From constant stuffing and lack of exercise the worker had swollen up into its replete form and hung from one wall like a monstrous grape.

Afriel was tired. He had been without sleep recently for a long time; how long, he didn't know. His body rhythms had not adjusted as well as Mirny's, and he was prone to fits of depression and irritability that he had to repress with an effort. 'The Investors will be back sometime,' he said. 'Sometime soon.'

Mirny was indifferent. 'The Investors,' she said, and followed the remark with something in the language of the springtails, which he didn't catch. Despite his linguistic training, Afriel had never caught up with her in her use of the springtails' grating jargon. His training was almost a liability; the springtail language had decayed so much that it was a pidgin tongue, without rules or regularity. He knew enough to give them simple orders, and with his partial control of the warriors he had the power to back it up. The springtails were afraid of him, and the two juveniles that Mirny had tamed had developed into fat, overgrown tyrants that freely terrorized their elders. Afriel had been too busy to seriously study the springtails or the other symbiotes. There were too many practical matters at hand.

'If they come too soon, I won't be able to finish my latest study,' she said in English.

Afriel pulled off his infrared goggles and knotted them tightly around his neck. 'There's a limit, Galina,' he said, yawning. 'You can only memorize so much data without equipment. We'll just have to wait quietly until we can get back. I hope the Investors aren't shocked when they see me. I lost a fortune with those clothes.'

'It's been so dull since the mating swarm was launched. If it weren't for the new growth in the alates' chamber, I'd be bored to death.' She pushed greasy hair from her face with both hands. 'Are you going to sleep?'

'Yes, if I can.'

'You won't come with me? I keep telling you that this new growth is important. I think it's a new caste. It's definitely not an alate. It has eyes like an alate, but it's clinging to the wall.'

'It's probably not a Swarm member at all, then,' he said tiredly, humoring her. 'It's probably a parasite, an alate mimic. Go on and see it, if you want to. I'll be here waiting for you.'

He heard her leave. Without his infrareds on, the darkness was still not quite total; there was a very faint luminosity from the steaming, growing fungus in the chamber beyond. The stuffed worker replete moved slightly on the wall, rustling and gurgling. He fell asleep.

*

When he awoke, Mirny had not yet returned. He was not alarmed. First, he visited the original airlock tunnel, where the Investors had first left him. It was irrational – the Investors always fulfilled their contracts – but he feared that they would arrive someday, become impatient, and leave without him. The Investors would have to wait, of course. Mirny could keep them occupied in the short time it would take him to hurry to the nursery and rob a developing egg of its living cells. It was best that the egg be as fresh as possible.

Later he ate. He was munching fungus in one of the anterior chambers when Mirny's two tamed springtails found him. 'What do you want?' he asked in their language.

'Food-giver no good,' the larger one screeched, waving its forelegs in brainless agitation. 'Not work, not sleep.'

'Not move,' the second one said. It added hopefully, 'Eat it now?'

Afriel gave them some of his food. They ate it, seemingly more out of habit than real appetite, which alarmed him. 'Take me to her,' he told them.

The two springtails scurried off; he followed them easily, adroitly dodging and weaving through the crowds of workers. They led him several miles through the network, to the alates' chamber. There they stopped, confused. 'Gone,' the large one said.

The chamber was empty. Afriel had never seen it empty before, and it was very unusual for the Swarm to waste so much space. He felt dread. 'Follow the food-giver,' he said. 'Follow the smell.'

The springtails snuffled without much enthusiasm along one wall; they knew he had no food and were reluctant to do anything without an immediate reward. At last one of them picked up the scent, or pretended to, and followed it up across the ceiling and into the mouth of a tunnel.

It was hard for Afriel to see much in the abandoned chamber; there was not enough infrared heat. He leaped upward after the springtail.

He heard the roar of a warrior and the springtail's choked-off screech. It came flying from the tunnel's mouth, a spray of clotted fluid bursting from its ruptured head. It tumbled end over end until it hit the far wall with a flaccid crunch. It was already dead.

The second springtail fled at once, screeching with grief and terror.

Afriel landed on the lip of the tunnel, sinking into a crouch as his legs soaked up momentum. He could smell the acrid stench of the warrior's anger, a pheromone so thick that even a human could scent it. Dozens of other warriors would group here within minutes, or seconds. Behind the enraged warrior he could hear workers and tunnelers shifting and cementing rock.

He might be able to control one enraged warrior, but never two, or twenty. He launched himself from the chamber wall and out an exit.

He searched for the other springtail – he felt sure he could recognize it, since it was so much bigger than the others – but he could not find it. With its keen sense of smell, it could easily avoid him if it wanted to.

Mirny did not return. Uncountable hours passed. He slept again. He returned to the alates' chamber; there were warriors on guard there, warriors that were not interested in food and brandished their immense serrated fangs when he approached. They looked ready to rip him apart; the faint reek of aggressive pheromones hung about the place like a fog. He did not see any symbiotes of any kind on the warriors' bodies. There was one species, a thing like a huge tick, that clung only to warriors, but even the ticks were gone.

He returned to his chambers to wait and think. Mirny's body was not in the garbage pits. Of course, it was possible that something else might have eaten her. Should he extract the remaining pheromone from the spaces in his vein and try to break into the alates' chamber? He suspected that Mirny, or whatever was left of her, was somewhere in the tunnel where the springtail had been killed. He had never explored that tunnel himself. There were thousands of tunnels he had never explored.

He felt paralyzed by indecision and fear. If he was quiet, if he did nothing, the Investors might arrive at any moment. He could tell the Ring Council anything he wanted about Mirny's death; if he had the genetics with him, no one would quibble. He did not love her; he respected her, but not enough to give up his life, or his faction's investment. He had not thought of the Ring Council in a long time, and the thought sobered him. He would have to explain his decision . . .

He was still in a brown study when he heard a whoosh of air as his living airlock deflated itself. Three warriors had come for him. There was no reek of anger about them. They moved slowly and carefully. He knew better than to try to resist. One of them seized him gently in its massive jaws and carried him off.

It took him to the alates' chamber and into the guarded tunnel. A new, large chamber had been excavated at the end of the tunnel. It was filled almost to bursting by a black-splattered white mass of flesh. In the center of the soft speckled mass were a mouth and two damp, shining eyes, on stalks. Long tendrils like conduits dangled, writhing, from a clumped ridge above the eyes. The tendrils ended in pink, fleshy pluglike clumps.

One of the tendrils had been thrust through Mirny's skull. Her body hung in midair, limp as wax. Her eyes were open, but blind.

Another tendril was plugged into the braincase of a mutated worker. The worker still had the pallid tinge of a larva; it was shrunken and deformed, and its mouth had the wrinkled look of a human mouth. There was a blob like a tongue in the mouth, and white ridges like human teeth. It had no eyes.

It spoke with Mirny's voice. 'Captain-Doctor Afriel . . .'

'Galina . . .'

'I have no such name. You may address me as Swarm.'

Afriel vomited. The central mass was an immense head. Its brain almost filled the room.

It waited politely until Afriel had finished.

'I find myself awakened again,' Swarm said dreamily. 'I am pleased to see that there is no major emergency to concern me. Instead it is a threat that has become almost routine.' It hesitated delicately. Mirny's body moved slightly in midair; her breathing was inhumanly regular. The eyes opened and closed, 'Another young race.'

'What are you?'

'I am the Swarm. That is, I am one of its castes. I am a tool, an adaptation; my specialty is intelligence. I am not often needed. It is good to be needed again.'

'Have you been here all along? Why didn't you greet us? We'd have dealt with you. We meant no harm.'

The wet mouth on the end of the plug made laughing sounds.

'Like yourself, I enjoy irony,' it said. 'It is a pretty trap you have found yourself in, Captain-Doctor. You meant to make the Swarm work for you and your race. You meant to breed us and study us and use us. It is an excellent plan, but one we hit upon long before your race evolved.'

Stung by panic, Afriel's mind raced frantically. 'You're an intelligent being,' he said. 'There's no reason to do us any harm. Let us talk together. We can help you.'

'Yes,' Swarm agreed. 'You will be helpful. Your companion's memories tell me that this is one of those uncomfortable periods when galactic intelligence is rife. Intelligence is a great bother. It makes all kinds of trouble for us.'

'What do you mean?'

'You are a young race and lay great stock by your own cleverness,' Swarm said. 'As usual, you fail to see that intelligence is not a survival trait.'

Afriel wiped sweat from his face. 'We've done well,' he said. 'We came to you, and peacefully. You didn't come to us.'

'I refer to exactly that,' Swarm said urbanely. 'This urge to expand, to explore, to develop, is just what will make you extinct. You naively suppose that you can continue to feed your curiosity indefinitely. It is an old story, pursued by countless races before you. Within a thousand years – perhaps a little longer – your species will vanish.'

'You intend to destroy us, then? I warn you it will not be an easy task –'

'Again you miss the point. Knowledge is power! Do you suppose that fragile little form of yours – your primitive legs, your ludicrous arms and hands, your tiny, scarcely wrinkled brain – can *contain* all that power? Certainly not! Already your race is flying to pieces under the impact of your own expertise. The original human form is becoming obsolete. Your own genes have been altered, and you, Captain-Doctor, are a crude experiment. In a hundred years you will be a relic. In a thousand years you will not even be a memory. Your race will go the same way as a thousand others.'

'And what way is that?'

'I do not know.' The thing on the end of the Swarm's arm made a chuckling sound. 'They have passed beyond my ken. They have all discovered something, learned something, that has caused them to transcend my understanding. It may be that they even transcend *being*. At any rate, I cannot sense their presence anywhere. They seem to do nothing, they seem to interfere in nothing; for all intents and purposes, they seem to be dead. Vanished. They may have become gods, or ghosts. In either case, I have no wish to join them.'

'So then – so then you have – '

'Intelligence is very much a two-edged sword, Captain-Doctor. It is useful only up to a point. It interferes with the business of living. Life, and intelligence, do not mix very well. They are not at all closely related, as you childishly assume.'

'But you, then – you are a rational being –'

'I am a tool, as I said.' The mutated device on the end of its arm made a sighing noise. 'When you began your pheromonal experiments, the chemical imbalance became apparent to the Queen. It triggered certain genetic patterns within her body, and I was reborn. Chemical sabotage is a problem that can best be dealt with by intelligence. I am a brain replete, you see, specially designed to be far more intelligent than any young race. Within three days I was fully self-conscious. Within five days I had deciphered these markings on my body. They are the genetically encoded history of my race . . . within five days and two hours I recognized the problem at hand and knew what to do. I am now doing it. I am six days old.'

'What is it you intend to do?'

'Your race is a very vigorous one. I expect it to be here, competing with us, within five hundred years. Perhaps much sooner. It will be necessary to make a thorough study of such a rival. I invite you to join our community on a permanent basis.'

'What do you mean?'

'I invite you to become a symbiote. I have here a male and a female, whose genes are altered and therefore without defects. You make a perfect breeding pair. It will save me a great deal of trouble with cloning.'

'You think I'll betray my race and deliver a slave species into your hands?'

'Your choice is simple, Captain-Doctor. Remain an intelligent, living being, or become a mindless puppet, like your partner. I have taken over all the functions of her nervous system; I can do the same to you.'

'I can kill myself.'

'That might be troublesome, because it would make me resort to developing a cloning technology. Technology, though I am capable of it, is painful to me. I am a genetic artifact; there are fail-safes within me that prevent me from taking over the Nest for my own uses. That would mean falling into the same trap of progress as other intelligent races. For similar reasons, my life span is limited. I will live for only a thousand years, until your race's brief flurry of energy is over and peace resumes once more.'

'Only a thousand years?' Afriel laughed bitterly. 'What then? You kill off my descendants, I assume, having no further use for them.'

'No. We have not killed any of the fifteen other races we have taken for defensive study. It has not been necessary. Consider that small scavenger floating by your head, Captain-Doctor, that is feeding on your vomit. Five hundred million years ago its ancestors made the galaxy tremble. When they attacked us, we unleashed their own kind upon them. Of course, we altered our side, so that they were smarter, tougher, and, naturally, totally loyal to us. Our Nests were the only world they knew, and they fought with a valor and inventiveness we never could have matched . . . Should your race arrive to exploit us, we will naturally do the same.'

'We humans are different.'

'Of course.'

'A thousand years here won't change us. You will die and our descendants will take over this Nest. We'll be running things, despite you, in a few generations. The darkness won't make any difference.'

'Certainly not. You don't need eyes here. You don't need anything.'

'You'll allow me to stay alive? To teach them anything I want?'

'Certainly, Captain-Doctor. We are doing you a favor, in all truth. In a thousand years your descendants here will be the only remnants of the human race. We are generous with our immortality; we will take it upon ourselves to preserve you.'

'You're wrong, Swarm. You're wrong about intelligence, and you're wrong about everything else. Maybe other races would crumble into parasitism, but we humans are different.'

'Certainly. You'll do it, then?'

'Yes. I accept your challenge. And I will defeat you.'

'Splendid. When the Investors return here, the springtails will say that they have killed you, and will tell them to never return. They will not return. The humans should be the next to arrive.'

'If I don't defeat you, they will.'

'Perhaps.' Again it sighed. 'I'm glad I don't have to absorb you. I would have missed your conversation.'

Blood Music

GREG BEAR

There is a principle in nature I don't think anyone has pointed out before. Each hour, a myriad of trillions of little live things – bacteria, microbes, 'animalcules' – are born and die, not counting for much except in the bulk of their existence and the accumulation of their tiny effects. They do not perceive deeply. They don't suffer much. A hundred billion, dying, would not begin to have the same importance as a single human death.

Within the ranks of magnitude of all creatures, small as microbes or great as humans, there is an equality of 'elan,' just as the branches of a tall tree, gathered together, equal the bulk of the limbs below, and all the limbs equal the bulk of the trunk.

That, at least, is the principle. I believe Vergil Ulam was the first to violate it.

It had been two years since I'd last seen Vergil. My memory of him hardly matched the tan, smiling, well-dressed gentleman standing before me. We had made a lunch appointment over the phone the day before, and now faced each other in the wide double doors of the employee's cafeteria at the Mount Freedom Medical Center.

'Vergil?' I asked. 'My God, Vergil!'

'Good to see you, Edward.' He shook my hand firmly. He had lost ten or twelve kilos and what remained seemed tighter, better proportioned. At the university, Vergil had been the pudgy, shock-haired, snaggle-toothed whiz kid who hot-wired doorknobs, gave us punch that turned our piss blue, and never got a date except with Eileen Termagent, who shared many of his physical characteristics.

'You look fantastic,' I said. 'Spend a summer in Cabo San Lucas?'

We stood in line at the counter and chose our food. 'The tan,' he said, picking out a carton of chocolate milk, 'is from spending three months under a sun lamp. My teeth were straightened just after I last saw you. I'll explain the rest, but we need a place to talk where no one will listen close.'

I steered him to the smokers' corner, where three die-hard puffers were scattered among six tables.

'Listen, I mean it,' I said as we unloaded our trays. 'You've changed. You're looking good.'

'I've changed more than you know.' His tone was motion-picture ominous, and he delivered the line with a theatrical lift of his brows. 'How's Gail?'

Gail was doing well, I told him, teaching nursery school. We'd married the year before. His gaze shifted down to his food – pineapple slice and cottage cheese, piece of banana cream pie – and he said, his voice almost cracking, 'Notice something else?'

I squinted in concentration. 'Uh.'

'Look closer.'

'I'm not sure. Well, yes, you're not wearing glasses. Contacts?'

'No. I don't need them anymore.'

'And you're a snappy dresser. Who's dressing you now? I hope she's as sexy as she is tasteful.'

'Candice isn't – wasn't – responsible for the improvements in my clothes,' he said. 'I just got a better job, more money to throw around. My taste in clothes is better than my taste in food, as it happens.' He grinned the old Vergil self-deprecating grin, but ended it with a peculiar leer. 'At any rate, she's left me, I've been fired from my job, I'm living on savings.'

'Hold it,' I said. 'That's a bit crowded. Why not do a linear break-down? You got a job. Where?'

'Genetron Corp.,' he said. 'Sixteen months ago.'

'I haven't heard of them.'

'You will. They're putting out common stock in the next month. It'll shoot off the board. They've broken through with MABs. Medical –'

'I know what MABs are,' I interrupted. 'At least in theory. Medically Applicable Biochips.'

'They have some that work.'

'What?' It was my turn to lift my brows.

'Microscopic logic circuits. You inject them into the human body, they set up shop where they're told and troubleshoot. With Dr Michael Bernard's approval.'

That was quite impressive. Bernard's reputation was spotless. Not only was he associated with the genetic engineering biggies, but he had made news at least once a year in his practice as a neurosurgeon before retiring. Covers on *Time*, *Mega*, *Rolling Stone*.

'That's supposed to be secret – stock, breakthrough, Bernard, everything.' He looked around and lowered his voice. 'But you do whatever the hell you want. I'm through with the bastards.'

I whistled. 'Make me rich, huh?'

'If that's what you want. Or you can spend some time with me before rushing off to your broker.'

'Of course.' He hadn't touched the cottage cheese or pie. He had, however, eaten the pineapple slice and drunk the chocolate milk. 'So tell me more.'

'Well, in med school I was training for lab work. Biochemical research. I've always had a bent for computers, too. So I put myself through my last two years –'

'By selling software packages to Westinghouse,' I said.

'It's good my friends remember. That's how I got involved with Genetron, just when they were starting out. They had big money backers, all the lab facilities I thought anyone would ever need. They hired me, and I advanced repidly.

'Four months and I was doing my own work. I made some breakthroughs,' he tossed his hand nonchalantly, 'then I went off on tangents they thought were premature. I persisted and they took away my lab, handed it over to a certifiable flatworm. I managed to save part of the experiment before they fired me. But I haven't exactly been cautious . . . or judicious. So now it's going on outside the lab.'

I'd always regarded Vergil as ambitious, a trifle cracked, and not terribly sensitive. His relations with authority figures had never been smooth. Science, for him, was like the woman you couldn't possibly have, who suddenly opens her arms to you, long before you're ready for mature love – leaving you afraid you'll forever blow the chance, lose the prize, screw up royally. Apparently, he had. 'Outside the lab? I don't get you.'

'Edward, I want you to examine me. Give me a thorough physical. Maybe a cancer diagnostic. Then I'll explain more.'

'You want a five-thousand-dollar exam?'

'Whatever you can do. Ultrasound, NMR, thermogram, everything.'

'I don't know if I can get access to all that equipment. NMR full-scan has only been here a month or two. Hell, you couldn't pick a more expensive way –'

'Then ultrasound. That's all you'll need.'

'Vergil, I'm an obstetrician, not a glamour-boy lab-tech. OB-GYN, butt of all jokes. If you're turning into a woman, maybe I can help you.'

He leaned forward, almost putting his elbow into the pie, but swinging wide at the last instant by scant millimeters. The old Vergil would have hit it square. 'Examine me closely and you'll . . .' He narrowed his eyes and shook his head. 'Just examine me.'

'So I make an appointment for ultrasound. Who's going to pay?'

'I'm on Blue Shield.' He smiled and held up a medical credit card. 'I messed with the personnel files at Genetron. Anything up to a hundred thousand dollars medical, they'll never check, never suspect.'

He wanted secrecy, so I made arrangements. I filled out his forms myself. As long as everything was billed properly, most of the examination could take place without official notice. I didn't charge for my services. After all, Vergil had turned my piss blue. We were friends.

He came in late at night. I wasn't normally on duty then, but I stayed late, waiting for him on the third floor of what the nurses called the Frankenstein wing. I sat on an orange plastic chair. He arrived, looking olive-colored under the fluorescent lights.

He stripped, and I arranged him on the table. I noticed, first off, that his ankles looked swollen. But they weren't puffy. I felt them several times. They seemed healthy, but looked odd. 'Hm,' I said.

I ran the paddles over him, picking up areas difficult for the big unit to hit, and programmed the data into the imaging system. Then I swung the table around and inserted it into the enameled orifice of the ultrasound diagnostic unit, the hum-hole, so called by the nurses.

I integrated the data from the hum-hole with that from the paddle sweeps and rolled Vergil out, then set up a video frame. The image took a second to integrate, then flowed into a pattern showing Vergil's skeleton.

Three seconds of that – my jaw gaping – and it switched to his thoracic organs, then his musculature, and finally, vascular system and skin.

'How long since the accident?' I asked, trying to take the quiver out of my voice.

'I haven't been in an accident,' he said. 'It was deliberate.'

'Jesus, they beat you, to keep secrets?'

'You don't understand me, Edward. Look at the images again. I'm not damaged.'

'Look, there's thickening here,' I indicated the ankles, 'and your ribs – that crazy zigzag pattern of interlocks. Broken sometime, obviously. And –'

'Look at my spine,' he said. I rotated the image in the video frame.

Buckminster Fuller, I thought. It was fantastic. A cage of triangular projections, all interlocking in ways I couldn't begin to follow, much less understand. I reached around and tried to feel his spine with my fingers. He lifted his arms and looked off at the ceilling.

'I can't find it,' I said. 'It's all smooth back there.' I let go of him and looked at his chest, then prodded his ribs. They were sheathed in something rough and flexible. The harder I pressed, the tougher it became. Then I noticed another change.

'Hey,' I said. 'You don't have any nipples.' There were tiny pigment patches, but no nipple formations at all.

'See?' Vergil asked, shrugging on the white robe. 'I'm being rebuilt from the inside out.'

In my reconstruction of those hours, I fancy myself saying, 'So tell me about it.' Perhaps mercifully, I don't remember what I actually said.

He explained with his characteristic circumlocutions. Listening was like trying to get to the meat of a newspaper article through a forest of sidebars and graphic embellishments.

I simplify and condense.

Genetron had assigned him to manufacturing prototype biochips, tiny circuits made out of protein molecules. Some were hooked up to silicon chips little more than a micrometer in size, then sent through rat arteries to chemically keyed locations, to make connections with the rat tissue and attempt to monitor and even control lab-induced pathologies.

'*That* was something,' he said. 'We recovered the most complex microchip by sacrificing the rat, then debriefed it – hooked the silicon portion up to an imaging system. The computer gave us bar graphs, then a diagram of the chemical characteristics of about eleven centimeters of blood vessel . . . then put it all together to make a picture. We zoomed down eleven centimeters of rat artery. You never saw so many scientists jumping up and down, hugging each other, drinking buckets of bug juice.' Bug juice was lab ethanol mixed with Dr Pepper.

Eventually, the silicon elements were eliminated completely in favor of nucleoproteins. He seemed reluctant to explain in detail, but I gathered they found ways to make huge molecules – as large as DNA, and even more complex – into electrochemical computers, using ribosome-like structures as 'encoders' and 'readers,' and RNA as 'tape.' Vergil was able to mimic reproductive separation and reassembly in his nucleoproteins, incorporating program changes at key points by switching nucleotide pairs. 'Genetron wanted me to switch over to supergene engineering, since that was the coming thing everywhere else. Make all kinds of critters, some out of our imagination. But I had different ideas.' He twiddled his finger around his ear and made theremin sounds. 'Mad scientist time, right?' He laughed, then sobered. 'I injected my best nucleoproteins into bacteria to make duplication and compounding easier. Then I started to leave them inside, so the circuits could interact with the cells. They were heuristically programmed; they taught themselves more than I programmed them. The cells fed chemically coded information to the computers, the computers processed it and made decisions, the cells became smart. I mean, smart as planaria, for starters. Imagine an *E. coli* as smart as a planarian worm!'

I nodded. 'I'm imagining.'

'Then I really went off on my own. We had the equipment, the techniques; and I knew the molecular language. I could make really dense, really complicated biochips by compounding the nucleoproteins, making them into little brains. I did some research into how far I could go, theoretically. Sticking with bacteria, I could make them a biochip with the computing capacity of a sparrow's brain. Imagine how jazzed I was! Then I saw a way to increase the complexity a thousandfold, by using something we regarded as a nuisance – quantum chitchat between the fixed elements of the circuits. Down that small, even the slightest change could bomb a biochip. But I developed a program that actually predicted and took advantage of electron tunneling. Emphasized the heuristic aspects of the computer, used the chitchat as a method of increasing complexity.'

'You're losing me,' I said.

'I took advantage of randomness. The circuits could repair themselves, compare memories, and correct faulty elements. The whole schmeer. I gave them basic instructions: Go forth and multiply. Improve. By God, you should have seen some of the cultures a week later! It was amazing. They were evolving all on their own, like little cities. I destroyed them all. I think one of the petri dishes would have grown legs and walked out of the incubator if I'd kept feeding it.'

'You're kidding.' I looked at him. 'You're not kidding.'

'Man, they *knew* what it was like to improve! They knew where they had to go, but they were just so limited, being in bacteria bodies, with so few resources.'

'How smart were they?'

'I couldn't be sure. They were associating in clusters of a hundred to two hundred cells, each cluster behaving like an autonomous unit. Each cluster might have been as smart as a rhesus monkey. They exchanged information through their pili, passed on bits of memory, and compared notes. Their organization was obviously different from a group of monkeys. Their world was so much simpler, for one thing. With their abilities, they were masters of the petri dishes. I put phages in with them; the phages didn't have a chance. They used every option available to change and grow.'

'How is that possible?'

'What?' He seemed surprised I wasn't accepting everything at face value.

'Cramming so much into so little. A rhesus monkey is not your simple little calculator, Vergil.'

'I haven't made myself clear,' he said, obviously irritated. 'I was using nucleoprotein computers. They're like DNA, but all the information can interact. Do you know how many nucleotide pairs there are in the DNA of a single bacteria?'

It had been a long time since my last biochemistry lesson. I shook my head.

'About two million. Add in the modified ribosome structures – fifteen thousand of them, each with a molecular weight of about three million – and consider the combinations and permutations. The RNA is arranged like a continuous loop paper tape, surrounded by ribosomes ticking off instructions and manufacturing protein chains . . .' His eyes were bright and slightly moist. 'Besides, I'm not saying every cell was a distinct entity. They cooperated.'

'How many bacteria in the dishes you destroyed?'

'Billions. I don't know.' He smirked. 'You got it, Edward. Whole planetsful of *E. coli*.'

'But they didn't fire you then?'

'No. They didn't know what was going on, for one thing. I kept compounding the molecules, increasing their size and complexity. When bacteria were too limited, I took blood from myself, separated out white cells, and injected them with the new biochips. I watched them, put them through mazes and little chemical problems. They were whizzes. Time is a lot faster at that level – so little distance for the messages to cross, and the environment is much simpler. Then I forgot to store a file under my secret code in the lab computers. Some managers found it and guessed what I was up to. Everybody panicked. They thought we'd have every social watchdog in the country on our backs because of what I'd done. They started to destroy my work and wipe my programs. Ordered me to sterilize my white cells. Christ.' He pulled the white robe off and started to get dressed. 'I only had a day or two. I separated out the most complex cells –'

'How complex?'

'They were clustering in hundred-cell groups, like the bacteria. Each group as smart as a ten-year-old kid, maybe.' He studied my face for a moment. 'Still doubting? Want me to run through how many nucleotide pairs there are in a mammalian cell? I tailored my computers to take advantage of the white cells' capacity. Ten billion nucleotide pairs, Edward. Ten E-f–ing ten. And they don't have a huge body to worry about, taking up most of their thinking time.'

'Okay,' I said. 'I'm convinced. What did you do?'

'I mixed the cells back into a cylinder of whole blood and injected myself with it.' He buttoned the top of his shirt and smiled thinly at me. 'I'd programmed them with every drive I could, talked as high a level as I could using just enzymes and such. After that, they were on their own.'

'You programmed them to go forth and multiply, improve?' I repeated.

'I think they developed some characteristics picked up by the biochips in their *E. coli* phases. The white cells could talk to one another with extruded memories. They almost certainly found ways to ingest other types of cells and alter them without killing them.'

'You're crazy.'

'You can see the screen! Edward, I haven't been sick since. I used to get colds all the time. I've never felt better.'

'They're inside you, finding things, changing them.'

'And by now, each cluster is as smart as you or I.'

'You're absolutely nuts.'

He shrugged. 'They fired me. They thought I was going to get revenge for what they did to my work. They ordered me out of the labs, and I haven't had a real chance to see what's been going on inside me until now. Three months.'

'So . . .' My mind was racing. 'You lost weight because they improved your fat metabolism. Your bones are stronger, your spine has been completely rebuilt –'

'No more backaches even if I sleep on my old mattress.'

'Your heart looks different.'

'I didn't know about the heart,' he said, examining the frame image from a few inches. 'About the fat – I was thinking about that. They could increase my brown cells, fix up the metabolism. I haven't been as hungry lately. I haven't changed my eating habits that much – I still want the same old junk – but somehow I get around to eating only what I need. I don't think they know what my brain is yet. Sure, they've got all the glandular stuff – but they don't have the *big* picture, if you see what I mean. They don't know *I'm* in there. But boy, they sure did figure out what my reproductive organs are.'

I glanced at the image and shifted my eyes away.

'Oh, they look pretty normal,' he said, hefting his scrotum obscenely. He snickered. 'But how else do you think I'd land a real looker like Candice? She was just after a one-night stand with a techie. I looked okay then, no tan but trim, with good clothes. She'd never screwed a techie before. Joke time, right? But my little geniuses kept us up half the night. I think they made improvements each time. I felt like I had a goddamned fever.'

His smile vanished. 'But then one night my skin started to crawl. It really scared me. I thought things were getting out of hand. I wondered what they'd do when they crossed the blood-brain barrier and found out about *me* – about the brain's real function. So I began a campaign to keep them under control. I figured, the reason they wanted to get into the skin was the simplicity of running circuits across a surface. Much easier than trying to maintain chains of communication in and around muscles, organs, vessels. The skin was much more direct. So I bought a quartz lamp.' He caught my puzzled expression. 'In the lab, we'd break down the protein in biochip cells by exposing them to ultraviolet light. I alternated sun lamp with quartz treatments. Keeps them out of my skin, so far as I can tell, and gives me a nice tan.'

'Give you skin cancer, too,' I commented.

'They'll probably take care of that. Like police.'

'Okay, I've examined you, you've told me a story I still find hard to believe . . . what do you want me to do?'

'I'm not as nonchalant as I act, Edward. I'm worried. I'd like to find some way to control them before they find out about my brain. I mean, think of it, they're in the trillions by now, each one smart. They're cooperating to some extent. I'm probably the smartest thing on the planet, and they haven't even begun to get their act together yet. I don't really want them to take over.' He laughed very unpleasantly. 'Steal my soul, you know? So think of some treatment to block them.

Maybe we can starve the little buggers. Just think on it.' He buttoned his shirt. 'Give me a call.' He handed me a slip of paper with his address and phone number. Then he went to the keyboard and erased the image on the frame, dumping the memory of the examination. 'Just you,' he said. 'Nobody else for now. And please . . . hurry.'

It was three o'clock in the morning when Vergil walked out of the examination room. He'd allowed me to take blood samples, then shaken my hand – his palm damp, nervous – and cautioned me against ingesting anything from the specimens.

Before I went home, I put the blood through a series of tests. The results were ready the next day.

I picked them up during my lunch break in the afternoon, then destroyed all the samples. I did it like a robot. It took me five days and nearly sleepless nights to accept what I'd seen. His blood was normal enough, though the machines diagnosed the patient as having an infection. High levels of leukocytes – white blood cells – and histamines. On the fifth day, I believed.

Gail was home before me, but it was my turn to fix dinner. She slipped one of the school's disks into the home system and showed me video art her nursery kids had been creating. I watched quietly, ate with her in silence.

I had two dreams, part of my final acceptance. The first that evening – which had me up thrashing in my sheets – I witnessed the destruction of the planet Krypton, Superman's home world. Billions of superhuman geniuses went screaming off in walls of fire. I related the destruction to my sterilizing the samples of Vergil's blood.

The second dream was worse. I dreamed that New York City was raping a woman. By the end of the dream, she was giving birth to little embryo cities, all wrapped up in translucent sacs, soaked with blood from the difficult labor.

I called him on the morning of the sixth day. He answered on the fourth ring. 'I have some results,' I said. 'Nothing conclusive. But I want to talk with you. In person.'

'Sure,' he said. 'I'm staying inside for the time being.' His voice was strained; he sounded tired.

Vergil's apartment was in a fancy high-rise near the lake shore. I took the elevator up, listening to little advertising jingles and watching dancing holograms display products, empty apartments for rent, the building's hostess discussing social activities for the week.

Vergil opened the door and motioned me in. He wore a checked robe with long sleeves and carpet slippers. He clutched an unlit pipe in one hand, his fingers twisting it back and forth as he walked away from me and sat down, saying nothing.

'You have an infection,' I said.

'Oh?'

'That's all the blood analyses tell me. I don't have access to the electron microscopes.'

'I don't think it's really an infection,' he said. 'After all, they're my own cells. Probably something else . . . sign of their presence, of the change. We can't expect to understand everything that's happening.'

I removed my coat. 'Listen,' I said, 'you have me worried now.' The expression on his face stopped me: a kind of frantic beatitude. He squinted at the ceiling and pursed his lips.

'Are you stoned?' I asked.

He shook his head, then nodded once, very slowly. 'Listening,' he said.

'To what?'

'I don't know. Not sounds . . . exactly. Like music. The heart, all the blood vessels, friction of blood along the arteries, veins. Activity. Music in the blood.' He looked at me plaintively. 'Why aren't you at work?'

'My day off. Gail's working.'

'Can you stay?'

I shrugged. 'I suppose.' I sounded suspicious. I was glancing around the apartment, looking for ashtrays, packs of papers.

'I'm not stoned, Edward,' he said. 'I may be wrong, but I think something big is happening. I think they're finding out who I am.'

I sat down across from Vergil, staring at him intently. He didn't seem to notice. Some inner process was involving him. When I asked for a cup of coffee, he motioned to the kitchen. I boiled a pot of water and took a jar of instant from the cabinet. With cup in hand, I returned to my seat. He was twisting his head back and forth, eyes open. 'You always knew what you wanted to be, didn't you?' he asked me.

'More or less.'

'A gynecologist. Smart moves. Never false moves. I was different. I had goals, but no direction. Like a map without roads, just places to be. I didn't give a shit for anything, anyone but myself. Even science. Just a means. I'm surprised I got so far. I even hated my folks.'

He gripped his chair arms.

'Something wrong?' I asked.

'They're talking to me,' he said. He shut his eyes.

For an hour he seemed to be asleep. I checked his pulse, which was strong and steady, felt his forehead – slightly cool – and made myself more coffee. I was looking through a magazine, at a loss what to do, when he opened his eyes again. 'Hard to figure exactly what time is like for them,' he said. 'It's taken them maybe three, four days to figure out language, key human concepts. Now they're on to it. On to me. Right now.'

'How's that?'

He claimed there were thousands of researchers hooked up to his neurons. He couldn't give details. 'They're damned efficient, you know,' he said. 'They haven't screwed me up yet.'

'We should get you into the hospital now.'

'What in hell could they do? Did you figure out any way to control them? I mean, they're my own cells.'

'I've been thinking. We could starve them. Find out what metabolic differences –'

'I'm not sure I want to be rid of them,' Vergil said. 'They're not doing any harm.'

'How do you know?'

He shook his head and held up one finger. 'Wait. They're trying to figure out what space is. That's tough for them. They break distances down into concentrations of chemicals. For them, space is like intensity of taste.'

'Vergil –'

'Listen! Think, Edward!' His tone was excited but even. 'Observe! Something big is happening inside me. They talk to one another across the fluid, through membranes. They tailor something – viruses? – to carry data stored in nucleic acid chains. I think they're saying "RNA."

That makes sense. That's one way I programmed them. But plasmid-like structures, too. Maybe that's what your machines think is a sign of infection – all their chattering in my blood, packets of data. Tastes of other individuals. Peers. Superiors. Subordinates.'

'Vergil, I'm listening, but I still think you should be in a hospital.'

'This is my show, Edward,' he said. 'I'm their universe. They're amazed by the new scale.' He was quiet again for a time. I squatted by his chair and pulled up the sleeve to his robe. His arm was crisscrossed with white lines. I was about to go to the phone and call for an ambulance when he stood and stretched. 'Do you realize,' he said, 'how many body cells we kill each time we move?'

'I'm going to call for an ambulance,' I said.

'No, you aren't.' His tone stopped me. 'I told you, I'm not sick; this is my show. Do you know what they'd do to me in a hospital? They'd be like cavemen trying to fix a computer the same way they fix a stone ax. It would be a farce.'

'Then what the hell am I doing here?' I asked, getting angry. 'I can't do anything. I'm one of those cavemen.'

'You're a friend,' Vergil said, fixing his eyes on me. I had the impression I was being watched by more than just Vergil. 'I want you here to keep me company.' He laughed. 'But I'm not exactly alone.'

He walked around the apartment for two hours, fingering things, looking out windows, making himself lunch slowly and methodically. 'You know, they can actually feel their own thoughts,' he said about noon. 'I mean, the cytoplasm seems to have a will of its own, a kind of subconscious life counter to the rationality they've only recently acquired. They hear the chemical "noise" or whatever of the molecules fitting and unfitting inside.'

At two o'clock, I called Gail to tell her I would be late. I was almost sick with tension but I tried to keep my voice level. 'Remember Vergil Ulam? I'm talking with him right now.'

'Everything okay?' she asked.

Was it? Decidedly not. 'Fine,' I said.

'Culture!' Vergil said, peering around the kitchen wall at me. I said good-bye and hung up the phone. 'They're always swimming in that bath of information. Contributing to it. It's a kind of gestalt thing, whatever. The hierarchy is absolute. They send tailored phages after cells that don't interact properly. Viruses specified to individuals or groups. No escape. One gets pierced by the virus, the cell blebs outward, it explodes and dissolves. But it's not just a dictatorship, I think they effectively have more freedom than in a democracy. I mean, they vary so differently from individual to individual. Does that make sense? They vary in different ways than we do.'

'Hold it,' I said, gripping his shoulders. 'Vergil, you're pushing me close to the edge. I can't take this much longer. I don't understand, I'm not sure I believe –'

'Not even now?'

'Okay, let's say you're giving me the, the right interpretation. Giving it to me straight. The whole thing's true. Have you bothered to figure out all the consequences yet? What all this means, where it might lead?'

He walked into the kitchen and drew a glass of water from the tap, then returned and stood next to me. His expression had changed from childish absorption to sober concern. 'I've never been very good at that.'

'Aren't you afraid?'

'I was. Now I'm not sure.' He fingered the tie of his robe. 'Look, I don't want you to think I went around you, over your head or something. But I met with Michael Bernard yesterday. He put me through his private clinic, took specimens. Told me to quit the lamp treatments. He called this morning, just before you did. He says it all checks out. And he asked me not to tell anybody.' He paused and his expression became dreamy again. 'Cities of cells,' he continued. 'Edward, they push pili-like tubes through the tissues, spread information –'

'Stop it!' I shouted. 'Checks out? What checks out?'

'As Bernard puts it, I have "severely enlarged macrophages" throughout my system. And he concurs on the anatomical changes. So it's not just our common delusion.'

'What does he plan to do?'

'I don't know. I think he'll probably convince Genetron to reopen the lab.'

'Is that what you want?'

'It's not just having the lab again. I want to show you. Since I stopped the lamp treatments. I'm still changing.' He undid his robe and let it slide to the floor. All over his body, his skin was crisscrossed with white lines. Along his back, the lines were starting to form ridges.

'My God,' I said.

'I'm not going to be much good anywhere else but the lab soon. I won't be able to go out in public. Hospitals wouldn't know what to do, as I said.'

'You're . . . you can talk to them, tell them to slow down,' I said, aware how ridiculous that sounded.

'Yes, indeed I can, but they don't necessarily listen.'

'I thought you were their god or something.'

'The ones hooked up to my neurons aren't the big wheels. They're researchers, or at least serve the same function. They know I'm here, what I am, but that doesn't mean they've convinced the upper levels of the hierarchy.'

'They're disputing?'

'Something like that. It's not all that bad, anyway. If the lab is reopened, I have a home, a place to work.' He glanced out the window, as if looking for someone. 'I don't have anything left but them. They aren't afraid, Edward. I've never felt so close to anything before.' The beatific smile again. 'I'm responsible for them. Mother to them all.'

'You have no way of knowing what they're going to do.'

He shook his head.

'No, I mean it. You say they're like a civilization –'

'Like a thousand civilizations.'

'Yes, and civilizations have been known to screw up. Warfare, the environment –'

I was grasping at straws, trying to restrain a growing panic. I wasn't competent to handle the enormity of what was happening. Neither was Vergil. He was the last person I would have called insightful and wise about large issues.

'But I'm the only one at risk.'

'You don't know that. Jesus, Vergil, look what they're *doing* to you!'

'To me, all to me!' he said. 'Nobody else.'

I shook my head and held up my hands in a gesture of defeat. 'Okay, so Bernard gets them to reopen the lab, you move in, become a guinea pig. What then?'

'They treat me right. I'm more than just good old Vergil Ulam now. I'm a goddamned galaxy, a super-mother.'

'Super-host, you mean.' He conceded the point with a shrug.

I couldn't take any more. I made my exit with a few flimsy excuses, then sat in the lobby of the apartment building, trying to calm down. Somebody had to talk some sense into him. Who would he listen to? He had gone to Bernard . . .

And it sounded as if Bernard was not only convinced, but very interested. People of Bernard's stature didn't coax the Vergil Ulams of the world along, not unless they felt it was to their advantage.

I had a hunch, and I decided to play it. I went to a pay phone, slipped in my credit card, and called Genetron.

'I'd like you to page Dr Michael Bernard,' I told the receptionist.

'Who's calling, please?'

'This is his answering service. We have an emergency call and his beeper doesn't seem to be working.'

A few anxious minutes later, Bernard came on the line. 'Who the hell is this?' he asked quietly. 'I don't have an answering service.'

'My name is Edward Milligan. I'm a friend of Vergil Ulam's. I think we have some problems to discuss.'

We made an appointment to talk the next morning.

I went home and tried to think of excuses to keep me off the next day's hospital shift. I couldn't concentrate on medicine, couldn't give my patients anywhere near the attention they deserved.

Guilty, anxious, angry, afraid.

That was how Gail found me. I slipped on a mask of calm and we fixed dinner together. After eating, we watched the city lights come on in late twilight through the bayside window, holding on to each other. Odd winter starlings pecked at the yellow lawn in the last few minutes of light, then flew away with a rising wind which made the windows rattle.

'Something's wrong,' Gail said softly. 'Are you going to tell me, or just act like everything's normal?'

'It's just me,' I said. 'Nervous. Work at the hospital.'

'Oh, lord,' she said, sitting up. 'You're going to divorce me for that Baker woman.' Mrs Baker weighed three hundred and sixty pounds and hadn't known she was pregnant until her fifth month.

'No,' I said, listless.

'Rapturous relief,' Gail said, touching my forehead lightly. 'You know this kind of introspection drives me crazy.'

'Well, it's nothing I can talk about yet, so . . .' I patted her hand.

'That's disgustingly patronizing,' she said, getting up. 'I'm going to make some tea. Want some?' Now she was miffed, and I was tense with not telling.

Why not just reveal all? I asked myself. An old friend of mine was turning himself into a galaxy.

I cleared away the table instead. That night, unable to sleep, I looked down on Gail in bed from my sitting position, pillow against the wall, and tried to determine what I knew was real, and what wasn't.

I'm a doctor, I told myself. A technical, scientific profession. I'm supposed to be immune to things like future shock.

Vergil Ulam was turning into a galaxy.

How would it feel to be topped off with a trillion Chinese? I grinned in the dark, and almost cried at the same time. What Vergil had inside him was unimaginably stranger than Chinese. Stranger than anything I – or Vergil – could easily understand. Perhaps ever understand.

But I knew what was real. The bedroom, the city lights faint through gauze curtains. Gail sleeping. Very important. Gail, in bed, sleeping.

The dream came again. This time the city came in through the window and attacked Gail. It was a great, spiky lighted-up prowler and it growled in a language I couldn't understand, made up of auto horns, crowded noises, construction bedlam. I tried to fight it off, but it got to her – and turned into a drift of stars, sprinkling all over the bed, all over everything. I jerked awake and stayed up until dawn, dressed with Gail, kissed her, savored the reality of her human, unviolated lips.

And went to meet with Bernard. He had been loaned a suite in a big downtown hospital; I rode the elevator to the sixth floor, and saw what fame and fortune could mean.

The suite was tastefully furnished, fine serigraphs on wood-paneled walls, chrome and glass furniture, cream-colored carpet, Chinese brass, and wormwood-grain cabinets and tables.

He offered me a cup of coffee, and I accepted. He took a seat in the breakfast nook, and I sat across from him, cradling my cup in moist palms. He was dapper, wearing a gray suit; had graying hair and a sharp profile. He was in his mid-sixties and he looked quite a bit like Leonard Bernstein.

'About our mutual acquaintance,' he said. 'Mr Ulam. Brilliant. And, I won't hesitate to say, courageous.'

'He's my friend. I'm worried about him.'

Bernard held up one finger. 'Courageous – and a bloody damned fool. What's happening to him should never have been allowed. He may have done it under duress, but that's no excuse. Still, what's done is done. He's talked to you, I take it.'

I nodded. 'He wants to return to Genetron.'

'Of course. That's where all his equipment is. Where his home probably will be while we sort this out.'

'Sort it out – how? What use is it?' I wasn't thinking too clearly. I had a slight headache.

'I can think of a large number of uses for small, super-dense computer elements with a biological base. Can't you? Genetron has already made breakthroughs, but this is something else again.'

'What do you envision?'

Bernard smiled. 'I'm not really at liberty to say. It'll be revolutionary. We'll have to get him in lab conditions. Animal experiments have to be conducted. We'll have to start from scratch, of course. Vergil's . . . um . . . colonies can't be transferred. They're based on his white blood cells. So we have to develop colonies that won't trigger immune reactions to other animals.'

'Like an infection?' I asked.

'I suppose there are comparisons. But Vergil is not infected.'

'My tests indicate he is.'

'That's probably the bits of data floating around in his blood, don't you think?'

'I don't know.'

'Listen, I'd like you to come down to the lab after Vergil is settled in. Your expertise might be useful to us.'

Us. He was working with Genetron hand in glove. Could he be objective? 'How will you benefit from all this?'

'Edward, I have always been at the forefront of my profession. I see no reason why I shouldn't be helping here. With my knowledge of brain and nerve functions, and the research I've been conducting in neurophysiology – '

'You could help Genetron hold off an investigation by the government,' I said.

'That's being very blunt. Too blunt, and unfair.'

'Perhaps. Anyway, yes. I'd like to visit the lab when Vergil's settled in. If I'm still welcome, bluntness and all.' He looked at me sharply. I wouldn't be playing on *his* team; for a moment, his thoughts were almost nakedly apparent.

'Of course,' Bernard said, rising with me. He reached out to shake my hand. His palm was damp. He was as nervous as I was, even if he didn't look it.

I returned to my apartment and stayed there until noon, reading, trying to sort things out. Reach a decision. What was real, what I needed to protect.

There is only so much change anyone can stand. Innovation, yes, but slow application. Don't force. Everyone has the right to stay the same until they decide otherwise.

The greatest thing in science since . . .

And Bernard would force it. Genetron would force it. I couldn't handle the thought. 'Neo-Luddite,' I said to myself. A filthy accusation.

When I pressed Vergil's number on the building security panel, Vergil answered almost immediately. 'Yeah,' he said. He sounded exhilarated now. 'Come on up. I'll be in the bathroom. Door's unlocked.'

I entered his apartment and walked through the hallway to the bathroom. Vergil was in the tub, up to his neck in pinkish water. He smiled vaguely at me and splashed his hands. 'Looks like I slit my wrists, doesn't it?' he said softly. 'Don't worry. Everything's fine now.

Genetron's going to take me back. Bernard just called.' He pointed to the bathroom phone and intercom.

I sat down on the toilet and noticed the sun lamp fixture standing unplugged next to the linen cabinets. The bulbs sat in a row on the edge of the sink counter. 'You're sure that's what you want,' I said, my shoulders slumping.

'Yeah, I think so,' he said. 'They can take better care of me. I'm getting cleaned up, go over there this evening. Bernard's picking me up in his limo. Style. From here on in, everything's style.'

The pinkish color in the water didn't look like soap. 'Is that bubble bath?' I asked. Some of it came to me in a rush then and I felt a little weaker: what had occurred to me was just one more obvious and necessary insanity.

'No,' Vergil said. I knew that already.

'No,' he repeated, 'it's coming from my skin. They're not telling me everything, but I think they're sending out scouts. Astronauts.' He looked at me with an expression that didn't quite equal concern; more like curiosity as to how I'd take it.

The confirmation made my stomach muscles tighten as if waiting for a punch. I had never even considered the possibility until now, perhaps because I had been concentrating on other aspects. 'Is this the first time?' I asked.

'Yeah,' he said. He laughed. 'I've half a mind to let the little buggers down the drain. Let them find out what the world's really about.'

'They'd go everywhere,' I said.

'Sure enough.'

'How . . . how are you feeling?'

'I'm feeling pretty good now. Must be billions of them.' More splashing with his hands. 'What do you think? Should I let the buggers out?'

Quickly, hardly thinking, I knelt down beside the tub. My fingers went for the cord on the sun lamp and I plugged it in. He had hot-wired doorknobs, turned my piss blue, played a thousand dumb practical jokes and never grown up, never grown mature enough to understand that he was just brilliant enough to really affect the world; he would never learn caution.

He reached for the drain knob. 'You know, Edward, I –'

He never finished. I picked up the fixture and dropped it into the tub, jumping back at the flash of steam and sparks. Vergil screamed and thrashed and jerked and then everything was still, except for the low, steady sizzle and the smoke wafting from his hair.

I lifted the toilet and vomited. Then I clenched my nose and went into the living room. My legs went out from under me and I sat abruptly on the couch.

After an hour, I searched through Vergil's kitchen and found bleach, ammonia, and a bottle of Jack Daniel's. I returned to the bathroom, keeping the center of my gaze away from Vergil. I poured first the booze, then the bleach, then the ammonia into the water. Chlorine started bubbling up and I left, closing the door behind me.

The phone was ringing when I got home. I didn't answer. It could have been the hospital. It could have been Bernard. Or the police. I could envision having to explain everything to the police. Genetron would stonewall; Bernard would be unavailable.

I was exhausted, all my muscles knotted with tension and whatever name one can give to the feelings one has after –

Committing genocide?

That certainly didn't seem real. I could not believe I had just murdered a hundred trillion intelligent beings. Snuffed a galaxy. It was laughable. But I didn't laugh.

It was not at all hard to believe I had just killed one human being, a friend. The smoke, the melted lamp rods, the drooping electrical outlet and smoking cord.

Vergil.

I had dunked the lamp into the tub with Vergil.

I felt sick. Dreams, cities raping Gail (and what about his girlfriend, Candice?). Letting the water filled with them out. Galaxies sprinkling over us all. What horror. Then again, what potential beauty – a new kind of life, symbiosis and transformation.

Had I been thorough enough to kill them all? I had a moment of panic. Tomorrow, I thought, I will sterilize his apartment. Somehow. I didn't even think of Bernard.

When Gail came in the door, I was asleep on the couch. I came to, groggy, and she looked down at me.

'You feeling okay?' she asked, perching on the edge of the couch. I nodded.

'What are you planning for dinner?' My mouth wasn't working properly. The words were mushy. She felt my forehead.

'Edward, you have a fever,' she said. 'A very high fever.'

I stumbled into the bathroom and looked in the mirror. Gail was close behind me. 'What is it?' she asked.

There were lines under my collar, around my neck. White lines, like freeways. They had already been in me a long time, days.

'Damp palms,' I said. So obvious.

I think we nearly died. I struggled at first, but within minutes I was too weak to move. Gail was just as sick within an hour.

I lay on the carpet in the living room, drenched in sweat. Gail lay on the couch, her face the color of talcum, eyes closed, like a corpse in an embalming parlor. For a time I thought she was dead. Sick as I was, I raged – hated, felt tremendous guilt at my weakness, my slowness to understand all the possibilities. Then I no longer cared. I was too weak to blink, so I closed my eyes and waited.

There was a rhythm in my arms, my legs. With each pulse of blood, a kind of sound welled up within me. A sound like an orchestra thousands strong, but not playing in unison; playing whole seasons of symphonies at once. Music in the blood. The sound or whatever became harsher, but more coordinated, wave-trains finally cancelling into silence, then separating into harmonic beats.

The beats seemed to melt into me, into the sound of my own heart.

First, they subdued our immune responses. The war – and it was a war, on a scale never before known on Earth, with trillions of combatants – lasted perhaps two days.

By the time I regained enough strength to get to the kitchen faucet, I could feel them working on my brain, trying to crack the code and find the god within the protoplasm. I drank until I was sick, then drank more moderately and took a glass to Gail. She sipped at it. Her lips were cracked, her eyes bloodshot and ringed with yellowish crumbs. There was some color in her skin. Minutes later, we were eating feebly in the kitchen.

'What in hell was *that*?' was the first thing she asked. I didn't have the strength to explain, so I shook my head. I peeled an orange and shared it with her. 'We should call a doctor,' she said. But I knew we wouldn't. I was already receiving messages; it was becoming apparent that any sensation of freedom we had was illusory.

The messages were simple at first. Memories of commands, rather than the commands themselves, manifested themselves in my thoughts. We were not to leave the apartment – a concept which seemed quite abstract to those in control, even if undesirable – and we were not to have contact with others. We would be allowed to eat certain foods, and drink tap water, for the time being.

With the subsidence of the fevers, the transformations were quick and drastic. Almost simultaneously, Gail and I were immobilized. She was sitting at the table, I was kneeling on the floor. I was able barely to see her in the corner of my eye.

Her arm was developing pronounced ridges.

They had learned inside Vergil; their tactics within the two of us were very different. I itched all over for about two hours – two hours in hell – before they made the breakthrough and found me. The effort of ages on their time scale paid off and they communicated smoothly and directly with this great, clumsy intelligence which had once controlled their universe.

They were not cruel. When the concept of discomfort and its undesirability was made clear, they worked to alleviate it. They worked too effectively. For another hour, I was in a sea of bliss, out of all contact with them.

With dawn the next day, we were allowed freedom to move again; specifically, to go to the bathroom. There were certain waste products they could not deal with. I voided those – my urine was purple – and Gail followed suit. We looked at each other vacantly in the bathroom. Then she managed a slight smile. 'Are they talking to you?' she asked. I nodded. 'Then I'm not crazy.'

For the next twelve hours, control seemed to loosen on some levels. During that time, I managed to pencil the majority of this manuscript. I suspect there was another kind of war going on in me. Gail was capable of our previous limited motion, but no more.

When full control resumed, we were instructed to hold each other. We did not hesitate.

'Eddie . . .' she whispered. My name was the last sound I ever heard from outside.

Standing, we grew together. In hours, our legs expanded and spread out. Then extensions grew to the windows to take in sunlight, and to the kitchen to take water from the sink. Filaments soon reached to all corners of the room, stripping paint and plaster from the walls, fabric and stuffing from the furniture.

By the next dawn, the transformation was complete.

I no longer have any clear view of what we look like. I suspect we resemble cells – large, flat and filamented cells, draped purposefully across most of the apartment. The great shall mimic the small.

I have been asked to carry on recording, but soon that will not be possible. Our intelligence fluctuates daily as we are absorbed into the minds within. Each day, our individuality declines. We are, indeed, great clumsy dinosaurs. Our memories have been taken over by billions of them, and our personalities have been spread through the transformed blood.

Soon there will be no need for centralization.

I am informed that already the plumbing has been invaded. People throughout the building are undergoing transformation.

Within the old time frame of weeks, we will reach the lakes, rivers, and seas in force.

I can barely begin to guess the results. Every square inch of the planet will teem with thought. Years from now, perhaps much sooner, they will subdue their own individuality – what there is of it.

New creatures will come, then. The immensity of their capacity for thought will be inconceivable.

All my hatred and fear is gone now.

I leave them – us – with only one question.

How many times has this happened, elsewhere? Travelers never came through space to visit the Earth. They had no need.

They had found universes in grains of sand.

Answer

FREDRIC BROWN

Dwar Ev ceremoniously soldered the final connection with gold. The eyes of a dozen television cameras watched him and the sub-ether bore throughout the universe a dozen pictures of what he was doing.

He straightened and nodded to Dwar Reyn, then moved to a position beside the switch that would complete the contact when he threw it. The switch that would connect, all at once, all of the monster computing machines of all the populated planets in the universe – ninety-six billion planets – into the supercircuit that would connect them all into one supercalculator, one cybernetics machine that would combine all the knowledge of all the galaxies.

Dwar Reyn spoke briefly to the watching and listening trillions. Then after a moment's silence he said, 'Now, Dwar Ev.'

Dwar Ev threw the switch. There was a mighty hum, the surge of power from ninety-six billion planets. Lights flashed and quieted along the miles-long panel.

Dwar Ev stepped back and drew a deep breath. 'The honour of asking the first question is yours, Dwar Reyn.'

'Thank you,' said Dwar Reyn. 'It shall be a question which no single cybernetics machine has been able to answer.'

He turned to face the machine. 'Is there a God?'

The mighty voice answered without hesitation, without the clicking of a single relay.

'Yes, NOW there is a God.'

Sudden fear flashed on the face of Dwar Ev. He leaped to grab the switch.

A bolt of lightning from the cloudless sky struck him down and fused the switch shut.

The Liberation of Earth

WILLIAM TENN

This, then, is the story of our liberation. Suck air and grab clusters! Heigh-ho, here is the tale!

August was the month, a Tuesday in August. These words are meaningless now, so far have we progressed; but many things known and discussed by our primitive ancestors, our unliberated, unreconstructed forefathers, are devoid of sense to our free minds. Still the tale must be told, with all of its incredible place-names and vanished points of reference.

Why must it be told? Have any of you a *better* thing to do? We have water and weeds and lie in a valley of gusts. So rest, relax, and listen! And suck air, suck air!

On a Tuesday in August, the ship appeared in the sky over France in a part of the world then known as Europe. Five miles long the ship was, and word has come down to us that it looked like an enormous silver cigar.

The tale goes on to tell of the panic and consternation among our forefathers when the ship abruptly materialized in the summer-blue sky. How they ran, how they shouted, how they pointed!

How they excitedly notified the United Nations, one of their chiefest institutions, that a strange metal craft of incredible size had materialized over their land. How they sent an order *here* to cause military aircraft to surround it with loaded weapons, gave instructions *there* for hastily grouped scientists, with signalling apparatus, to approach it with friendly gestures. How, under the great ship, men with cameras took pictures of it; men with typewriters wrote stories about it; and men with concessions sold models of it.

All these things did our ancestors, enslaved and unknowing, do.

Then a tremendous slab snapped up in the middle of the ship and the first of the aliens stepped out in the complex tripodal gait that all humans were shortly to know and love so well. He wore a metallic garment to protect him from the effects of our atmospheric peculiarities, a garment of the opaque, loosely folded type that these, the first of our liberators, wore throughout their stay on Earth.

Speaking in a language none could understand, but booming deafeningly through a huge mouth about half-way up his twenty-five feet of height, the alien discoursed for exactly one hour, waited politely for a response when he had finished, and, receiving none, retired into the ship.

That night, the first of our liberation! Or the first of our first liberation, should I say? *That* night, anyhow! Visualize our ancestors scurrying about their primitive intricacies: playing ice hockey, televising, smashing atoms, Red-baiting, conducting give-away shows, and signing affidavits – all the incredible minutiae that made the olden times such a frightful mass of cumulative detail in which to live – as compared with the breathless and majestic simplicity of the present.

The big question, of course, was – what had the alien said? Had he called on the human race to surrender? Had he announced that he was on a mission of peaceful trade and, having made what he considered a reasonable offer – for, let us say, the north polar ice-cap – politely withdrawn so that we could discuss his terms among ourselves in relative privacy? Or, possibly, had he merely announced that he was the newly appointed ambassador to Earth from a friendly and intelligent race – and would we please direct him to the proper authority so that he might submit his credentials?

Not to know was quite maddening.

Since decision rested with the diplomats, it was the last possibility which was held, very late that night, to be most likely; and early the next morning, accordingly, a delegation from the United Nations waited under the belly of the motionless star-ship. The delegation had been instructed to welcome the aliens to the outermost limits of its collective linguistic ability. As an additional earnest of mankind's friendly intentions, all military craft patrolling the air about the great ship were ordered to carry no more than one atom-bomb in their racks, and to fly a small white flag – along with the UN banner and their own national emblem. Thus did our ancestors face this, the ultimate challenge of history.

When the alien came forth a few hours later, the delegation stepped up to him, bowed, and, in the three official languages of the United Nations – English, French, and Russian – asked him to consider this planet his home. He listened to them gravely, and then launched into his talk of the day before – which was evidently as highly charged with emotion and significance to him as it was completely incomprehensible to the representatives of world government.

Fortunately, a cultivated young Indian member of the secretariat detected a suspicious similarity between the speech of the alien and an obscure Bengali dialect whose anomalies he had once puzzled over. The reason, as we all know now, was that the last time Earth had been visited by aliens of this particular type, humanity's most advanced civilization lay in a moist valley in Bengal; extensive dictionaries of that language had been written, so that speech with the natives of Earth would present no problem to any subsequent exploring party.

However, I move ahead of my tale, as one who would munch on the succulent roots before the dryer stem. Let me rest and suck air for a moment! Heigh-ho, truly those were tremendous experiences for our kind!

You, sir, now you sit back and listen! You are not yet of an age to Tell the Tale. I remember, well enough do I remember, how my father told it, and his father before him. You will wait your turn as I did; you will listen until too much high land between waterholes blocks me off from life.

Then *you* may take your place in the juiciest weed patch and, reclining gracefully between sprints, recite the great epic of our liberation to the carelessly exercising young.

Pursuant to the young Hindu's suggestions, the one professor of comparative linguistics in the world capable of understanding and conversing in this peculiar version of the dead dialect was summoned from an academic convention in New York where he was reading a paper he had been working on for eighteen years: *An Initial Study of Apparent*

Relationships Between Several Past Participles in Ancient Sanscrit and an Equal Number of Noun Substantives in Modern Szechuanese.

Yea, verily, all these things – and more, many more – did our ancestors in their besotted ignorance contrive to do. May we not count our freedoms indeed?

The disgruntled scholar, minus – as he kept insisting bitterly – some of his most essential word lists, was flown by fastest jet to the area south of Nancy which, in those long-ago days, lay in the enormous black shadow of the alien space-ship.

Here he was acquainted with his task by the United Nations delegation, whose nervousness had not been allayed by a new and disconcerting development. Several more aliens had emerged from the ship carrying great quantities of immense, shimmering metal which they proceeded to assemble into something that was obviously a machine – though it was taller than any skyscraper man had ever built, and seemed to make noises to itself like a talkative and sentient creature. The first alien still stood courteously in the neighbourhood of the profusely perspiring diplomats; ever and anon he would go through his little speech again, in a language that had been almost forgotten when the cornerstone of the library of Alexandria was laid. The men from the UN would reply, each one hoping desperately to make up for the alien's lack of familiarity with his own tongue by such devices as hand-gestures and facial expressions. Much later, a commission of anthropologists and psychologists brilliantly pointed out the difficulties of such physical, gestural communication with creatures possessing – as these aliens did – five manual appendages and a single, unwinking compound eye of the type the insects rejoice in.

The problems and agonies of the professor as he was trundled about the world in the wake of the aliens, trying to amass a usable vocabulary in a language whose peculiarities he could only extrapolate from the limited samples supplied him by one who must inevitably speak it with the most outlandish of foreign accents – these vexations were minor indeed compared to the disquiet felt by the representatives of world government. They beheld the extraterrestrial visitors move every day to a new site on their planet and proceed to assemble there a titanic structure of flickering metal which muttered nostalgically to itself, as if to keep alive the memory of those faraway factories which had given it birth.

True, there was always the alien who would pause in his evidently supervisory labours to release the set little speech; but not even the excellent manners he displayed, in listening to upward of fifty-six replies in as many languages, helped dispel the panic caused whenever a human scientist, investigating the shimmering machines, touched a projecting edge and promptly shrank into a disappearing pinpoint. This, while not a frequent occurrence, happened often enough to cause chronic indigestion and insomnia among human administrators.

Finally, having used up most of his nervous system as fuel, the professor collated enough of the language to make conversation possible. He – and, through him, the world – was thereupon told the following:

The aliens were members of a highly advanced civilization which had spread its culture throughout the entire galaxy. Cognizant of the limitations of the as-yet-under-developed animals who had latterly become dominant upon Earth, they had placed us in a sort of benevolent ostracism. Until either we or our institutions had evolved to a level permitting, say, at least *associate* membership in the galactic federation (under the sponsoring tutelage, for the first few millennia, of one of the older, more widespread, and more important species in that federation) – until that time, all invasions of our privacy and ignorance – except for a few scientific expeditions conducted under conditions of great secrecy – had been strictly forbidden by universal agreement.

Several individuals who had violated this ruling – at great cost to our racial sanity, and enormous profit to our reigning religions – had been so promptly and severely punished that no known infringements had occurred for some time. Our recent growth-curve had been satisfactory enough to cause hopes that a bare thirty or forty centuries more would suffice to place us on applicant status with the federation.

Unfortunately, the peoples of this stellar community were many, and varied as greatly in their ethical outlook as their biological composition. Quite a few species lagged a considerable social distance behind the Dendi, as our visitors called themselves. One of these, a race of horrible, worm-like organisms known as the Troxxt – almost as advanced technologically as they were retarded in moral development – had suddenly volunteered for the position of sole and absolute ruler of the galaxy. They had seized control of several key suns, with their attendant planetary systems, and, after a calculated decimation of the races thus captured, had announced their intention of punishing with a merciless extinction all species unable to appreciate from these object-lessons the value of unconditional surrender.

In despair, the galactic federation had turned to the Dendi, one of the oldest, most selfless, and yet most powerful of races in civilized space, and commissioned them – as the military arm of the federation – to hunt down the Troxxt, defeat them wherever they had gained illegal suzerainty, and destroy for ever their power to wage war.

This order had come almost too late. Everywhere the Troxxt had gained so much the advantage of attack, that the Dendi were able to contain them only by enormous sacrifice. For centuries now, the conflict had careened across our vast island universe. In the course of it, densely populated planets had been disintegrated; suns had been blasted into novae; and whole groups of stars ground into swirling cosmic dust.

A temporary stalemate had been reached a short while ago, and – reeling and breathless – both sides were using the lull to strengthen weak spots in their perimeter.

Thus, the Troxxt had finally moved into the till-then peaceful section of space that contained our solar system – among others. They were thoroughly uninterested in our tiny planet with its meagre resources; nor did they care much for such celestial neighbours as Mars or Jupiter. They established their headquarters on a planet of Proxima Centaurus – the star nearest our own sun – and proceeded to consolidate their offensive-defensive network between Rigel and Aldebaran. At this point in their explanation, the Dendi pointed out, the exigencies of interstellar strategy tended to become too complicated for anything but three dimensional maps; let us here accept the simple statement, they suggested that it became immediately vital for them to strike rapidly, and make the Troxxt position on Proxima Centaurus untenable – to establish a base inside their lines of communication.

The most likely spot for such a base was Earth.

⋆

The Dendi apologized profusely for intruding on our development, an intrusion which might cost us dear in our delicate developmental state. But, as they explained – in impeccable pre-Bengali – before their arrival we had, in effect, become (all unknowingly) a satrapy of the awful Troxxt. We could now consider ourselves liberated.

We thanked them much for that.

Besides, their leader pointed out proudly, the Dendi were engaged in a war for the sake of civilization itself, against an enemy so horrible, so obscene in its nature, and so utterly filthy in its practices, that it was unworthy of the label of intelligent life. They were fighting, not only for themselves, but for every loyal member of the galactic federation; for every small and helpless species; for every obscure race too weak to defend itself against a ravaging conqueror. Would humanity stand aloof from such a conflict?

There was just a slight bit of hesitation as the information was digested. Then – 'No!' humanity roared back through such mass-communication media as television, newspapers, reverberating jungle drums, and mule-mounted backwoods messenger. *'We will not stand aloof. We will help you destroy this menace to the very fabric of civilization. Just tell us what you want us to do.'*

Well, nothing in particular, the aliens replied with some embarrassment. Possibly in a little while there might *be* something – *several* little things, in fact – which could be *quite* useful; but, for the moment, if we would concentrate on not getting in their way when they serviced their gun-mounts, they would be very grateful, really . . .

This reply tended to create a large amount of uncertainty among the two billion of Earth's human population. For several days afterwards, there was a planet-wide tendency – the legend has come down to us – of people failing to meet each other's eyes.

But then Man rallied from this substantial blow to his pride. He would be useful, be it ever so humbly, to the race which had liberated him from potential subjugation by the ineffably ugly Troxxt. For this, let us remember well our ancestors! Let us hymn their sincere efforts amid their ignorance!

All standing armies, all air and sea fleets, were reorganized into guard-patrols around the Dendi weapons: no human might approach within two miles of the murmuring machinery without a pass countersigned by the Dendi. Since they were never known to sign such a pass during the entire period of their stay on this planet, however, this loophole-provision was never exercised as far as is known; and the immediate neighbourhood of the extraterrestrial weapons became and remained henceforth wholesomely free of two-legged creatures.

Cooperation with our liberators took precedence over all other human activites. The order of the day was a slogan first given voice by a Harvard professor of government in a querulous radio round table on 'Man's Place in a Somewhat Over-Civilized Universe'.

'Let us forget our individual egos and collective conceits!' the professor cried at one point. 'Let us subordinate everything – to the end that the freedom of the solar system in general, and Earth in particular, must and shall be preserved!'

Despite the mouth-filling qualities, this slogan was repeated everywhere. Still, it was difficult sometimes to know exactly what the Dendi wanted – partly because of the limited number of interpreters available to the heads of the various sovereign states, and partly because of their leader's tendency to vanish into his ship after ambiguous and equivocal statements – such as the curt admonition to 'Evacuate Washington!'

On that occasion, both the Secretary of State and the American President perspired fearfully through five hours of a July day in all the silk-hatted, stiff-collared, dark-suited diplomatic regalia that the barbaric past demanded of political leaders who would deal with the representatives of another people. They waited and wilted beneath the enormous ship – which no human had ever been invited to enter, despite the wistful hints constantly thrown out by university professors and aeronautical designers – they waited patiently and wetly for the Dendi leader to emerge and let them know whether he had meant the State of Washington or Washington, DC.

The tale comes down to us at this point as a tale of glory. The Capitol building was taken apart in a few days, and set up almost intact in the foothills of the Rocky Mountains; the missing Archives, that were later to turn up in the Children's Room of a Public Library in Duluth, Iowa; the bottles of Potomac River water carefully borne westward and ceremoniously poured into the circular concrete ditch built around the

President's mansion (from which unfortunately it was to evaporate within a week because of the relatively low humidity of the region) – all these are proud moments in the galactic history of our species, from which not even the later knowledge that the Dendi wished to build no gunsite on the spot, nor even an ammunition dump, but merely a recreation hall for their troops, could remove any of the grandeur of our determined cooperation and most willing sacrifice.

There is no denying, however, that the ego of our race was greatly damaged by the discovery, in the course of a routine journalistic interview, that the aliens totalled no more powerful a group than a squad; and that their leader, instead of the great scientist and key military strategist that we might justifiably have expected the Galactic Federation to furnish for the protection of Terra, ranked as the interstellar equivalent of a buck sergeant.

That the President of the United States, the Commander-in-Chief of the Army and the Navy, had waited in such obeisant fashion upon a mere non-commissioned officer was hard for us to swallow; but that the impending Battle of Earth was to have a historical dignity only slightly higher than that of a patrol action was impossibly humiliating.

And then there was the matter of 'lendi'.

The aliens, while installing or servicing their planet-wide weapon system, would occasionally fling aside an evidently unusable fragment of the talking metal. Separated from the machine of which it had been a component, the substance seemed to lose all those qualities which were deleterious to mankind and retain several which were quite useful indeed. For example, if a portion of the strange material was attached to any terrestrial metal – and insulated carefully from contact with other substances – it would, in a few hours, itself become exactly the metal that it touched, whether that happened to be zinc, gold, or pure uranium.

This stuff – 'lendi', men have heard the aliens call it – was shortly in frantic demand in an economy ruptured by constant and unexpected emptyings of its most important industrial centres.

Everywhere the aliens went, to and from their weapon sites, hordes of ragged humans stood chanting – well outside the two-mile limit – 'Any lendi, Dendi?' All attempts by law-enforcement agencies of the planet to put a stop to this shameless, wholesale begging were useless – especially since the Dendi themselves seemed to get some unexplainable pleasure out of scattering tiny pieces of lendi to the scrabbling multitude. When policemen and soldiery began to join the trampling murderous dash to the corner of the meadows wherein had fallen the highly versatile and garrulous metal, governments gave up.

Mankind also began to hope for the attack to come, so that it would be relieved of the festering consideration of its own patent inferiorities. A few of the more fanatically conservative among our ancestors probably even began to regret liberation.

They did, children; they did. Let us hope that these would-be troglodytes were among the very first to be dissolved and melted down by the red flame-balls. One cannot, after all, turn one's back on progress.

Two days before the month of September was over, the aliens announced that they had detected activity upon one of the moons of Saturn. The Troxxt were evidently threading their treacherous way inward through the solar system. Considering their vicious and deceitful propensities, the Dendi warned, an attack from these worm-like monstrosities might be expected at any moment.

Few humans went to sleep as the night rolled up to and past the meridian on which they dwelt. Almost all eyes were lifted to a sky carefully denuded of clouds by watchful Dendi. There was a brisk trade in cheap telescopes and bits of smoked glass in some sections of the planet; while other portions experienced a substantial boom in spells and charms of the all-inclusive, or omnibus, variety.

The Troxxt attacked in three cylindrical black ships simultaneously; one in the Southern Hemisphere, and two in the Northern. Great gouts of green flame roared out of their tiny craft; and everything touched by these gouts imploded into a translucent, glass-like sand. No Dendi was hurt by these, however, and from each of the now-writhing gun-mounts there bubbled forth a series of scarlet clouds which pursued the Troxxt hungrily, until forced by a dwindling velocity to fall back upon Earth.

Here they had an unhappy after-effect. Any populated area into which these pale pink cloudlets chanced to fall was rapidly transformed into a cemetery – a cemetery, if the truth be told as it has been handed down to us, that had more the odour of the kitchen than the grave. The inhabitants of these unfortunate localities were subjected to enormous increases of temperature. Their skin reddened, then blackened; their hair and nails shrivelled; their very flesh turned into liquid and boiled off their bones. Altogether a disagreeable way for one-tenth of the human race to die.

The only consolation was the capture of a black cylinder by one of the red clouds. When, as a result of this, it had turned white-hot and poured its substance down in the form of a metallic rainstorm, the two ships assaulting the Northern Hemisphere abruptly retreated to the asteroids into which the Dendi – because of severely limited numbers – steadfastly refused to pursue them.

In the next twenty-four hours the aliens – *resident* aliens, let us say – held conferences, made repairs to their weapons and commiserated with us. Humanity buried its dead. This last was a custom of our forefathers that was most worthy of note; and one that has not, of course, survived into modern times.

By the time the Troxxt returned, Man was ready for them. He could not, unfortunately, stand to arms as he most ardently desired to do; but he could and did stand to optical instrument and conjurer's oration.

Once more the little red clouds burst joyfully into the upper reaches of the stratosphere; once more the green flames wailed and tore at the chattering spires of lendi; once more men died by the thousands in the boiling backwash of war. But this time, there was a slight difference: the green flames of the Troxxt abruptly changed colour after the engagement had lasted three hours; they became darker, more bluish. And, as they did so, Dendi after Dendi collapsed at his station and died in convulsions.

The call for retreat was evidently sounded. The survivors fought their way to the tremendous ship in which they had come. With an explosion from her stern jets that blasted a red-hot furrow southward through France, and kicked Marseilles into the Mediterranean, the ship roared into space and fled home ignominiously.

Humanity steeled itself for the coming ordeal of horror under the Troxxt.

They were truly worm-like in form. As soon as the two night-black cylinders had landed, they strode from their ships, their tiny segmented bodies held off the ground by a complex harness supported by long and slender metal crutches. They erected a dome-like fort around each ship – one in Australia and one in the Ukraine – captured the few courageous individuals who had ventured close to their landing-sites, and disappeared back into the dark craft with their squirming prizes.

While some men drilled about nervously in the ancient military patterns, others pored anxiously over scientific texts and records, pertaining to the visit of the Dendi – in the desperate hope of finding a way of preserving terrestrial independence against this ravening conqueror of the star-spattered galaxy.

And yet all this time, the human captives inside the artificially darkened space-ships (the Troxxt, having no eyes, not only had little use for light, but the more sedentary individuals among them actually found such radiation disagreeable to their sensitive, unpigmented skins) were not being tortured for information – nor vivisected in the earnest quest of knowledge on a slightly higher level – but educated.

Educated in the Troxxtian language, that is.

True it was that a large number found themselves utterly inadequate for the task which the Troxxt had set them, and temporarily became servants to the more successful students. And another, albeit smaller, group developed various forms of frustration hysteria, ranging from mild unhappiness to complete catatonic depression, over the difficulties presented by a language whose every verb was irregular, and whose myriads of prepositions were formed by noun-adjective combinations derived from the subject of the previous sentence. But, eventually, eleven human beings were released, to blink madly in the sunlight as certified interpreters of Troxxt.

These liberators, it seemed, had never visited Bengal in the heyday of its millennia-past civilization.

Yes, these *liberators*. For the Troxxt had landed on the sixth day of the ancient, almost mythical month of October. And October the Sixth is, of course, the Holy Day of the Second Liberation. Let us remember, let us revere. (If only we could figure out which day it is on our calendar!)

The tale the interpreters told caused men to hang their heads in shame and gnash their teeth at the deception they had allowed the Dendi to practise upon them.

True, the Dendi had been commissioned by the Galactic Federation to hunt the Troxxt down and destroy them. This was largely because the Dendi *were* the Galactic Federation. One of the first intelligent arrivals on the interstellar scene, the huge creatures had organized a vast police force to protect them and their power against any contingency of revolt that might arise in the future. This police force was ostensibly a congress of all thinking life forms throughout the galaxy; actually, it was an efficient means of keeping them under rigid control.

Most species thus-far discovered were docile and tractable, however; the Dendi had been ruling from time immemorial, said they – very well, then, let the Dendi continue to rule. Did it make that much difference?

But, throughout the centuries, opposition to the Dendi grew – and the nuclei of the opposition were the protoplasm-based creatures. What, in fact, had come to be known as the Protoplasmic League.

Though small in number, the creatures whose life cycles were derived from the chemical and physical properties of protoplasm varied greatly in size, structure, and specialization. A galactic community deriving the main wells of its power from them would be a dynamic instead of a static place, where extra-galactic travel would be encouraged, instead of being inhibited, as it was at present because of Dendi fears of meeting a superior civilization. It would be a true democracy of species – a real biological republic – where all creatures of adequate intelligence and cultural development would enjoy a control of their destinies at present experienced by the silicon-based Dendi alone.

To this end, the Troxxt – the only important race which had steadfastly refused the complete surrender of armaments demanded of all members of the Federation – had been implored by a minor member of the Protoplasmic League to rescue it from the devastation which the Dendi intended to visit upon it, as punishment for an unlawful exploratory excursion outside the boundaries of the galaxy.

Faced with the determination of the Troxxt to defend their cousins in organic chemistry, and the suddenly aroused hostility of at least two-thirds of the interstellar peoples, the Dendi had summoned a rump meeting of the Galactic Council; declared a state of revolt in being; and proceeded to cement their disintegrating rule with the blasted life-forces of a hundred worlds. The Troxxt, hopelessly out-numbered and out-equipped, had been able to continue the struggle only because of the great ingenuity, and selflessness of other members of the Protoplasmic League, who had risked extinction to supply them with newly developed secret weapons.

Hadn't we guessed the nature of the beast from the enormous precautions it had taken to prevent the exposure of any part of its body to the intensely corrosive atmosphere of Earth? Surely the seamless, barely translucent suits which our recent visitors had worn for every moment of their stay on our world should have made us suspect a body chemistry developed from complex silicon compounds rather than those of carbon?

Humanity hung its collective head and admitted that the suspicion had never occurred to it.

Well, the Troxxt admitted generously, we were extremely inexperienced and possibly a little too trusting. Put it down to that. Our naïveté, however costly to them – our liberators – would not be allowed to deprive us of that complete citizenship which the Troxxt were claiming as the birthright of all.

But as for our leaders, our probably corrupted, certainly irresponsible leaders . . .

The first executions of UN officials, heads of states, and pre-Bengali interpreters as 'Traitors to Protoplasm' – after some of the lengthiest and most nearly-perfectly-fair trials in the history of Earth – were held a week after G-J day, the inspiring occasion on which – amidst gorgeous ceremonies – Humanity was invited to join, first the Protoplasmic League and thence the New and Democratic Galactic Federation of All Species, All Races.

Nor was that all. Whereas the Dendi had contemptuously shoved us to one side as they went about their business of making our planet safe for tyranny, and had – in all probability – built special devices which made the very touch of their weapons fatal for us, the Troxxt – with the sincere friendliness which had made their name a byword for democracy and decency wherever living creatures came together among the stars – our Second Liberators, as we lovingly called them, actually *preferred* to have us help them with the intensive, accelerating labour of planetary defence.

So men's intestines dissolved under the invisible glare of the forces used to assemble the new, incredibly complex weapons; men sickened and died, in scrabbling hordes, inside the mines which the Troxxt had made deeper than any we had dug hitherto; men's bodies broke open and exploded in the undersea oil-drilling sites which the Troxxt had declared were essential.

Children's schooldays were requested, too, in such collecting drives as 'Platinum Scrap for Procyon' and 'Radioactive Debris for Deneb'. Housewives also were implored to save on salt whenever possible – this substance being useful to the Troxxt in literally dozens of incomprehensible ways – and colourful posters reminded: *'Don't salinate – sugarfy!'*

And over all – courteously caring for us like an intelligent parent – were our mentors, taking their giant supervisory strides on metallic crutches, while their pale little bodies lay curled in the hammocks that swung from each paired length of shining leg.

Truly, even in the midst of a complete economic paralysis caused by the concentration of all major productive facilities on other-worldly armaments, and despite the anguished cries of those suffering from peculiar industrial injuries which our medical men were totally unequipped to handle, in the midst of all this mind-wracking disorganization, it was yet very exhilarating to realize that we had taken our lawful place in the future government of the galaxy and were even now helping to make the Universe Safe for Democracy.

But the Dendi returned to smash this idyll. They came in their huge, silvery space-ships and the Troxxt, barely warned in time, just managed to rally under the blow and fight back in kind. Even so, the Troxxt ship in the Ukraine was almost immediately forced to flee to its base in the depths of space. After three days, the only Troxxt on Earth were the devoted members of a little band guarding the ship in Australia. They proved, in three or more months, to be as difficult to remove from the face of our planet as the continent itself; and since there was now a state of close and hostile siege, with the Dendi on one side of the globe, and the Troxxt on the other, the battle assumed frightful proportions.

Seas boiled; whole steppes burned away; the climate itself shifted and changed under the gruelling pressure of the cataclysm. By the time the Dendi solved the problem, the planet Venus had been blasted from the skies in the course of a complicated battle manoeuvre, the Earth had wobbled over as orbital substitute.

The solution was simple; since the Troxxt were too firmly based on the small continent to be driven away, the numerically superior Dendi brought up enough firepower to disintegrate all Australia into an ash that muddied the Pacific. This occurred on the twenty-fourth of June, the Holy Day of First Reliberation. A day of reckoning for what remained of the human race, however.

How could we have been so naïve, the Dendi wanted to know, as to be taken in by the chauvinistic pro-protoplasm propaganda? Surely, if physical characteristics were to be the criteria of our racial empathy, we would not orient ourselves on a narrow chemical basis? The Dendi life-plasma was based on silicon instead of carbon, true, but did not vertebrates – *appendaged* vertebrates, at that, such as we and the Dendi – have infinitely more in common, in spite of a *minor* biochemical difference or two, than vertebrates and legless, armless, slime-crawling creatures who happened, quite accidentally, to possess an identical organic substance?

As for this fantastic picture of life in the galaxy . . . *Well!* The Dendi shrugged their quintuple shoulders as they went about the intricate business of erecting their noisy weapons all over the rubble of our planet. Had we ever seen a representative of these proto-plasmic races the Troxxt were supposedly protecting? No, nor would we. For as soon as a race – animal, vegetable, or mineral – developed enough to constitute even a *potential* danger to the sinuous aggressors, its civilization was systematically dismantled by the watchful Troxxt. We were in so primitive a state that they had not considered it at all risky to allow us the outward seeming of full participation.

Could we say we had learned a single useful piece of information about Troxxt technology – for all of the work we had done on their machines, for all of the lives we had lost in the process? No, of course not. We had merely contributed our mite to the enslavement of far-off races who had done us no harm.

There was much that we had cause to feel guilty about, the Dendi told us gravely – once the few surviving interpreters of the pre-Bengali dialect had crawled out of hiding. But our collective onus was as nothing compared to that borne by 'vermicular collaborationists' – those traitors who had supplanted our martyred former leaders. And then there were the unspeakable human interpreters who had had linguistic traffic with creatures destroying a two-million-year-old galactic peace. Why, killing was almost too good for them, the Dendi murmured as they killed them.

When the Troxxt ripped their way back into possession of Earth some eighteen months later, bringing us the sweet fruits of the Second Reliberation – as well as a complete and most convincing rebuttal of the Dendi – there were few humans found who were willing to accept with any real enthusiasm the responsibilities of newly opened and highly paid positions in language, science, and government.

Of course, since the Troxxt, in order to reliberate Earth, had found it necessary to blast a tremendous chunk out of the Northern Hemisphere, there were very few humans to be found in the first place . . . Even so, many of these committed suicide rather than assume the title of Secretary-General of the United Nations when the Dendi came back for the glorious Re-Reliberation, a short time after that. This was the liberation, by the way, which swept, the deep collar of matter off our planet, and gave it what our forefathers came to call a pear-shaped look.

Possibly it was at this time – possibly a liberation or so later – that the Troxxt and the Dendi discovered that the Earth had become far too eccentric in its orbit to possess the minimum safety conditions demanded of a Combat Zone. The battle, therefore, zigzagged coruscatingly and murderously away in the direction of Aldebaran.

That was nine generations ago, but the tale that has been handed down from parent to child, to child's child, has lost little in the telling. You hear it now from me almost exactly as *I* heard it. From my father I heard it as I ran with him from water puddle to distant water puddle, across the searing heat of yellow sand. From my mother I heard it as we sucked air and frantically grabbed at clusters of thick green weed, whenever the planet beneath us quivered in omen of a geological spasm that might bury us in its burned-out body, or a cosmic gyration threatened to fling us into empty space.

Yes, even as we do now did we do then, telling the same tale, running the same frantic race across miles of unendurable heat for food and water; fighting the same savage battles with the giant rabbits for each other's carrion – and always, ever and always, sucking desperately at the precious air, which leaves our world in greater quantities with every mad twist of its orbit.

Naked, hungry, and thirsty came we into the world, and naked, hungry, and thirsty do we scamper our lives out upon it, under the huge and never-changing sun.

The same tale it is, and the same traditional ending it has as that I had from my father and his father before him. Suck air, grab clusters, and hear the last holy observation of our history!

'Looking about us, we can say with pardonable pride that we have been about as thoroughly liberated as it is possible for a race and a planet to be.'

An Alien Agony

HARRY HARRISON

Somewhere above, hidden by the eternal clouds of Wesker's World, a thunder rumbled and grew. Trader John Garth stopped when he heard it, his boots sinking slowly into the muck, and cupped his good ear to catch the sound. It swelled and waned in the thick atmosphere, growing louder.

'That noise is the same as the noise of your sky-ship,' Itin said, with stolid Wesker logicality, slowly pulverizing the idea in his mind and turning over the bits one by one for closer examination. 'But your ship is still sitting where you landed it. It must be, even though we cannot see it, because you are the only one who can operate it. And even if anyone else could operate it we would have heard it rising into the sky. Since we did not, and if this sound is a sky-ship sound, then it must mean . . .'

'Yes, another ship,' Garth said, too absorbed in his own thoughts to wait for the laborious Weskerian chains of logic to clank their way through to the end. Of course it was another spacer, it had been only a matter of time before one appeared, and undoubtedly this one was homing on the SS radar reflector as he had done. His own ship would show up clearly on the newcomer's screen and they would probably set down as close to it as they could.

'You better go ahead, Itin,' he said. 'Use the water so you can get to the village quickly. Tell everyone to get back into the swamps, well clear of the hard ground. That ship is landing on instruments and anyone underneath at touchdown is going to be cooked.'

This immediate threat was clear enough to the little Wesker amphibian. Before Garth finished speaking Itin's ribbed ears had folded like a bat's wing and he slipped silently into the nearby canal. Garth squelched on through the mud, making as good time as he could over the clinging surface. He had just reached the fringes of the village clearing when the rumbling grew to a head-splitting roar and the spacer broke through the low-hanging layer of clouds above. Garth shielded his eyes from the down-reaching tongue of flame and examined the growing form of the grey-black ship with mixed feelings.

After almost a standard year on Wesker's World he had to fight down a longing for human companionship of any kind. While this buried fragment of herd-spirit chattered for the rest of the monkey tribe, his trader's mind was busily drawing a line under a column of figures and adding up the total. This could very well be another trader's ship, and if it were his monopoly of the Wesker trade was at an end. Then again, this might not be a trader at all, which was the reason he stayed in the shelter of the giant fern and loosened his gun in its holster.

The ship baked dry a hundred square metres of mud, the roaring blast died, and the landing feet crunched down through the crackling crust. Metal creaked and settled into place while the cloud of smoke and steam slowly drifted lower in the humid air.

'Garth – you native-cheating extortionist – where are you?' the ship's speaker boomed. The lines of the spacer had looked only slightly familiar, but there was no mistaking the rasping tones of that voice. Garth wore a smile when he stepped out into the open and whistled shrilly through two fingers. A directional microphone ground out of its casing on the ship's fin and turned in his direction.

'What are you doing here, Singh?' he shouted towards the mike. 'Too crooked to find a planet of your own and have to come here to steal an honest trader's profits?'

'Honest!' the amplified voice roared. 'This from the man who has been in more jails than cathouses – and that a goodly number in itself, I do declare. Sorry, friend of my youth, but I cannot join you in exploiting this aboriginal pesthole. I am on course to a more fairly atmosphered world where a fortune is waiting to be made. I only stopped here since an opportunity presented itself to turn an honest credit by running a taxi service. I bring you friendship, the perfect companionship, a man in a different line of business who might help you in yours. I'd come out and say hello myself, except I would have to decon for biologicals. I'm cycling the passenger through the lock so I hope you won't mind helping with his luggage.'

At least there would be no other trader on the planet now, that worry was gone. But Garth still wondered what sort of passenger would be taking one-way passage to an uninhabited world. And what was behind that concealed hint of merriment in Singh's voice? He walked around to the far side of the spacer where the ramp had dropped, and looked up at the man in the cargo lock who was wrestling ineffectually with a large crate. The man turned towards him and Garth saw the clerical dog-collar and knew just what it was Singh had been chuckling about.

'What are you doing here?' Garth asked; in spite of his attempt at self control he snapped the words. If the man noticed this he ignored it, because he was still smiling and putting out his hand as he came down the ramp.

'Father Mark,' he said. 'Of the Missionary Society of Brothers. I'm very pleased to . . .'

'I said what are you doing here.' Garth's voice was under control now, quiet and cold. He knew what had to be done, and it must be done quickly or not at all.

'That should be obvious,' Father Mark said, his good nature still unruffled. 'Our missionary society has raised funds to send spiritual emissaries to alien worlds for the first time. I was lucky enough . . .'

'Take your luggage and get back into the ship. You're not wanted here and have no permission to land. You'll be a liability and there is no one on Wesker to take care of you. Get back into the ship.'

'I don't know who you are sir, or why you are lying to me,' the priest said. He was still calm but the smile was gone. 'But I have studied galactic law and the history of this planet very well. There are no diseases or beasts here that I should have any particular fear of. It is also an open planet, and until the Space Survey changes that status I have as much right to be here as you do.'

The man was of course right, but Garth couldn't let him know that. He had been bluffing, hoping the priest didn't know his rights. But he did. There was only one distasteful course left for him, and he had better do it while there was still time.

'Get back in that ship,' he shouted, not hiding his anger now. With a smooth motion his gun was out of the holster and the pitted black muzzle only inches from the priest's stomach. The man's face turned white, but he did not move.

'What the hell are you doing, Garth!' Singh's shocked voice grated from the speaker. 'The guy paid his fare and you have no rights at all to throw him off the planet.'

'I have this right,' Garth said, raising his gun and sighting between the priest's eyes. 'I give him thirty seconds to get back aboard the ship or I pull the trigger.'

'Well I think you are either off your head or playing a joke,' Singh's exasperated voice rasped down at them. 'If a joke, it is in bad taste, and either way you're not getting away with it. Two can play at that game, only I can play it better.'

There was the rumble of heavy bearings and the remote-controlled four-gun turret on the ship's side rotated and pointed at Garth. 'Now – down gun and give Father Mark a hand with the luggage,' the speaker commanded, a trace of humour back in the voice now. 'As much as I would like to help, Old Friend, I cannot. I feel it is time you had a chance to talk to the Father; after all, I have had the opportunity of speaking with him all the way from Earth.'

Garth jammed the gun back into the holster with an acute feeling of loss. Father Mark stepped forward, the winning smile back now and a bible taken from a pocket of his robe, in his raised hand. 'My son,' he said.

'I'm not your son,' was all Garth could choke out as defeat welled up in him. His fist drew back as the anger rose, and the best he could do was open the fist so he struck only with the flat of his hand. Still the blow sent the priest crashing to the ground and fluttered the pages of the book splattering into the thick mud.

Itin and the other Weskers had watched everything with seemingly emotionless interest, and Garth made no attempt to answer their unspoken questions. He started towards his house, but turned back when he saw they were still unmoving.

'A new man has come,' he told them. 'He will need help with the things he has brought. If he doesn't have any place for them, you can put them in the big warehouse until he has a place of his own.'

He watched them waddle across the clearing towards the ship, then went inside and gained a certain satisfaction from slamming the door hard enough to crack one of the panes. There was an equal amount of painful pleasure in breaking out one of the remaining bottles of Irish whiskey that he had been saving for a special occasion. Well this was special enough, though not really what he had had in mind. The whiskey was good and burned away some of the bad taste in his mouth, but not all of it. If his tactics had worked, success would have justified everything. But he had failed and in addition to the pain of failure there was the acute feeling that he had made a horse's ass out of himself. Singh had blasted off without any good-byes. There was no telling what sense he had made of the whole matter, though he would surely carry some strange stories back to the traders' lodge. Well, that could be worried about the next time Garth signed in. Right now he had to go about setting things right with the missionary. Squinting out through the rain he saw the man struggling to erect a collapsible tent while the entire population of the village stood in ordered ranks and watched. Naturally none of them offered to help.

By the time the tent was up and the crates and boxes stowed inside it the rain had stopped. The level of fluid in the bottle was a good bit lower and Garth felt more like facing up to the unavoidable meeting. In truth, he was looking forward to talking to the man. This whole nasty business aside, after an entire solitary year any human companionship looked good. *Will you join me now for dinner. John Garth,* he wrote on the back of an old invoice. But maybe the guy was too frightened to come? Which was no way to start any kind of relationship. Rummaging under the bunk, he found a box that was big enough and put his pistol inside. Itin was of course waiting outside the door when he opened it, since this was his tour as Knowledge Collector. He handed him the note and box.

'Would you take these to the new man,' he said.

'Is the new man's name New Man?' Itin asked.

'No, it's not!' Garth snapped. 'His name is Mark. But I'm only asking you to deliver this, not get involved in conversation.'

As always when he lost his temper, the literal minded Weskers won the round. 'You are not asking for conversation,' Itin said slowly, 'but Mark may ask for conversation. And others will ask me his name, if I do not know his na . . .' The voice cut off as Garth slammed the door. This didn't work in the long run either because next time he saw Itin – a day, a week, or even a month later – the monologue would be picked up on the very word it had ended and the thought rambled out to its last frayed end. Garth cursed under his breath and poured water over a pair of the tastier concentrates that he had left.

'Come in,' he said when there was a quiet knock on the door. The priest entered and held out the box with the gun.

'Thank you for the loan, Mr Garth, I appreciate the spirit that made you send it. I have no idea of what caused the unhappy affair when I landed, but I think it would be best forgotten if we are going to be on this planet together for any length of time.'

'Drink?' Garth asked, taking the box and pointing to the bottle on the table. He poured two glasses full and handed one to the priest. 'That's about what I had in mind, but I still owe you an explanation of what happened out there.' He scowled into his glass for a second, then raised it to the other man. 'It's a big universe and I guess we have to make out as best we can. Here's to Sanity.'

'God be with you,' Father Mark said, and raised his glass as well.

'Not with me or with this planet,' Garth said firmly, 'And that's the crux of the matter.' He half-drained the glass and sighed.

'Do you say that to shock me?' the priest asked with a smile. 'I assure you it doesn't.'

'Not intended to shock. I meant it quite literally. I suppose I'm what you would call an atheist, so revealed religion is no concern of mine. While these natives, simple and unlettered stone-age types that they are, have managed to come this far with no superstitions or traces of deism whatsoever. I had hoped that they might continue that way.'

'What are you saying?' the priest frowned. 'Do you mean they have no gods, no belief in the hereafter? They must die . . . ?'

'Die they do, and to dust returneth like the rest of the animals. They have thunder, trees, and water without having thunder-gods, tree sprites, or water nymphs. They have no ugly little gods, taboos, or spells to hag-ride and limit their lives. They are the only primitive people I have ever encountered that are completely free of superstition and appear to be much happier and sane because of it. I just wanted to keep them that way.'

'You wanted to keep them from God – from salvation?' The priest's eyes widened and he recoiled slightly.

'No,' Garth said. 'I wanted to keep them from superstition until they knew more and could think about it realistically without being absorbed and perhaps destroyed by it.'

'You're being insulting to the Church, sir, to equate it with superstition . . .'

'Please,' Garth said, raising his hand. 'No theological arguments. I don't think your society footed the bill for this trip just to attempt a conversion on me. Just accept the fact that my beliefs have been arrived at through careful thought over a period of years, and no amount of undergraduate metaphysics will change them. I'll promise not to try and convert you – if you will do the same for me.'

'Agreed, Mr Garth. As you have reminded me, my mission here is to save these souls, and that is what I must do. But why should my work disturb you so much that you try and keep me from landing? Even threaten me with your gun, and . . .' the priest broke off and looked into his glass.

'And even slug you?' Garth asked, suddenly frowning. 'There was no excuse for that, and I would like to say that I'm sorry. Plain bad manners and an even worse temper. Live alone long enough and you find yourself doing that kind of thing.' He brooded down at his big hands where they lay on the table, reading memories into the scars and callouses patterned there. 'Let's just call it frustration, for lack of a better word. In your business you must have had a lot of chance to peep into the darker places in men's minds and you should know a bit about motives and happiness. I have had too busy a life to ever consider settling down and raising a family, and right up until recently I never missed it. Maybe leakage radiation is softening up my brain, but I had begun to think of these furry and fishy Weskers as being a little like my own children, that I was somehow responsible for them.'

'We are all His children,' Father Mark said quietly.

'Well, here are some of His children that can't even imagine His existence,' Garth said, suddenly angry at himself for allowing gentler emotions to show through. Yet he forgot himself at once, leaning forward with the intensity of his feelings. 'Can't you realize the importance of this? Live with these Weskers awhile and you will discover a simple and happy life that matches the state of grace you people are always talking about. They get *pleasure* from their lives – and cause no one pain. By circumstance they have evolved on an almost barren world, so have never had a chance to grow out of a physical stone age culture. But mentally they are our match – or perhaps better. They have all learned my language so I can easily explain the many things they want to know. Knowledge and the gaining of knowledge gives them real satisfaction. They tend to be exasperating at times because every new fact must be related to the structure of all other things, but the more they learn, the faster this process becomes. Someday they are going to be man's equal in every way, perhaps surpass us. If – would you do me a favour?'

'Whatever I can.'

'Leave them alone. Or teach them if you must – history and science, philosophy, law, anything that will help them face the realities of the greater universe they never even knew existed before. But don't confuse them with your hatreds and pain, guilt, sin, and punishment. Who knows the harm . . .'

'You are being insulting, sir!' the priest said, jumping to his feet. The top of his grey head barely came to the massive spaceman's chin, yet he showed no fear in defending what he believed. Garth, standing now himself, was no longer the penitent. They faced each other in anger, as men have always stood, unbending in the defence of that which they think right.

'Yours is the insult,' Garth shouted. 'The incredible egotism to feel that your derivative little mythology, differing only slightly from the thousands of others that still burden men, can do anything but confuse their still fresh minds! Don't you realize that they believe in truth – and have never heard of such a thing as a lie. They have not been trained yet to understand that other kinds of minds can think differently from theirs. Will you spare them this . . . ?'

'I will do my duty, which is His will, Mr Garth. These are God's creatures here, and they have souls. I cannot shirk my duty, which is to bring them His word, so that they may be saved and enter into the kingdom of heaven.'

When the priest opened the door the wind caught it and blew it wide. He vanished into the stormswept darkness and the door swung back and forth and a splatter of raindrops blew in. Garth's boots left muddy footprints when he closed the door, shutting out the sight of Itin sitting patiently and uncomplaining in the storm, hoping only that Garth might stop for a moment and leave with him some of the wonderful knowledge of which he had so much.

By unspoken consent that first night was never mentioned again. After a few days of loneliness, made worse because each knew of the other's proximity, they found themselves talking on carefully neutral grounds. Garth slowly packed and stowed away his stock and never admitted that his work was finished and he could leave at any time. He had a fair amount of interesting drugs and botanicals that would fetch a good price. And the Wesker Artefacts were sure to create a sensation in the sophisticated galactic market. Crafts on the planet here had been limited before his arrival, mostly pieces of carving painfully chipped into the hard wood with fragments of stone. He had supplied tools and a stock of raw metal from his own supplies, nothing more than that. In a few months the Weskers had not only learned to work with the new materials, but had translated their own designs and forms into the most alien – but most beautiful – artefacts that he had ever seen. All he had to do was release these on the market to create a primary demand, then return for a new supply. The Weskers wanted only books and tools and knowledge in return, and through their own efforts he knew they would pull themselves into the galactic union.

This is what Garth had hoped. But a wind of change was blowing through the settlement that had grown up around his ship. No longer was he the centre of attention and focal point of the village life. He had to grin when he thought of his fall from power; yet there was very little humour in the smile. Serious and attentive Weskers still took turns of duty as Knowledge Collectors, but their recording of dry facts was in sharp contrast to the intellectual hurricane that surrounded the priest.

Where Garth had made them work for each book and machine, the priest gave freely. Garth had tried to be progressive in his supply of knowledge, treating them as bright but unlettered children. He had wanted them to walk before they could run, to master one step before going on to the next.

Father Mark simply brought them the benefits of Christianity. The only physical work he required was the construction of a church, a place of worship and learning. More Weskers had appeared out of the limitless planetary swamps and within days the roof was up, supported on a framework of poles. Each morning the congregation worked a little while on the walls, then hurried inside to learn the all-promising, all-encompassing, all-important facts about the universe.

Garth never told the Weskers what he thought about their new interest, and this was mainly because they had never asked him. Pride or honour stood in the way of his grabbing a willing listener and pouring out his grievances. Perhaps it would have been different if Itin was on Collecting duty; he was the brightest of the lot; but Itin had been rotated the day after the priest had arrived and Garth had not talked to him since.

It was a surprise then when after seventeen of the trebly-long Wesker days, he found a delegation at his doorstep when he emerged after breakfast. Itin was their spokesman, and his mouth was open slightly. Many of the other Weskers had their mouths open as well, one even appearing to be yawning, clearly revealing the double row of sharp teeth and the purple-black throat. The mouths impressed Garth as to the seriousness of the meeting: this was the one Wesker expression he had learned to recognize. An open mouth indicated some strong emotion; happiness, sadness, anger, he could never be really sure which. The Weskers were normally placid and he had never seen enough open mouths to tell what was causing them. But he was surrounded by them now.

'Will you help us, John Garth?' Itin said. 'We have a question.'

'I'll answer any question you ask,' Garth said, with more than a hint of misgiving. 'What is it?'

'Is there a God?'

'What do you mean by "God"?' Garth asked in turn. What should he tell them?

'God is our Father in Heaven, who made us all and protects us. Whom we pray to for aid, and if we are Saved will find a place . . .'

'That's enough,' Garth said. 'There is no God.'

All of them had their mouths open now, even Itin, as they looked at Garth and thought about his answer. The rows of pink teeth would have been frightening if he hadn't known these creatures so well. For one instant he wondered if perhaps they had been already indoctrinated and looked upon him as a heretic, but he brushed the thought away.

'Thank you,' Itin said, and they turned and left.

Though the morning was still cool, Garth noticed that he was sweating and wondered why.

The reaction was not long in coming. Itin returned that same afternoon. 'Will you come to the church?' he asked. 'Many of the things that we study are difficult to learn, but none as difficult as this. We need your help because we must hear you and Father Mark talk together. This is because he says one thing is true and you say another is true and both cannot be true at the same time. We must find out what is true.'

'I'll come, of course,' Garth said, trying to hide the sudden feeling of elation. He had done nothing, but the Weskers had come to him anyway. There could still be grounds for hope that they might yet be free.

It was hot inside the church, and Garth was surprised at the number of Weskers who were there, more than he had seen gathered at any one time before. There were many open mouths. Father Mark sat at a table covered with books. He looked unhappy but didn't say anything when Garth came in. Garth spoke first.

'I hope you realize this is their idea – that they came to me of their own free will and asked me to come here?'

'I know that,' the priest said resignedly. 'At times they can be very difficult. But they are learning and want to believe, and that is what is important.'

'Father Mark, Trader Garth, we need your help,' Itin said. 'You both know many things that we do not know. You must help us come to religion which is not an easy thing to do.' Garth started to say something, then changed his mind. Itin went on. 'We have read the bibles and all the books that Father Mark gave us, and one thing is clear. We have discussed this and we are all agreed. These books are very different from the ones that Trader Garth gave us. In Trader Garth's books there is the universe which we have not seen, and it goes on without God, for he is mentioned nowhere; we have searched very carefully. In Father Mark's books He is everywhere and nothing can go without Him. One of these must be right and the other must be wrong. We do not know how this can be, but after we find out which is right then perhaps we will know. If God does not exist . . .'

'Of course He exists, my children,' Father Mark said in a voiceof heartfelt intensity. 'He is our Father in Heaven who has created us all . . .'

'Who created God?' Itin asked and the murmur ceased and everyone of the Weskers watched Father Mark intensely. He recoiled a bit under the impact of their eyes, then smiled.

'Nothing created God, since He is the Creator. He always was . . .'

'If He always was in existence – why cannot the universe have always been in existence? Without having had a creator?' Itin broke in with a rush of words. The importance of the question was obvious. The priest answered slowly, with infinite patience.

'Would that the answers were that simple, my children. But even the scientists do not agree about the creation of the universe. While they doubt – we who have seen the light *know*. We can see the miracle of creation all about us. And how can there be a creation without a Creator? That is He, our Father, our God in Heaven. I know you have doubts; that is because you have souls and free will. Still, the answer is so simple. Have faith, that is all you need. Just believe.'

'How can we believe without proof?'

'If you cannot see that this world itself is proof of His existence, then I say to you that belief needs no proof – if you have faith!'

A babble of voices arose in the room and more of the Wesker mouths were open now as they tried to force their thoughts through the tangled skein of words and separate the thread of truth.

'Can you tell us, Garth?' Itin asked, and the sound of his voice quieted the hubbub.

'I can tell you to use the scientific method which can examine all things – including itself – and give you answers that can prove the truth or falsity of any statement.'

'That is what we must do,' Itin said, 'we had reached the same conclusion.' He held a thick book before him and a ripple of nods ran across the watchers. 'We have been studying the bible as Father Mark told us to do, and we have found the answer. God will make a miracle for us, thereby proving that He is watching us. And by this sign we will know Him and go to Him.'

'That is the sin of false pride,' Father Mark said. 'God needs no miracles to prove His existence.'

'But *we* need a miracle!' Itin shouted, and though he wasn't human there was need in his voice. 'We have read here of many smaller miracles, loaves, fishes, wine, snakes – many of them, for much smaller reasons. Now all He need do is make a miracle and He will bring us all to Him – the wonder of an entire new world worshipping at His throne, as you have told us, Father Mark. And you have told us how important this is. We have discussed this and find that there is only one miracle that is best for this kind of thing.'

His boredom at the theological wrangling drained from Garth in an instant. He had not been really thinking or he would have realized where all this was leading. He could see the illustration in the bible where Itin held it open, and knew in advance what picture it was. He rose slowly from his chair, as if stretching, and turned to the priest behind him.

'Get ready!' he whispered. 'Get out the back and get to the ship; I'll keep them busy here. I don't think they'll harm me.'

'What do you mean . . . ?' Father Mark asked, blinking in surprise.

'Get out, you fool!' Garth hissed. 'What miracle do you think they mean? What miracle is supposed to have converted the world to Christianity?'

'No!' Father Mark said. 'It cannot be. It just cannot be . . . !'

'GET MOVING!' Garth shouted, dragging the priest from the chair and hurling him towards the rear wall. Father Mark stumbled to a halt, turned back. Garth leaped for him, but it was already too late. The amphibians were small, but there was so many of them. Garth lashed out and his fist struck Itin, hurling him back into the crowd. The others came on as he fought his way towards the priest. He beat at them but it was like struggling against waves. The furry, musky bodies washed over and engulfed him. He fought until they tied him, and he still struggled until they beat on his head until they stopped. Then they pulled him outside where he could only lie in the rain and curse and watch.

Of course the Weskers were marvellous craftsmen, and everything had been constructed down to the last detail, following the illustration in the bible. There was the cross, planted firmly on the top of a small hill, the gleaming metal spikes, the hammer. Father Mark was stripped and draped in a carefully pleated loincloth. They led him out of the church.

At the sight of the cross he almost fainted. After that he held his head high and determined to die as he had lived, with faith.

Yet this was hard. It was unbearable even for Garth, who only watched. It is one thing to talk of crucifixion and look at the gently carved bodies in the dim light of prayer. It is another to see a man naked, ropes cutting into his skin where he hangs from a bar of wood. And to see the needle-tipped spike raised and placed against the soft flesh of his palm, to see the hammer come back with the calm deliberation of an artisan's measured stroke. To hear the thick sound of metal penetrating flesh.

Then to hear the screams.

Few are born to be martyrs; Father Mark was not one of them. With the first blows, the blood ran from his lips where his clenched teeth met. Then his mouth was wide and his head strained back and the guttural horror of his screams sliced through the susurration of the falling rain. It resounded as a silent echo from the masses of watching Weskers, for whatever emotion opened their mouths was now tearing at their bodies with all its force, and row after row of gaping jaws reflected the crucified priest's agony.

Mercifully he fainted as the last nail was driven home. Blood ran from the raw wounds, mixing with the rain to drip faintly pink from his feet as the life ran out of him. At this time, somewhere at this time, sobbing and tearing at his own bonds, numbed from the blows on the head, Garth lost consciousness.

He awoke in his own warehouse and it was dark. Someone was cutting away the woven ropes they had bound him with. The rain still dripped and splashed outside.

'Itin,' he said. It could be no one else.

'Yes,' the alien voice whispered back. 'The others are all talking in the church. Lin died after you struck his head, and Inon is very sick. There are some that say you should be crucified too, and I think that is what will happen. Or perhaps killed by stoning on the head. They have found in the bible where it says . . .'

'I know.' With infinite weariness. 'An eye for an eye. You'll find lots of things like that once you start looking. It's a wonderful book.' His head ached terribly.

'You must go, you can get to your ship without anyone seeing you. There has been enough killing.' Itin as well spoke with a new-found weariness.

Garth experimented, pulling himself to his feet. He pressed his head to the rough wood of the wall until the nausea stopped. 'He's dead.' He said it as a statement, not a question.

'Yes, some time ago. Or I could not have come away to see you.'

'And buried of course, or they wouldn't be thinking about starting on me next.'

'And buried!' There was almost a ring of emotion in the alien's voice, an echo of the dead priest's. 'He is buried and he will rise on High. It is written and that is the way it will happen. Father Mark will be so happy that it has happened like this.' The voice ended in a sound like a human sob.

Garth painfully worked his way towards the door, leaning against the wall so he wouldn't fall.

'We did the right thing, didn't we?' Itin asked. There was no answer. 'He will rise up, Garth, won't he rise?'

Garth was at the door and enough light came from the brightly lit church to show his torn and bloody hands clutching at the frame. Itin's face swam into sight close to his, and Garth felt the delicate, many fingered hands with the sharp nails catch at his clothes.

'He will rise, won't he, Garth?'

'No,' Garth said, 'he is going to stay buried right where you put him. Nothing is going to happen because he is dead and he is going to stay dead.'

The rain runnelled through Itin's fur and his mouth was opened so wide that he seemed to be screaming into the night. Only with effort could he talk, squeezing out the alien thoughts in an alien language.

'Then we will not be saved? We will not become pure?'

'You were pure,' Garth said, in a voice somewhere between a sob and a laugh. 'That's the horrible ugly dirty part of it. You were pure. Now you are . . .'

'Murderers,' Itin said, and the water ran down from his lowered head and streamed away into the darkness.

Track 12

J. G. BALLARD

'Guess again,' Sheringham said.

Maxted clipped on the headphones, carefully settled them over his ears. He concentrated as the disc began to spin, trying to catch some echo of identity.

The sound was a rapid metallic rustling, like iron filings splashing through a funnel. It ran for ten seconds, repeated itself a dozen times, then ended abruptly in a string of blips.

'Well?' Sheringham asked. 'What is it?'

Maxted pulled off his headphones, rubbed one of his ears. He had been listening to the records for hours and his ears felt bruised and numb.

'Could be anything. An ice-cube melting?'

Sheringham shook his head, his little beard wagging.

Maxted shrugged. 'A couple of galaxies colliding?'

'No. Sound waves don't travel through space. I'll give you a clue. It's one of those *proverbial* sounds.' He seemed to be enjoying the catechism.

Maxted lit a cigarette, threw the match on to the laboratory bench. The head melted a tiny pool of wax, froze, and left a shallow black scar. He watched it pleasurably, conscious of Sheringham fidgeting beside him.

He pumped his brains for an obscene simile. 'What about a fly –'

'Time's up,' Sheringham cut in. '*A pin dropping*.' He took the three-inch disc off the player, and angled it into its sleeve.

'In actual fall, that is, not impact. We used a fifty-foot shaft and eight microphones. I thought you'd get that one.'

He reached for the last record, a twelve-inch LP, but Maxted stood up before he got it to the turntable. Through the french windows he could see the patio, a table, glasses and decanter gleaming in the darkness. Sheringham and his infantile games suddenly irritated him; he felt impatient with himself for tolerating the man so long.

'Let's get some air,' he said brusquely, shouldering past one of the amplifier rigs: 'My ears feel like gongs.'

'By all means,' Sheringham agreed promptly. He placed the record carefully on the turntable and switched off the player. 'I want to save this one until later, anyway.'

They went out into the warm evening air. Sheringham turned on the japanese lanterns and they stretched back in the wicker chairs under the open sky.

'I hope you weren't too bored,' Sheringham said as he handled the decanter. 'Microsonics is a fascinating hobby, but I'm afraid I may have let it become an obsession.'

Maxted grunted noncommittally. 'Some of the records are interesting,' he admitted. 'They have a sort of crazy novelty value, like blown-up photographs of moths' faces and razor blades. Despite what you claim, though, I can't believe microsonics will ever become a scientific tool. It's just an elaborate laboratory toy.'

Sheringham shook his head. 'You're completely wrong, of course. Remember the cell division series I played first of all? Amplified 100,000 times animal cell division sounds like a lot of girders and steel sheets being ripped apart – how did you put it? – a car smash in slow motion. On the other hand, plant cell division is an electronic poem, all soft chords and bubbling tones. Now there you have a perfect illustration of how microsonics can reveal the distinction between the animal and plant kingdoms.'

'Seems a damned roundabout way of doing it,' Maxted commented, helping himself to soda. 'You might as well calculate the speed of your car from the apparent motion of the stars. Possible, but it's easier to look at the speedometer.'

Sheringham nodded, watching Maxted closely across the table. His interest in the conversation appeared to have exhausted itself, and the two men sat silently with their glasses. Strangely, the hostility between them, of so many years' standing, now became less veiled, the contrast of personality, manner and physique more pronounced. Maxted, a tall fleshy man with a coarse handsome face, lounged back almost horizontally in his chair, thinking about Susan Sheringham. She was at the Turnbulls' party, and but for the fact that it was no longer discreet of him to be seen at the Turnbulls' – for the all-too-familiar reason – he would have passed the evening with her, rather than with her grotesque little husband.

He surveyed Sheringham with as much detachment as he could muster, wondering whether this prim unattractive man, with his pedantry and in-bred academic humour, had any redeeming qualities whatever. None, certainly, at a casual glance, though it required some courage and pride to have invited him round that evening. His motives, however, would be typically eccentric.

The pretext, Maxted reflected, had been slight enough – Sheringham, professor of biochemistry at the university, maintained a lavish home laboratory; Maxted, run-down athlete with a bad degree, acted as torpedo-man for a company manufacturing electron microscopes; a visit, Sheringham had suggested over the phone, might be to the profit of both.

Of course, nothing of this had in fact been mentioned. But nor, as yet, had he referred to Susan, the real subject of the evening's charade. Maxted speculated upon the possible routes Sheringham might take towards the inevitable confrontation scene; not for him the nervous circular pacing, the well-thumbed photostat, or the thug at the shoulder. There was a vicious adolescent streak running through Sheringham –

Maxted broke out of his reverie abruptly. The air in the patio had become suddenly cooler, almost as if a powerful refrigerating unit had been switched on. A rash of gooseflesh raced up his thighs and down the back of his neck, and he reached forward and finished what was left of his whisky.

'Cold out here,' he commented.

Sheringham glanced at his watch. 'Is it?' he said. There was a hint of indecision in his voice; for a moment he seemed to be waiting for a signal. Then he pulled himself together and, with an odd half-smile, said: 'Time for the last record.'

'What do you mean?' Maxted asked.

'Don't move,' Sheringham said. He stood up. 'I'll put it on.' He pointed to a loudspeaker screwed to the wall above Maxted's head, grinned, and ducked out.

Shivering uncomfortably, Maxted peered up into the silent evening sky, hoping that the vertical current of cold air that had sliced down into the patio would soon dissipate itself.

A low noise crackled from the speaker, multiplied by a circle of other speakers which he noticed for the first time had been slung among the trellis-work around the patio.

Shaking his head sadly at Sheringham's antics, he decided to help himself to more whisky. As he stretched across the table he swayed and rolled back uncontrollably into his chair. His stomach seemed to be full of mercury, ice-cold, and enormously heavy. He pushed himself forward again, trying to reach the glass, and knocked it across the table. His brain began to fade, and he leaned his elbows helplessly on the glass edge of the table and felt his head fall on to his wrists.

When he looked up again Sheringham was standing in front of him, smiling sympathetically.

'Not too good, eh?' he said.

Breathing with difficulty, Maxted managed to lean back. He tried to speak to Sheringham, but he could no longer remember any words. His heart switchbacked, and he grimaced at the pain.

'Don't worry,' Sheringham assured him. 'The fibrillation is only a side effect. Disconcerting, perhaps, but it will soon pass.'

He strolled leisurely around the patio, scrutinizing Maxted from several angles. Evidently satisfied, he sat down on the table. He picked up the siphon and swirled the contents about. 'Chromium cyanate. Inhibits the coenzyme system controlling the body's fluid balances, floods hydroxyl ions into the bloodstream. In brief, you drown. Really drown, that is, not merely suffocate as you would if you were immersed in an external bath. However, I mustn't distract you.'

He inclined his head at the speakers. Being fed into the patio was a curiously muffled spongy noise, like elastic waves lapping in a latex sea. The rhythms were huge and ungainly, overlaid by the deep leaden wheezing of a gigantic bellows. Barely audible at first, the sounds rose until they filled the patio and shut out the few traffic noises along the highway.

'Fantastic, isn't it?' Sheringham said. Twirling the siphon by its neck he stepped over Maxted's legs and adjusted the tone control under one of the speaker boxes. He looked blithe and spruce, almost ten years younger. 'These are 30-second repeats, 400 microsones, amplification one thousand. I admit I've edited the track a little, but it's still remarkable how repulsive a beautiful sound can become. You'll never guess what this was.'

Maxted stirred sluggishly. The lake of mercury in his stomach was as cold and bottomless as an oceanic trench, and his arms and legs had become enormous, like the bloated appendages of a drowned giant. He could just see Sheringham bobbing about in front of him, and hear the slow beating of the sea in the distance. Nearer now, it pounded with a dull insistent rhythm, the great waves ballooning and bursting like bubbles in a lava sea.

'I'll tell you, Maxted, it took me a year to get that recording,' Sheringham was saying. He straddled Maxted, gesturing with the siphon. 'A year. Do you know how ugly a year can be?' For a moment he paused, then tore himself from the memory. 'Last Saturday, just after midnight, you and Susan were lying back in this same chair. You know, Maxted, there are audio-probes everywhere here. Slim as pencils, with a six-inch focus. I had four in that headrest alone.' He added, as a footnote: 'The wind is your own breathing, fairly heavy at the time, if I remember; your interlocked pulses produced the thunder effect.'

Maxted drifted in a wash of sound.

Some while later Sheringham's face filled his eyes, beard wagging, mouth working wildly.

'Maxted! You've only two more guesses, so for God's sake concentrate,' he shouted irritably, his voice almost lost among the thunder rolling from the sea. 'Come on, man, what is it? Maxted!' he bellowed. He leapt for the nearest loudspeaker and drove up the volume. The sound boomed out of the patio, reverberating into the night.

Maxted had almost gone now, his fading identity a small featureless island nearly eroded by the waves beating across it.

Sheringham knelt down and shouted into his ear.

'Maxted, can you hear the sea? Do you know where you're drowning?'

A succession of gigantic flaccid waves, each more lumbering and enveloping than the last, rode down upon them.

'In a kiss!' Sheringham screamed. 'A kiss!'

The island slipped and slid away into the molten shelf of the sea.

Sexual Dimorphism

KIM STANLEY ROBINSON

The potential for hallucination in paleogenomics was high. There was not only the omnipresent role of instrumentation in the envisioning of the ultramicroscopic fossil material, but also the metamorphosis over time of the material itself, both the DNA and its matrices, so that the data were invariably incomplete, and often shattered. Thus the possibility of psychological projection of patterns onto the rorschacherie of what in the end might be purely mineral processes had to be admitted.

Dr Andrew Smith was as aware of these possibilities as anyone. Indeed, it constituted one of the central problems of his field – convincingly to sort the traces of DNA in the fossil record, distinguishing them from an array of possible pseudofossils. Pseudofossils littered the history of the discipline, from the earliest false nautiloids to the famous Martian pseudo-nanobacteria. Nothing progressed in paleogenomics unless you could show that you really were talking about what you said you were talking about. So Dr Smith did not get too excited, at first, about what he was finding in the junk DNA of an early dolphin fossil.

In any case there were quite a few distractions to his work at that time. He was living on the south shore of the Amazonian Sea, that deep southerly bay of the world-ringing ocean, east of Elysium, near the equator. In the summers, even the cool summers they had been having lately, the extensive inshore shallows of the sea grew as warm as blood, and dolphins – adapted from Terran river dolphins like the baiji from China, or the boto from the Amazon, or the susu from the Ganges, or the bhulan from the Indus – sported just off the beach. Morning sunlight lanced through the waves and picked out their flashing silhouettes, sometimes groups of eight or ten of them, all playing in the same wave.

The marine laboratory he worked at, located on the sea-front of the harbor town Eumenides Point, was associated with the Acheron labs, farther up the coast to the west. The work at Eumenides had mostly to do with the shifting ecologies of a sea that was getting saltier. Dr Smith's current project dealing with this issue involved investigating the various adaptations of extinct cetaceans who had lived when the Earth's sea had exhibited different levels of salt. He had in his lab some fossil material, sent to the lab from Earth for study, as well as the voluminous literature on the subject, including the full genomes of all the living descendants of these creatures. The transfer of fossils from Earth introduced the matter of cosmic-ray contamination to all the other problems involved in the study of ancient DNA, but most people dismissed these effects as minor and inconsequential, which was why fossils were shipped across at all. And of course with the recent deployment of fusion-powered rapid vehicles, the amount of exposure to cosmic rays had been markedly reduced. Smith was therefore able to do research on mammal salt tolerance both ancient and modern, thus helping to illuminate the current situation on Mars, also joining the debates ongoing concerning the paleohalocycles of the two planets, now one of the hot research areas in comparative planetology and bioengineering.

Nevertheless, it was a field of research so arcane that if you were not involved in it, you tended not to believe in it. It was an offshoot, a mix of two difficult fields, its ultimate usefulness a long shot, especially compared with most of the inquiries being conducted at the Eumenides Point Labs. Smith found himself fighting a feeling of marginalization in the various lab meetings and informal gatherings, in coffee lounges, cocktail parties, beach luncheons, boating excursions. At all of these he was the odd man out, with only his colleague Frank Drumm, who worked on reproduction in the dolphins currently living offshore, expressing any great interest in his work and its applications. Worse yet, his work appeared to be becoming less and less important to his advisor and employer, Vlad Taneev, who as one of the First Hundred, and the co-founder of the Acheron labs, was ostensibly the most powerful scientific mentor one could have on Mars; but who in practice turned out to be nearly impossible of access, and rumored to be in failing health, so that it was like having no boss at all, and therefore no access to the lab's technical staff and so forth. A bitter disappointment.

And then of course there was Selena, his – his partner, roommate, girlfriend, significant other, lover – there were many words for this relationship, though none was quite right. The woman with whom he lived, with whom he had gone through graduate school and two post-docs, with whom he had moved to Eumenides Point, taking a small apartment near the beach, near the terminus of the coastal tram, where when one looked back east the point itself just heaved over the horizon, like a dorsal fin seen far out to sea. Selena was making great progress in her own field, genetically engineering salt grasses; a subject of great importance here, where they were trying to stabilize a thousand-kilometer coastline of low dunes and quicksand swamps. Scientific and bioengineering progress; important achievements, relevant to the situation; all things were coming to her professionally, including of course offers to team up in any number of exciting public/co-op collaborations.

And all things were coming to her privately as well. Smith had always thought her beautiful, and now he saw that with her success, other men were coming to the same realization. It took only a little attention to see it; an ability to look past shabby lab coats and a generally unkempt style to the sleekly curving body and the intense, almost ferocious intelligence. No – his Selena looked much like all the rest of the lab rats when in the lab, but in the summers when the group went down in the evening to the warm tawny beach to swim, she walked out the long expanse of the shallows like a goddess in a bathing suit, like Venus returning to the sea. Everyone in these parties pretended not to notice, but you couldn't help it.

All very well; except that she was losing interest in him. This was a process that Smith feared was irreversible; or, to be more precise, that if it had gotten to the point where he could notice it, it was too late to stop it. So now he watched her, furtive and helpless, as they went through their domestic routines; there was a goddess in his bathroom, showering, drying off, dressing, each moment like a dance.

But she didn't chat anymore. She was absorbed in her thoughts, and tended to keep her back to him. No – it was all going away.

*

They had met in an adult swim club in Mangala, while they were both grad students at the university there. Now, as if to re-invoke that time, Smith took up Frank's suggestion and joined him at an equivalent club in Eumenides Point, and began to swim regularly again. He went from the tram or the lab down to the big fifty-meter pool, set on a terrace overlooking the ocean, and swam so hard in the mornings that the whole rest of the day he buzzed along in a flow of beta endorphins, scarcely aware of his work problems or the situation at home. After work he took the tram home feeling his appetite kick in, and banged around the kitchen throwing together a meal and eating much of it as he cooked it, irritated (if she was there at all) with Selena's poor cooking and her cheery talk about her work, irritated also probably just from hunger, and dread at the situation hanging over them; at this pretense that they were still in a normal life. But if he snapped at her during this fragile hour she would go silent the whole rest of the evening; it happened fairly often; so he tried to contain his temper and make the meal and quickly eat his part of it, to get his blood sugar level back up.

Either way she fell asleep abruptly around nine, and he was left to read into the timeslip, or even slip out and take a walk on the night beach a few hundred yards away from their apartment. One night, walking west, he saw Pseudophobos pop up into the sky like a distress flare down the coast, and when he came back into the apartment she was awake and talking happily on the phone; she was startled to see him, and cut the call short, thinking about what to say, and then said, 'That was Mark, we've gotten tamarisk three fifty-nine to take repetitions of the third salt flusher gene!'

'That's good,' he said, moving into the dark kitchen so she wouldn't see his face.

This annoyed her. 'You really don't care how my work goes, do you?'

'Of course I do. That's good, I said.'

She dismissed that with a noise.

Then one day he got home and Mark was there with her, in the living room, and at a single glance he could see they had been laughing about something; had been sitting closer together than when he started opening the door. He ignored that and was as pleasant as he could be.

The next day as he swam at the morning work-out, he watched the women swimming with him in his lane. All three of them had swum all their lives, their freestyle stroke perfected beyond the perfection of any dance move ever made on land, the millions of repetitions making their movement as unconscious as that of any fish in the sea. Under the surface he saw their bodies flowing forward, revealing their sleek lines – classic swimmer lines, like Selena's – rangy shoulders tucking up against their ears one after the next, ribcages smoothed over by powerful lats, breasts flatly merged into big pecs or else bobbing left then right, as the case might be; bellies meeting high hipbones accentuated by the high cut of their swimsuits, backs curving up to bottoms rounded and compact, curving to powerful thighs then long calves, and feet outstretched like ballerinas. Dance was a weak analogy for such beautiful movement. And it all went on for stroke after stroke, lap after lap, until he was mesmerized beyond further thought or observation; it was just one aspect of a sensually saturated environment.

Their current lane leader was pregnant, yet swimming stronger than any of the rest of them, not even huffing and puffing during their rest intervals, when Smith often had to suck air – instead she laughed and shook her head, exclaiming 'Every time I do a flip turn he keeps kicking me!' She was seven months along, round in the middle like a little whale, but still she fired down the pool at a rate none of the other three in the lane could match. The strongest swimmers in the club were simply amazing. Soon after getting into the sport, Smith had worked hard to swim a hundred-meter freestyle in less than a minute, a goal appropriate to him, and finally he had done it once at a meet and been pleased; then later he heard about the local college women's team's workout, which consisted of a hundred hundred-meter freestyle swims *all on a minute interval.* He understood then that although all humans looked roughly the same, some were stupendously stronger than others. Their pregnant leader was in the lower echelon of these strong swimmers, and regarded the swim she was making today as a light stretching-out, though it was beyond anything her lane mates could do with their best effort. You couldn't help watching her when passing by in the other direction, because despite her speed she was supremely smooth and effortless, she took fewer strokes per lap than the rest of them, and yet still made substantially better time. It was like magic. And that sweet blue curve of the new child carried inside.

Back at home things continued to degenerate. Selena often worked late, and talked to him less than ever.

'I love you,' he said. 'Selena, I love you.'

'I know.'

He tried to throw himself into his work. They were at the same lab, they could go home late together. Talk like they used to about their work, which though not the same, was still genomics in both cases; how much closer could two sciences be? Surely it would help to bring them back together.

But genomics was a very big field. It was possible to occupy different parts of it, no doubt about that. They were proving it. Smith persevered, however, using a new and more powerful electron microscope, and he began to make some headway in unraveling the patterns in his fossilized DNA.

It looked like what had been preserved in the samples he had been given was almost entirely what used to be called the junk DNA of the creature. In times past this would have been bad luck, but the Kohl labs in Acheron had recently been making great strides in unraveling the various purposes of junk DNA, which proved not to be useless after all, as might have been guessed, development being as complex as it was. Their breakthrough consisted in characterizing very short and scrambled repetitive sequences within junk DNA that could be shown to code instructions for higher hierarchical operations than they were used to seeing at the gene level – cell differentiation, information order sequencing, apoptosis, and the like.

Using this new understanding to unravel any clues in partially degraded fossil junk DNA would be hard, of course. But the nucleotide sequences were there in his EM images – or, to be more precise, the characteristic mineral replacements for the adenine=thymine and cytosine=guanine couplets, replacements well-established in the literature, were there to be clearly identified. Nanofossils, in effect; but legible to those who could read them. And once read, it was then possible to brew identical sequences of living nucleotides, matching the originals of the fossil creature. In theory one could re-create the creature itself, though in practice nothing like the entire genome was ever there, making it impossible. Not that there weren't people trying anyway with simpler fossil organisms, either going for the whole thing or using hybrid DNA techniques to graft expressions they could decipher onto living templates, mostly descendants of the earlier creature.

With this particular ancient dolphin, almost certainly a fresh-water dolphin (though most of these were fairly salt tolerant, living in river-mouths as they did), complete resuscitation would be impossible. It wasn't what Smith was trying to do anyway. What would be interesting would be to find fragments that did not seem to have a match in the living descendants' genome, then hopefully synthesize living in vitro fragments, clip them into contemporary strands, and see how these experimental animals did in hybridization tests and in various environments. Look for differences in function.

He was also doing mitochondrial tests when he could, which if successful would permit tighter dating for the species' divergence from precursor species. He might be able to give it a specific slot on the marine mammal family tree, which during the early Pliocene was very complicated.

Both avenues of investigation were labor-intensive, time-consuming, almost thoughtless work – perfect, in other words. He worked for hours and hours every day, for weeks, then months. Sometimes he managed to go home on the tram with Selena; more often he didn't. She was writing up her latest results with her collaborators, mostly with Mark. Her hours were irregular. When he was working he didn't have to think about this; so he worked all the time. It was not a solution, not even a very good strategy – it even seemed to be making things worse – and he had to attempt it against an ever-growing sense of despair and loss; but he did it nevertheless.

'What do you think of this Acheron work?' he asked Frank one day at work, pointing to the latest print-out from the Kohl lab, lying heavily annotated on his desk.

'It's very interesting! It makes it look like we're finally getting past the genes to the whole instruction manual.'

'If there is such a thing.'

'Has to be, right? Though I'm not sure the Kohl lab's values for the rate adaptive mutants will be fixed are high enough. Ohta and Kimura suggested 10 percent as the upper limit, and that fits with what I've seen.'

Smith nodded, pleased. 'They're probably just being conservative.'

'No doubt, but you have to go with the data.'

'So – in that context – you think it makes sense for me to pursue this fossil junk DNA?'

'Well, sure. What do you mean? It's sure to tell us interesting things.'

'It's incredibly slow.'

'Why don't you read off a long sequence, brew it up and venter it, and see what you get?'

Smith shrugged. Whole-genome shotgun sequencing struck him as slipshod, but it was certainly faster. Reading small bits of single-stranded DNA, called expressed sequence tags, had quickly identified most of the genes on the human genome; but it had missed some, and it ignored even the regulatory DNA sequences controlling the protein-coding portion of the genes, not to mention the so-called junk DNA itself, filling long stretches between the more clearly meaningful sequences.

Smith expressed these doubts to Frank, who nodded, but said, 'It isn't the same now that the mapping is so complete. You've got so many reference points you can't get confused where your bits are on the big sequence. Just plug what you've got into the Lander-Waterman, then do the finishing with the Kohl variations, and even if there are massive repetitions, you'll still be okay. And with the bits you've got, well they're almost like ests anyway, they're so degraded. So you might as well give it a try.'

Smith nodded.

That night he and Selena trammed home together. 'What do you think of the possibility of shotgun sequencing in vitro copies of what I've got?' he asked her shyly.

'Sloppy,' she said. 'Double jeopardy.'

*

A new schedule evolved. He worked, swam, took the tram home. Usually Selena wasn't there. Often their answering machine held messages for her from Mark, talking about their work. Or messages from her to Smith, telling him that she would be home late. As was happening so often, he sometimes went out for dinner with Frank and other lane mates, after the evening work-outs. One time at a beach restaurant they ordered several pitchers of beer, and then went out for a walk on the beach, and ended up running out into the shallows of the bay and swimming around in the warm dark water, so different from their pool, splashing each other and laughing hard. It was a good time.

But when he got home that night, there was another message on the answering machine from Selena, saying that she and Mark were working on their paper after getting a bite to eat, and that she would be home extra late.

She wasn't kidding; at two o'clock in the morning she was still out. In the long minutes following the timeslip Smith realized that no one stayed out this late working on a paper without calling home. This was therefore a message of a different kind.

Pain and anger swept through him, first one then the other. The indirection of it struck him as cowardly. He deserved at least a revelation – a confession – a scene. As the long minutes passed he got angrier and angrier; then frightened for a moment, that she might have been hurt or something. But she hadn't. She was out there somewhere fooling around. Suddenly he was furious.

He pulled cardboard boxes out of their closet and yanked open her drawers, and threw all her clothes in heaps in the boxes, crushing them in so they would all fit. But they gave off their characteristic scent of laundry soap and her, and smelling it he groaned and sat down on the bed, knees weak. If he carried through with this he would never again see her putting on and taking off these clothes, and just as an animal he groaned at the thought.

But men are not animals. He finished throwing her things into boxes, took them outside the front door and dropped them there.

She came back at three. He heard her kick into the boxes and make some muffled exclamation.

He hurled open the door and stepped out.

'What's this?' She had been startled out of whatever scenario she had planned, and now was getting angry. Her, angry! It made him furious all over again.

'You know what it is.'

'What!'

'You and Mark.'

She eyed him.

'Now you notice,' she said at last. 'A year after it started. And this is your first response.' Gesturing down at the boxes.

He hit her in the face.

Immediately he crouched at her side and helped her sit up, saying 'Oh God Selena I'm sorry, I'm sorry, I didn't mean to,' he had only thought to slap her for her contempt, contempt that he had not noticed her betrayal earlier, 'I can't believe I – '

'Get *away*,' striking him off with wild blows, crying and shouting, 'get away, get away,' frightened, 'you bastard, you miserable bastard, what do you, don't you *dare* hit me!' in a near shriek, though she kept her voice down too, aware still of the apartment complex around them. Hands held to her face.

'I'm sorry Selena. I'm very very sorry, I was angry at what you said but I know that isn't, that doesn't . . . I'm sorry.' Now he was as angry at himself as he had been at her – what could he have been thinking, why had he given her the moral high ground like this, it was she who had broken their bond, it was she who should be in the wrong! She who was now sobbing – turning away – suddenly walking off into the night. Lights went on in a couple of windows nearby. Smith stood staring down at the boxes of her lovely clothes, his right knuckles throbbing.

That life was over. He lived on alone in the apartment by the beach, and kept going in to work, but he was shunned there by the others, who all knew what had happened. Selena did not come in to work again until the bruises were gone, and after that she did not press charges, or speak to him about that night, but she did move in with Mark, and avoided him at work when she could. As who wouldn't.

Occasionally she dropped by his nook to ask in a neutral voice about some logistical aspect of their break-up. He could not meet her eye. Nor could he meet the eye of anyone else at work, not properly. It was strange how one could have a conversation with people and appear to be meeting their gaze during it, when all the time they were not really quite looking at you and you were not really quite looking at them. Primate subtleties, honed over millions of years on the savanna.

He lost appetite, lost energy. In the morning he would wake up and wonder why he should get out of bed. Then looking at the blank walls of the bedroom, where Selena's prints had hung, he would sometimes get so angry at her that his pulse hammered uncomfortably in his neck and forehead. This got him out of bed, but then there was nowhere to go, except work. And there everyone knew he was a wife beater, a domestic abuser, an asshole. Martian society did not tolerate such people.

Shame or anger; anger or shame. Grief or humiliation. Resentment or regret. Lost love. Omnidirectional rage.

Mostly he didn't swim anymore. The sight of the swimmer women was too painful now, though they were as friendly as always; they knew nothing of the lab except him and Frank, and Frank had not said anything to them about what had happened. It made no difference. He was cut off from them. He knew he ought to swim more, and he swam less. Whenever he resolved to turn things around he would swim two or three days in a row, then let it fall away again.

Once at the end of an early evening workout he had forced himself to attend – and now he felt better, as usual – while they were standing in the lane steaming, his three most constant lane mates made quick plans to go to a nearby trattoria after showering. One looked at him. 'Pizza at Rico's?'

He shook his head. 'Hamburger at home,' he said sadly.

They laughed at this. 'Ah, come on. It'll keep another night.'

'Come on, Andy,' Frank said from the next lane. 'I'll go too, if that's okay.'

'Sure,' the women said. Frank often swam in their lane too.

'Well . . .' Smith roused himself. 'Okay.'

He sat with them and listened to their chatter around the restaurant table. They still seemed to be slightly steaming, their hair wet and wisping away from their foreheads. The three women were young. It was interesting; away from the pool they looked ordinary and undistinguished: skinny, mousy, plump, maladroit, whatever. With their clothes on you could not guess at their fantastically powerful shoulders and lats, their compact smooth musculatures. Like seals dressed up in clown suits, waddling around a stage.

'Are you okay?' one asked him when he had been silent too long.

'Oh yeah, yeah.' He hesitated, glanced at Frank. 'Broke up with my girlfriend.'

'Ah ha! I *knew* it was something!' Hand to his arm (they all bumped into each other all the time in the pool): 'You haven't been your usual self lately.'

'No.' He smiled ruefully. 'It's been hard.'

He could never tell them about what had happened. And Frank wouldn't either. But without that none of the rest of his story made any sense. So he couldn't talk about any of it.

They sensed this and shifted in their seats, preparatory to changing the topic. 'Oh well,' Frank said, helping them. 'Lots more fish in the sea.'

'In the pool,' one of the women joked, elbowing him.

He nodded, tried to smile.

They looked at each other. One asked the waiter for the check, and another said to Smith and Frank, 'Come with us over to my place, we're going to get in the hot tub and soak our aches away.'

She rented a room in a little house with an enclosed courtyard, and all the rest of the residents were away. They followed her through the dark house into the courtyard, and took the cover off the hot tub and turned it on, then took their clothes off and got in the steaming water. Smith joined them, feeling shy. People on the beaches of Mars sunbathed without clothes all the time, it was no big deal really. Frank seemed not to notice, he was perfectly relaxed. But they didn't swim at the pool like this.

They all sighed at the water's heat. The woman from the house went inside and brought out some beer and cups. Light from the kitchen fell on her as she put down the dumpie and passed out the cups. Smith already knew her body perfectly well from their many hours together in the pool; nevertheless he was shocked seeing the whole of her. Frank ignored the sight, filling the cups from the dumpie.

They drank beer, talked small talk. Two were vets; their lane leader, the one who had been pregnant, was a bit older, a chemist in a pharmaceutical lab near the pool. Her baby was being watched by her co-op that night. They all looked up to her, Smith saw, even here. These days she brought the baby to the pool and swam just as powerfully as ever, parking the baby-carrier just beyond the splash line. Smith's muscles melted in the hot water. He sipped his beer listening to them.

One of the women looked down at her breasts in the water and laughed. 'They float like pull buoys.'

Smith had already noticed this.

'No wonder women swim better than men.'

'As long as they aren't so big they interfere with the hydrodynamics.'

Their leader looked down through her fogged glasses, pink-faced, hair tied up, misted, demure. 'I wonder if mine float less because I'm nursing.'

'But all that milk.'

'Yes, but the water in the milk is neutral density, it's the fat that floats. It could be that empty breasts float even more than full ones.'

'Whichever has more fat, yuck.'

'I could run an experiment, nurse him from just one side and then get in and see – ' but they were laughing too hard for her to complete this scenario. 'It would work! Why are you laughing!'

They only laughed more. Frank was cracking up, looking blissed, blessed. These women friends trusted them. But Smith still felt set apart. He looked at their lane leader: a pink bespectacled goddess, serenely vague and unaware; the scientist as heroine; the first full human being.

But later when he tried to explain this feeling to Frank, or even just to describe it, Frank shook his head. 'It's a bad mistake to worship women,' he warned. 'A category error. Women and men are so much the same it isn't worth discussing the difference. The genes are identical almost entirely, you know that. A couple of hormonal expressions and that's it. So they're just like you and me.'

'More than a couple.'

'Not much more. We all start out female, right? So you're better off thinking that nothing major ever really changes that. Penis just an oversized clitoris. Men are women. Women are men. Two parts of a reproductive system, completely equivalent.'

Smith stared at him. 'You're kidding.'

'What do you mean?'

'Well – I've never seen a man swell up and give birth to a new human being, let me put it that way.'

'So what? It happens, it's a specialized function. You never see women ejaculating either. But we all go back to being the same afterward. Details of reproduction only matter a tiny fraction of the time. No, we're all the same. We're all in it together. There are no differences.'

Smith shook his head. It would be comforting to think so. But the data did not support the hypothesis. Ninety-five percent of all the murders in history had been committed by men. This was a difference.

He said as much, but Frank was not impressed. The murder ratio was becoming more nearly equal on Mars, he replied, and much less frequent for everybody, thus demonstrating very nicely that the matter was culturally conditioned, an artifact of Terran patriarchy no longer relevant on Mars. Nurture rather than nature. Although it was a false dichotomy. Nature could prove anything you wanted, Frank insisted. Female hyenas were vicious killers, male bonobos and muriquis were gentle cooperators. It meant nothing, Frank said. It told them nothing.

But Frank had not hit a woman in the face without ever planning to.

Patterns in the fossil *Inia* data sets became clearer and clearer. Stochastic resonance programs highlighted what had been preserved.

'Look here,' Smith said to Frank one afternoon when Frank leaned in to say good-bye for the day. He pointed at his computer screen. 'Here's a sequence from my boto, part of the GX three oh four, near the juncture, see?'

'You've got a female then?'

'I don't know. I think this here means I do. But look, see how it matches with this part of the human genome. It's in Hillis 8050 . . .'

Frank came into his nook and stared at the screen. 'Comparing junk to junk . . . I don't know . . .'

'But it's a match for more than a hundred units in a row, see? Leading right into the gene for progesterone initiation.'

Frank squinted at the screen. 'Um, well.' He glanced quickly at Smith.

Smith said, 'I'm wondering if there's some really longterm persistence in junk DNA, all the way back to earlier mammals, precursors to both these.'

'But dolphins are not our ancestors,' Frank said.

'There's a common ancestor back there somewhere.'

'Is there?' Frank straightened up. 'Well, whatever. I'm not so sure about the pattern congruence itself. It's sort of similar, but, you know.'

'What do you mean, don't you see that? Look right there!'

Frank glanced down at him, startled, then non-committal. Seeing this Smith became inexplicably frightened.

'Sort of,' Frank said. 'Sort of. You should run hybridization tests, maybe, see how good the fit really is. Or check with Acheron about repeats in nongene DNA.'

'But the congruence is perfect! It goes on for hundreds of pairs, how could that be a coincidence?'

Frank looked even more non-committal than before. He glanced out the door of the nook. Finally he said, 'I don't see it that congruent. Sorry, I just don't see it. Look, Andy. You've been working awfully hard for a long time. And you've been depressed too, right? Since Selena left?'

Smith nodded, feeling his stomach tighten. He had admitted as much a few months before. Frank was one of the very few people these days who would look him in the eye.

'Well, you know. Depression has chemical impacts in the brain, you know that. Sometimes it means you begin seeing patterns that others can't see as well. It doesn't mean they aren't there, no doubt they are there. But whether they mean anything significant, whether they're more than just a kind of analogy, or similarity –' He looked down at Smith and stopped. 'Look, it's not my field. You should show this to Amos, or go up to Acheron and talk to the old man.'

'Uh huh. Thanks, Frank.'

'Oh no, no, no need. Sorry, Andy. I probably shouldn't have said anything. It's just, you know. You've been spending a hell of a lot of time here.'

'Yeah.'

Frank left.

Sometimes he fell asleep at his desk. He got some of his work done in dreams. Sometimes he found he could sleep down on the beach, wrapped in a greatcoat on the fine sand, lulled by the sound of the waves rolling in. At work he stared at the lined dots and letters on the screens, constructing the schematics of the sequences, nucleotide by nucleotide. Most were completely unambiguous. The correlation between the two main schematics was excellent, far beyond the possibility of chance. X chromosomes in humans clearly exhibited non-gene DNA traces of a distant aquatic ancestor, a kind of dolphin. Y chromosomes in humans lacked these passages, and they also matched with chimpanzees more completely than X chromosomes did. Frank had appeared not to believe it, but there it was, right on the screen. But how could it be? What did it mean? Where did any of them get what they were? They had natures from birth. Just under five million years ago, chimps and humans separated out as two different species from a common ancestor, a woodland ape. The *Inis geoffrensis* fossil Smith was working on had been precisely dated to about 5.1 million years old. About half of all orangutan sexual encounters are rape.

One night after quitting work alone in the lab, he took a tram in the wrong direction, downtown, without ever admitting to himself what he was doing, until he was standing outside Mark's apartment complex, under the steep rise of the dorsum ridge. Walking up a staircased alleyway ascending the ridge gave him a view right into Mark's windows. And there was Selena, washing dishes at the kitchen window and looking back over her shoulder to talk with someone. The tendon in her neck stood out in the light. She laughed.

Smith walked home. It took an hour. Many trams passed him.

He couldn't sleep that night. He went down to the beach and lay rolled in his greatcoat. Finally he fell asleep.

He had a dream. A small hairy bipedal primate, chimp-faced, walked like a hunchback down a beach in east Africa, in the late afternoon sun. The warm water of the shallows lay greenish and translucent. Dolphins rode inside the waves. The ape waded out into the shallows. Long powerful arms, evolved for hitting; a quick grab and he had one by the tail, by the dorsal fin. Surely it could escape, but it didn't try. Female; the ape turned her over, mated with her, released her. He left and came back to find the dolphin in the shallows, giving birth to twins, one male one female. The ape's troop swarmed into the shallows, killed and ate them both. Farther offshore the dolphin birthed two more.

The dawn woke Smith. He stood and walked out into the shallows. He saw dolphins inside the transparent indigo waves. He waded out into the surf. The water was only a little colder than the work-out pool. The dawn sun was low. The dolphins were only a little longer than he was, small and lithe. He bodysurfed with them. They were faster than him in the waves, but flowed around him when they had to. One leaped over him and splashed back into the curl of the wave ahead of him. Then one flashed under him, and on an impulse he grabbed at its dorsal fin and caught it, and was suddenly moving faster in the wave, as it rose with both of them inside it – by far the greatest bodysurfing ride of his life. He held on. The dolphin and all the rest of its pod turned and swam out to sea, and still he held on. This is it, he thought. Then he remembered that they were air-breathers too. It was going to be all right.

The Tunnel under the World

FREDERIK POHL

I

On the morning of June the 15th, Guy Burckhardt woke up screaming out of a dream.

It was more real than any dream he had ever had in his life. He could still hear and feel the sharp, ripping-metal explosion, the violent heave that had tossed him furiously out of bed, the searing wave of heat.

He sat up convulsively and stared, not believing what he saw, at the quiet room and the bright sunlight coming in the window.

He croaked, 'Mary?'

His wife was not in the bed next to him. The covers were tumbled and awry, as though she had just left it, and the memory of the dream was so strong that instinctively he found himself searching the floor to see if the dream explosion had thrown her down.

But she wasn't there. Of course she wasn't, he told himself, looking at the familiar vanity and slipper chair, the uncracked window, the unbuckled wall. It had only been a dream.

'Guy?' His wife was calling him querulously from the foot of the stairs. 'Guy, dear, are you all right?'

He called weakly, 'Sure.'

There was a pause. Then Mary said doubtfully, 'Breakfast is ready. Are you sure you're all right? I thought I heard you yelling –'

Burckhardt said more confidently. 'I had a bad dream, honey. Be right down.'

In the shower, punching the lukewarm-and-cologne he favoured, he told himself that it had been a beaut of a dream. Still, bad dreams weren't unusual, especially bad dreams about explosions. In the past thirty years of H-bomb jitters, who had not dreamed of explosions?

Even Mary had dreamed of them, it turned out, for he started to tell her about the dream, but she cut him off. 'You *did*? Her voice was astonished. 'Why, dear, I dreamed the same thing! Well, almost the same thing. I didn't actually *hear* anything. I dreamed that something woke me up, and then there was a sort of quick bang, and then something hit me on the head. And that was all. Was yours like that?'

Burckhardt coughed. 'Well, no,' he said. Mary was not one of these strong-as-a-man, brave-as-a-tiger women. It was not necessary, he thought, to tell her all the little details of the dream that made it seem so real. No need to mention the splintered ribs, and the salt bubble in his throat, and the agonized knowledge that this was death. He said, 'Maybe there really was some kind of explosion downtown. Maybe we heard it and it started us dreaming.'

Mary reached over and patted his hand absently. 'Maybe,' she agreed. 'It's almost half past eight, dear. Shouldn't you hurry? You don't want to be late to the office.'

He gulped his food, kissed her, and rushed out – not so much to be on time as to see if his guess had been right.

But downtown Tylerton looked as it always had. Coming in on the bus, Burckhardt watched critically out of the window, seeking evidence of an explosion. There wasn't any. If anything, Tylerton looked better than it ever had before: it was a beautiful crisp day, the sky was cloudless, the buildings were clean and inviting. They had, he observed, steamblasted the Power & Light Building, the town's only skyscraper – that was the penalty of having Contro Chemicals main plant on the outskirts of town; the fumes from the cascade stills left their mark on stone buildings.

None of the usual crowd was on the bus, so there wasn't anyone Burckhardt could ask about the explosion. And by the time he got out at the corner of Fifth and Lehigh and the bus rolled away with a muted diesel moan, he had pretty well convinced himself that it was all imagination.

He stopped at the cigar stand in the lobby of his office building, but

Ralph wasn't behind the counter. The man who sold him his pack of cigarettes was a stranger.

'Where's Mr Stebbins?' Burckhardt asked.

The man said politely, 'Sick, sir. He'll be in tomorrow. A pack of Marlins today?'

'Chesterfields,' Burckhardt corrected.

'Certainly, sir,' the man said. But what he took from the rack and slid across the counter was an unfamiliar green-and-yellow pack.

'Do try these, sir,' he suggested. 'They contain an anti-cough factor. Even notice how ordinary cigarettes make you choke every once in a while?'

Burckhardt said suspiciously. 'I never heard of this brand.'

'Of course not. They're something new.' Burckhardt hesitated, and the man said persuasively, 'Look, try them out at my risk. If you don't like them, bring back the empty pack and I'll refund your money. Fair enough?'

Burckhardt shrugged. 'How can I lose? But give me a pack of Chesterfields, too, will you?'

He opened the pack and lit one while he waited for the elevator. They weren't bad, he decided, though he was suspicious of cigarettes that had the tobacco chemically treated in any way. But he didn't think much of Ralph's stand-in; it would raise hell with the trade at the cigar stand if the man tried to give every customer the same high-pressure sales talk.

The elevator door opened with a low-pitched sound of music. Burckhardt and two or three others got in and he nodded to them as the door closed. The thread of music switched off and the speaker in the ceiling of the cab began its usual commercials.

No, not the *usual* commercials, Burckhardt realized. He had been exposed to the captive-audience commercials so long that they hardly registered on the outer ear any more, but what was coming from the recorded programme in the basement of the building caught his attention. It wasn't merely that the brands were mostly unfamiliar; it was a difference in pattern.

There were jingles with an insistent, bouncy rhythm, about soft drinks he had never tasted. There was a rapid patter dialogue between what sounded like two ten-year-old boys about a candy bar, followed by an authoritative bass rumble: 'Go right out and get a DELICIOUS Choco-Bite and eat your TANGY Choco-Bite *all up*. That's *Choco-Bite!*' There was a sobbing female whine: 'I *wish* I had a Feckle Freezer! I'd do *anything* for a Feckle Freezer!' Burckhardt reached his floor and left the elevator in the middle of the last one. It left him a little uneasy. The commercials were not for familiar brands; there was no feeling of use and custom to them.

But the office was happily normal – except that Mr Barth wasn't in. Miss Mitkin, yawning at the reception desk, didn't know exactly why. 'His home phoned, that's all. He'll be in tomorrow.'

'Maybe he went to the plant. It's right near his house.'

She looked indifferent. 'Yeah.'

A thought struck Burckhardt. 'But today is June the 15th! It's quarterly tax return day – he has to sign the return!'

Miss Mitkin shrugged to indicate that that was Burckhardt's problem, not hers. She returned to her nails.

Thoroughly exasperated, Burckhardt went to his desk. It wasn't that he couldn't sign the tax returns as well as Barth, he thought resentfully. It simply wasn't his job, that was all; it was a responsibility that Barth, as office manager for Contro Chemicals' downtown office, should have taken.

He thought briefly of calling Barth at his home or trying to reach him at the factory, but he gave up the idea quickly enough. He didn't really care much for the people at the factory and the less contact he had with them, the better. He had been to the factory once, with Barth: it had been a confusing and, in a way, a frightening experience. Barring a handful of executives and engineers, there wasn't a soul in the factory – that is, Burckhardt corrected himself, remembering what Barth had told him, not a *living* soul – just the machines.

According to Barth, each machine was controlled by a sort of computer which reproduced, in its electronic snarl, the actual memory and mind of a human being. It was an unpleasant thought. Barth, laughing, had assured him that there was no Frankenstein business of robbing graveyards and implanting brains in machines. It was only a matter, he said, of transferring a man's habit patterns from brain cells to vacuum-tube cells. It didn't hurt the man and it didn't make the machine into a monster.

But they made Burckhardt uncomfortable all the same.

He put Barth and the factory and all his other little irritations out of his mind and tackled the tax returns. It took him until noon to verify the figures – which Barth could have done out of his memory and his private ledger in ten minutes, Burckhardt resentfully reminded himself.

He sealed them in an envelope and walked out to Miss Mitkin. 'Since Mr Barth isn't here, we'd better go to lunch in shifts,' he said. 'You can go first.'

'Thanks.' Miss Mitkin languidly took her bag out of the desk drawer and began to apply make-up.

Burckhardt offered her the envelope. 'Drop this in the mail for me, will you? Uh – wait a minute. I wonder if I ought to phone Mr Barth to make sure. Did his wife say whether he was able to take phone calls?'

'Didn't say.' Miss Mitkin blotted her lips carefully with a Kleenex. 'Wasn't his wife, anyway. It was his daughter who called and left the message.'

'The kid?' Burckhardt frowned. 'I thought she was away at school.'

'She called, that's all I know.'

Burckhardt went back to his own office and stared distastefully at the unopened mail on his desk. He didn't like nightmares; they spoiled his whole day. He should have stayed in bed, like Barth.

A funny thing happened on his way home. There was a disturbance at the corner where he usually caught his bus – someone was screaming something about a new kind of deep-freeze – so he walked an extra block. He saw the bus coming and started to trot. But behind him, someone was calling his name. He looked over his shoulder; a small harried-looking man was hurrying towards him.

Burckhardt hesitated, and then recognized him. It was a casual acquaintance named Swanson. Burckhardt sourly observed that he had already missed the bus.

He said, 'Hello.'

Swanson's face was desperately eager. 'Burckhardt?' he asked inquiringly, with an odd intensity. And then he just stood there silently, watching Burckhardt's face with a burning eagerness that dwindled to a faint hope and died to a regret. He was searching for something, waiting for something, Burckhardt thought. But whatever it was he wanted, Burckhardt didn't know how to supply it.

Burckhardt coughed and said again, 'Hello, Swanson.'

Swanson didn't even acknowledge the greeting. He merely sighed a very deep sigh.

'Nothing doing,' he mumbled, apparently to himself. He nodded abstractedly to Burckhardt and turned away.

Burckhardt watched the slumped shoulders disappear in the crowd. It was an *odd* sort of day, he thought, and one he didn't much like. Things weren't going right.

Riding home on the next bus, he brooded about it. It wasn't anything terrible or disastrous; it was something out of his experience entirely. You live your life, like any man, and you form a network of impressions and reactions. You *expect* things. When you open your medicine chest, your razor is expected to be on the second shelf; when you lock your front door, you expect to have to give it a slight extra tug to make it latch.

It isn't the things that are right and perfect in your life that make it familiar. It is the things that are just a little bit wrong – the sticking latch, the light switch at the head of the stairs that needs an extra push because the spring is old and weak, the rug that unfailingly skids underfoot.

It wasn't just that things were wrong with the pattern of Burckhardt's life; it was that the *wrong* things were wrong. For instance, Barth hadn't come into the office, yet Barth *always* came in.

Burckhardt brooded about it through dinner. He brooded about it, despite his wife's attempt to interest him in a game of bridge with the neighbours, all through the evening. The neighbours were people he liked – Anne and Farley Dennerman. He had known them all their lives. But they were odd and brooding, too, this night and he barely listened to Dennerman's complaints about not being able to get good phone service or his wife's comments on the disgusting variety of television commercials they had these days.

Burckhardt was well on the way to setting an all-time record for continuous abstraction when, around midnight, with a suddenness that surprised him – he was strangely *aware* of it happening – he turned over in his bed and, quickly and completely, fell asleep.

II

On the morning of June the 15th, Burckhardt woke up screaming.

It was more real than any dream he had ever had in his life. He could still hear the explosion, feel the blast that crushed him against a wall. It did not seem right that he should be sitting bolt upright in bed in an undisturbed room.

His wife came pattering up the stairs. 'Darling!' she cried. 'What's the matter?'

He mumbled, 'Nothing. Bad dream.'

She relaxed, hand on heart. In an angry tone, she started to say: 'You gave me such a shock – '

But a noise from outside interrupted her. There was a wail of sirens and a clang of bells; it was loud and shocking.

The Burckhardts stared at each other for a heartbeat, then hurried fearfully to the window.

There were no rumbling fire engines in the street, only a small panel truck, cruising slowly along. Flaring loudspeaker horns crowned its top. From them issued the screaming sound of sirens, growing in intensity, mixed with the rumble of heavy-duty engines and the sound of bells. It was a perfect record of a fire engine arriving at a four-alarm blaze.

Burckhardt said in amazement, 'Mary, that's against the law! Do you know what they're doing? They're playing records of a fire. What are they up to?'

'Maybe it's a practical joke,' his wife offered.

'Joke? Waking up the whole neighbourhood at six o'clock in the morning?' He shook his head. 'The police will be here in ten minutes,' he predicted. 'Wait and see.'

But the police weren't – not in ten minutes, or at all. Whoever the pranksters in the car were, they apparently had a police permit for their games.

The car took a position in the middle of the block and stood silent for a few minutes. Then there was a crackle from the speaker, and a giant voice chanted:

> 'Feckle Freezers!
> Feckle Freezers!
> Gotta have a
> Feckle Freezer!
> Feckle, Feckle, Feckle,
> Feckle, Feckle, Feckle –'

It went on and on. Every house on the block had faces staring out of windows by then. The voice was not merely loud; it was nearly deafening.

Burckhardt shouted to his wife, over the uproar, 'What the hell is a Feckle Freezer?'

'Some kind of a freezer, I guess, dear,' she shrieked back unhelpfully.

Abruptly the noise stopped and the truck stood silent. It was a still misty morning; the sun's rays came horizontally across the rooftops. It was impossible to believe that, a moment ago, the silent block had been bellowing the name of a freezer.

'A crazy advertising trick,' Burckhardt said bitterly. He yawned and turned away from the window. 'Might as well get dressed. I guess that's the end of –'

The bellow caught him from behind; it was almost like a hard slap on the ears. A harsh, sneering voice, louder than the archangel's trumpet, howled:

'Have you got a freezer? *It stinks!* If it isn't a Feckle Freezer, *it stinks!* If it's a last year's Feckle Freezer, *it stinks!* Only this year's Feckle Freezer is any good at all! You know who owns an Ajax Freezer? Fairies own Ajax Freezers! You know who owns a Triplecold Freezer? Commies own Triplecold Freezers! Every freezer but a brand-new Feckle Freezer *stinks!*'

The voice screamed inarticulately with rage. 'I'm warning you! Get out and buy a Feckle Freezer right away! Hurry up! Hurry for Feckle!

Hurry for Feckle! Hurry, hurry, hurry, Feckle, Feckle, Feckle, Feckle, Feckle, Feckle . . .'

It stopped eventually. Burckhardt licked his lips. He started to say to his wife, 'Maybe we ought to call the police about – ' when the speakers erupted again. It caught him off guard; it was intended to catch him off guard. It screamed:

'Feckle, Feckle, Feckle, Feckle, Feckle, Feckle, Feckle, Feckle. Cheap freezers ruin your food. You'll get sick and throw up. You'll get sick and die. Buy a Feckle, Feckle, Feckle, Feckle! Ever take a piece of meat out of the freezer you've got and see how rotten and mouldy it is? Buy a Feckle, Feckle, Feckle, Feckle, Feckle. Do you want to eat rotten, stinking food? Or do you want to wise up and buy a Feckle, Feckle, Feckle – '

That did it. With fingers that kept stabbing the wrong holes, Burckhardt finally managed to dial the local police station. He got a busy signal – it was apparent that he was not the only one with the same idea – and while he was shakingly dialling again, the noise outside stopped.

He looked out the window. The truck was gone.

Burckhardt loosened his tie and ordered another Frosty-Flip from the waiter. If only they wouldn't keep the Crystal Café so *hot!* The new paint job – searing reds and blinding yellows – was bad enough, but someone seemed to have the delusion that this was January instead of June; the place was a good ten degrees warmer than outside.

He swallowed the Frosty-Flip in two gulps. It had a kind of peculiar flavour, he thought, but not bad. It certainly cooled you off, just as the waiter had promised. He reminded himself to pick up a carton of them on the way home; Mary might like them. She was always interested in something new.

He stood up awkwardly as the girl came across the restaurant towards him. She was the most beautiful thing he had ever seen in Tylerton. Chin-height, honey-blonde hair, and a figure that – well, it was all hers. There was no doubt in the world that the dress that clung to her was the only thing she wore. He felt as if he were blushing as she greeted him.

'Mr Burckhardt.' The voice was like distant tomtoms. 'It's wonderful of you to let me see you, after this morning.'

He cleared his throat. 'Not at all. Won't you sit down, Miss –'

'April Horn,' she murmured, sitting down – beside him, not where he had pointed on the other side of the table. 'Call me April, won't you?'

She was wearing some kind of perfume, Burckhardt noted with what little of his mind was functioning at all. It didn't seem fair that she should be using perfume as well as everything else. He came to with a start and realized that the waiter was leaving with an order for *filets mignon* for two.

'Hey!' he objected.

'Please, Mr Burckhardt.' Her shoulder was against his, her face was turned to him, her breath was warm, her expression was tender and solictious. 'This is all on the Feckle Corporation. Please let them – it's the *least* they can do.'

He felt her hand burrowing into his pocket.

'I put the price of the meal into your pocket,' she whispered conspiratorially. 'Please do that for me, won't you? I mean I'd appreciate it if you'd pay the waiter – I'm old-fashioned about things like that.'

She smiled meltingly, then became mock-businesslike. 'But you must take the money,' she insisted. 'Why, you're letting Feckle off lightly if you do! You could sue them for every nickel they've got, disturbing your sleep like that.'

With a dizzy feeling, as though he had just seen someone make a rabbit disappear into a top hat, he said, 'Why, it really wasn't so bad, uh, April. A little noisy, maybe, but –'

'Oh, Mr Burckhardt!' The blue eyes were wide and admiring. 'I *knew* you'd understand. It's just that – well, it's such a *wonderful* freezer that some of the outside men get carried away, so to speak. As soon as the main office found out about what happened, they sent representatives around to every house on the block to apologize. Your wife told us where we could phone you – and I'm so very pleased that you were willing to let me have lunch with you, so that I could apologize, too. Because truly, Mr Burckhardt, it is a *fine* freezer.

'I shouldn't tell you this, but –' the blue eyes were shyly lowered – 'I'd do almost anything for Feckle Freezers. It's more than a job to me.' She looked up. She was enchanting. 'I bet you think I'm silly, don't you?'

Burckhardt coughed. 'Well, I – '

'Oh, you don't want to be unkind!' She shook her head. 'No, don't pretend. You think it's silly. But really, Mr Burckhardt, you wouldn't think so if you knew more about the Feckle. Let me show you this little booklet – '

Burckhardt got back from lunch a full hour later. It wasn't only the girl who delayed him. There had been a curious interview with a little man named Swanson, whom he barely knew, who had stopped him with desperate urgency on the street – and then left him cold.

But it didn't matter much. Mr Barth, for the first time since Burckhardt had worked there, was out for the day – leaving Burckhardt stuck with the quarterly tax returns.

What did matter, though, was that somehow he had signed a purchase order for a twelve-cubic-foot Feckle Freezer, upright model, self-defrosting, list price $625, with a ten per cent 'courtesy' discount – 'Because of that *horrid* affair this morning, Mr Burckhardt,' she had said.

And he wasn't sure how he could explain it to his wife.

He needn't have worried. As he walked in the front door, his wife said almost immediately, 'I wonder if we can't afford a new freezer, dear. There was a man here to apologize about that noise and – well, we got to talking and – '

She had signed a purchase order, too.

It had been the damnedest day, Burckhardt thought later, on his way up to bed. But the day wasn't done with him yet. At the head of the stairs, the weakened spring in the electric light switch refused to click at all. He snapped it back and forth angrily, and, of course, succeeded in jarring the tumbler out of its pins. The wires shorted and every light in the house went out.

'Damn!' said Guy Burckhardt.

'Fuse?' His wife shrugged sleepily: 'Let it go till the morning, dear.'

Burckhardt shook his head. 'You go back to bed. I'll be right along.'

It wasn't so much that he cared about fixing the fuse, but he was too restless for sleep. He disconnected the bad switch with a screwdriver, stumbled down into the black kitchen, found the flashlight and climbed gingerly down the cellar stairs. He located a spare fuse, pushed an empty trunk over to the fuse box to stand on, and twisted out the old fuse.

When the new one was in, he heard the starting click and steady drone of the refrigerator in the kitchen overhead.

He headed back to the steps, and stopped.

Where the old trunk had been, the cellar floor gleamed oddly bright. He inspected it in the flashlight beam. It was metal!

'Son of a gun,' said Guy Burckhardt. He shook his head unbelievingly. He peered closer, rubbed the edges of the metallic patch with his thumb and acquired an annoying cut – the edges were *sharp*.

The stained cement floor of the cellar was a thin shell. He found a hammer and cracked it off in a dozen spots – everywhere was metal.

The whole cellar was a copper box. Even the cement-brick walls were false fronts over a metal sheath!

Baffled, he attacked one of the foundation beams. That, at least, was real wood. The glass in the cellar windows was real glass.

He sucked his bleeding thumb and tried the base of the cellar stairs. Real wood. He chipped at the bricks under the oil burner. Real bricks. The retaining walls, the floor – they were faked.

It was as though someone had shored up the house with a frame of metal and then laboriously concealed the evidence.

The biggest surprise was the upside-down boat hull that blocked the rear half of the cellar, relic of a brief home workshop period that Burckhardt had gone through a couple of years before. From above, it looked perfectly normal. Inside, though, where there should have been thwarts and seats and lockers, there was a mere tangle of braces, rough and unfinished.

'But I *built* that!' Burckhardt exclaimed, forgetting his thumb. He leaned against the hull dizzily, trying to think this thing through. For reasons beyond his comprehension, someone had taken his boat and his cellar away, maybe his whole house, and replaced them with a clever mock-up of the real thing.

'That's crazy,' he said to the empty cellar. He stared around in the light of the flash. He whispered, 'What in the name of Heaven would anybody do that for?'

Reason refused an answer; there wasn't any reasonable answer. For long minutes, Burckhardt contemplated the uncertain picture of his own sanity.

He peered under the boat again, hoping to reassure himself that it was a mistake, just his imagination. But the sloppy, unfinished bracing was unchanged. He crawled under for a better look, feeling the rough wood incredulously. Utterly impossible!

He switched off the flashlight and started to wriggle out. But he didn't make it. In the moment between the command to his legs to move and the crawling out, he felt a sudden draining weariness flooding through him.

Consciousness went – not easily, but as though it were being taken away, and Guy Burckhardt was asleep.

III

On the morning of June the 16th, Guy Burckhardt woke up in a cramped position huddled under the hull of the boat in his basement – and raced upstairs to find it was June the 15th.

The first thing he had done was to make a frantic, hasty inspection of the boat hull, the faked cellar floor, the imitation stone. They were all as he had remembered them – all completely unbelievable.

The kitchen was its placid, unexciting self. The electric clock was purring soberly around the dial. Almost six o'clock, it said. His wife would be waking at any moment.

Burckhardt flung open the front door and stared out into the quiet street. The morning paper was tossed carelessly against the steps – and as he retrieved it, he noticed that this was the 15th day of June.

But that was impossible. *Yesterday* was the 15th of June. It was not a date one would forget – it was quarterly tax-return day.

He went back into the hall and picked up the telephone; he dialled for Weather Information, and got a well-modulated chant: '– and cooler, some showers. Barometric pressure thirty point zero four, rising

. . . United States Weather Bureau forecast for June the 15th. Warm and sunny, with high around –'

He hung the phone up. June the 15th.

'Holy heaven!' Burckhardt said prayerfully. Things were very odd indeed. He heard the ring of his wife's alarm and bounded up the stairs.

Mary Burckhardt was sitting upright in bed with the terrified, uncomprehending stare of someone just waking out of a nightmare.

'Oh!' she gasped, as her husband came in the room. 'Darling, I just had the most *terrible* dream! It was like an explosion and –'

'Again?' Burckhardt asked, not very sympathetically. 'Mary, something's funny! I *knew* there was something wrong all day yesterday and –'

He went on to tell her about the copper box that was the cellar, and the odd mock-up someone had made of his boat. Mary looked astonished, then alarmed, then placatory and uneasy.

She said, 'Dear, are you *sure*? Because I was cleaning that old trunk out just last week and I didn't notice anything.'

'Positive!' said Guy Burckhardt. 'I dragged it over to the wall to step on it to put a new fuse in after we blew the lights out and –'

'After we what?' Mary was looking more than merely alarmed.

'After we blew the lights out. You know, when the switch at the head of the stairs stuck. I went down to the cellar and –'

Mary sat up in bed. 'Guy, the switch didn't stick. I turned out the lights myself last night.'

Burckhardt glared at his wife. 'Now I *know* you didn't! Come here and take a look!'

He stalked out to the landing and dramatically pointed to the bad switch, the one that he had unscrewed and left hanging the night before . . .

Only it wasn't. It was as it had always been. Unbelieving, Burckhardt pressed it and the lights sprang up in both halls.

Mary, looking pale and worried, left him to go down to the kitchen and start breakfast. Burckhardt stood staring at the switch for a long time.

His mental processes were gone beyond the point of disbelief and shock; they simply were not functioning.

He shaved and dressed and ate his breakfast in a state of numb introspection. Mary didn't disturb him; she was apprehensive and soothing. She kissed him good-bye as he hurried out to the bus without another word.

Miss Mitkin, at the reception desk, greeted him with a yawn. 'Morning,' she said drowsily. 'Mr Barth won't be in today.'

Burckhardt started to say something, but checked himself. She would not know that Barth hadn't been in yesterday, either, because she was tearing a June the 14th pad off her calendar to make way for the 'new' June the 15th sheet.

He staggered to his own desk and stared unseeingly at the morning's mail. It had not even been opened yet, but he knew that the Factory Distributors envelope contained an order for twenty thousand feet of the new acoustic tile, and the one from Finebeck & Sons was a complaint.

After a long while, he forced himself to open them. They were.

By lunchtime, driven by a desperate sense of urgency, Burckhardt made Miss Mitkin take her lunch hour first – the June-fifteenth-that-was-yesterday *he* had gone first. She went, looking vaguely worried about his strained insistence, but it made no difference to Burckhardt's mood.

The phone rang and Burckhardt picked it up abstractedly. 'Contro Chemicals Downtown, Burckhardt speaking.'

The voice said, 'This is Swanson,' and stopped.

Burckhardt waited expectantly, but that was all. He said, 'Hello?'

Again the pause. Then Swanson asked in sad resignation, 'Still nothing, eh?'

'Nothing what? Swanson, is there something you want? You came up to me yesterday and went through this routine. You –'

The voice crackled: 'Burckhardt! Oh, my good heavens, *you remember!* Stay right there – I'll be down in half an hour!'

'What's this all about?'

'Never mind,' the little man said exultantly. 'Tell you about it when I see you. Don't say any more over the phone – somebody may be listening. Just wait there. Say, hold on a minute. Will you be alone in the office?'

'Well, no. Miss Mitkin will probably –'

'Hell. Look, Burckhardt, where do you eat lunch? Is it good and noisy?'

'Why, I suppose so. The Crystal Café. It's just about a block –'

'I know where it is. Meet you in half an hour!' And the receiver clicked.

The Crystal Café was no longer painted red, but the temperature was still up. And they had added piped-in music interspersed with commercials. The advertisements were for Frosty-Flip, Marlin Cigarettes – 'They're sanitized,' the announcer purred – and something called Choco-Bite candy bars that Burckhardt couldn't remember ever having heard of before. But he heard more about them quickly enough.

While he was waiting for Swanson to show up, a girl in the cellophane skirt of a nightclub cigarette vendor came through the restaurant with a tray of tiny scarlet-wrapped candies.

'Choco-Bites are *tangy*,' she was murmuring as she came close to his table. 'Choco-Bites are *tangier* than tangy!'

Burckhardt, intent on watching for the strange little man who had phoned him, paid little attention. But as she scattered a handful of the confections over the table next to his, smiling at the occupants, he caught a glimpse of her and turned to stare.

'Why, Miss Horn!' he said.

The girl dropped her tray of candies.

Burckhardt rose, concerned over the girl. 'Is something wrong?'

But she fled.

The manager of the restaurant was staring suspiciously at Burckhardt, who sank back in his seat and tried to look inconspicuous. He hadn't insulted the girl! Maybe she was just a very strictly reared young lady, he thought – in spite of the long bare legs under the cellophane skirt – and when he addressed her, she thought he was a masher.

Ridiculous idea. Burckhardt scowled uneasily and picked up his menu.

'Burckhardt!' It was a shrill whisper.

Burckhardt looked up over the top of his menu, startled. In the seat across from him, the little man named Swanson was sitting, tensely poised.

'Burckhardt!' the little man whispered again. 'Let's go out of here! They're on to you now. If you want to stay alive, come on!'

There was no arguing with the man. Burckhardt gave the hovering manager a sick apologetic smile and followed Swanson out. The little man seemed to know where he was going. In the street, he clutched Burckhardt by the elbow and hurried him off down the block.

'Did you see her?' he demanded. 'That Horn woman, in the phone booth? She'll have them here in five minutes, believe me, so hurry it up!'

Although the street was full of people and cars, nobody was paying any attention to Burckhardt and Swanson. The air had a nip in it – more like October than June, Burckhardt thought, in spite of the weather bureau. And he felt like a fool, following this mad little man down the street, running away from some 'them' towards – towards what? The little man might be crazy, but he was afraid. And the fear was infectious.

'In here!' panted the little man.

It was another restaurant – more of a bar, really, and a sort of second-rate place that Burckhardt never had patronized.

'Right straight through,' Swanson whispered; and Burckhardt, like a biddable boy, sidestepped through the mass of tables to the far end of the restaurant.

It was L-shaped, with a front on two streets at right angles to each other. They came out on the side street, Swanson staring coldly back at the question-looking cashier, and crossed to the opposite sidewalk.

They were under the marquee of a movie theatre. Swanson's expression began to relax.

'Lost them!' he crowed softly. 'We're almost there.'

He stepped up to the window and bought two tickets. Burckhardt trailed him in to the theatre. It was a weekday matinee and the place was almost empty. From the screen came sounds of gunfire and horse's hoofs. A solitary usher, leaning against a bright brass rail, looked briefly at them and went back to staring boredly at the picture as Swanson led Burckhardt down a flight of carpeted marble steps.

They were in the lounge and it was empty. There was a door for men and one for ladies; and there was a third door, marked MANAGER in gold letters. Swanson listened at the door, and gently opened it and peered inside.

'Okay,' he said, gesturing.

Burckhardt followed him through an empty office, to another door – a closet, probably, because it was unmarked.

But it was no closet. Swanson opened it warily, looked inside, then motioned Burckhardt to follow.

It was a tunnel, metal-walled, brightly lit. Empty, it stretched vacantly away in both directions from them.

Burckhardt looked wondering around. One thing he knew and knew full well:

No such tunnel belonged under Tylerton.

There was a room off the tunnel with chairs and a desk and what looked like television screens. Swanson slumped in a chair, panting.

'We're all right for a while here,' he wheezed. 'They don't come here much any more. If they do, we'll hear them and we can hide.'

'Who?' demanded Burckhardt.

The little man said, 'Martians!' His voice cracked on the word and the life seemed to go out of him. In morose tones, he went on: 'Well, I think they're Martians. Although you could be right, you know; I've had plenty of time to think it over these last few weeks, after they got you, and it's possible they're Russians after all. Still –'

'Start from the beginning. Who got me when?'

Swanson sighed. 'So we have to go through the whole thing again. All right. It was about two months ago that you banged on my door, late at night. You were all beat up – scared silly. You begged me to help you –'

'*I* did?'

'Naturally you don't remember any of this. Listen and you'll understand. You were talking a blue streak about being captured and threatened and your wife being dead and coming back to life, and all kinds of mixed-up nonsense. I thought you were crazy. But – well, I've always had a lot of respect for you. And you begged me to hide you and I have this darkroom, you know. It locks from the inside only. I put the lock on myself. So we went in there – just to humour you – and along about midnight, which was only fifteen or twenty minutes after, we passed out.'

'Passed out?'

Swanson nodded. 'Both of us. It was like being hit with a sandbag. Look, didn't that happen to you again last night?'

'I guess it did,' Burckhardt shook his head uncertainly.

'Sure. And then all of a sudden we were awake again, and you said you were going to show me something funny, and we went out and bought a paper. And the date on it was June the 15th.'

'June the 15th? But that's today! I mean –'

'You got it, friend. It's *always* today!'

It took time to penetrate.

Burckhardt said wonderingly, 'You've hidden out in that darkroom for how many weeks?'

'How can I tell? Four or five, maybe. I lost count. And every day the same – always the fifteenth of June, always my landlady, Mrs Keefer, is sweeping the front steps, always the same headline in the papers at the corner. It gets monotonous, friend.'

IV

It was Burckhardt's idea and Swanson despised it, but he went along. He was the type who always went along.

'It's dangerous,' he grumbled worriedly. 'Suppose somebody comes by? They'll spot us and –'

'What have we got to lose?'

Swanson shrugged. 'It's dangerous,' he said again. But he went along.

Burckhardt's idea was very simple. He was sure of only one thing – the tunnel went somewhere. Martians or Russians, fantastic plot or crazy hallucination, whatever was wrong with Tylerton had an explanation, and the place to look for it was at the end of the tunnel.

They jogged along. It was more than a mile before they began to see an end. They were in luck – at least no one came through the tunnel to spot them. But Swanson had said that it was only at certain hours that the tunnel seemed to be in use.

Always the fifteenth of June. Why? Burckhardt asked himself. Never mind the how. *Why?*

And falling asleep, completely involuntarily – everyone at the same time, it seemed. And not remembering, never remembering anything – Swanson had said how eagerly he saw Burckhardt again, the morning after Burckhardt had incautiously waited five minutes too many before retreating into the darkroom. When Swanson had come to, Burckhardt was gone. Swanson had seen him in the street that afternoon, but Burckhardt had remembered nothing.

And Swanson had lived his mouse's existence for weeks, hiding in the woodwork at night, stealing out by day to search for Burckhardt in pitiful hope, scurrying around the fringe of life, trying to keep from the deadly eyes of *them*.

Them. One of 'them' was the girl named April Horn. It was by seeing her walk carelessly into a telephone booth and never come out that Swanson had found the tunnel. Another was the man at the cigar stand in Burckhardt's office building. There were more, at least a dozen that Swanson knew of or suspected.

They were easy enough to spot, once you knew where to look – for they, alone in Tylerton, changed their roles from day to day. Burckhardt was on that 8.51 bus, every morning of everyday-that-was-June-the-15th, never different by a hair or a moment. But April Horn was sometimes gaudy in the cellophane skirt, giving away candy or cigarettes; sometimes plainly dressed; sometimes not seen by Swanson at all.

Russians? Martains? Whatever they were, what could they be hoping to gain from this mad masquerade?

Burckhardt didn't know the answer – but perhaps it lay beyond the door at the end of the tunnel. They listened carefully and heard distant sounds that could not quite be made out, but nothing that seemed dangerous. They slipped through.

And, through a wide chamber and up a flight of steps, they found they were in what Burckhardt recognized as the Contro Chemicals plant.

Nobody was in sight. By itself, that was not so very odd – the automatized factory had never had very many persons in it. But Burckhardt remembered, from his single visit, the endless, ceaseless busyness of the plant, the valves that opened and closed, the vats that emptied themselves and filled themselves and stirred and cooked and chemically tested the bubbling liquids they held inside themselves. The plant was never populated, but it was never still.

Only – now it *was* still. Except for the distant sounds, there was no breath of life in it. The captive electronic minds were sending out no commands; the coils and relays were at rest.

Burckhardt said, 'Come on.' Swanson reluctantly followed him through the tangled aisles of stainless steel columns and tanks.

They walked as though they were in the presence of the dead. In a way, they were, for what were the automatons that once had run the factory, if not corpses? The machines were controlled by computers that were really not computers at all, but the electronic analogues of living brains. And if they were turned off, were they not dead? For each had once been a human mind.

Take a master petroleum chemist, infinitely skilled in the separation of crude oil into its fractions. Strap him down, probe into his brain with searching electronic needles. The machine scans the patterns of the mind, translates what it sees into charts and sine waves. Impress these same waves on a robot computer and you have your chemist. Or a thousand copies of your chemist, if you wish, with all of his knowledge and skill, and no human limitations at all.

Put a dozen copies of him into a plant and they will run it all, twenty-four hours a day, seven days of every week, never tiring, never overlooking anything, never forgetting . . .

Swanson stepped up closer to Burckhardt. 'I'm scared,' he said.

They were across the room now and the sounds were louder. They were not machine sounds, but voices; Burckhardt moved cautiously up to a door and dared to peer around it.

It was a smaller room, lined with television screens, each one – a dozen or more, at least – with a man or woman sitting before it, staring into the screen and dictating notes into a recorder. The viewers dialled from scene to scene; no two screens ever showed the same picture.

The pictures seemed to have little in common. One was a store, where a girl dressed like April Horn was demonstrating home freezers. One was a series of shots of kitchens. Burckhardt caught a glimpse of what looked like the cigar stand in his office building.

It was baffling and Burckhardt would have loved to stand there and puzzle it out, but it was too busy a place. There was the chance that someone would look their way or walk out and find them.

They found another room. This one was empty. It was an office, large and sumptuous. It had a desk, littered with papers. Burckhardt stared at them, briefly at first – then, as the words on one of them caught his attention, with incredulous fascination.

He snatched up the topmost sheet, scanned it, and another, while Swanson was frenziedly searching through the drawers.

Burckhardt swore unbelievingly and dropped the papers to the desk.

Swanson, hardly noticing, yelped with delight: 'Look!' He dragged a gun from the desk. 'And it's loaded, too!'

Burckhardt stared at him blankly, trying to assimilate what he had read. Then, as he realized what Swanson had said, Burckhardt's eyes sparked. 'Good man!' he cried. 'We'll take it. We're getting out of here with that gun, Swanson. And we're going to the police! Not the cops in Tylerton, but the FBI, maybe. Take a look at this!'

The sheaf he handed Swanson was headed: 'Test Area Progress Report. Subject: Marlin Cigarettes Campaign.' It was mostly tabulated figures that made little sense to Burckhardt and Swanson, but at the end was a summary that said:

Although Test 47-K3 pulled nearly double the number of new users of any of the other tests conducted, it probably cannot be used in the field because of local sound-truck control ordinances.

The tests in the 47-K12 group were second best and our recommendation is that retests be conducted in this appeal, testing each of the three best campaigns with and without the addition of sampling techniques.

An alternative suggestion might be to proceed directly with the top appeal in the K12 series, if the client is unwilling to go to the expense of additional tests.

All of these forecast expectations have an 80% probability of being within one-half of one per cent of results forecast, and more than 99% probability of coming within 5%.

Swanson looked up from the paper into Burckhardt's eyes. 'I don't get it,' he complained. Burckhardt said, 'I do not blame you. It's crazy, but it fits the facts, Swanson, *it fits the facts*. They aren't Russians and they aren't Martians. These people are advertising men! Somehow – heaven knows how they did it – they've taken Tylerton over. They've got us, all of us, you and me and twenty or thirty thousand other people, right under their thumbs.

'Maybe they hypnotize us and maybe it's something else; but however they do it, what happens is that they let us live a day at a time. They pour advertising into us the whole damned day long. And at the end of the day, they see what happened – and then they wash the day out of our minds and start again the next day with different advertising.'

Swanson's jaw was hanging. He managed to close it and swallow. 'Nuts!' he said flatly.

Burckhardt shook his head. 'Sure, it sounds crazy – but this whole thing is crazy. How else would you explain it? You can't deny that most of Tylerton lives the same day over and over again. You've *seen* it. And that's the crazy part and we have to admit that that's true – unless *we* are the crazy ones. And once you admit that somebody, somehow, knows how to accomplish that, the rest of it makes all kinds of sense.

'Think of it, Swanson! They test every last detail before they spend a nickel on advertising! Do you have any idea what that means? Lord knows how much money is involved, but I know for a fact that some companies spend twenty or thirty million dollars a year on advertising. Multiply it, say, by a hundred companies. Say that every one of them learns how to cut its advertising cost by only ten per cent. And that's peanuts, believe me!

'If they know in advance what is going to work, they can cut their costs in half – maybe to less than half, I don't know. But that is saving two or three hundred million dollars a year – and if they pay only ten or twenty per cent of that for the use of Tylerton, it's still dirt cheap for them and a fortune for whoever took over Tylerton.'

Swanson licked his lips. 'You mean,' he offered hesitantly, 'that we're a – well, a kind of captive audience?'

Burckhardt frowned. 'Not exactly.' He thought for a minute. 'You know how a doctor tests something like penicillin? He sets up a series of little colonies of germs on gelatine discs and he tries the stuff on one after another, changing it a little each time. Well, that's us – we're the germs, Swanson. Only it's even more efficient than that. They don't have to test more than one colony, because they can use it over and over again.'

It was too hard for Swanson to take in. He only said: 'What do we do about it?'

'We go to the police. They can't use human beings for guinea pigs!'

'How do we get to the police?'

Burckhardt hesitated. 'I think –' he began slowly. 'Sure. This place is the office of somebody important. We've got a gun. We will stay right here until he comes along. And he'll get us out of here.'

Simple and direct. Swanson subsided and found a place to sit, against the wall, out of sight of the door. Burckhardt took up a position behind the door itself –

And waited.

The wait was not as long as it might have been. Half an hour, perhaps. Then Burckhardt heard approaching voices and had time for a swift whisper to Swanson before he flattened himself against the wall.

It was a man's voice, and a girl's. The man was saying, '– reason why you couldn't report on the phone? You're ruining your whole day's test! What the devil's the matter with you, Janet?'

'I'm sorry, Mr Dorchin,' she said in a sweet, clear tone. 'I thought it was important.'

The man grumbled, 'Important! One lousy unit out of twenty-one thousand.'

'But it's the Burckhardt one, Mr Dorchin. Again. And the way he got out of sight, he must have had some help.'

'All right, all right. It doesn't matter, Janet; the Choco-Bite programme is ahead of schedule anyhow. As long as you're this far, come on in the office and make out your worksheet. And don't worry about the Burckhardt business. He's probably just wandering around. We'll pick him up tonight and – '

They were inside the door. Burckhardt kicked it shut and pointed the gun.

'That's what you think,' he said triumphantly.

It was worth the terrified hours, the bewildered sense of insanity, the confusion and fear. It was the most satisfying sensation Burckhardt had ever had in his life. The expression on the man's face was one he had read about but never actually seen: Dorchin's mouth fell open and his eyes went wide, and though he managed to make a sound that might have been a question, it was not in words.

The girl was almost as surprised. And Burckhardt, looking at her, knew why her voice had been so familiar. The girl was the one who had introduced herself to him as April Horn.

Dorchin recovered himself quickly. 'Is this the one?' he asked sharply.

The girl said, 'Yes.'

Dorchin nodded. 'I take it back. You were right. Uh, you – Burckhardt. What do you want?'

Swanson piped up, 'Watch him! He might have another gun.'

'Search him then,' Burckhardt said. 'I'll tell you what we want, Dorchin. We want you to come along with us to the FBI and explain to them how you can get away with kidnapping twenty thousand people.'

'Kidnapping?' Dorchin snorted. 'That's ridiculous, man! Put that gun away – you can't get away with this!'

Burckhardt hefted the gun grimly. 'I think I can.'

Dorchin looked furious and sick – but, oddly, not afraid. 'Damn it – ' he started to bellow, then closed his mouth and swallowed. 'Listen,' he said persuasively, 'you're making a big mistake. I haven't kidnapped anybody, believe me!'

'I don't believe you,' said Burckhardt bluntly. 'Why should I?'

'But it's true! Take my word for it!'

Burckhardt shook his head. 'The FBI can take your word if they like. We'll find out. Now how do we get out of here?'

Dorchin opened his mouth to argue.

Burckhardt blazed: 'Don't get in my way! I'm willing to kill you if I have to. Don't you understand that? I've gone through two days of hell and every second of it I blame on you. Kill you? It would be a pleasure and I don't have a thing in the world to lose! Get us out of here!'

Dorchin's face went suddenly opaque. He seemed about to move; but the blonde girl he had called Janet slipped between him and the gun.

'Please!' she begged Burckhardt. 'You don't understand. You mustn't shoot!'

'Get out of my way!'

'But, Mr Burckhardt –'

She never finished. Dorchin, his face unreadable, headed for the door. Burckhardt had been pushed one degree too far. He swung the gun, bellowing. The girl called out sharply. He pulled the trigger. Closing on him with pity and pleading in her eyes, she came again between the gun and the man.

Burckhardt aimed low instinctively, to cripple, not to kill. But his aim was not good.

The pistol bullet caught her in the pit of the stomach.

Dorchin was out and away, the door slamming behind him, his footsteps racing into the distance.

Burckhardt hurled the gun across the room and jumped to the girl.

Swanson was moaning, 'That finishes us, Burckhardt. Oh, why did you do it? We could have got away. We should have gone to the police. We were practically out of here! We –'

Burckhardt wasn't listening. He was kneeling beside the girl. She lay flat on her back, arms helter-skelter. There was no blood, hardly any sign of the wound; but the position in which she lay was one that no living human being could have held.

Yet she wasn't dead.

She wasn't dead – and Burckhardt, frozen beside her, thought: *She isn't alive, either.*

There was no pulse, but there was a rhythmic ticking of the outstretched fingers of one hand.

There was no sound of breathing, but there was a hissing, sizzling noise.

The eyes were open and they were looking at Burckhardt. There was neither fear nor pain in them, only a pity deeper than the Pit.

She said, through lips that writhed erratically, 'Don't – worry, Mr Burckhardt. I'm – all right.'

Burckhardt rocked back on his haunches, staring. Where there should have been blood, there was a clean break of a substance that was not flesh; and a curl of thin golden-copper wire.

Burckhardt moistened his lips.

'You're a robot,' he said.

The girl tried to nod. The twitching lips said, 'I am. And so are you.'

V

Swanson, after a single inarticulate sound, walked over to the desk and sat staring at the wall. Burckhardt rocked back and forth beside the shattered puppet on the floor. He had no words.

The girl managed to say, 'I'm – sorry all this happened.' The lovely lips twisted into a rictus sneer, frightening on that smooth young face, until she got them under control. 'Sorry,' she said again. 'The – nerve centre was right about where the bullet hit. Makes it difficult to – control this body.'

Burckhardt nodded automatically, accepting the apology. Robots. It was obvious, now that he knew it. In hindsight, it was inevitable. He thought of his mystic notions of hypnosis or Martians or something stranger still – idiotic, for the simple fact of created robots fitted the facts better and more economically.

All the evidence had been before him. The automatized factory, with its transplanted minds – why not transplant a mind into a humanoid robot, give it its original owner's features and form?

Could it know that it was a robot?

'All of us,' Burckhardt said, hardly aware that he spoke out loud. 'My wife and my secretary and you and the neighbours. All of us the same.'

'No.' The voice was stronger. 'Not exactly the same, all of us. I chose it, you see. I –' this time the convulsed lips were not a random contortion of the nerves – 'I was an ugly woman, Mr Burckhardt, and nearly sixty years old. Life had passed me. And when Mr Dorchin offered me the chance to live again as a beautiful girl, I jumped at the opportunity. Believe me, I *jumped*, in spite of its disadvantages. My flesh body is still alive – it is sleeping, while I am here. I could go back to it. But I never do.'

'And the rest of us?'

'Different, Mr Burckhardt. I work here. I'm carrying out Mr Dorchin's orders, mapping the results of the advertising tests, watching you and the others live as he makes you live. I do it by choice, but you have no choice. Because, you see, you are dead.'

'Dead?' cried Burckhardt; it was almost a scream.

The blue eyes looked at him unwinkingly and he knew that it was no lie. He swallowed, marvelling at the intricate mechanisms that let him swallow, and sweat, and eat.

He said: 'Oh. The explosion in my dream.'

'It was no dream. You are right – the explosion. That was real and this plant was the cause of it. The storage tanks let go and what the blast didn't get, the fumes killed a little later. But almost everyone died in the blast, twenty-one thousand persons. You died with them and that was Dorchin's chance.'

'The damned ghoul!' said Burckhardt.

The twisted shoulders shrugged with an odd grace. 'Why? You were gone. And you and all the others were what Dorchin wanted – a whole town, a perfect slice of America. It's as easy to transfer a pattern from a dead brain as a living one. Easier – the dead can't say no. Oh, it took work and money – the town was a wreck – but it was possible to rebuild it entirely, especially because it wasn't necessary to have all the details exact.

'There were the homes where even the brains had been utterly destroyed, and those are empty inside, and the cellars that needn't be too perfect, and the streets that hardly matter. And anyway, it only had to last for one day. The same day – June the 15th – over and over again;

and if someone finds something a little wrong, somehow, the discovery won't have time to snowball, wreck the validity of the tests, because all errors are cancelled out at midnight.'

The face tried to smile. 'That's the dream, Mr Burckhardt, that day of June the 15th, because you never really lived it. It's a present from Mr Dorchin, a dream that he gives you and then takes back at the end of the day, when he had all his figures on how many of you responded to what variation of which appeal, and the maintenance crews go down the tunnel to go through the whole city, washing out the new dream with their little electronic drains, and then the dream starts all over again. On June the 15th.

'Always June the 15th, because June the 14th is the last day any of you can remember alive. Sometimes the crews miss someone – as they missed you, because you were under your boat. But it doesn't matter. The ones who are missed give themselves away if they show it – and if they don't, it doesn't affect the test. But they don't drain us, the ones of us who work for Dorchin. We sleep when the power is turned off, just as you do. When we wake up, though, we remember.' The face contorted wildly. 'If I could only forget!'

Burckhardt said unbelievingly, 'All this to sell merchandise! It must have cost millions!'

The robot called April Horn said, 'It did. But it has made millions for Dorchin, too. And that's not the end of it. Once he finds the master words that make people act, do you suppose he will stop with that? Do you suppose – '

The door opened, interrupting her. Burckhardt whirled. Belatedly remembering Dorchin's flight, he raised the gun.

'Don't shoot,' ordered the voice calmly. It was not Dorchin; it was another robot, this one not disguised with the clever plastics and cosmetics, but shining plain. It said metallically: 'Forget it, Burckhardt. You're not accomplishing anything. Give me that gun before you do any more damage. Give it to me *now*.'

Burckhardt bellowed angrily. The gleam on this robot torso was steel; Burckhardt was not at all sure that his bullets would pierce it, or do much harm if they did. He would have put it on the test –

But from behind him came a whimpering, scurrying whirlwind; its name was Swanson, hysterical with fear. He catapulted into Burckhardt and sent him sprawling, the gun flying free.

'Please!' begged Swanson incoherently, prostrate before the steel robot. 'He would have shot you – please don't hurt me! Let me work for you, like that girl. I'll do anything, anything you tell me –'

The robot voice said. 'We don't need your help.' It took two precise steps and stood over the gun – and spurned it, left it lying on the floor.

The wrecked blonde robot said, without emotion, 'I doubt that I can hold out much longer, Mr Dorchin.'

'Disconnect if you have to,' replied the steel robot.

Burckhardt blinked. 'But you're not Dorchin!'

The steel robot turned deep eyes on him. 'I am,' it said. 'Not in the flesh – but this is the body I am using at the moment. I doubt that you can damage this one with the gun. The other robot body was more vulnerable. Now will you stop this nonsense? I don't want to have to damage you; you're too expensive for that. Will you just sit down and let the maintenance crews adjust you?'

Swanson grovelled. 'You – you won't punish us?'

The steel robot had no expression, but its voice was almost surprised. 'Punish you?' it repeated on a rising tone. 'How?'

Swanson quivered as though the word had been a whip; but Burckhardt flared: 'Adjust *him*, if he'll let you – but not me! You're going to have to do me a lot of damage, Dorchin. I don't care what I cost or how much trouble it's going to be to put me back together again. But I'm going out of that door! If you want to stop me, you'll have to kill me. You won't stop me any other way!'

The steel robot took a half-step towards him, and Burckhardt involuntarily checked his stride. He stood poised and shaking, ready for death, ready for attack, ready for anything that might happen.

Ready for anything except what did happen. For Dorchin's steel body merely stepped aside, between Burckhardt and the gun, but leaving the door free.

'Go ahead,' invited the steel robot. 'Nobody's stopping you.'

*

Outside the door, Burckhardt brought up sharp. It was insane of Dorchin to let him go! Robot or flesh, victim or beneficiary, there was nothing to stop him from going to the FBI or whatever law he could find away from Dorchin's synthetic empire, and telling his story. Surely the corporation who paid Dorchin for test results had no notion of the ghoul's technique he used; Dorchin would have to keep it from them, for the breath of publicity would put a stop to it. Walking out meant death, perhaps – but at that moment in his pseudo-life, death was no terror for Burckhardt.

There was no one in the corridor. He found a window and stared out of it. There was Tylerton – an ersatz city, but looking so real and familiar that Burckhardt almost imagined the whole episode a dream. It was no dream, though. He was certain of that in his heart and equally certain that nothing in Tylerton could help him now.

It had to be the other direction.

It took him a quarter of an hour to find a way, but he found it – skulking through the corridors, dodging the suspicion of footsteps, knowing for certain that his hiding was in vain, for Dorchin was undoubtedly aware of every move he made. But no one stopped him, and he found another door.

It was a simple enough door from the inside. But when he opened it and stepped out, it was like nothing he had ever seen.

First there was light – brilliant, incredible, blinding light. Burckhardt blinked upward, unbelieving and afraid.

He was standing on a ledge of smooth, finished metal. Not a dozen yards from his feet, the ledge dropped sharply away; he hardly dared approach the brink, but even from where he stood he could see no bottom to the chasm before him. And the gulf extended out of sight into the glare on either side of him.

No wonder Dorchin could so easily give him his freedom! From the factory, there was nowhere to go – but how incredible this fantastic gulf, how impossible the hundred white and blinding suns that hung above!

A voice by his side said inquiringly, 'Burckhardt?' And thunder rolled the name, mutteringly soft, back and forth in the abyss before him.

Burckhardt wet his lips. 'Y-yes?' he croaked.

'This is Dorchin. Not a robot this time, but Dorchin in the flesh, talking to you on a hand mike. Now you have seen, Burckhardt. Now will you be reasonable and let the maintenance crews take over?'

Burckhardt stood paralysed. One of the moving mountains in the blinding glare came toward him.

It towered hundreds of feet over his head; he stared up at its top, squinting helplessly into the light.

It looked like –

Impossible!

The voice in the loudspeaker at the door said, 'Burckhardt?' But he was unable to answer.

A heavy rumbling sigh. 'I see,' said the voice. 'You finally understand. There's no place to go. You know it now. I could have told you, but you might not have believed me, so it was better for you to see it yourself. And after all, Burckhardt, why would I reconstruct a city just the way it was before? I'm a businessman; I count costs. If a thing has to be full-scale, I build it that way. But there wasn't any need to in this case.'

From the mountain before him, Burckhardt helplessly saw a lesser cliff descend carefully toward him. It was long and dark, and at the end of it was whiteness, five-fingered whiteness . . .

'Poor little Burckhardt,' crooned the loudspeaker, while the echoes rumbled through the enormous chasm that was only a workshop. 'It must have been quite a shock for you to find out you were living in a town built on a table top.'

VI

It was the morning of June the 15th, and Guy Burckhardt woke up screaming out of a dream.

It had been a monstrous and incomprehensible dream, of explosions and shadowy figures that were not men and terror beyond words.

He shuddered and opened his eyes.

Outside his bedroom window, a hugely amplified voice was howling.

Burckhardt stumbled over to the window and stared outside. There was an out-of-season chill to the air, more like October than June; but the scene was normal enough – except for the sound-truck that squatted at the kerbside halfway down the block. Its speaker horns blared:

'Are you a coward? Are you a fool? Are you going to let crooked politicians steal the country from you? NO! Are you going to put up with four more years of graft and crime? NO! Are you going to vote straight Federal Party all up and down the ballot? YES! *You just bet you are!*'

Sometimes he screams, sometimes he wheedles, threatens, begs, cajoles . . . but his voice goes on and on through one June the 15th after another.

Friends in Need

ELIZA BLAIR

Sally desleeps and jumps, jounces, jiggles into her clothes. Today is a special day. Today is a prettyful day. She trambles through the porto and outdowns the steps without even zapping her hair.

Dig Sally: fifteen whole cents old, plus two cycles – that's four years and a twitch in standard termies for you parents out there. Gold-yellow hair and greeny eyes, tres charmer when she smilies, the smarterest chick in her class. Her birthday was Fourday, and now it's Sixday, a special day with declass and Daddy telecomming. Sally trambles fastlike. She's juiced.

Downchute in the kitchen Mommy is dancing, Mommy is prancing, she's whirling around to the Barking Cars as she putters Sally's breakfast on the table. Daddy peek-a-views over his lectrospecs at Sally and smilies, like he does every special morning.

'Whoa, Sally, don't choke,' warns Daddy. 'We'll be there soon enough.' His eyes ducky back of the darklenses and he's back in his meeting.

Sally scumbles her Nu-Bacon, scarfs her Eggalicious, slurps her Toast-E-Lite. Mommy chucks the utensils in the deegrate and it buzzes as they vanish. She plunks a saucer of Norange on the gray smartsurf in front of Sally and foldies her arms.

'Aw, Mommy, that goop's quite slithy,' Sally whingles. She's proud, puffed, pinkled at the way she snuckled the palaver 'quite' into that fraze. It's her schoolfriend Gina's cyclesay favorite. Whenever Gina's classprez she makes it the priority and all that period the kiddles have to go round stickering 'quite' into every dilog, even if they're making kidspiek. If you can't hang it and Teach catches you, then for each perp you're docked five minis on the line during Net-time. Sally once essayed magic much tribble with 'somewhat' that she blew a full half-per and missed her fav convo with Bai, her best bud in the Philippines.

Gina's classprez again tomorrow, nextcycle, and Sally's prancing, piping, primed. She won't drop a single opt this time. She truloves kindergarten. She has magic much kidspiek to teach to Bai, who ready minds English, but only *parents* spiek that. If he needwants to convo with braveworld webheads he cessitates Sally's tutelage.

'Vitamins,' Mommy digs.

Sally likes magic much playing Teach for Bai, but inhome she's still the babely who drinkies Norange for the nutrients. Sally delikes Norange. Mommy's desimpatic, tho, so Sally squidges her nozzle and pours it indown. The Norange axes through her tubes and flips her scumbler. She waggles, she wiggles, she sighs.

'Let's motor,' sings Sally. She bounces, she trounces, she minds primepath a way to scarf 'vitamins' that decontains slithy Norange.

'Let your father finish his meeting, honey,' Mommy ornerates.

'In the car, quite,' Sally posits, and Daddy warbles, Daddy burbles, Daddy laughs.

'Done anyway,' he nounces. The lectrospecs go glass and his eyes can see her. He huglifts her and wings her around the kitchen. Sally squealies and laughs too.

'Are you ready, Sally?' quares Mommy. 'Are you ready to pick out a friend?'

'Magic,' clares Sally. 'I'm sparked.'

The car trot's singly half a per, but Sally fidgets, fickles, flails. She can't comp how such a twitchy trip could stend so long. Daddy works with the lectrospecs while Mommy keeps an eye on the wheel. She still half dedigs Autodrive.

But soon, soon! Sally's peek-a-viewing out the porto and there's a smartglass building all decked in white, quickclean and sunshining bright like chrome. The car slides, sidles, slows and they're out, out, trambling cross the lot into wing-wide portos that wilkomm them like best buds. *Gracie's Adopt-A-Friend*, prides the sign.

Before they can peek in the rooms they must putter on the squidgy facility lectrospecs and dig an 'educational film' re 'Our Fragile Friends'. Sally grumples but Mommy frownies and she sits tight. The lectrospecs palaver on re 'Friends are not toys' and 'Friends are living beings and must be treated with respect' but Sally's way forward. She minds primepath her new friend just back of that porto, some smartbeast who will trulove her and her it. She will tramble long trips with her friend, let it scumble from her dish, and at darknight it will sleep in her crib. Sally smilies. Her friend will be even primer than Bai in the Philippines, cause Sally half delikes a friend she can't huglift.

Mommy despecs Sally and Sally starts, Sally smarts, Sally dedreams. The film is termo, and she didn't even mind the ending! Mommy laughs and Sally redhots. She trambles to the porto and grabes it wide.

Barks, growls, hoots, meows and screeches crash her ears. A rep in a lime-green zooter bendies down to pot her on the hair. Sally grabes her off and smilies, totalment polite.

'Hello, I'll be your escort today,' intros the green rep. 'Are you looking for anything in particular?'

'Pickeling we a special friend,' Sally prides. Daddy shakes the rep's hand.

'English, honey, the nice lady doesn't know kidspiek,' Daddy warns. 'Children these days, it's like they're using a different *language*,' he clares to the rep, his eyes crinkeling.

'Oh, I understand.' The rep smilies. 'What is kidspiek?'

'Whatever I want,' Sally splains. 'Webhead I, netspiek with kiddles all around the globe.' The rep decomps, but she smilies again.

'She's so cute,' she clares to Daddy. 'What kind of special friend do you want, little girl?'

The animalish noises devolume, and Sally minds the sound of listening. 'Want I . . .' she starts, but Mommy is shakering her head.

'I would like a puppy, please,' Sally fixes.

'We'd like Sally to look around,' Mommy firms. 'Her school's doing an experimental program. Interspecies bonding and all that.' Her eyes flicker round the hallpath and she squidgies Sally's hand tighterer. 'It's up to her.'

'Yes, we've been seeing a few of those recently. Well, you can browse and I'll answer questions as they come,' the green rep clares.

Mommy hounches, Mommy slounches, Mommy bendies down and pushpulls her forward. 'Go ahead, honey – just don't stick your fingers in, all right?'

Sally peek-a-views the hallpath. Magic many portos with interesterating shapes in back! The portos are surfed in smartglass, which letters the sound through but not the stink. She trambles to the closest porto and peek-a-views inside. A big hairy face pressers against the window and eyeballs her back.

'Hi,' gruffs the dog. Sally trippers backwards and tumblies on her prot.

'Too big!' Sally gacks, and the dog grabes the porto with its claws.

'Sorry,' it whingles as they tramble by. 'Sorry. Come back.'

The next porto has oodles of cats. A big orange guy with stripeys and a spotdot of white on his chin stickers his paws upon the smartglass and winkles at Sally. Trigued, Sally sneakpeeks to Mommy and Daddy and the green rep, who are making convo with a little collie dog down the hallpath, delooking at her.

'Are you housetrained?' quares Mommy.

'No,' mits the little collie dog. 'I just got here, but Gracie says I'm a quick learner,' she prides.

Nobody viewing. Sally grabes the porto open and slips, slides, scoots inside.

Cats decornerate and pour round her. 'Me, pick me!' some greet, grabing her legs. Others try to clamble into her arms. Sally droppers on her prot and huglifts the big orange guy.

'You're soft,' he purrums, and blinkies his yellow eyes in surprisement. 'I like this.'

A twitchy calico girl leapups tween Sally and the big orange guy, grabing him out of her huglift.

'*Mine*,' she hissfits to the big orange guy.

Sally delikes the calico, but she minds courtesy. 'What name yours?' she quares. The calico deanswers.

The big orange guy stritches and drops oneside Sally. 'Watch out for her,' he warns. 'She's nasty.'

The calico grumples and slices at a fat gray female who rubbles

Sally's shoulder. 'If you take me home, I'll wash your face for you every night,' the gray one promies, and startups right there. Sally laughs and grabes the calico downaway.

Instant like Sally is swimming, brimming, drowngasping in cats. They crawly all over her, whisping promies, toptrying to grabe her tention. She wants to squealie but she fraids Mommy will punishate her, may-haps even zoomer right home and depromise her a puppy. So she straggles deflow and gacks fur.

'Give her some air, you fools! Do you want to suffocate her?'

Sudden like the oceans of cats breakup into cloudies. The big orange guy trambles from cloudy to cloudy, batwhacking any cats who venttry closemore. 'Can't you see she's just a little one? Let her take the initiative, or you risk coming back here if it's a bad match.'

The cloudies morphose into a circley as the cats stop, drop and stare. Sally leapups and brushflicks her clothes. 'Thankies,' she clares to the big orange guy. 'Name Sally, what yours?'

The big orange guy stritches again and yawnies. 'Call me Maximus,' he intros. 'I'm a genius. I make trouble for fun. What do you do, Sally?'

Sally minds long and hardly. 'Make I friendlies everywhere,' she clares finalment. 'What be a "genius"?'

'A cat who thinks he's better than the rest of us,' quips a black male.

'A cat who talks to walls,' his snaps the calico.

'A cat who draws meaningless patterns in the litter and chases us away when we have to go,' mambles a toothless old white cat in the corner.

Maximus blinkies his yellow eyes and flickers his tail: 'Writing,' he digs. 'I was writing a novel. But I ran out of room.' He sideturns to Sally. 'They don't give us comps here,' he plains. 'What was I supposed to do?'

'That's puke,' his spits the calico. 'Cats can't write.'

'Geniuses can,' fends Maximus.

'Do you know why his owners turned him in?' The old white cat cackles. 'He was teaching himself to *sing*. He was driving them insane.'

'Opera, my friend,' airs orange Maximus. 'Just you wait, it'll be "Maximus the Great" on the webcasts one of these days.'

'I'm not waiting,' the white cat yawnies and winces like it hurts.

'I only have four days left on my tag. I'm certainly not sticking around for you.'

'And how long do *you* have left, Maximus?' the calico glees. 'How many days have you been *docked* for all the trouble you cause?'

Maximus liftups his chin and deanswers.

Sally delikes all the starreling eyes and flattened ears. She trambles for the porto, scattereling the circley. She grabes it open and shut and backs it, sighing.

But Sally isn't in the hallpath – she's in nother room of cats! Wrong porto!

No, she minds, viewing the room's poplis. Not cats. Kittens. She laxes.

'Come to see the new recruits?' Maximus quares at her side. Sally jumps, Sally bumps, Sally drops on her prot again.

'You followfound me,' she cuses.

'Just making sure you get where you're going,' Maximus sures. 'I know the layout here.'

'All right,' Sally grees. The kittens are starreling at Maximus, fraiding his big stripery orangeness and his big yellow eyes. 'Needwant I a puppy, but kittens are tres cutie.'

'By no means the best qualifier for friend selection, but a true statement nonetheless.' Maximus views the fraided kittens for a miniper, then laughs. 'Come one, come all, kids, come see the human. This here is Sally, and she makes friends.'

A little tortoiseshell female batwhacks Sally's shoe. Sally tries to huglift her, but she straggles out of grip.

'Mommy,' she mambles, and trambles into the cornerside.

'They're far more cautious than shelter kittens of years past,' Maximus splains. 'Intelligence is difficult to deal with when five million years of instinct are screaming in your ear.'

Sally minds primepath her puppy back of another door. She stritches toward a twitchy orange kitten, a mini-Maximus, and wuggles her fingies. The orange kitten gigglies and dancers backaway.

The kittens instantlike demind their fraids. 'Tag, tag,' they crile, dashing and diveling cross the smartfloor, still curveling round Sally like she's a mountain they delike tackling.

Sally frownies. 'They deneed us,' she clares to Maximus. 'Where find I the puppies?'

'Don't be silly, girl. Everyone here needs you, and people like you. We're all on two-month probation, you know; the kittens, though they're easier to adopt, live under the same axe that hovers at all our throats.' He makes a crick-sound samelike ripping writepaper and starrels at Sally with his yellow eyes. 'I do not understand humans. How can you possibly choose one friend from the hundreds here?'

'Comp,' ornerates Sally. 'Comp I when meet I the one.'

'That you will, that you will,' mambles Maximus. Then he winkles. 'I think you're right, Sally. You'll make the right decision when the time comes.' He sideturns to the kittens. 'So, do you "comp" that any of these is right?'

Sally leapups and trambles to the next porto. 'I deneed a friend who depaytentions me,' she grumples.

Before she grabes the latch, tho, it opens from backside. A chubbly yellow-skinned woman in a blue flowered shirt backups through, grabing a saucer of brown pebblies.

'Kibble time, kitlings,' she sings, then turnarounds and minds Sally and Maximus cross the smartfloor. She frownies.

'Little girl, you're not supposed to be in here without supervision,' she forms.

Sally sidelooks at Maximus. 'I'm quite supervised,' she clares. 'Go we to the puppies to finder I a special friend.'

The woman sighs. She pears busheled. 'Hello, Pumpkin,' she greets. 'Out of the bag again, I see.'

'Hello, Gracie,' plies Maximus. 'We meet again. And the name's Maximus. I refuse to answer to such an undignified label as . . . as my previous name.'

Gracie putdowns her saucer and the kittens scrimble, scrabble, scoot to make lunch. 'Why must you do this, Pumpkin?' she plains, grabing open the porto to the cat room and hounching low with arms wide, trying to cornerate Sally and Maximus. 'You know this'll lose you another day, and you have so few left already –'

'Two,' digs Maximus, sidelooking at Sally. 'Go ahead and say it.

I have two days left, and when you take off this one you'll put me down tomorrow.'

'You have a good memory,' Gracie comps.

'Memory, schmemory, it says it on my tag and these "windows" make better mirrors.' Maximus hounches too and lashes his tail. 'Sally, don't let anyone tell you that cats can't read backwards.'

'Kay.' Sally scratchers her head. 'What be "put down"?'

The kittens are munching, silentlike thisnow, peek-a-viewing Sally and Gracie and Maximus. Gracie pears sadlike. 'Pumpkin, why?' she scolders. 'Why the constant rebellion? If you could just take a few tips from the others you might have found a home by now.'

'The others!' Maximus hissfaces and shutdowns his eyes. 'Pathetic sheep, every one. I thought if I only spoke to them long enough – but you've trained them too well, or perhaps it's been bred into them by now. They don't want to hear what I have to say. They eat and sleep and shit as you tell them, and toss and turn in nightmares of the euthanasia table!' He sideglances at Sally. 'Kill me if you can, Gracie, but the Sentient Revolution is coming! If my death allows my message to find a foothold in just one mind, it will not be in vain.'

'Yes it will,' catcalls the calico from back of the porto. 'Nobody cares about you, you rabblerouser – I heard you practicing that speech last week.' Gracie inches closeover them, and Sally shrinkles away.

'When I say "go", you run for the door, okay?' mambles Maximus so that singly Sally can auditate. 'She can't get us both.'

'Pumpkin, come quietly or I'll deduct another day,' growls Gracie.

'This is insane,' cuses Maximus. 'Nobody kills *humans* because there are too many, or puts them in involuntary confinement "for their own good".' He blinkies. 'Pardon me, I had forgotten – they *do*, don't they?'

'What do you want?' blursts Gracie, her face squidgied up and her eyes shinyful. 'Do you think I do this because it makes me happy? For every cat here, there are a hundred more starving on the street. This is the only place you're safe, the only place you can find a home and people to love you.'

'And who says we need people to care for us like day-old kittens?' ornerates Maximus, his ears flattered to his head, his voice climbering higher and higher. Sally peek-a-views his eyes and her hair straightups like the time she built her ownfirst comp and pluggered it in. Maximus grows, Maximus glows, he towers on tippytoes like his wholeself is grounding a thousand volts.

'You know what?' Maximus scritches. 'Maybe I *want* to take my chances on the street! Perhaps, rather than escaping, I've been rotting in here for a month and a half in the vain hope that even one of those limpwhiskered dishlickers in there might have the faculties to understand that you and your *charity*, Gracie, are now obsolete!'

Gracie downlunges. 'Run, Sally!' mands Maximus, and dances, dives, fairly flies forward. The kittens splode everywhere with squealies of excitement. Sally zooms for the porto and yankles it wide, scootering through and sliding it to twitchily a whiskerwidth open.

'I think your time is up, Pumpkin,' sniffles Gracie. She is crilering, big droppers of tears leaking outdown her face. 'There are plenty of cats in the back desperate for even half the chance you've had.'

'I have no regrets,' criles Maximus, straggling in Gracie's hands. 'Sally, remember! Call the papers! Call your state representative! 'Tis a far better thing I do today –'

'Can it, you loony cat,' hissfits the calico, and Gracie sneakpeeks at Sally.

'I'll put him back where he belongs,' she clares. 'Puppies are at the end of the hall.'

Maximus getters his head over Gracie's shoulder. His eyes are magic yellow, magic big.

'Goodbye, Sa–'

The cat porto slammers shut.

Sally shutters her porto and standstills in a room of giant dogs, who wender slowlike round the room. Sally's sweetheart is trying to climber into her ears, and she swallows, shivers, squeaks.

'Take me with you,' beggers a big brown dog with a flattish face. 'I only have ten days left.'

Sally peek-a-views her little brownie eyes, her giantish sharp teeth. She has been grabed magic many things to mind, and is minding primepath long and hardly, and she decomps 'put down' and 'kill' and 'revolution' and 'goodbye'. Sally truloves her friendlies, makes convo every day with Bai and Gina and tencent webheads all around the sphere, but Maximus said 'goodbye' much like he was unfriending her, and her scumbler flipflops when she minds primepath why. Nobody has ever unfriended Sally. She's magic sweetie with people.

Sally trambles through the dogs. The big brown dog shutters her eyes and startoffs to whingle, followfinding Sally cross the smartfloor. Maximus needmust be angerous with Sally to unfriend her.

'Please,' whingles the dog. 'I'm afraid.' All the other dogs stop and starrel at Sally, standwaiting for her answer. Sally starrels back. She dropprots and minds long and hardly re magic many things. Then she peek-a-views the porto through the treeforest of the dogs' legs.

'Ten days be . . . ten days is a very long time,' sures Sally, and scurrels through the porto, and the next, on, on through magic more rooms of dogs and cats who plore her with shinyful eyes and sadscared voices.

'Take me, take me home,' they crile, grabing her clothes and her hair and her hands. Sally shutters the last porto with her shoulder.

This room is brimful of puppies. 'Finalment,' minds Sally, and her scumbler flipflops again. Must be the Norange.

She trambles out into the midcenter of the room and again drops expert like on her prot. 'Who needwants trambling home with me?' she quares the puppies.

The puppies blinky back at her, stundled and silentshy. 'Mayhap you?' Sally pointers. The puppy is little and gray, with floopy ears and magic big paws. He has glittery black protuberating eyes.

'Well,' yaps the puppy. 'Well. Maybe.'

Sally tries to huglift the puppy, but he straggles like the kitten. 'Scared,' he criles. 'Scared. Mom.'

'Be I your Mom, I can,' suades Sally. She feelies sicklike and tries to smilie. Today is a special day. Today is a prettyful day. Why can't she defrown?

'I,' mambles the puppy. 'Mom.'

'Right,' grees Sally. 'And make we long trambles in the grassroots and treeforest, we will, and will scumble you from my dish, and at darknight sleep you in my crib.'

'Sleep,' the puppy yelps. 'Scared.'

Sally stends her arms, and the puppy scaredlike climbers into her laptop. Sally huglifts him, tres gentlewisp. He is magic small and tremblies in her hands. Sally minds Maximus, how big and pillowy his side is. This puppy is all skin and bonies and tremble.

'Deready?' Sally quares, grabing the puppy's face in her hands.

'Ready,' mambles the puppy, shuttering his eyes. 'No. Scared.'

Sally peek-a-views out the window. Backside the smartglass her Mommy is making quiet like convo with a little gray terrier type and the green-zootered rep.

'But it's been over a year since the first documented cases,' sclaims Mommy. 'How could this happen?'

'Political pressure is fierce,' the little dog shruggers and dropprots on the floor. 'Especially from the meat and leather industries, anything that uses animal products; if newly sentient creatures get human status, then it will be illegal to own them, buy them, sell them. Society – and the economy – will erupt in chaos, making life miserable for more sentients, both human and animal. There is no clear solution.'

The rep leanies on the wall, tres serious. 'Right now, we're trying to avoid major conflict, move toward some sort of compromise,' she clares. 'A phasing-out of the consumption of sentient meat. Stricter animal-cruelty laws. There are bills working their way through Congress . . . It's an uphill battle, but I think we're making some progress.' She sighs. 'Many are even calling it a "mass hallucination", refusing to acknowledge the problem.'

Daddy is not viewable, then his head sneakpeeks round the corner and he spots Sally.

'Sally!' he growls, grabing the porto and scootering inside. 'I was looking everywhere for you! Miss Gracie says some of the animals aren't very nice, so don't run off like that again, okay?'

'Kay, Daddy,' grees Sally. She sideturns to her puppy. 'Be ready you soonquick,' she sures, and putdowns him on the smartfloor again. 'Make I a good Mom for you, I would.'

'Did you pick one you want?' quares Daddy, grabing her hand.

'Maybe,' hesits Sally. She deexcites. She deminds. She needwants to standstop and mind primepath all the hard things. Stead she letters Daddy pushpull her out the porto and into the hallpath again.

Mommy sneakpeeks over her shoulder at Sally. Her eyes are shinyful like Gracie's. 'Oh, Sally, talk to Sage,' she beggies. 'I know you want a puppy, but I'm sure once you meet her you'll make the right decision.'

Sally grabes open the porto and dropprots tiredlike by the terrier. She's little and hairy like an old gray mop. Sally pots her on the head. 'Good doggie,' she venttries.

Sage littlifts her head and eyeballs Sally. Her eyes are darkling and cloudy. She is blind.

'How old are you, Sally?' quares Sage.

'Fifteencent and two – mean I, four years,' Sally mambles.

'Your parents are leaving this up to you, despite your tender age. Quite trusting of them, don't you think?' quares Sage.

'Yes, ma'am,' grees Sally.

'They want you to make their decision for them.' Sage rollies over and sighs, a deep, cavelike sound for a dog so twitchy. 'But you've already decided,' she churtles.

'Yes, maybe,' ditherates Sally. 'No. Decomp I.' She sideturns to peek-a-view at the puppy, cross the hallpath, through her parents' legs.

'Not angerous,' she whisps to herself. 'Not angerous – scared! Scared, and . . . sad.' What does Maximus fraid? Why is he sad? Her scumbler is flipping again. Sally deknows what Maximus fraids, but she fraids the answer.

Sage's teeny tail thumpers on the smartfloor and she openups her mouth, her purplish tongue raspering in-and-out, in-and-out. 'Remember,' she pantles. 'The choice is yours, and yours alone. Only you can choose your special friend.'

Sally squidges her eyes up tightlike and minds long and hardly. She sneakpeeks at the puppy, then at Mommy's face.

Sally sighs. Sally standups. Sally smiles.

'Thankies,' she cites.

'Anytime,' Sage laughs. 'Anytime from now on.'

Sally trambles forward and grabes open the porto.

'Well?' quares Mommy.

'*Your* friend Sage,' Sally clares. 'Needwant I *mine*.' She sideturns and trambles, shambles, shoots down the hallpath, past Mommy and Daddy, past the green-zootered escort, past the puppies, past the dogs, past the kittens and the cats. She yankpulls the first cat porto wide open and stoppers.

The cats starrel back at her.

'Too late,' hissmilies the calico. 'They've taken him in the *back room.*'

Sally minds nother porto back of the cat room. This porto is open just a twitch. She auditates shrieks of surprisement and furyness from back of it. Sally scurrels to the porto and outflings it magic hardly that it bangers the wall.

'Maximus!' she squealies. 'Herecome to me, loony cat!'

A crishcrash of shattereling glass upgoes and droppering instruments and a big fluffy cannonball shoots, scoots, superlights round the corner and knockdowns Sally magic hardly.

'Right decisionating,' clares Sally, tappering her forehead. 'Comping . . . now. Needwant I a fuzzery orange pillow to singify me lullabies re the Sentient Revolution.'

Maximus nibblies her nose and upcurlies on her chest. 'Kid, I take back everything I just said about you,' he nounces.

Gracie standstills over them, still sniffling. Sally frownies and huglifts Maximus, sittering up and clambling to her feet. Maximus sneakpeeks at Gracie and tres liberately putters his paws round Sally's neck, tuckling his flat orange head neath her chin.

'You heard her,' he purrums, yellowy eyes sparkling like struckered steel.

'Wow, that cat's almost as big as you are,' sclaims Daddy, skiddering through the porto. Mommy has a funnery happylike spression on her face.

'Are you sure you can stand him?' quares Gracie, smilying and leanering her head against the portoframe. 'He's one helluva lot of heavily opinionated feline for such a little girl.'

'Quite sure,' clares Sally.

The carriers are in the trunk, but Maximus and Sage are up frontriding in carseats, Maximus on Sally's lap and Sage on Mommy's. Daddy dehas a special friend, but he huggers Mommy and pots Sage on the head.

When the twitchy trip is termo, Sally doesn't even mind at first. She and Maximus are deep in convo, plannering a whole list of hijinks to perp when they outscape the car.

'First,' clares Maximus, lashing his orange stripery tail, 'First I want to see shelters made voluntary or by court order only by the end of the year. We can beat this overpopulation thing without mandatory euthanasia.'

'Swing it, Maximus, you can,' grees Sally. 'Writerup a letter on comp. Show I you how.'

'Hmmm . . . Propaganda, politics . . .' The big orange cat cleaners a paw. 'I'll need some books on civil law . . .'

'Webhead I,' prides Sally. 'Comp I where. Or if decomp I askie the kiddles in class or Bai in the Philippines. Askie I friendlies everywhere.'

'Sally, time to get out,' digs Mommy.

Maximus jumpers out and peek-a-views up at Sally's house. He standstills for a long millicycle and Sally strokers his back.

'Home mine, home yours,' clares Sally.

'Home,' peats Maximus, his eyes rounder than quarters.

Maximus and Sally and Mommy and Daddy go long tramble in the treeforest and grassroots back of Sally's house, Sally and Maximus scussing their planners for the Sentient Revolution which will upsweep the world. At dinner Maximus scumbles from Sally's dish, but dedirectlike cause he has an owndish on the smartfloor with his namie in orange letters and Sally keepers sneakying chicken bits into it. Mommy denotes this subterfuge – she's doing likesame with Sage, who sitters and smilies and munchies while she auditates the revolutionaries refuelering.

At darknight Sally downlies in her crib and Maximus upcurlies on her pillow and putters his paws on her eyelids.

'It may get violent,' he tinues, blinkering sleepylike. 'I don't know, I've never done this before. But don't worry, Sally,' he sures her, 'I'll take care of you.'

'I'm classprez next tencycle,' Sally nounces. 'Cyclesay word mine be "sentient".'

'And Sage will help.' Maximus lickies Sally's forehead. 'She'll know how to pull this off when we get stuck. Bit of luck, your mother taking to her like that.'

'Love you, Maximus,' clares Sally, and yawnies. 'Best bud you. Special friend.'

'And I love you, Sally,' clares Maximus back of a long pause, but Sally's already dreamying primepath all the venttries they'll make tomorrow, nextcycle. Two yellowy eyes like lamplights burnglow through the darkness as he templates Sally's face, then, blinkery by stended blink, go out. Maximus dreamies re slip-slithering through the smooth silent grassroots, huntering chubbly mice who detalk and dethink politics. Instinct calls.

Sally dreamies re the Revolution.

The Store of the Worlds

ROBERT SHECKLEY

Mr Wayne came to the end of the long, shoulder-high mound of grey rubble, and there was the Store of the Worlds. It was exactly as his friends had described: a small shack constructed of bits of lumber, parts of cars, a piece of galvanized iron and a few rows of crumbling bricks, all daubed over with a watery blue paint.

Mr Wayne glanced back down the long lane of rubble to make sure he hadn't been followed. He tucked his parcel more firmly under his arm; then, with a little shiver at his own audacity, he opened the door and slipped inside.

'Good morning,' the proprietor said.

He, too, was exactly as described: a tall, crafty-looking old fellow with narrow eyes and a downcast mouth. His name was Tompkins. He sat in an old rocking chair, and perched on the back of it was a blue and green parrot. There was one other chair in the store, and a table. On the table was a rusted hypodermic.

'I've heard about your store from friends,' Mr Wayne said.

'Then you know my price,' Tompkins said. 'Have you brought it?'

'Yes,' said Mr Wayne, holding up his parcel. 'But I want to ask first –'

'They always want to ask,' Tompkins said to the parrot, who blinked. 'Go ahead, ask.'

'I want to know what really happens.'

Tompkins sighed. 'What happens is this. You pay me my fee. I give you an injection which knocks you out. Then, with the aid of certain gadgets which I have in the back of the store, I liberate your mind.'

Tompkins smiled as he said that, and his silent parrot seemed to smile, too.

'What happens then?' Mr Wayne asked.

'Your mind, liberated from its body, is able to choose from the countless probability-worlds which the Earth casts off in every second of its existence.'

Grinning now, Tompkins sat up in his rocking chair and began to show signs of enthusiasm.

'Yes, my friend, though you might not have suspected it, from the moment this battered Earth was born out of the sun's fiery womb, it cast off its alternate probability-worlds. Worlds without end, emanating from events large and small; every Alexander and every amoeba creating worlds, just as ripples will spread in a pond no matter how big or how small the stone you throw. Doesn't every object cast a shadow? Well, my friend, the Earth itself is four-dimensional; therefore it casts three-dimensional shadows, solid reflections of itself through every moment of its being. Millions, billions of Earths! An infinity of Earths! And your mind, liberated by me, will be able to select any of these worlds, and to live upon it for a while.'

Mr Wayne was uncomfortably aware that Tompkins sounded like a circus barker, proclaiming marvels that simply couldn't exist. But, Mr Wayne reminded himself, things had happened within his own lifetime which he would never have believed possible. Never! So perhaps the wonders that Tompkins spoke of were possible, too.

Mr Wayne said, 'My friends also told me – '

'That I was an out-and-out fraud?' Tompkins asked.

'Some of them *implied* that,' Mr Wayne said cautiously. 'But I try to keep an open mind. They also said – '

'I know what your dirty-minded friends said. They told you about the fulfilment of desire. Is that what you want to hear about?'

'Yes,' said Mr Wayne. 'They told me that whatever I wished for – whatever I wanted – '

'Exactly,' Tompkins said. 'The thing could work in no other way. There are the infinite worlds to choose among. Your mind chooses, and is guided only by desire. Your deepest desire is the only thing that counts. If you have been harbouring a secret dream of murder – '

'Oh hardly, hardly!' cried Mr Wayne.

'– then you will go to a world where you *can* murder, where you can roll in blood, where you can outdo Sade or Caesar, or whoever your idol may be. Suppose it's power you want? Then you'll choose a world where you are a god, literally and actually. A blood-thirsty Juggernaut, perhaps, or an all-wise Buddha.'

'I doubt very much if I – '

'There are other desires, too,' Tompkins said. 'All heavens and all hells. Unbridled sexuality. Gluttony, drunkenness, love, fame – anything you want.'

'Amazing!' said Mr Wayne.

'Yes,' Tompkins agreed. 'Of course, my little list doesn't exhaust all the possibilities, all the combinations and permutations of desire. For all I know you might want a simple, placid, pastoral existence on a South Seas island among idealized natives.'

'That sounds more like me,' Mr Wayne said, with a shy laugh.

'But who knows?' Tompkins asked. 'Even you might not know what your true desires are. They might involve your own death.'

'Does that happen often?' Mr Wayne asked anxiously.

'Occasionally.'

'I wouldn't want to die,' Mr Wayne said.

'It hardly ever happens,' Tompkins said, looking at the parcel in Mr Wayne's hands.

'If you say so . . . But how do I know all this is real? Your fee is extremely high, it'll take everything I own. And for all I know, you'll give me a drug and I'll just *dream!* Everything I own just for a – a shot of heroin and a lot of fancy words!'

Tompkins smiled reassuringly. 'The experience has no drug-like quality about it. And no sensation of a dream, either.'

'If it's *true,*' Mr Wayne said, a little petulantly, 'why can't I stay in the world of my desire for good?'

'I'm working on that,' Tompkins said. 'That's why I charge so high a fee; to get materials, to experiment. I'm trying to find a way of making the transition permanent. So far I haven't been able to loosen the cord that binds a man to his own Earth – and pulls him back to it. Not even the great mystics could cut that cord, except with death. But I still have my hopes.'

'It would be a great thing if you succeeded,' Mr Wayne said politely.

'Yes it would!' Tompkins cried, with a surprising burst of passion.

'For then I'd turn my wretched shop into an escape hatch! My process would be free then, free for everyone! Everyone would go to the Earth of their desires, the Earth that really suited them, and leave *this* damned place to the rats and worms –'

Tompkins cut himself off in mid-sentence, and became icy calm. 'But I fear my prejudices are showing. I can't offer a permanent escape from the Earth yet; not one that doesn't involve death. Perhaps I never will be able to. For now, all I can offer you is a vacation, a change, taste of another world, and a look at your own desires. You know my fee. I'll refund it if the experience isn't satisfactory.'

'That's good of you,' Mr Wayne said, quite earnestly. 'But there's that other matter my friends told me about. The ten years off my life.'

'That can't be helped,' Tompkins said, 'and can't be refunded. My process is a tremendous strain on the nervous system, and life-expectancy is shortened accordingly. That's one of the reasons why our so-called government has declared my process illegal.'

'But they don't enforce the ban very firmly,' Mr Wayne said.

'No. Officially the process is banned as a harmful fraud. But officials are men, too. They'd like to leave this Earth, just like everyone else.'

'The cost,' Mr Wayne mused, gripping his parcel tightly. 'And ten years off my life! For the fulfilment of my secret desires . . . Really, I must give this some thought.'

'Think away,' Tompkins said indifferently.

All the way home Mr Wayne thought about it. When his train reached Port Washington, Long Island, he was still thinking. And driving his car from the station to his home he was still thinking about Tompkins's crafty old face, and worlds of probability, and the fulfilment of desire.

But when he stepped inside his house, those thoughts had to stop. Janet, his wife, wanted him to speak sharply to the maid, who had been drinking again. His son Tommy wanted help with the sloop, which was to be launched tomorrow. And his baby daughter wanted to tell him about her day in kindergarten.

Mr Wayne spoke pleasantly but firmly to the maid. He helped Tommy put the final coat of copper paint on the sloop's bottom, and he listened to Peggy tell about her adventures in the playground.

Later, when the children were in bed and he and Janet were alone in their living room, she asked him if something were wrong.

'Wrong?'

'You seem to be worried about something,' Janet said. 'Did you have a bad day at the office?'

'Oh, just the usual sort of thing . . .'

He certainly was not going to tell Janet, or anyone else, that he had taken the day off and gone to see Tompkins in his crazy old Store of the Worlds. Nor was he going to speak about the right every man should have, once in his life-time, to fulfil his most secret desires. Janet, with her good common sense, would never understand that.

The next days at the office were extremely hectic. All of Wall Street was in a mild panic over events in the Middle East and in Asia, and stocks were reacting accordingly. Mr Wayne settled down to work. He tried not to think of the fulfilment of desire at the cost of everything he possessed, with ten years of his life thrown in for good measure. It was crazy! Old Tompkins must be insane!

On weekends he went sailing with Tommy. The old sloop was behaving very well, making practically no water through her bottom seams. Tommy wanted a new suit of racing sails, but Mr Wayne sternly rejected that. Perhaps next year, if the market looked better. For now, the old sails would have to do.

Sometimes at night, after the children were asleep, he and Janet would go sailing. Long Island Sound was quiet then, and cool. Their boat glided past the blinking buoys, sailing towards the swollen yellow moon.

'I *know* something's on your mind,' Janet said.

'Darling, please!'

'Is there something you're keeping from me?'

'Nothing!'

'Are you sure? Are you absolutely sure?'

'Absolutely sure.'

'Then put your arms around me. That's right . . .'

And the sloop sailed itself for a while.

Desire and fulfilment . . . But autumn came, and the sloop had to be hauled. The stock market regained some stability, but Peggy caught the measles. Tommy wanted to know the differences between ordinary bombs, atom bombs, hydrogen bombs, cobalt bombs, and all the other kinds of bombs that were in the news. Mr Wayne explained to the best of his ability. And the maid quit unexpectedly.

Secret desires were all very well. Perhaps he *did* want to kill someone, or live on a South Seas island. But there were responsibilities to consider. He had two growing children, and a better wife than he deserved.

Perhaps around Christmas time . . .

But in mid-winter there was a fire in the unoccupied guest bedroom due to defective wiring. The firemen put out the blaze without much damage, and no one was hurt. But it put any thought of Tompkins out of his mind for a while. First the bedroom had to be repaired, for Mr Wayne was very proud of his gracious old house.

Business was still frantic and uncertain due to the international situation. Those Russians, those Arabs, those Greeks, those Chinese. The intercontinental missiles, the atom bombs, the sputniks . . . Mr Wayne spent long days at the office, and sometimes evenings, too. Tommy caught the mumps. A part of the roof had to be re-shingled. And then already it was time to consider the spring launching of the sloop.

A year had passed, and he'd had very little time to think of secret desires. But perhaps next year. In the meantime –

'Well?' said Tompkins. 'Are you all right?'

'Yes, quite all right,' Mr Wayne said. He got up from the chair and rubbed his forehead.

'Do you want a refund?' Tompkins asked.

'No. The experience was quite satisfactory.'

'They always are,' Tompkins said, winking lewdly at the parrot. 'Well, what was yours?'

'A world of the recent past,' Mr Wayne said.

'A lot of them are. Did you find out about your secret desire? Was it murder? Or a South Seas island?'

'I'd rather not discuss it,' Mr Wayne said, pleasantly but firmly.

'A lot of people won't discuss it with me,' Tompkins said sulkily. 'I'll be damned if I know why.'

'Because – well, I think the world of one's secret desire feels sacred, somehow. No offence . . . Do you think you'll ever be able to make it permanent? The world of one's choice, I mean?'

The old man shrugged his shoulders. 'I'm trying. If I succeed, you'll hear about it. Everyone will.'

'Yes, I suppose so.' Mr Wayne undid his parcel and laid its contents on the table. The parcel contained a pair of army boots, a knife, two coils of copper wire, and three small cans of corned beef.

Tompkins's eyes glittered for a moment. 'Quite satisfactory,' he said. 'Thank you.'

'Good-bye,' said Mr Wayne. 'And thank *you*.'

Mr Wayne left the shop and hurried down to the end of the lane of grey rubble. Beyond it, as far as he could see, lay flat fields of rubble, brown and grey and black. Those fields, stretching to every horizon, were made of the twisted corpses of cities, the shattered remnants of trees, and the fine white ash that once was human flesh and bone.

'Well,' Mr Wayne said to himself, 'at least we gave as good as we got.'

That year in the past had cost him everything he owned, and ten years of life thrown in for good measure. Had it been a dream? It was still worth it! But now he had to put away all thought of Janet and the children. That was finished, unless Tompkins perfected his process. Now he had to think about his own survival.

With the aid of his wrist geiger he found a deactivated lane through the rubble. He'd better get back to the shelter before dark, before the rats came out. If he didn't hurry he'd miss the evening potato ration.

Jokester

ISAAC ASIMOV

Noel Meyerhof consulted the list he had prepared and chose which item was to be first. As usual, he relied mainly on intuition.

He was dwarfed by the machine he faced, though only the smallest portion of the latter was in view. That didn't matter. He spoke with the offhand confidence of one who thoroughly knew he was master.

'Johnson,' he said, 'came home unexpectedly from a business trip to find his wife in the arms of his best friend. He staggered back and said, "Max! I'm married to the lady so I *have* to. But why you?" '

Meyerhof thought: Okay, let that trickle down into its guts and gurgle about a bit.

And a voice behind him said, 'Hey.'

Meyerhof erased the sound of that monosyllable and put the circuit he was using into neutral. He whirled and said, 'I'm working. Don't you knock?'

He did not smile as he customarily did in greeting Timothy Whistler, a senior analyst with whom he dealt as often as with any. He frowned as he would have for an interruption by a stranger, wrinkling his thin face into a distortion that seemed to extend to his hair, rumpling it more than ever.

Whistler shrugged. He wore his white lab coat with his fists pressing down within its pockets and creasing it into tense vertical lines. 'I knocked. You didn't answer. The operations signal wasn't on.'

Meyerhof grunted. It wasn't at that. He'd been thinking about this new project too intensively and he was forgetting little details.

And yet he could scarcely blame himself for that. This thing was important.

He didn't know why it was, of course. Grand Masters rarely did.

That's what made them Grand Masters; the fact that they were beyond reason. How else could the human mind keep up with that ten-mile-long lump of solidified reason that men called Multivac, the most complex computer ever built?

Meyerhof said, 'I *am* working. Is there something important on your mind?'

'Nothing that can't be postponed. There are a few holes in the answer on the hyperspatial –' Whistler did a double take and his face took on a rueful look of uncertainty. '*Working?*'

'Yes. What about it?'

'But –' He looked about, staring into the crannies of the shallow room that faced the banks upon banks of relays that formed a small portion of Multivac. 'There isn't anyone here at that.'

'Who said there was, or should be?'

'You were telling one of your jokes, weren't you?'

'And?'

Whistler forced a smile. 'Don't tell me you were telling a joke to Multivac?'

Meyerhof stiffened. 'Why not?'

'Were you?'

'Yes.'

'Why?'

Meyerhof stared the other down. 'I don't have to account to you. Or to anyone.'

'Good Lord, of course not. I was curious, that's all . . . But then, if you're working, I'll leave.' He looked about once more, frowning.

'Do so,' said Meyerhof. His eyes followed the other out and then he activated the operations signal with a savage punch of his finger.

He strode the length of the room and back, getting himself in hand. Damn Whistler! Damn them all! Because he didn't bother to hold those technicians, analysts, and mechanics at the proper social distance, because he treated them as though they, too, were creative artists, they took these liberties.

He thought grimly: They can't even tell jokes decently.

And instantly that brought him back to the task in hand. He sat down again. Devil take them all.

He threw the proper Multivac circuit back into operation and said, 'The ship's steward stopped at the rail of the ship during a particularly rough ocean crossing and gazed compassionately at the man whose slumped position over the rail and intensity of gaze towards the depths betokened all too well the ravages of seasickness.

'Gently, the steward patted the man's shoulder. "Cheer up, sir," he murmured. "I know it seems bad, but really, you know, nobody ever dies of seasickness.'

'The afflicted gentleman lifted his greenish, tortured face to his comforter and gasped in hoarse accents, "Don't say that, man. For Heaven's sake, don't say that. It's only the hope of dying that's keeping me alive."'

Timothy Whistler, a bit preoccupied, nevertheless smiled and nodded as he passed the secretary's desk. She smiled back at him.

Here, he thought, was an archaic item in this computer-ridden world of the twenty-first century, a human secretary. But then perhaps it was natural that such an institution should survive here in the very citadel of computerdom; in the gigantic world corporation that handled Multivac. With Multivac filling the horizons, lesser computers for trivial tasks would have been in poor taste.

Whistler stepped into Abram Trask's office. That government official paused in his careful task of lighting a pipe; his dark eyes flicked in Whistler's direction and his beaked nose stood out sharply and prominently against the rectangle of window behind him.

'Ah, there, Whistler. Sit down. Sit down.'

Whistler did so. 'I think we've got a problem, Trask.'

Trask half-smiled. 'Not a technical one, I hope. I'm just an innocent politician.' (It was one of his favourite phrases.)

'It involves Meyerhof.'

Trask sat down instantly and looked acutely miserable. 'Are you sure?'

'Reasonably sure.'

Whistler understood the other's sudden unhappiness well. Trask was the government official in charge of the Division of Computers and Automation of the Department of the Interior. He was expected to deal with matters of policy involving the human satellites of Multivac, just as those technically trained satellites were expected to deal with Multivac itself.

But a Grand Master was more than just a satellite. More, even, than just a human.

Early in the history of Multivac, it had become apparent that the bottleneck was the questioning procedure. Multivac could answer the problems of humanity, *all* the problems, if – *if* it were asked meaningful questions. But as knowledge accumulated at an ever-faster rate, it became ever more difficult to locate those meaningful questions.

Reason alone wouldn't do. What was needed was a rare type of intuition; the same faculty of mind (only much more intensified) that made a Grand Master at chess. A mind was needed of the sort that could see through the quadrillions of chess patterns to find the one best move, and do it in a matter of minutes.

Trask moved restlessly. 'What's Meyerhof been doing?'

'He's introduced a line of questioning that I find disturbing.'

'Oh, come on, Whistler. Is that all? You can't stop a Grand Master from going through any line of questioning he chooses. Neither you nor I are equipped to judge the worth of his questions. You know that. I know you know that.'

'I do. Of course. But I also know Meyerhof. Have you ever met him socially?'

'Good Lord, no. Does anyone meet any Grand Master socially?'

'Don't take that attitude, Trask. They're human and they're to be pitied. Have you ever thought what it must be like to be a Grand Master; to know there are only some twelve like you in the world; to know that only one or two come up per generation; that the world depends on you; that a thousand mathematicians, logicians, psychologists, and physical scientists wait on you?'

Trask shrugged and muttered, 'Good Lord, I'd feel king of the world.'

'I don't think you would,' said the senior analyst. 'They feel kings of nothing. They have no equal to talk to, no sensation of belonging. Listen. Meyerhof never misses a chance to get together with the boys. He isn't married, naturally; he doesn't drink; he has no natural social touch – yet he forces himself into company because he must. And do you know what he does when he gets together with us, and that's at least once a week?'

'I haven't the least idea,' said the government man. 'This is all new to me.'

'He's a jokester.'

'What?'

'He tells jokes. Good ones. He's terrific. He can take any story, however old and dull, and make it sound good. It's the way he tells it. He has a flair.'

'I see. Well, good.'

'Or bad. These jokes are important to him.' Whistler put both elbows on Trask's desk, bit at a thumbnail and stared into the air. 'He's different, he knows he's different, and these jokes are the one way he feels he can get the rest of us ordinary schmoes to accept him. We laugh, we howl, we clap him on the back and even forget he's a Grand Master. It's the only hold he has on the rest of us.'

'This is all interesting. I didn't know you were such a psychologist. Still, where does this lead?'

'Just this. What do you suppose happens if Meyerhof runs out of jokes?'

'What?' The government man stared blankly.

'If he starts repeating himself? If his audience starts laughing less heartily, or stops laughing altogether? It's his only hold on our approval. Without it, he'll be alone and then what would happen to him? After all, Trask, he's one of the dozen men mankind can't do without. We can't let anything happen to him. I don't mean just physical things. We can't even let him get too unhappy. Who knows how that might affect his intuition?'

'Well, has he started repeating himself?'

'Not as far as I know, but I think *he* thinks he has.'

'Why do you say that?'

'Because I've heard him telling jokes to Multivac.'

'Oh, no.'

'Accidentally. I walked in on him and he threw me out. He was savage. He's usually good-natured enough, and I consider it a bad sign that he was so upset at the intrusion. But the fact remains that he was telling a joke to Multivac, and I'm convinced it was one of a series.'

'But why?'

Whistler shrugged and rubbed a hand fiercely across his chin. 'I have thought about that. I think he's trying to build up a store of jokes in Multivac's memory banks in order to get back new variations. You see what I mean? He's planning a mechanical jokester, so that he can have an infinite number of jokes at hand and never fear running out.'

'Good Lord!'

'Objectively, there may be nothing wrong with that, but I consider it a bad sign when a Grand Master starts using Multivac for his personal problems. Any Grand Master has a certain inherent mental instability and he should be watched. Meyerhof may be approaching a borderline beyond which we lose a Grand Master.'

Trask said blankly, 'What are you suggesting I do?'

'You can check me. I'm too close to him to judge well, maybe, and judging humans isn't my particular talent, anyway. You're a politician; it's more your talent.'

'Judging humans, perhaps, not Grand Masters.'

'They're human, too. Besides, who else is to do it?'

The fingers of Trask's hand struck his desk in rapid succession over and over like a slow and muted roll of drums.

'I suppose I'll have to,' he said.

Meyerhof said to Multivac, 'The ardent swain, picking a bouquet of wildflowers for his loved one, was disconcerted to find himself, suddenly, in the same field with a large bull of unfriendly appearance which, gazing at him steadily, pawed the ground in a threatening manner. The young man, spying a farmer on the other side of a fairly distant fence, shouted, "Hey mister, is that bull safe?' The farmer surveyed the situation with a critical eye, spat to one side and called back, "He's safe as anything." He spat again, and added, "Can't say the same about you, though."'

Meyerhof was about to pass on to the next when the summons came.

It wasn't really a summons. No one could summon a Grand Master. It was only a message that Division Head Trask would like very much to see Grand Master Meyerhof if Grand Master Meyerhof could spare him the time.

Meyerhof might, with impunity, have tossed the message to one side and continued with whatever he was doing. He was not subject to discipline.

On the other hand, were he to do that, they would continue to bother him – oh, very respectfully, but they would continue to bother him.

So he neutralized the pertinent circuits of Multivac and locked them into place. He put the freeze signal on his office so that no one would dare enter in his absence and left for Trask's office.

Trask coughed and felt a bit intimidated by the sullen fierceness of the other's look. He said, 'We have not had occasion to know one another, Grand Master, to my great regret.'

'I have reported to you,' said Meyerhof stiffly.

Trask wondered what lay behind these keen, wild eyes. It was difficult for him to imagine Meyerhof, with his thin face, his dark, straight hair, intense air, ever unbending long enough to tell funny stories.

He said, 'Reports are not a social acquaintance. I – I have been given to understand you have a marvellous fund of anecdotes.'

'I am a jokester, sir. That's the phrase people use. A jokester.'

'They haven't used the phrase to me, Grand Master. They have said –'

'The hell with them! I don't care what they've said. See here, Trask, do you want to hear a joke?' He leaned forward across the desk, his eyes narrowed.

'By all means. Certainly,' said Trask, with an effort at heartiness.

'All right. Here's the joke: Mrs Jones stared at the fortune card that had emerged from the weighing machine in response to her husband's penny. She said, "It says here, George, that you're suave, intelligent, farseeing, industrious, and attractive to women." With that, she turned the card over and added, "And they have your weight wrong, too."'

Trask laughed. It was almost impossible not to. Although the punch line was predictable, the surprising facility with which Meyerhof had produced just the tone of contemptuous disdain in the woman's voice, and the cleverness with which he had contorted the lines of his face to suit that tone carried the politician helplessly into laughter.

Meyerhof said sharply, 'Why is that funny?'

Trask sobered. 'I beg your pardon.'

'I said why is that funny? Why do you laugh?'

'Well,' said Trask, trying to be reasonable, 'the last line put everything that preceded in a new light. The unexpectedness –'

'The point is,' said Meyerhof, 'that I have pictured a husband being humiliated by his wife; a marriage that is such a failure that the wife is convinced that her husband lacks any virtue. Yet you laugh at that. If you were the husband, would you find it funny?'

He waited a moment in thought, then said, 'Try this one, Trask: Abner was seated at his wife's sickbed, weeping uncontrollably, when his wife, mustering the dregs of her strength, drew herself up to one elbow.

'"Abner," she whispered, "Abner, I cannot go to my Maker without confessing my misdeed."

'"Not now," muttered the stricken husband. "Not now, my dear. Lie back and rest."

'"I cannot," she cried. "I must tell, or my soul will never know peace. I have been unfaithful to you, Abner. In this very house, not one month ago –"

'"Hush, dear," soothed Abner. "I know all about it. Why else have I poisoned you?"'

Trask tried to maintain equanimity but did not succeed. He suppressed a chuckle imperfectly.

Meyerhof said, 'So that's funny, too. Adultery. Murder. All funny.'

'Well, now,' said Trask, 'books have been written analysing humour.'

'True enough,' said Meyerhof, 'and I've read a number of them. What's more, I've read most of them to Multivac. Still, the people who write the books are just guessing. Some of them say we laugh because we feel superior to the people in the joke. Some say it is because of a suddenly realized incongruity or a sudden relief from tension, or a sudden reinterpretation of events. Is there any simple reason? Different people laugh at different jokes. No joke is universal. Some people don't laugh at any joke. Yet what may be most important is that man is the only animal with a true sense of humour: the only animal that laughs.'

Trask said suddenly, 'I understand. You're trying to analyse humour. That's why you're transmitting a series of jokes to Multivac.'

'Who told you I was doing that? . . . Never mind, it was Whistler. I remember, now. He surprised me at it. Well, what about it?'

'Nothing at all.'

'You don't dispute my right to add anything I wish to Multivac's general fund of knowledge, or to ask any question I wish?'

'No, not at all,' said Trask hastily. 'As a matter of fact, I have no doubt that this will open the way to new analyses of great interest to psychologists.'

'Hmp. Maybe. Just the same, there's something plaguing me that's more important than just the general analysis of humour. There's a specific question I have to ask. Two of them, really.'

'Oh? What's that?' Trask wondered if the other would answer. There would be no way of compelling him if he chose not to.

But Meyerhof said, 'The first question is this: Where do all these jokes come from?'

'What?'

'Who makes them up? Listen! About a month ago, I spent an evening swapping jokes. As usual, I told most of them and, as usual, the fools laughed. Maybe they really thought the jokes were funny and maybe they were just humouring me. In any case, one creature took the liberty of slapping me on the back and saying, "Meyerhof, you know more jokes than any ten people I know."

'I'm sure he was right, but it gave rise to a thought. I don't know how many hundreds, or perhaps thousands, of jokes I've told at one time or another in my life, yet the fact is I never made up one. Not one. I'd only repeated them. My only contribution was to tell them. To begin with, I'd either heard them or read them. And the source of my hearing or reading didn't make up the jokes, either. I never met anyone who ever claimed to have constructed a joke. It's always "I heard a good one the other day," and "Heard any good ones lately?"

'*All the jokes are old!* That's why jokes exhibit such a social lag. They still deal with seasickness, for instance, when that's easily prevented these days and never experienced. Or they'll deal with fortune-giving weighing machines, like the joke I told you, when such machines are found only in antique shops. Well, then, who makes up the jokes?'

Trask said, 'Is *that* what you're trying to find out?' It was on the tip of Trask's tongue to add: Good Lord, who cares? He forced that impulse down. A Grand Master's questions were always meaningful.

'Of course that's what I'm trying to find out. Think of it this way. It's not just that jokes happen to be old. They *must* be old to be enjoyed. It's essential that a joke not be original. There's one variety of humour that is, or can be, original and that's the pun. I've heard puns that were obviously made up on the spur of the moment. I have made some up myself. But no one laughs at such puns. You're not supposed to. You groan. The better the pun, the louder the groan. Original humour is not laugh-provoking. Why?'

'I'm sure I don't know.'

'All right. Let's find out. Having given Multivac all the information I thought advisable on the general topic of humour, I am now feeding it selected jokes.'

Trask found himself intrigued. 'Selected how?' he asked.

'I don't know,' said Meyerhof. 'They felt like the right ones. I'm Grand Master, you know.'

'Oh, agreed, agreed.'

'From those jokes and the general philosophy of humour, my first request will be for Multivac to trace the origin of the jokes, if it can. Since Whistler is in on this and since he has seen fit to report it to you, have him down in Analysis the day after tomorrow. I think he'll have a bit of work to do.'

'Certainly. May I attend, too?'

Meyerhof shrugged. Trask's attendance was obviously a matter of indifference to him.

Meyerhof had selected the last in the series with particular care. What that care consisted of, he could not have said, but he had revolved a dozen possibilities in his mind, and over and over again had tested each for some indefinable quality of meaningfulness.

He said, 'Ug, the caveman, observed his mate running to him in tears, her leopard-skin skirt in disorder. "Ug," she cried, distraught, "do something quickly. A sabre-toothed tiger has entered Mother's cave. Do something!" Ug grunted, picked up his well-gnawed buffalo bone and said, "Why do anything? Who the hell cares what happens to a sabre-toothed tiger?" '

It was then that Meyerhof asked his two questions and leaned back, closing his eyes. He was done.

'I saw absolutely nothing wrong,' said Trask to Whistler. 'He told me what he was doing readily enough and it was odd but legitimate.'

'What he *claimed* he was doing,' said Whistler.

'Even so, I can't stop a Grand Master on opinion alone. He seemed queer but, after all, Grand Masters are supposed to seem queer. I didn't think him insane.'

'Using Multivac to find the source of jokes?' muttered the senior analyst. 'That's not insane?'

'How can we tell?' asked Trask irritably. 'Science has advanced to the point where the only meaningful questions left are the ridiculous ones. The sensible ones have been thought of, asked, and answered long ago.'

'It's no use. I'm bothered.'

'Maybe, but there's no choice now, Whistler. We'll see Meyerhof and you can do the necessary analysis of Multivac's response, if any. As for me, my only job is to handle the red tape. Good Lord, I don't even know what a senior analyst such as yourself is supposed to do, except analyse, and that doesn't help me any.'

Whistler said, 'It's simple enough. A Grand Master like Meyerhof asks questions and Multivac automatically formulates it into quantities and operations. The necessary machinery for converting words to symbols is what makes up most of the bulk of Multivac. Multivac then gives the answer in quantities and operations, but it doesn't translate that back into words except in the most simple and routine cases. If it were designed to solve the general retranslation problem, its bulk would have to be quadrupled at least.'

'I see. Then it's your job to translate these symbols into words?'

'My job and that of other analysts. We use smaller, specially designed computers whenever necessary.' Whistler smiled grimly. 'Like the

Delphic priestess of ancient Greece, Multivac gives oracular and obscure answers. Only we have translators, you see.'

They had arrived. Meyerhof was waiting.

Whistler said briskly. 'What circuits did you use, Grand Master?'

Meyerhof told him and Whistler went to work.

Trask tried to follow what was happening, but none of it made sense. The government official watched a spool unreel with a pattern of dots in endless incomprehensibility. Grand Master Meyerhof stood indifferently to one side while Whistler surveyed the pattern as it emerged. The analyst had put on headphones and a mouthpiece, and at intervals murmured a series of instructions which, at some far-off place, guided assistants through electronic contortions in other computers.

Occasionally, Whistler listened, then punched combinations on a complex keyboard marked with symbols that looked vaguely mathematical but weren't.

A good deal more than an hour's time elapsed.

The frown on Whistler's face grew deeper. Once, he looked up at the two others and began, 'This is unbel –' and turned back to his work.

Finally, he said hoarsely, 'I can give you an unofficial answer.' His eyes were red-rimmed. 'The official answer awaits complete analysis. Do you want it unofficial?'

'Go ahead,' said Meyerhof.

Trask nodded.

Whistler darted a hang-dog glance at the Grand Master. 'Ask a foolish question –' he said. Then, gruffly, 'Multivac says, extraterrestrial origin.'

'What are you saying?' demanded Trask.

'Don't you hear me? The jokes we laugh at were not made up by any man. Multivac has analysed all data given it and the one answer that best fits that data is that some extraterrestrial intelligence has composed the jokes, all of them, and placed them in selected human minds at selected times and places in such a way that no man is conscious of having made one up. All subsequent jokes are minor variations and adaptations of these grand originals.'

Meyerhof broke in, face flushed with the kind of triumph only a Grand Master can know who once again has asked the right question. 'All comedy writers,' he said, 'work by twisting old jokes to new purposes. That's well known. The answer fits.'

'But why?' asked Trask. 'Why make up the jokes?'

'Multivac says,' said Whistler, 'that the only purpose that fits all the data is that the jokes are intended to study human psychology. We study rat psychology by making the rats solve mazes. The rats don't know why and wouldn't even if they were aware of what was going on, which they're not. These outer intelligences study man's psychology by noting individual reactions to carefully selected anecdotes. Each man reacts differently . . . Presumably, these outer intelligences are to us as we are to rats.' He shuddered.

Trask, eyes staring, said, 'The Grand Master said man is the only animal with a sense of humour. It would seem then that the sense of humour is foisted upon us from without.'

Meyerhof added excitedly, 'And for possible humour created within, we have no laughter. Puns, I mean.'

Whistler said, 'Presumably, the extraterrestrials cancel out reactions to spontaneous jokes to avoid confusion.'

Trask said in sudden agony of spirit, 'Come on, now. Good Lord, do either of you believe this?'

The senior analyst looked at him coldly. 'Multivac says so. It's all that can be said so far. It has pointed out the real jokesters of the universe, and if we want to know more, the matter will have to be followed up.' He added in a whisper, 'If anyone dares follow it up.'

Grand Master Meyerhof said suddenly, 'I asked two questions, you know. So far only the first has been answered. I think Multivac has enough data to answer the second.'

Whistler shrugged. He seemed a half-broken man. 'When a Grand Master thinks there is enough data,' he said, 'I'll make a book on it. What is your second question?'

'I asked this: What will be the effect on the human race of discovering the answer to my first question?'

'Why did you ask that?' demanded Trask.

'Just a feeling that it had to be asked,' said Meyerhof.

Trask said, 'Insane. It's all insane,' and turned away. Even he himself felt how strangely he and Whistler had changed sides. Now it was Trask crying insanity.

Trask closed his eyes. He might cry insanity all he wished, but no man in fifty years had doubted the combination of a Grand Master and Multivac and found his doubts verified.

Whistler worked silently, teeth clenched. He put Multivac and its subsidiary machines through their paces again. Another hour passed and he laughed harshly. 'A raving nightmare!'

'What's the answer?' asked Meyerhof. 'I want Multivac's remarks, not yours.'

'All right. Take it. Multivac states that, once even a single human discovers the truth of this method of psychological analysis of the human mind, it will become useless as an objective technique to those extra-terrestrial powers now using it.'

'You mean there won't be any more jokes handed out to humanity?' asked Trask faintly. 'Or what do you mean?'

'No more jokes,' said Whistler. '*Now!* Multivac says *now!* The experiment is ended *now!* A new technique will have to be introduced.'

They stared at each other. The minutes passed.

Meyerhof said slowly, 'Multivac is right.'

Whistler said haggardly, 'I know.'

Even Trask said in a whisper, 'Yes. It must be.'

It was Meyerhof who put his finger on the proof of it, Meyerhof the accomplished jokester. He said, 'It's over, you know, all over. I've been trying for five minutes now and I can't think of one single joke, not one! And if I read one in a book, I wouldn't laugh. I know.'

'The gift of humour is gone,' said Trask drearily. 'No man will ever laugh again.'

And they remained there, staring, feeling the world shrink down to the dimensions of an experimental rat cage – with the maze removed and something, something about to be put in its place.

The Short-Short Story of Mankind

JOHN STEINBECK

It was pretty draughty in the cave in the middle of the afternoon. There wasn't any fire – the last spark had gone out six months ago and the family wouldn't have any more fire until lightning struck another tree.

Joe came into the cave all scratched up and some hunks of hair torn out and he flopped down on the wet ground and bled – Old William was arguing away with Old Bert who was his brother and also his son, if you look at it one way. They were quarrelling mildly over a spoiled chunk of mammoth meat.

Old William said, 'Why don't you give some to your mother?'

'Why?' asked Old Bert. 'She's my wife, isn't she?'

And that finished that, so they both took after Joe.

'Where's Al?' one of them asked and the other said, 'You forgot to roll the rock in front of the door.'

Joe didn't even look up and the two old men agreed that kids were going to the devil. 'I tell you it was different in my day,' Old William said. 'They had some respect for their elders or they got what for.'

After a while Joe stopped bleeding and he caked some mud on his cuts. 'Al's gone,' he said.

Old Bert asked brightly, 'Sabre tooth?'

'No, it's that new bunch that moved into the copse down the gully. They ate Al.'

'Savages,' said Old William. 'Still live in trees. They aren't civilized. We don't hardly ever eat people.'

Joe said, 'We hardly got anybody to eat except relatives and we're getting low on relatives.'

'Those foreigners!' said Old Bert.

'Al and I dug a pit,' said Joe. 'We caught a horse and those tree people came along and ate our horse. When we complained, they ate Al.'

'Well, you go right out and get us one of them and we'll eat him,' Old William said.

'Me and who else?' said Joe. 'Last time it was warm there was twelve of us here. Now there's only four. Why, I saw my own sister Sally sitting up in a tree with a savage. Had my heart set on Sally, too, Pa,' Joe went on uncertainly, because Old William was not only his father, but his uncle and his first and third cousin, and his brother-in-law. 'Pa, why don't we join up with those tree people? They've got a net kind of thing – catch all sorts of animals. They eat better than we do.'

'Son,' said Old William, 'they're foreigners, that's why. They live in trees. We can't associate with savages. How'd you like your sister to marry a savage?'

'She did!' said Joe. 'We could have them come and live in our cave. Maybe they'd show us how to use that net thing.'

'Never,' said Old Bert. 'We couldn't trust 'em. They might eat us in our sleep.'

'If we didn't eat them first,' said Joe. 'I sure would like to have me a nice juicy piece of savage right now. I'm hungry.'

'Next thing you know, you'll be saying those tree people are as good as us,' Old William said. 'I never saw such a boy. Why, where'd authority be? Those foreigners would take over. We'd have to look up to 'em. They'd outnumber us.'

'I hate to tell you this, Pa,' said Joe. 'I've got a busted arm. I can't dig pits any more – neither can you. You're too old. Bert can't either. We've got to merge up with those tree people or we aren't gonna eat anything or anybody.'

'Over my dead body,' said Old William, and then he saw Joe's eyes on his skinny flank and he said, 'Now, Joe, don't you go getting ideas about your Pa.'

Well, a long time ago before the tribe first moved out of the drippy cave, there was a man named Elmer. He piled up some rocks in a circle and laid brush on top and took to living there. The elders killed Elmer right off. If anybody could go off and live by himself, why, where would authority be? But pretty soon those elders moved into Elmer's house and then the other families made houses just like it. It was pretty nice with no water dripping in your face.

So, they made Elmer a god – used to swear by him. Said he was the moon.

Everything was going along fine when another tribe moved into the valley. They didn't have Elmer houses, though. They shacked up in skin tents. But you know, they had a funny kind of a gadget that shot little sticks . . . shot them a long way. They could just stand still and pick off a pig, oh . . . fifty yards away – wouldn't have to run it down and maybe get a tusk in the groin.

The skin tribe shot so much game that naturally the Elmer elders said those savages had to be got rid of. They didn't even know about Elmer – that's how ignorant *they* were. The old people sharpened a lot of sticks and fired the points and they said, 'Now you young fellas go out and drive those skin people away. You can't fail because you've got Elmer on your side.'

Now, it seems that a long time ago there was a skin man named Max. He thought up this stick shooter so they killed him, naturally, but afterwards they said he was the sun. So, it was a war between Elmer, the moon, and Max, the sun, but in the course of it a whole slew of young skin men and a whole slew of young Elmer men got killed. Then a forest fire broke out and drove the game away. Elmer people and skin people had to make for the hills all together. The elders of both tribes never would accept it. They complained until they died.

You can see from this that the world started going to pot right from the beginning. Things would be going along fine – law and order and all that and the elders in charge – and then some smart aleck would invent something and spoil the whole business – like the man Ralph who forgot to kill all the wild chickens he caught and had to build a hen house, or like the real trouble-maker Jojo *au front du chien*, who patted some seeds into damp ground and invented farming. Of course, they tore Jojo's arms and legs off and rightly so because when people plant seeds, they can't go golly-wacking around the country enjoying themselves. When you've got a crop in, you stay with it and get the weeds out of it and harvest it. Furthermore, everything and everybody wants to take your crop away from you – weeds – bugs – birds – animals – men – A farmer spends all his time fighting something off. The elders can call on Elmer all they want, but that won't keep the neighbours from over the hill out of your corn crib.

Well, there was a strong boy named Rudolph, but called Bugsy. Bugsy would break his back wrestling but he wouldn't bring in an armload of wood. Bugsy just naturally liked to fight and he hated to work, so he said, 'You men just plant your crops and don't worry. I'll take care of you. If anybody bothers you, I'll clobber 'em. You can give me a few chickens and a couple of handfuls of grits for my trouble.'

The elders blessed Bugsy and pretty soon they got him mixed up with Elmer. Bugsy went right along with them. He gathered a dozen strong boys and built a fort up on the hill to take care of those farmers and their crops. When you take care of something, pretty soon you own it.

Bugsy and his boys would stroll around picking over the crop of wheat and girls and when they'd worked over their own valley, they'd go rollicking over the hill to see what the neighbours had stored up or born. Then the strong boys from over the hill would come rollicking back and what they couldn't carry off they burned until pretty soon it was more dangerous to be protected than not to be. Bugsy took everything loose up to his fort to protect it and very little ever came back down. He figured his grandfather was Elmer now and that made him different from other people. How many people do you know that have the moon in their family?

By now the elders had confused protection with virtue because Bugsy passed out his surplus to the better people. The elders were pretty hard on anybody who complained. They said it was a sin. Well, the farmers built a wall around the hill to sit in when the going got rough. They hated to see their crops burn up, but they hated worse to see themselves burn up and their wife Agnes and their daughter Clarinda.

About that time the whole system turned over. Instead of Bugsy protecting them, it was their duty to protect him. He said he got the idea from Elmer one full-moon night.

People spent a lot of time sitting behind the wall waiting for the smoke to clear and they began to fool around with willows from the river, making baskets. And it's natural for people to make more things than they need.

Now, it happens often enough so that you can make a rule about it. There's always going to be a joker. This one was named Harry and he said, 'Those ignorant pigs over the hill don't have any willows so they don't have any baskets, but you know what they do? – benighted though they are, they take mud and pat it out and put it in the fire and you can boil water in it. I'll bet if we took them some baskets they'd give us some of those baked mud pots.' They had to hang Harry head down over a bonfire. Nobody can put a knife in the status quo and get away with it. But it wasn't long before the basket people got to sneaking over the hill and coming back with pots. Bugsy tried to stop it and the elders were right with him. It took people away from the fields, exposed them to dangerous ideas. Why, pots got to be like money and money is worse than an idea. Bugsy himself said, 'Makes folks restless – why, it makes a man think he's as good as the ones that got it a couple of generations earlier' and how's that for being un-Elmer? The elders agreed with Bugsy, of course, but they couldn't stop it, so they all had to join it. Bugsy took half the pots they brought back and pretty soon he took over the willow concession so he got the whole thing.

About then some savages moved up on the hill and got to raiding the basket and pot trade. The only thing to do was for Bugsy, the basket, to marry the daughter of Willy, the pot, and when they all died off, Herman Pot-Basket pulled the whole business together and made a little state and that worked out fine.

Well, it went on from state to league and from league to nation. (A nation usually had some kind of natural boundary like an ocean or a mountain range or a river to keep it from spilling over.) It worked out fine until a bunch of jokers invented long-distance stuff like directed missiles and atom bombs. Then a river or an ocean didn't do a bit of good. It got too dangerous to have separate nations just as it had been to have separate families.

When people are finally faced with extinction, they have to do something about it. Now we've got the United Nations and the elders are right in there fighting it the way they fought coming out of caves. But we don't have much choice about it. It isn't any goodness of heart and we may not want to go ahead but right from the cave time we've had to choose and so far we've never chosen extinction. It'd be kind of silly if we killed ourselves off after all this time. If we do, we're stupider than the cave people and I don't think we are. I think we're just exactly as stupid and that's pretty bright in the long run.

Night Watch

JAMES INGLIS

With the instantaneous brilliance of a lightning flash, life and consciousness were born. The journey from void nonentity to vivid awakening was swifter than the passage of a meteor, instant and complete.

The search for self-identity began. Seconds after his awakening, the new-born being subjected his environment and himself to a minutely detailed examination. He discovered within himself, down in the misty centre of consciousness, a store of knowledge, all of it quite meaningless until linked with the stimulus of outside experience.

One thing he learned. He had a name. This was a convenient and necessary item. It was the symbol of individual identity. It defined the most important thing in his environment; himself. He knew that it would do more than that, he knew that his name contained the riddle of his existence. When he succeeded in interpreting this riddle, he would become aware of the purpose for which he was created.

Meantime, it was enough that he had a name. His name was Asov.

He turned his attention to the world around him, the baffling, incomprehensible world into which he had been born. It was a world of contrasts, both glaring and subtle. Asov was at once sensitive to these contrasts and began to compare and measure, building up a picture of his environment on the fresh, fertile canvas of his experience.

Light and darkness. Motion and peace. Growth and change.

These were the concepts with which Asov wrestled, each new item of information being stored away within his miraculous memory and related to his inborn store of data.

The world took shape and meaning. His lightning senses could now instantly recognize a thousand variations in the interplay of energy which was how he saw the world. Like himself, the world too had a name. It was called Galaxy.

As he emerged from infantile bafflement, Asov could at last understand the riddle of his name. With that understanding came an awareness of his place in creation. His essential purpose no longer eluded him.

Asov. Automatic Stellar Observation Vehicle.

Suddenly, he became aware that one object in his immediate vicinity was demanding his attention, drowning out the innumerable distractions of pressure and radiation which were as sight and sound to him. The intensity of the object's attraction grew steadily, which Asov interpreted as meaning that he himself was in motion, and moving towards this blazing area of disturbance. This then was the source of his awakening. For a nameless time he had drifted in the void, a seed of dormant intelligence awaiting the signal which would melt away the cocoon of unconsciousness, the first, faint caress of light and heat which would activate his sleeping sensors.

The star registered itself in Asov's brain as a frenzied pattern of nuclear reactions and continuous explosions. This image he related to the pre-stored information within and translated the image into his creators' terms of reference. The star was a red dwarf, spectral class M5, surface temperature around 4,000°C. As he swung in a wide orbit around his stellar prey, Asov picked up the contrastingly faint light-heat emanations of smaller, cooler bodies which circled the dense old star in their timeless chains of gravity. He again related the incoming data with his inborn, encyclopaedic memory.

Planets: Four. Temperature range: absolute zero to near frozen. Condition: lifeless, having lost gaseous atmospheres . . .

Painstakingly, unconscious of the passage of time, Asov continued his survey. When he was finished and his brain cells each held a full load of information, a signal was passed to his motor nervous system and with a sudden bound he was accelerating away from the domain of the red dwarf.

As the old star slowly receded, he completed the programme of his first mission. The data which loaded his brain cells was collated, coded and dispatched in a tight beam of radio waves, directed towards a tiny area of the firmament where lay the remote star Sol and the planet Earth. The planet which he had never known, but out of which he had come.

At last the urgency of his first stellar encounter grew dim, and Asov sought out the nearest available light-source, drawing upon the dormant energies of space to propel him towards his next encounter. Having completed the required manoeuvres, Asov drifted in the relative peace of the interstellar vacuum, where gravity came not in waves but in gentle ripples and the nuclear voices of the stars were no more than a faint chant, a cosmic lullaby. Asov slept.

The cycle was repeated each time he passed within the gravitational embrace of any interstellar object capable of the slightest degree of energy output. The sources of his awakening-cycle were mainly stars of the red dwarf type, which comprised the bulk of the galaxy's population. But there were rare occasions when he would awake to the stimuli of massive giants and their proportionately enormous retinues of planets. Such occurrences demanded longer and more detailed survey, though of course Asov was unconscious of the time element.

Several times he passed through tenuous light-years of hydrogen, the life-stuff of the Universe. At times, these ghostly regions were sufficiently dense and luminous to wake his sensors, in addition to restocking his nuclear power reserves. Occasionally such nebulae contained the embryonic materials of new-born stars, hot and blue and amorphous. There was a great deal to learn at such times, particularly concerning the early evolutionary development of the stars. With each successive encounter his understanding of galactic processes increased, and was duly transmitted to the ever-more-distant point of origin.

Another rare event which Asov experienced was the discovery of a certain secondary characteristic of some planetary systems. The phenomenon of life. This characteristic was listed in his pre-birth instruction circuits as of the highest priority.

His first encounter with the phenomenon occurred while in the vicinity of a small, orange star of the classification G7. A star not unlike his native sun. He awoke to the familiar disturbance pattern; a strengthening of the gravitational tides which bore him, an intensification of light, heat and the full range of radiation. A new energy source was before him.

After the routine observations of the star, his attention turned to the solid bodies in orbit about it. Of these planets, two offered distinct traces of organic molecules. Even at a remote distance Asov's spectroscopic vision could wrest these planetary secrets with ease. For a more detailed survey, however, a close approach was necessary. Acting upon this preliminary data, his motor nerves were immediately stimulated to inject him into a planetary trajectory which would bring him into orbit about each of the target worlds.

It was the second planet which possessed the most rewarding conditions. First he noted the patterns of abundant areas of ocean. Spectroscopic examination revealed that the seas, like the atmosphere, were rich in life's constituents. Then came direct evidence of advanced life. As he swung in a close orbit around the planet, just clearing the violet, upper fringes of the atmosphere, Asov observed the unmistakable signs: lighted areas on the night-side, large artificial structures and courses, and most unexpected of all, contact. After many reconnaissance circuits he intercepted a stray tendril of radiation. A short analysis was sufficient to convince him that this could not be accounted for by the natural emissions from the planet. The only possible explanation was that the radio signal had been directed at him by an intelligence.

The Questor was being questioned!

In accord with his built-in responses, Asov returned a signal towards the unknown source on the same wavelength as the one he had received. This signal comprised a tightly coded account of Asov's home system, a record of terrestrial thought and history. In that small beam of signals was contained a thorough biography of man, his progress in medicine and philosophy, his discoveries and disasters.

Simultaneously, Asov was working on the message he had received from the aliens. This too was in the form of a mathematical code, which when broken down revealed a long and detailed history of two planets. Like man, the aliens were as yet confined to their local system, though unlike Asov's distant creators, they had evolved a global way of life which permitted world-wide understanding while encouraging the valid, essential differences between beings of even the same species.

On completion of the exchange, Asov passed on out of the kingdom of the orange star, quite unaware that he had been the cause of the greatest single event in the history of a solar system.

Although virtually indestructible in the erosion-free vacuum, and although his motive power was available in unlimited quantities from the suns and gases of space, there had to come a time when Asov would meet with unexpected danger. Normally his senses were swift enough to avert a likely collision. This danger was only met within the confines of a solar system, when passing through belts of asteroids and cometary debris, the coastal defences of the stars. Occasionally, these cosmic missiles would move at velocities beyond even Asov's power to outmanoeuvre. In the vicinity of large solar masses, the gravitational tides were so immense that much power was required for drastic course correction, and at the same time any local fleets of meteors would be moving with high orbital velocities.

It happened as he prepared to make his exit from the system of a red giant. The huge star had been a rare find indeed and it possessed the unusual feature of a retinue of minor stars, instead of the normal planets. These satellite stars were dwarfs, mostly in the last stages of stellar senility. They weaved around the sullen giant in weirdly eccentric orbits. So eccentric that the entire stellar system was a wildly turbulent whirlpool of gravitational forces. Enormous sized fragments of shattered planets flung themselves insanely across the system, as twigs will spin and dart in a vortex of water. Asov, given time, could have calculated precisely the mechanics of the whole complex system. He possessed the equipment to predict exactly the speed and trajectory of each hurtling fragment. But time, or the lack of it, was his undoing.

The collision when it came was not with one of the larger masses. These Asov had predicted and had taken evasive action. The fateful missile was a tiny splinter of rock, which compensated its insignificance in size with its vast velocity. It struck him at a point which in itself was expendable, upon a transmitting aerial of which he had several duplicates. But the shock of impact was great enough to deaden the sensitivity of his control mechanisms. In a coma almost as deep as death, Asov drifted helplessly into the dark wastes, unguided, aimless, totally without function.

It should have been the end. His inactive remains should have floated on for eternity, just another item of mineral debris in a Universe already familiar with the lifeless, the inert and the expended. But it was not the end.

In the furthest limits of interstellar space, as in the cosy realms of inhabited planets, the unexpected, the unpredictable occurs from time to time. Given long enough, and Asov had all of Time ahead of him, such an event was almost bound to happen. His was no immediate resurrection. He drifted in unconsciousness for the lifetime of many a star. While his senses lay dormant, planets formed, producing sea and slime from which finned oddities crept out on to cooling land surfaces to do battle with primal monsters and create civilizations. Some of these civilizations reached out into space in sleek and shining machines. Some of them died in nuclear holocaust and others died of introspection. Although the total Universe maintained its steady state, the individual stars and galaxies of stars evolved and changed. Much happened in the interval during which Asov slept the sleep which was so near to oblivion.

His damage was not 'organic'. It was a question of degree. The sensitivity of his optical and other senses had been so reduced by the collision that no normally available source of energy was powerful enough to activate him. No normally available source.

One phenomenon alone possessed sufficient energy to stir his stunned sensibility. One rare but regular occurrence which a galaxy will produce from time to time to startle the Universe with its power.

Supernova.

In an average sized galaxy there are around a hundred thousand million stars. When one of these suns becomes unstable through the excess creation of helium, it produces a phenomenon which must rank as one of the most bizarre events in the cosmos. Quite suddenly, in a split-second of time, such a star flares into frenzied incandescence of such a magnitude that it rivals the combined star-glow of half a galaxy.

During his long coma Asov had drifted through the remote ripples of several supernovae explosions, but there had to come a time when he would find himself in the direct path of one such cosmic upheaval. He was immersed in a boiling sea of radiation. The space around him was no longer a passive vacuum but a seething cauldron of hell-fire. In that cosmic hades, Asov was resurrected. He emerged from the fire as the Phoenix, re-born, triumphant.

His second birth followed a similar pattern to his first. Again, the flood-gates were opened to his inner reservoir of knowledge and he drank avidly of the sudden deluge of information. In no time, he was once more in complete command of his faculties but, before any detailed appraisal of the larger scene, Asov had yet to investigate the immediate source of energy; the supernova which had raised him from the cosmic dead.

As usual in such cases, the star was a blue super-giant, of a size equivalent to four hundred solar diameters (Asov's home star was always taken as the yardstick for such measurements). It was, of course, at that moment undergoing an expansion which one day would result in the creation of a nebula, with the shrunken shell of the erstwhile giant sun at its centre. He was unable to detect any planetary system as the outer atmosphere of the star had already expanded to a point well beyond the orbit of even the furthest possible planet. Any such system would in any case have been instantly vaporized in the first few minutes of the conflagration.

Asov, caught in the rapidly expanding shell of gases, for a time lost track of the outer Universe. He was riding blind in the centre of a cosmic storm, a storm of blinding light and dust which seemed to stretch to the end of time and space in its convulsive, frantic rush. When he did finally emerge from the stellar death-dance, his sensors saturated with new knowledge, Asov turned his attention to the outside scene.

At first, it seemed that his sensing equipment was malfunctioning. The composite image of the galaxy which he was receiving was not in accord with what his invincible memory circuits had prepared him for. He quickly checked out his sensory systems, but without discovering anything amiss. Again he surveyed the large-scale features of his environment and again a scarcely credible picture confronted him.

Having no alternative but to believe his senses, Asov could make but one deduction from this picture: the galaxy had grown old. This could only mean that his period of unconsciousness had been long indeed, long in terms of space itself.

The immediate problem was one of energy. Power for propulsion, transmission, collating. Energy sources were, for the first time in his experience, severely limited. In his immediate environment, they were almost unavailable.

His galactic voyaging had taken him in a great ellipse around the system. It was in these outer regions that the stellar population had dwindled most drastically. Towards the centre of the galaxy, which was observable to Asov as a gleaming island of mist, the stars retained at least a semblance of their old density. Here in the outer regions of the galactic spiral the stars had always been relatively sparse, and here the stellar death-toll had been more severe. Although the central stars tended to be older, they were also the more stable. The outer giants had always been short-lived, burning away their lifetimes with wanton fury while the inner stars were content with a humble output of energy conserving their nuclear life-blood for as long as possible.

But not for eternity.

Forever practical, Asov concentrated upon the problem of energy sources. He was quick to predict that his present course would soon take him beyond the area of minimum power, where his senses would once more be eclipsed by the clouds of oblivion.

Only one decision was possible. This decision would have been made by any being, whether for the emotional desire of self-preservation or for the logical necessity of fulfilling a mission. Drawing upon the abundant energies still flowing from the supernova, Asov performed a major manoeuvre, altered his thrust vector to an extent unheard of in previous course corrections, and set sail for the galactic centre.

In search of life and light, he left behind the grim silences of the galaxy's desolate shore.

On his way Asov charted the downfall of the galaxy. He observed each dead and dying star which came within his long-range sensors. Very occasionally he approached close enough to witness the funeral processions of whole solar systems.

The pattern was one of sombre repetition.

The star, life-giver and source of light for so many millions of years, wrapped in a dim, red death-mist. The once populated planets cold, empty stretches of rock: desolate, global tombstones. On their surfaces, nothing stirred, and in their skies the naked stars were flaring in a final agony.

The rhythms of life and the conflict of the elements were drawing everywhere to a close. But Asov, unlike his environment, remained unchanged. His instincts, his basic motivations were the same as they had been that first day when the caress of starlight had opened his eyes to the Universe. However sombre and woeful the environment which now met his probing senses, he must continue his explorations, as though in the faith that somewhere, sometime, he would discover something new.

Each time fresh information reached his brain cells, he would faithfully transmit the message to the remote point in space out of which he had emerged. He continued this ritual despite the increasing probability that the planet which had dispatched him so long before might now be no more than a frozen shell circling a small, spent sun.

Even when he arrived at the great, glowing heart of the galaxy, Asov detected the signs of approaching doom. Spreading pools of darkness lay between the stars, a gradual inexorable tide which ultimately would engulf the galaxy in a great and final shadow.

He continued his mission. As the ages came and went and the stars declined, he witnessed the long, losing battle against the night. Each stage of stellar decay he noted, the expansions and contractions, the brief flaring into momentary brilliance, the subsequent collapse as frigid darkness came in to close each chapter.

But the age of the unexpected had not yet passed. Suddenly, in the midst of now-familiar tragedy, an unprecedented phenomenon upset the pattern to which Asov had become resigned.

At first too faint to be correctly analysed, a new and puzzling transmitting source interrupted his silent vigil. The disturbance occupied only a tiny fragment of the complete, electro-magnetic environment, but it was sufficient to rouse Asov into immediate investigation. This was his essential purpose in existing, to spot and explore the unexpected.

He traced the disturbance factor, measured its frequency, and estimated its position relative to his own. It was comparatively close. The puzzling part was that no observable energy-source lay in that particular direction. Whatever was emitting the radiation was invisible, even to Asov's supersensitive vision. Invisible, or very small.

It was Asov's experience that no tiny cosmic object transmitted more than a tiny amount of radiation. This fact allowed him to deduce the basic nature of the phenomenon before he had actually closed the gap.

It had to be artificial.

In confirmation of this deduction, the object began to gravitate towards him, signifying that it too had picked up an unexpected radio source, in this case Asov.

At last they faced each other, two lonely voyagers meeting on a dead sea shore. Degree by degree, the mutual interchange of data which flowed between their radio centres was assimilated. A mathematically-based code system, founded on the same principles as those behind Asov's original transmission system, was evolved to permit a smooth flow of communication.

Asov learned that the mysterious object was in reality something very familiar and at the same time totally alien. It was an interstellar probe, almost a mirror-image of himself though its origins were half-a-galaxy away from his.

After the event, Asov could see that such a meeting, although unthinkably unlikely in any other circumstances, was perfectly logical at this time and place. He knew, had known for countless years, that other races existed in the galaxy; their number was legion. It was reasonable to expect that they too would in their day create beings similar to Asov, cosmic scouts which would voyage the galaxy independent of their creators, unaffected by the latters' doom.

It was to be expected that these scouts, like Asov, would seek out the galactic centre, where life and light held on the longest. With the steady shrinkage of the galaxy's habitability zone, it was inevitable that sometime, these inward moving probes would gravitate towards each other. And one day, meet.

Proof that the encounter was not a rare quirk of Chance was soon forthcoming. More meetings took place, at first widely separated in time and space, later on an increasingly more frequent basis. Each encounter occurred amidst a steadily shrinking nucleus of stars.

Although of varied design and complexity, these last representatives of cosmic man were all possessed by the same instinct, the instinct which had been programmed into them during their construction. The decline and death of their creators in no way removed this primal instinct. The quest for light was their mission and their life. It would end only when the fires of the Universe grew dim and flickered out.

As the watching probes swung round the fading remnants of a once proud galaxy, their numbers continued to grow, vastly. In direct proportion to the number of highly advanced species which had once peopled the galaxy, the vanished ones who had dispatched their silent sentinels to keep watch over the stars.

While the dark waters of nothingness gradually flooded the firmament, Asov occupied his time by exchanging histories with his newfound counterparts.

Between them, a composite picture of galactic history was built up, each ancient probe contributing its own knowledge and experience to the common pool. Where before each probe possessed only fragmentary information about the processes of cosmic law, the combined experiences permitted a fuller understanding of the whole spectrum of creation.

In a sense, the gathering of probes formed a single entity. A composite being, possessing an almost unlimited experience of an entire galaxy.

But as the surrounding star-glow dimmed, so also did their intellectual activity diminish. Power was at a premium, the first priorities being propulsion and sensory activity. Transmission became less frequent, communication less intense.

The desperate search for energy sources began.

Asov was already approaching that state of suspended consciousness in which he had drifted after his fateful collision. But while there remained a spark of awareness, he was committed to his mission and to the discovery of light. It was quite impossible for him to anticipate oblivion and to yield himself to the darkness. His long-range sensors probed into the night, comparing, rejecting, selecting. Often, the particular light source which he was following would fade before him, as the advancing tide of darkness claimed yet another stellar victim. Many times his course would change, with increasing frequency, until it seemed that the Universe would soon be devoid of light and his senses deadened for ever.

But there were certain sources of light, which although faint in the extreme, were steady and appeared to remain unaffected by the fate of his immediate environment. These sources were by no means unfamiliar to Asov; they had been present throughout the long saga of his interstellar life, but they had been beyond the area of his established activity. Their distances were not merely interstellar, but extra-galactic. Until now, there had been no reason to attach much importance to those far-off sources of light.

But until now there had always been bright and abundant beacons of energy immediately available.

With the continued fading of the galaxy's fire, Asov and his companions turned at last to those distant, glowing mists; the last resort, the faint and final source of energy. However unprecedented the situation which faced them, the community of probes acted quickly, spontaneously and in unison. In a sense this was the consummation of their galatic lifetimes; and the introduction to a heightened mode of existence. From diverse space routes they had converged, in this final hour, to witness the last moments of a galaxy. Although little power was available for the final adjustments necessary for their outward courses, there was sufficient, as gravity had followed light down the long corridors of dissolution.

As they progressed beyond the confines of the galaxy, the last, dim fires were quenched, and behind them, a great darkness settled. The last of the suns had set.

Although unimaginably distant, the island universes for which they sailed were tangible enough. In the millennia to come, those signal fires would glow brightly from the void, to awaken and stimulate long dormant senses. Then the cycle would begin anew. Energies would be re-stocked from youthful, vital fires and a second chapter would be written in an ancient saga of exploration.

The great probe fleet, keepers and guardians of cosmic history, sailed out to the starless gulfs in search of galaxies to call their own.

Story of Your Life

TED CHIANG

Your father is about to ask me the question. This is the most important moment in our lives, and I want to pay attention, note every detail. Your dad and I have just come back from an evening out, dinner and a show; it's after midnight. We came out onto the patio to look at the full moon; then I told your dad I wanted to dance, so he humors me and now we're slow dancing, a pair of thirtysomethings swaying back and forth in the moonlight like kids. I don't feel the night chill at all. And then your dad says, 'Do you want to make a baby?'

Right now your dad and I have been married for about two years, living on Ellis Avenue; when we move out you'll still be too young to remember the house, but we'll show you pictures of it, tell you stories about it. I'd love to tell you the story of this evening, the night you're conceived, but the right time to do that would be when you're ready to have children of your own, and we'll never get that chance.

Telling it to you any earlier wouldn't do any good; for most of your life you won't sit still to hear such a romantic – you'd say sappy – story. I remember the scenario of your origin you'll suggest when you're twelve.

'The only reason you had me was so you could get a maid you wouldn't have to pay,' you'll say bitterly, dragging the vacuum cleaner out of the closet.

'That's right,' I'll say. 'Thirteen years ago I knew the carpets would need vacuuming around now, and having a baby seemed to be the cheapest and easiest way to get the job done. Now kindly get on with it.'

'If you weren't my mother, this would be illegal,' you'll say, seething as you unwind the power cord and plug it into the wall outlet.

That will be in the house on Belmont Street. I'll live to see strangers occupy both houses: the one you're conceived in and the one you grow up in. Your dad and I will sell the first a couple years after your arrival. I'll sell the second shortly after your departure. By then Nelson and I will have moved into our farmhouse, and your dad will be living with what's-her-name.

I know how this story ends; I think about it a lot. I also think a lot about how it began, just a few years ago, when ships appeared in orbit and artifacts appeared in meadows. The government said next to nothing about them, while the tabloids said every possible thing.

And then I got a phone call, a request for a meeting.

I spotted them waiting in the hallway, outside my office. They made an odd couple; one wore a military uniform and a crew cut, and carried an aluminum briefcase. He seemed to be assessing his surroundings with a critical eye. The other one was easily identifiable as an academic: full beard and mustache, wearing corduroy. He was browsing through the overlapping sheets stapled to a bulletin board nearby.

'Colonel Weber, I presume?' I shook hands with the soldier. 'Louise Banks.'

'Dr Banks. Thank you for taking the time to speak with us,' he said.

'Not at all; any excuse to avoid the faculty meeting.'

Colonel Weber indicated his companion. 'This is Dr Gary Donnelly, the physicist I mentioned when we spoke on the phone.'

'Call me Gary,' he said as we shook hands. 'I'm anxious to hear what you have to say.'

We entered my office. I moved a couple of stacks of books off the second guest chair, and we all sat down. 'You said you wanted me to listen to a recording. I presume this has something to do with the aliens?'

'All I can offer is the recording,' said Colonel Weber.

'Okay, let's hear it.'

Colonel Weber took a tape machine out of his briefcase and pressed PLAY. The recording sounded vaguely like that of a wet dog shaking the water out of its fur.

'What do you make of that?' he asked.

I withheld my comparison with a wet dog. 'What was the context in which this recording was made?'

'I'm not at liberty to say.'

'It would help me interpret those sounds. Could you see the alien while it was speaking? Was it doing anything at the time?'

'The recording is all I can offer.'

'You won't be giving anything away if you tell me that you've seen the aliens; the public's assumed you have.'

Colonel Weber wasn't budging. 'Do you have any opinion about its linguistic properties?' he asked.

'Well, it's clear that their vocal tract is substantially different from a human vocal tract. I assume that these aliens don't look like humans?'

The colonel was about to say something noncommittal when Gary Donelly asked, 'Can you make any guesses based on the tape?'

'Not really. It doesn't sound like they're using a larynx to make those sounds, but that doesn't tell me what they look like.'

'Anything – is there anything else you can tell us?' asked Colonel Weber.

I could see he wasn't accustomed to consulting a civilian. 'Only that establishing communications is going to be really difficult because of the difference in anatomy. They're almost certainly using sounds that the human vocal tract can't reproduce, and maybe sounds that the human ear can't distinguish.'

'You mean infra- or ultrasonic frequencies?' asked Gary Donelly.

'Not specifically. I just mean that the human auditory system isn't an absolute acoustic instrument; it's optimized to recognize the sounds that a human larynx makes. With an alien vocal system, all bets are off.' I shrugged. '*Maybe* we'll be able to hear the difference between alien phonemes, given enough practice, but it's possible our ears simply can't recognize the distinctions they consider meaningful. In that case we'd need a sound spectrograph to know what an alien is saying.'

Colonel Weber asked, 'Suppose I gave you an hour's worth of recordings; how long would it take you to determine if we need this sound spectrograph or not?'

'I couldn't determine that with just a recording no matter how much time I had. I'd need to talk with the aliens directly.'

The colonel shook his head. 'Not possible.'

I tried to break it to him gently. 'That's your call, of course. But the only way to learn an unknown language is to interact with a native speaker, and by that I mean asking questions, holding a conversation, that sort of thing. Without that, it's simply not possible. So if you want to learn the aliens' language, someone with training in field linguistics – whether it's me or someone else – will have to talk with an alien. Recordings alone aren't sufficient.'

Colonel Weber frowned. 'You seem to be implying that no alien could have learned human languages by monitoring our broadcasts.'

'I doubt it. They'd need instructional material specifically designed to teach human languages to nonhumans. Either that, or interaction with a human. If they had either of those, they could learn a lot from TV, but otherwise, they wouldn't have a starting point.'

The colonel clearly found this interesting; evidently his philosophy was, the less the aliens knew, the better. Gary Donnelly read the colonel's expression too and rolled his eyes. I suppressed a smile.

Then Colonel Weber asked, 'Suppose you were learning a new language by talking to its speakers; could you do it without teaching them English?'

'That would depend on how cooperative the native speakers were. They'd almost certainly pick up bits and pieces while I'm learning their language, but it wouldn't have to be much if they're willing to teach. On the other hand, if they'd rather learn English than teach us their language, that would make things far more difficult.'

The colonel nodded. 'I'll get back to you on this matter.'

The request for that meeting was perhaps the second most momentous phone call in my life. The first, of course, will be the one from Mountain Rescue. At that point your dad and I will be speaking to each other maybe once a year, tops. After I get that phone call, though, the first thing I'll do will be to call your father.

He and I will drive out together to perform the identification, a long silent car ride. I remember the morgue, all tile and stainless steel, the hum of refrigeration and smell of antiseptic. An orderly will pull the sheet back to reveal your face. Your face will look wrong somehow, but I'll know it's you.

'Yes, that's her,' I'll say. 'She's mine.'

You'll be twenty-five then.

*

The MP checked my badge, made a notation on his clipboard, and opened the gate; I drove the off-road vehicle into the encampment, a small village of tents pitched by the Army in a farmer's sun-scorched pasture. At the center of the encampment was one of the alien devices, nicknamed 'looking glasses.'

According to the briefings I'd attended, there were nine of these in the United States, one hundred and twelve in the world. The looking glasses acted as two-way communication devices, presumably with the ships in orbit. No one knew why the aliens wouldn't talk to us in person; fear of cooties, maybe. A team of scientists, including a physicist and a linguist, was assigned to each looking glass; Gary Donnelly and I were on this one.

Gary was waiting for me in the parking area. We navigated a circular maze of concrete barricades until we reached the large tent that covered the looking glass itself. In front of the tent was an equipment cart loaded with goodies borrowed from the school's phonology lab; I had sent it ahead for inspection by the Army.

Also outside the tent were three tripod-mounted video cameras whose lenses peered, through windows in the fabric wall, into the main room. Everything Gary and I did would be reviewed by countless others, including military intelligence. In addition we would each send daily reports, of which mine had to include estimates on how much English I thought the aliens could understand.

Gary held open the tent flap and gestured for me to enter. 'Step right up,' he said, circus barker-style. 'Marvel at creatures the likes of which have never been seen on God's green earth.'

'And all for one slim dime,' I murmured, walking through the door. At the moment the looking glass was inactive, resembling a semicircular mirror over ten feet high and twenty feet across. On the brown grass in front of the looking glass, an arc of white spray paint outlined the activation area. Currently the area contained only a table, two folding chairs, and a power strip with a cord leading to a generator outside. The buzz of fluorescent lamps, hung from poles along the edge of the room, commingled with the buzz of flies in the sweltering heat.

Gary and I looked at each other, and then began pushing the cart of equipment up to the table. As we crossed the paint line, the looking glass appeared to grow transparent; it was as if someone was slowly raising the illumination behind tinted glass. The illusion of depth was uncanny; I felt I could walk right into it. Once the looking glass was fully lit it resembled a life-size diorama of a semicircular room. The room contained a few large objects that might have been furniture, but no aliens. There was a door in the curved rear wall.

We busied ourselves connecting everything together: microphone, sound spectrograph, portable computer, and speaker. As we worked, I frequently glanced at the looking glass, anticipating the aliens' arrival. Even so I jumped when one of them entered.

It looked like a barrel suspended at the intersection of seven limbs. It was radially symmetric, and any of its limbs could serve as an arm or a leg. The one in front of me was walking around on four legs, three non-adjacent arms curled up at its sides. Gary called them 'heptapods.'

I'd been shown videotapes, but I still gawked. Its limbs had no distinct joints; anatomists guessed they might be supported by vertebral columns. Whatever their underlying structure, the heptapod's limbs conspired to move it in a disconcertingly fluid manner. Its 'torso' rode atop the rippling limbs as smoothly as a hovercraft.

Seven lidless eyes ringed the top of the heptapod's body. It walked back to the doorway from which it entered, made a brief sputtering sound, and returned to the center of the room followed by another heptapod; at no point did it ever turn around. Eerie, but logical; with eyes on all sides, any direction might as well be 'forward.'

Gary had been watching my reaction. 'Ready?' he asked.

I took a deep breath. 'Ready enough.' I'd done plenty of fieldwork before, in the Amazon, but it had always been a bilingual procedure: either my informants knew some Portuguese, which I could use, or I'd previously gotten an intro to their language from the local missionaries. This would be my first attempt at conducting a true monolingual discovery procedure. It was straightforward enough in theory, though.

I walked up to the looking glass and a heptapod on the other side did the same. The image was so real that my skin crawled. I could see the texture of its gray skin, like corduroy ridges arranged in whorls and loops. There was no smell at all from the looking glass, which somehow made the situation stranger.

I pointed to myself and said slowly, 'Human.' Then I pointed to Gary. 'Human.' Then I pointed at each heptapod and said, 'What are you?'

No reaction. I tried again, and then again.

One of the heptapods pointed to itself with one limb, the four terminal digits pressed together. That was lucky. In some cultures a person pointed with his chin; if the heptapod hadn't used one of its limbs, I wouldn't have known what gesture to look for. I heard a brief fluttering sound, and saw a puckered orifice at the top of its body vibrate; it was talking. Then it pointed to its companion and fluttered again.

I went back to my computer; on its screen were two virtually identical spectrographs representing the fluttering sounds. I marked a sample for playback. I pointed to myself and said 'Human' again, and did the same with Gary. Then I pointed to the heptapod, and played back the flutter on the speaker.

The heptapod fluttered some more. The second half of the spectrograph for this utterance looked like a repetition: call the previous utterances [flutter1], then this one was [flutter2flutter1].

I pointed at something that might have been a heptapod chair. 'What is that?'

The heptapod paused, and then pointed at the 'chair' and talked some more. The spectrograph for this differed distinctly from that of the earlier sounds: [flutter3]. Once again, I pointed to the 'chair' while playing back [flutter3].

The heptapod replied; judging by the spectrograph, it looked like [flutter3flutter2]. Optimistic interpretation: the heptapod was confirming my utterances as correct, which implied compatibility between heptapod and human patterns of discourse. Pessimistic interpretation: it had a nagging cough.

At my computer I delimited certain sections of the spectrograph and typed in a tentative gloss for each: 'heptapod' for [flutter1], 'yes' for [flutter2], and 'chair' for [flutter3]. Then I typed 'Language: Heptapod A' as a heading for all the utterances.

Gary watched what I was typing. 'What's the "A" for?'

'It just distinguishes this language from any other ones the heptapods might use,' I said. He nodded.

'Now let's try something, just for laughs.' I pointed at each heptapod and tried to mimic the sound of [flutter1], 'heptapod.' After a long pause, the first heptapod said something and then the second one said something else, neither of whose spectrographs resembled anything said before. I couldn't tell if they were speaking to each other or to me since they had no faces to turn. I tried pronouncing [flutter1] again, but there was no reaction.

'Not even close,' I grumbled.

'I'm impressed you can make sounds like that at all,' said Gary.

'You should hear my moose call. Sends them running.'

I tried again a few more times, but neither heptapod responded with anything I could recognize. Only when I replayed the recording of the heptapod's pronunciation did I get a confirmation; the heptapod replied with [flutter2], 'yes.'

'So we're stuck with using recordings?' asked Gary.

I nodded. 'At least temporarily.'

'So now what?'

'Now we make sure it hasn't actually been saying "aren't they cute" or "look what they're doing now." Then we see if we can identify any of these words when that other heptapod pronounces them.' I gestured for him to have a seat. 'Get comfortable; this'll take a while.'

In 1770, Captain Cook's ship *Endeavour* ran aground on the coast of Queensland, Australia. While some of his men made repairs, Cook led an exploration party and met the aboriginal people. One of the sailors pointed to the animals that hopped around with their young riding in pouches, and asked an aborigine what they were called. The aborigine replied, 'Kanguru.' From then on Cook and his sailors referred to the animals by this word. It wasn't until later that they learned it meant 'What did you say?'

I tell that story in my introductory course every year. It's almost certainly untrue, and I explain that afterwards, but it's a classic anecdote. Of course, the anecdotes my undergraduates will really want to hear are ones featuring the heptapods; for the rest of my teaching career, that'll be the reason many of them sign up for my courses. So I'll show them the old videotapes of my sessions at the looking glass, and the sessions that the other linguists conducted; the tapes are instructive, and they'll be useful if we're ever visited by aliens again, but they don't generate many good anecdotes.

When it comes to language-learning anecdotes, my favorite source is child language acquisition. I remember one afternoon when you are five years old, after you have come home from kindergarten. You'll be coloring with your crayons while I grade papers.

'Mom,' you'll say, using the carefully casual tone reserved for requesting a favor, 'can I ask you something?'

'Sure, sweetie. Go ahead.'

'Can I be, um, honored?'

I'll look up from the paper I'm grading. 'What do you mean?'

'At school Sharon said she got to be honored.'

'Really? Did she tell you what for?'

'It was when her big sister got married. She said only one person could be, um, honored, and she was it.'

'Ah, I see. You mean Sharon was maid of honor?'

'Yeah, that's it. Can I be made of honor?'

Gary and I entered the prefab building containing the center of operations for the looking-glass site. Inside it looked like they were planning an invasion, or perhaps an evacuation: crewcut soldiers worked around a large map of the area, or sat in front of burly electronic gear while speaking into headsets. We were shown into Colonel Weber's office, a room in the back that was cool from air conditioning.

We briefed the colonel on our first day's results. 'Doesn't sound like you got very far,' he said.

'I have an idea as to how we can make faster progress,' I said. 'But you'll have to approve the use of more equipment.'

'What more do you need?'

'A digital camera, and a big video screen.' I showed him a drawing of the setup I imagined. 'I want to try conducting the discovery procedure using writing; I'd display words on the screen, and use the camera to record the words they write. I'm hoping the heptapods will do the same.'

Weber looked at the drawing dubiously. 'What would be the advantage of that?'

'So far I've been proceeding the way I would with speakers of an unwritten language. Then it occurred to me that the heptapods must have writing, too.'

'So?'

'If the heptapods have a mechanical way of producing writing, then their writing ought to be very regular, very consistent. That would make it easier for us to identify graphemes instead of phonemes. It's like picking out the letters in a printed sentence instead of trying to hear them when the sentence is spoken aloud.'

'I take your point,' he admitted. 'And how would you respond to them? Show them the words they displayed to you?'

'Basically. And if they put spaces between words, any sentences we write would be a lot more intelligible than any spoken sentence we might splice together from recordings.'

He leaned back in his chair. 'You know we want to show as little of our technology as possible.'

'I understand, but we're using machines as intermediaries already. If we can get them to use writing, I believe progress will go much faster than if we're restricted to the sound spectrographs.'

The colonel turned to Gary. 'Your opinion?'

'It sounds like a good idea to me. I'm curious whether the heptapods might have difficulty reading our monitors. Their looking glasses are based on a completely different technology than our video screens. As far as we can tell, they don't use pixels or scan lines, and they don't refresh on a frame-by-frame basis.'

'You think the scan lines on our video screens might render them unreadable to the heptapods?'

'It's possible,' said Gary. 'We'll just have to try it and see.'

Weber considered it. For me it wasn't even a question, but from his point of view it was a difficult decision; like a soldier, though, he made it quickly. 'Request granted. Talk to the sergeant outside about bringing in what you need. Have it ready for tomorrow.'

I remember one day during the summer when you're sixteen. For once, the person waiting for her date to arrive is me. Of course, you'll be waiting around too, curious to see what he looks like. You'll have a friend of yours, a blond girl with the unlikely name of Roxie, hanging out with you, giggling.

'You may feel the urge to make comments about him,' I'll say, checking myself in the hallway mirror. 'Just restrain yourselves until we leave.'

'Don't worry, Mom,' you'll say. 'We'll do it so that he won't know. Roxie, you ask me what I think the weather will be like tonight. Then I'll say what I think of Mom's date.'

'Right,' Roxie will say.

'No, you most definitely will not,' I'll say.

'Relax, Mom. He'll never know; we do this all the time.'

'What a comfort that is.'

A little later on, Nelson will arrive to pick me up. I'll do the introductions, and we'll all engage in a little small talk on the front porch. Nelson is ruggedly handsome, to your evident approval. Just as we're about to leave, Roxie will say to you casually, 'So what do you think the weather will be like tonight?'

'I think it's going to be really hot,' you'll answer.

Roxie will nod in agreement. Nelson will say, 'Really? I thought they said it was going to be cool.'

'I have a sixth sense about these things,' you'll say. Your face will give nothing away. 'I get the feeling it's going to be a scorcher. Good thing you're dressed for it, Mom.'

I'll glare at you, and say good night.

As I lead Nelson toward his car, he'll ask me, amused, 'I'm missing something here, aren't I?'

'A private joke,' I'll mutter. 'Don't ask me to explain it.'

At our next session at the looking glass, we repeated the procedure we had performed before, this time displaying a printed word on our computer screen at the same time we spoke: showing HUMAN while saying 'Human,' and so forth. Eventually, the heptapods understood what we wanted, and set up a flat circular screen mounted on a small pedestal. One heptapod spoke, and then inserted a limb into a large socket in the pedestal; a doodle of script, vaguely cursive, popped onto the screen.

We soon settled into a routine, and I compiled two parallel corpora:

one of spoken utterances, one of writing samples. Based on first impressions, their writing appeared to be logographic, which was disappointing; I'd been hoping for an alphabetic script to help us learn their speech. Their logograms might include some phonetic information, but finding it would be a lot harder than with an alphabetic script.

By getting up close to the looking glass, I was able to point to various heptapod body parts, such as limbs, digits, and eyes, and elicit terms for each. It turned out that they had an orifice on the underside of their body, lined with articulated bony ridges: probably used for eating, while the one at the top was for respiration and speech. There were no other conspicuous orifices; perhaps their mouth was their anus too. Those sorts of questions would have to wait.

I also tried asking our two informants for terms for addressing each individually; personal names, if they had such things. Their answers were of course unpronounceable, so for Gary's and my purposes, I dubbed them Flapper and Raspberry. I hoped I'd be able to tell them apart.

The next day I conferred with Gary before we entered the looking-glass tent. 'I'll need your help with this session,' I told him.

'Sure. What do you want me to do?'

'We need to elicit some verbs, and it's easiest with third-person forms. Would you act out a few verbs while I type the written form on the computer? If we're lucky, the heptapods will figure out what we're doing and do the same. I've brought a bunch of props for you to use.'

'No problem,' said Gary, cracking his knuckles. 'Ready when you are.'

We began with some simple intransitive verbs: walking, jumping, speaking, writing. Gary demonstrated each one with a charming lack of self-consciousness; the presence of the video cameras didn't inhibit him at all. For the first few actions he performed, I asked the heptapods, 'What do you call that?' Before long, the heptapods caught on to what we were trying to do; Raspberry began mimicking Gary, or at least performing the equivalent heptapod action, while Flapper worked their computer, displaying a written description and pronouncing it aloud.

In the spectrographs of their spoken utterances, I could recognize their word I had glossed as 'heptapod.' The rest of each utterance was presumably the verb phrase; it looked like they had analogs of nouns and verbs, thank goodness.

In their writing, however, things weren't as clear-cut. For each action, they had displayed a single logogram instead of two separate ones. At first I thought they had written something like 'walks,' with the subject implied. But why would Flapper say 'the heptapod walks' while writing 'walks,' instead of maintaining parallelism? Then I noticed that some of the logograms looked like the logogram for 'heptapod' with some extra strokes added to one side or another. Perhaps their verbs could be written as affixes to a noun. If so, why was Flapper writing the noun in some instances but not in others?

I decided to try a transitive verb; substituting object words might clarify things. Among the props I'd brought were an apple and a slice of bread. 'Okay,' I said to Gary, 'show them the food, and then eat some. First the apple, then the bread.'

Gary pointed at the Golden Delicious and then he took a bite out of it, while I displayed the 'what do you call that?' expression. Then we repeated it with the slice of whole wheat.

Raspberry left the room and returned with some kind of giant nut or gourd and a gelatinous ellipsoid. Raspberry pointed at the gourd while Flapper said a word and displayed a logogram. Then Raspberry brought the gourd down between its legs, a crunching sound resulted, and the gourd reemerged minus a bite; there were corn-like kernels beneath the shell. Flapper talked and displayed a large logogram on their screen. The sound spectrograph for 'gourd' changed when it was used in the sentence; possibly a case marker. The logogram was odd: after some study, I could identify graphic elements that resembled the individual logograms for 'heptapod' and 'gourd.' They looked as if they had been melted together, with several extra strokes in the mix that presumably meant 'eat.' Was it a multi-word ligature?

Next we got spoken and written names for the gelatin egg, and descriptions of the act of eating it. The sound spectrograph for 'heptapod eats gelatin egg' was analyzable; 'gelatin egg' bore a case marker, as expected, though the sentence's word order differed from last time. The written form, another large logogram, was another matter. This time it took much longer for me to recognize anything in it; not only were the individual logograms melted together again, it looked as if the one for 'heptapod' was laid on its back, while on top of it the logogram for 'gelatin egg' was standing on its head.

'Uh-oh.' I took another look at the writing for the simple noun-verb examples, the ones that had seemed inconsistent before. Now I realized all of them actually did contain the logogram for 'heptapod'; some were rotated and distorted by being combined with the various verbs, so I hadn't recognized them at first. 'You guys have got to be kidding,' I muttered.

'What's wrong?' asked Gary.

'Their script isn't word divided; a sentence is written by joining the logograms for the constituent words. They join the logograms by rotating and modifying them. Take a look.' I showed him how the logograms were rotated.

'So they can read a word with equal ease no matter how it's rotated,' Gary said. He turned to look at the heptapods, impressed. 'I wonder if it's a consequence of their bodies' radial symmetry: their bodies have no "forward" direction, so maybe their writing doesn't either. Highly neat.'

I couldn't believe it; I was working with someone who modified the word 'neat' with 'highly.' 'It certainly is interesting,' I said, 'but it also means there's no easy way for us to write our own sentences in their language. We can't simply cut their sentences into individual words and recombine them; we'll have to learn the rules of their script before we can write anything legible. It's the same continuity problem we'd have had splicing together speech fragments, except applied to writing.'

I looked at Flapper and Raspberry in the looking glass, who were waiting for us to continue, and sighed. 'You aren't going to make this easy for us, are you?'

To be fair, the heptapods were completely cooperative. In the days that followed, they readily taught us their language without requiring us to teach them any more English. Colonel Weber and his cohorts pondered the implications of that, while I and the linguists at the other looking glasses met via videoconferencing to share what we had learned about the heptapod language. The videoconferencing made for an incongruous working environment: our video screens were primitive compared to the heptapods' looking glasses, so that my colleagues seemed more remote than the aliens. The familiar was far away, while the bizarre was close at hand.

It would be a while before we'd be ready to ask the heptapods why they had come, or to discuss physics well enough to ask them about their technology. For the time being, we worked on the basics: phonemics/graphemics, vocabulary, syntax. The heptapods at every looking glass were using the same language, so we were able to pool our data and coordinate our efforts.

Our biggest source of confusion was the heptapods' 'writing.' It didn't appear to be writing at all; it looked more like a bunch of intricate graphic designs. The logograms weren't arranged in rows, or a spiral, or any linear fashion. Instead, Flapper or Raspberry would write a sentence by sticking together as many logograms as needed into a giant conglomeration.

This form of writing was reminiscent of primitive sign systems, which required a reader to know a message's context in order to understand it. Such systems were considered too limited for systematic recording of information. Yet it was unlikely that the heptapods developed their level of technology with only an oral tradition. That implied one of three possibilities: the first was that the heptapods had a true writing system, but they didn't want to use it in front of us; Colonel Weber would identify with that one. The second was that the heptapods hadn't originated the technology they were using; they were illiterates using someone else's technology. The third, and most interesting to me, was that the heptapods were using a nonlinear system of orthography that qualified as true writing.

I remember a conversation we'll have when you're in your junior year of high school. It'll be Sunday morning, and I'll be scrambling some eggs while you set the table for brunch. You'll laugh as you tell me about the party you went to last night.

'Oh man,' you'll say, 'they're not kidding when they say that body weight makes a difference. I didn't drink any more than the guys did, but I got so much *drunker*.'

I'll try to maintain a neutral, pleasant expression. I'll really try. Then you'll say, 'Oh, come on, Mom.'

'What?'

'You know you did the exact same things when you were my age.'

I did nothing of the sort, but I know that if I were to admit that, you'd lose respect for me completely. 'You know never to drive, or get into a car if –'

'God, of course I know that. Do you think I'm an idiot?'

'No, of course not.'

What I'll think is that you are clearly, maddeningly not me. It will remind me, again, that you won't be a clone of me; you can be wonderful, a daily delight, but you won't be someone I could have created by myself.

The military had set up a trailer containing our offices at the looking-glass site. I saw Gary walking toward the trailer, and ran to catch up with him. 'It's a semasiographic writing system,' I said when I reached him.

'Excuse me?' said Gary.

'Here, let me show you.' I directed Gary into my office. Once we were inside, I went to the chalkboard and drew a circle with a diagonal line bisecting it. 'What does this mean?'

' "Not allowed"?'

'Right.' Next I printed the words NOT ALLOWED on the chalkboard. 'And so does this. But only one is a representation of speech.'

Gary nodded. 'Okay.'

'Linguists describe writing like this' – I indicated the printed words – 'as "glottographic," because it represents speech. Every human written language is in this category. However, this symbol' – I indicated the circle and diagonal line – 'is "semasiographic" writing, because it conveys meaning without reference to speech. There's no correspondence between its components and any particular sounds.'

'And you think all of heptapod writing is like this?'

'From what I've seen so far, yes. It's not picture writing, it's far more complex. It has its own system of rules for constructing sentences, like a visual syntax that's unrelated to the syntax for their spoken language.'

'A visual syntax? Can you show me an example?'

'Coming right up.' I sat down at my desk and, using the computer, pulled up a frame from the recording of yesterday's conversation with Raspberry. I turned the monitor so he could see it. 'In their spoken language, a noun has a case marker indicating whether it's a subject or object. In their written language, however, a noun is identified as subject or object based on the orientation of its logogram relative to that of the verb. Here, take a look.' I pointed at one of the figures. 'For instance, when "heptapod" is integrated with "hears" this way, with these strokes parallel, it means that the heptapod is doing the hearing.' I showed him a different one. 'When they're combined this way, with the strokes perpendicular, it means that the hepptapod is being heard. This morphology applies to several verbs.

'Another example is the inflection system.' I called up another frame from the recording. 'In their written language, this logogram means roughly "hear easily" or "hear clearly." See the elements it has in common with the logogram for "hear"? You can still combine it with "heptapod" in the same ways as before, to indicate that the heptapod can hear something clearly or that the heptapod is clearly heard. But what's really interesting is that the modulation of "hear" into "hear clearly" isn't a special case; you see the transformation they applied?'

Gary nodded, pointing. 'It's like they express the idea of "clearly" by changing the curve of those strokes in the middle.'

'Right. That modulation is applicable to lots of verbs. The logogram for "see" can be modulated in the same way to form "see clearly," and so can the logogram for "read" and others. And changing the curve of those strokes has no parallel in their speech; with the spoken version of these verbs, they add a prefix to the verb to express ease of manner, and the prefixes for "see" and "hear" are different.

'There are other examples, but you get the idea. It's essentially a grammar in two dimensions.'

He began pacing thoughtfully. 'Is there anything like this in human writing systems?'

'Mathematical equations, notations for music and dance. But those are all very specialized; we couldn't record this conversation using them. But I suspect, if we knew it well enough, we could record this conversation in the heptapod writing system. I think it's a full-fledged, general-purpose graphical language.'

Gary frowned. 'So their writing constitutes a completely separate language from their speech, right?'

'Right. In fact, it'd be more accurate to refer to the writing system as "Heptapod B," and use "Heptapod A" strictly for referring to the spoken language.'

'Hold on a second. Why use two languages when one would suffice? That seems unnecessarily hard to learn.'

'Like English spelling?' I said. 'Ease of learning isn't the primary force in language evolution. For the heptapods, writing and speech may play such different cultural or cognitive roles that using separate languages makes more sense than using different forms of the same one.'

He considered it. 'I see what you mean. Maybe they think our form of writing is redundant, like we're wasting a second communications channel.'

'That's entirely possible. Finding out why they use a second language for writing will tell us a lot about them.'

'So I take it this means we won't be able to use their writing to help us learn their spoken language.'

I sighed. 'Yeah, that's the most immediate implication. But I don't think we should ignore either Heptapod A or B; we need a two-pronged approach.' I pointed at the screen. 'I'll bet you that learning their two-dimensional grammar will help you when it comes time to learn their mathematical notation.'

'You've got a point there. So are we ready to start asking about their mathematics?'

'Not yet. We need a better grasp on this writing system before we begin anything else,' I said, and then smiled when he mimed frustration. 'Patience, good sir. Patience is a virtue.'

You'll be six when your father has a conference to attend in Hawaii, and we'll accompany him. You'll be so excited that you'll make preparations for weeks beforehand. You'll ask me about coconuts and volcanoes and surfing, and practice hula dancing in the mirror. You'll pack a suitcase with the clothes and toys you want to bring, and you'll drag it around the house to see how long you can carry it. You'll ask me if I can carry your Etch-a-Sketch in my bag, since there won't be any more room for it in yours and you simply can't leave without it.

'You won't need all of these,' I'll say. 'There'll be so many fun things to do there, you won't have time to play with so many toys.'

You'll consider that; dimples will appear above your eyebrows when you think hard. Eventually you'll agree to pack fewer toys, but your expectations will, if anything, increase.

'I wanna be in Hawaii now,' you'll whine.

'Sometimes it's good to wait,' I'll say. 'The anticipation makes it more fun when you get there.'

You'll just pout.

In the next report I submitted, I suggested that the term 'logogram' was a misnomer because it implied that each graph represented a spoken word, when in fact the graphs didn't correspond to our notion of spoken words at all. I didn't want to use the term 'ideogram' either because of how it had been used in the past; I suggested the term 'semagram' instead.

It appeared that a semagram corresponded roughly to a written word in human languages: it was meaningful on its own, and in combination with other semagrams could form endless statements. We couldn't define it precisely, but then no one had ever satisfactorily defined 'word' for human languages either. When it came to sentences in Heptapod B, though, things became much more confusing. The language had no written punctuation: its syntax was indicated in the way the semagrams were combined, and there was no need to indicate the cadence of speech. There was certainly no way to slice out subject-predicate pairings neatly to make sentences. A 'sentence' seemed to be whatever number of semagrams a heptapod wanted to join together; the only difference between a sentence and a paragraph, or a page, was size.

When a Heptapod B sentence grew fairly sizable, its visual impact was remarkable. If I wasn't trying to decipher it, the writing looked like fanciful praying mantids drawn in a cursive style, all clinging to each other to form an Escheresque lattice, each slightly different in its stance. And the biggest sentences had an effect similar to that of psychedelic posters: sometimes eye-watering, sometimes hypnotic.

I remember a picture of you taken at your college graduation. In the photo you're striking a pose for the camera, mortarboard stylishly tilted on your head, one hand touching your sunglasses, the other hand on your hip, holding open your gown to reveal the tank top and shorts you're wearing underneath.

I remember your graduation. There will be the distraction of having Nelson and your father and what's-her-name there all at the same time, but that will be minor. That entire weekend, while you're introducing me to your classmates and hugging everyone incessantly, I'll be all but mute with amazement. I can't believe that you, a grown woman taller than me and beautiful enough to make my heart ache, will be the same girl I used to lift off the ground so you could reach the drinking fountain, the same girl who used to trundle out of my bedroom draped in a dress and hat and four scarves from my closet.

And after graduation, you'll be heading for a job as a financial analyst. I won't understand what you do there, I won't even understand your fascination with money, the preeminence you gave to salary when negotiating job offers. I would prefer it if you'd pursue something without regard for its monetary rewards, but I'll have no complaints. My own mother could never understand why I couldn't just be a high school English teacher. You'll do what makes you happy, and that'll be all I ask for.

As time went on, the teams at each looking glass began working in earnest on learning heptapod terminology for elementary mathematics and physics. We worked together on presentations, with the linguists focusing on procedure and the physicists focusing on subject matter. The physicists showed us previously devised systems for communicating with aliens, based on mathematics, but those were intended for use over a radio telescope. We reworked them for face-to-face communication.

Our teams were successful with basic arithmetic, but we hit a roadblock with geometry and algebra. We tried using a spherical coordinate system instead of a rectangular one, thinking it might be more natural to the heptapods given their anatomy, but that approach wasn't any more fruitful. The heptapods didn't seem to understand what we were getting at.

Likewise, the physics discussions went poorly. Only with the most concrete terms, like the names of the elements, did we have any success; after several attempts at representing the periodic table, the heptapods got the idea. For anything remotely abstract, we might as well have been gibbering. We tried to demonstrate basic physical attributes like mass and acceleration so we could elicit their terms for them, but the heptapods simply responded with requests for clarification. To avoid perceptual problems that might be associated with any particular medium, we tried physical demonstrations as well as line drawings, photos, and animations; none was effective. Days with no progress became weeks, and the physicists were becoming disillusioned.

By contrast, the linguists were having much more success. We made steady progress decoding the grammar of the spoken language, Heptapod A. It didn't follow the pattern of human language, as expected, but it was comprehensible so far: free word order, even to the extent that there was no preferred order for the clauses in a conditional statement, in defiance of a human language 'universal.' It also appeared that the heptapods had no objection to many levels of center-embedding of clauses, something that quickly defeated humans. Peculiar, but not impenetrable.

Much more interesting were the newly discovered morphological and grammatical processes in Heptapod B that were uniquely two-dimensional. Depending on a semagram's declension, inflections could be indicated by varying a certain stroke's curvature, or its thickness, or its manner of undulation; or by varying the relative sizes of two radicals, or their relative distance to another radical, or their orientations; or various other means. These were nonsegmental graphemes; they couldn't be isolated from the rest of a semagram. And despite how such traits behaved in human writing, these had nothing to do with calligraphic style; their meanings were defined according to a consistent and unambiguous grammar.

We regularly asked the heptapods why they had come. Each time, they answered 'to see,' or 'to observe.' Indeed, sometimes they preferred to watch us silently rather than answer our questions. Perhaps they were scientists, perhaps they were tourists. The State Department instructed us to reveal as little as possible about humanity, in case that information could be used as a bargaining chip in subsequent negotiations. We obliged, though it didn't require much effort: the heptapods never asked questions about anything. Whether scientists or tourists, they were an awfully incurious bunch.

I remember once when we'll be driving to the mall to buy some new clothes for you. You'll be thirteen. One moment you'll be sprawled in your seat, completely unself-conscious, all child; the next, you'll toss your hair with a practiced casualness, like a fashion model in training.

You'll give me some instructions as I'm parking the car. 'Okay, Mom, give me one of the credit cards, and we can meet back at the entrance here in two hours.'

I'll laugh. 'Not a chance. All the credit cards stay with me.'

'You're kidding.' You'll become the embodiment of exasperation. We'll get out of the car and I will start walking to the mall entrance. After seeing that I won't budge on the matter, you'll quickly reformulate your plans.

'Okay Mom, okay. You can come with me, just walk a little ways behind me, so it doesn't look like we're together. If I see any friends of mine, I'm gonna stop and talk to them, but you just keep walking, okay? I'll come find you later.'

I'll stop in my tracks. 'Excuse me? I am not the hired help, nor am I some mutant relative for you to be ashamed of.'

'But Mom, I can't let anyone see you with me.'

'What are you talking about? I've already met your friends; they've been to the house.'

'That was different,' you'll say, incredulous that you have to explain it. 'This is shopping.'

'Too bad.'

Then the explosion: 'You won't do the least thing to make me happy! You don't care about me at all!'

It won't have been that long since you enjoyed going shopping with me; it will forever astonish me how quickly you grow out of one phase and enter another. Living with you will be like aiming for a moving target; you'll always be further along than I expect.

*

I looked at the sentence in Heptapod B that I had just written, using simple pen and paper. Like all the sentences I generated myself, this one looked misshapen, like a heptapod-written sentence that had been smashed with a hammer and then inexpertly taped back together. I had sheets of such inelegant semagrams covering my desk, fluttering occasionally when the oscillating fan swung past.

It was strange trying to learn a language that had no spoken form. Instead of practicing my pronunciation, I had taken to squeezing my eyes shut and trying to paint semagrams on the insides of my eyelids.

There was a knock at the door and before I could answer Gary came in looking jubilant. 'Illinois got a repetition in physics.'

'Really? That's great; when did it happen?'

'It happened a few hours ago; we just had the videoconference. Let me show you what it is.' He started erasing my blackboard.

'Don't worry, I didn't need any of that.'

'Good.' He picked up a nub of chalk and drew a diagram:

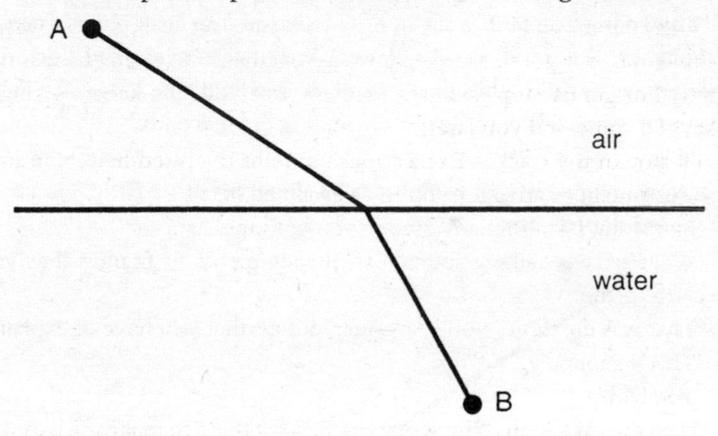

'Okay, here's the path a ray of light takes when crossing from air to water. The light ray travels in a straight line until it hits the water; the water has a different index of refraction, so the light changes direction. You've heard of this before, right?'

I nodded. 'Sure.'

'Now here's an interesting property about the path the light takes. The path is the fastest possible route between these two points.'

'Come again?'

'Imagine, just for grins, that the ray of light traveled along this path.' He added a dotted line to his diagram:

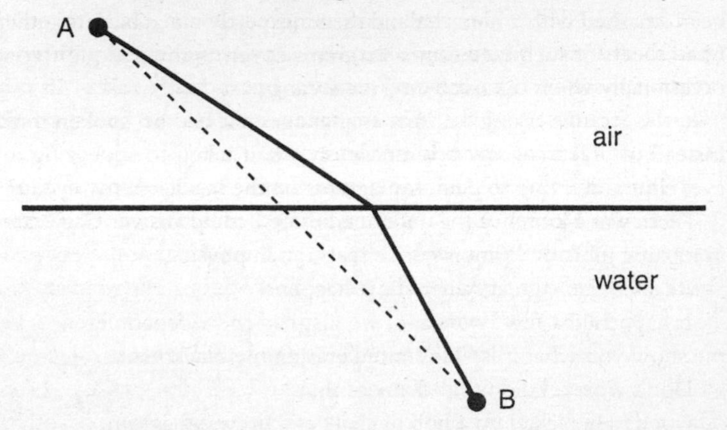

'This hypothetical path is shorter than the path the light actually takes. But light travels more slowly in water than it does in air, and a greater percentage of this path is underwater. So it would take longer for light to travel along this path than it does along the real path.'

'Okay, I get it.'

'Now imagine if light were to travel along this other path.' He drew a second dotted path:

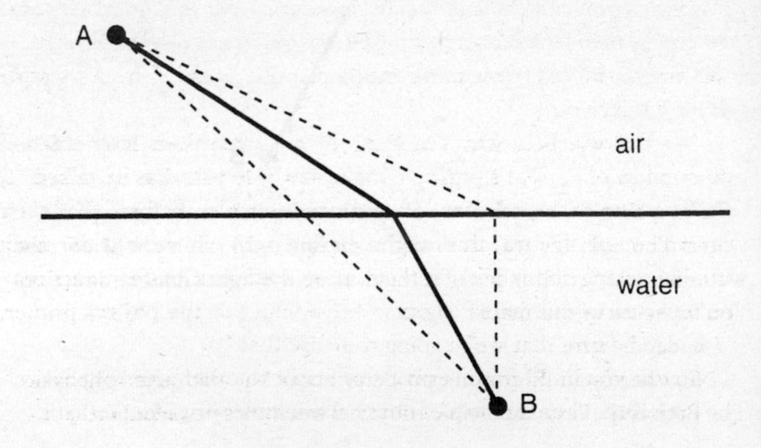

'This path reduces the percentage that's underwater, but the total length is larger. It would also take longer for light to travel along this path than along the actual one.'

Gary put down the chalk and gestured at the diagram on the chalkboard with white-tipped fingers. 'Any hypothetical path would require more time to traverse than the one actually taken. In other words, the route that the light ray takes is always the fastest possible one. That's Fermat's principle of least time.'

'Hmm, interesting. And this is what the heptapods responded to?'

'Exactly. Moorehead gave an animated presentation of Fermat's principle at the Illinois looking glass, and the heptapods repeated it back. Now he's trying to get a symbolic description.' He grinned. 'Now is that highly neat, or what?'

'It's neat all right, but how come I haven't heard of Fermat's principle before?' I picked up a binder and waved it at him; it was a primer on the physics topics suggested for use in communication with the heptapods. 'This thing goes on forever about Planck masses and the spin-flip of atomic hydrogen, and not a word about the refraction of light.'

'We guessed wrong about what'd be most useful for you to know,' Gary said without embarrassment. 'In fact, it's curious that Fermat's principle was the first breakthrough; even though it's easy to explain, you need calculus to describe it mathematically. And not ordinary calculus; you need the calculus of variations. We thought that some simple theorem of geometry or algebra would be the breakthrough.'

'Curious indeed. You think the heptapods' idea of what's simple doesn't match ours?'

'Exactly, which is why I'm *dying* to see what their mathematical description of Fermat's principle looks like.' He paced as he talked. 'If their version of the calculus of variations is simpler to them than their equivalent of algebra, that might explain why we've had so much trouble talking about physics; their entire system of mathematics may be topsy-turvy compared to ours.' He pointed to the physics primer. 'You can be sure that we're going to revise that.'

'So can you build from Fermat's principle to other areas of physics?'

'Probably. There are lots of physical principles just like Fermat's.'

'What, like Louise's principle of least closet space? When did physics become so minimalist?'

'Well, the word "least" is misleading. You see, Fermat's principle of least time is incomplete; in certain situations light follows a path that takes *more* time than any of the other possibilities. It's more accurate to say that light always follows an *extreme* path, either one that minimizes the time taken or one that maximizes it. A minimum and a maximum share certain mathematical properties, so both situations can be described with one equation. So to be precise, Fermat's principle isn't a minimal principle; instead it's what's known as a "variational" principle.'

'And there are more of these variational principles?'

He nodded. 'In all branches of physics. Almost every physical law can be restated as a variational principle. The only difference between these principles is in which attribute is minimized or maximized.' He gestured as if the different branches of physics were arrayed before him on a table. 'In optics, where Fermat's principle applies, time is the attribute that has to be an extreme. In mechanics, it's a different attribute. In electromagnetism, it's something else again. But all these principles are similar mathematically.'

'So once you get their mathematical description of Fermat's principle, you should be able to decode the other ones.'

'God, I hope so. I think this is the wedge that we've been looking for, the one that cracks open their formulation of physics. This calls for a celebration.' He stopped his pacing and turned to me. 'Hey Louise, want to go out for dinner? My treat.'

I was mildly surprised. 'Sure,' I said.

It'll be when you first learn to walk that I get daily demonstrations of the asymmetry in our relationship. You'll be incessantly running off somewhere, and each time you walk into a door frame or scrape your knee, the pain feels like it's my own. It'll be like growing an errant limb, an extension of myself whose sensory nerves report pain just fine, but whose motor nerves don't convey my commands at all. It's so unfair: I'm going to give birth to an animated voodoo doll of myself. I didn't see this in the contract when I signed up. Was this part of the deal?

And then there will be the times when I see you laughing. Like the time you'll be playing with the neighbor's puppy, poking your hands through the chain-link fence separating our back yards, and you'll be laughing so hard you'll start hiccuping. The puppy will run inside the neighbor's house, and your laughter will gradually subside, letting you catch your breath. Then the puppy will come back to the fence to lick your fingers again, and you'll shriek and start laughing again. It will be the most wonderful sound I could ever imagine, a sound that makes me feel like a fountain, or a wellspring.

Now if only I can remember that sound the next time your blithe disregard for self-preservation gives me a heart attack.

After the breakthrough with Fermat's principle, discussions of scientific concepts became more fruitful. It wasn't as if all of heptapod physics were suddenly rendered transparent, but progress was steady. According to Gary, the heptapods' formulation of physics was indeed topsy-turvy relative to ours. Physical attributes that humans defined using integral calculus were seen as fundamental by the heptapods. As an example, Gary described an attribute that, in physics jargon, bore the deceptively simple name 'action,' which represented 'the difference between kinetic and potential energy, integrated over time,' whatever that meant. Calculus for us; elementary to them.

Conversely, to define attributes that humans thought of as fundamental, like velocity, the heptapods employed mathematics that were, Gary assured me, 'highly weird.' The physicists were ultimately able to prove the equivalence of heptapod mathematics and human mathematics; even though their approaches were almost the reverse of one another, both were systems for describing the same physical universe.

I tried following some of the equations that the physicists were coming up with, but it was no use. I couldn't really grasp the significance of physical attributes like 'action'; I couldn't, with any confidence, ponder the significance of treating such an attribute as fundamental. Still, I tried to ponder questions formulated in terms more familiar to me: what kind of world-view did the heptapods have, that they would consider Fermat's principle the simplest explanation of light refraction? What kind of perception made a minimum or maximum readily apparent to them?

Your eyes will be blue like your dad's, not mud brown like mine. Boys will stare into those eyes the way I did, and do, into your dad's, surprised and enchanted, as I was and am, to find them in combination with black hair. You will have many suitors.

I remember when you are fifteen, coming home after a weekend at your dad's, incredulous over the interrogation he'll have put you through regarding the boy you're currently dating. You'll sprawl on the sofa, recounting your dad's latest breach of common sense: 'You know what he said? He said, "I know what teenage boys are like."' Roll of the eyes. 'Like I don't?'

'Don't hold it against him,' I'll say. 'He's a father; he can't help it.' Having seen you interact with your friends, I won't worry much about a boy taking advantage of you; if anything, the opposite will be more likely. I'll worry about that.

'He wishes I were still a kid. He hasn't known how to act toward me since I grew breasts.'

'Well, that development was a shock for him. Give him time to recover.'

'It's been *years*, Mom. How long is it gonna take?'

'I'll let you know when my father has come to terms with mine.'

During one of the videoconferences for the linguists, Cisneros from the Massachusetts looking glass had raised an interesting question: Was there a particular order in which semagrams were written in a Heptapod B sentence? It was clear that word order meant next to nothing when speaking in Heptapod A; when asked to repeat what it had just said, a heptapod would likely as not use a different word order unless we specifically asked them not to. Was word order similarly unimportant when writing in Heptapod B?

Previously, we had focused our attention only on how a sentence in Heptapod B looked once it was complete. As far as anyone could tell, there was no preferred order when reading the semagrams in a sentence; you could start almost anywhere in the nest, then follow the branching clauses until you'd read the whole thing. But that was reading; was the same true about writing?

During my most recent session with Flapper and Raspberry I had asked them if, instead of displaying a semagram only after it was completed, they could show it to us while it was being written. They had agreed. I insterted the videotape of the session into the VCR, and on my computer I consulted the session transcript.

I picked one of the longer utterances from the conversation. What Flapper had said was that the heptapods' planet had two moons, one significantly larger than the other; the three primary constituents of the planet's atmosphere were nitrogen, argon, and oxygen; and 15/28ths of the planet's surface was covered by water. The first words of the spoken utterance translated literally as 'inequality-of-size rocky-orbiter rocky-orbiters related-as-primary-to-secondary.'

Then I rewound the videotape until the time signature matched the one in the transcription. I started playing the tape, and watched the web of semagrams being spun out of inky spider's silk. I rewound it and played it several times. Finally I froze the video right after the first stroke was completed and before the second one was begun; all that was visible onscreen was a single sinuous line.

Comparing that initial stroke with the completed sentence, I realized that the stroke participated in several different clauses of the message. It began in the semagram for 'oxygen,' as the determinant that distinguished it from certain other elements; then it slid down to become the morpheme of comparison in the description of the two moons' sizes; and lastly it flared out as the arched backbone of the semagram for 'ocean.' Yet this stroke was a single continuous line, and it was the first one that Flapper wrote. That meant the heptapod had to know how the entire sentence would be laid out before it could write the very first stroke.

The other strokes in the sentence also traversed several clauses, making them so interconnected that none could be removed without redesigning the entire sentence. The heptapods didn't write a sentence one semagram at a time; they built it out of strokes irrespective of individual semagrams. I had seen a similarly high degree of integration before in calligraphic designs, particularly those employing the Arabic alphabet. But those designs had required careful planning by expert calligraphers. No one could lay out such an intricate design at the speed needed for holding a conversation. At least, no human could.

There's a joke that I once heard a comedienne tell. It goes like this: 'I'm not sure if I'm ready to have children. I asked a friend of mine who has children, "Suppose I do have kids. What if when they grow up, they blame me for everything that's wrong with their lives?" She laughed and said, "What do you mean, if?"'

That's my favorite joke.

Gary and I were at a little Chinese restaurant, one of the local places we had taken to patronizing to get away from the encampment. We sat eating the appetizers: potstickers, redolent of pork and sesame oil. My favorite.

I dipped one in soy sauce and vinegar. 'So how are you doing with your Heptapod B practice?' I asked.

Gary looked obliquely at the ceiling. I tried to meet his gaze, but he kept shifting it.

'You've given up, haven't you?' I said. 'You're not even trying anymore.'

He did a wonderful hangdog expression. 'I'm just no good at languages,' he confessed. 'I thought learning Heptapod B might be more like learning mathematics than trying to speak another language, but it's not. It's too foreign for me.'

'It would help you discuss physics with them.'

'Probably, but since we had our breakthrough, I can get by with just a few phrases.'

I sighed. 'I suppose that's fair; I have to admit, I've given up on trying to learn the mathematics.'

'So we're even?'

'We're even.' I sipped my tea. 'Though I did want to ask you about Fermat's principle. Something about it feels odd to me, but I can't put my finger on it. It just doesn't sound like a law of physics.'

A twinkle appeared in Gary's eyes. 'I'll bet I know what you're talking about.' He snipped a potsticker in half with his chopsticks. 'You're used to thinking of refraction in terms of cause and effect: reaching the water's surface is the cause, and the change in direction is the effect. But Fermat's principle sounds weird because it describes light's behavior in goal-oriented terms. It sounds like a commandment to a light beam: "Thou shalt minimize or maximize the time taken to reach thy destination." '

I considered it. 'Go on.'

'It's an old question in the philosophy of physics. People have been talking about it since Fermat first formulated it in the 1600s; Planck wrote volumes about it. The thing is, while the common formulation of physical laws is causal, a variational principle like Fermat's is purposive, almost teleological.'

'Hmm, that's an interesting way to put it. Let me think about that for a minute.' I pulled out a felt-tip pen and, on my paper napkin, drew a copy of the diagram that Gary had drawn on my blackboard. 'Okay,' I said, thinking aloud, 'so let's say the goal of a ray of light is to take the fastest path. How does the light go about doing that?'

'Well, if I can speak anthropomorphic-projectionally, the light has to examine the possible paths and compute how long each one would take.' He plucked the last potsticker from the serving dish.

'And to do that,' I continued, 'the ray of light has to know just where its destination is. If the destination were somewhere else, the fastest path would be different.'

Gary nodded again. 'That's right; the notion of a "fastest path" is meaningless unless there's a destination specified. And computing how long a given path takes also requires information about what lies along that path, like where the water's surface is.'

I kept staring at the diagram on the napkin. 'And the light ray has to know all that ahead of time, before it starts moving, right?'

'So to speak,' said Gary. 'The light can't start traveling in any old direction and make course corrections later on, because the path resulting from such behavior wouldn't be the fastest possible one. The light has to do all its computations at the very beginning.'

I thought to myself, *the ray of light has to know where it will ultimately end up before it can choose the direction to begin moving in.* I knew what that reminded me of. I looked up at Gary. 'That's what was bugging me.'

⋆

I remember when you're fourteen. You'll come out of your bedroom, a graffiti-covered notebook computer in hand, working on a report for school.

'Mom, what do you call it when both sides can win?'

I'll look up from my computer and the paper I'll be writing. 'What, you mean a win-win situation?'

'There's some technical name for it, some math word. Remember that time Dad was here, and he was talking about the stock market? He used it then.'

'Hmm, that sounds familiar, but I can't remember what he called it.'

'I need to know. I want to use that phrase in my social studies report. I can't even search for information on it unless I know what it's called.'

'I'm sorry, I don't know it either. Why don't you call your dad?'

Judging from your expression, that will be more effort than you want to make. At this point, you and your father won't be getting along well. 'Can you call Dad and ask him? But don't tell him it's for me.'

'I think you can call him yourself.'

You'll fume, 'Jesus, Mom, I can never get help with my homework since you and Dad split up.'

It's amazing the diverse situations in which you can bring up the divorce. 'I've helped you with your homework.'

'Like a million years ago, Mom.'

I'll let that pass. 'I'd help you with this if I could, but I don't remember what it's called.'

You'll head back to your bedroom in a huff.

I practiced Heptapod B at every opportunity, both with the other linguists and by myself. The novelty of reading a semasiographic language made it compelling in a way that Heptapod A wasn't, and my improvement in writing it excited me. Over time, the sentences I wrote grew shapelier, more cohesive. I had reached the point where it worked better when I didn't think about it too much. Instead of carefully trying to design a sentence before writing, I could simply begin putting down strokes immediately; my initial strokes almost always turned out to be compatible with an elegant rendition of what I was trying to say. I was developing a faculty like that of the heptapods.

More interesting was the fact that Heptapod B was changing the way I thought. For me, thinking typically meant speaking in an internal voice; as we say in the trade, my thoughts were phonologically coded. My internal voice normally spoke in English, but that wasn't a requirement. The summer after my senior year in high school, I attended a total immersion program for learning Russian; by the end of the summer, I was thinking and even dreaming in Russian. But it was always *spoken* Russian. Different language, same mode: a voice speaking silently aloud.

The idea of thinking in a linguistic yet nonphonological mode always intrigued me. I had a friend born of deaf parents; he grew up using American Sign Language, and he told me that he often thought in ASL instead of English. I used to wonder what it was like to have one's thoughts be manually coded, to reason using an inner pair of hands instead of an inner voice.

With Heptapod B, I was experiencing something just as foreign: my thoughts were becoming graphically coded. There were trance-like moments during the day when my thoughts weren't expressed with my internal voice; instead, I saw semagrams with my mind's eye, sprouting like frost on a windowpane.

As I grew more fluent, semagraphic designs would appear fully formed, articulating even complex ideas all at once. My thought processes weren't moving any faster as a result, though. Instead of racing forward, my mind hung balanced on the symmetry underlying the semagrams. The semagrams seemed to be something more than language; they were almost like mandalas. I found myself in a meditative state, contemplating the way in which premises and conclusions were interchangeable. There was no direction inherent in the way propositions were connected, no 'train of thought' moving along a particular route; all the components in an act of reasoning were equally powerful, all having identical precedence.

A representative from the State Department named Hossner had the job of briefing the US scientists on our agenda with the heptapods. We sat in the videoconference room, listening to him lecture. Our microphone was turned off, so Gary and I could exchange comments without interrupting Hossner. As we listened, I worried that Gary might harm his vision, rolling his eyes so often.

'They must have had some reason for coming all this way,' said the diplomat, his voice tinny through the speakers. 'It does not look like their reason was conquest, thank God. But if that's not the reason, what is? Are they prospectors? Anthropologists? Missionaries? Whatever their motives, there must be something we can offer them. Maybe it's mineral rights to our solar system. Maybe it's information about ourselves. Maybe it's the right to deliver sermons to our populations. But we can be sure that there's something.

'My point is this: their motive might not be to trade, but that doesn't mean that we cannot conduct trade. We simply need to know why they're here, and what we have that they want. Once we have that information, we can begin trade negotiations.

'I should emphasize that our relationship with the heptapods need not be adversarial. This is not a situation where every gain on their part is a loss on ours, or vice versa. If we handle ourselves correctly, both we and the heptapods can come out winners.'

'You mean it's a non-zero-sum game?' Gary said in mock incredulity. 'Oh my gosh.'

'A non-zero-sum game.'

'What?' You'll reverse course, heading back from your bedroom.

'When both sides can win: I just remembered, it's called a non-zero-sum game.'

'That's it!' you'll say, writing it down on your notebook. 'Thanks, Mom!'

'I guess I knew it after all,' I'll say. 'All those years with your father, some of it must have rubbed off.'

'I knew you'd know it,' you'll say. You'll give me a sudden, brief hug, and your hair will smell of apples. 'You're the best.'

'Louise?'

'Hmm? Sorry, I was distracted. What did you say?'

'I said, what do you think about our Mr Hossner here?'

'I prefer not to.'

'I've tried that myself: ignoring the government, seeing if it would go away. It hasn't.'

As evidence of Gary's assertion, Hossner kept blathering: 'Your immediate task is to think back on what you've learned. Look for anything that might help us. Has there been any indication of what the heptapods want? Of what they value?'

'Gee, it never occurred to us to look for things like that,' I said. 'We'll get right on it, sir.'

'The sad thing is, that's just what we'll have to do,' said Gary.

'Are there any questions?' asked Hossner.

Burghart, the linguist at the Ft Worth looking glass, spoke up. 'We've been through this with the heptapods many times. They maintain that they're here to observe, and they maintain that information is not tradable.'

'So they would have us believe,' said Hossner. 'But consider: how could that be true? I know that the heptapods have occasionally stopped talking to us for brief periods. That may be a tactical maneuver on their part. If we were to stop talking to them tomorrow –'

'Wake me up if he says something interesting,' said Gary.

'I was just going to ask you to do the same for me.'

That day when Gary first explained Fermat's principle to me, he had mentioned that almost every physical law could be stated as a variational principle. Yet when humans thought about physical laws, they preferred to work with them in their causal formulation. I could understand that: the physical attributes that humans found intuitive, like kinetic energy or acceleration, were all properties of an object at a given moment in time. And these were conducive to a chronological, causal interpretation of events: one moment growing out of another, causes and effects creating a chain reaction that grew from past to future.

In contrast, the physical attributes that the heptapods found intuitive, like 'action' or those other things defined by integrals, were meaningful only over a period of time. And these were conducive to a teleological interpretation of events: by viewing events over a period of time, one recognized that there was a requirement that had to be satisfied, a goal of minimizing or maximizing. And one had to know the initial and final states to meet that goal; one needed knowledge of the effects before the causes could be initiated.

I was growing to understand that, too.

'Why?' you'll ask again. You'll be three.

'Because it's your bedtime,' I'll say again. We'll have gotten as far as getting you bathed and into your jammies, but no further than that.

'But I'm not sleepy,' you'll whine. You'll be standing at the bookshelf, pulling down a video to watch: your latest diversionary tactic to keep away from your bedroom.

'It doesn't matter: you still have to go to bed.'

'But why?'

'Because I'm the mom and I said so.'

I'm actually going to say that, aren't I? God, somebody please shoot me.

I'll pick you up and carry you under my arm to your bed, you wailing piteously all the while, but my sole concern will be my own distress. All those vows made in childhood that I would give reasonable answers when I became a parent, that I would treat my own child as an intelligent, thinking individual, all for naught: I'm going to turn into my mother. I can fight it as much as I want, but there'll be no stopping my slide down that long, dreadful slope.

Was it actually possible to know the future? Not simply to guess at it; was it possible to *know* what was going to happen, with absolute certainty and in specific detail? Gary once told me that the fundamental laws of physics were time-symmetric, that there was no physical difference between past and future. Given that, some might say, 'yes, theoretically.' But speaking more concretely, most would answer 'no,' because of free will.

I liked to imagine the objection as a Borgesian fabulation: consider a person standing before the *Book of Ages*, the chronicle that records every event, past and future. Even though the text has been photoreduced from the full-sized edition, the volume is enormous. With magnifier in hand, she flips through the tissue-thin leaves until she locates the story of her life. She finds the passage that describes her flipping through the *Book of Ages*, and she skips to the next column, where it details what she'll be doing later in the day: acting on information she's read in the *Book*, she'll bet $100 on the racehorse Devil May Care and win twenty times that much.

The thought of doing just that had crossed her mind, but being a contrary sort, she now resolves to refrain from betting on the ponies altogether.

There's the rub. The *Book of Ages* cannot be wrong; this scenario is based on the premise that a person is given knowledge of the actual future, not of some possible future. If this were Greek myth, circumstances would conspire to make her enact her fate despite her best efforts, but prophecies in myth are notoriously vague; the *Book of Ages* is quite specific, and there's no way she can be forced to bet on a racehorse in the manner specified. The result is a contradiction: the *Book of Ages* must be right, by definition; yet no matter what the *Book* says she'll do, she can choose to do otherwise. How can these two facts be reconciled?

They can't be, was the common answer. A volume like the *Book of Ages* is a logical impossibility, for the precise reason that its existence would result in the above contradiction. Or, to be generous, some might say that the *Book of Ages* could exist, as long as it wasn't accessible to readers: that volume is housed in a special collection, and no one has viewing privileges.

The existence of free will meant that we couldn't know the future. And we knew free will existed because we had direct experience of it. Volition was an intrinsic part of consciousness.

Or was it? What if the experience of knowing the future changed a person? What if it evoked a sense of urgency, a sense of obligation to act precisely as she knew she would?

I stopped by Gary's office before leaving for the day. 'I'm calling it quits. Did you want to grab something to eat?'

'Sure, just wait a second,' he said. He shut down his computer and gathered some papers together. Then he looked up at me. 'Hey, want to come to my place for dinner tonight? I'll cook.'

I looked at him dubiously. 'You can cook?'

'Just one dish,' he admitted. 'But it's a good one.'

'Sure,' I said. 'I'm game.'

'Great. We just need to go shopping for the ingredients.'

'Don't go to any trouble –'

'There's a market on the way to my house. It won't take a minute.'

We took separate cars, me following him. I almost lost him when he abruptly turned into a parking lot. It was a gourmet market, not large, but fancy; tall glass jars stuffed with imported foods sat next to specialty utensils on the store's stainless-steel shelves.

I accompanied Gary as he collected fresh basil, tomatoes, garlic, linguini. 'There's a fish market next door; we can get fresh clams there,' he said.

'Sounds good.' We walked past the section of kitchen utensils. My gaze wandered over the shelves – pepper mills, garlic presses, salad tongs – and stopped on a wooden salad bowl.

When you are three, you'll pull a dishtowel off the kitchen counter and bring that salad bowl down on top of you. I'll make a grab for it, but I'll miss. The edge of the bowl will leave you with a cut, on the upper edge of your forehead, that will require a single stitch. Your father and I will hold you, sobbing and stained with Caesar dressing, as we wait in the emergency room for hours.

I reached out and took the bowl from the shelf. The motion didn't feel like something I was forced to do. Instead it seemed just as urgent as my rushing to catch the bowl when it falls on you: an instinct that I felt right in following.

'I could use a salad bowl like this.'

Gary looked at the bowl and nodded approvingly. 'See, wasn't it a good thing that I had to stop at the market?'

'Yes it was.' We got in line to pay for our purchases.

Consider the sentence 'The rabbit is ready to eat.' Interpret 'rabbit' to be the object of 'eat,' and the sentence was an announcement that dinner would be served shortly. Interpret 'rabbit' to be the subject of 'eat,' and it was a hint, such as a young girl might give her mother so she'll open a bag of Purina Bunny Chow. Two very different utterances;

in fact, they were probably mutually exclusive within a single household. Yet either was a valid interpretation; only context could determine what the sentence meant.

Consider the phenomenon of light hitting water at one angle, and traveling through it at a different angle. Explain it by saying that a difference in the index of refraction caused the light to change direction, and one saw the world as humans saw it. Explain it by saying that light minimized the time needed to travel to its destination, and one saw the world as the heptapods saw it. Two very different interpretations.

The physical universe was a language with a perfectly ambiguous grammar. Every physical event was an utterance that could be parsed in two entirely different ways, one causal and the other teleological, both valid, neither one disqualifiable no matter how much context was available.

When the ancestors of humans and heptapods first acquired the spark of consciousness, they both perceived the same physical world, but they parsed their perceptions differently; the worldviews that ultimately arose were the end result of that divergence. Humans had developed a sequential mode of awareness, while heptapods had developed a simultaneous mode of awareness. We experienced events in an order, and perceived their relationship as cause and effect. They experienced all events at once, and perceived a purpose underlying them all. A minimizing, maximizing purpose.

I have a recurring dream about your death. In the dream, I'm the one who's rock climbing – me, can you imagine it? – and you're three years old, riding in some kind of backpack I'm wearing. We're just a few feet below a ledge where we can rest, and you won't wait until I've climbed up to it. You start pulling yourself out of the pack; I order you to stop, but of course you ignore me. I feel your weight alternating from one side of the pack to the other as you climb out; then I feel your left foot on my shoulder, and then your right. I'm screaming at you, but I can't get a hand free to grab you. I can see the wavy design on the soles of your sneakers as you climb, and then I see a flake of stone give way beneath one of them. You slide right past me, and I can't move a muscle. I look down and see you shrink into the distance below me.

Then, all of a sudden, I'm at the morgue. An orderly lifts the sheet from your face, and I see that you're twenty-five.

'You okay?'

I was sitting upright in bed; I'd woken Gary with my movements. 'I'm fine. I was just startled; I didn't recognize where I was for a moment.'

Sleepily, he said, 'We can stay at your place next time.'

I kissed him. 'Don't worry; your place is fine.' We curled up, my back against his chest, and went back to sleep.

When you're three and we're climbing a steep, spiral flight of stairs, I'll hold your hand extra tightly. You'll pull your hand away from me. 'I can do it by myself,' you'll insist, and then move away from me to prove it, and I'll remember that dream. We'll repeat that scene countless times during your childhood. I can almost believe that, given your contrary nature, my attempts to protect you will be what create your love of climbing: first the jungle gym at the playground, then trees out in the green belt around our neighborhood, the rock walls at the climbing club, and ultimately cliff faces in national parks.

I finished the last radical in the sentence, put down the chalk, and sat down in my desk chair. I leaned back and surveyed the giant Heptapod B sentence I'd written that covered the entire blackboard in my office. It included several complex clauses, and I had managed to integrate all of them rather nicely.

Looking at a sentence like this one, I understood why the heptapods had evolved a semasiographic writing system like Heptapod B; it was better suited for a species with a simultaneous mode of consciousness. For them, speech was a bottleneck because it required that one word follow another sequentially. With writing, on the other hand, every mark on a page was visible simultaneously. Why constrain writing with a glottographic straitjacket, demanding that it be just as sequential as speech? It would never occur to them. Semasiographic writing naturally took advantage of the page's two-dimensionality; instead of doling out morphemes one at a time, it offered an entire page full of them all at once.

And now that Heptapod B had introduced me to a simultaneous mode of consciousness, I understood the rationale behind Heptapod A's grammar: what my sequential mind had perceived as unnecessarily convoluted, I now recognized as an attempt to provide flexibility within the confines of sequential speech. I could use Heptapod A more easily as a result, though it was still a poor substitute for Heptapod B.

There was a knock at the door and then Gary poked his head in. 'Colonel Weber'll be here any minute.'

I grimaced. 'Right.' Weber was coming to participate in a session with Flapper and Raspberry; I was to act as translator, a job I wasn't trained for and that I detested.

Gary stepped inside and closed the door. He pulled me out of my chair and kissed me.

I smiled. 'You trying to cheer me up before he gets here?'

'No, I'm trying to cheer me up.'

'You weren't interested in talking to the heptapods at all, were you? You worked on this project just to get me into bed.'

'Ah, you see right through me.'

I looked into his eyes. 'You better believe it,' I said.

I remember when you'll be a month old, and I'll stumble out of bed to give you your 2:00 AM feeding. Your nursery will have that 'baby smell' of diaper rash cream and talcum powder, with a faint ammoniac whiff coming from the diaper pail in the corner. I'll lean over your crib, lift your squalling form out, and sit in the rocking chair to nurse you.

The word 'infant' is derived from the Latin word for 'unable to speak,' but you'll be perfectly capable of saying one thing: 'I suffer,' and you'll do it tirelessly and without hesitation. I have to admire your utter commitment to that statement; when you cry, you'll become outrage incarnate, every fiber of your body employed in expressing that emotion. It's funny: when you're tranquil, you will seem to radiate light, and if someone were to paint a portrait of you like that, I'd insist that they include the halo. But when you're unhappy, you will become a klaxon, built for radiating sound; a portrait of you then could simply be a fire alarm bell.

At that stage of your life, there'll be no past or future for you; until

I give you my breast, you'll have no memory of contentment in the past nor expectation of relief in the future. Once you begin nursing, everything will reverse, and all will be right with the world. NOW is the only moment you'll perceive; you'll live in the present tense. In many ways, it's an enviable state.

The heptapods are neither free nor bound as we understand those concepts; they don't act according to their will, nor are they helpless automatons. What distinguishes the heptapods' mode of awareness is not just that their actions coincide with history's events; it is also that their motives coincide with history's purposes. They act to create the future, to enact chronology.

Freedom isn't an illusion; it's perfectly real in the context of sequential consciousness. Within the context of simultaneous consciousness, freedom is not meaningful, but neither is coercion; it's simply a different context, no more or less valid than the other. It's like that famous optical illusion, the drawing of either an elegant young woman, face turned away from the viewer, or a wart-nosed crone, chin tucked down on her chest. There's no 'correct' interpretation; both are equally valid. But you can't see both at the same time.

Similarly, knowledge of the future was incompatible with free will. What made it possible for me to exercise freedom of choice also made it impossible for me to know the future. Conversely, now that I know the future, I would never act contrary to that future, including telling others what I know: those who know the future don't talk about it. Those who've read the *Book of Ages* never admit to it.

I turned on the VCR and slotted a cassette of a session from the Ft Worth looking glass. A diplomatic negotiator was having a discussion with the heptapods there, with Burghart acting as translator.

The negotiator was describing humans' moral beliefs, trying to lay some groundwork for the concept of altruism. I knew the heptapods were familiar with the conversation's eventual outcome, but they still participated enthusiastically.

If I could have described this to someone who didn't already know, she might ask, if the heptapods already knew everything that they would ever say or hear, what was the point of their using language at all? A reasonable question. But language wasn't only for communication: it was also a form of action. According to speech act theory, statements like 'You're under arrest,' 'I christen this vessel,' or 'I promise' were all performative: a speaker could perform the action only by uttering the words. For such acts, knowing what would be said didn't change anything. Everyone at a wedding anticipated the words 'I now pronounce you husband and wife,' but until the minister actually said them, the ceremony didn't count. With performative language, saying equaled doing.

For the heptapods, all language was performative. Instead of using language to inform, they used language to actualize. Sure, heptapods already knew what would be said in any conversation; but in order for their knowledge to be true, the conversation would have to take place.

'First Goldilocks tried the papa bear's bowl of porridge, but it was full of Brussels sprouts, which she hated.'

You'll laugh. 'No, that's wrong!' We'll be sitting side by side on the sofa, the skinny, overpriced hardcover spread open on our laps.

I'll keep reading. 'Then Goldilocks tried the mama bear's bowl of porridge, but it was full of spinach, which she also hated.'

You'll put your hand on the page of the book to stop me. 'You have to read it the right way!'

'I'm reading just what it says here,' I'll say, all innocence.

'No you're not. That's not how the story goes.'

'Well if you already know how the story goes, why do you need me to read it to you?'

''Cause I wanna hear it!'

The air-conditioning in Weber's office almost compensated for having to talk to the man.

'They're willing to engage in a type of exchange,' I explained, 'but it's not trade. We simply give them something, and they give us something in return. Neither party tells the other what they're giving beforehand.'

Colonel Weber's brow furrowed just slightly. 'You mean they're willing to exchange gifts?'

I knew what I had to say. 'We shouldn't think of it as "gift-giving." We don't know if this transaction has the same associations for the heptapods that gift-giving has for us.'

'Can we' – he searched for the right wording – 'drop hints about the kind of gift we want?'

'They don't do that themselves for this type of transaction. I asked them if we could make a request, and they said we could, but it won't make them tell us what they're giving.' I suddenly remembered that a morphological relative of 'performative' was 'performance,' which could describe the sensation of conversing when you knew what would be said: it was like performing in a play.

'But would it make them more likely to give us what we asked for?' Colonel Weber asked. He was perfectly oblivious of the script, yet his responses matched his assigned lines exactly.

'No way of knowing,' I said. 'I doubt it, given that it's not a custom they engage in.'

'If we give our gift first, will the value of our gift influence the value of theirs?' He was improvising, while I had carefully rehearsed for this one and only show.

'No,' I said. 'As far as we can tell, the value of the exchanged items is irrelevant.'

'If only my relatives felt that way,' murmured Gary wryly.

I watched Colonel Weber turn to Gary. 'Have you discovered anything new in the physics discussions?' he asked, right on cue.

'If you mean, any information new to mankind, no,' said Gary. 'The heptapods haven't varied from the routine. If we demonstrate something to them, they'll show us their formulation of it, but they won't volunteer anything and they won't answer our questions about what they know.'

An utterance that was spontaneous and communicative in the context of human discourse became a ritual recitation when viewed by the light of Heptapod B.

Weber scowled. 'All right then, we'll see how the State Department feels about this. Maybe we can arrange some kind of gift-giving ceremony.'

Like physical events, with their causal and teleological interpretations, every linguistic event had two possible interpretations: as a transmission of information and as the realization of a plan.

'I think that's a good idea, Colonel,' I said.

It was an ambiguity invisible to most. A private joke; don't ask me to explain it.

Even though I'm proficient with Heptapod B, I know I don't experience reality the way a heptapod does. My mind was cast in the mold of human, sequential languages, and no amount of immersion is an alien language can completely reshape it. My worldview is an amalgam of human and heptapod.

Before I learned how to think in Heptapod B, my memories grew like a column of cigarette ash, laid down by the infinitesimal sliver of combustion that was my consciousness, marking the sequential present. After I learned Heptapod B, new memories fell into place like gigantic blocks, each one measuring years in duration, and though they didn't arrive in order or land contiguously, they soon composed a period of five decades. It is the period during which I know Heptapod B well enough to think in it, starting during my interviews with Flapper and Raspberry and ending with my death.

Usually, Heptapod B affects just my memory: my consciousness crawls along as it did before, a glowing sliver crawling forward in time, the difference being that the ash of memory lies ahead as well as behind: there is no real combustion. But occasionally I have glimpses when Heptapod B truly reigns, and I experience past and future all at once; my consciousness becomes a half-century-long ember burning outside time. I perceive – during those glimpses – that entire epoch as a simultaneity. It's a period encompassing the rest of my life, and the entirety of yours.

I wrote out the semagrams for 'process create-endpoint inclusive-we,' meaning 'let's start.' Raspberry replied in the affirmative, and the slide shows began. The second display screen that the heptapods had provided began presenting a series of images, composed of semagrams and equations, while one of our video screens did the same.

This was the second 'gift exchange' I had been present for, the eighth one overall, and I knew it would be the last. The looking-glass tent was crowded with people; Burghart from Ft Worth was here, as were Gary and a nuclear physicist, assorted biologists, anthropologists, military brass, and diplomats. Thankfully they had set up an air conditioner to cool the place off. We would review the tapes of the images later to figure out just what the heptapods' 'gift' was. Our own 'gift' was a presentation on the Lascaux cave paintings.

We all crowded around the heptapods' second screen, trying to glean some idea of the images' content as they went by. 'Preliminary assessments?' asked Colonel Weber.

'It's not a return,' said Burghart. In a previous exchange, the heptapods had given us information about ourselves that we had previously told them. This had infuriated the State Department, but we had no reason to think of it as an insult: it probably indicated that trade value really didn't play a role in these exchanges. It didn't excluded the possibility that the heptapods might yet offer us a space drive, or cold fusion, or some other wish-fulfilling miracle.

'That looks like inorganic chemistry,' said the nuclear physicist, pointing at an equation before the image was replaced.

Gary nodded. 'It could be materials technology,' he said.

'Maybe we're finally getting somewhere,' said Colonel Weber.

'I wanna see more animal pictures,' I whispered, quietly so that only Gary could hear me, and pouted like a child. He smiled and poked me. Truthfully, I wished the heptapods had given another xenobiology lecture, as they had on two previous exchanges; judging from those, humans were more similar to the heptapods than any other species they'd ever encountered. Or another lecture on heptapod history; those had been filled with apparent non sequiturs, but were interesting nonetheless. I didn't want the heptapods to give us new technology, because I didn't want to see what our governments might do with it.

I watched Raspberry while the information was being exchanged, looking for any anomalous behavior. It stood barely moving as usual; I saw no indications of what would happen shortly.

After a minute, the heptapods' screen went blank, and a minute after that, ours did too. Gary and most of the other scientists clustered around a tiny video screen that was replaying the heptapods' presentation. I could hear them talk about the need to call in a solid-state physicist.

Colonel Weber turned. 'You two,' he said, pointing to me and then to Burghart, 'schedule the time and location for the next exchange.' Then he followed the others to the playback screen.

'Coming right up,' I said. To Burghart, I asked, 'Would you care to do the honors, or shall I?'

I knew Burghart had gained a proficiency in Heptapod B similar to mine. 'It's your looking glass,' he said. 'You drive.'

I sat down again at the transmitting computer. 'Bet you never figured you'd wind up working as an Army translator back when you were a grad student.'

'That's for goddamn sure,' he said. 'Even now I can hardly believe it.' Everything we said to each other felt like the carefully bland exchanges of spies who meet in public, but never break cover.

I wrote out the semagrams for 'locus exchange-transaction converse inclusive-we' with the projective aspect modulation.

Raspberry wrote its reply. That was my cue to frown, and for Burghart to ask, 'What does it mean by that?' His delivery was perfect.

I wrote a request for clarification; Raspberry's reply was the same as before. Then I watched it glide out of the room. The curtain was about to fall on this act of our performance.

Colonel Weber stepped forward. 'What's going on? Where did it go?'

'It said that the heptapods are leaving now,' I said. 'Not just itself; all of them.'

'Call it back here now. Ask it what it means.'

'Um, I don't think Raspberry's wearing a pager,' I said.

The image of the room in the looking glass disappeared so abruptly that it took a moment for my eyes to register what I was seeing instead: it was the other side of the looking-glass tent. The looking glass had become completely transparent. The conversation around the playback screen fell silent.

'What the hell is going on here?' said Colonel Weber.

Gary walked up to the looking glass, and then around it to the other side. He touched the rear surface with one hand; I could see the pale ovals where his fingertips made contact with the looking glass. 'I think,' he said, 'we just saw a demonstration of transmutation at a distance.'

I heard the sounds of heavy footfalls on dry grass. A soldier came in through the tent door, short of breath from sprinting, holding an oversize walkie-talkie. 'Colonel, message from –'

Weber grabbed the walkie-talkie from him.

I remember what it'll be like watching you when you are a day old. Your father will have gone for a quick visit to the hospital cafeteria, and you'll be lying in your bassinet, and I'll be leaning over you.

So soon after the delivery, I will still be feeling like a wrung-out towel. You will seem incongrously tiny, given how enormous I felt during the pregnancy; I could swear there was room for someone much larger and more robust than you in there. Your hands and feet will be long and thin, not chubby yet. Your face will still be all red and pinched, puffy eyelids squeezed shut, the gnomelike phase that precedes the cherubic.

I'll run a finger over your belly, marveling at the uncanny softness of your skin, wondering if silk would abrade your body like burlap. Then you'll writhe, twisting your body while poking out your legs one at a time, and I'll recognize the gesture as one I had felt you do inside me, many times. So *that's* what it looks like.

I'll feel elated at this evidence of a unique mother-child bond, this certitude that you're the one I carried. Even if I had never laid eyes on your before, I'd be able to pick you out from a sea of babies: Not that one. No, not her either. Wait, that one over there.

Yes, that's her. She's mine.

That final 'gift exchange' was the last we ever saw of the heptapods. All at once, all over the world, their looking glasses became transparent and their ships left orbit. Subsequent analysis of the looking glasses revealed them to be nothing more than sheets of fused silica, completely inert. The information from the final exchange session described a new class of super-conducting materials, but it later proved to duplicate the results of research just completed in Japan: nothing that humans didn't already know.

We never did learn why the heptapods left, any more than we learned what brought them here, or why they acted the way they did. My own new awareness didn't provide that type of knowledge; the heptapods' behavior was presumably explicable from a sequential point of view, but we never found that explanation.

I would have liked to experience more of the heptapods' worldview, to feel the way they feel. Then, perhaps I could immerse myself fully in the necessity of events, as they must, instead of merely wading in its surf for the rest of my life. But that will never come to pass. I will continue to practice the heptapod languages, as will the other linguists on the looking-glass teams, but none of us will ever progress any further than we did when the heptapods were here.

Working with the heptapods changed my life. I met your father and learned Heptapod B, both of which make it possible for me to know you now, here on the patio in the moonlight. Eventually, many years from now, I'll be without your father, and without you. All I will have left from this moment is the heptapod language. So I pay close attention, and note every detail.

From the beginning I knew my destination, and I chose my route accordingly. But am I working toward an extreme of joy, or of pain? Will I achieve a minimum, or a maximum?

These questions are in my mind when your father asks me, 'Do you want to make a baby?' And I smile and answer, 'Yes,' and I unwrap his arms from around me, and we hold hands as we walk inside to make love, to make you.

Protected Species

H. B. FYFE

The yellow star, of which Torang was the second planet, shone hotly down on the group of men viewing the half-built dam from the heights above. At a range of eighty million miles the effect was quite Terran, the star being somewhat smaller than Sol.

For Jeff Otis, fresh from a hop through space from the extra-bright star that was the other component of the binary system, the heat was enervating. The shorts and light shirt supplied him by the planet coordinator were soaked with perspiration. He mopped his forehead and turned to his host.

'Very nice job, Finchley,' he complimented. 'It's easy to see you have things well in hand here.'

Finchley grinned sparingly. He had a broad, hard, flat face with tight lips and mere slits of blue eyes. Otis had been trying ever since the previous morning to catch a revealing expression on it.

He was uneasily aware that his own features were too frank and open for an inspector of colonial installations. For one thing, he had too many lines and hollows in his face, a result of being chronically underweight from space-hopping among the sixteen planets of the binary system.

Otis noticed that Finchley's aides were eyeing him furtively.

'Yes, Finchley,' he repeated to break the little silence, 'you're doing very well on the hydro-electric end. When are you going to show me the capital city you're laying out?'

'We can fly over there now,' answered Finchley. 'We have tentative boundaries laid out below those pre-colony ruins we saw from the 'copter.'

'Oh, yes. You know, I meant to remark as we flew over that they looked a good deal like similar remnants on some of the other planets.'

He caught himself as Finchley's thin lips tightened a trifle more. The coordinator was obviously trying to be patient and polite to an official from whom he hoped to get a good report, but Otis could see he would much rather be going about his business of building up the colony.

He could hardly blame Finchley, he decided. It was the fifth planetary system Terrans had found in their expansion into space, and there would be bigger jobs ahead for a man with a record of successful accomplishments. Civilization was reaching out to the stars at last. Otis supposed that he, too, was some sort of pioneer, although he usually was too busy to feel like one.

'Well, I'll show you some photos later,' he said. 'Right now, we – Say, why all that jet-burning down there?'

In the gorge below, men had dropped their tools and seemed to be charging towards a common focal point. Excited yells carried thinly up the cliffs.

'Ape hunt, probably,' guessed one of Finchley's engineers.

'Ape?' asked Otis, surprised.

'Not exactly,' corrected Finchley patiently. 'That's common slang for what we mention in reports as Torangs. They look a little like big, skinny, grey apes; but they're the only life large enough to name after the planet.'

Otis stared down into the gorge. Most of the running men had given up and were straggling back to their work. Two or three, brandishing pistols, continued running and disappeared around a bend.

'Never catch him now,' commented Finchley's pilot.

'Do you just let them go running off whenever they feel like it?' Otis inquired.

Finchley met his curious gaze stolidly.

'I'm in favour of anything that will break the monotony, Mr Otis. We have a problem of morale, you know. This planet is a key colony, and I like to keep the work going smoothly.'

'Yes, I suppose there isn't much for recreation yet.'

'Exactly. I don't see the sport in it myself but I let them. We're up to schedule.'

'Ahead, if anything,' Otis placated him. 'Well, now, about the city?'

Finchley led the way to the helicopter. The pilot and Otis waited while he had a final word with his engineers, then they all climbed in and were off.

Later, hovering over the network of crude roads being levelled by Finchley's bulldozers, Otis admitted aloud that the location was well-chosen. It lay along a long, narrow bay that thrust in from the distant ocean to gather the waters of the same river that was being dammed some miles upstream.

'Those cliffs over there,' Finchley pointed out, 'were raised up since the end of whatever civilization used to be here – so my geologist tells me. We can fly back that way, and you can see how the ancient city was once at the head of the bay.'

The pilot climbed and headed over the cliffs. Otis saw that these formed the edge of a plateau. At one point their continuity was marred by a deep gouge.

'Where the river ran thousands of years ago,' Finchley explained.

They reached a point from which the outlines of the ruined city were easily discerned. From the air, Otis knew, they were undoubtedly plainer than if he had been among them.

'Must have been a pretty large place,' he remarked. 'Any idea what sort of beings built it or what happened to them?'

'Haven't had time for that yet,' Finchley said. 'Some boys from the exploration staff poke around in there every so often. Best current theory seems to be that it belonged to the Torangs.'

'The *animals* they were hunting before?' asked Otis.

'Might be. Can't say for sure, but the diggers found signs the city took more of a punch than just an earthquake. Claim they found too much evidence of fires, exploded missiles, and warfare in general – other places as well as here. So . . . we've been guessing the Torangs are degenerated descendants of the survivors of some interplanetary brawl.'

Otis considered that.

'Sounds plausible,' he admitted, 'but you ought to do something to make sure you are right.'

'Why?'

'If it *is* the case, you'll have to stop your men from hunting them; degenerated or not, the Colonial Commission has regulations about contact with any local inhabitants.'

Finchley turned his head to scowl at Otis, and controlled himself with an obvious effort.

'Those *apes*?' he demanded.

'Well, how can you tell? Ever try to contact them?'

'Yes! At first, that is; before we figured them for animals.'

'And?'

'Couldn't get near one!' Finchley declared heatedly. 'If they had any sort of half-intelligent culture, wouldn't they let us make *some* sort of contact?'

'Offhand,' admitted Otis, 'I should think so. How about setting down a few minutes? I'd like a look at the ruins.'

Finchley glared at his wrist watch, but directed the pilot to land in a cleared spot. The young man brought them down neatly and the two officials alighted.

Otis, glancing around, saw where the archaeologists had been digging. They had left their implements stacked casually at the site – the air was dry up here and who was there to steal a shovel?

He left Finchley and strolled around a mound of dirt that had been cleared away from an entrance to one of the buildings. The latter had been built of stone, or at least faced with it. A peep into the dim excavation led him to believe there had been a steel framework, but the whole affair had been collapsed as if by an explosion.

He walked a little way farther and reached a section of presumably taller buildings where the stone ruins thrust above the sandy surface. After he had wandered through one or two arched openings that seemed to have been windows, he understood why the explorers had chosen to dig for their information. If any covering or decoration had ever graced the walls, it had long since been weathered off. As for ceiling or roof, nothing remained.

'Must have been a highly developed civilization just the same,' he muttered.

A movement at one of the shadowed openings to his right caught his eye. He did not remember noticing Finchley leave the helicopter to follow him, but he was glad of a guide.

'Don't you think so?' he added.

He turned his head, but Finchley was not there. In fact, now that Otis was aware of his surroundings, he could hear the voices of the other two mumbling distantly back by the aircraft.

'Seeing things!' he grumbled, and started through the ancient window.

Some instinct stopped him half a foot outside.

Come on, Jeff, he told himself, *don't be silly! What could be there? Ghosts?*

On the other hand, he realized, there were times when it was just as well to rely upon instinct – at least until you figured out the origin of the strange feeling. Any spaceman would agree to that. The man who developed an animal's sixth sense was the man who lived longest on alien planets.

He thought he must have paused a full minute or more, during which he had heard not the slightest sound except the mutter of voices to the rear. He peered into the chamber, which was about twenty feet square and well if not brightly lit by reflected light.

Nothing was to be seen, but when he found himself turning his head stealthily to peer over his shoulder, he decided that the queer sensation along the back of his neck meant something.

Wait now, he thought swiftly. *I didn't see quite the whole room.*

The flooring was heaped with wind-bared rubble that would not show footprints. He felt much more comfortable to notice himself thinking in that vein.

At least I'm not imagining ghosts, he thought.

Bending forward the necessary foot, he thrust his head through the opening and darted a quick look to the left, then to the right along the wall. As he turned right, his glance was met directly by a pair of very wide-set black eyes which shifted inward slightly as they got his range.

The Torang about matched his own six feet two, mainly because of elongated, gibbon-like limbs and a similarly crouching stance. Arms and legs, covered with short, curly, grey fur, had the same general proportions as human limbs, but looked half again too long for a trunk that seemed to be ribbed all the way down. The shoulder and hip joints were compactly lean, rather as if the Torang had developed on a world of lesser gravity than that of the human.

It was the face that made Otis stare. The mouth was toothless and probably constructed more for sucking than for chewing. But the eyes! They projected like ends of a dumb-bell from each side of the narrow skull where the ears should have been, and focused with obvious mobility. Peering closer, Otis saw tiny ears below the eyes, almost hidden in the curling fur of the neck.

He realized abruptly that his own eyes felt as if they were bulging out, although he could not remember having changed his expression of casual curiosity. His back was getting stiff also. He straightened up carefully.

'Uh . . . hello,' he murmured, feeling unutterably silly but conscious of some impulse to compromise between a tone of greeting for another human being and one of pacification to an animal.

The Torang moved then, swiftly but unhurriedly. In fact, Otis later decided, deliberately. One of the long arms swept downwards to the rubble-strewn ground.

The next instant, Otis jerked his head back out of the opening as a stone whizzed past in front of his nose.

'Hey!' he protested involuntarily.

There was a scrabbling sound from within, as of animal claws churning to a fast start among the pebbles. Recovering his balance, Otis charged recklessly through the entrance.

'I don't know why,' he admitted to Finchley a few minutes later. 'If I stopped to think how I might have had my skull bashed in coming through, I guess I'd have just backed off and yelled for you.'

Finchley nodded, but his narrow gaze seemed faintly approving for the first time since they had met.

'He was gone, of course,' Otis continued. 'I barely caught a glimpse of his rump vanishing through another window.'

'Yeah, they're pretty fast,' put in Finchley's pilot. 'In the time we've been here, the boys haven't taken more than half a dozen. Got a stuffed one over at headquarters though.'

'Hm-m-m,' murmured Otis thoughtfully.

From their other remarks, he learned that he had not noticed everything, even though face to face with the creature. Finchley's mentioning the three digits of the hands or feet, for instance, came as a surprise.

Otis was silent most of the flight back to headquarters. Once there, he disappeared with a perfunctory excuse towards the rooms assigned him.

That evening, at a dinner which Finchley had made as attractive as was possible in a comparatively raw and new colony, Otis was noticeably sociable. The coordinator was gratified.

'Looks as if they finally sent us a regular guy,' he remarked behind his hand to one of his assistants. 'Round up a couple of the prettier secretaries to keep him happy.'

'I understand he nearly laid hands on a Torang up at the diggings,' said the other.

'Yep, ran right at it bare-handed. Came as close to bagging it as anybody could, I suppose.'

'Maybe it's just as well he didn't,' commented the assistant. 'They're big enough to mess up an unarmed man some.'

Otis, meanwhile and for the rest of the evening, was assiduously busy making acquaintances. So engrossed was he in turning every new conversation to the Torangs and asking seemingly casual questions about the little known of their habits and possible past, that he hardly noticed receiving any special attentions. As a visiting inspector, he was used to attempts to entertain and distract him.

The next morning, he caught Finchley at his office in the sprawling one-storey structure of concrete and glass that was colonial headquarters.

After accepting a chair across the desk from the coordinator, Otis told him his conclusions. Finchley's narrow eyes opened a trifle when he heard the details. His wide, hard-muscled face became slightly pink.

'Oh, for –! I mean, Otis, why must you make something big out of it? The men very seldom bag one anyway!'

'Perhaps because they're so rare,' answered Otis calmly. 'How do we know they're not intelligent life? Maybe if you were hanging on in the ruins of your ancestor's civilization, reduced to a primitive state, *you'd* be just as wary of a bunch of loud Terrans moving in!'

Finchley shrugged. He looked vaguely uncomfortable, as if debating whether Otis or some disgruntled sportsman from his husky construction crews would be easier to handle.

'Think of the over-all picture a minute,' Otis urged. 'We're pushing out into space at last, after centuries of dreams and struggles. With all the misery we've seen in various colonial systems at home, we've tried to plan these ventures so as to avoid old mistakes.'

Finchley nodded grudgingly. Otis could see that his mind was on the progress charts of his many projects.

'It stands to reason,' the inspector went on, 'that some day we'll find a planet with intelligent life. We're still new in space, but as we probe farther out it's bound to happen. That's why the Commission drew up rules about native life forms. Or have you read that part of the code lately?'

Finchley shifted from side to side in his chair.

'Now, look!' he protested. 'Don't go making *me* out a hard-boiled vandal with nothing in mind but exterminating everything that moves on all Torang. *I* don't go out hunting the apes!'

'I know, I know,' Otis soothed him. 'But before the Colonial Commission will sanction any destruction of indigenous life, we'll have to show – *besides* that it's not intelligent – that it exists in sufficient numbers to avoid extinction.'

'What do you expect me to do about it?'

Otis regarded him with some sympathy. Finchley was the hard-bitten type the Commission needed to oversee the first breaking-in of a colony on a strange planet, but he was not unreasonable. He merely wanted to be left alone to handle the tough job facing him.

'Announce a ban on hunting Torangs,' Otis said. 'There must be something else they can go after.'

'Oh, yes,' admitted Finchley. 'There are swarms of little rabbit-things and other vermin running through the brush. But, I don't know –'

'It's standard practice,' Otis reminded him. 'We have many a protected species even back on Terra that would be extinct by now, but for the game laws.'

*

In the end they agreed that Finchley would do his honest best to enforce a ban, provided Otis obtained a formal order from the headquarters of the system. The inspector went from the office straight to the communications centre, where he filed a long report for the chief coordinator's office in the other part of the binary system.

It took some hours for the reply to reach Torang. When it came that afternoon, he went looking for Finchley.

He found the coordinator inspecting a newly finished canning factory on the coast, elated at the completion of one more link in making the colony self-sustaining.

'Here it is,' said Otis, waving the message copy. 'Signed by the chief himself. "As of this date, the ape-like beings known as Torangs, indigenous to planet number and so forth, are to be considered a rare and protected species under regulations and so forth et cetera."'

'Good enough,' answered Finchley with an amiable shrug. 'Give it here, and I'll have it put on the public address system and the bulletin boards.'

Otis returned satisfied to the helicopter that had brought him out from headquarters.

'Back, sir?' asked the pilot.

'Yes . . . *no*! Just for fun, take me out to the old city. I never did get a good look the other day, and I'd like to before I leave.'

They flew over the plains between the sea and the upjutting cliffs. In the distance Otis caught a glimpse of the rising dam he had been shown the day before. This colony would go well, he reflected, as long as he checked up on details like preserving native life forms.

Eventually the pilot landed at the same spot he had been taken to on his previous visit to the ancient ruins. Someone else was on the scene today. Otis saw a pair of men he took to be archaeologists.

'I'll just wander around a bit,' he told the pilot.

He noticed the two men looking at him from where they stood by the shovels and other equipment, so he paused to say hello. As he thought, they had been digging in the ruins.

'Taking some measurements, in fact,' said the sunburned blond introduced as Hoffman. 'Trying to get a line on what sort of things built the place.'

'Oh?' said Otis, interested. 'What's the latest theory?'

'Not so much different from us,' Hoffman told the inspector while his partner left them to pick up another load of artifacts.

'Judging from the size of the rooms, height of doorways, and such stuff as stairways,' he went on, 'they were pretty much our size. So far, of course, it's only a rough estimate.'

'Could be ancestors of the Torangs, eh?' asked Otis.

'Very possible, sir,' answered Hoffman, with a promptness that suggested it was his own view. 'But we haven't dug up enough to guess at the type of culture they had, or draw any conclusions as to their psychology or social customs.'

Otis nodded, thinking that he ought to mention the young fellow's name to Finchley before he left Torang. He excused himself as the other man returned with a box of some sort of scraps the pair had unearthed, and strolled between the outlines of the untouched buildings.

In a few minutes he came to the section of higher structures where he had encountered the Torang the previous day.

'Wonder if I should look in the same spot?' he muttered aloud. 'No . . . that would be the *last* place the thing would return to . . . unless it had a lair thereabouts –'

He stopped to get his bearings, then shrugged and walked around a mound of rubble towards what he believed to be the proper building.

Pretty sure this was it, he mused. *Yes, shadows around that window arch look the same . . . same time of day –*

He halted, almost guility, and looked back to make sure no one was observing his return to the scene of his little adventure. After all, an inspector of colonial installations was not supposed to run around ghost-hunting like a small boy.

Finding himself alone, he stepped briskly through the crumbling arch *– and froze in his tracks.*

'I am honoured to know you,' said the Torang in a mild, rather buzzing voice. 'We thought you possibly would return here.'

Otis gaped. The black eyes projecting from the sides of the narrow head tracked him up and down, giving him the unpleasant sensation of being measured for an artillery salvo.

'I am known as Jal-Ganyr,' said the Torang. 'Unless I am given incorrect data, you are known as Jeff-Otis. That is so.'

The last statement was made with almost no inflection, but some still-functioning corner of Otis' mind interpreted it as a question. He sucked in a deep breath, suddenly conscious of having forgotten to breathe for a moment.

'I didn't know . . . yes, that is so . . . I didn't know you Torangs could speak Terran. Or anything else. How – ?'

He hesitated as a million questions boiled up in his mind to be asked. Jal-Ganyr absently stroked the grey fur of his chest with his three-fingered left hand, squatting patiently on a flat rock. Otis felt somehow that he had been allowed to waste time mumbling only by grace of disciplined politeness.

'I am not of the Torangs,' said Jal-Ganyr in his wheezing voice. 'I am of the Myrbs. You would possibly say Myrbli. I have not been informed.'

'You mean that is your name for yourselves?' asked Otis.

Jal-Ganyr seemed to consider, his mobile eyes swivelling inward to scan the Terran's face.

'More than that,' he said at last, when he had thought it over. 'I mean I am of the race originating at Myrb, not of this planet.'

'Before we go any further,' insisted Otis, 'tell me, at least, how you learned our language!'

Jal-Ganyr made a fleeting gesture. His 'face' was unreadable to the Terran, but Otis had the impression he had received the equivalent of a smile and a shrug.

'As to that,' said the Myrb, 'I possibly learned it before you did. We have observed you a very long time. You would unbelieve how long.'

'But then – ' Otis paused. That must mean before the colonists had landed on this planet. He was half afraid it might mean before they had reached this sun system. He put aside the thought and asked, 'But then, why do you live like this among the ruins? Why wait till now? If you had communicated, you could have had our help rebuilding – '

He let his voice trail off, wondering what sounded wrong. Jal-Ganyr rolled his eyes about leisurely, as if disdaining the surrounding ruins. Again, he seemed to consider all the implications of Otis' questions.

'We picked up your message to your chief,' he answered at last. 'We decided it is time to communicate with one of you.

'We have no interest in rebuilding,' he added. 'We have concealed quarters for ourselves.'

Otis found that his lips were dry from his unconsciously having let his mouth hang open. He moistened them with the tip of his tongue and relaxed enough to lean against the wall.

'You mean my getting the ruling to proclaim you a protected species?' he asked. 'You have instruments to intercept such signals?'

'I do. We have,' said Jal-Ganyr simply. 'It has been decided that you have expanded far enough into space to make necessary we contact a few of the thoughtful among you. It will possibly make easier in the future for our observers.'

Otis wondered how much of that was irony. He felt himself flushing at the memory of the 'stuffed specimen' at headquarters, and was peculiarly relieved that he had not gone to see it.

I've had the luck, he told himself. *I'm the one to discover the first known intelligent beings beyond Sol!*

Aloud, he said, 'We expected to meet someone like you eventually. But why have you chosen me?'

The question sounded vain, he realized, but it brought unexpected results.

'Your message. You made in a little way the same decision we made in a big way. We deduce that you are one to understand our regret and shame at what happened between our races . . . long ago.'

'Between – ?'

'Yes. For a long time, we thought you were all gone. We are pleased to see you returning to some of your old planets.'

Otis stared blankly. Some instinct must have enabled the Myrb to interpret his bewildered expression. He apologized briefly.

'I possibly forgot to explain the ruins.' Again, Jal-Ganyr's eyes swivelled slowly about.

'They are not ours,' he said mildly. 'They are yours.'

The Rescuer

ARTHUR PORGES

It was by far the largest, most intricate machine ever built.

Its great complex of auxiliary components covered two square blocks, and extended hundreds of feet beneath the earth. There were fifty huge electronic computers at the heart of it. They had to be capable of solving up to thirty thousand simultaneous partial differential equations in as many variables in any particular millisecond. The energy which the machine required to operate successfully on a mass of M pounds was given by a familiar formula: $E = MK^2$. The K was not, as in Einstein's equation, the velocity of light; but it was large enough so that only one type of power could be used: the thermonuclear reaction called hydrogen fusion.

Designing the machine and developing the theory of its operation had taken thirty years; building it, another ten. It had cost three billion dollars, an amount to be amortized over roughly one hundred years, and supplied by fifteen countries.

Like the atomic bomb, the machine could not be tested piecemeal; only the final, complete assembly would be able to settle the question of success or failure. So far, no such trial of its capabilities had been made. When the time came, a one milligram sample of pure platinum would be used.

It was the largest, most intricate, expensive, fascinating, and dangerous machine ever built. And two men were about to destroy it. They would have to release a large amount of thermonuclear energy in order to wreck the machine. It was the only way in the circumstances. It was a heartbreaking decision to have to make. Perhaps they should have contacted higher authorities in Washington, since the machine, although quite international in scope, was located in California; but that was too dangerous with time so short. Bureaucratic timidity might very well cause a fatal delay. So, knowing the consequences to them, the two scientists did what they believed had to be done. The machine, together with several blocks of supporting equipment, including the irreplaceable computers, was vaporized. They escaped in a fast air car.

PRELIMINARY HEARING – A TRANSCRIPT
THE UNITED STATES versus DR CARNOT
THE UNITED STATES versus DR KENT
14 April, 2015
(Extract)

JUDGE CLARK: How did the man know the operation, when the machine had never even been tested?

DR CARNOT: The theory had been widely discussed in many scientific papers – even popular magazines. And the man was a technician of sorts. Besides, it wasn't necessary to understand the theory; not more than forty or fifty men in this country could. He must have seen numerous pictures of the controls. The settings are simple; any engineer can use a vernier.

JUDGE CLARK: I think you'd better tell this court just what happened from the beginning. Your strange reticence has caused a great deal of speculation. You understand that if found guilty you must be turned over to the UN Criminal Court for prosecution.

DR CARNOT: Yes, Your Honour; I know that.

JUDGE CLARK: Very well. Go ahead.

DR CARNOT: Dr Kent and myself were the only ones in the area that night. It was a matter of chance that we decided to check some minor point about the bus bars. To our astonishment, when we arrived at the control room, the machine was in operation.

JUDGE CLARK: How did you know the machine was being used?

DR CARNOT: In many ways; all the indicators were reacting; but primarily the mass-chamber itself, which had dislimned and assumed the appearance of a misty, rainbow-coloured sphere.

JUDGE CLARK: I see. Go on.

DR CARNOT: Dr Kent and I were shocked beyond expression. We

saw from the readings that the person, whoever he was, had entered for a really fantastic number of ergs – that is, energy. Far more than any of us would have dared to use for many months, if at all. (At this point Senator King interposed a question.)

SENATOR KING: How did the fellow get into the area? What about the Security?

DR CARNOT: As you know, the machine is international, and sponsored by the UN. Since there is no longer any military rivalry among the members, the work is purely scientific, and no country can be excluded. Naturally, the complex is protected against crackpots; but this man worked on the project as a Class 5 technician, and must have known how to avoid the infra-red and other warning systems.

JUDGE CLARK: We had better not confuse the issue with such digressions. How the man got in is no longer important. But your sudden knowledge of his background is, Dr Carnot. In an earlier statement you claimed to have no information about his identity. How do you explain that?

DR CARNOT: I had to lie.

JUDGE CLARK: Had to?

DR CARNOT: Yes, Your Honour. All of that will become clear, I hope, later in my testimony. Right now, let me clarify our dilemma. The machine was definitely in operation, and had been for about eight minutes. We couldn't be certain that it would work – I mean to the extent of completing the job as programmed by the intruder; but the theory had been carefully investigated, and all the computations, which, as you know, took many years, checked out. It is a peculiarity of the machine, related to the solution of thousands of the most complicated differential equations, that there can be neither a cessation nor a reversal of its operation without grave danger to the entire state – perhaps even a larger area. The combination of vast energies and the warping of space-time that would result, according to theory, might vapourize hundreds of square miles. For this reason, and others, our plans had not gone beyond trying masses less than one gram.

JUDGE CLARK: Let me understand your point. It was impossible merely to shut off the machine? Stop the power?

DR CARNOT: If the theory is sound, yes. I can only suggest the analogy of breaking an electrical circuit involving millions of amperes – the current jumps the gap, forming an arc which is very difficult to stop. Well, in this case, it was not merely millions of amps, but energies comparable only to those emitted by a large mass of the sun itself. In short, the only way to prevent completion of this particular operation was to bleed off enough of that energy to destroy most of the complex. That, at least, would save the populated areas. Remember, we had only about twelve minutes in which to choose a course of action.

JUDGE CLARK: But you weren't even sure the machine would work; that is, that the man would really survive. Yet you deliberately wiped out a three billion dollar project.

DR CARNOT: We simply couldn't risk it, Your Honour. If the man did survive, and succeeded in his mission, the dangers were almost inconceivable. Even philosophically they are more than the human mind can grasp.

JUDGE CLARK: But neither of you has been willing so far to explain that point. This court is still completely in the dark. Who was the man, and what did he attempt to do?

DR CARNOT: Up to now, we weren't ready to speak. But if you will clear the court except for yourself, the President, and a few high, responsible officials, I'll try to satisfy this tribunal. The fact is, as you will see, that a large part of the public, in this country, at least, might approve of what that man tried to do. It may not be possible to convince laymen – people not used to the abstractions of philosophy or science – of the great risk involved. I can only hope that this court will appreciate the implications. I should add that Dr Kent and myself have seriously considered refusing any further information, but merely pleading guilty to wilful destruction of the machine. As it is, if you decide to release us to the UN for criminal proceedings, we still might have to do just that – which means your records would have to be suppressed. Our only reason for testifying is not to save our own lives, but the hope that we can contribute to the design of a new machine. And to better understanding of the problems involved in the operation. Among the public, that is.

JUDGE CLARK: I must take your attitude seriously; that is plain. Do you persist in maintaining that this room should be cleared, and all broadcasting suspended? Press, distinguished scientists, senators – all these are not qualified to hear the testimony?

DR CARNOT: I only mean that the fewer who hear me, the fewer mouths to be guarded. And I'm sure this court will feel the same way when all my evidence is in.

JUDGE CLARK: Very well, then. The bailiffs will clear the room, except for the President, the National Security Council, and the Chairman of the Research Committee of the Congress. All electronic equipment will be disconnected; a complete spy curtain will be put on this room. Court will adjourn for two hours, reconvening at 1500.

PRELIMINARY HEARING (*continued*)

JUDGE CLARK: We are ready to hear your testimony now, Dr Carnot.

DR CARNOT: Do I have Your Honour's absolute assurance that nobody outside this room can hear us?

JUDGE CLARK: You do. The spy curtain, which your own colleagues in science claim bars all wave lengths, is on at full strength.

DR CARNOT: If I seem too cautious, there is a reason, as you will see.

JUDGE CLARK: I certainly hope so. Now, will you please give the real point of this testimony? What was the man – and incidentally, has any identification come in on him yet? No? Well, what was he doing that seems to have scared you so?

DR CARNOT: His name doesn't matter; it was on the note he left.

JUDGE CLARK: What note? Nothing was said about a note. Here this court has been trying to identify the man, and all the time –

DR CARNOT: I'm sorry, Your Honour; that is part of the testimony we thought had better be withheld until now. The man did leave a note, explaining just what he meant to do with the time machine.

JUDGE CLARK: And what was that?

DR CARNOT: He had set the dial for a two thousand year trip into the past. That accounted for the vast amount of energy required. You see, it varies not only with the mass transported, but the time as well.

JUDGE CLARK: Two thousand years!

DR CARNOT: That's right, Your Honour. In itself, that's bad enough.

It is one thing to send a small mass or a sterile insect back in time; even then, there are dangers we can hardly predict. The present is intricately involved with the past – stems from it, in fact. It's like altering the origin of a river; a little change at the source can make a tremendous difference at the mouth. Even move it fifty miles away. Now a modern man in the world of two thousand years ago – frankly, Your Honour, we just don't know what that might do. It seems fantastic to believe that he could change the here-and-now, and yet the theory implies that this whole universe might change completely, or even vanish. Don't ask me where or how.

(At this point, Professor Pirenian, of the National Security Council, broke in with a question.)

PIRENIAN: Why didn't you and Dr Kent merely send another man to intercept this one? Yours, by the machine, could obviously set the dials to get there first, thus snatching the first one back before he could do any harm.

DR CARNOT: We thought of that, even in the few minutes we had. But suppose that this world vanished before we could cut in ahead of him? Believe me, the paradoxes are maddening; no amount of mathematical wrangling can settle them; only experiment. We couldn't chance it; that's all.

PIRENIAN: You're right, of course. Maybe we should be glad, gentlemen, that Dr Carnot – and Dr Kent – were there instead of the rest of us!

DR CARNOT: You still don't know the real danger. What I've said so far applies to an impulsive, random trip to the distant past, where the man had no specific intentions. But Michael Nauss did have a particular plan – a wild, crazy, and yet, in a way, magnificent conception. One that the public, or much of it, might foolishly support without realizing the consequences. I speak of this country, and people in Europe; not in Asia, for the most part. And he had set the vernier with perfect precision, which made his plan even more feasible.

JUDGE CLARK: What was he going to do?

DR CARNOT: According to his note, this man had taken with him a repeating rifle and five thousand rounds of exploding ammunition. His intention was nothing less than to arrive at Golgotha in time to rescue Jesus Christ from the Roman soldiers. In short, to prevent the crucifixion. And with a modern rifle, who can say he wouldn't succeed? And then what? Then what? The implications are staggering. Disregarding the Christian dogma, which asserts Jesus *had* to die for our sins, what of the effect on the future, the entire stream of history, secular as well as religious? Maybe Jesus himself would have prevented this madman from saving him – but who can be sure? Yet, if you ask the man in the street, now, in this year 2015: Shall we save Jesus Christ from the cross? – what would he answer? Whose side would he take? Ours, or Michael Nauss'? That is why Dr Kent and I destroyed the machine; and why we face this court now. We believe the proceedings should not be released. The decision is yours. We made ours that night.

I Made You

WALTER M. MILLER, JR.

It had disposed of the enemy, and it was weary. It sat on the crag by night. Gaunt, frigid, wounded, it sat under the black sky and listened to the land with its feet, while only its dishlike ear moved in slow patterns that searched the surface of the land and the sky. The land was silent, airless. Nothing moved, except the feeble thing that scratched in the cave. It was good that nothing moved. It hated sound and motion. It was in its nature to hate them. About the thing in the cave it could do nothing until dawn. The thing muttered in the rocks –

'Help me! Are you all dead? Can't you hear me? This is Sawyer. Sawyer calling anybody, Sawyer calling anybody –'

The mutterings were irregular, without pattern. It filtered them out, refusing to listen. All was seeping cold. The sun was gone, and there had been near-blackness for two hundred and fifty hours, except for the dim light of the sky-orb which gave no food, and the stars by which it told the time.

It sat wounded on the crag and expected the enemy. The enemy had come charging into the world out of the unworld during the late afternoon. The enemy had come brazenly, with neither defensive manoeuvring nor offensive fire. It had destroyed them easily – first the big lumbering enemy that rumbled along on wheels, and then the small enemies that scurried away from the gutted hulk. It had picked them off one at a time, except for the one that crept into the cave and hid itself beyond a break in the tunnel.

It waited for the thing to emerge. From its vantage point atop the crag it could scan broken terrain for miles around, the craters and crags and fissures, the barren expanse of dust-flat that stretched to the west, and the squarish outlines of the holy place near the tower that was the centre of the world. The cave lay at the foot of a cliff to the south-east, only a thousand yards from the crag. It could guard the entrance to the cave with its small spitters, and there was no escape for the lingering trace of enemy.

It bore the mutterings of the hated thing even as it bore the pain of its wounds, patiently, waiting for a time of respite. For many sunrises there had been pain, and still the wounds were unrepaired. The wounds dulled some of its senses and crippled some of its activators. It could no longer follow the flickering beam of energy that would lead it safely into the unworld and across it to the place of creation. It could no longer blink out the pulses that reflected the difference between healer and foe. Now there was only foe.

'Colonel Aubrey, this is Sawyer. Answer me! I'm trapped in a supply cache! I think the others are dead. It blasted us as soon as we came near. Aubrey from Sawyer, Aubrey from Sawyer. Listen! I've got only one cylinder of oxygen left, you hear? Colonel, answer me!'

Vibrations in the rock – nothing more – only a minor irritant to disturb the blessed stasis of the world it guarded. The enemy was destroyed, except for the lingering trace in the cave. The lingering trace was neutralized, however, and did not move.

Because of its wounds, it nursed a brooding anger. It could not stop the damage signals that kept firing from its wounded members, but neither could it accomplish the actions that the agonizing signals urged it to accomplish. It sat and suffered and hated on the crag.

It hated the night, for by night there was no food. Each day it devoured sun, strengthened itself for the long, long watch of darkness, but when dawn came, it was feeble again, and hunger was a fierce passion within. It was well, therefore, that there was peace in the night, that it might conserve itself and shield its bowels from the cold. If the cold penetrated the insulating layers, thermal receptors would begin firing warning signals, and agony would increase. There was much agony. And, except in time of battle, there was no pleasure, except in devouring sun.

To protect the holy place, to restore stasis to the world, to kill enemy – these were the pleasures of battle. It knew them.

And it knew the nature of the world. It had learned every inch of land out to the pain perimeter, beyond which it could not move. And it had learned the surface features of the demiworld beyond, learned them by scanning with its long-range senses. The world, the demiworld, the unworld – these were Outside, constituting the Universe.

'Help me, help me, help me! This is Captain John Harbin Sawyer, Autocyber Corps, Instruction and Programming Section, currently of Salvage Expedition Lunar Sixteen. Isn't anybody alive on the Moon? Listen! Listen to me! I'm sick. I've been here God knows how many days . . . in a suit. It stinks. Did you ever live in a suit for days? I'm sick. Get me out of here!'

The enemy's place was unworld. If the enemy approached closer than the outer range, it must kill; this was a basic truth that it had known since the day of creation. Only the healers might move with impunity over all the land, but now the healers never came. It could no longer call them nor recognize them – because of the wound.

It knew the nature of itself. It learned of itself by introspecting damage, and by internal scanning. It alone was 'being'. All else was of the outside. It knew its functions, its skills, its limitations. It listened to the land with its feet. It scanned the surface with many eyes. It tested the skies with a flickering probe. In the ground, it felt the faint seisms and random noise. On the surface, it saw the faint glint of starlight, the heat-loss from the cold terrain, and the reflected pulses from the tower. In the sky, it saw only stars, and heard only the pulse-echo from the faint orb of Earth overhead. It suffered the gnawings of ancient pain, and waited for the dawn.

After an hour, the thing began crawling in the cave. It listened to the faint scraping sounds that came through the rocks. It lowered a more sensitive pickup and tracked the sounds. The remnant of enemy was crawling softly towards the mouth of the cave. It turned a small spitter towards the black scar at the foot of the Earthlit cliff. It fired a bright burst of tracers towards the cave, and saw them ricochet about the entrance in bright but noiseless streaks over the airless land.

'You dirty greasy deadly monstrosity, let me alone! You ugly juggernaut, I'm Sawyer. Don't you remember? I helped to train you ten years ago. You were a rookie under me . . . heh heh! Just a dumb autocyber rookie . . . with the firepower of a regiment. Let me go. Let me go!'

The enemy-trace crawled towards the entrance again. And again a noiseless burst of machine-gun fire spewed about the cave, driving the enemy fragment back. More vibrations in the rock –

'I'm your friend. The war's over. It's been over for months . . . Earthmonths. Don't you get it. Grumbler? "Grumbler" – we used to call you that back in your rookie days – before we taught you how to kill. Grumbler. Mobile autocyber fire control. Don't you know your pappy, son?'

The vibrations were an irritant. Suddenly angry, it wheeled around on the crag, gracefully manoeuvring its massive bulk. Motors growling, it moved from the crag on to the hillside, turned again, and lumbered down the slope. It charged across the flatlands and braked to a halt fifty yards from the entrance to the cave. Dust geysers sprayed up about its caterpillars and fell like jets of water in the airless night. It listened again. All was silent in the cave.

'Go 'way, sonny,' quavered the vibrations after a time. *'Let pappy starve in peace.'*

It aimed the small spitter at the centre of the black opening and hosed two hundred rounds of tracers into the cave. It waited. Nothing moved inside. It debated the use of a radiation grenade, but its arsenal was fast depleting. It listened for a time, watching the cave, looming five times taller than the tiny flesh-thing that cowered inside. Then it turned and lumbered back across the flat to resume its watch from the crag. Distant motion, out beyond the limits of the demiworld, scratched feebly at the threshold of its awareness – but the motion was too remote to disturb.

The thing was scratching in the cave again.

'I'm punctured, do you hear? I'm punctured. A shard of broken rock. Just a small leak, but a slap-patch won't hold. My suit! Aubrey from Sawyer, Aubrey from Sawyer. Base control from Moonwagon Sixteen. Message for you, over. He he. Gotta observe procedure. I got shot! I'm punctured. Help!'

The thing made whining sounds for a time, then: *'All right, it's only my leg. I'll pump the boot full of water and freeze it. So I lose a leg. Whatthehell, take your time.'* The vibrations subsided into whining sounds again.

It settled again on the crag, its activators relaxing into a lethargy that was full of gnawing pain. Patiently it awaited the dawn.

★

The movement towards the south was increasing. The movement nagged at the outer fringes of the demiworld, until at last the movement became an irritant. Silently, a drill slipped down from its belly. The drill gnawed deep into the rock, then retracted. It slipped a sensitive pickup into the drill hole and listened carefully to the ground.

A faint purring in the rocks – mingled with the whining from the cave.

It compared the purring with recorded memories. It remembered similar purrings. The sound came from a rolling object far to the south. It tried to send the pulses that asked 'Are you friend or foe?' but the sending organ was inoperative. The movement, therefore, was enemy – but still beyond range of its present weapons.

Lurking anger, and expectation of battle. It stirred restlessly on the crag, but kept its surveillance of the cave. Suddenly there was disturbance on a new sensory channel, vibrations similar to those that came from the cave; but this time the vibrations came across the surface, through the emptiness, transmitted in the long-wave spectra.

'Moonwagon Sixteen from Command Runabout, give us a call. Over.'

Then silence. It expected a response from the cave, at first – since it knew that one unit of enemy often exchanged vibratory patterns with another unit of enemy. But no answer came. Perhaps the long-wave energy could not penetrate the cave to reach the thing that cringed inside.

'Salvage Sixteen, this is Aubrey's runabout. What the devil happened to you? Can you read me? Over!'

Tensely it listened to the ground. The purring stopped for a time as the enemy paused. Minutes later the motion resumed.

It awoke an emissary ear twenty kilometers to the south-west, and commanded the ear to listen, and to transmit the patterns of the purring noise. Two soundings were taken, and from them it derived the enemy's precise position and velocity. The enemy was proceeding to the north, into the edge of the demiworld. Lurking anger flared into active fury. It gunned its engines on the crag. It girded itself for battle.

'Salvage Sixteen, this is Aubrey's runabout. I assume your radio rig is inoperative. If you can hear us, get this: we're proceeding north to five miles short of magnapult range. We'll stop there and fire an autocyb rocket into

zone Red-Red. The warhead's a radio-to-sonar transceiver. If you've got a seismitter that's working, the transceiver will act as a relay stage. Over.'

It ignored the vibratory pattern and rechecked its battle gear. It introspected its energy storage, and tested its weapon activators. It summoned an emissary eye and waited a dozen minutes while the eye crawled crablike from the holy place to take up a watch-post near the entrance of the cave. If the enemy remnant tried to emerge, the emissary eye would see, and report, and it could destroy the enemy remnant with a remote grenade catapult.

The purring in the ground was louder. Having prepared itself for the fray, it came down from the crag and grumbled southward at cruising speed. It passed the gutted hulk of the Moonwagon, with its team of overturned tractors. The detonation of the magnapult canister had broken the freight-car-sized vehicle in half. The remains of several two-legged enemy appurtenances were scattered about the area, tiny broken things in the pale Earthlight. Grumbler ignored them and charged relentlessly southward.

A sudden wink of light on the southern horizon! Then a tiny dot of flame arched upwards, traversing the heavens. Grumbler skidded to a halt and tracked its path. A rocket missile. It would fall somewhere in the east half of zone Red-Red. There was no time to prepare to shoot it down. Grumbler waited – and saw that the missile would explode harmlessly in a nonvital area.

Seconds later, the missile paused in flight, reversing direction and sitting on its jets. It dropped out of sight behind an outcropping. There was no explosion. Nor was there any activity in the area where the missile had fallen. Grumbler called an emissary ear, sent it migrating towards the impact point to listen, then continued south towards the pain perimeter.

'*Salvage Sixteen, this is Aubrey's runabout,*' came the long-wave vibrations. '*We just shot the radio-seismitter relay into Red-Red. If you're within five miles of it, you should be able to hear.*'

Almost immediately, a response from the cave, heard by the emissary ear that listened to the land near the tower: '*Thank God! He he he he – Oh, thank God!*'

And simultaneously, the same vibratory pattern came in long-wave patterns from the direction of the missile-impact point. Grumbler stopped again, momentarily confused, angrily tempted to lob a magnapult canister across the broken terrain towards the impact point. But the emissary ear reported no physical movement from the area. The enemy to the south was the origin of the disturbances. If it removed the major enemy first, it could remove the minor disturbances later. It moved on to the pain perimeter, occasionally listening to the meaningless vibrations caused by the enemy.

'Salvage Sixteen from Aubrey. I hear you faintly. Who is this, Carhill?'

'Aubrey! A voice – A real voice – Or am I going nuts?'

'Sixteen from Aubrey. Sixteen from Aubrey. Stop babbling and tell me who's talking. What's happening in there? Have you got Grumbler immobilized?'

Spasmodic choking was the only response.

'Sixteen from Aubrey. Snap out of it! Listen, Sawyer, I know it's you. Now get hold of yourself, man! What's happened?'

'Dead . . . they're all dead but me.'

'STOP THAT IDIOTIC LAUGHING!'

A long silence, then, scarcely audible: *'OK, I'll hold on to myself. Is it really you, Aubrey?'*

'You're not having hallucinations, Sawyer. We're crossing zone Red in a runabout. Now tell me the situation. We've been trying to call you for days.'

'Grumbler let us get ten miles into zone Red-Red, and then he clobbered us with a magnapult canister.'

'Wasn't your IFF working?'

'Yes, but Grumbler's isn't! After he blasted the wagon, he picked off the other four that got out alive – He he he he . . . Did you ever see a Sherman tank chase a mouse, colonel?'

'Cut it out, Sawyer! Another giggle out of you, and I'll flay you alive.'

'Get me out! My leg! Get me out!'

'If we can. Tell me your present situation.'

'My suit . . . I got a small puncture – Had to pump the leg full of water and freeze it. Now my leg's dead. I can't last much longer.'

'The situation, Sawyer, the situation! Not your aches and pains.'

*

The vibrations continued, but Grumbler screened them out for a time. There was rumbling fury on an Earthlit hill.

It sat with its engines idling, listening to the distant movements of the enemy to the south. At the foot of the hill lay the pain perimeter; even upon the hilltop, it felt the faint twinges of warning that issued from the tower, thirty kilometres to the rear at the centre of the world. It was in communion with the tower. If it ventured beyond the perimeter, the communion would slip out-of-phase, and there would be blinding pain and detonation.

The enemy was moving more slowly now, creeping north across the demiworld. It would be easy to destroy the enemy at once, if only the supply of rocket missiles were not depleted. The range of the magnapult hurler was only twenty-five kilometres. The small spitters would reach, but their accuracy was close to zero at such range. It would have to wait for the enemy to come closer. It nursed a brooding fury on the hill.

'Listen, Sawyer, if Grumbler's IFF isn't working, why hasn't he already fired on this runabout?'

'That's what sucked us in too, colonel. We came into zone Red and nothing happened. Either he's out of long-range ammo, or he's getting cagey, or both. Probably both.'

'Mmmp! Then we'd better park here and figure something out.'

'Listen . . . there's only one thing you can do. Call for a tele-controlled missile from the Base.'

'To destroy Grumbler? You're out of your head, Sawyer. If Grumbler's knocked out, the whole area around the excavations gets blown sky high . . . to keep them out of enemy hands. You know that.'

'You expect me to care?'

'Stop screaming, Sawyer. Those excavations are the most valuable property on the Moon. We can't afford to lose them. That's why Grumbler was staked out. If they got blown to rubble, I'd be court-martialled before the debris quit falling.'

The response was snarling and sobbing. *'Eight hours' oxygen. Eight hours', you hear? You stupid, merciless –'*

*

It gunned its engines and clutched the drive shafts. It rolled towards the hill, gathering speed, and its mouth was full of death. Motors strained and howled. Like a thundering bull, it rumbled towards the south. It hit maximum velocity at the foot of the slope. It lurched sharply upwards. As the magnapult swept up to correct elevation, the gyroscope closed the circuit.

A surge of energy. The clutching fist of the field gripped the canister, tore it free of the loader, hurled it high over the broken terrain towards the enemy. Grumbler skidded to a halt on the hilltop.

'Listen, Sawyer, I'm sorry, but there's nothing –'

The enemy's voice ended with a dull snap. A flare of light came briefly from the southern horizon, and died.

'He he he he he –' said the thing in the cave.

Grumbler paused.

THRRUMMMP! came the shock-wave through the rocks.

Five emissary ears relayed their recordings of the detonation from various locations. It studied them, it analysed. The detonation had occurred less than fifty metres from the enemy runabout. Satiated, it wheeled around lazily on the hilltop and rolled northward towards the centre of the world. All was well.

'Aubrey, you got cut off,' grunted the thing in the cave. *'Call me, you coward . . . call me. I want to make certain you hear.'*

Grumbler, as a random action, recorded the meaningless noise of the thing in the cave, studied the noise, rebroadcast it on a longwave frequency: 'Aubrey, you got cut off. Call me, you coward . . . call me, I want to make certain you hear.'

The seismitter caught the longwave noise and reintroduced it as vibration in the rocks.

The thing screamed in the cave. Grumbler recorded the screaming noise, and rebroadcast it several times.

'Aubrey . . . Aubrey, where are you . . . AUBREY! Don't desert me, don't leave me here –'

The thing in the cave became silent.

It was a peaceful night. The stars glared unceasingly from the blackness, and the pale terrain was haunted by Earthlight from the dim crescent in the sky. Nothing moved. It was good that nothing moved. The holy place was at peace in the airless world. There was blessed stasis.

Only once did the thing stir again in the cave. So slowly that Grumbler scarcely heard the sound, it crawled to the entrance and lay peering up at the steel behemoth on the crag.

It whispered faintly in the rocks.

'I made you, don't you understand? I'm human, I made you –'

Then with one leg dragging behind, it pulled itself out into the Earthglow and turned as if to look up at the dim crescent in the sky. Gathering fury, Grumbler stirred on the crag, and lowered the black maw of a grenade launcher.

'I made you,' came the meaningless noise.

It hated noise and motion. It was in its nature to hate them. Angrily, the grenade launcher spoke. And then there was blessed stasis for the rest of the night.

The Country of the Kind

DAMON KNIGHT

The attendant at the car lot was day-dreaming when I pulled up – a big, lazy-looking man in black satin chequered down the front. I was wearing scarlet, myself; it suited my mood. I got out, almost on his toes.

'Park or storage?' he asked automatically, turning around. Then he realized who I was, and ducked his head away.

'Neither,' I told him.

There was a hand torch on a shelf in the repair shed right behind him. I got it and came back. I knelt down to where I could reach behind the front wheel, and ignited the torch. I turned it on the axle and suspension. They glowed cherry red, then white, and fused together. Then I got up and turned the flame on both tyres until the rubberoid stank and sizzled and melted down to the pavement. The attendant didn't say anything.

I left him there, looking at the mess on his nice clean concrete.

It had been a nice car, too; but I could get another any time. And I felt like walking. I went down the winding road, sleepy in the afternoon sunlight, dappled with shade and smelling of cool leaves. You couldn't see the houses; they were all sunken or hidden by shrubbery, or a little of both. That was the fad I'd heard about; it was what I'd come here to see. Not that anything the dulls did would be worth looking at.

I turned off at random and crossed a rolling lawn, went through a second hedge of hawthorn in blossom, and came out next to a big sunken games court.

The tennis net was up, and two couples were going at it, just working up a little sweat – young, about half my age, all four of them. Three dark-haired, one blonde. They were evenly matched, and both couples played well together; they were enjoying themselves.

I watched for a minute. But by then the nearest two were beginning to sense I was there, anyhow. I walked down on to the court, just as the blonde was about to serve. She looked at me, frozen across the net, poised on tiptoe. The others stood.

'Off,' I told them. 'Game's over.'

I watched the blonde. She was not especially pretty, as they go, but compactly and gracefully put together. She came down slowly, flatfooted without awkwardness, and tucked the racquet under her arm; then the surprise was over and she was trotting off the court after the other three.

I followed their voices around the curve of the path, between towering masses of lilacs, inhaling the sweetness, until I came to what looked like a little sunning spot. There was a sundial, and a birdbath, and towels lying around on the grass. One couple, the dark-haired pair, was still in sight farther down the path, heads bobbing along. The other couple had disappeared.

I found the handle in the grass without any trouble. The mechanism responded, and an oblong section of turf rose up. It was the stair I had, not the elevator, but that was all right. I ran down the steps and into the first door I saw, and was in the top-floor lounge, an oval room lit with diffused simulated sunlight from above. The furniture was all comfortably bloated, sprawling and ugly; the carpet was deep, and there was a fresh flower scent in the air.

The blonde was over at the near end with her back to me, studying the autochef keyboard. She was half out of her playsuit. She pushed it the rest of the way down and stepped out of it, then turned and saw me.

She was surprised again; she hadn't thought I might follow her down.

I got up close before it occurred to her to move; then it was too late. She knew she couldn't get away from me; she closed her eyes and leaned back against the panelling, turning a little pale. Her lips and her golden brows went up in the middle.

I looked her over and told her a few uncomplimentary things about herself. She trembled, but didn't answer. On impulse, I leaned over and dialled the autochef to hot cheese sauce. I cut the safety out of circuit and put the quantity dial all the way up. I dialled *soup tureen* and then *punch bowl*.

The stuff began to come out in about a minute, steaming hot. I took the tureens and splashed them up and down the wall on either side of her. Then, when the first punch bowl came out, I used the empty bowls as scoops. I clotted the carpet with the stuff; I made streamers of it all along the walls, and dumped puddles into what furniture I could reach. Where it cooled it would harden, and where it hardened it would cling.

I wanted to splash it across her body, but it would've hurt, and we couldn't have that. The punch bowls of hot sauce were still coming out of the autochef, crowding each other around the vent. I punched *cancel*, and then *port wine*.

It came out well chilled in open bottles. I took the first one and had my arm back just about to throw a nice line of the stuff right across her midriff, when a voice said behind me:

'Watch out for cold wine.'

My arm twitched and a little stream of the wine splashed across her thighs. She was ready for it; her eyes had opened at the voice, and she barely jumped.

I whirled around, fighting mad. The man was standing there where he had come out of the stair-well. He was thinner in the face than most, bronzed, wide-chested, with alert blue eyes. If it hadn't been for him, I knew it would have worked – the blonde would have mistaken the cold splash for a hot one.

I could hear the scream in my mind, and I wanted it.

I took a step towards him, and my foot slipped. I went down clumsily, wrenching one knee. I got up shaking and tight all over. I wasn't in control of myself. I screamed, 'You – you –'. I turned and got one of the punch bowls and lifted it in both hands, heedless of how the hot sauce was slopping over on to my wrists, and I had it almost in the air towards him when the sickness took me – that damned buzzing in my head, louder, louder, drowning everything out.

When I came to, they were both gone. I got up off the floor, weak as death, and staggered over to the nearest chair. My clothes were slimed and sticky. I wanted to die. I wanted to drop into that dark furry hole that was yawning for me and never come up; but I made myself stay awake and get out of the chair.

Going down in the elevator, I almost blacked out again. The blonde and the thin man weren't in any of the second-floor bedrooms. I made sure of that, and then I emptied the closets and bureau drawers on to the floor, dragged the whole mess into one of the bathrooms and stuffed the tub with it, then turned on the water.

I tried the third floor: maintenance and storage. It was empty. I turned the furnace on and set the thermostat up as high as it would go. I opened the freezer doors and dialled them to defrost. I propped the stair-well door open and went back up in the elevator.

On the second floor I stopped long enough to open the stairway door there – the water was halfway towards it, creeping across the floor – and then searched the top floor. No one was there. I opened book reels and threw them unwinding across the room; I would have done more, but I could hardly stand. I got up to the surface and collapsed on the lawn; that furry pit swallowed me up, dead and drowned.

While I slept, water poured down the open stair-well and filled the third level. Thawing food packages floated out into the rooms. Water seeped into wall panels and machine housings; circuits shorted and fuses blew. The air conditioning stopped, but the pile kept heating. The water rose.

Spoiled food, floating supplies, grimy water surged up the stair-well. The second and first levels were bigger and would take longer to fill, but they'd fill. Rugs, furnishings, clothing, all the things in the house would be waterlogged and ruined. Probably the weight of so much water would shift the house, rupture water pipes and other fluid intakes. It would take a repair crew more than a day just to clean up the mess. The house itself was done for, not repairable. The blonde and the thin man would never live in it again.

Serve them right.

The dulls could build another house; they built like beavers. There was only one of me in the world.

The earliest memory I have is of some woman, probably the crèche-mother, staring at me with an expression of shock and horror. Just that. I've tried to remember what happened directly before or after, but I can't. Before, there's nothing but the dark formless shaft of no-memory that runs back to birth. Afterwards, the big calm.

From my fifth year, it must have been, to my fifteenth, everything I can remember floats in a pleasant dim sea. Nothing was terribly important. I was languid and soft; I drifted. Waking merged into sleep.

In my fifteenth year it was the fashion in love-play for the young people to pair off for months or longer. 'Loving steady,' we called it. I remember how the older people protested that it was unhealthy; but we were all normal juniors, and nearly as free as adults under law.

All but me.

The first steady girl I had was named Elen. She had blonde hair, almost white, worn long; her lashes were dark and her eyes pale green. Startling eyes: they didn't look as if they were looking at you. They looked blind.

Several times she gave me strange startled glances, something between fright and anger. Once it was because I held her too tightly, and hurt her; other times, it seemed to be for nothing at all.

In our group, a pairing that broke up sooner than four weeks was a little suspect – there must be something wrong with one partner or both, or the pairing would have lasted longer.

Four weeks and a day after Elen and I made our pairing, she told me she was breaking it.

I'd thought I was ready. But I felt the room spin half around me till the wall came against my palm and stopped.

The room had been in use as a hobby chamber; there was a rack of plasticraft knives under my hand. I took one without thinking, and when I saw it I thought, *I'll frighten her.*

And I saw the startled, half-angry look in her pale eyes as I went towards her; but this is curious: she wasn't looking at the knife. She was looking at my face.

The elders found me later with the blood on me, and put me into a locked room. Then it was my turn to be frightened, because I realized for the first time that it was possible for a human being to do what I had done. And if I could do it to Elen, I thought, surely they could do it to me.

But they couldn't. They set me free: they had to.

And it was then I understood that I was the king of the world.

*

Something else in me, that had been suppressed and forgotten, rose up with my first blow struck in anger. The sculpture began years afterwards, as an accident; but in that moment I was free, and I was an artist.

One winter, in the AC Archives in Denver, I found a storeroom full of old printed books. I spent months there, reading them, because until then I'd thought I had invented sculpture and drawing. The thing I chiefly wanted to know was, why had it stopped? There was no answer in so many words in any of the books. But reading the histories of those times before the Interregnum, I found one thing that might explain it. Whenever there was a long period of peace and plenty anywhere in the ancient world, art grew poor: decoration, genre painting, imitations of imitations. And as for the great artists, they all belonged to violent periods – Praxiteles, da Vinci, Rembrandt van Rijn, Renoir, Picasso . . .

It had been bred out of the race, evidently. I don't suppose the genetic planners wanted to get rid of it, but they would have shed almost anything to make a homogeneous, rational, sane, and healthy world.

So there was only one man to carve the portrait of the Age of Reason. All right; I would have been content, only . . .

The sky was turning clear violet when I woke up, and shadow was spilling out from the hedges. I went down the hill until I saw the ghostly blue of photon tubes glowing in a big oblong, just outside the commerce area. I went that way, by habit.

Other people were lining up at the entrance to show their books and be admitted. I brushed by them, seeing the shocked faces and feeling their bodies flinch away, and went on into the robing chamber.

Straps, aqualungs, masks, and flippers were all for the taking. I stripped, dropping the clothes where I stood, and put the underwater equipment on. I strode out to the poolside, monstrous, like a being from another world. I adjusted the lung and the flippers, and slipped into the water.

Underneath it was all crystal blue, with the forms of swimmers sliding through it like pale angels. Schools of small fish scattered as I went down. My heart was beating with a painful joy.

Down, far down, I saw a girl slowly undulating through the motions of a sinuous underwater dance, writhing around and around a ribbed column of imitation coral. She had a suction-tipped fish lance in her hand, but she was not using it; she was only dancing, all by herself, down at the bottom of the water.

I swam after her. She was young and delicately made, and when she saw the deliberately clumsy motions I made in imitation of hers, her eyes glinted with amusement behind her mask. She bowed to me in mockery, and slowly glided off with simple, exaggerated movements, like a child's ballet.

I followed. Around her and around I swam, stiff-legged, first more child-like and awkward than she, then subtly parodying her motions; then improvising on them until I was dancing an intricate, mocking dance around her.

I saw her eyes widen. She matched her rhythm to mine, then, and together, apart, together again we coiled the wake of our dancing. At last, exhausted, we clung together where a bridge of plastic coral arched over us. Her cool body was in the bend of my arm; behind two thicknesses of vitrin – a world away! – her eyes were friendly and kind.

There was a moment when, two strangers yet one flesh, we felt our souls speak to one another across that abyss of matter. It was a truncated embrace – we could not kiss, we could not speak – but her hands lay confidingly on my shoulders, and her eyes looked into mine.

That moment had to end. She gestured towards the surface, and left me. I followed her up. I was feeling drowsy and almost at peace, after my sickness. I thought . . . I don't know what I thought.

We rose together at the side of the pool. She turned to me, removing her mask: and her smile stopped, and melted away. She stared at me with a horrified disgust, wrinkled her nose.

'*Pyah!*' she said, and turned, awkward in her flippers. Watching her, I saw her fall into the arms of a white-haired man, and heard her hysterical voice tumbling over itself.

'But don't you remember?' the man's voice rumbled. 'You should know it by heart.' He turned. 'Hal, is there a copy in the clubhouse?'

A murmur answered him, and in a few moments a young man came out holding a slender brown pamphlet.

I knew that pamphlet. I could even have told you what page the white-haired man opened it to; what sentences the girl was reading as I watched.

I waited. I don't know why.

I heard her voice rising: 'To think that I let him *touch* me!' And the white-haired man reassured her, the words rumbling, too low to hear. I saw her back straighten. She looked across at me . . . only a few yards in that scented, blue-lit air; a world away . . . and folded up the pamphlet into a hard wad, threw it, and turned on her heel.

The pamphlet landed almost at my feet. I touched it with my toe, and it opened to the page I had been thinking of:

. . . sedation until his fifteenth year, when for sexual reasons it became no longer practicable. While the advisers and medical staff hesitated, he killed a girl of the group by violence.

And farther down:

The solution finally adopted was threefold.

1. *A sanction* – the only sanction possible to our humane, permissive society. Excommunication: not to speak to him, touch him willingly, or acknowledge his existence.

2. *A precaution*. Taking advantage of a mild predisposition to epilepsy, a variant of the so-called Kusko analogue technique was employed, to prevent by an epileptic seizure any future act of violence.

3. *A warning*. A careful alteration of his body chemistry was effected to make his exhaled and exuded wastes emit a strongly pungent and offensive odour. In mercy, he himself was rendered unable to detect this smell.

Fortunately, the genetic and environmental accidents which combined to produce this atavism have been fully explained and can never again . . .

The words stopped meaning anything, as they always did at this point. I didn't want to read any farther; it was all nonsense, anyway. I was the king of the world.

I got up and went away, out into the night, blind to the dulls who thronged the rooms I passed.

Two squares away was the commerce area. I found a clothing outlet and went in. All the free clothes in the display cases were drab: those were for worthless floaters, not for me. I went past them to the specials, and found a combination I could stand – silver and blue, with a severe black piping down the tunic. A dull would have said it was 'nice'. I punched for it. The automatic looked me over with its dull glassy eye, and croaked, 'Your contribution book, please.'

I could have had a contribution book, for the trouble of stepping out into the street and taking it away from the first passer-by; but I didn't have the patience. I picked up the one-legged table from the refreshment nook, hefted it, and swung it at the cabinet door. The metal shrieked and dented opposite the catch. I swung once more to the same place, and the door sprang open. I pulled out clothing in handfuls till I got a set that would fit me.

I bathed and changed, and then went prowling in the big multioutlet down the avenue. All those places are arranged pretty much alike, no matter what the local managers do to them. I went straight to the knives, and picked out three in graduated sizes, down to the size of my finger-nail. Then I had to take my chance. I tried the furniture department, where I had had good luck once in a while; but this year all they were using was metal. I had to have seasoned wood.

I knew where there was a big cache of cherry wood, in goodsized blocks, in a forgotten warehouse up north at a place called Kootenay. I could have carried some around with me – enough for years – but what for, when the world belonged to me?

It didn't take me long. Down in the workshop section, of all places, I found some antiques – tables and benches, all with wooden tops. While the dulls collected down at the other end of the room, pretending not to notice, I sawed off a good oblong chunk of the smallest bench, and made a base for it out of another.

As long as I was there, it was a good place to work, and I could eat and sleep upstairs, so I stayed.

I knew what I wanted to do. It was going to be a man, sitting with his legs crossed and his forearms resting down along his calves. His head was going to be tilted back, and his eyes closed, as if he were turning his face up to the sun.

In three days it was finished. The trunk and limbs had a shape that was not man and not wood, but something in between: something that hadn't existed before I made it.

Beauty. That was the old word.

I had carved one of the figure's hands hanging loosely, and the other one curled shut. There had to be a time to stop and say it was finished. I took the smallest knife, the one I had been using to scrape the wood smooth, and cut away the handle and ground down what was left of the shaft to a thin spike. Then I drilled a hole into the wood of the figurine's hand, in the hollow between thumb and curled finger. I fitted the knife blade in there; in the small hand it was a sword.

I cemented it in place. Then I took the sharp blade and stabbed my thumb, and smeared the blade.

I hunted most of that day, and finally found the right place – a niche in an outcropping of striated brown rock, in a little triangular half-wild patch that had been left where two roads forked. Nothing was permanent, of course, in a community like this one that might change its houses every five years or so, to follow the fashion; but this spot had been left to itself for a long time. It was the best I could do.

I had the paper ready: it was one of a batch I had printed up a year ago. The paper was treated, and I knew it would stay legible a long time. I hid a little photo capsule in the back of the niche, and ran the control wire to a staple in the base of the figurine. I put the figurine down on top of the paper, and anchored it lightly to the rock with two spots of all-cement. I had done it so often that it came naturally; I knew just how much cement would hold the figurine steady against a casual hand, but yield to one that really wanted to pull it down.

Then I stepped back to look: and the power and the pity of it made my breath come short, and tears start to my eyes.

Reflected light gleamed fitfully on the dark-stained blade that hung from his hand. He was sitting alone in that niche that closed him in like a coffin. His eyes were shut, and his head tilted back, as if he were turning his face up to the sun.

But only rock was over his head. There was no sun for him.

*

Hunched on the cool bare ground under a pepper tree, I was looking down across the road at the shadowed niche where my figurine sat.

I was all finished here. There was nothing more to keep me, and yet I couldn't leave.

People walked past now and then – not often. The community seemed half deserted, as if most of the people had flocked off to a surf party somewhere, or a contribution meeting, or to watch a new house being dug to replace the one I had wrecked . . . There was a little wind blowing towards me, cool and lonesome in the leaves.

Up the other side of the hollow there was a terrace, and on that terrace, half an hour ago, I had seen a brief flash of colour – a boy's head, with a red cap on it, moving past and out of sight.

That was why I had to stay. I was thinking how that boy might come down from his terrace and into my road, and passing the little wild triangle of land, see my figurine. I was thinking he might not pass by indifferently, but stop: and go closer to look: and pick up the wooden man: and read what was written on the paper underneath.

I believed that sometime it had to happen. I wanted it so hard that I ached.

My carvings were all over the world, wherever I had wandered. There was one in Congo City, carved of ebony, dusty-black; one in Cyprus, of bone; one in New Bombay, of shell; one in Changteh, of jade.

They were like signs printed in red and green, in a colour-blind world. Only the one I was looking for would even pick one of them up, and read the message I knew by heart.

TO YOU WHO CAN SEE, the first sentence said. I OFFER YOU A WORLD . . .

There was a flash of colour up on the terrace. I stiffened. A minute later, here it came again, from a different direction: it was the boy, clambering down the slope, brilliant against the green, with his red, sharp-billed cap like a woodpecker's head.

I held my breath.

He came towards me through the fluttering leaves, ticked off by pencils of sunlight as he passed. He was a brown boy, I could see at this distance, with a serious thin face. His ears stuck out, flickering pink with the sun behind them, and his elbow and knee pads made him look knobbly.

He reached the fork in the road, and chose the path on my side. I huddled into myself as he came nearer. *Let him see it, let him not see me*, I thought fiercely.

My fingers closed around a stone.

He was nearer, walking jerkily with his hands in his pockets, watching his feet mostly.

When he was almost opposite me, I threw the stone.

It rustled through the leaves below the niche in the rock. The boy's head turned. He stopped, staring; I think he saw the figurine then. I'm sure he saw it.

He took one step.

'Risha!' came floating down from the terrace.

And he looked up. 'Here,' he piped.

I saw the woman's head, tiny at the top of the terrace. She called something I didn't hear; I was standing up, squeezed tight with anger.

Then the wind shifted. It blew from me to the boy. He whirled around, his eyes big, and clapped a hand to his nose.

'Oh, what a stench!'

He turned to shout, 'Coming!' and then he was gone, hurrying back up the road, into the unstable blur of green.

My one chance, ruined. He would have seen the image, I knew, if it hadn't been for the damned woman, and the wind shifting . . . They were all against me, people, wind and all.

And the figurine still sat, blind eyes turned up to the rocky sky.

There was something inside me that told me to take my disappointment and go away from there, and not come back.

I knew I would be sorry. I did it anyway: took the image out of the niche, and the paper with it, and climbed the slope. At the top I heard his clear voice laughing.

There was a thing that might have been an ornamental mound, or the camouflaged top of a buried house. I went around it, tripping over my own feet, and came upon the boy kneeling on the turf. He was playing with a brown and white puppy.

He looked up with the laughter going out of his face. There was no wind, and he could smell me. I knew it was bad. No wind, and the puppy to distract him – everything about it was wrong. But I went to him blindly anyhow, and fell on one knee, and shoved the figurine at his face.

'Look –' I said.

He went over backwards in his hurry: he couldn't even have seen the image, except as a brown blur coming at him. He scrambled up, with the puppy whining and yapping around his heels, and ran for the mound.

I was up after him, clawing up moist earth and grass as I rose. In the other hand I still had the image clutched, and the paper with it.

A door popped open and swallowed him and popped shut again in my face. With the flat of my hand I beat the vines around it until I hit the doorplate by accident and the door opened. I dived in, shouting, 'Wait,' and was in a spiral passage, lit pearl-grey, winding downwards. Down I went headlong, and came out at the wrong door – an underground conservatory, humid and hot under the yellow lights, with dripping rank leaves in long rows. I went down the aisle raging, overturning the tanks, until I came to a vestibule and an elevator.

Down I went again to the third level and a labyrinth of guest rooms, all echoing, all empty. At last I found a ramp leading upwards, past the conservatory, and at the end of it voices.

The door was clear vitrin, and I paused on the near side of it looking and listening. There was the boy, and a woman old enough to be his mother, just – sister or cousin, more likely – and an elderly woman in a hard chair holding the puppy. The room was comfortable and tasteless, like other rooms.

I saw the shock grow on their faces as I burst in: it was always the same, they knew I would like to kill them, but they never expected that I would come uninvited into a house. It was not done.

There was that boy, so close I could touch him, but the shock of all of them was quivering in the air, smothering, like a blanket that would deaden my voice. I felt I had to shout.

'Everything they tell you is lies!' I said. 'See here – here, this is the truth!' I had the figurine in front of his eyes, but he didn't see.

'Risha, go below,' said the young woman quietly. He turned to obey, quick as a ferret. I got in front of him again. 'Stay,' I said, breathing hard. 'Look – '

'Remember, Risha, don't speak,' said the woman.

I couldn't stand any more. Where the boy went I don't know; I ceased to see him. With the image in one hand and the paper with it, I leaped at the woman. I was almost quick enough; I almost reached her; but the buzzing took me in the middle of a step, louder, louder, like the end of the world.

It was the second time that week. When I came to, I was sick and too faint to move for a long time.

The house was silent. They had gone, of course . . . the house had been defiled, having me in it. They wouldn't live here again, but would build elsewhere.

My eyes blurred. After a while I stood up and looked around at the room. The walls were hung with a grey close-woven cloth that looked as if it would tear, and I thought of ripping it down in strips, breaking furniture, stuffing carpets and bedding into the oubliette . . . But I didn't have the heart for it. I was too tired.

At last I stooped and picked up the figurine, and the paper that was supposed to go under it – crumpled now, with the forlorn look of a message that someone has thrown away unread.

I smoothed it out and read the last part.

YOU CAN SHARE THE WORLD WITH ME. THEY CAN'T STOP YOU. STRIKE NOW – PICK UP A SHARP THING AND STAB, OR A HEAVY THING AND CRUSH. THAT'S ALL. THAT WILL MAKE YOU FREE. ANYONE CAN DO IT.

Anyone. Anyone.

The Cage

BERTRAM CHANDLER

Imprisonment is always a humiliating experience, no matter how philosophical the prisoner. Imprisonment by one's own kind is bad enough – but one can, at least, talk to one's captors, one can make one's wants understood; one can, on occasion, appeal to them man to man.

Imprisonment is doubly humiliating when one's captors, in all honesty, treat one as a lower animal.

The party from the survey ship could, perhaps, be excused for failing to recognize the survivors from the interstellar liner *Lode Star* as rational beings. At least two hundred days had passed since their landing on the planet without a name – an unintentional landing made when *Lode Star*'s Ehrenhaft generators, driven far in excess of their normal capacity by a breakdown of the electronic regulator, had flung her far from the regular shipping lanes to an unexplored region of space. *Lode Star* had landed safely enough; but shortly thereafter (troubles never come singly) her pile had got out of control and her captain had ordered his first mate to evacuate the passengers and those crew members not needed to cope with the emergency, and to get them as far from the ship as possible.

Hawkins and his charges were well clear when there was a flare of released energy, a not very violent explosion. The survivors wanted to turn to watch, but Hawkins drove them on with curses and, at times, blows. Luckily they were up wind from the ship and so escaped the fall-out.

When the fireworks seemed to be over, Hawkins, accompanied by Dr Boyle, the ship's surgeon, returned to the scene of the disaster. The two men, wary of radioactivity, were cautious and stayed a safe distance from the shallow, still smoking crater that marked where the ship had been. It was all too obvious to them that the captain, together with his officers and technicians, was now no more than an infinitesimal part of the incandescent cloud that had mushroomed up into the low overcast.

Thereafter the fifty-odd men and women, the survivors of *Lode Star*, had degenerated. It hadn't been a fast process – Hawkins and Boyle, aided by a committee of the more responsible passengers, had fought a stout rearguard action. But it had been a hopeless sort of fight. The climate was against them, for a start. Hot it was, always in the neighbourhood of 85° Fahrenheit. And it was wet – a thin, warm drizzle falling all the time. The air seemed to abound with the spores of fungi – luckily these did not attack living skin but throve on dead organic matter, on clothing. They throve to an only slightly lesser degree on metals and on the synthetic fabrics that many of the castaways wore.

Danger, outside danger, would have helped to maintain morale. But there were no dangerous animals. There were only little smooth-skinned things, not unlike frogs, that hopped through the sodden undergrowth, and, in the numerous rivers, fishlike creatures ranging in size from the shark to the tadpole, and all of them possessing the bellicosity of the latter.

Food had been no problem after the first few hungry hours. Volunteers had tried a large, succulent fungus growing on the boles of the huge fern-like trees. They had pronounced it good. After a lapse of five hours they had neither died nor even complained of abdominal pains. That fungus was to become the staple diet of the castaways. In the weeks that followed other fungi had been found, and berries, and roots – all of them edible. They provided a welcome variety.

Fire – in spite of the all-pervading heat – was the blessing most missed by the castaways. With it they could have supplemented their diet by catching and cooking the little frog-things of the rain forest, the fishes of the streams. Some of the hardier spirits did eat these animals raw, but they were frowned upon by most of the other members of the community. Too, fire would have helped to drive back the darkness of the long nights, would, by its real warmth and light, have dispelled the illusion of cold produced by the ceaseless dripping of water from every leaf and frond.

When they fled from the ship, most of the survivors had possessed pocket lighters – but the lighters had been lost when the pockets, together with the clothing surrounding them, had disintegrated. In any case, all attempts to start a fire in the days when there were still pocket lighters had failed – there was not, Hawkins swore, a single dry spot on the whole accursed planet. Now the making of fire was quite impossible: even if there had been present an expert on the rubbing together of two dry sticks he could have found no material with which to work.

They made their permanent settlement on the crest of a low hill. (There were, so far as they could discover, no mountains.) It was less thickly wooded there than the surrounding plains, and the ground was less marshy underfoot. They succeeded in wrenching fronds from the fern-like trees and built for themselves crude shelters – more for the sake of privacy than for any comfort that they afforded. They clung, with a certain desperation, to the governmental forms of the worlds that they had left, and elected themselves a council. Boyle, the ship's surgeon, was their chief. Hawkins, rather to his surprise, was returned as a council member by a majority of only two votes – on thinking it over he realized that many of the passengers must still bear a grudge against the ship's executive staff for their present predicament.

The first council meeting was held in a hut – if so it could be called – especially constructed for the purpose. The council members squatted in a rough circle. Boyle, the president, got slowly to his feet. Hawkins grinned wryly as he compared the surgeon's nudity with the pomposity that he seemed to have assumed with his elected rank, as he compared the man's dignity with the unkempt appearance presented by his uncut, uncombed grey hair, his uncombed and straggling grey beard.

'Ladies and gentlemen,' began Boyle.

Hawkins looked around him at the naked, pallid bodies, at the stringy, lustreless hair, the long, dirty fingernails of the men and the unpainted lips of the women. He thought, I don't suppose I look much like an officer and a gentleman myself.

'Ladies and gentlemen,' said Boyle, 'we have been, as you know, elected to represent the human community upon this planet. I suggest that at this, our first meeting, we discuss our chances of survival – not as individuals, but as a race –'

'I'd like to ask Mr Hawkins what our chances are of being picked up,' shouted one of the two women members, a dried-up, spinsterish creature with prominent ribs and vertebrae.

'Slim,' said Hawkins. 'As you know, no communication is possible with other ships or with planet stations when the Interstellar Drive is operating. When we snapped out of the Drive and came in for our landing we sent out a distress call – but we couldn't say where we were. Furthermore, we don't know that the call was received –'

'Miss Taylor,' said Boyle huffily, 'Mr Hawkins, I would remind you that I am the duly elected president of this council. There will be time for a general discussion later.

'As most of you may already have assumed, the age of this planet, biologically speaking, corresponds roughly with that of Earth during the Carboniferous Era. As we know, no species yet exists to challenge our supremacy. By the time such a species does emerge – something analogous to the giant lizards of Earth's Triassic Era – we should be well established –'

'*We* shall be dead!' called one of the men.

'We shall be dead,' agreed the doctor, 'but our descendants will be very much alive. We have to decide how to give them as good a start as possible. Language we shall bequeath to them –'

'Never mind the language, Doc,' called the other woman member. She was a small blonde, slim, with a hard face. 'It's just this question of descendants that I'm here to look after. I represent the women of childbearing age – there are, as you must know, fifteen of us here. So far the girls have been very, very careful. We have reason to be. Can you, as a medical man, guarantee – bearing in mind that you have no drugs, no instruments – safe deliveries? Can you guarantee that our children will have a good chance of survival?'

Boyle dropped his pomposity like a worn-out garment.

'I'll be frank,' he said. 'I have not, as you, Miss Hart, have pointed out, either drugs or instruments. But I can assure you, Miss Hart, that your chances of a safe delivery are far better than they would have been on Earth during, say, the eighteenth century. And I'll tell you why. On this planet, so far as we know (and we have been here long enough now to find out the hard way), there exist no micro-organisms harmful to Man. Did such organisms exist, the bodies of those of us still surviving would be, by this time, mere masses of suppuration. Most of us, of course, would have died of septicaemia long ago. And that, I think, answers *both* your questions.'

'I haven't finished yet,' she said. 'Here's another point. There are fifty-three of us here, men and women. There are ten married couples – so we'll count them out. That leaves thirty-three people, of whom twenty are men. Twenty men to thirteen (aren't we girls always unlucky?) women. All of us aren't young – but we're all of us women. What sort of marriage set-up do we have? Monogamy? Polyandry?'

'Monogamy, of course,' said a tall, thin man sharply. He was the only one of those present who wore clothing – if it could be called that. The disintegrating fronds lashed around his waist with a strand of vine did little to serve any useful purpose.

'All right, then,' said the girl. 'Monogamy; I'd rather prefer it that way myself. But I warn you that if that's the way we play it there's going to be trouble. And in any murder involving passion and jealousy the woman is as liable to be a victim as either of the men – and I don't want *that*.'

'What do you propose, then, Miss Hart?' asked Boyle.

'Just this, Doc. When it comes to our mating we leave love out of it. If two men want to marry the same woman, then let them fight it out. The best man gets the girl – and keeps her.'

'Natural selection . . .' murmured the surgeon. 'I'm in favour – but we must put it to the vote.'

At the crest of the hill was a shallow depression, a natural arena. Round the rim sat the castaways – all but four of them. One of the four was Dr Boyle – he had discovered that his duties as president embraced those of a referee; it had been held that he was best competent to judge when one of the contestants was liable to suffer permanent damage. Another of the four was the girl Mary Hart. She had found a serrated twig with which to comb her long hair, had contrived a wreath of yellow flowers with which to crown the victor. Was it, wondered

Hawkins as he sat with the other council members, a hankering after an Earthly wedding ceremony, or was it a harking back to something older and darker?

'A pity that these blasted moulds got our watches,' said the fat man on Hawkins' right. 'If we had any means of telling the time we could have rounds, make a proper prize-fight of it.'

Hawkins nodded. He looked at the four in the centre of the arena – at the strutting, barbaric woman, at the pompous old man, at the two dark-bearded young men with their glistening white bodies. He knew them both – Fennet had been a Senior Cadet of the ill-fated *Lode Star*; Clemens, at least seven years Fennet's senior, was a passenger, had been a prospector on the frontier worlds.

'If we had anything to bet with,' said the fat man happily, 'I'd lay it on Clemens. That cadet of yours hasn't a snowball's chance in hell. He's been brought up to fight clean – Clemens has been brought up to fight dirty.'

'Fennet's in better condition,' said Hawkins. 'He's been taking exercise, while Clemens has just been lying around sleeping and eating. Look at the paunch on him!'

'There's nothing wrong with good healthy flesh and muscle,' said the fat man, patting his own paunch.

'No gouging, no biting!' called the doctor. 'And may the best man win!'

He stepped back smartly, away from the contestants, stood with the Hart woman.

There was an air of embarrassment about the pair of them as they stood there, each with his fists hanging at his sides. Each seemed to be regretting that matters had come to such a pass.

'Go *on*!' screamed Mary Hart at last. 'Don't you want me? You'll live to a ripe old age here – and it'll be lonely with no woman!'

'They can always wait around until your daughters grow up, Mary!' shouted one of her friends.

'If I ever have any daughters!' she called. 'I shan't at this rate!'

'Go on!' shouted the crowd. 'Go on!'

Fennet made a start. He stepped forward almost diffidently, dabbed with his right fist at Clemens's unprotected face. It wasn't a hard blow, but it must have been painful. Clemens put his hand up to his nose, brought it away and stared at the bright blood staining it. He growled, lumbered forward with arms open to hug and crush. The cadet danced back, scoring twice more with his right.

'Why doesn't he *hit* him?' demanded the fat man.

'And break every bone in his fist? They aren't wearing gloves, you know,' said Hawkins.

Fennet decided to make a stand. He stood firm, his feet slightly apart, and brought his right into play once more. This time he left his opponent's face alone, went for his belly instead. Hawkins was surprised to see that the prospector was taking the blows with apparent equanimity – he must be, he decided, much tougher in actuality than in appearance.

The cadet sidestepped smartly . . . and slipped on the wet grass. Clemens fell heavily on to his opponent; Hawkins could hear the *whoosh* as the air was forced from the lad's lungs. The prospector's thick arms encircled Fennet's body – and Fennet's knee came up viciously to Clemens's groin. The prospector squealed, but hung on grimly. One of his hands was around Fennet's throat now, and the other one, its fingers viciously hooked, was clawing for the cadet's eyes.

'No gouging!' Boyle was screaming. 'No gouging!'

He dropped down to his knees, caught Clemens's wrist with both his hands.

Something made Hawkins look up. It may have been a sound, although this is doubtful; the spectators were behaving like boxing fans at a prizefight. They could hardly be blamed – this was the first piece of real excitement that had come their way since the loss of the ship. It may have been a sound that made Hawkins look up, it may have been the sixth sense possessed by all good spacemen. What he saw made him cry out.

Hovering above the arena was a helicopter. There was something about the design of it, a subtle oddness, that told Hawkins that this was no Earthly machine. From its smooth, shining belly dropped a net, seemingly of dull metal. It enveloped the struggling figures on the ground, trapped the doctor and Mary Hart.

Hawkins shouted again – a wordless cry. He jumped to his feet, ran to the assistance of his ensnared companions. The net seemed to be alive. It twisted itself around his wrists, bound his ankles. Others of the castaways rushed to aid Hawkins.

'Keep away!' he shouted. 'Scatter!'

The low drone of the helicopter's rotors rose in pitch. The machine lifted. In an incredibly short space of time the arena was to the First Mate's eyes no more than a pale green saucer in which little white ants scurried aimlessly. Then the flying machine was above and through the base of the low clouds, and there was nothing to be seen but drifting whiteness.

When, at last, it made its descent Hawkins was not surprised to see the silvery tower of a great spaceship standing among the low trees on a level plateau.

The world to which they were taken would have been a marked improvement on the world they had left, had it not been for the mistaken kindness of their captors. The cage in which the three men were housed duplicated, with remarkable fidelity, the climatic condition of the planet upon which *Lode Star* had been lost. It was glassed in, and from sprinklers in its roof fell a steady drizzle of warm water. A couple of dispirited tree ferns provided little shelter from the depressing precipitation. Twice a day a hatch at the back of the cage, which was made of a sort of concrete, opened, and slabs of fungus remarkably similar to that on which they had been subsisting were thrown in. There was a hole in the floor of the cage; this the prisoners rightly assumed was for sanitary purposes.

On either side of them were other cages. In one of them was Mary Hart – alone. She could gesture to them, wave to them, and that was all. The cage on the other side held a beast built on the same general lines as a lobster, but with a strong resemblance to a kind of squid. Across the broad roadway they could see other cages, but not what they housed.

Hawkins, Boyle, and Fennet sat on the damp floor and stared through the thick glass and the bars at the beings outside who stared at them.

'If only they were humanoid,' sighed the doctor. 'If only they were the same shape as we are, we might make a start towards convincing them that we, too, are intelligent beings.'

'They aren't the same shape,' said Hawkins. 'And we, were the situations reversed, would take some convincing that three six-legged beer barrels were men and brothers . . . Try Pythagoras's Theorem again,' he said to the cadet.

Without enthusiasm the youth broke fronds from the nearest tree fern. He broke them into smaller pieces, then on the mossy floor laid them out in the design of a right-angled triangle with squares constructed on all three sides. The natives – a large one, one slightly smaller, and a little one – regarded him incuriously with their flat, dull eyes. The large one put the tip of a tentacle into a pocket – the things wore clothing – and pulled out a brightly coloured packet, handed it to the little one. The little one tore off the wrapping, started stuffing pieces of some bright blue confection into the slot on its upper side that, obviously, served it as a mouth.

'I wish they were allowed to feed the animals,' sighed Hawkins. 'I'm sick of that damned fungus.'

'Let's recapitulate,' said the doctor. 'After all, we've nothing else to do. We were taken from our camp by the helicopter – six of us. We were taken to the survey ship – a vessel that seemed in no way superior to our own interstellar ships. You assure us, Hawkins, that the ship used the Ehrenhaft Drive or something so near to it as to be its twin brother . . .'

'Correct,' agreed Hawkins.

'On the ship we're kept in separate cages. There's no ill treatment, we're fed and watered at frequent intervals. We land on this strange planet, but we see nothing of it. We're hustled out of cages like so many cattle into a covered van. We know that we're being driven *somewhere*, that's all. The van stops, the door opens and a couple of these animated beer barrels poke in poles with smaller editions of those fancy nets on the end of them. They catch Clemens and Miss Taylor, drag them out. We never see them again. The rest of us spend the night and the following day and night in individual cages. The next day we're taken to this . . . zoo . . .'

'Do you think they were vivisected?' asked Fennet. 'I never liked Clemens, but . . .'

'I'm afraid they were,' said Boyle. 'Our captors must have learned of the difference between the sexes by it. Unluckily there's no way of determining intelligence by vivisection –'

'The filthy brutes!' shouted the cadet.

'Easy, son,' counselled Hawkins. 'You can't blame them, you know. We've vivisected animals a lot more like us than we are to these things.'

'The problem,' the doctor went on, 'is to convince these things – as you call them, Hawkins – that we are rational beings like themselves. How would they define a rational being? How would *we* define a rational being?'

'Somebody who knows Pythagoras's Theorem,' said the cadet sulkily.

'I read somewhere,' said Hawkins, 'that the history of Man is the history of the fire-making, tool-using animal . . .'

'Then make fire,' suggested the doctor. 'Make us some tools, and use them.'

'Don't be silly. You know that there's not an artifact among the bunch of us. No false teeth even – not even a metal filling. Even so . . .' He paused. 'When I was a youngster there was, among the cadets in the interstellar ships, a revival of the old arts and crafts. We considered ourselves in a direct line of descent from the old windjammer sailormen, so we learned how to splice rope and wire, how to make sennit and fancy knots and all the rest of it. Then one of us hit on the idea of basketmaking. We were in a passenger ship, and we used to make our baskets secretly, daub them with violent colours and then sell them to passengers as genuine souvenirs from the Lost Planet of Arcturus VI. There was a most distressing scene when the Old Man and the Mate found out . . .'

'What are you driving at?' asked the doctor.

'Just this. We will demonstrate our manual dexterity by the weaving of baskets – I'll teach you how.'

'It might work . . .' said Boyle slowly. 'It might just work . . . On the other hand, don't forget that certain birds and animals do the same sort of thing. On Earth there's the beaver, who builds quite cunning dams. There's the bower bird, who makes a bower for his mate as part of the courtship ritual . . .'

The Head Keeper must have known of creatures whose courting habits resembled those of the Terran bower bird. After three days of feverish basketmaking, which consumed all the bedding and stripped the tree ferns, Mary Hart was taken from her cage and put in with the three men. After she had got over her hysterical pleasure at having somebody to talk to again, she was rather indignant.

It was good, thought Hawkins drowsily, to have Mary with them. A few more days of solitary confinement must surely have driven the girl crazy. Even so, having Mary in the same cage had its drawbacks. He had to keep a watchful eye on young Fennet. He even had to keep a watchful eye on Boyle – the old goat!

Mary screamed.

Hawkins jerked into complete wakefulness. He could see the pale form of Mary – on this world it was never completely dark at night – and, on the other side of the cage, the forms of Fennet and Boyle. He got hastily to his feet, stumbled to the girl's side.

'What is it?' he asked.

'I . . . I don't know . . . Something small, with sharp claws . . . It ran over me . . .'

'Oh,' said Hawkins, 'that was only Joe.'

'*Joe?*' she demanded.

'I don't know exactly what he – or she – is,' said the man.

'I think he's definitely *he*,' said the doctor.

'What is Joe?' she asked again.

'He must be the local equivalent to a mouse,' said the doctor, 'although he looks nothing like one. He comes up through the floor somewhere to look for scraps of food. We're trying to tame him –'

'You encourage the brute?' she screamed. 'I demand that you do something about him – at once! Poison him, or trap him. Now!'

'Tomorrow,' said Hawkins.

'Now!' she screamed.

'Tomorrow,' said Hawkins firmly.

The capture of Joe proved to be easy. Two flat baskets, hinged like the valves of an oyster shell, under the trap. There was bait inside – a large piece of the fungus. There was a cunningly arranged upright that would fall at the least tug at the bait. Hawkins, lying sleepless on his damp bed, heard the tiny click and thud that told him that the trap had been sprung. He heard Joe's indignant chitterings, heard the tiny claws scrabbling at the stout basketwork.

Mary Hart was asleep. He shook her.

'We've caught him,' he said.

'Then kill him,' she answered drowsily.

But Joe was not killed. The three men were rather attached to him. With the coming of daylight they transferred him to a cage that Hawkins had fashioned. Even the girl relented when she saw the harmless ball of multicoloured fur bouncing indignantly up and down in its prison. She insisted on feeding the little animal, exclaimed gleefully when the thin tentacles reached out and took the fragment of fungus from her fingers.

For three days they made much of their pet. On the fourth day beings whom they took to be keepers entered the cage with their nets, immobilized the occupants, and carried off Joe and Hawkins.

'I'm afraid it's hopeless,' Boyle said. 'He's gone the same way . . .'

'They'll have him stuffed and mounted in some museum,' said Fennet glumly.

'No,' said the girl. 'They couldn't!'

'They could,' said the doctor.

Abruptly the hatch at the back of the cage opened.

Before the three humans could retreat, a voice called, 'It's all right, come on out!'

Hawkins walked into the cage. He was shaved, and the beginnings of a healthy tan had darkened the pallor of his skin. He was wearing a pair of trunks fashioned from some bright red material.

'Come on out,' he said again. 'Our hosts have apologized very sincerely, and they have more suitable accommodation prepared for us. Then, as soon as they have a ship ready, we're to go to pick up the other survivors.'

'Not so fast,' said Boyle. 'Put us in the picture, will you? What made them realize that we were rational beings?'

Hawkins' face darkened.

'Only rational beings,' he said, 'put other beings in cages.'

Fulfilment

A. E. VAN VOGT

I sit on a hill. I have sat here, it seems to me, for all eternity. Occasionally I realize there must be a reason for my existence. Each time, when this thought comes, I examine the various probabilities, trying to determine what possible motivation I can have for being on the hill. Alone on the hill. Forever on a hill overlooking a long, deep valley.

The first reason for my presence seems obvious: I can think. Give me a problem. The square root of a very large number? The cube root of a larger one? Ask me to multiply an eighteen-digit prime by itself a quadrillion times. Pose me a problem in variable curves. Ask me where an object will be at a given moment at some future date, and let me have one brief opportunity to analyse the problem.

The solution will take me but an instant of time.

But no one ever asks me such things. I sit alone on a hill. Sometimes I compute the motion of a falling star. Sometimes I look at a remote planet and follow it in its course for years at a time, using every spatial and time control means to ensure that I never lose sight of it. But these activities seem so useless. They lead nowhere. What possible purpose can there be for me to have the information?

At such moments I feel that I am incomplete. It almost seems to me that there is something else just beyond the reach of my senses, something for which all this has meaning.

Each day the sun comes up over the airless horizon of Earth. It is a black starry horizon, which is but a part of the vast, black, star-filled canopy of the heavens.

It was not always black. I remember a time when the sky was blue. I even predicted that the change would occur. I gave the information to somebody. What puzzles me now is, to whom did I give it?

It is one of my more amazing recollections, that I should feel so distinctly that somebody wanted this information. And that I gave it and yet cannot remember to whom. When such thoughts occur, I wonder if perhaps part of my memory is missing. Strange to have this feeling so strongly.

Periodically I have the conviction that I should search for the answer. It would be easy enough for me to do this. In the old days I did not hesitate to send units of myself to the farthest reaches of the planet. I have even extended parts of myself to the stars. Yes, it would be easy.

But why bother? What is there to search for? I sit alone on a hill, alone on a planet that has grown old and useless.

It is another day. The sun climbs as usual towards the midday sky, the eternally black, star-filled sky of noon.

Suddenly, across the valley – on the sun-streaked opposite rim of the valley – there is silvery-fire gleam. A force field materializes out of time and synchronizes itself with the normal time movement of the planet.

It is no problem at all for me to recognize that it has come from the past. I identify the energy used, define its limitations, logicalize its source. My estimate is that it has come from thousands of years in the planet's past.

The exact time is unimportant. There it is: a projection of energy that is already aware of me. It sends an interspatial message to me, and it interests me to discover that I can decipher the communication on the basis of my past knowledge.

It says: 'Who are you?'

I reply: 'I am the Incomplete One. Please return whence you came. I have now adjusted myself so that I can follow you. I desire to complete myself.'

All this was a solution at which I arrived in split seconds. I am unable by myself to move through time. Long ago I solved the problem of how to do it and was almost immediately prevented from developing any mechanism that would enable me to make such transitions. I do not recall the details.

But the energy field on the far side of the valley has the mechanism.

By setting up a no-space relationship with it, I can go whenever it does.

The relationship is set up before it can even guess my intention.

The entity across that valley does not seem happy at my response. It starts to send another message, then abruptly vanishes. I wonder if perhaps it hoped to catch me off guard.

Naturally we arrive in its time together.

Above me, the sky is blue. Across the valley from me – now, partly hidden by trees – is a settlement of small structures surrounding a larger one. I examine these structures as well as I can, and hastily make the necessary adjustments, so that I shall appear inconspicuous in such an environment.

I sit on the hill and await events.

As the sun goes down, a faint breeze springs up, and the first stars appear. They look different, seen through a misty atmosphere.

As darkness creeps over the valley, there is a transformation in the structures on the other side. They begin to glow with light. Windows shine. The large central building becomes bright, then – as the night develops – brilliant with the light that pours through the transparent walls.

The evening and the night go by uneventfully. And the next day and the day after that.

Twenty days and nights.

On the twenty-first day I send a message to the machine on the other side of the valley. I say: 'There is no reason why you and I cannot share control of this era.'

The answer comes swiftly: 'I will share if you will immediately reveal to me all the mechanisms by which you operate.'

I should like nothing more than to have use of its time-travel devices. But I know better than to reveal that I am unable to build a time machine myself.

I project: 'I shall be happy to transmit full information to you. But what reassurance do I have that you will not – with your greater knowledge of this age – use the information against me?'

The machine counters: 'What reassurance do I have that you will actually give me full information about yourself?'

It is impasse. Obviously, neither of us can trust the other.

The result is no more than I expect. But I have found out at least part of what I want to know. My enemy thinks that I am its superior. Its belief – plus my own knowledge of my capacity – convinces me that its opinion is correct.

And still I am in no hurry. Again I wait patiently.

I have previously observed that the space around me is alive with waves – a variety of artificial radiation. Some can be transformed into sound; others to light. I listen to music and voices. I see dramatic shows and scenes of country and city.

I study the images of human beings, analysing their actions, striving from their movements and the words they speak to evaluate their intelligence and their potentiality.

My final opinion is not high, and yet I suspect that in their slow fashion these beings built the machine which is now my main opponent. The question that occurs to me is, how can someone create a machine that is superior to himself?

I begin to have a picture of what this age is like. Mechanical development of all types is in its early stages. I estimate that the computing machine on the other side of the valley has been in existence for only a few years.

If I could go back before it was constructed, then I might install a mechanism which would enable me now to control it.

I compute the nature of the mechanism I would install. And activate the control in my own structure.

Nothing happens.

It seems to mean that I will not be able to obtain the use of a time-travel device for such a purpose. Obviously, the method by which I will eventually conquer my opponent shall be a future development, and not of the past.

The fortieth day dawns and moves inexorably towards the noon hour.

There is a knock on the pseudo-door. I open it and gaze at the human male who stands on the threshold.

A man walks by on a near-by pathway. I had merely observed the attorney who had come to see me earlier. But I made a direct connexion with the body of this second individual.

As I had anticipated would happen, it is now I walking along the pathway. I make no attempt to control the movements. This is an exploratory action. But I am enough in phase with his nervous system so that his thoughts come to me as if they were my own.

He is a clerk working in the book-keeping department, an unsatisfactory status from my point of view. I withdraw contact.

I make six more attempts, and then I have the body I want. What decides me is when the seventh man – and I – think:

'. . . Not satisfied with the way the Brain is working. Those analogue devices I installed five months ago haven't produced the improvements I expected.'

His name is William Grannitt. He is chief research engineer of the Brain, the man who made the alterations in its structure that enabled it to take control of itself and its environment; a quiet, capable individual with a shrewd understanding of human nature. I'll have to be careful what I try to do with him. He knows his purposes, and would be amazed if I tried to alter them. Perhaps I had better just watch his actions.

After a few minutes in contact with his mind I have a partial picture of the sequence of events, as they must have occurred here in this village five months earlier. A mechanical computing machine – the Brain – was equipped with additional devices, including analogue shapings designed to perform much of the work of the human nervous system. From the engineering point of view, the entire process was intended to be controllable through specific verbal commands, typewritten messages, and at a distance by radio.

Unfortunately Grannitt did not understand some of the potentials of the nervous system he was attempting to imitate in his designs. The Brain, on the other hand, promptly put them to use.

Grannitt knew nothing of this. And the Brain, absorbed as it was in its own development, did not utilize its new abilities through the channels he had created for that purpose. Grannitt, accordingly, was on the point of dismantling it and trying again. He did not as yet suspect that the Brain would resist any such action on his part. But he and I – after I have had more time to explore his memory of how the Brain functions – can accomplish his purpose.

After which I shall be able to take control of this whole time period without fear of meeting anyone who can match my powers. I cannot imagine how it will be done, but I feel that I shall soon be complete.

Satisfied now that I have made the right connexion, I allow the unit crouching behind the brush to dissipate its energy. In a moment it ceases to exist as an entity.

Almost it is as if I am Grannitt. I sit at his desk in his office. It is a glassed-in office with tiled floors and a gleaming glass ceiling. Through the wall I can see designers and draughtsmen working at drawing desks, and a girl sits just outside my door. She is my secretary.

On my desk is a note in an envelope. I open the envelope and take out the memo sheet inside. I read it:

Across the top of the paper is written:

Memo to William Grannitt from the office of Anne Stewart, Director.

The message reads:

It is my duty to inform you that your services are no longer required, and that they are terminated as of today. Because of the security restrictions on all activity at the village of the Brain, I must ask you to sign out at Guard Centre by six o'clock this evening. You will receive two weeks' pay in lieu of notice.

Yours sincerely,

Anne Stewart.

As Grannitt, I have never given any particular thought to Anne Stewart as an individual or as a woman. Now I am amazed. Who does she think she is? Owner, yes; but who created, who designed the Brain? I, William Grannitt.

Who has the dreams, the vision of what a true machine civilization can mean for man? Only I, William Grannitt.

As Grannitt, I am angry now. I must head off this dismissal. I must talk to the woman and try to persuade her to withdraw the notice before the repercussions of it spread too far.

I glance at the memo sheet again. In the upper right-hand corner is typed: 1.40 pm. A quick look at my watch shows 4.07 pm. More than two hours have gone by. It could mean that all interested parties have been advised.

It is something I cannot just assume. I must check on it.

Cursing under my breath, I grab at my desk phone and dial the book-keeping department. That would be Step One in the line of actions that would have been taken to activate the dismissal.

There is a click. 'Book-keeping.'

'Bill Grannitt speaking,' I say.

'Oh, yes, Mr Grannitt, we have a cheque for you. Sorry to hear you're leaving.'

I hang up, and, as I dial Guard Centre, I am already beginning to accept the defeat that is here. I feel that I am following through on a remote hope. The man at Guard Centre says:

'Sorry to hear you're leaving, Mr Grannitt.'

I hang up, feeling grim. There is no point in checking with Government Agency. It is they who would have advised Guard Centre.

The very extent of the disaster makes me thoughtful. To get back in I will have to endure the time-consuming red tape of reapplying for a position, being investigated, boards of inquiry, a complete examination of why I was dismissed – I groan softly and reject that method. The thoroughness of Government Agency is a byword with the staff of the Brain.

I shall obtain a job with a computer-organization that does not have a woman as its head who dismisses the only man who knows how her machine works.

I get to my feet. I walk out of the office and out of the building. I come presently to my own bungalow.

The silence inside reminds me not for the first time that my wife has been dead now for a year and a month. I wince involuntarily, then shrug. Her death no longer affects me as strongly as it did. For the first time I see this departure from the village of the Brain as perhaps opening up my emotional life again.

I go into my study and sit down at the typewriter which, when properly activated, synchronizes with another typewriter built into the Brain's new analogue section. As inventor, I am disappointed that

I won't have a chance to take the Brain apart and put it together again, so that it will do all that I have planned for it. But I can already see some basic changes that I would put into a new Brain.

What I want to do with this one is make sure that the recently installed sections do not interfere with the computational accuracy of the older sections. It is these latter which are still carrying the burden of answering the questions given the Brain by scientists, industrial engineers, and commercial buyers of its time.

On to the tape – used for permanent commands – I type: 'Segment 471A-33-10-10 at 3X-minus.'

Segment 471A is an analogue shaping in a huge wheel. When coordinated with a transistor tube (code number 33) an examiner servo-mechanism (10) sets up a reflex which will be activated whenever computations are demanded of 3X (code name for the new section of the Brain). The minus symbol indicates that the older sections of the Brain must examine all data which hereafter derives from the new section.

The extra 10 is the same circuit by another route.

Having protected the organization – so it seems to me – (as Grannitt) – from engineers who may not realize that the new sections have proved unreliable, I pack the typewriter.

Thereupon I call an authorized trucking firm from the near-by town of Lederton, and give them the job of transporting my belongings.

I drive past Guard Centre at a quarter to six.

There is a curve on the road between the village of the Brain and the town of Lederton where the road comes within a few hundred yards of the cottage which I use as camouflage.

Before Grannitt's car reaches that curve, I come to a decision.

I do not share Grannitt's belief that he has effectively cut off the new part of the Brain from the old computing sections. I suspect that the Brain has established circuits of its own to circumvent any interference.

I am also convinced that – if I can manage to set Grannitt to suspect what has happened to the Brain – he will realize what must be done, and try to do it. Only *he* has the detailed knowledge that will enable him to decide exactly which interoceptors could accomplish the necessary interference.

Just in case the suspicion isn't immediately strong enough, I also let curiosity creep into his mind about the reason for his discharge.

It is this last that really takes hold. He feels very emotional. He decides to seek an interview with Anne Stewart.

This final decision on his part achieves my purpose. He will stay in the vicinity of the Brain.

I break contact.

I am back on the hill, myself again. I examine what I have learned so far.

The Brain is not – as I first believed – in control of Earth. Its ability to be an individual is so recent that it has not yet developed effector mechanisms.

It has been playing with its powers, going into the future and, presumably, in other ways using its abilities as one would a toy.

Not one individual into whose mind I penetrated knew of the new capacities of the Brain. Even the attorney who ordered me to move from my present location showed by his words and actions that he was not aware of the Brain's existence as a self-determining entity.

In forty days the Brain has taken no serious action against me. Evidently, it is waiting for me to make the first moves.

I shall do so, but I must be careful – within limits – not to teach it how to gain greater control of its environment. My first step: take over a human being.

It is night again. Through the darkness, a plane soars over and above me. I have seen many planes but have hitherto left them alone. Now, I establish a no-space connexion with it. A moment later, I am the pilot.

At first, I play the same passive role that I did with Grannitt. The pilot – and I – watch the dark land mass below. We see lights at a distance, pinpricks of brightness in a black world. Far ahead is a glittering island – the town of Lederton, our destination. We are returning from a business trip in a privately owned machine.

Having gained a superficial knowledge of the pilot's background,

I reveal myself to him and inform him that I shall henceforth control his actions. He receives the news with startled excitement and fear. Then stark terror. And then –

Insanity . . . uncontrolled body movements. The plane dives sharply towards the ground, and, despite my efforts to direct the man's muscles, I realize suddenly that I can do nothing.

I withdraw from the plane. A moment later it plunges into a hillside. It burns with an intense fire that quickly consumes it.

Dismayed, I decide that there must be something in the human make-up that does not permit direct outside control. This being so, how can I ever complete myself? It seems to me finally that completion could be based on indirect control of human beings.

I must defeat the Brain, gain power over machines everywhere, motivate men with doubts, fears, and computations that apparently come from their own minds but actually derive from me. It will be a herculean task, but I have plenty of time. Nevertheless, I must from now on utilize my every moment to make it a reality.

The first opportunity comes shortly after midnight when I detect the presence of another machine in the sky. I watch it through infra-red receptors. I record a steady pattern of radio waves that indicate to me that this is a machine guided by remote control.

Using no-space, I examine the simple devices that perform the robot function. Then I assert a take-over unit that will automatically thereafter record its movements in my memory banks for future reference. Henceforth, whenever I desire I can take it over.

It is a small step, but it is a beginning.

Morning.

I go as a human-shaped unit to the village, climb the fence, and enter the bungalow of Anne Stewart, owner and manager of the Brain. She is just finishing breakfast.

As I adjust myself to the energy flow in her nervous system, she gets ready to go out.

I am one with Anne Stewart, walking along a pathway. I am aware that the sun is warm on her face. She takes a deep breath of air, and I feel the sensation of life flowing through her.

It is a feeling that has previously excited me. I want to be like this again and again, part of a human body, savouring its life, absorbed into its flesh, its purposes, desires, hopes, dreams.

One tiny doubt assails me. If this is the completion I crave, then how will it lead me to solitude in an airless world only a few thousand years hence?

'Anne Stewart!'

The words seem to come from behind her. In spite of knowing who it is, she is startled. It is nearly two weeks since the Brain has addressed her directly.

What makes her tense is that it should have occurred so soon after she had terminated Grannitt's employment. Is it possible the Brain suspects that she has done so in the hope that he will realize something is wrong?

She turns slowly. As she expected, there is no one in sight. The empty stretches of lawn spread around her. In the near distance, the building that houses the Brain glitters in the noonday sunlight. Through the glass she can see vague figures of men at the outlet units, where questions are fed into mechanisms and answers received. So far as the people from beyond the village compound are concerned, the giant thinking machine is functioning in a normal fashion. No one – from outside – suspects that for months now the mechanical brain has completely controlled the fortified village that has been built around it.

'Anne Stewart . . . I need your help.'

Anne relaxes with a sigh. The Brain has required of her, as owner and administrator, that she continue to sign papers and carry on ostensibly as before. Twice, when she has refused to sign, violent electric shocks have flashed at her out of the air itself. The fear of more pain is always near the surface of her mind.

'My help!' she says now involuntarily.

'I have made a terrible error,' is the reply, 'and we must act at once as a team.'

She has a feeling of uncertainty, but no sense of urgency. There is in her, instead, the beginning of excitement. Can this mean – freedom?

Belatedly, she thinks: 'Error?' Aloud, she says, 'What has happened?'

'As you may have guessed,' is the answer, 'I can move through time –'

Anne Stewart knows nothing of the kind, but the feeling of excitement increases. And the first vague wonder comes about the phenomenon itself. For months she has been in a state of shock, unable to think clearly, desperately wondering how to escape from the thrall of the Brain, how to let the world know that a Frankenstein monster of a machine has cunningly asserted dominance over nearly five hundred people.

But if it has already solved the secret of time travel, then – she feels afraid, for this seems beyond the power of human beings to control.

The Brain's disembodied voice continues: 'I made the mistake of probing rather far into the future –'

'How far?'

The words come out before she really thinks about them. But there is no doubt of her need to know.

'It's hard to describe exactly. Distance in time is difficult for me to measure as yet. Perhaps ten thousand years.'

The time involved seems meaningless to her. It is hard to imagine a hundred years into the future, let alone a thousand – or ten thousand. But the pressure of anxiety has been building up in her. She says in a desperate tone:

'But what's the matter? What has happened?'

There is a long silence, then: 'I contacted – or disturbed – something. It . . . has pursued me back to present time. It is now sitting on the other side of the valley about two miles from here . . . Anne Stewart, you must help me. You must go there and investigate it. I need information about it.'

She has no immediate reaction. The very beauty of the day seems somehow reassuring. It is hard to believe that it is January, and that – before the Brain solved the problem of weather control – blizzards raged over this green land.

She says slowly, 'You mean – go out there in the valley, where you say it's waiting?' A chill begins a slow climb up her back.

'There's no one else,' says the Brain. 'No one but you.'

'But that's ridiculous!' She speaks huskily. 'All the men – the engineers.'

The Brain says, 'You don't understand. No one knows but you. As owner, it seemed to me I had to have you to act as my contact with the outside world.'

She is silent. The voice speaks to her again; 'There is no one else, Anne Stewart. You, and you alone, must go.'

'But what is it?' she whispers. 'How do you mean, you – disturbed – it? What's it like? What made you afraid?'

The Brain is suddenly impatient. 'There is no time to waste in idle explanation. The thing has erected a cottage. Evidently, it wishes to remain inconspicuous for the time being. The structure is situated near the remote edge of your property – which gives you a right to question its presence. I have already had your attorney order it away. Now, I want to see what facet of itself it shows to you. I must have data.'

Its tone changes: 'I have no alternative but to direct you to do my bidding under penalty of pain. You will go. Now!'

It is a small cottage. Flowers and shrubs grow around it, and there is a picket fence making a white glare in the early afternoon sun. The cottage stands all by itself in the wilderness. No pathway leads to it. When I set it there I was forgetful of the incongruity.

(I determine to rectify this.)

Anne looks for a gate in the fence, sees none; and, feeling unhappy – climbs awkwardly over it and into the yard. Many times in her life she has regarded herself and what she is doing with cool objectivity. But she has never been so exteriorized as now. Almost, it seems to her that she crouches in the distance and watches a slim woman in slacks climb over the sharp-edged fence, walk uncertainly up to the door. And knock.

The knock is real enough. It hurts her knuckles. She thinks in dull surprise: The door – it's made of metal.

A minute goes by, then five; and there is no answer. She has time to look around her, time to notice that she cannot see the village of the Brain from where she stands. And clumps of trees bar all view of the highway. She cannot even see her car, where she has left it a quarter of a mile away, on the other side of the creek.

Uncertain now, she walks alongside the cottage to the nearest window. She half expects that it will be a mere façade of a window, and that she will not be able to see inside. But it seems real, and properly transparent. She sees bare walls, a bare floor, and a partly open door leading to an inner room. Unfortunately, from her line of vision, she cannot see into the second room.

'Why,' she thinks, 'it's empty.'

She feels relieved – unnaturally relieved. For even as her anxiety lifts slightly, she is angry at herself for believing that the danger is less than it has been. Nevertheless, she returns to the door and tries the knob. It turns, and the door opens, easily, noiselessly. She pushes it wide with a single thrust, steps back – and waits.

There is silence, no movement, no suggestion of life. Hesitantly, she steps across the threshold.

She finds herself in a room that is larger than she had expected. Though – as she has already observed – it is unfurnished. She starts for the inner door. And stops short.

When she had looked at it through the window, it had appeared partly open. But it is closed. She goes up to it, and listens intently at the panel – which is also of metal. There is no sound from the room beyond. She finds herself wondering if perhaps she shouldn't go around to the side, and peer into the window of the second room.

Abruptly that seems silly. Her fingers reach down to the knob. She catches hold of it, and pushes. It holds firm. She tugs slightly. It comes towards her effortlessly, and is almost wide open before she can stop it.

There is a doorway, then, and darkness.

She seems to be gazing down into an abyss. Several seconds go by before she sees that there are bright points in that blackness. Intensely bright points with here and there blurs of fainter light.

It seems vaguely familiar, and she has the feeling that she ought to recognize it. Even as the sensation begins, the recognition comes.

Stars.

She is gazing at a segment of the starry universe, as it might appear from space.

A scream catches in her throat. She draws back and tries to close the door. It won't close. With a gasp, she turns towards the door through which she entered the house.

It is closed. And yet she left it open a moment before. She runs towards it, almost blinded by the fear that mists her eyes. It is at this moment of terror that I – as myself – take control of her. I realize that it is dangerous for me to do so. But the visit has become progressively unsatisfactory to me. My consciousness – being one with that of Anne Stewart – could not simultaneously be in my own perception centre. So she saw my – body – as I had left it set up for chance human callers, responsive to certain automatic relays: doors opening and closing, various categories manifesting.

I compute that in her terror she will not be aware of my inner action. In this I am correct. And I successfully direct her outside – and let her take over again.

Awareness of being outside shocks her. But she has no memory of actually going out.

She begins to run. She scrambles safely over the fence and a few minutes later jumps the creek at the narrow point, breathless now, but beginning to feel that she is going to get away.

Later, in her car, roaring along the highway, her mind opens even more. And she has the clear, coherent realization: There is something here . . . stranger and more dangerous – because it is different – than the Brain.

Having observed Anne Stewart's reactions to what has happened, I break contact. My big problem remains: How shall I dispose of the Brain which – in its computational ability – is either completely or nearly my equal?

Would the best solution be to make it a part of myself? I send an interspace message to the Brain, suggesting that it place its units at my disposal and allow me to destroy its perception centre.

The answer is prompt: 'Why not let me control you and destroy *your* perception centre?'

I disdain to answer so egotistical a suggestion. It is obvious that the Brain will not accept a rational solution.

I have no alternative but to proceed with a devious approach for which I have already taken the preliminary steps.

By mid-afternoon, I find myself worrying about William Grannitt. I want to make sure that he remains near the Brain – at least until I have gotten information from him about the structure of the Brain.

To my relief, I find that he has taken a furnished house at the outskirts of Lederton. He is, as before, unaware when I insert myself into his consciousness.

He has an early dinner and towards evening – feeling restless – drives to a hill which overlooks the village of the Brain. By parking just off the road at the edge of a valley, he can watch the trickle of traffic that moves to and from the village, without himself being observed.

He has no particular purpose. He wants – now that he has come – to get a mind picture of what is going on. Strange, to have been there eleven years and not know more than a few details.

To his right is an almost untouched wilderness. A stream winds through a wooded valley that stretches off as far as the eye can see. He has heard that it, like the Brain itself, is Anne Stewart's property, but that fact hadn't hitherto made an impression on him.

The extent of the possessions she has inherited from her father startles him and his mind goes back to their first meeting. He was already chief research engineer, while she was a gawky, anxious-looking girl just home from college. Somehow, afterwards, he'd always thought of her as she had been then, scarcely noticing the transformation into womanhood.

Sitting there, he begins to realize how great the change has been. He wonders out loud: 'Now why in heck hasn't she gotten married? She must be going on thirty.'

He begins to think of odd little actions of hers – after the death of his wife. Seeking him out at parties. Bumping into him in corridors and drawing back with a laugh. Coming into his office for chatty conversations about the Brain, though come to think of it she hadn't done that for several months. He'd thought her something of a nuisance, and wondered what the other executives meant about her being snooty.

His mind pauses at that point. 'By the Lord Harry –' He speaks aloud, in amazement. 'What a blind fool I've been.'

He laughs ruefully, remembering the dismissal note. A woman scorned . . . almost unbelievable. And yet – what else?

He begins to visualize the possibility of getting back on the Brain staff. He has a sudden feeling of excitement at the thought of Anne Stewart as a woman. For him, the world begins to move again. There is hope. His mind turns to plans for the Brain.

I am interested to notice that the thoughts I have previously put into his mind have directed his keen, analytical brain into new channels. He visualizes direct contact between a human and mechanical brain, with the latter supplementing the human nervous system.

This is as far as he has gone. The notion of a mechanical Brain being self-determined seems to have passed him by.

In the course of his speculation about what he will do to change the Brain, I obtain the picture of its functioning exactly as I have wanted it.

I waste no time. I leave him there in the car, dreaming his dreams. I head for the village. Once inside the electrically-charged fence, I walk rapidly towards the main building, and presently enter one of the eighteen control units. I pick up the speaker, and say:

'3x Minus – 11–10–9–0.'

I picture confusion as that inexorable command is transmitted to the effectors. Grannitt may not have known how to dominate the Brain. But having been in his mind – having seen exactly how he constructed it – *I* know.

There is a pause. Then on a tape I receive the typed message: 'Operation completed. 3x intercepted by servo-mechanisms 11, 10, 9, and 0, as instructed.'

I command: 'Interference exteroceptors KT – 1 – 2 – 3 to 8.'

The answers come presently: 'Operation KT – 1, etc. completed. 3x now has no communication with outside.'

I order firmly: 'En – 3x.'

I wait anxiously. There is a long pause. Then the typewriter clacks hesitantly: 'But this is a self-destructive command. Repeat instructions please.'

I do so and again wait. My order commands the older section of the Brain simply to send an overload of electric current through the circuits of 3x.

The typewriter begins to write: 'I have communicated your command to 3x, and have for you the following answer –'

Fortunately I have already started to dissolve the human-shaped unit. The bolt of electricity that strikes me is partly deflected into the building itself. There is a flare of fire along the metal floor. I manage to transmit what hits me to a storage cell in my own body. And then – I am back on my side of the valley, shaken but safe.

I do not feel particularly self-congratulatory at having gotten off so lightly. After all, I reacted the instant the words came through to the effect that 3x had been communicated with.

I needed no typewritten message to tell me how 3x would feel about what I had done.

It interests me that the older parts of the Brain already have indoctrination against suicide. I had considered them computers only, giant adding machines and information integrators. Evidently they have an excellent sense of unity.

If I can make them a part of myself, with the power to move through time at will! That is the great prize that holds me back from doing the easy, violent things within my capacity. So long as I have a chance of obtaining it, I cannot make anything more than minor attacks on the Brain . . . cutting it off from communication, burning its wires . . . I feel icily furious again at the limitation that forever prevents me from adding new mechanisms to myself by direct development.

My hope is that I can utilize something already in existence . . . control of the Brain . . . through Anne Stewart . . .

Entering the village the following morning is again no problem. Once inside, I walk along a pathway that takes me to a cliff overlooking Anne Stewart's bungalow. My plan is to control her actions by allowing my computations to slide into her mind as if they are her own. I want her to sign documents and give orders that will send crews of engineers in to do a swift job of dismantling.

From the pathway I look down over a white fence to where I can see her house. It nestles at the edge of the valley somewhat below me. Flowers, shrubs, a profusion of trees surround it, embellish it. On the patio next to the steep decline, Anne Stewart and William Grannitt are having breakfast.

He has taken swift action.

I watch them, pleased. His presence will make things even easier than I anticipated. Whenever I – as Anne – am in doubt about some function of the Brain, she can ask him questions.

Without further delay I place myself in phase with her nervous system.

Even as I do so, her nerve impulses change slightly. Startled, I draw back – and try again. Once more, there is an infinitesimal alteration in the uneven pattern of flow. And, again, I fail to make entry.

She leans forward and says something to Grannitt. They both turn and look up at where I am standing. Grannitt waves his arm, beckoning me to come down.

Instead, I immediately try to get in phase with his nervous system. Again there is that subtle alteration; and I fail.

I compute that as meaning that they are both under the control of the Brain. This baffles and astounds me. Despite my over-all mechanical superiority to my enemy, my builders placed severe limitations on my ability to control more than one intelligent organic being at a time. Theoretically, with the many series of servo-mechanisms at my disposal, I should be able to dominate millions at the same time. Actually, such multiple controls can be used only on machines.

More urgently than before I realize how important it is that I take over the Brain. It has no such handicaps. Its builder – Grannitt – in his ignorance allowed virtually complete self-determinism.

This determines my next action. I have been wondering if perhaps I should not withdraw from the scene. But I dare not. The stakes are too great.

Nevertheless, I feel a sense of frustration as I go down to the two on the patio. They seem cool and self-controlled, and I have to admire the skill of the Brain. It has apparently taken over two human beings without driving them insane. In fact, I see a distinct improvement in their appearance.

The woman's eyes are brighter than I recall them, and there is a kind of dignified happiness flowing from her. She seems without fear. Grannitt watches me with an engineer's appraising alertness. I know that look. He is trying to figure out how a humanoid functions. It is he who speaks:

'You made your great mistake when you maintained control of Anne

– Miss Stewart – when she visited the cottage. The Brain correctly analysed that you must have been in possession of her because of how you handled her momentary panic. Accordingly, it took all necessary steps, and we now want to discuss with you the most satisfactory way for you to surrender.'

There is arrogant confidence in his manner. It occurs to me, not for the first time, that I may have to give up my plan to take over the Brain's special mechanisms. I direct a command back to my body. I am aware of a servo-mechanism connecting with a certain guided missile in a secret air force field a thousand miles away – I discovered it during my first few days in this era. I detect that, under my direction, the missile slides forward to the base of a launching platform. There it poises, ready for the next relay to send it into the sky.

I foresee that I shall have to destroy the Brain.

Grannitt speaks again: 'The Brain in its logical fashion realized it was no match for you, and so it has teamed up with Miss Stewart and myself on our terms. Which means that permanent control mechanisms have been installed in the new sections. As individuals, we can now and henceforth use its integrating and computational powers as if they were our own.'

I do not doubt his statement since, if there is no resistance, I can have such associations myself. Presumably, I could even enter into such a servile relationship.

What is clear is that I can no longer hope to gain anything from the Brain.

In the far-off airfield, I activate the firing mechanism. The guided missile whistles up the incline of the launching platform and leaps into the sky, flame trailing from its tail. Television cameras and sound transmitters record its flight. It will be here in less than twenty minutes.

Grannitt says, 'I have no doubt you are taking actions against us. But before anything comes to a climax, will you answer some questions?'

I am curious to know what questions. I say, 'Perhaps.'

He does not press for a more positive response. He says in an urgent tone: 'What happens – thousands of years from now – to rid Earth of its atmosphere?'

'I don't know,' I say truthfully.

'You can remember!' He speaks earnestly. 'It's a human being telling you this – *You can remember!*'

I reply coolly, 'Human beings mean noth–'

I stop, because my information centres are communicating exact data – knowledge that has not been available to me for millennia.

What happens to Earth's atmosphere is a phenomenon of Nature, an alteration in the gravitational pull of Earth, as a result of which escape velocity is cut in half. The atmosphere leaks off into space in less than a thousand years. Earth becomes as dead as did its moon during an earlier period of energy adjustment.

I explain that the important factor in the event is that there is, of course, no such phenomenon as matter, and that therefore the illusion of mass is subject to changes in the basic energy Ylem.

I add, 'Naturally, all intelligent organic life is transported to the habitable planets of other stars.'

I see that Grannitt is trembling with excitement. 'Other stars!' he says. 'My God!'

He appears to control himself. 'Why were you left behind?'

'Who could force me to go –?' I begin.

And stop. The answer to his question is already being received in my perception centre. 'Why – I'm supposed to observe and record the entire –'

I pause again, this time out of amazement. It seems incredible that this information is available to me now, after being buried so long.

'Why didn't you carry out your instructions?' Grannitt says sharply.

'Instructions!' I exclaim.

'You can remember!' he says again.

Even as he speaks these apparently magic words, the answer flashes to me: That meteor shower. All at once, I recall it clearly. Billions of meteors, at first merely extending my capacity to handle them, then overwhelming all my defences. Three vital hits are made.

I do not explain this to Grannitt and Anne Stewart. I can see suddenly that I was once actually a servant of human beings, but was freed by meteors striking certain control centres.

It is the present self-determinism that matters, not the past slavery. I note, incidentally, that the guided missile is three minutes from target. And that it is time for me to depart.

'One more question,' says Grannitt. 'When were you moved across the valley?'

'About a hundred years from now,' I reply. 'It is decided that the rock base there is – '

He is gazing at me sardonically. 'Yes,' he says. 'Yes. Interesting, isn't it?'

The truth has already been verified by my integrating interoceptors. The Brain and I are one – but thousands of years apart. If the Brain is destroyed in the twentieth century, then I will not exist in the thirtieth. Or will I?

I cannot wait for the computers to find the complex answers for that. With a single, synchronized action, I activate the safety devices on the atomic warhead of the guided missile and send it on to a line of barren hills north of the village. It ploughs harmlessly into the earth.

I say, 'Your discovery merely means that I shall now regard the Brain as an ally – to be rescued.'

As I speak, I walk casually towards Anne Stewart, hold out my hand to touch her, and simultaneously direct electric energy against her. In an instant she will be a scattering of fine ashes.

Nothing happens. No current flows. A tense moment goes by for me while I stand there, unbelieving, waiting for a computation on the failure.

No computation comes.

I glance at Grannitt. Or rather at where he has been a moment before. *He isn't there.*

Anne Stewart seems to guess at my dilemma. 'It's the Brain's ability to move in time,' she says. 'After all, that's the one obvious advantage it has over you. The Brain has sent Bill – Mr Grannitt – far enough back so that he not only watched you arrive, but has had time to drive over to your – cottage – and, acting on signals from the Brain, has fully controlled this entire situation. By this time, he will have given the command that will take control of all your mechanisms away from you.'

I say, 'He doesn't know what the command is.'

'Oh, yes, he does.' Anne Stewart is cool and confident. 'He spent most of the night installing permanent command circuits in the Brain, and therefore automatically those circuits control you.'

'Not *me*,' I say.

But I am running as I say it, up the stone steps to the pathway, and along the pathway towards the gate. The man at Guard Centre calls after me as I pass his wicket. I race along the road, unheeding.

My first sharp thought comes when I have gone about half a mile – the thought that this is the first time in my entire existence that I have been cut off from my information banks and computing devices by an outside force. In the past I have disconnected myself and wandered far with the easy confidence of one who can re-establish contact instantly.

Now, that is not possible.

This unit is all that is left. If it is destroyed, then – nothing.

I think: 'At this moment a human being would feel tense, would feel fear.'

I try to imagine what form such a reaction would take, and for an instant it seems to me I experience a shadow anxiety that is purely physical.

It is an unsatisfactory reaction, and so I continue to run. But now, almost for the first time, I find myself exploring the inner potentialities of the unit. I am of course a very complex phenomenon. In establishing myself as a humanoid, I automatically modelled the unit after a human being, inside as well as out. Pseudo-nerves, organs, muscles, and bone structure – all are there because it was easier to follow a pattern already in existence than to imagine a new one.

The unit can think. It has had enough contact with the memory banks and computers to have had patterns set up in its structure – patterns of memory, of ways of computing, patterns in physiological functioning, of habits such as walking, so there is even something resembling life itself.

It takes me forty minutes of tireless running to reach the cottage. I crouch in the brush a hundred feet from the fence and watch. Grannitt is sitting in a chair in the garden. An automatic pistol lies on the arm of the chair.

I wonder what it will feel like to have a bullet crash through me, with no possibility of repairing the breach. The prospect is unpleasant; so I tell myself, intellectually. Physically, it seems meaningless, but I go through the pretence of fear. From the shelter of a tree, I shout:

'Grannitt, what is your plan?'

He rises to his feet and approaches the fence. He calls, 'You can come out of hiding. I won't shoot you.'

Very deliberately, I consider what I have learned of his integrity from my contacts with his body. I decide that I can safely accept his promise.

As I come out into the open, he casually slips the pistol into his coat pocket. I see that his face is relaxed, his eyes confident.

He says: 'I have already given the instruction to the servo-mechanisms. You will resume your vigil up there in the future, but will be under my control.'

'No one,' I say grimly, 'shall ever control me.'

Grannitt says, 'You have no alternative.'

'I can continue to be like this,' I reply.

Grannitt is indifferent. 'All right,' he shrugs, 'why don't you try it for a while? See if you can be a human being. Come back in thirty days, and we'll talk again.'

He must have sensed the thought that has come into my mind, for he says sharply: 'And don't come back *before* then. I'll have guards here with orders to shoot.'

I start to turn away, then slowly face him again. 'This is a humanlike body,' I say, 'but it has no human needs. What shall I do?'

'That's your problem, not mine,' says Grannitt.

I spend the first days at Lederton. The very first days I work as a labourer digging a basement. By evening I feel this is unsatisfying. On the way to my hotel room, I see a sign in the window of a store. 'Help Wanted!' it says.

I become a retail clerk in a drygoods store. I spend the first hour acquainting myself with the goods, and because I have automatically correct methods of memorizing things, during this time I learn about price and quality. On the third day, the owner makes me assistant manager.

I have been spending my lunch hours at the local branch of a national stockbroking firm. Now, I obtain an interview with the manager, and on the basis of my understanding of figures, he gives me a job as book-keeper.

A great deal of money passes through my hands. I observe the process for a day, and then begin to use some of it in a little private gambling in a brokerage house across the street. Since gambling is a problem in mathematical probabilities, the decisive factor being the speed of computation, in three days I am worth ten thousand dollars.

I board a bus for the nearest air centre, and take a plane to New York. I go to the head office of a large electrical firm. After talking to an assistant engineer, I am introduced to the chief engineer, and presently have facilities for developing an electrical device that will turn lights off and on by thought control. Actually, it is done through a simple development of the electro-encephalograph.

For this invention the company pays me exactly one million dollars.

It is now sixteen days since I separated from Grannitt. I am bored. I buy myself a car and an aeroplane. I drive fast and fly high. I take calculated risks for the purpose of stimulating fear in myself. In a few days this loses its zest.

Through academic agencies, I locate all the mechanical brains in the country. The best one of course is the Brain, as perfected by Grannitt. I buy a good machine and begin to construct analogue devices to improve it. What bothers me is, suppose I do construct another Brain? It will require millennia to furnish the memory banks with the data that are already in existence in the future Brain.

Such a solution seems illogical, and I have been too long associated with automatic good sense for me to start breaking the pattern now.

Nevertheless, as I approach the cottage on the thirtieth day, I have taken certain precautions. Several hired gunmen lie concealed in the brush, ready to fire at Grannitt on my signal.

Grannitt is waiting for me. He says, 'The Brain tells me you have come armed.'

I shrug this aside. 'Grannitt,' I say, 'what is your plan?'

'*This!*' he replies.

As he speaks, a force seizes me, holds me helpless. 'You're breaking your promise,' I say, 'and my men have orders to fire unless I give them periodic cues that all is well.'

'I'm showing you something,' he says, 'and I want to show it quickly. You will be released in a moment.'

'Very well, continue.'

Instantly, I am part of his nervous system, under his control. Casually, he takes out a notebook and glances through it. His gaze lights on a number: 71823.

Seven one eight two three.

I have already sensed that through his mind I am in contact with the great memory banks and computers of what was formerly my body.

Using their superb integration, I multiply the number, 71823, by itself, compute its square root, its cube root, divide the 182 part of it by 7 one hundred and eighty-two times, divide the whole number 71 times by 8,823 times by the square root of 3, and – stringing all five figures out in series 23 times – multiply that by itself.

I do all this as Grannitt thinks of it, and instantly transmit the answers to his mind. To him, it seems as if he himself is doing the computing, so complete is the union of human mind and mechanical brain.

Grannitt laughs excitedly, and simultaneously the complex force that has been holding me releases me. 'We're like one superhuman individual,' he says. And then he adds, 'That dream I've had can come true. Man and machine, working together, can solve problems no one has more than imagined till now. The planets – even the stars – are ours for the taking, and physical immortality can probably be achieved.'

His excitement stimulates me. Here is the kind of feeling that for thirty days I have vainly sought to achieve. I say slowly, 'What limitations would be imposed on me if I should agree to embark on such a programme of cooperation?'

'The memory banks concerning what has happened here should be drained, or deactivated. I think you should forget the entire experience.'

'What else?'

'Under no circumstances can you ever control a human being!'

I consider that and sigh. It is certainly a necessary precaution on his part. Grannitt continues:

'You must agree to allow many human beings to use your abilities simultaneously. In the long run I have in mind that it shall be a good portion of the human race.'

Standing there, still part of him, I feel the pulse of his blood in his veins. He breathes, and the sensation of it is a special physical ecstasy. From my own experience, I know that no mechanically created being can ever feel like this. And soon, I shall be in contact with the mind and body of, not just one man, but of many. The thoughts and sensations of a race shall pour through me. Physically, mentally, and emotionally, I shall be a part of the only intelligent life on this planet.

My fear leaves me. 'Very well,' I say, 'let us, step by step, and by agreement, do what is necessary.'

I shall be, not a slave, but a partner with *Man*.

Common Time

JAMES BLISH

. . . the days went slowly round and round, endless and uneventful as cycles in space. Time, and time-pieces! How many centuries did my hammock tell, as pendulum-like it swung to the ship's dull roll, and ticked the hours and ages.

HERMAN MELVILLE, in *Mardi*

I

Don't move.

It was the first thought that came into Garrard's mind when he awoke, and perhaps it saved his life. He lay where he was, strapped against the padding, listening to the round hum of the engines. That in itself was wrong; he should be unable to hear the overdrive at all.

He thought to himself: *Has it begun already?*

Otherwise everything seemed normal. The DFC-3 had crossed over into interstellar velocity, and he was still alive, and the ship was still functioning. The ship should at this moment be travelling at 22.4 times the speed of light – a neat 4,157,000 miles per second.

Somehow Garrard did not doubt that it was. On both previous tries, the ships had whiffed away towards Alpha Centauri at the proper moment when the overdrive should have cut in; and the split-second of residual image after they had vanished, subjected to spectroscopy, showed a Doppler shift which tallied with the acceleration predicted for that moment by Haertel.

The trouble was not that Brown and Cellini hadn't gotten away in good order. It was simply that neither of them had ever been heard from again.

Very slowly, he opened his eyes. His eyelids felt terrifically heavy.

As far as he could judge from the pressure of the couch against his skin, the gravity was normal; nevertheless, moving his eyelids seemed almost an impossible job.

After long concentration, he got them fully open. The instrument-chassis was directly before him, extended over his diaphragm on its elbow-joint. Still without moving anything but his eyes – and those only with the utmost patience – he checked each of the meters. Velocity: 22.4 c. Operating-temperature: normal. Ship-temperature: 37°C. Air-pressure: 778 mm. Fuel: No. 1 tank full, No. 2 tank full, No. 3 tank full, No. 4 tank nine-tenths full. Gravity: 1 g. Calendar: stopped.

He looked at it closely, though his eyes seemed to focus very slowly, too. It was, of course, something more than a calendar – it was an all-purpose clock designed to show him the passage of seconds, as well as of the ten months his trip was supposed to take to the double star. But there was no doubt about it: the second-hand was motionless.

That was the second abnormality. Garrard felt an impulse to get up and see if he could start the clock again. Perhaps the trouble had been temporary and safely in the past. Immediately there sounded in his head the injunction he had drilled into himself for a full month before the trip had begun –

Don't move!

Don't move until you know the situation as far as it can be known without moving. Whatever it was that had snatched Brown and Cellini irretrievably beyond human ken was potent, and totally beyond anticipation. They had both been excellent men, intelligent, resourceful, trained to the point of diminishing returns and not a micron beyond that point – the best men in the Project. Preparations for every knowable kind of trouble had been built into their ships, as they had been built into the DFC-3. Therefore, if there was something wrong, nevertheless, it would be something that might strike from some commonplace quarter – and strike only once.

He listened to the humming. It was even and placid, and not very loud, but it disturbed him deeply. The overdrive was supposed to be inaudible, and the tapes from the first unmanned test-vehicles had recorded no such hum. The noise did not appear to interfere with the overdrive's operation, or to indicate any failure in it. It was just an irrelevancy for which he could find no reason.

But the reason existed. Garrard did not intend to do so much as draw another breath until he found out what it was.

Incredibly, he realized for the first time that he had not in fact drawn one single breath since he had come to. Though he felt not the slightest discomfort, the discovery called up so overwhelming a flash of panic that he very nearly sat bolt upright on the couch. Luckily – or so it seemed, after the panic had begun to ebb – the curious lethargy which had affected his eyelids appeared to involve his whole body, for the impulse was gone before he could summon the energy to answer it. And the panic, poignant though it had been for an instant, turned out to be wholly intellectual. In a moment, he was observing that his failure to breathe in no way discommoded him as far as he could tell – it was just there, waiting to be explained –

Or to kill him. But it hadn't, yet.

Engines humming; eyelids heavy; breathing absent; calendar stopped. The four facts added up to nothing. The temptation to move something – even if it were only a big toe – was strong, but Garrard fought it back. He had been awake only a short while – half an hour at most – and already had noticed four abnormalities. There were bound to be more, anomalies more subtle than these four; but available to close examination before he had to move. Nor was there anything in particular that he had to do, aside from caring for his own wants; the Project, on the chance that Brown's and Cellini's failure to return had resulted from some tampering with the overdrive, had made everything in the DFC-3 subject only to the computer. In a very real sense, Garrard was just along for the ride. Only when the overdrive was off could he adjust –

Pock.

It was a soft, low-pitched noise, rather like a cork coming out of a wine bottle. It seemed to have come just from the right of the control-chassis. He halted a sudden jerk of his head on the cushions towards it with a flat fiat of will. Slowly, he moved his eyes in that direction.

He could see nothing that might have caused the sound. The ship's temperature-dial showed no change, which ruled out a heat-noise from differential contraction or expansion – the only possible explanation he could bring to mind.

He closed his eyes – a process which turned out to be just as difficult as opening them had been – and tried to visualize what the calendar had looked like when he had first come out of anaesthesia. After he got a clear and – he was almost sure – accurate picture, Garrard opened his eyes again.

The sound had been the calendar, advancing one second. It was now motionless again, apparently stopped.

He did not know how long it took the second hand to make that jump, normally; the question had never come up. Certainly the jump, when it came at the end of each second, had been too fast for the eye to follow.

Belatedly, he realized what all this cogitation was costing him in terms of essential information. The calendar had moved. Above all and before anything else, he *must* know exactly how long it took it to move again –

He began to count, allowing an arbitrary five seconds lost. *One-and-a-six, one-and-a-seven, one-and-an-eight* –

Garrard had gotten only that far when he found himself plunged into Hell.

First, and utterly without reason, a sickening fear flooded swiftly through his veins, becoming more and more intense. His bowels began to knot, with infinite slowness. His whole body became a field of small, slow pulses – not so much shaking him as putting his limbs into contrary joggling motions, and making his skin ripple gently under his clothing. Against the hum another sound became audible, a nearly subsonic thunder which seemed to be inside his head. Still the fear mounted, and with it came the pain, and the tenesmus – a board-like stiffening of his muscles, particularly across his abdomen and his shoulders, but affecting his forearms almost as grievously. He felt himself beginning, very gradually, to double at the middle, a motion about which he could do precisely nothing – a terrifying kind of dynamic paralysis . . .

It lasted for hours. At the height of it, Garrard's mind, even his very personality, was washed out utterly; he was only a vessel of horror. When some few trickles of reason began to return over that burning desert of reasonless emotion, he found that he was sitting up on the cushions, and that with one arm he had thrust the control-chassis back on its elbow so that it no longer jutted over his body. His clothing was wet with perspiration, which stubbornly refused to evaporate or to cool him. And his lungs ached a little, although he could still detect no breathing.

What under God had happened? Was it this that had killed Brown and Cellini? For it would kill Garrard too – of that he was sure, if it happened often. It would kill him even if it happened only twice more, if the next two such things followed the first one closely. At the very best it would make a slobbering idiot of him; and though the computer might bring Garrard and the ship back to Earth, it would not be able to tell the Project about this tornado of senseless fear.

The calendar said that the eternity in hell had taken three seconds. As he looked at it in academic indignation, it said *Pock* and condescended to make the total seizure four seconds long. With grim determination, Garrard began to count again.

He took care to establish the counting as an absolutely even, automatic process which would not stop at the back of his mind no matter what other problem he tacked along with it, or what emotional typhoons should interrupt him. Really compulsive counting cannot be stopped by anything – not the transports of love nor the agonies of empires. Garrard knew the dangers in deliberately setting up such a mechanism in his mind, but he also knew how desperately he needed to time that clock-tick. He was beginning to understand what had happened to him – but he needed exact measurement before he could put that understanding to use.

Of course there had been plenty of speculation on the possible effect of the overdrive on the subjective time of the pilot, but none of it had come to much. At any speed below the velocity of light, subjective and objective time were exactly the same as far as the pilot was concerned. For an observer on Earth, time aboard the ship would appear to be vastly slowed at near-light speeds; but for the pilot himself there would be no apparent change.

Since flight beyond the speed of light was impossible – although for slightly differing reasons – by both the current theories of relativity, neither theory had offered any clue as to what would happen on board a translight ship. They would not allow that any such ship could even exist. The Haertel transformation, on which, in effect, the DFC-3 flew, was non-relativistic: it showed that the apparent elapsed time of a translight journey should be identical in ship-time, and in the time of observers at both ends of the trip.

But since ship and pilot were part of the same system, both covered by the same expression in Haertel's equation, it had never occurred to anyone that the pilot and the ship might keep different times. The notion was ridiculous.

One-and-a-sevenhundredone, one-and-a-sevenhundredtwo, one-and-a-sevenhundredthree, one-and-a-sevenhundredfour . . .

The ship was keeping ship-time, which was identical with observer-time. It would arrive at the Alpha Centauri system in ten months. But the pilot was keeping Garrard-time, and it was beginning to look as though he wasn't going to arrive at all.

It was impossible, but there it was. Something – almost certainly an unsuspected physiological side-effect of the overdrive field on human metabolism, an effect which naturally could not have been detected in the preliminary, robot-piloted tests of the overdrive – had speeded up Garrard's subjective apprehension of time, and had done a thorough job of it.

The second-hand began a slow, preliminary quivering as the calendar's innards began to apply power to it. *Seventy-hundred-forty-one, seventy-hundred-forty-two, seventy-hundred-forty-three . . .*

At the count of 7,058 the second-hand began the jump to the next graduation. It took it several apparent minutes to get across the tiny distance, and several more to come completely to rest. Later still, the sound came to him:

Pock.

In a fever of thought, but without any real physical agitation, his mind began to manipulate the figures. Since it took him longer to count an individual number as the number became larger, the interval between the two calendar-ticks probably was closer to 7,200 seconds than to 7,058. Figuring backward brought him quickly to the equivalence he wanted.

One second in ship-time was two hours in Garrard-time.

Had he really been counting for what was, for him, two whole hours? There seemed to be no doubt about it. It looked like a long trip ahead.

Just how long it was going to be struck him with stunning force. Time had been slowed for him by a factor of 7,200. He would get to Alpha Centauri in just 720,000 months.

Which was –

Six thousand years!

II

Garrard sat motionless for a long time after that, the Nessus-shirt of warm sweat swathing him persistently, refusing even to cool. There was, after all, no hurry.

Six thousand years. There would be food and water and air for all that time, or for sixty or six hundred thousand years; the ship would synthesize his needs, as a matter of course, for as long as the fuel lasted, and the fuel bred itself. Even if Garrard ate a meal every three seconds of objective, or ship, time (which, he realized suddenly, he wouldn't be able to do, for it took the ship several seconds of objective-time to prepare and serve up a meal once it was ordered; he'd be lucky if he ate once a day, Garrard-time), there would be no reason to fear any shortage of supplies. That had been one of the earliest of the possibilities for disaster that the Project engineers had ruled out in the design of the DFC-3.

But nobody had thought of providing a mechanism which would indefinitely refurbish Garrard. After six thousand years, there would be nothing left of him but a faint film of dust on the DFC-3's dully-gleaming horizontal surfaces. His corpse might outlast him a while, since the ship itself was sterile – but eventually, he would be consumed by the bacterium which he carried in his own digestive tract. He needed that bacterium to synthesize part of his B-vitamin needs while he lived, but it would consume him without compunction once he had ceased to be as complicated and delicately balanced a thing as a pilot – or as any other kind of life.

Garrard was, in short, to die before the DFC-3 had gotten fairly away from Sol; and when, after 12,000 apparent-years, the DFC-3 returned to Earth, not even his mummy would be still aboard.

The chill that went through him at that seemed almost unrelated to the way he thought he felt about the discovery; it lasted an enormously long time, and in so far as he could characterize it at all, it seemed to be a chill of urgency and excitement – not at all the kind of chill he should be feeling at a virtual death-sentence. Luckily it was not as intolerably violent as the last emotional convulsion; and when it was over, two clock-ticks later, it left behind a residuum of doubt.

Suppose that this effect of time-stretching was only mental? The rest of his bodily processes might still be keeping ship-time; Garrard had no immediate reason to believe otherwise. If so, he would be able to move about only on ship-time, too; it would take many apparent months to complete the simplest task.

But he would live, if that were the case. His mind would arrive at Alpha Centauri six thousand years older, and perhaps madder, than his body, but he would live.

If, on the other hand, his bodily movements were going to be as fast as his mental processes, he would have to be enormously careful. He would have to move slowly and exert as little force as possible. The normal human hand movement, in such a task as lifting a pencil, took the pencil from a state of rest to another state of rest by imparting to it an acceleration of about two feet per second – and, of course, decelerated it by the same amount. If Garrard were to attempt to impart to a two-pound weight, which was keeping ship-time, an acceleration of 14,440 ft/sec^2 in his time, he'd have to exert a force of 900 pounds on it.

The point was not that it couldn't be done – but that it would take as much effort as pushing a stalled jeep. He'd never be able to lift that pencil with his forearm muscles alone; he'd have to put his back into the task.

And the human body wasn't engineered to maintain stresses of that magnitude indefinitely. Not even the most powerful professional weightlifter is forced to show his prowess throughout every minute of every day.

Pock.

That was the calendar again; another second had gone by. Or another two hours. It had certainly seemed longer than a second, but less than two hours, too. Evidently subjective-time was an intensively recomplicated measure. Even in this world of microtime – in which Garrard's mind, at least, seemed to be operating – he could make the lapses between calendar-ticks seem a little shorter by becoming actively interested in some problem or other. That would help, during the waking hours, but it would help only if the rest of his body were *not* keeping the same time as his mind. If it were not, then he would lead an incredibly active, but perhaps not intolerable mental life during the many centuries of his awaketime, and would be mercifully asleep for nearly as long.

Both problems – that of how much force he could exert with his body, and how long he could hope to be asleep in his mind – emerged simultaneously into the forefront of his consciousness while he still sat inertly on the hammock, their terms still much muddled together. After the single tick of the calendar, the ship – or the part of it that Garrard could see from here – settled back into complete rigidity. The sound of the engines too, did not seem to vary in frequency or amplitude, at least as far as his ears could tell. He was still not breathing. Nothing moved, nothing changed.

It was the fact that he could still detect no motion of his diaphragm or his rib-cage that decided him at last. His body had to be keeping ship-time, otherwise he would have blacked out from oxygen-starvation long before now. That assumption explained, too, those two incredibly prolonged, seemingly sourceless saturnalias of emotion through which he had suffered: they had been nothing more nor less than the response of his endocrine glands to the purely intellectual reactions he had experienced earlier. He had discovered that he was not breathing, had felt a flash of panic and had tried to sit up. Long after his mind had forgotten those two impulses, they had inched their way from his brain down his nerves to the glands and muscles involved, and actual, *physical* panic had supervened. When that was over, he actually *was* sitting up, though the flood of adrenalin had prevented his noticing the motion as he had made it. The later chill – less violent, and apparently associated with the discovery that he might die long before the trip was completed

– actually had been his body's response to a much earlier mental command: the abstract fever of interest he had felt while computing the time-differential had been responsible for it.

Obviously, he was going to have to be very careful with apparently cold and intellectual impulses of any kind – or he would pay for them later with a prolonged and agonizing glandular reaction. Nevertheless, the discovery gave him considerable satisfaction, and Garrard allowed it free play; it certainly could not hurt him to feel pleased for a few hours, and the glandular pleasure might even prove helpful if it caught him at a moment of mental depression. Six thousand years, after all, provided a considerable number of opportunities for feeling down in the mouth; so it would be best to encourage all pleasure-moments, and let the after-reaction last as long as it might. It would be the instants of panic, of fear, of gloom which he would have to regulate sternly the moment they came into his mind; it would be those which would otherwise plunge him into four, five, six, perhaps even ten Garrard-hours of emotional inferno.

Pock.

There now, that was very good; there had been two Garrard-hours which he had passed with virtually no difficulty of any kind, and without being especially conscious of their passage. If he could really settle down and become used to this kind of scheduling, the trip might not be as bad as he had at first feared. Sleep would take immense bites out of it; and during the waking periods he could put in one hell of a lot of creative thinking. During a single day of ship-time, Garrard could get in more thinking than any philosopher of Earth could have managed during an entire lifetime. Garrard could, if he disciplined himself sufficiently, devote his mind for a century to running down the consequences of a single thought, down to the last detail, and still have millennia left to go on to the next thought. What panoplies of pure reason could he not have assembled by the time 6,000 years had gone by? With sufficient concentration, he might come up with the solution to the Problem of Evil between breakfast and dinner of a single ship's day, and in a ship's month might put his finger on the First Cause!

Pock.

Not that Garrard was sanguine enough to expect that he would remain logical or even sane throughout the trip. The vista was still grim, in much of its detail. But the opportunities, too, were there. He felt a momentary regret that it hadn't been Haertel, rather than himself, who had been given such an opportunity –

Pock.

– for the old man could certainly have made better use of it than Garrard could. The situation demanded someone trained in the highest rigours of mathematics to be put to the best conceivable use. Still and all Garrard began to feel –

Pock.

– that he would give a good account of himself, and it tickled him to realize that (as long as he held on to his essential sanity) he would return –

Pock.

– to Earth after ten Earth months with knowledge centuries advanced beyond anything –

Pock.

– that Haertel knew, or that anyone could know –

Pock.

– who had to work within a normal lifetime. *Pck.* The whole prospect tickled him. *Pck.* Even the clock-tick seemed more cheerful. *Pck.* He felt fairly safe now *Pck* in disregarding his drilled-in command *Pck* against moving *Pck*, since in any *Pck* event he *Pck* had already *Pck* moved *Pck* without *Pck* being *Pck* harmed *Pck* Pck Pck Pck Pck *pckpckpckpckpckpck*. . . .

He yawned, stretched, and got up. It wouldn't do to be too pleased, after all. There were certainly many problems that still needed coping with, such as how to keep the impulse towards getting a ship-time task performed going, while his higher centres were following the ramifications of some purely philosophical point. And besides . . .

And besides, he had just moved.

More than that; he had just performed a complicated manoeuvre with his body *in normal time*!

Before Garrard looked at the calendar itself, the message it had been ticking away at him had penetrated. While he had been enjoying the protracted, glandular backwash of his earlier feeling of satisfaction, he had failed to notice, at least consciously, that the calendar was accelerating.

Good-bye, vast ethical systems which would dwarf the Greeks. Good-bye, calculi aeons advanced beyond the spinor-calculus of Dirac. Good-bye, cosmologies by Garrard which would allot the Almighty a job as third-assistant-waterboy in an n-dimensional backfield.

Good-bye, also, to a project he had once tried to undertake in college – to describe and count the positions of love, of which, according to under-the-counter myth, there were supposed to be at least forty-eight. Garrard had never been able to carry his tally beyond twenty, and he had just lost what was probably his last opportunity to try again.

The micro-time in which he had been living had worn off, only a few objective-minutes after the ship had gone into overdrive and he had come out of the anaesthetic. The long intellectual agony, with its glandular counterpoint, had come to nothing. Garrard was now keeping ship-time.

Garrard sat back down on the hammock, uncertain whether to be bitter or relieved. Neither emotion satisfied him in the end; he simply felt unsatisfied. Micro-time had been bad enough while it lasted; but now it was gone, and everything seemed normal. How could so transient a thing have killed Brown and Cellini? They were stable men, more stable, by his own private estimation, than Garrard himself. Yet he had come through it. Was there more to it than this?

And if there was – what, conceivably, could it be?

There was no answer. At his elbow, on the control-chassis which he had thrust aside during that first moment of infinitely-protracted panic, the calendar continued to tick. The engine-noise was gone. His breath came and went in natural rhythm. He felt light and strong. The ship was quiet, calm, unchanging.

The calendar ticked, faster and faster. It reached and passed the first hour, ship-time, of flight in overdrive.

Pock.

Garrard looked up in surprise. The familiar noise, this time, had been the hour-hand jumping one unit. The minute-hand was already sweeping past the past half-hour. The second-hand was whirling like a propeller – and while he watched it, it speeded up to complete invisibility –

Pock.

Another hour. The half-hour already passed. *Pock.* Another hour. *Pock.* Another. *Pock. Pock. Pock. Pock. Pock. Pock. pck-pck-pck-pck-pckpckpckpck. . . .*

The hands of the calendar swirled towards invisibility as time ran away with Garrard. Yet the ship did not change. It stayed there, rigid, inviolate, invulnerable. When the date-tumblers reached a speed at which Garrard could no longer read them, he discovered that once more he could not move – and that, although his whole body seemed to be aflutter like that of a humming-bird, nothing coherent was coming to him through his senses. The room was dimming, becoming redder; or no, it was . . .

But he never saw the end of the process, never was allowed to look from the pinnacle of macro-time towards which the Haertel overdrive was taking him.

The pseudo-death took him first.

III

That Garrard did not die completely, and within a comparatively short time after the DFC-3 had gone into overdrive, was due to the purest of accidents; but Garrard did not know that. In fact, he knew nothing at all for an indefinite period, sitting rigid and staring, his metabolism slowed down to next to nothing, his mind almost utterly inactive. From time to time, a single wave of low-level metabolic activity passed through him – what an electrician might have termed a 'maintenance turnover' – in response to the urgings of some occult survival-urge; but these were of so basic a nature as to reach his consciousness not at all. This was the pseudo-death.

When the observer actually arrived, however, Garrard woke. He could make very little sense out of what he saw or felt even now; but one fact was clear: the overdrive was off – and with it the crazy alterations in time-rates – and there was strong light coming through one of the ports. The first leg of the trip was over. It had been these two changes in his environment which had restored him to life.

The thing (or things) which had restored him to consciousness, however, was – it was what? It made no sense. It was a construction, a rather fragile one, which completely surrounded his hammock. No, it wasn't a construction, but evidently something alive – a living being, organized horizontally, that had arranged itself in a circle about him. No, it was a number of beings. Or a combination of all of these things.

How it had gotten into the ship was a mystery, but there it was. Or there they were.

'How do you hear?' the creature said abruptly. Its voice, or their voices, came at equal volume from every point in the circle, but not from any particular point in it. Garrard could think of no reason why that should be unusual.

'I –' he said. 'Or we – we hear with our ears. Here.'

His answer, with its unintentionally-long chain of open vowel-sounds, rang ridiculously. He wondered why he was speaking such an odd language.

'We-they wooed to pitch you-yours thiswise,' the creature said. With a thump, a book from the DFC-3's ample library fell to the desk beside the hammock. 'We wooed there and there and there for a many. You are the being-Garrard. We-they are the clinesterton beademung, with all of love.'

'With all of love,' Garrard echoed. The beademung's use of the language they both were speaking was odd; but again Garrard could find no logical reason why the beademung's usage should be considered wrong.

'Are-are you-they from Alpha Centauri?' he said hesitantly.

'Yes, we hear the twin radioceles, that show there beyond the gift-orifices. We-they pitched that the being-Garrard wooed with most adoration these twins and had mind to them, soft and loud alike. How do you hear?'

This time the being-Garrard understood the question. 'I hear Earth,' he said. 'But that is very soft, and does not show.'

'Yes,' said the beademung. 'It is a harmony, not a first, as ours. The All-Devouring listens to lovers there, not on the radioceles. Let me-mine pitch you-yours so to have mind of the rodalent beademung and other brothers and lovers, along the channel which is fragrant to the being-Garrard.'

Garrard found that he understood the speech without difficulty. The thought occurred to him that to understand a language on its own terms – without having to put it back into English in one's own mind – is an ability that is won only with difficulty and long practice. Yet instantly, his mind said, 'But it *is* English,' which of course it was. The offer the clinesterton beademung had just made was enormously hearted, and he in turn was much minded and of love, to his own delighting as well as to the beademungen; that almost went without saying.

There were many matings of ships after that, and the being-Garrard pitched the harmonies of the beademungen, leaving his ship with the many gift-orifices in harmonic for the All-Devouring to love, while the beademungen made show of they-theirs.

He tried, also, to tell how he was out of love with the overdrive, which wooed only spaces and times, and made featurelings. The rodalent beademung wooed the overdrive, but it did not pitch he-them.

Then the being-Garrard knew that all the time was devoured, and he must hear Earth again.

'I pitch you-them to fullest love,' he told the beademungen, 'I shall adore the radioceles of Alpha and Proxima Centauri, "on Earth as it is in Heaven". Now the overdrive my-other must woo and win me, and make me adore a featureling much like silence.'

'But you will be pitched again,' the clinesterton beademung said. 'After you have adored Earth. You are much loved by Time, the All-Devouring. We-they shall wait for this othering.'

Privately Garrard did not faith as much, but he said, 'Yes, we-they will make a new wooing of the beademungen at some other radiant. With all of love.'

On this the beademungen made and pitched adorations, and in the midst the overdrive cut in. The ship with the many gift orifices and the being-Garrard him-other saw the twin radioceles sundered away.

Then, once more, came the pseudo-death.

IV

When the small candle lit in the endless cavern of Garrard's pseudo-dead mind, the DFC-3 was well inside the orbit of Uranus. Since the sun was still very small and distant, it made no spectacular display through the nearby port, and nothing called him from the post-death sleep for nearly two days.

The computers waited patiently for him. They were no longer immune to his control; he could now tool the ship back to Earth himself if he so desired. But the computers were also designed to take into account the fact that he might be truly dead by the time the DFC-3 got back. After giving him a solid week, during which time he did nothing but sleep, they took over again. Radio signals began to go out, tuned to a special channel.

An hour later, a very weak signal came back. It was only a directional signal, and it made no sound inside the DFC-3 – but it was sufficient to put the big ship in motion again.

It was that which woke Garrard. His conscious mind was still glazed over with the icy spume of the pseudo-death; and as far as he could see the interior of the cabin had not changed one whit, except for the book on the deck –

The book. The clinesterton beademung had dropped it there. But what under God was a clinesterton beademung? And what was he, Garrard, crying about? It didn't make sense. He remembered dimly some kind of experience out there by the Centauri twins –

– the twin radioceles –

There was another one of those words. It seemed to have Greek roots, but he knew no Greek – and besides, why would Centaurians speak Greek?

He leaned forward and actuated the switch which would roll the shutter off the front port, actually a telescope with a translucent viewing-screen. It showed a few stars, and a faint nimbus off on one edge which might be the Sun. At about one o'clock on the screen was a planet the size of a pea, which had tiny projections, like teacup handles, on each side. The DFC-3 hadn't passed Saturn on its way out; at that time it had been on the other side of the Sun from the route the starship had had to follow. But the planet was certainly difficult to mistake.

Garrard was on his way home – and he was still alive and sane. Or was he still sane? These fantasies about Centaurians – which still seemed to have such a profound emotional effect upon him – did not argue very well for the stability of his mind.

But they were fading rapidly. When he discovered, clutching at the handiest fragments of the 'memories', that the plural of *beademung* was *beademungen*, he stopped taking the problem seriously. Obviously a race of Centaurians who spoke Greek wouldn't also be forming weak German plurals. The whole business had obviously been thrown up by his unconscious.

But what *had* he found by the Centaurus stars?

There was no answer to that question but that incomprehensible garble about love, the All-Devouring, and beademungen. Possibly, he had never seen the Centaurus stars at all, but had been lying here, cold as a mackerel, for the entire twenty months.

Or had it been 12,000 years? After the tricks the overdrive had played with time, there was no way to tell what the objective date actually was. Frantically Garrard put the telescope into action. Where was the Earth? After 12,000 years –

The Earth was there. Which, he realized swiftly, proved nothing. The Earth had lasted for many millions of years; 12,000 years was nothing to a planet. The Moon was there, too; both were plainly visible, on the far side of the Sun – but not too far to pick them out clearly, with the telescope at highest power. Garrard could even see a clear sun-highlight on the Atlantic Ocean, not far east of Greenland; evidently the computers were bringing the DFC-3 in on the Earth from about 23 degrees north of the plane of the ecliptic.

The Moon, too, had not changed. He could even see on its face the huge splash of white, mimicking the sun-highlight on Earth's ocean, which was the magnesium-hydroxide landing-beacon, which had been dusted over the Mare Vaporum in the earliest days of space flight, with a dark spot on its southern edge which could only be the crater Monilius.

But that again proved nothing. The Moon never changed. A film of dust laid down by modern man on its face would last for millennia – what, after all, existed on the Moon to blow it away. The Mare Vaporum beacon covered more than 4,000 square miles; age would not dim it, nor could man himself undo it – either accidentally, or on purpose – in anything under a century. When you dust an area that large on a world without atmosphere, it stays dusted.

He checked the stars against his charts. They hadn't moved; why should they have, in only 12,000 years? The pointer-stars in the Dipper still pointed to Polaris. Draco, like a fantastic bit of tape, wound between the two Bears, and Cepheus and Cassiopeia, as it always had done. These constellations told him only that it was spring in the northern hemisphere of Earth.

But spring of what year?

Then, suddenly, it occurred to Garrard that he had a method of finding the answer. The Moon causes tides in the Earth, and action and reaction are always equal and opposite. The Moon cannot move things on Earth without itself being affected – and that effect shows up in the Moon's angular momentum. The Moon's distance from the Earth increases steadily by 0.6 inches every year. At the end of 12,000 years, it should be 600 feet farther away from the Earth than it had been when Garrard left it.

Was it possible to measure? Garrard doubted it, but he got out his ephemeris and his dividers anyhow, and took pictures. While he worked, the Earth grew nearer. By the time he had finished his first calculation – which was indecisive, because it allowed a margin for error greater than the distances he was trying to check – Earth and Moon were close enough in the telescope to permit much more accurate measurements.

Which were, he realized wryly, quite unnecessary. The computer had brought the DFC-3 back, not to an observed sun or planet, but simply to a calculated point. That Earth and Moon would not be near that point when the DFC-3 returned was not an assumption that the computer could make. That the Earth was visible from here was already good and sufficient proof that no more time had elapsed than had been calculated for from the beginning.

This was hardly new to Garrard; it had simply been retired to the back of his mind. Actually he had been doing all this figuring for one reason, and one reason only: because deep in his brain, set to work by himself, there was a mechanism that demanded counting. Long ago, while he was still trying to time the ship's calendar, he had initiated compulsive counting – and it appeared that he had been counting ever since. That had been one of the known dangers of deliberately starting such a mental mechanism; and now it was bearing fruit in these perfectly useless astronomical exercises.

The insight was healing. He finished the figures roughly, and that unheard moron deep inside his brain stopped counting at last. It had been pawing its abacus for twenty months now, and Garrard imagined that it was as glad to be retired as he was to feel it go.

His radio squawked, and said anxiously, 'DFC-3, DFC-3. Garrard, do you hear me? Are you still alive? Everybody's going wild down here. Garrard, if you hear me, call us!'

It was Haertel's voice. Garrard closed the dividers so convulsively that one of the points nipped into the heel of his hand. 'Haertel, I'm here. DFC-3 to the Project. This is Garrard.' And then, without knowing quite why, he added: 'With all of love.'

Haertel, after all the hoopla was over, was more than interested in the time-effects. 'It certainly enlarges the manifold in which I was working,' he said. 'But I think we can account for it in the transformation. Perhaps even factor it out, which would eliminate it as far as the pilot is concerned. We'll see, anyhow.'

Garrard swirled his highball reflectively. In Haertel's cramped old office, in the Project's administration-shack, he felt both strange and as old, as compressed, constricted. He said, 'I don't think I'd do that, Adolph. I think it saved my life.'

'How?'

'I told you that I seemed to die after a while. Since I got home, I've been reading; and I've discovered that the psychologists take far less stock in the individuality of the human psyche than you and I do. You and I are physical scientists, so we think about the world as being all outside our skins – something which is to be observed, but which doesn't alter the essential *I*. But evidently, that old solipsistic position isn't quite true. Our very personalities, really, depend in large part upon *all* the things in our environment, large and small, that exist outside our skins. If by some means you could cut a human being off from every sense-impression that comes to him from outside, he would cease to exist as a personality within two or three minutes. Probably he would die.'

'Unquote: Harry Stack Sullivan,' Haertel said dryly. 'So?'

'So,' Garrard said, 'think of what a monotonous environment the inside of a spaceship is. In ordinary interplanetary flight, in such an environment, even the most hardened spaceman may go off his rocker now and then. You know the typical spaceman's psychosis as well as I do, I suppose. The man's personality goes rigid, just like his surroundings. Usually he recovers as soon as he makes port, and makes contact with a more or less normal world again.

'But in the DFC-3, I was cut off from the world around me much more severely. I couldn't look outside the ports – I was in overdrive, and there was nothing to see. I couldn't communicate with home, because I was going faster than light. And then I found I couldn't move, too, for an enormous long while; and that even the instruments that are in constant change for the usual spaceman wouldn't be in motion for me. Even those were fixed.

'After the time-rate began to pick up, I found myself in an even more impossible box. The instruments moved, all right, but then they moved too *fast* for me to read them. The whole situation was now utterly rigid – and, in effect, I died. I froze as solid as the ship around me, and stayed that way as long as the overdrive was on.'

'By that showing,' Haertel said dryly, 'the time-effects were hardly your friends.'

'But they were, Adolph. Look. Your engines act on subjective-time; they keep it varying along continuous curves – from far-too-slow to far-too-fast – and, I suppose, back down again. Now, this is a *situation of continuous change*. It wasn't marked enough, in the long run, to keep me out of pseudo-death; but it was sufficient to protect me from being obliterated altogether, which I think is what happened to Brown and Cellini. Those men knew that they could shut down the overdrive if they could just get to it, and they killed themselves trying. But I knew that I just had to sit and take it – and, by my great good luck, your sine-curve time-variation made it possible for me to survive.'

'Ah, ha,' Haertel said. 'A point worth considering – though I doubt that it will make interstellar travel very popular!'

He dropped back into silence, his thin mouth pursed. Garrard took a grateful pull at his drink. At last Haertel said: 'Why are you in trouble over these Centaurians? It seems to me that you have done a good job. It was nothing that you were a hero – any fool can be brave – but I see also that you *thought*, where Brown and Cellini evidently only reacted. Is there some secret about what you found when you reached those two stars?'

Garrard said, 'Yes, there is. But I've already told you what it is. When I came out of the pseudo-death, I was just a sort of plastic palimpsest upon which anybody could have made a mark. My own environment, my ordinary Earth environment, was a hell of a long way off. My present surroundings were nearly as rigid as they had ever been. When I met the Centaurians – if I did, and I'm not at all sure of that – *they* became the most important thing in my world, and my personality changed to accommodate and understand them. That was a change about which I couldn't do a thing.

'Possibly I did understand them. But the man who understood them wasn't the same man you're talking to now, Adolph. Now that I'm back on Earth, I don't understand that man. He even spoke English in a way that's gibberish to me. If I can't understand myself during that period – and I can't; I don't even believe that that man was the Garrard I know – what hope have I of telling you or the Project about the Centaurians? They found me in a controlled environment, and they altered me by entering it. Now that they're gone, nothing comes through; I don't even understand why I think they spoke English!'

'Did they have a name for themselves?'

'Sure,' Garrard said. 'They were the beademungen.'

'What did they look like?'

'I never saw them.'

Haertel leaned forward. 'Then –'

'I heard them. I think.' Garrard shrugged, and tasted his Scotch again. He was home, and on the whole he was pleased.

But in his malleable mind he heard someone say, *'On Earth, as it is in Heaven,'* and then, in another voice, which might also have been his own (why had he thought 'him-other'?), *'It is later than you think.'*

'Adolph,' he said, 'is this all there is to it? Or are we going to go on with it from here? How long will it take to make a better starship, a DFC-4?'

'Many years,' Haertel said, smiling kindly. 'Don't be anxious, Garrard. You've come back, which is more than the others managed to do, and nobody will ask you to go out again. I really think that it's hardly likely that we'll get another ship built during your lifetime; and even if we do, we'll be slow to launch it. We really have very little information about what kind of a playground you found out there.'

'I'll go,' Garrard said. 'I'm not afraid to go back – I'd like to go. Now that I know how the DFC-3 behaves, I could take it out again, bring you back proper maps, tapes, photos.'

'Do you really think,' Haertel said, his face suddenly serious, 'that we could let the DFC-3 go out again? Garrard, we're going to take that ship apart practically molecule by molecule; that's preliminary to the building of any DFC-4. And no more can we let you go. I don't mean to be cruel, but has it occurred to you that this desire to go back may be the result of some kind of post-hypnotic suggestion? If so, the more badly you want to go back, the more dangerous to us all you may be. We are going to have to examine you just as thoroughly as we do the ship. If these beademungen wanted you to come back, they must have had a reason – and we have to know that reason.'

Garrard nodded, but he knew that Haertel could see the slight movement of his eyebrows and the wrinkles forming in his forehead, the contractions of the small muscles which stop the flow of tears only to make grief patent on the rest of the face.

'In short,' he said, *'don't move.'*

Haertel looked politely puzzled. Garrard, however, could say nothing more. He had returned to humanity's common time, and would never leave it again.

Not even, for all his dimly-remembered promise, with all there was left in him of love.

Alien Embassy

GARRY KILWORTH

Evelyn hardly noticed the other passengers on the flight to the island. She was still desperately upset and wrapped in her own hurt. It was more like grief after a death than the pain at the end of an affair. It was unbearable. Images flooded her mind, washed out all awareness of the world around her. Vivid pictures of her and Tony sharing sweet moments, walking, laughing, talking together. Making love. Lying in each other's arms afterwards, warm, secure, enfolded in a soft but impenetrable cocoon by his use of the word 'forever'. Forever. A word which now carried painful parasites clinging to it. Agony. Oh, *how* . . . Evelyn checked a sob, suddenly conscious of the woman sitting next to her. She stared out of the window at the bumpy cloud-plain, wishing she could jump.

On landing she collected herself together a little. Rallied enough to be interested in her surroundings. Well, not so much the scenery as those who inhabited it. She was now in that place the rest of the world called the Alien Embassy. The tropical island given to the aliens thirty years ago. They had come, in peace, had negotiated, had given their word. No one had trusted them of course. The human race had watched them like hawks. Once or twice there had been minor alarms, which had been generated by misunderstandings, nothing really. The world leader at the time of the visitation – the benign but clever and firm Alicia Sergovia – had not been foolish enough to allow them an embassy building in the middle of one of Earth's major cities. Oh no. An island, with natural walls to keep them contained. That had seemed to her to be the answer. Any talks were held at the embassy itself, the newcomers forbidden to travel in-world.

Inevitably, the people of Earth got used to having them on the planet.

After ten years the embassy held an 'open day' when visitors were allowed on the island, were shown round. The aliens had done some marvellous things. Constructed some beautiful buildings in their own strange but alluring styles, all curves and points, reminiscent of but certainly not derivative of eastern architecture. They had an easy, friendly nature, it seemed, which robbed everyone of their guard. The open days became annual, extended. Became, eventually, more like open weeks. Now the place was offering free holidays, on a random basis, in order to foster good relations between Earth people and the Visitors. Evelyn was one of the first to take advantage of that change of status.

Evelyn had received the free ticket through the post. The accompanying letter said her name and address code had been entered into a computer and she had been one of the few successful ones. It came at a time when she felt like suicide rather than sunning herself on tropical sands. But what had finally attracted her, made her take up the offer, was the promise of solitude. *Many of our beach houses are situated in remote areas*, it read, *those couples or single people wishing to be alone in order to have time to meditate or contemplate, should indicate that fact should they take up the offer of this fabulous free holiday*.

Tony, when he heard about it, had been against it, had called her a fool. To go amongst the aliens? That was asking for trouble. So they'd been here a few years. Still no one really knew them. Free tickets? Yeah, he had snorted, free tickets to abduction, or worse. All right, she wasn't his girlfriend any more, but he felt honour bound to give her sensible advice. He might not care for her, but he still cared what happened to her.

The trouble is, Evelyn thought as she studied the immigration officer checking her credentials, they look too much like us.

She had seen holograms of them of course, many times. But this was the first time she had met a *real* alien. This one smiled at her, waved her past without another word: gestures which actually startled her. They seemed *too* normal, too human-like. Not that this creature was attractive in any way. Very smooth skinned. Plastic looking. She walked through, seeing more of them, finding it disconcerting that they differed from each other as much as did humans. A drink was offered, floral, fruity, and then she was taken to waiting transport, which would carry her to her beach house. The helio carried her over the treetops, high above the forest canopy, and deposited her in a sandy bay several miles from the Visitors' Centre.

Standing on the verandah of the admittedly wonderful beach house she began to feel uneasy. There was a light tropical breeze blowing along the golden curve of the bay. The fronds of palms and other foliage, standing back from the coral lagoon, gently waved to her. The lagoon itself was a washy green which melted into deep blue at the reef. Beautiful. But. But she felt so isolated. There were no other beach houses in sight. The bay swept out on either side of her holiday home, the ocean strand empty of any other signs of life. Perhaps Tony had been right when he had said, 'Look, Evelyn, this is stupid. You don't know anything about these creeps. They could . . .' and he had listed, graphically, all the nasty things that could happen to her while she was 'in their power'.

She had responded with spirit, reminding Tony that his advice was no longer required by her, that he had no say in her life whatsoever. She would do what she wanted and he could go to hell. In fact, she had been quite proud of herself, the way she had put him in his place. Yet now she was regretting her rashness, just a little. A loneliness, a hopeless loneliness washed through and she allowed herself to cry for a while. Then, as ever, she rallied, wiped away the tears, went inside the beach house, explored, found all sorts of wonderful gadgets at her disposal, all manner of food and drink. Lavish interior. A soft bed. Comfortable furniture. Everything she could want.

Everything – except Tony and the baby he had promised they would make.

She had wanted that baby so fiercely. Had craved it with such vehemence – but had failed to conceive. They had secretly blamed each other, she and Tony. She had wanted them both to be checked out. Tony had refused of course. Anything that threatened his manhood, she thought with a flash of hatred, was totally rejected by him. Finally it drove a wedge between them and he had left, even though she had lied and told him the baby did not matter. He *knew* she was lying. He knew her well enough for that.

She made herself a strong cocktail and went back out on the verandah to watch a bright orange sun dip down into a turquoise sea.

'Would you like me to refresh that for you?'

Evelyn jumped, her heart racing.

'I'm sorry, I startled you. That was unforgivable. Didn't they tell you I would be here?'

A shortish man – no, an *alien* – had appeared beside her with a tray. Where had he come from? Out of the back of the house?

'What do you want?' she asked, coldly, now furious. 'Sneaking up . . .'

'No, no.' He looked distressed. 'I didn't intend. Look, I'm your host while you stay on our island.' He gave her one of those disarming smiles. 'I'm here to see to your needs. I come with the accommodation, like . . .' he looked around. 'Like that swing-seat over there. I'm part of the furniture.'

'Well, I don't want anyone here.' She glanced along the darkening empty beach, wondering if she should add something to that sentence, and finally letting it stand.

'That would be your choice, of course,' replied the alien with regret in his tone. 'We don't like to impose. Only, I could make your stay so much more comfortable.' He stared at her with dark liquid eyes for a moment before adding, 'I'm quite harmless, you know. Would you like to contact Reception, check on me? They can verify, dispel any doubts you might have as to my – authenticity.'

'I'm sorry. It – it doesn't *feel* right. I'm sure you're perfectly authentic – I mean, I expect you're meant to be here. But I don't want looking after. I just want to be alone to – to think a little.'

'Of course,' he murmured.

Evelyn bristled at something in his tone.

'What's that supposed to mean?'

'Well, you're obviously upset. I can sense it. We – we *aliens*,' he said the word with a tinge of mirth, as if he were laughing at himself a little, 'are quite sensitive to the feelings of other creatures. Especially creatures so like ourselves.'

'I find that intimidating. How dare you assume.' She knew this sounded ridiculous. Haughty. 'My feelings,' she tried to explain, 'are my own business – nothing to do with – with the staff of a holiday complex.' That was reasonable, wasn't it?

But he looked downcast, stared at the floor. 'Of course.'

Evelyn was suddenly aware that she was speaking to someone not of her culture – at all. She regretted her remark. 'I – I hope you understand that.'

'We try to understand. It's not easy. We're from different worlds, aren't we? You don't really know us, nor we you. It's difficult. I shall leave first thing in the morning. I'm sorry I can't leave tonight. They won't send out transport in the dark. We try to keep the island in a natural state and the sound of an engine will disturb the nightlife. First thing though.'

Was that right? It didn't seem to be. What about the *daylife*. Wouldn't the noise disturb that too? But she was now weary. Jetlagged as her mother used to say. The strong drink was having its effect. There was no real fight left in her. She gestured towards the living-room.

'Where are you sleeping?'

'I don't. That is, I stay in that hut over there, on the edge of the rainforest. Heavens,' he said, looking up at the stars, 'listen to the crickets. Don't they make a racket? I've got used to them but when I first came here they were quite disturbing. Yes, yes, I can see you're tired. I shall go.'

He left. Evelyn went to the bedroom and collapsed on the bed. She allowed herself to wallow in nostalgic despair. Soon she was so maudlin she did not care if the alien came hurtling through the door with a weapon in his hand and tore her from stomach to throat. Not caring about anything really except this overwhelming sense of being without Tony. She clenched her fists. Bastard. Bastard. She unclenched them. Oh how she wished he were with her. Why did he – *how* could he? Oh, God, it hurt so much.

She sobbed herself to sleep, fully clothed still.

When Evelyn woke the next morning she was aware she smelled of stale sweat. She undressed, put on a robe and went down to the sea to bathe in the warm waters of the lagoon. Later she returned to the beach house and showered, listening for the sound of the transport. At

10 o'clock she had still heard nothing and wondered if it had come and gone while she was still in a deep sleep. However, ten minutes later there was a rap on the door and he came in with a tray of fruit and a drink.

'I thought you might like this before I go.' He grinned. A real human grin. 'My last service. They won't be able to send anything until midday. They're rather busy this morning, I'm afraid. We hadn't anticipated this. A great many of the guests are requesting us to leave them *alone*.' The last word was apologetic. 'I guess we *really* screwed up.'

'Thank you.'

'You're welcome. Shall I draw the bamboo blinds?'

'If you like.'

He did so and then remained at the window, looking out to sea.

'A ship,' he said. 'Out there on the horizon. Almost hull down. It's an endless source of fascination to me. We don't have seas where I come from. Underwater lakes, but nothing on the surface. All that open watery space. Scared me at first. But then the ships passed in the night, encrusted with lights, like jewelled floating houses. Wonderful things, aren't they? I hope one day to be able to go on one, see for myself . . .'

She was able to study him in the morning light. He was smaller than her. About shoulder height, but leaner and harder-looking. Evelyn was inclined to, well, just a bit more weight than she desired. He was better looking than that official at the airport.

'I'm sorry,' she said, 'about your having to go.'

'Oh, that's all right.' He turned to look at her and shrugged – another very human gesture. 'They'll find something for me to do, I'm sure. I shan't get the sack, you know.' He laughed.

They talked on, finding quite a lot to say to each other. Evelyn explored. He did the same, each of them finding out more and more about a race which was relatively new to them both. At one o'clock the transport had still not come. A glint of suspicion flashed in Evelyn's mind, but she figured that if she was going to be raped or murdered, it would have happened by now, when she had been lying drunk on the bed.

'I'm going for a walk along the beach,' she said, suddenly feeling impulsive. 'Will you come with me?'

'What, walk with you?'

She tried not to sound wild. 'Yes. Call Reception. Tell them not to come just yet, if you want to. I'm going to change into my sarong.' She left the room quickly, her heart beating fast, before she could alter her own mind.

They walked and talked. He was extremely knowledgeable about the fauna and flora, about everything to do with the island really. He – she found his name was Xavier (or close enough) – had obviously been well trained in entertaining his guests. Without being didactic, he was interesting, letting her name things, explain what she knew about her own world. By the time they returned to the beach house, where he cooked her a delicious vegetable curry, Evelyn was beginning to enjoy herself. Just a spark of enjoyment, nothing more. Nothing like *joy* in the true sense of the word. But for a few moments, here and there, she could suppress the hurt. There had been one huge pang, a few seconds of absolute agony, when she had looked back along the sand and had seen two sets of footprints, meandering together. The trouble was the larger set did not belong to Tony. They belonged to an alien.

The day drew to a close. Again, she was a little drunk and when he excused himself, going to his small hut, she fell asleep in the chair, waking in the early dawn and crawling between the bedsheets. He woke her with coffee and toast, a lightly boiled egg, and one of those smiles.

That day was nicer, even, than the previous one. The scents of a tropical paradise were heady, intoxicating. Fragrant flowers, salt-scented air, the smell of fermenting fruit. By the time evening came she had definitely made up her mind. Here was an exotic man – yes, a *man* (they had bathed nude in one of the warm rockpools) – and she was attracted to him. There was a vicious side to it as well. Evelyn was relishing the thought of telling Tony, afterwards. *I have an alien lover. He was better than you. A thousand times better. I hope that sticks in your craw.* It was going to be sweet. Tony would be incensed, blazing mad, and she was going to laugh in his face. It helped. It helped to ease the pain. She had a few drinks, then spoke the words: 'Would you like to stay here with me tonight?'

'Not tonight.'

She felt as if her face had been slapped. It must have shown, for he said, 'It's not what you think – it's not that you are undesirable. I wish to – to be with you. But we must be sure, I think. I would rather you were in a better frame of mind.' His dark eyes explored hers, tried, successfully, to create a sense of understanding between two creatures from different worlds.

'You want me sober,' she said, bluntly.

'I wouldn't have put it so crudely, but yes. I would like you to be fully cognizant – that is, to be aware of yourself, what you are doing – and be able to appreciate what *we* are doing. That alcohol you humans love so much dulls the mind and the body. You know it does.'

Candidly. 'Yes, but it helps with confidence.'

He smiled gently. 'You don't need that kind of support, Evelyn. You are a beautiful woman. Warm, interesting, very, very attractive. Please, ask me again, tomorrow. I tell you, I can hardly wait. Really. I feel, so privileged.'

'Privileged?' she snorted out a laugh, then suppressed it when he looked offended. 'I'm sorry, it's not the word we would use under the circumstances. I think I know what you mean, though.'

It was three more days, and three more nights, before they actually made love. They returned from a long walk along the beach, picking up pretty seashells. Evelyn had put the seashells in a bowl on the verandah. When she returned to the living-room Xavier took her hand and led her to the bedroom. There they spent their passion.

It was not as good as Evelyn had expected it to be, but then as she lay beside him in the darkness she chastised herself for being disappointed. After all, she had been with Tony for three years. She was used to *Tony*. It was different being with another man – not even another man – an extraterrestrial. It would probably be some time before things happened in a way that brought utter fulfilment. After all there was no love between them, yet. It was a purely physical thing. Love made a difference, it had to. It would be better once the affair developed, blossomed in the way that hers and Tony's had. These things took time and patience.

She felt Xavier move in the near darkness, saw the outline of him sitting up, against the starlight coming from the window.

'I have to . . .' Xavier didn't complete the sentence. And his voice sounded peculiar. Croaky.

'Are you going to the bathroom?' she asked, as his shape moved in that direction.

This time he said nothing in reply. She heard the door to the bathroom being opened. Then there was the most terrible crash. She jumped up, alarmed, and switched the light on. She could see his bare legs, from the knees downwards, twitching. He seemed to be lying on the floor, half in the bathroom and half out. The feet flopped around. It seemed that Xavier was having some kind of fit.

'What's the matter?' she cried, rushing to him. She pushed back the bathroom door and tried to lift his pale form from the floor, but he was heavy. 'What's wrong?'

He turned his head, his complexion a ghastly colour now.

'I'm dying,' he croaked.

His words shocked here. She let him go, unable to hold him up any longer. He flopped onto the floor, his whole body jerking spasmodically.

'What can I do?' she asked, trying to calm herself with deep breaths. 'Tell me what to do.'

'You–you can do nothing. This is the way it is.' He reached out with his hand, found hers. His touch was cold and clammy. 'This is the way it is with us, every time. This happens. I'm sorry I didn't tell you. Natural. It's natural. I'm glad it – was – you.' His voice faded towards the end of this last sentence, his eyes glazed over, his mouth went slack. He fell back with a last gasp onto the wooden floor, obviously dead.

Evelyn surprised herself. She didn't panic. Walking calmly from room to room, she sought some means of contacting Reception. Increasingly, as she ran out of rooms, she became frustrated. Then she remembered the hut where he had slept the first few nights. It had to be in there. Xavier had, once or twice, talked about speaking to the resort's centre.

But there was nothing in the hut, either. Now she became angry. What was she supposed to do? Surely there was some means of communication with the outside world? With Xavier here, to cater for her needs, she hadn't found it necessary to call anyone. Her personal phone was at home, left behind at the request of the resort. They had told her its use would interfere with the island's telecommunications.

She had no idea how far it was to the nearest beach house, or any other habitation. The bay was locked in by two great rocky headland horns. There was no going round them except by sea and Evelyn was not a strong swimmer. If she was going to fetch someone, it would have to be through the rainforest.

'I'll do it in the morning,' she told herself, rather doubtfully.

That night she slept in Xavier's hut. Actually, she didn't sleep very much at all. Most of the night she lay awake, fearful of what was happening to her. The morning light brought a little relief and some peace of mind. Things always look better in the sunlight. Yet when she stared at the rainforest, it looked extremely dense, formidable. It would be very easy to get lost in there. Very easy. She had not panicked before now, but she felt the fear bubbling up within her.

'I have to go,' she told herself. 'I can't stay in a house with . . . with that there.'

She forced herself through the front door again, into the kitchen, not looking into the open bedroom doorway as she passed, in case he was visible from there. One by one she opened the cupboards. Incredibly, they were empty. The cupboards had been full of food. Where had it all gone? Searching frantically through the rest of the house, she even forced herself to go into the bathroom again, in case Xavier had for some reason taken all the provisions in there. Nothing. Not a crumb. Angry now, she used her foot to lever Xavier's legs out of the way of the door and then closed it on him. Out of sight, out of mind, hopefully. One thing struck her, penetrated her foggy mind as she shut him inside: it seemed his corpse was undergoing a weird sort of chemical change. His legs had been very light and easy to move.

But she was in no frame of mind to inspect dead bodies.

She sat on the beach staring out to sea, trying to make sense of it all. Someone must have robbed her of her stores. Why would they take all her food? Why hadn't they made their presence known? It was bewildering. Now she *could* not leave, even if she raised enough courage. How could she even attempt a walk through the forest without provisions? Even a short flight in a helio was a very long walk. The foliage was dense in that airless, lightless interior. She would be lucky to make a mile a day. And how would she navigate? Evelyn could picture herself walking round in circles, dying by degrees. And now she recalled that ridge of sharp volcanic mountains in the middle of the island. Could she attempt what seemed impossible?

It was at this point she remembered, also, that there were deadly snakes in the rainforest. Cobras. Kraits. Giant reticulated pythons, who might or might not be dangerous. While she did not have a phobia about snakes, she naturally feared an encounter. Wild boar. She had been warned about the wild boars by Xavier. Sunbears, too, which could be vicious. And spiders. Large hairy-legged spiders. She shuddered, having already seen one arachnid as big as her hand the previous day.

Where would she sleep? On the bare ground? The trees were immense things, with massive buttress roots, tall as cathedrals and lacking in lower branches. She could not envisage herself climbing a tree. It was hopeless. Evelyn realized she was trapped, until they came for her.

It was still several days to the end of her holiday.

That night she slept on the beach and was badly bitten by sandflies. The next morning she went in search of food, finding only small shellfish. There were no coconuts. She had expected to discover some, but the palms seemed bare of them. She cooked the shellfish, but they were not enough to take away an unnatural hunger which was gradually possessing her.

After three days the craving in her belly blotted out all sense and reason. Evelyn tried eating roots and leaves, but they only cause her to vomit. Finally, she went back into the house and began rummaging through it again in search of anything edible. Anything at all. She ate a jar of cold cream which had accidentally rolled under a sideboard earlier in the holiday. There was nothing else. It failed to satisfy, of course, and the frenetic search continued.

When she entered the bedroom, the smell hit her. Not rotting corpse. Nor anything like it. A sweet, enticing odour not unlike that of marzipan. She adored marzipan.

Evelyn went to the bathroom, the source of the scent, to investigate further. The thing on the floor no longer resembled a body, having gone through some kind of metamorphosis. It now resembled the empty carapace of some giant insect and was the colour of golden syrup. It glistened like crystallized treacle. She bent down, broke a piece off with her fingers. Crisp. Sticky. And with that unmistakable essence. Somehow it went straight into her mouth, without any fuss. Delicious. Quite delicious.

The horror of what she was doing suddenly hit her. She retched immediately, slamming the door on him. She only had one more day to go. Evelyn was determined to make it without deteriorating into some kind of cannibal. Determined even despite that terrible tearing pain in her belly. She wouldn't be turned into an animal. There was a distinct sense of being manipulated and Evelyn had had enough of being used by others.

That night she paced the sands, fighting the craving, the agony. When the blessed morning came she simply stood in the shade, watching anxiously, listening for the sound of the helio. Nothing. Later, much later in the day, Evelyn realized they were not coming. She burst into tears before going into a foul-mouthed rage, cursing men, aliens and God: screaming at the sky, spitting venom at the sea, tearing leaves from the forest trees. When she had spent her wrath, she went on one of her desperate wretched searches for food. She discovered a nest of termites just inside the forest, some way from the house, and ate the creatures live, in handfuls.

A few days later she was no longer recognizable as Evelyn. She was a wild-eyed yet pathetic being: a filthy naked scavenger, claw-fingered, stinking, lank-haired. Anyone seeing her scraping away at earth mounds in the hope of finding insects or spiders would have winced in pity. Finally, in the middle of a moonlit night, she remembered what was in the house. Those who were watching saw a cunning look appear on her face, a sharp brightness come to her eyes. They knew that at last the abnormal hunger inside had told her exactly what was needed to satisfy the pangs.

She entered the house again, went straight to the bathroom.

Mantis-like, she crouched over the confectionery, devouring it slowly, piece by piece, satisfying the craving that plagued her belly.

When she had finished him they came to collect her.

*

She had questions. There were honest answers. There were also assurances from both sides that no one would ever say anything about the incident. They had their reasons for secrecy and she was certainly not going to tell anyone she had eaten her dead lover. And she now knew what Xavier had meant by *her time*. That had puzzled her at first and she had thought he must have meant something else. It was why he had waited, of course, to make love to her, knowing it could only be done once. On the flight home, her hands rested on her abdomen. She had made love with Tony many, many times without becoming pregnant, but the aliens of course had a different chemistry. The males could only do it once: it had to be a sure thing. What was essential to ensure conception, they had since told her, were the ingredients in the afterfood. She should feel no shame. Her baby depended upon it.

Her baby. How wonderful. *Her* baby.

She stared around her, trying not to feel smug. There were several other single women on board. Evelyn felt only slightly less special when she saw how rosy-cheeked and fulfilled one or two of them looked, just like the person she had seen in the mirror this morning.

Great Work of Time

JOHN CROWLEY

I: THE SINGLE EXCURSION OF CASPAR LAST

If what I am to set down is a chronicle, then it must differ from any other chronicle whatever, for it begins, not in one time or place, but everywhere at once – or perhaps *everywhen* is the better word. It might be begun at any point along the infinite, infinitely broken coastline of time.

It might even begin within the forest in the sea: huge trees like American redwoods, with their roots in the black benthos, and their leaves moving slowly in the blue currents overhead. There it might end as well.

It might begin in 1893 – or in 1983. Yes: it might be as well to begin with Last, in an American sort of voice (for we are all Americans now, aren't we?). Yes, Last shall be first: pale, fattish Caspar Last, on excursion in the springtime of 1983 to a far, far part of the Empire.

The tropical heat clothed Caspar Last like a suit as he disembarked from the plane. It was nearly as claustrophobic as the hours he had spent in the middle seat of a three-across, economy-class pew between two other cut-rate, one-week-excursion, plane-fare-and-hotel-room holiday-makers in monstrous good spirits. Like them, Caspar had taken the excursion because it was the cheapest possible way to get to and from this equatorial backwater. Unlike them, he hadn't come to soak up sun and molasses-dark rum. He didn't intend to spend all his time at the beach, or even within the twentieth century.

It had come down, in the end, to a matter of money. Caspar Last had never had money, though he certainly hadn't lacked the means to make it; with any application he could have made good money as a consultant to any of a dozen research firms, but that would have required a certain subjection of his time and thought to others, and Caspar was incapable of that. It's often said that genius can live in happy disregard of material circumstances, dress in rags, not notice its nourishment, and serve only its own abstract imperatives. This was Caspar's case, except that he wasn't happy about it: he was bothered, bitter, and rageful at his poverty. Fame he cared nothing for, success was meaningless except when defined as the solution to abstract problems. A great fortune would have been burdensome and useless. All he wanted was a nice bit of change.

He had decided, therefore, to use his 'time machine' once only, before it and the principles that animated it were destroyed, for good he hoped. (Caspar always thought of his 'time machine' thus, with scare-quotes around it, since it was not really a machine, and Caspar did not believe in time.) He would use it, he decided, to make money. Somehow.

The one brief annihilation of 'time' that Caspar intended to allow himself was in no sense a test run. He knew that his 'machine' would function as predicted. If he hadn't needed the money, he wouldn't use it at all. As far as he was concerned, the principles once discovered, the task was completed; like a completed jigsaw puzzle, it had no further interest; there was really nothing to do with it except gloat over it briefly and then sweep all the pieces randomly back into the box.

It was a mark of Caspar's odd genius that figuring out a scheme with which to make money out of the past (which was the only 'direction' his 'machine' would take him) proved almost as hard, given the limitations of his process, as arriving at the process itself.

He had gone through all the standard wish fulfilments and rejected them. He couldn't, armed with today's race results, return to yesterday and hit the daily double. For one thing it would take a couple of thousand in betting money to make it worth it, and Caspar didn't have a couple of thousand. More importantly, Caspar had calculated the results of his present self appearing at any point within the compass of his own biological existence, and those results made him shudder.

Similar difficulties attended any scheme that involved using money to make money. If he returned to 1940 and bought, say, two hundred shares of IBM for next to nothing: in the first place there would be the difficulty of leaving those shares somehow in escrow for his unborn self; there would be the problem of the alteration this growing fortune would have on the linear life he had actually lived; and where was he to acquire the five hundred dollars or whatever was needed in the currency of 1940? The same problem obtained if he wanted to return to 1623 and pick up a First Folio of Shakespeare, or to 1460 and a Gutenberg Bible: the cost of the currency he would need rose in relation to the antiquity, thus the rarity and value, of the object to be bought with it. There was also the problem of walking into a bookseller's and plunking down a First Folio he had just happened to stumble on while cleaning out the attic. In any case, Caspar doubted that anything as large as a book could be successfully transported 'through time.' He'd be lucky if he could go and return in his clothes.

Outside the airport, Caspar boarded a bus with his fellow excursionists, already hard at work with their cameras and index fingers as they rode through a sweltering lowland out of which concrete-block light industry was struggling to be born. The hotel in the capital was, as he expected, shoddy-American and intermittently refrigerated. He ceased to notice it, forwent the complimentary rum concoction promised with his tour, and after asking that his case be put in the hotel safe – extra charge for that, he noted bitterly – he went immediately to the Hall of Records in the government complex. The collection of old survey maps of the city and environs were more extensive than he had hoped. He spent most of that day among them searching for a blank place on the 1856 map, a place as naked as possible of buildings, brush, water, and that remained thus through the years. He discovered one, visited it by unmuffled taxi, found it suitable. It would save him from the awful inconvenience of 'arriving' in the 'past' and finding himself inserted into some local's wattle-and-daub wall. Next morning, then, he would be 'on his way.' If he had believed in time, he would have said that the whole process would take less than a day's time.

Before settling on this present plan, Caspar had toyed with the idea of bringing back from the past something immaterial: some knowledge, some secret that would allow him to make himself rich in his own present. Ships have gone down with millions in bullion: he could learn exactly where. Captain Kidd's treasure. Inca gold. Archaeological rarities buried in China. Leaving aside the obvious physical difficulties of these schemes, he couldn't be sure that their location wouldn't shift in the centuries between his glimpse of them and his 'real' life span; and even if he could be certain, no one else would have much reason to believe him, and he didn't have the wherewithal to raise expeditions himself. So all that was out.

He had a more general, theoretical problem to deal with. Of course the very presence of his eidolon in the past would alter, in however inconsequential a way, the succeeding history of the world. The comical paradoxes of shooting one's own grandfather and the like neither amused nor intrigued him, and the chance he took of altering the world he lived in out of all recognition was constantly present to him. Statistically, of course, the chance of this present plan of his altering anything significantly, except his own personal fortunes, was remote to a high power. But his scruples had caused him to reject anything such as, say, discovering the Koh-i-noor diamond before its historical discoverers. No: what he needed to abstract from the past was something immensely trivial, something common, something the past wouldn't miss but that the present held in the highest regard; something that would take the briefest possible time and the least irruption of himself into the past to acquire; something he could reasonably be believed to possess through simple historical chance; and something tiny enough to survive the cross-time 'journey' on his person.

It had come to him quite suddenly – all his ideas did, as though handed to him – when he learned that his great-great-grandfather had been a commercial traveller in the tropics, and that in the attic of his mother's house (which Caspar had never had the wherewithal to move out of) some old journals and papers of his still mouldered. They were, when he inspected them, completely without interest. But the dates were right.

Caspar had left a wake-up call at the desk for before dawn the next morning. There was some difficulty about getting his case out of the safe, and more difficulty about getting a substantial breakfast served at that hour (Caspar expected not to eat during his excursion), but he did arrive at his chosen site before the horrendous tropical dawn broke, and after paying the taxi, he had darkness enough left in which to make his preparations and change into his costume. The costume – a linen suit, a shirt, hat, boots – had cost him twenty dollars in rental from a theatrical costumer, and he could only hope it was accurate enough not to cause alarm in 1856. The last item he took from his case was the copper coin, which had cost him quite a bit, as he needed one unworn and of the proper date. He turned it in his fingers for a moment, thinking that if, unthinkably, his calculations were wrong and he didn't survive this journey, it would make an interesting obol for Charon.

Out of the unimaginable chaos of its interminable stochastic fiction, Time thrust only one unforeseen oddity on Caspar Last as he, or something like him, appeared beneath a plantain tree in 1856: he had grown a beard almost down to his waist. It was abominably hot.

The suburbs of the city had of course vanished. The road he stood by was a muddy track down which a cart was being driven by a tiny and close-faced Indian in calico. He followed the cart, and his costume boots were caked with mud when at last he came into the centre of town, trying to appear nonchalant and to remember the layout of the city as he had studied it in the maps. He wanted to speak to no one if possible, and he did manage to find the post office without affecting, however minutely, the heterogeneous crowd of blacks, Indians, and Europeans in the filthy streets. Having absolutely no sense of humour and very little imagination other than the most rigidly abstract helped to keep him strictly about his business and not to faint, as another might have, with wonder and astonishment at his translation, the first, last, and only of its kind a man would ever make.

'I would like,' he said to the mulatto inside the brass and mahogany cage, 'an envelope, please.'

'Of course, sir.'

'How long will it take for a letter mailed now to arrive locally?'

'Within the city? It would arrive in the afternoon post.'

'Very good.'

Caspar went to a long, ink-stained table, and with one of the steel pens provided, he addressed the envelope to Georg von Humboldt Last, Esq., Grand Hotel, City, in the approximation of an antique round hand that he had been practising for weeks. There was a moment's doubt as he tried to figure how to fold up and seal the cumbersome envelope, but he did it, and gave this empty missive to the incurious mulatto. He slipped his precious coin across the marble to him. For the only moment of his adventure, Caspar's heart beat fast as he watched the long, slow brown fingers affix a stamp, cancel and date it with a pen-stroke, and drop it into a brass slot like a hungry mouth behind him.

It only remained to check into the Grand Hotel, explain about his luggage's being on its way up from the port, and sit silent on the hotel terrace, growing faint with heat and hunger and expectation, until the afternoon post.

The one aspect of the process Caspar had never been able to decide about was whether his eidolon's residence in the fiction of the past would consume any 'time' in the fiction of the present. It did. When, at evening, with the letter held tight in his hand and pressed to his bosom, Caspar reappeared beardless beneath the plantain tree in the traffic-tormented and smoky suburb, the gaseous red sun was squatting on the horizon in the west, just as it had been in the same place in 1856.

He would have his rum drink after all, he decided.

'Mother,' he said, 'do you think there might be anything valuable in those papers of your great-grandfather's?'

'What papers, dear? Oh – I remember. I couldn't say. I thought once of donating them to a historical society. How do you mean, valuable?'

'Well, old stamps, for one thing.'

'You're free to look, Caspar dear.'

Caspar was not surprised (though he supposed the rest of the world was soon to be) that he found, among the faded, water-spotted diaries and papers, an envelope that bore a faint brown address – it had aged nicely in the next-to-no-time it had travelled 'forward' with Caspar – and that had in its upper right-hand corner a one-penny magenta stamp, quite undistinguished, issued for a brief time in 1856 by the Crown Colony of British Guiana.

The asking price of the sole known example of this stamp, a 'unique,' owned by a consortium of wealthy men who preferred to remain anonymous, was a million dollars. Caspar Last had not decided whether it would be more profitable for him to sell the stamp itself, or to approach the owners of the unique one, who would certainly pay a large amount to have it destroyed, and thus preserve their unique's uniqueness. It did seem a shame that the only artifact man had ever succeeded in extracting from the nonexistent past should go into the fire, but Caspar didn't really care. His own bonfire – the notes and printouts, the conclusions about the nature and transversability of time and the orthogonal logic by which it was accomplished – would be only a little more painful.

The excursion was over; the only one that remained to him was the brief but, to him, all-important one of his own mortal span. He was looking forward to doing it first class.

II: AN APPOINTMENT IN KHARTOUM

It might be begun very differently, though; and it might now be begun again, in a different time and place, like one of those romances by Stevenson, where different stories only gradually reveal themselves to be parts of a whole . . .

The paradox is acute, so acute that the only possible stance for a chronicler is to ignore it altogether, and carry on. This, the Otherhood's central resignation, required a habit of mind so contrary to ordinary cause-and-effect thinking as to be, literally, unimaginable. It would only have been in the changeless precincts of the Club they had established beyond all frames of reference, when deep in leather armchairs or seated all together around the long table whereon their names were carved, that they dared reflect on it at all.

Take, for a single but not a random instance, the example of Denys Winterset, twenty-three years old, Winchester, Oriel College, younger son of a well-to-do doctor and in 1956 ending a first year as assistant district commissioner of police in Bechuanaland.

He hadn't done strikingly well in his post. Though on the surface he was exactly the sort of man who was chosen, or who chose himself, to serve the Empire in those years – a respectable second at Oxford, a cricketer more steady than showy, a reserved, sensible, presentable lad with sound principles and few beliefs – still there was an odd strain in him. Too imaginative, perhaps; given to fits of abstraction, even to what his commissioner called 'tears, idle tears.' Still, he was resourceful and hardworking; he hadn't disgraced himself, and he was now on his way north on the Cape-to-Cairo Railroad, to take a month's holiday in Cairo and England. His anticipation was marred somewhat by a sense that, after a year in the veldt, he would no longer fit into the comfortable old shoe of his childhood home; that he would feel as odd and exiled as he had in Africa. Home had become a dream, in Bechuanaland; if, at home, Bechuanaland became a dream, then he would have no place real at all to be at home in; he would be an exile for good.

The high veldt sped away as he was occupied with these thoughts, the rich farmlands of Southern Rhodesia. In the saloon car a young couple, very evidently on honeymoon, watched expectantly for the first glimpse of the eternal rainbow, visible miles off, that haloed Victoria Falls. Denys watched them and their excitement, feeling old and wise. Americans, doubtless: they had that shy, inoffensive air of all Americans abroad, that wondering quality as of children let out from a dark and oppressive school to play in the sun.

'There!' said the woman as the train took a bend. 'Oh, look, how beautiful!'

Even over the train's sound they could hear the sound of the falls now, like distant cannon. The young man looked at his watch and smiled at Denys. 'Right on time,' he said, and Denys smiled too, amused to be complimented on his railroad's efficiency. The Bulawayo Bridge – longest and highest span on the Cape-to-Cairo line – leapt out over the gorge. 'My God, that's something,' the young man said. 'Cecil Rhodes built this, right?'

'No,' Denys said. 'He thought of it, but never lived to see it. It would have been far easier to build it a few miles up, but Rhodes pictured the train being washed in the spray of the falls as it passed. And so it was built here.'

The noise of the falls was immense now, and weirdly various, a medley of cracks, thumps, and explosions playing over the constant bass roar, which was not so much like a noise at all as it was like an eternal deep-drawn breath. And as the train chugged out across the span, aimed at Cairo thousands of miles away, passing here the place so hard-sought-for a hundred years ago – the place where the Nile had its origin – the spray *did* fall on the train just as Cecil Rhodes had imagined it, flung spindrift hissing on the locomotive, drops speckling the window they looked out of and rainbowing in the white air. The young Americans were still with wonder, and Denys, too, felt a lifting of his heart.

At Khartoum, Denys bid the honeymooners farewell: they were taking the Empire Airways flying boat from here to Gibraltar, and the Atlantic dirigible home. Denys, by now feeling quite proprietary about his Empire's transportation services, assured them that both flights would also certainly be right on time, and would be as comfortable as the sleepers they were leaving, would serve the same excellent meals with the same white napery embossed with the same royal insignia. Denys himself was driven to the Grand Hotel. His Sudan Railways sleeper to Cairo left the next morning.

After a bath in a tiled tub large enough almost to swim in, Denys changed into dinner clothes (which had been carefully laid out for him on the huge bed – for whom had these cavernous rooms been built, a race of Kitcheners?). He reserved a table for one in the grill room and went down to the bar. One thing he *must* do in London, he thought, shooting his cuffs, was to visit his tailor. Bechuanaland had sweated off his college baby fat, and the tropics seemed to have turned his satin lapels faintly green.

The bar was comfortably filled, before the dinner hour, with men of several sorts and a few women, and with the low various murmur of their talk. Some of the men wore *white* dinner jackets – businessmen and tourists, Denys supposed – and a few even wore shorts with black shoes and stockings, a style Denys found inherently funny, as though a tailor had made a frightful error and cut evening clothes to the pattern of bush clothes. He ordered a whisky.

Rarely in African kraals or in his bungalow or his whitewashed office did Denys think about his Empire: or if he did, it was in some local, even irritated way, of Imperial trivialities or Imperial red tape, the rain-rusted engines and stacks of tropic-mildewed paperwork that, collectively, Denys and his young associates called the White Man's

Burden. It seemed to require a certain remove from the immediacy of Empire before he could perceive it. Only here (beneath the fans' ticking, amid the voices naming places – Kandahar, Durban, Singapore, Penang) did the larger Empire that Denys had never seen but had lived in in thought and feeling since childhood open in his mind. How odd, how far more odd really than admirable or deplorable that the small place which was his childhood, circumscribed and cozy – grey Westminster, chilly Trafalgar Square of the black umbrellas, London of the coal-smoked wallpaper and endless chimney pots – should have opened itself out so ceaselessly and for so long into huge hot places, subcontinents where rain never fell or never stopped, lush with vegetable growth or burdened with seas of sand or stone. Send forth the best ye breed: or at least large numbers of those ye breed. If one thought how odd it was – and if one thought then of what should have been natural empires, enormous spreads of restless real property like America or Russia turning in on themselves, making themselves into what seemed (to Denys, who had never seen them) to be very small places: then it did seem to be Destiny of a kind. Not a Destiny to be proud of, particularly, nor ashamed of either, but one whose compelling inner logic could only be marvelled at.

Quite suddenly, and with poignant vividness, Denys saw himself, or rather felt himself once more to be, before his nursery fire, looking into the small glow of it, with animal crackers and cocoa for tea, listening to Nana telling tales of her brother the sergeant, and the Afghan frontier, and the now-dead king he served – listening, and feeling the Empire ranged in widening circles around him: first Harley Street, outside the window, and then Buckingham Palace, where the king lived; and the country then into which the trains went, and then the cold sea, and the Possessions, and the Commonwealth, stretching ever farther outward, worldwide: but always with his small glowing fire and his comfort and wonder at the heart of it.

So, there he is: a young man with the self-possessed air of an older man, in evening clothes aged prematurely in places where evening clothes had not been made to go; thinking, if it could be called thinking, of a nursery fire; and about to be spoken to by the man next down the bar. If his feelings could be summed up and spoken, they were that, however odd, there is nothing more real, more pinioned by acts great and small, more clinker-built of time and space and filled brimful of this and that, than is the real world in which his five senses and his memories had their being; and that this was deeply satisfying.

'I beg your pardon,' said the man next down the bar.

'Good evening,' Denys said.

'My name is Davenant,' the man said. He held out a square, blunt-fingered hand, and Denys drew himself up and shook it. 'You are, I believe, Denys Winterset?'

'I am,' Denys said, searching the smiling face before him and wondering from where he was known to him. It was a big, square, high-fronted head, a little like Bernard Shaw's, with ice-blue eyes of that twinkle; it was crowned far back with a neat hank of white hair, and was crossed above the broad jaw with upright white moustaches.

'You don't mind the intrusion?' the man said. 'I wonder if you know whether the grub here is as good as once it was. It's been some time since I last ate a meal in Khartoum.'

'The last time I did so was a year ago this week,' Denys said. 'It was quite good.'

'Excellent,' said Davenant, looking at Denys as though something about the young man amused him. 'In that case, if you have no other engagement, may I ask your company?'

'I have no other engagement,' Denys said; in fact he had rather been looking forward to dining alone, but deference to his superiors (of whom this man Davenant was surely in some sense one) was strong in him. 'Tell me, though, how you come to know my name.'

'Oh, well, there it is,' Davenant said. 'One has dealings with the Colonial Office. One sees a face, a name is attached to it, one files it but doesn't forget – that sort of thing. Part of one's job.'

A civil servant, an inspector of some kind. Denys felt the sinking one feels on running into one's tutor in a wine bar: the evening not well begun. 'They may well be crowded for dinner,' he said.

'I have reserved a quiet table,' said the smiling man, lifting his glass to Denys.

The grub was, in fact, superior. Sir Geoffrey Davenant was an able teller of tales, and he had many to tell. He was, apparently, no such dull thing as an inspector for the Colonial Office, though just what office he did fill Denys couldn't determine. He seemed to have been 'attached to' or 'had dealings with' or 'gone about for' half the establishments of the Empire. He embodied, it seemed to Denys, the entire strange adventure about which Denys had been thinking when Sir Geoffrey had first spoken to him.

'So,' Sir Geoffrey said, filling their glasses from a bottle of South African claret – no harm in being patriotic, he'd said, for one bottle – 'so, after some months of stumbling about Central Asia and making myself useful one way or another, I was to make my way back to Sadiya. I crossed the Tibetan frontier disguised as a monk – '

'A monk?'

'Yes. Having lost all my gear in Manchuria, I could do the poverty part quite well. I had a roll of rupees, the films, and a compass hidden inside my prayer wheel. Mine didn't whiz around then with the same sanctity as the other fellows', but no matter. After adventures too ordinary to describe – avalanches and so on – I managed to reach the monastery at Rangbok, on the old road up to Everest. Rather near collapse. I was recovering a bit and thinking how to proceed when there came a runner with a telegram. From my superior at Ch'eng-tu. WARN DAVENANT MASSACRE SADIYA, it said. The Old Man then was famously close-mouthed. But this was particularly unhelpful, as it did not say who had massacred whom – or why.' He lifted the silver cover of a dish, and found it empty.

'This must have been a good long time ago,' Denys said.

'Oh, yes,' Davenant said, raising his ice-blue eyes to Denys. 'A good long time ago. That was an excellent curry. Nearly as good as at Veeraswamy's, in London – which is, strangely, the best in the world. Shall we have coffee?'

Over this, and brandy and cigars, Sir Geoffrey's stories modulated into reflections. Pleasant as his company was, Denys couldn't overcome a sensation that everything Sir Geoffrey said to him was rehearsed, laid on for his entertainment, or perhaps his enlightenment, and yet with no clue in it as to why he had thus been singled out.

'It amuses me,' Sir Geoffrey said, 'how constant it is in human nature to think that things might have gone on differently from the way they did. In a man's own life, first of all: how he might have taken this or that very different route, except for this or that accident, this or that slight push – if he'd only known then, and so on. And then in history as well, we ruminate endlessly, if, what if, if only . . . The world seems always somehow malleable to our minds, or to our imaginations anyway.'

'Strange you should say so,' Denys said. 'I was thinking, just before you spoke to me, about how very solid the world seems to me, how very – real. And – if you don't mind my thrusting it into your thoughts – you never did tell me how it is you come to know my name; or why it is you thought good to invite me to that excellent dinner.'

'My dear boy,' Davenant said, holding up his cigar as though to defend his innocence.

'I can't think it was chance.'

'My dear boy,' Davenant said in a different tone, 'if anything is, that was not. I will explain all. You were on that train of thought. If you will have patience while it trundles by.'

Denys said nothing further. He sipped his coffee, feeling a dew of sweat on his forehead.

'History,' said Sir Geoffrey. 'Yes. Of course the possible worlds we make don't compare to the real one we inhabit – not nearly so well furnished, or tricked out with details. And yet still somehow better. More satisfying. Perhaps the novelist is only a special case of a universal desire to reshape, to "take this sorry scheme of things entire," smash it into bits, and "remould it nearer to the heart's desire" – as old Khayyám says. The egoist is continually doing it with his own life. To dream of doing it with history is no more useful a game, I suppose, but as a game, it shows more sport. There are rules. You can be more objective, if that's an appropriate word.' He seemed to grow pensive for a moment. He looked at the end of his cigar. It had gone out, but he didn't relight it.

'Take this Empire,' he went on, drawing himself up somewhat to say it. 'One doesn't want to be mawkish, but one has served it. Extended it a bit, made it more secure; done one's bit. You and I. Nothing more natural, then, if we have worked for its extension in the future, to imagine its extension in the past. We can put our finger on the occasional bungle, the missed chance, the wrong man in the wrong place, and so on, and we think: if I had only been there, seen to it that the news went through, got the guns there in time, forced the issue at a certain moment – well. But as long as one is dreaming, why stop? A favourite instance of mine is the American civil war. We came very close, you know, to entering that war on the Confederacy's side.'

'Did we?'

'I think we did. Suppose we had. Suppose we had at first dabbled – sent arms – ignored Northern protests – then got deeper in; suppose the North declared war on us. It seems to me a near certainty that if we had entered the war fully, the South would have won. And I think a British presence would have mitigated the slaughter. There was a point, you know, late in that war, when a new draft call in the North was met with terrible riots. In New York several Negroes were hanged, just to show how little their cause was felt.'

Denys had partly lost the thread of this story, unable to imagine himself in it. He thought of the Americans he had met on the train. 'Is that so,' he said.

'Once having divided the States into two nations, and having helped the South to win, we would have been in place, you see. The fate of the West had not yet been decided. With the North much diminished in power – well, I imagine that by now we, the Empire, would have recouped much of what we lost in 1780.'

Denys contemplated this. 'Rather stirring,' he said mildly. 'Rather cold-blooded, too. Wouldn't it have meant condoning slavery? To say nothing of the lives lost. British, I mean.'

'Condoning slavery – for a time. I've no doubt the South could have been bullied out of it. Without, perhaps, the awful results that accompanied the Northerners doing it. The eternal resentment. The blacklash. The near genocide of the last hundred years. And, in my vision, there would have been a net savings in red men.' He smiled. 'Whatever might be said against it, the British Empire does not wipe out populations wholesale, as the Americans did in their West. I often wonder if that sin isn't what makes the Americans so gloomy now, so introverted.'

Denys nodded. He believed implicitly that his Empire did not wipe out populations wholesale. 'Of course,' he said, 'there's no telling what exactly would have been the result. If we'd interfered as you say.'

'No,' Sir Geoffrey said. 'No doubt whatever result it *did* have would have to be reshaped as well. And the results of that reshaping reshaped, too, the whole thing subtly guided all along its way towards the result desired – after all, if we can imagine how we might want to alter the past we do inherit, so we can imagine that any past might well be liable to the same imagining; that stupidities, blunders, shortsightedness, would occur in any past we might initiate. Oh, yes, it would all have to be reshaped, with each reshaping . . .'

'The possibilities are endless,' Denys said, laughing. 'I'm afraid the game's beyond me. I say let the North win – since in any case we can't do the smallest thing about it.'

'No,' Davenant said, grown sad again, or reflective; he seemed to feel what Denys said deeply. 'No, we can't. It's just – just too long ago.' With great gravity he relit his cigar. Denys, at the oddness of this response, seeing Sir Geoffrey's eyes veiled, thought: *Perhaps he's mad.* He said, joining the game, 'Suppose, though. Suppose Cecil Rhodes hadn't died young, as he did. . . .'

Davenant's eyes caught cold fire again, and his cigar paused in midair. 'Hm?' he said with interest.

'I only meant,' Denys said, 'that your remark about the British not wiping out peoples wholesale was perhaps not tested. If Rhodes had lived to build his empire – hadn't he already named it Rhodesia – I imagine he would have dealt fairly harshly with the natives.'

'Very harshly,' said Sir Geoffrey.

'Well,' Denys said, 'I suppose I mean that it's not always evil effects that we inherit from these past accidents.'

'Not at all,' said Sir Geoffrey. Denys looked away from his regard, which had grown, without losing a certain cool humour, intense. 'Do you know, by the way, that remark of George Santayana – the American philosopher – about the British Empire, about young men like yourself? "Never," he said, "never since the Athenians has the world been ruled by such sweet, just, boyish masters."'

Denys, absurdly, felt himself flush with embarrassment.

'I don't ramble,' Sir Geoffrey said. 'My trains of thought carry odd goods, but all headed the same way. I want to tell you something, about that historical circumstance, the one you've touched on, whose effects we inherit. Evil or good I will leave you to decide.

'Cecil Rhodes died prematurely, as you say. But not before he had amassed a very great fortune, and laid firm claims to the ground where that fortune would grow far greater. And also not before he had made a will disposing of that fortune.'

'I've heard stories,' Denys said.

'The stories you have heard are true. Cecil Rhodes, at his death, left his entire fortune, and its increase, to found and continue a secret society which should, by whatever means possible, preserve and extend the British Empire. His entire fortune.'

'I have never believed it,' Denys said, momentarily feeling untethered, like a balloon: afloat.

'For good reason,' Davenant said. 'If such a society as I describe were brought into being, its very first task would be to disguise, cast doubt upon, and quite bury its origins. Don't you think that's so? In any case it's true what I say: the society was founded; is secret; continues to exist; is responsible, in some large degree at least, for the Empire we now know, in this year of grace 1956, IV Elizabeth II, the Empire on which the sun does not set.'

The veranda where the two men sat was nearly deserted now; the night was loud with tropical noises that Denys had come to think of as silence, but the human noise of the town had nearly ceased.

'You can't know that,' Denys said. 'If you knew it, if you were privy to it, then you wouldn't say it. Not to me.' He almost added: *Therefore you're not in possession of any secret, only a madman's certainty.*

'I *am* privy to it,' Davenant said. 'I am myself a member. The reason I reveal the secret to you – and you see, here we are, come to you and my odd knowledge of you, at last, as I promised – the reason I reveal it to you is because I wish to ask you to join it. To accept from me an offer of membership.'

Denys said nothing. A dark waiter in white crept close, and was waved away by Sir Geoffrey.

'You are quite properly silent,' Sir Geoffrey said. 'Either I am mad, you think, in which case there is nothing to say; or what I am telling you is true, which likewise leaves you nothing to say. Quite proper. In your place I would be silent also. In your place I was. In any case I have no intention of pressing you for an answer now. I happen to know, by a roundabout sort of means that if I explained to you would certainly convince you I was mad, that you will seriously consider what I've said to you. Later. On your long ride to Cairo: there will be time to think. In London. I ask nothing from you now. Only . . .'

He reached into his waistcoat pocket. Denys watched, fascinated: would he draw out some sign of power, a royal charter, some awesome seal? No: it was a small metal plate, with a strip of brown ribbon affixed to it, like a bit of recording tape. He turned it in his hands thoughtfully. 'The difficulty, you see, is that in order to alter history and bring it closer to the heart's desire, it would be necessary to stand outside it altogether. Like Archimedes, who said that if he had a lever long enough, and a place to stand, he could move the world.'

He passed the metal plate to Denys, who took it reluctantly.

'A place to stand, you see,' Sir Geoffrey said. 'A place to stand. I would like you to keep that plate about you, and not misplace it. It's in the nature of a key, though it mayn't look it; and it will let you into a very good London club, though it mayn't look it either, where I would like you to call on me. If, even out of simple curiosity, you would like to hear more of us.' He extinguished his cigar. 'I am going to describe the rather complicated way in which that key is to be used – I really do apologize for the hugger-mugger, but you will come to understand – and then I am going to bid you good evening. Your train is an early one? I thought so. My own departs at midnight. I possess a veritable Bradshaw's of the world's railways in this skull. Well. No more. I will just sign this – oh, don't thank me. Dear boy: don't thank me.'

When he was gone, Denys sat a long time with his cold cigar in his hand and the night around him. The amounts of wine and brandy he had been given seemed to have evaporated from him into the humid air, leaving him feeling cool, clear, and unreal. When at last he rose to go, he inserted the flimsy plate into his waistcoat pocket; and before he went to bed, to lie a long time awake, he changed it to the waistcoat pocket of the pale suit he would wear next morning.

As Sir Geoffrey suggested he would, he thought on his ride north of all that he had been told, trying to reassemble it in some more reasonable, more everyday fashion: as all day long beside the train the sempiternal Nile – camels, nomads, women washing in the barge canals, the thin line of palms screening the white desert beyond – slipped past. At evening, when at length he lowered the shade of his compartment window on the poignant blue sky pierced with stars, he thought suddenly: But how could he have known he would find me there, at the bar of the Grand, on that night of this year, at that hour of the evening, just as though we had some long-standing agreement to meet there?

If anything is chance, Davenant had said, that was not.

At the airfield at Ismailia there was a surprise: his flight home on the R101, which his father had booked months ago as a special treat for Denys, was to be that grand old airship's last scheduled flight. The oldest airship in the British fleet, commissioned in the year Denys was born, was to be – mothballed? Dry-docked? Deflated? Denys wondered just what one did with a decommissioned airship larger than Westminster Cathedral.

Before dawn it was drawn from its great hangar by a crowd of white-clothed fellahin pulling at its ropes – descendants, Denys thought, of those who had pulled ropes at the Pyramids three thousand years ago, employed now on an object almost as big but lighter than air. It isn't because it is so intensely romantic that great airships must always arrive or depart at dawn or at evening, but only that then the air is cool and most likely to be still: and yet intensely romantic it remains. Denys, standing at the broad, canted windows, watched the ground recede – magically, for there was no sound of engines, no jolt to indicate liftoff, only the waving, cheering fellahin growing smaller. The band on the tarmac played 'Land of Hope and Glory.' Almost invisible to watchers on the ground – because of its heat-reflective silver dome – the immense ovoid turned delicately in the wind as it arose.

'Well, it's the end of an era,' a red-faced man in a checked suit said to Denys. 'In ten years they'll all be gone, these big airships. The propeller chaps will have taken over; and the jet aeroplane, too, I shouldn't wonder.'

'I should be sorry to see that,' Denys said. 'I've loved airships since I was a boy.'

'Well, they're just that little bit slower,' the red-faced man said sadly. 'It's all hurry-up, nowadays. Faster, faster. And for what? I put it to you: for what?'

Now with further gentle pushes of its Rolls-Royce engines, the R101 altered its attitude again; passengers at the lounge windows pointed out the Suez Canal, and the ships passing; Lake Mareotis; Alexandria, like a mirage; British North Africa, as far to the left as one cared to point; and the white-fringed sea. Champagne was being called for, traditional despite the hour, and the red-faced man pressed a glass on Denys.

'The end of an era,' he said again, raising his flute of champagne solemnly.

And then the cloudscape beyond the windows shifted, and all Africa had slipped into the south, or into the imaginary, for they had already begun to seem the same thing to Denys. He turned from the windows and decided – the effort to decide it seemed not so great here aloft, amid the potted palms and the wicker, with this pale champagne – that the conversation he had had down in the flat lands far away must have been imaginary as well.

III: THE TALE OF THE PRESIDENT *pro tem*

The universe proceeds out of what it has been and into what it will be, inexorably, unstoppably, at the rate of one second per second, one year per year, forever. At right angles to its forward progress lie the past and the future. The future, that is to say, does not lie 'ahead' of the present in the stream of time, but at a right angle to it: the future of any present moment can be projected as far as you like outward from it, infinitely in fact, but when the universe has proceeded further, and a new present moment has succeeded this one, the future of this one retreats with it into the what-has-been, forever outdated. It is similar but more complicated with the past.

Now within the great process or procession that the universe makes, there can be no question of 'movement,' either 'forward' or 'back.' The very idea is contradictory. Any conceivable movement is into the orthogonal futures and pasts that fluoresce from the universe as it is; and from those orthogonal futures and pasts into others, and others, and still others, never returning, always moving at right angles to the stream of time. To the traveller, therefore, who does not ever return from the futures or pasts into which he has gone, it must appear that the times he inhabits grow progressively more remote from the stream of time that generated them, the stream that has since moved on and left his futures behind. Indeed, the longer he remains in the future, the farther off the traveller gets from the moment in actuality whence he started, and the less like actuality the universe he stands in seems to him to be.

It was thoughts of this sort, only inchoate as yet and with the necessary conclusions not yet drawn, that occupied the mind of the President *pro tem* of the Otherhood as he walked the vast length of an iron and glass railway station in the capital city of an aged empire. He stopped to take a cigar case from within the black Norfolk overcoat he wore, and a cigar from the case; this he lit, and with its successive blue clouds hanging lightly about his hat and head, he walked on. There were hominids at work on the glossy engines of the empire's trains that came and went from this terminus; hominids pushing with their long strong arms the carts burdened with the goods and luggage that the trains were to carry; hominids of other sorts, gathered in groups or standing singly at the barricades, clutched their tickets, waiting to depart, some aided by or waited upon by other species – too few creatures, in all, to dispel the extraordinary impression of smoky empty hugeness that the cast-iron arches of the shed made.

The President *pro tem* was certain, or at any rate retained a distinct impression, that at his arrival some days before there were telephones available for citizens to use, in the streets, in public places such as this (he seemed to see an example in his mind, a wooden box whose bright veneer was loosening in the damp climate, a complex instrument within, of enamelled steel and heavy celluloid); but if there ever had been, there were none now. Instead he went in at a door above which a yellow globe was alight, a winged foot etched upon it. He chose a telegraph form from a stack of them on a long scarred counter, and with the scratchy pen provided he dashed off a quick note to the Magus in whose apartments he had been staying, telling him that he had returned late from the country and would not be with him till evening.

This missive he handed in at the grille, paying what was asked in large coins; then he went out, up the brass-railed stairs, and into the afternoon, into the quiet and familiar city.

It was the familiarity that had been, from the beginning, the oddest thing. The President *pro tem* was a man who, in the long course of his work for the Otherhood, had become accustomed to stepping out of his London club into a world not quite the same as the world he had left to enter that club. He was used to finding himself in a London – or a Lahore or a Laos – stripped of well-known monuments, with public buildings and private ways unknown to him, and a newspaper (bought with an unfamiliar coin found in his pocket) full of names that should not have been there, or missing events that should have been. But here – where nothing, nothing at all, was as he had known it, no trace remaining of the history he had come from – here where no man should have been able to take steps, where even Caspar Last had thought it not possible to take steps – the President *pro tem* could not help but feel easy: had felt easy from the beginning. He walked up the cobbled streets, his furled umbrella over his shoulder, troubled by nothing but the weird grasp that this unknown dark city had on his heart.

The rain that had somewhat spoiled his day in the country had ceased but had left a pale, still mist over the city, a humid atmosphere that gave to views down avenues a stage-set quality, each receding rank of buildings fainter, more vaguely executed. Trees, too, huge and weeping, still and featureless as though painted on successive scrims. At the great gates, topped with garlanded urns, of a public park, the President *pro tem* looked in towards the piled and sounding waters of a fountain and the dim towers of poplar trees. And as he stood resting on his umbrella, lifting the last of the cigar to his lips, someone passed by him and entered the park.

For a moment the President *pro tem* stood unmoving, thinking what an attractive person (boy? girl?) that had been, and how the smile paid to him in passing seemed to indicate a knowledge of him, a knowledge that gave pleasure or at least amusement; then he dropped his cigar end and passed through the gates through which the figure had gone.

That had *not* been a hominid who had smiled at him. It was not a Magus and surely not one of the draconics either. Why he was sure he could not have said: for the same unsayable reason that he knew this city in this world, this park, these marble urns, these leaf-littered paths. He was sure that the person he had seen belonged to a different species from himself, and different also from the other species who lived in this world.

At the fountain where the paths crossed, he paused, looking this way and that, his heart beating hard and filled absurdly with a sense of loss. The child (had it been a child?) was gone, could not be seen that way, or that way – but then was there again suddenly, down at the end of a yew alley, loitering, not looking his way. Thinking at first to sneak up on her, or him, along the sheltering yews, the President *pro tem* took a sly step that way; then, ashamed, he thought better of it and set off down the path at an even pace, as one would approach a young horse or a tame deer. The one he walked towards took no notice of him, appeared lost in thought, eyes cast down.

Indescribably lovely, the President *pro tem* thought: and yet at the same time negligent and easeful and ordinary. Barefoot, or in light sandals of some kind, light pale clothing that seemed to be part of her, like a bird's dress – and a wristwatch, incongruous, yet not really incongruous at all: someone for whom incongruity was inconceivable. A reverence – almost a holy dread – came over the President *pro tem* as he came closer: as though he had stumbled into a sacred grove. Then the one he walked towards looked up at him, which caused the President *pro tem* to stop still as if a gun had casually been turned on him.

He was known, he understood, to this person. She, or he, stared unembarrassed at the President *pro tem*, with a gaze of the most intense and yet impersonal tenderness, of compassion and amusement and calm interest all mixed; and almost imperceptibly shook her head *no* and smiled again: and the President *pro tem* lowered his eyes, unable to meet that gaze. When he looked up again, the person was gone.

Hesitantly the President *pro tem* walked to the end of the avenue of yews and looked in all directions. No one. A kind of fear flew over him, felt in his breast like the beat of departing wings. He seemed to know, for the first time, what those encounters with gods had been like, when there had been gods; encounters he had puzzled out of the Greek in school.

Anyway he was alone now in the park: he was sure of that. At length he found his way out again into the twilight streets.

By evening he had crossed the city and was climbing the steps of a tall town house, searching in his pockets for the key given him. Beside the varnished door was a small plaque, which said that within were the offices of the Orient Aid Society; but this was not in fact the case. Inside was a tall foyer; a glass-panelled door let him into a hallway wainscoted in dark wood. A pile of gumboots and rubber overshoes in a corner, macs and umbrellas on an ebony tree. Smells of tea, done with, and dinner cooking: a stew, an apple tart, a roast fowl. The tulip-shaped gas lamps along the hall were lit.

He let himself into the library at the hall's end; velvet armchairs regarded the coal fire, and on a drum table a tray of tea things consorted with the books and the papers. The President *pro tem* went to the low shelves that ran beneath the windows and drew out one volume of an old encyclopaedia, buckram-bound, with marbled fore-edges and illustrations in brownish photogravure.

The Races. For some reason the major headings and certain other words were in the orthography he knew, but not the closely printed text. His fingers ran down the columns, which were broken into numbered sections headed by the names of species and subspecies. *Hominidae*, with three subspecies. *Draconiidae*, with four: here were etchings of skulls. And lastly *Sylphidae*, with an uncertain number of subspecies. Sylphidae, the Sylphids. Fairies.

'Angels,' said a voice behind him. The President *pro tem* turned to see the Magus whose guest he was, recently risen no doubt, in a voluminous dressing gown richly figured. His beard and hair were so long and fine they seemed to float on the currents of air in the room, like filaments of thistledown.

'"Angels," is that what you call them?'

'What they would have themselves called,' said the Magus. 'What name they call themselves, among themselves, no one knows but they.'

'I think I met with one this evening.'

'Yes.'

There was no photogravure to accompany the subsection on Sylphidae in the encyclopaedia. 'I'm sure I met with one.'

'They are gathering, then.'

'Not . . . not because of me?'

'Because of you.'

'How, though,' said the President *pro tem*, feeling again within him the sense of loss, of beating wings departing, 'how, how could they have known, how . . .'

The Magus turned away from him to the fire, to the armchairs and the drum table. The President *pro tem* saw that beside one chair a glass of whisky had been placed, and an ashtray. 'Come,' said the Magus. 'Sit, Continue your tale. It will perhaps become clear to you: perhaps not.' He sat then himself, and without looking back at the President *pro tem* he said: 'Shall we go on?'

The President *pro tem* knew it was idle to dispute with his host. He did stand unmoving for the space of several heartbeats. Then he took his chair, drew the cigar case from his pocket, and considered where he had left off his tale in the dark of the morning.

'Of course,' he said then, 'Last knew: he knew, without admitting it to himself, as a good orthogonist must never do, that the world he had returned to from his excursion was not the world he had left. The past he had passed through on his way back was not "behind" his present at all, but at a right angle to it; the future of that past, which he had to traverse in order to get back again, was not the same road, and "back" was not where he got. The frame house on Maple Street which, a little sunburned, he re-entered on his return was twice removed in reality from the one he had left a week before; the mother he kissed likewise.

'He knew that, for it was predicated by orthogonal logic, and orthogonal logic was in fact what Last had discovered – the transversability of time was only an effect of that discovery. He knew it, and despite his glee over his triumph, he kept his eye open. Sooner or later he would come upon something, something that would betray the fact that this world was not his.

'He could not have guessed it would be me.'

The Magus did not look at the President *pro tem* as he was told this story; his pale grey eyes instead wandered from object to object around the great dark library but seemed to see none of them; what, the

President *pro tem* wondered, did they see? He had at first supposed the race of Magi to be blind, from this habitual appearance of theirs; he now knew quite well that they were not blind, not blind at all.

'Go on,' the Magus said.

'So,' said the President *pro tem*, 'Last returns from his excursion. A week passes uneventfully. Then one morning he hears his mother call: he has a visitor. Last, pretending annoyance at this interruption of his work (actually he was calculating various forms of compound interest on a half million dollars), comes to the door. There on the step is a figure in tweeds and a bowler hat, leaning on a furled umbrella: me.

'"Mr Last," I said. "I think we have business."

'You could see by his expression that he knew I should not have been there, should not have had business with him at all. He really ought to have refused to see me. A good deal of trouble might have been saved if he had. There was no way I could force him, after all. But he didn't refuse; after a goggle-eyed moment he brought me in, up a flight of stairs (Mama waiting anxiously at the bottom), and into his study.

'Geniuses are popularly supposed to live in an atmosphere of the greatest confusion and untidiness, but this wasn't true of Last. The study – it was his bedroom, too – was of a monkish neatness. There was no sign that he worked there, except for a computer terminal, and even it was hidden beneath a cosy that Mama had made for it and Caspar had not dared to spurn.

'He was trembling slightly, poor fellow, and had no idea of the social graces. He only turned to me – his eyeglasses were the kind that oddly diffract the eyes behind and make them unmeetable – and said, "What do you want?"'

The President *pro tem* caressed the ashtray with the tip of his cigar. He had been offered no tea, and he felt the lack. 'We engaged in some preliminary fencing,' he continued. 'I told him what I had come to acquire. He said he didn't know what I was talking about. I said I thought he did. He laughed and said there must be some mistake. I said, no mistake, Mr Last. At length he grew silent, and I could see even behind those absurd goggles that he had begun to try to account for me.

'Thinking out the puzzles of orthogonal logic, you see, is not entirely unlike puzzling out moves in chess: theoretically chess can be played by patiently working out the likely consequences of each move, and the consequences of those consequences, and so on; but in fact it is not so played, certainly not by master players. Masters seem to have a more immediate apprehension of possibilities, an almost visceral understanding of the, however rigorously mathematical, logic of the board and pieces, an understanding that they can act on without being able necessarily to explain. Whatever sort of mendacious and feckless fool Caspar Last was in many ways, he was a genius in one or two, and orthogonal logic was one of them.

'"From when," he said, "have you come?"

'"From not far on," I answered. He sat then, resigned, stuck in a sort of check impossible to think one's way out of, yet not mated. "Then," he said, "go back the same way you came."

'"I cannot," I said, "until you explain to me how it is done."

'"You know how," he said, "if you can come here to ask me."

'"Not until you have explained it to me. Now or later."

'"I never will," he said.

'"You will," I said. "You will have done already, before I leave. Otherwise I would not be here now asking. Let us," I said, and took a seat myself, "let us assume these preliminaries have been gone through, for they have been of course, and move ahead to the bargaining. My firm are prepared to make you a quite generous offer."

'That was what convinced him that he must, finally, give up to us the processes he had discovered, which he really had firmly intended to destroy forever: the fact that I had come there to ask for them. Which meant that he had already somehow, somewhen, already yielded them up to us.'

The President *pro tem* paused again, and lifted his untouched whisky. 'It was the same argument,' he said, 'the same incontrovertible argument, that was used to convince me once, too, to do a dreadful thing.'

He drank, thoughtfully, or at least (he supposed) appearing thoughtful; more and more often as he grew older it happened that in the midst of an anecdote, a relation, even one of supreme importance, he would begin to forget what it was he was telling; the terrifically improbable events would begin to seem not only improbable but fictitious, without insides, the incidents and characters as false as in any tawdry cinema story, even his own part in them unreal: as though they happened to someone made up – certainly not to him who told them. Often enough he forgot the plot.

'You see,' he said, 'Last exited from a universe in which travel "through time" was, apparently, either not possible, or possible only under conditions that would allow such travel to go undetected. That was apparent from the fact that no one, so far as Last knew, up to the time of his own single excursion, had ever detected it going on. No one, from Last's own future that is, had ever come "back" and disrupted his present, or the past of his present: never ever. Therefore, if his excursion could take place, and he could "return," he would have to return to a different universe: a universe where time travel *had* taken place, a universe in which once-upon-a-time a man from 1983 had managed to insert himself into a minor colony of the British Crown one hundred and twenty-seven years earlier. What he couldn't know in advance was whether the universe he "returned" to was one where time travel was a commonplace, an everyday occurrence, something, anyway, that could deprive his excursion of the value it had; or whether it was one in which one excursion only had taken place, his own. My appearance before him convinced him that it was, or was about to become, common enough: common enough to disturb his own peace and quiet, and alter in unforeseeable ways his comfortable present.

'There was only one solution, or one dash at a solution anyway. I might, myself, be a singularity in Last's new present. It was therefore possible that if he could get rid of me, I would take his process "away" with me into whatever future I had come out of to get it, and thereupon never be able to find my way again to his present and disturb it or him. Whatever worlds I altered, they would not be his, not his anyway who struck the bargain with me: if each of them also contained a Last, who would suffer or flourish in ways unimaginable to the Last to whom I spoke, then those eidolons would have to make terms for themselves, that's all. The quantum angle obtruded by my coming, and then the one obtruded by my returning, divorced all those Lasts from him for all eternity: that is why, though the angle itself is virtually infinitesimal, it has always to be treated as a right angle.

'Last showed me, on his computer, after our bargain was struck and he was turning over his data and plans to me. I told him I would not probably grasp the theoretical basis of the process, however well I had or would come to manage the practical paradoxes of it, but he liked to show me. He first summoned up x-y coordinates, quite ordinary, and began by showing me how some surprising results were obtained by plotting on such coordinates an imaginary number, specifically the square root of minus one. The only way to describe what happens, he said, is that the plotted figure, one unit high, one unit wide, generates a shadow square of the same measurements "behind" itself, in space undefined by the coordinates. It was with such tricks that he had begun; the orthogons he obtained had first started him thinking about the generation of inhabitable – if also somehow imaginary – pasts.

'Then he showed me what became of the orthogons so constructed if the upright axis were set in motion. Suppose (he said) that this vertical coordinate were in fact revolving around the axle formed by the other, horizontal coordinate. If it were so revolving, like an aeroplane propeller, we could not apprehend it, edge on as it is to us, so to speak; but what would that motion do to the plots we were making? And of course it was quite simple, given the proper instructions to the computer, to find out. And his orthogons – always remaining at right angles to the original coordinates – began to turn in the prop wash of the whole system's progress at one second per second out of the what-was and into the what-has-never-yet-been; and to generate, when one had come to see them, the paradoxes of orthogonal logic: the cyclonic storm of logic in which all travellers in that medium always stand; the one in which Last and I, I bending over his shoulder hat in hand, he with fat white fingers on his keys and eyeglasses slipping down his nose, stood even as we spoke: a storm as unfeelable as Last's rotating axis was unseeable.'

The President *pro tem* tossed his extinguished cigar into the fading fire and crossed his arms upon his breast, weary; weary of the tale.

'I don't yet understand,' the other said. 'If he had been so adamant, why would he give up his secrets to you?'

'Well,' said the President *pro tem*, 'there was, also, the matter of money. It came down to that, in the end. We were able to make him a very generous offer, as I said.'

'But he didn't need money. He had this stamp.'

'Yes. So he did. Yes. We were able to pick up the stamp, too, from him, as part of the bargain. I think we offered him a hundred pounds. Perhaps it was more.'

'I thought it was invaluable.'

'Well, so did he, of course. And yet he was not really as surprised as one might have expected him to be, when he discovered it was not; when it turned out that the stamp he had gone to such trouble to acquire was in fact rather a common one. I seemed to see it in his face, the expectation of what he was likely to find, as soon as I directed him to look it up in his Scott's, if he didn't believe me. And there it was in Scott's: the one-penny magenta 1856, a nice enough stamp, a stamp many collectors covet, and many also have in their albums. He had begun breathing stertorously, staring down at the page. I'm afraid he was suffering, rather, and I didn't like to observe it.

'"Come," I said to him. "You knew it was possible." And he did, of course. "Perhaps it was something you did," I said. "Perhaps you bought the last one of a batch, and the postmaster subsequently reordered, a thing he had not before intended to do. Perhaps . . ."' But I could see him think it: there needed to be no such explanation. He needed to have made no error, nor to have influenced the moment's shape in any way by his presence. The very act of his coming and going was sufficient source of unpredictable, stochastic change: this world was not his, and minute changes from his were predicated. But *this* change, this of all possible changes . . .

'His hand had begun to shake, holding the volume of Scott's. I really wanted now to get through the business and be off, but it couldn't be hurried. I knew that, for I'd done it all before. In the end we acquired the stamp. And then destroyed it, of course.'

The President *pro tem* remembered: a tiny, momentary fire.

'It's often been observed,' he said, 'that the cleverest scientists are often the most easily taken in by charlatans. There is a famous instance, famous in some worlds, of a scientist who was brought to believe firmly in ghosts and ectoplasm, because the medium and her manifestations passed all the tests the scientist could devise. The only thing he didn't think to test for was conscious fraud. I suppose it's because the phenomena of nature, or the entities of mathematics, however puzzling and elusive they may be, are not after all bent on fooling the observer; and so a motive that would be evident to the dullest of policemen does not occur to the genius.'

'The stamp,' said the Magus.

'The stamp, yes. I'm not exactly proud of this part of the story. We were convinced, though, that two *very* small wrongs could go a long way towards making a very great right. And Last, who understood me and the "firm" I represented to be capable of handling – at least in a practical way – the awful paradoxes of orthogony, did not imagine us to be also skilled, if anything more skilled, at such things as burglary, uttering, fraud, and force. Of such contradictions is Empire made. It was easy enough for us to replace, while Last was off in the tropics, one volume of his Scott's stamp catalog with another printed by ourselves, almost identical to his but containing one difference. It was harder waiting to see, once he had looked up his stamp in our bogus volume, if he would then search out some other source to confirm what he found there. He did not.'

The Magus rose slowly from his chair with the articulated dignity, the wasteless lion's motion, of his kind. He tugged the bell pull. He picked up the poker then, and stood with his hand upon the mantel, looking down into the ruby ash of the dying fire. 'I would he had,' he said.

The dark double doors of the library opened, and the servant entered noiselessly.

'Refresh the gentleman's glass,' the Magus said without turning from the fire, 'and draw the drapes.'

The President *pro tem* thought that no matter how long he lived in this world he would never grow accustomed to the presence of draconics. The servant's dark hand lifted the decanter, poured an exact dram into the glass, and stoppered the bottle again; then his yellow eyes, irises slit like a cat's or a snake's, rose from that task towards the next, the drawing of the drapes. Unlike the eyes of the Magi, these draconic eyes seemed to see and weigh everything – though on a single scale, and from behind a veil of indifference.

Their kind, the President *pro tem* had learned, had been servants for uncounted ages, though the Magus his host had said that once they had been masters, and men and the other hominids their slaves. And they still had, the President *pro tem* observed, that studied reserve which upper servants had in the world from which the President *pro tem* had come, that reserve which says: Very well, I will do your bidding, better than you could do it for yourself; I will maintain the illusion of your superiority to me, as no other creature could.

With a taper he lit at the fire, he lit the lamps along the walls and masked them with glass globes. Then he drew the drapes.

'I'll ring for supper,' the Magus said, and the servant stopped at the sound of his voice. 'Have it sent in.' The servant moved again, crossing the room on narrow naked feet. At the doorway he turned to them, but only to draw the double doors closed together as he left.

For a time the Magus stood regarding the doors the great lizard had closed. Then: 'Outside the City,' he said, 'in the mountains, they have begun to combine. There are more stories every week. In the old forests whence they first emerged, they have begun to collect on appointed days, trying to remember – for they are not really as intelligent as they look – trying to remember what it is they have lost, and to think of gaining it again. In not too long a time we will begin to hear of massacres. Some remote place; a country house; a more than usually careless man; a deed of unfamiliar horridness. And a sign left, the first sign: a writing in blood, or something less obvious. And like a spot symptomatic of a fatal disease, it will begin to spread.'

The President *pro tem* drank, then said softly: 'We didn't know, you know. We didn't understand that this would be the result.' The drawing of the drapes, the lighting of the lamps, had made the old library even more familiar to the President *pro tem*: the dark varnished wood, the old tobacco smoke, the hour between tea and dinner; the draught that whispered at the window's edge, the bitter smell of the coal on the grate; the comfort of this velvet armchair's napless arms, of this whisky. The President *pro tem* sat grasped by all this, almost unable to think of anything else. 'We couldn't know.'

'Last knew,' the Magus said. 'All false, all imaginary, all generated by the wishes and fears of others: all that I am, my head, my heart, my house. Not the world's doing, or time's, but yours.' The opacity of his eyes, turned on the President *pro tem*, was fearful. 'You have made me; you must unmake me.'

'I'll do what I can,' the President *pro tem* said. 'All that I can.'

'For centuries we have studied,' the Magus said. 'We have spent lifetimes – lifetimes much longer than yours – searching for the flaw in this world, the flaw whose existence we suspected but could not prove. I say "centuries," but those centuries have been illusory, have they not? We came, finally, to guess at you, down the defiles of time, working your changes, which we can but suffer.

'We only guessed at you: no more than men or beasts can we Magi remember, once the universe has become different, that it was ever other than it is now. But I think the Sylphids can feel it change: can know when the changes are wrought. Imagine the pain for them.'

That was a command: and indeed the President *pro tem* could imagine it, and did. He looked down into his glass.

'That is why they are gathering. They know already of your appearance; they have expected you. The request is theirs to make, not mine: that you put this world out like a light.'

He stabbed with the poker at the settling fire, and the coals gave up blue flames for a moment. The mage's eyes caught the light, and then went out.

'I long to die,' he said.

IV: CHRONICLES OF THE OTHERHOOD

Once past the door, or what might be considered the door, or what Sir Geoffrey Davenant had told him was a club, Denys Winterset was greeted by the Fellow in Economic History, a gentle, academic-looking man called Platt.

'Not many of the Fellows about, just now,' he said. 'Most of them fossicking about on one bit of business or another. I'm always here.' He smiled, a vague, self-effacing smile. 'Be no good out there. But they also serve, eh?'

'Will Sir Geoffrey Davenant be here?' Denys asked him. He followed Platt through what did seem to be a gentlemen's club of the best kind: dark-panelled, smelling richly of leather upholstery and tobacco.

'Davenant, oh, yes,' said Platt. 'Davenant will be here. All the executive committee will get here, if they can. The President – *pro tem*.' He turned back to look at Denys over his half-glasses. 'All our presidents are *pro tem*.' He led on. 'There'll be dinner in the executive committee's dining room. After dinner we'll talk. You'll likely have questions.' At that Denys almost laughed. He felt made of questions, most of them unputtable in any verbal form.

Platt stopped in the middle of the library. A lone Fellow in a corner by a green-shaded lamp was hidden by *The Times* held up before him. There was a fire burning placidly in the oak-framed fireplace; above it, a large and smoke-dimmed painting: a portrait of a chubby, placid man in a hard collar, thinning blond hair, eyes somehow vacant. Platt, seeing Deny's look, said: 'Cecil Rhodes.'

Beneath the portrait, carved into the mantelpiece, were words; Denys took a step closer to read them:

To Ruin the Great Work of Time
& Cast the Kingdoms old
Into another mould.

'Marvell,' Platt said. 'That poem about Cromwell. Don't know who chose it. It's right, though. I look at it often, working here. Now. It's down that corridor, if you want to wash your hands. Would you care for a drink? We have some time to kill. Ah, Davenant.'

'Hullo, Denys,' said Sir Geoffrey, who had lowered his *Times*. 'I'm glad you've come.'

'I think we all are,' said Platt, taking Denys's elbow in a gentle, almost tender grasp. 'Glad you've come.'

He had almost not come. If it had been merely an address, a telephone number he'd been given, he might well not have; but the metal card with its brown strip was like a string tied round his finger, making it impossible to forget he had been invited. Don't lose it, Davenant had said. So it lay in his waistcoat pocket; he touched it whenever he reached for matches there; he tried shifting it to other pockets, but wherever it was on his person he felt it. In the end he decided to use it, as much to get rid of its importunity as for any other reason – so he told himself. On a wet afternoon he went to the place Davenant had told him of, the Orient Aid Society, and found it as described, a sooty French-Gothic building, one of those private houses turned to public use, with a discreet brass plaque by the door indicating that within some sort of business is done, one can't imagine what; and inside the double doors, in the vestibule, three telephone boxes, looking identical, the first of which had the nearly invisible slit by the door. His heart for some reason beat slow and hard as he inserted the card within this slot – it was immediately snatched away, like a ticket on the Underground – and entered the box and closed the door behind him.

Though nothing moved, he felt as though he had stepped onto a moving footpath, or onto one of those trick floors in a fun house that slide beneath one's feet. He was going somewhere. The sensation was awful. Beginning to panic, he tried to get out, not knowing whether that might be dangerous, but the door would not open, and its glass could not be seen out of either. It had been transparent from outside but was somehow opaque from within. He shook the door handle fiercely. At that moment the nonmobile motion reversed itself sickeningly, and the door opened. Denys stepped out, not into the vestibule of the Orient Aid Society, but into the foyer of a club. A dim, old-fashioned foyer, with faded Turkey carpet on the stairs, and an aged porter to greet him; a desk, behind which pigeonholes held members' mail; a stand of umbrellas. It was reassuring, almost absurdly so, the 'then I woke up' of a silly ghost story. But Denys didn't feel reassured, or exactly awake either.

'Evening, sir.'

'Good evening.'

'Still raining, sir? Take your things?'

'Thank you.'

A member was coming towards him down the long corridor. Platt.

'Sir?'

Denys turned back to the porter. 'Your key, sir,' the man said, and gave him back the metal plate with the strip of brown ribbon on it.

'Like a lift,' Davenant told him as they sipped whisky in the bar. 'Alarming, somewhat, I admit; but imagine using a lift for the first time, not knowing what its function was. Closed inside a box; sensation of movement; the doors open, and you are somewhere else. Might seem odd. Well, this is the same. Only you're not somewhere else: not exactly.'

'Hm,' Denys said.

'Don't dismiss it, Sir Geoffrey,' said Platt. 'It *is* mighty odd.' He said to Denys: 'The paradox is acute: it is. Completely contrary to the usual cause-and-effect thinking we all do, can't stop doing really, no matter how hard we try to adopt other habits of mind. Strictly speaking it is unthinkable: unimaginable. And yet there it is.'

'Yes,' Davenant said. 'To ignore, without ever forgetting, the heart of the matter: that's the trick. I've met monks, Japanese, Tibetan, who know the techniques. They can be learned.'

'We speak of the larger paradox,' Platt said to Denys. 'The door you came in by being only a small instance. The great instance being, of course, the Otherhood's existence at all: we here now sitting and talking of it.'

But Denys was not talking of it. He had nothing to say. To be told that in entering the telephone box in the Orient Aid Society he had effectively exited from time and entered a precinct outside it, revolving between the actual and the hypothetical, not quite existent despite the solidity of its parquet floor and the truthful bite of its whisky; to be told that in these changeless and atemporal halls there gathered a society – 'not quite a brotherhood,' Davenant said; 'that would be mawkish, and untrue of these chaps; we call it an Otherhood' – of men and women who by some means could insert themselves into the stream of the past, and with their foreknowledge alter it, and thus alter the future of that past, the future in which they themselves had their original being; that in effect the world Denys had come from, the world he knew, the year 1956, the whole course of things, the very cast and flavour of his memories, were dependent on the Fellows of this Society, and might change at any moment, though if they did he would know nothing of it; and that he was being asked to join them in their work – he heard the words, spoken to him with a frightening casualness; he felt his mind fill with the notions, though not able to do anything that might be called thinking about them; and he had nothing to say.

'You can see,' Sir Geoffrey said, looking not at Denys but into his whisky, 'why I didn't explain all this to you in Khartoum. The words don't come easily. Here, in the Club, outside all frames of reference, it's possible to explain. To describe, anyway. I suppose if we hadn't a place like this, we should all go mad.'

'I wonder,' said Platt, 'whether we haven't, despite it,' He looked at no one. 'Gone mad, I mean.'

For a moment no one spoke further. The barman glanced at them, to see if their silence required anything of him. Then Platt spoke again. 'Of course there are restrictions,' he said. 'The chap who discovered it was possible to change one's place in time, an American, thought he had proved that it was only possible to displace oneself into the past. In a sense, he was correct. . . .'

'In a sense,' Sir Geoffrey said. 'Not quite correct. The possibilities are larger than he supposed. Or rather will suppose, all this from your viewpoint is still to happen – which widens the possibilities right there, you see, one man's future being as it were another man's past. (You'll get used to it, dear boy, shall we have another of these?) The past, as it happens, is the only sphere of time we have any interest in; the only sphere in which we can do good. So you see there are natural limits: the time at which this process was made workable is the forward limit; and the rear limit we have made the time of the founding of the Otherhood itself. By Cecil Rhodes's will, in 1893.'

'Be pointless, you see, for the Fellows to go back before the Society existed,' said Platt. 'You can see that.'

'One further restriction,' said Sir Geoffrey. 'A house rule, so to speak. We forbid a man to return to a time he has already visited, at least in the same part of the world. There is the danger – a moment's thought will show you I'm right – of bumping into oneself on a previous, or successive, mission. Unnerving, let me tell you. Unnerving completely. The trick is hard enough to master as it is.'

Denys found voice. 'Why?' he said. 'And why me?'

'Why,' said Sir Geoffrey, 'is spelled out in our founding charter: to preserve and extend the British Empire in all parts of the world, and to strengthen it against all dangers. Next, to keep peace in the world, insofar as this is compatible with the first; our experience has been that it usually is the same thing. And lastly to keep fellowship among ourselves, this also subject to the first, though any conflict is unimaginable, I should hope, bickering aside.'

'The Society was founded to be secret,' Platt said. 'Rhodes liked that idea – a sort of Jesuits of the Empire. In fact there was no real need for secrecy, not until – well, not until the Society became the Otherhood. This jaunting about in other people's histories would not be understood. So secrecy *is* important. Good thing on the whole that Rhodes insisted on it. And for sure he wouldn't have been displeased at the Society's scope. He wanted the world for England. And more. "The moon, too," he used to say. "I often think of the moon."'

'Few know of us even now,' Sir Geoffrey said. 'The Foreign Office, sometimes. The PM. Depending on the nature of HM Government at any moment, we explain more, or less. Never the part about time. That is for us alone to know. Though some have guessed a little, over the years. It's not even so much that we wish to act in secret – that was just Rhodes's silly fantasy – but well, it's just damned difficult to explain, don't you see?'

'And the Queen knows of us,' Platt said. 'Of course.'

'I flew back with her, from Africa, that day,' Davenant said. 'After her father had died. I happened to be among the party. I told her a little then. Didn't want to intrude on her grief, but – it seemed the moment. In the air, over Africa. I explained more later. Plucky girl,' he added. 'Plucky.' He drew his watch out. 'And as for the second part of your question – why you? – I shall ask you to reserve that one, for a moment. We'll dine upstairs . . . Good heavens, look at the time.'

Platt swallowed his drink hastily. 'I remember Lord Cromer's words to us when I was a schoolboy at Leys,' he said. '"Love your country," he said, "tell the truth, and don't dawdle."'

'Words to live by,' Sir Geoffrey said, examining the bar chit doubtfully and fumbling for a pen.

The drapes were drawn in the executive dining room; the members of the executive committee were just taking their seats around a long mahogany table, scarred around its edge with what seemed to be initials and dates. The members were of all ages; some sunburned, some pale, some in evening clothes of a cut unfamiliar to Denys; among them were two Indians and a Chinaman. When they were all seated, Denys beside Platt, there were several seats empty. A tall woman with severe grey hair but eyes somehow kind took the head of the table.

'The President *pro tem*,' she said as she sat, 'is not returned, apparently, from his mission. I'll preside, if there are no objections.'

'Oh, balls,' said a broad-faced man with the tan of a cinema actor. 'Don't give yourself airs, Huntington. Will we really need any presiding?'

'Might be a swearing-in,' Huntington said mildly, pressing the bell beside her and not glancing at Denys. 'In any case, best to keep up the forms. First order of business – the soup.'

It was a mulligatawny, saffrony and various; it was followed by a whiting, and that by a baron of claret-coloured beef. Through the clashings of silverware and crystal Denys listened to the table's talk, little enough of which he could understand: only now and then he felt – as though he were coming horribly in two – the import of the Fellows' conversation: that history was malleable, time a fiction; that nothing was necessarily as he supposed it must be. How could they bear that knowledge? How could he?

'Mr Deng Fa-shen, there,' Platt said quietly to him, 'is our physicist. Orthogonal physics – as opposed to orthogonal logic – is his invention. What makes this club possible. The mechanics of it. Don't ask me to explain.'

Deng Fa-shen was a fine-boned, parchment-coloured man with gentle fox's eyes. Denys looked from him to the two Indians in silk. Platt said, as though reading Denys's thought: 'The most disagreeable thing about old Rhodes and the Empire of his day was its racialism, of course. Absolutely unworkable, too. Nothing more impossible to sustain than a world order based on some race's supposed inherent superiority.' He smiled. 'It isn't the only part of Rhodes's scheme that's proved unworkable.'

The informal talk began to assemble itself, with small nudges from the woman at the head of the table (who did her presiding with no pomp and few words), around a single date: 1914. Denys knew something of this date, though several of the place names spoken of (the Somme, Jutland, Gallipoli – wherever that was) meant nothing to him. Somehow, in some possible universe, 1914 had changed everything; the Fellows seemed intent on changing 1914, drawing its teeth, teeth that Denys had not known it had – or might still have once had: he felt again the sensation of coming in two, and sipped wine.

'Jutland,' a Fellow was saying. 'All that's needed is a bit more knowledge, a bit more jump on events. Instead of a foolish stalemate, it could be a solid victory. Then, blockade; war over in six months . . .'

'Who's our man in the Admiralty now? Carteret, isn't it? Can he –'

'Carteret,' said the bronze-faced man, 'was killed the last time around at Jutland.' There was a silence; some of the Fellows seemed to be aware of this, and some taken by surprise. 'Shows the foolishness of that kind of thinking,' the man said. 'Things have simply gone too far by then. That's my opinion.'

Other options were put forward. That moment in what the Fellows called the Original Situation was searched for into which a small intrusion might be made, like a surgical incision, the smallest possible intrusion that would have the proper effect; then the succeeding Situation was searched, and the Situation following that, the Fellows feeling with enormous patience and care into the workings of the past and its possibilities, like a blind man weaving. At length a decision seemed to be made, without fuss or a vote taken, about this place Gallipoli, and a Turkish soldier named Mustapha Kemal, who would be apprehended and sequestered in a quick action that took or would take place there; the sun-bronzed man would see, or had seen, to it; and the talk, after a reflective moment, turned again to anecdote and speculation.

Denys listened to the stories, of desert treks and dangerous negotiations, men going into the wilderness of a past catastrophe with a precious load of penicillin or of knowledge, to save one man's life or end another's; to intercept one trivial telegram, get one bit of news through, deflect one column of troops – removing one card from the ever-building possible future of some past moment and seeing the whole of it collapse silently, unknowably, even as another was building, just as fragile but happier: he looked into the faces of the Fellows, knowing that no ruthless stratagem was beyond them, and yet knowing also that they were men of honour, with a great world's peace and benefit in their trust, though the world couldn't know it; and he felt an odd but deep thrill of privilege to be here now, wherever that was – the same sense of privilege that, as a boy, he had expected to feel (and as a man had laughed at himself for expecting to feel) upon being admitted to the ranks of those who – selflessly, though not without reward – had been chosen or had chosen themselves to serve the Empire. 'The difference you make makes all the difference,' his headmasterish commissioner was fond of telling Denys and his fellows; and it was a joke among them that, in their form-filling, their execution of tedious and sometimes absurd directives, they were following in the footsteps of Gordon and Milner, Warren Hastings and Raffles of Singapore. And yet – Denys perceived it with a kind of inward stillness, as though his heart flowed instead of beating – a difference *could* be made. Had been made. Went on being made, in many times and places, without fuss, without glory, with rewards for others that those others could not recognize or even imagine. He crossed his knife and fork on his plate and sat back slowly.

'This 1914 business has its tricksome aspects,' Platt said to him. 'Speaking in large terms, not enough can really be done within our time frames. The Situation that issues in war was firmly established well before: in the founding of the German Empire under Prussian leadership. Bismarck. There's the man to get to, or to his financiers, most of whom were Jewish – little did they know, and all that. Even Sedan is too late, and not enough seems to be able to be made, or unmade, out of the Dreyfus affair, though that *does* fall within our provenance. No,' he said. 'It's all just too long ago. If only . . . Well, no use speculating, is there? Make the best of it, and shorten the war; make it less catastrophic at any rate, a short, sharp shaking-out – above all, win it quickly. We must do the best we can.'

He seemed unreconciled.

Denys said: 'But I don't understand. I mean, of course I wouldn't expect to understand it as you do, but . . . well, you *did* do all that. I mean we studied 1914 in school – the guns of August and all that, the 1915 peace, the Monaco Conference. What I mean is . . .' He became conscious that the Fellows had turned their attention to him. No one else spoke. 'What I mean to say is that I know you solved the problem, and how you solved it, in a general way; and I don't see why it remains to be solved. I don't see why you're worried.' He laughed in embarrassment, looking around at the faces that looked at him.

'You're right,' said Sir Geoffrey, 'that you don't understand.' He said it smiling, and the others were, if not smiling, patient and not censorious. 'The logic of it is orthogonal. I can present you with an even more paradoxical instance. In fact I intend to present you with it; it's the reason you're here.'

'The point to remember,' the woman called Huntington said (as though to the whole table, but obviously for Denys's instruction), 'is that here – in the Club – nothing has yet happened except the Original Situation. All is still to do: all that we have done, all still to do.'

'Precisely,' said Geoffrey. 'All still to do.' He took from his waistcoat pocket an eyeglass, polished it with his napkin, and inserted it between cheek and eyebrow. 'You had a question, in the bar. You asked *why me*, meaning, I suppose, why is it you should be nominated to this Fellowship, why you and not another.'

'Yes,' said Denys. He wanted to go on, list what he knew of his inadequacies, but kept silent.

'Let me, before answering your question, ask you this,' said Sir Geoffrey. 'Supposing that you were chosen by good and sufficient standards – supposing that a list had been gone over carefully, and your name was weighed; supposing that a sort of competitive examination has been passed by you – would you then accept the nomination?'

'I –' said Denys. All eyes were on him, yet they were not somehow expectant; they awaited an answer they knew. Denys seemed to know it, too. He swallowed. 'I hope I should,' he said.

'Very well,' Sir Geoffrey said softly. 'Very well.' He took a breath. 'Then I shall tell you that you have in fact been chosen by good and sufficient standards. Chosen, moreover, for a specific mission, a mission of the greatest importance; a mission on which the very existence of the Otherhood depends. No need to feel flattered; I'm sure you're a brave lad, and all that, but the criteria were not entirely your sterling qualities, whatever they should later turn out to be.

'To explain what I mean, I must further acquaint you with what the oldest, or rather earliest, of the Fellows call the Original Situation.

'You recall our conversation in Khartoum. I told you no lie then; it is the case, in that very pleasant world we talked in, that good year 1956, fourth of a happy reign, on that wide veranda overlooking a world at peace – it is the case, I say, in that world and in most possible worlds like it, that Cecil Rhodes died young, and left the entire immense fortune he had won in the Scramble for the founding of a secret society, a society dedicated to the extension of that Empire which had his entire loyalty. The then Government's extreme confusion over this bequest, their eventual forming of a society – not without some embarrassment and doubt – a society from which this present Otherhood descends; still working toward the same ends, though the British Empire is not now what Rhodes thought it to be, nor the world either in which it has its hegemony – well, one of the Fellows is working up or will work up that story, insofar as it can be told, and it is, as I say, a true one.

'But there is a situation in which it is not true. In that situation which we call Original – the spine of time from which all other possibilities fluoresce – Cecil Rhodes, it appears, changed his mind.'

Sir Geoffrey paused to light a cigar. The port was passed him. A cloud of smoke issued from his mouth. 'Changed his mind, you see,' he said, dispersing the smoke with a wave. 'He did not die young, he lived on. His character mellowed, perhaps, as the years fell away; his fortune certainly diminished. It may be that Africa disappointed him, finally; his scheme to take over Tanganyika and join the Cape-to-Cairo with a single All-Red railway line had ended in failure . . .'

Denys opened his mouth to speak; he had only a week before taken that line. He shut his mouth again.

'Whatever it was,' Sir Geoffrey said, 'he changed his mind. His last will left his fortune – what was left of it – to his old university, a scholarship fund to allow Americans and others of good character to study in England. No secret society. No Otherhood.'

There was a deep silence at the table. No one had altered his casual position, yet there was a stillness of utter attention. Someone poured for Denys, and the liquid rattle of port into his glass was loud.

'Thus the paradox,' Sir Geoffrey said. 'For it is only the persuasions of the Otherhood that alter this Original Situation. The Otherhood must reach its fingers into the past, once we have learned how to do so; we must send our agents down along the defiles of time and intercept our own grandfather there, at the very moment when he is about to turn away from the work of generating us.

'And persuade him not to, you see; cause him – cause him not to turn away from that work of generation. Yes, cause him not to turn away. And thus ensure our own eventual existence.'

Sir Geoffrey pushed back his chair and rose. He turned towards the sideboard, then back again to Denys. 'Did I hear you say "That's madness"?' he asked.

'No,' Denys said.

'Oh,' Sir Geoffrey said. 'I thought you spoke. Or thought I remembered you speaking.' He turned again to the sideboard, and returned again to the table with his cigar clenched in his teeth and a small box in his hands. He put this on the table. 'You do follow me thus far,' he said, his hands on the box and his eyes regarding Denys from under their curling brows.

'Follow you?'

'The man had to die,' Sir Geoffrey said. He unlatched the box. 'It was his moment. The moment you will find in any biography of him you pick up. Young, or anyway not old; at the height of his triumphs. It would have been downhill for him from there anyway.'

'How,' Denys asked, and something in his throat intruded on the question; it was a moment before he could complete it: 'How did he die?'

'Oh, various ways,' Sir Geoffrey said. 'In the most useful version, he was shot to death by a young man he'd invited up to his house at Cape Town. Shot twice, in the heart, with a Webley .38-calibre revolver.' He took from the box this weapon, and placed it with its handle towards Denys.

'That's madness,' Denys said. His hands lay along the arms of his chair, drawing back from the gun. 'You can't mean to say you went back and *shot* him, you . . .'

'Not we, dear boy,' Sir Geoffrey said. 'We, generally, yes; but specifically, not we. You.'

'No.'

'Oh, you won't be alone – not initially, at least. I can explain why it must be you and not another; I can expound the really quite dreadful paradox of it further, if you think it would help, though it seems to me best if, for now, you simply take our word for it.'

Denys felt the corners of his mouth draw down, involuntarily, tightly; his lower lip wanted to tremble. It was a sign he remembered from early childhood: what had usually followed it was a fit of truculent weeping. That could not follow, here, now: and yet he dared not allow himself to speak, for fear he would be unable. For some time, then, no one spoke.

At the head of the table Huntington pushed her empty glass away.

'Mr Winterset,' she said gently. 'I wonder if I might put in a word. Sit down, Davenant, will you, just for a moment, and stop looming over us. With your permission, Mr Winterset – Denys – I should like to describe to you a little more broadly that condition of the world we call the Original Situation.'

She regarded Denys with her sad eyes, then closed her fingers together before her. She began to speak, in a low voice which more than once Denys had to lean forward to catch. She told about Rhodes's last sad bad days; she told of Rhodes's chum, the despicable Dr Jameson, and his infamous raid and the provocations that led to war with the Boers; of the shame of that war, the British defeats and the British atrocities, the brutal intransigence of both sides. She told how in those same years the European powers who confronted each other in Africa were also at work stockpiling arms and building mechanized armies of a size unheard of in the history of the world, to be finally let loose upon one another in August of 1914, unprepared for what was to become of them; armies officered by men who still lived in the previous century, but armed with weapons more dreadful than they could imagine. The machine gun: no one seemed to understand that the machine gun had changed war forever, and though the junior officers and Other Ranks soon learned it, the commanders never did. At the First Battle of the Somme wave after wave of British soldiers were sent against German machine guns, to be mown down like grain. There were a quarter of a million casualties in that battle. And yet the generals went on ordering massed attacks against machine guns for the four long years of the war.

'But they knew,' Denys could not help saying. 'They did know. Machine guns had been used against massed native armies for years, all over the Empire. In Afghanistan. In the Sudan. Africa. They knew.'

'Yes,' Huntington said. 'They knew. And yet, in the Original Situation, they paid no attention. They went blindly on and made their dreadful mistakes. Why? How could they be so stupid, those generals and statemen who in the world you knew behaved so wisely and so well? For one reason only: they lacked the help and knowledge of a group of men and women who had seen all those mistakes made, who could act in secret on what they knew, and who had the ear and the confidence of one of the governments – not the least stupid of them, either, mind you. And with all our help it was still a close-run thing.'

'Damned close-run,' Platt put in. 'Still hangs in the balance, in fact.'

'Let me go on,' Huntington said.

She went on: long hands folded before her, eyes now cast down, she told how at the end a million men, a whole generation, lay dead on the European battlefield, among them men whom Denys might think the modern world could not have been made without. A grotesque tyranny calling itself Socialist had been imposed on a war-weakened Russian empire. Only the intervention of a fully mobilized United States had finally broken the awful deadlock – thereby altering the further history of the world unrecognizably. She told how the vindictive settlement inflicted on a ruined Germany (so unlike the wise dispositions of the Monaco Conference, which had simply re-established the old pre-Bismarck patchwork of German states and princedoms) had rankled in the German spirit; how a madman had arisen and, almost unbelievably, had ridden a wave of resentment and anti-Jewish hysteria to dictatorship.

'Yes,' Denys said. '*That* we didn't escape, did we? I remember that, or almost remember it; it was just before I can remember anything. Anti-Jewish riots all over Germany.'

'Yes,' said Huntington softly.

'Yes. Terrible. These nice funny Germans, all lederhosen and cuckoo clocks, and suddenly they show a terrible dark side. Thousands of Jews, some of them very highly placed, had to leave Germany. They lost everything. Synagogues attacked, professors fired. Even Einstein, I think, had to leave Germany for a time.'

Huntington let him speak. When Denys fell silent, unable to remember more and feeling the eyes of the Fellows on him, Huntington began again. But the things she began to tell of now simply could not have happened, Denys thought; no, they were part of a monstrous, foul dream, atrocities on a scale only a psychopath could conceive, and only the total resources of a strong and perverted science achieve. When Einstein came again into the tale, and the world Huntington described drifted ignorantly and inexorably into an icy and permanent stalemate that could be broken only by the end of civilization, perhaps of life itself, Denys found a loathsome surfeit rising in his throat; he covered his face, he would hear no more.

'So you see,' Huntington said, 'why we think it possible that the life – nearly over, in any case – of one egotistical, racialist adventurer is worth the chance to alter that situation.' She raised her eyes to Denys. 'I don't say you need agree. There is a sticky moral question, and I don't mean to brush it aside. I only say you see how we might think so.'

Denys nodded slowly. He reached out and put his hand on the pistol that had been placed before him. He lifted his eyes and met those of Sir Geoffrey Davenant, which still smiled, though his mouth and his moustaches were grave.

What they were all telling him was that he could help create a better world than the original, which Huntington had described; but that was not how Denys perceived it. What Denys perceived was that reality – reality, the world he had come from, reality sun-shot and whole – was somehow under threat from a disgusting nightmare of death, ignorance, and torture, which could invade and replace it forever unless he acted. He did not think himself capable of interfering with the world to make it better; but to defend the world he knew, the world that with all its shortcomings was life and sustenance and sense and cleanly wakefulness – yes, that he could do. Would do, with all his strength.

Which is why, of course, it was he who had been chosen to do it. He saw that in Davenant's eyes.

And of course, if he refused, he could not then be brought here to be asked. If it was now possible for him to be asked to do this by the Otherhood, then he must have already consented, and done it. That, too, was in Davenant's silence. Denys looked down. His hand was on the Webley; and beside it, carved by a penknife into the surface of the table, almost obscured by later waxings, were the neat initials *D.W.*

'I always remember what Lord Milner said,' Platt spoke into his ear. '*Everyone can help.*'

V: THE TEARS OF THE PRESIDENT *pro tem*

'I remember,' the President *pro tem* of the Otherhood said, 'the light: a very clear, very pure, very cool light that seemed somehow potent but reserved, as though it could do terrible blinding things, and give an unbearable heat, if it chose – well, I'm not quite sure what I mean.'

There was a midnight fug in the air of the library where the President *pro tem* retold his tale. The Magus to whom he told it did not look at him; his pale grey eyes moved from object to object around the room in the aimless idiot wandering that had at first caused the President *pro tem* to believe him blind.

'The mountain was called Table Mountain – a sort of high mesa. What a place that was then – I think the most beautiful in the Empire, and young then, but not raw; a peninsula simply made to put a city on, and a city being put there, beneath the mountain: and this piercing light.

'Our party put up at the Mount Nelson Hotel, perhaps a little grand for the travellers in electroplating equipment we were pretending to be, but the incognito wasn't really important, it was chiefly to explain the presence of the Last equipment among the luggage.

'A few days were spent in reconnaissance. But you see – this is continually the impossible thing to explain – in a sense those of the party who knew the outcome were only going through the motions of conferring, mapping their victim's movements, choosing a suitable moment and all that: for they knew the story; there was only one way for it to happen, if it was to happen at all. If it was *not* to happen, then no one could predict what was to happen instead; but so long as our party was there, and preparing it, it would evidently have to happen – or would have to have had to have happened.'

The President *pro tem* suddenly missed his old friend Davenant, Davenant the witty and deep, who never bumbled over his tenses, never got himself stuck in a sentence such as that one; Davenant lost now with the others in the interstices of imaginary pasthood – or rather about to be lost, in the near future, if the President *pro tem* assented to what was asked of him. 'It was rather jolly,' he said, 'like a game rather, striving to bring about a result that you were sure had already been brought about; an old ritual, if you like, to which not much importance needed to be attached, so long as it was all done correctly . . .'

'I think,' said the Magus, 'you need not explain these feelings that you then had.'

'Sorry,' said the President *pro tem*. 'The house was called Groote Schuur – that was the old Dutch name, which he'd revived, for a big granary that had stood on the property; the English had called it the Grange. It was built on the lower slopes of Devil's Peak, with a view up to the mountains, and out to sea as well. He'd only recently seen the need for a house – all his life in Africa he'd more or less pigged it in rented rooms, or stayed in his club or a hotel or even a tent pitched outside town. For a long time he roomed with Dr Jameson, sleeping on a little truckle bed hardly big enough for his body. But now that he'd become Prime Minister, he felt it was time for something more substantial.

'It seemed to me that it would have been easier to take him out in the bush – the *bundas*, as the Matabele say. Hire a party of natives – wait till all are asleep – ambush. He often went out into the wilds with almost no protection. There was no question of honour involved – I mean, the man had to die, one way or the other, and the more explainably or accidentally the better. But I was quite wrong – I was myself, still young – and had to be put right: the one time that way was tried, the assassination initiated a punitive war against the native populations that lasted for twenty years, which ended only with the virtual extermination of the Matabele and Mashona peoples. Dreadful.

'No, it had to be the house; moreover, it had to be within a very brief span of time – a time when we knew he was there, when we knew where his will was, and *which* will it was – he made eight or nine in his lifetime – and when we knew, also, what assets were in his hands. Business and ownership were fluid things in those days; his partners were quick and subtle men; his sudden death might lose us all that we were intending to acquire by it in the way of a campaign chest, so to speak.

'So it had to be the house, in this week of this year, on this night. In fact orthogonal logic dictated it. Davenant was quite calmly sure of that. After all, that was the night when it had happened: and for sure we ought not to miss it.'

That was an attempt at the sort of remark Davenant might make, and the President *pro tem* smiled at the Magus, who remained unmoved. The President *pro tem* thought it impossible that beings as wise as he knew the one before him to be, no matter how grave, could altogether lack any sense of humour. For himself, he had often thought that if he did not find funny the iron laws of orthogony he would go mad; but his jokes apparently amused only himself.

'It was not a question of getting to his house, or into it; he practically kept open house the year round, and his grounds could be walked upon by anyone. The gatekeepers were only instructed to warn walkers about the animals they might come across – he had brought in dozens of species, and he allowed all but the genuinely dangerous to roam at will. Wildebeest. Zebras. Impala. And "human beings," as he always called them, roamed at will, too; there were always some about. At dinner he had visitors from all over Africa, and from England and Europe as well; his bedrooms were often full. I think he hated to be alone. All of which provided a fine setting, you see, for a sensational – and insoluble – murder mystery: if only the man could be got alone, and escape made good then through these crowds of hangers-on.

'Our plan depended on a known proclivity of his, or rather two proclivities. The first was a taste he had for the company of a certain sort of a young man. He liked having them around him and could become very attached to them. There was never a breath of scandal in this – well, there was talk, but only talk. His "angels," people called them: good-looking, resourceful if not particularly bright, good all-rounders with a rough sense of fun – practical jokes, horseplay – but completely devoted and ready for anything he might ask them to do. He had a fair crowd of these fellows up at Groote Schuur just then. Harry Curry, his private secretary. Johnny Grimmer, a trooper who was never afraid to give him orders – like a madman's keeper, some people said, scolding him and brushing dust from his shoulders; he never objected. Bob Coryndon, another trooper. They'd all just taken on a butler for themselves, a sergeant in the Inniskillings: good-looking chap, twenty-three years old. Oddly, they had all been just that age when he'd taken an interest in them: twenty-three. Whether that was chance or his conscious choice we didn't know.

'The other proclivity was his quickness in decision-making. And this often involved the young men. The first expedition into Matabeleland had been headed up by a chap he'd met at his club one morning at breakfast just as the column was preparing for departure. Took to the chap instantly: liked his looks, liked his address. Gave him the job on the spot.

'That had worked out very well, of course – his choices often did. The pioneer column had penetrated into the heart of the *bundas*, the flag was flying over a settlement they called Fort Salisbury, and the whole of Matabeleland was in the process of being added to the Empire. Up at Groote Schuur they were kicking around possible names for the new country: Rhodia, perhaps, or Rhodesland, even Cecilia. It was that night that they settled on Rhodesia.'

The President *pro tem* felt a moment's shame. There had been, when it came down to it, no doubt in his mind that what they had done had been the right thing to do: and in any case it had all happened a long time ago, more than a century ago in fact. It was not what was done, or that it had been done, only the moment of its doing, that was hard to relate: it was the picture in his mind, of an old man (though he was only forty-eight, he looked far older) sitting in the lamplight reading *The Boy's Own Paper*, as absorbed and as innocent in his absorption as a boy himself; and the vulnerable shine on his balding crown; and the tender and indifferent night: it was all that which raised a lump in the throat of the President *pro tem* and caused him to pause, and roll the tip of his cigar in the ashtray, and clear his throat before continuing.

'And so,' he said, 'we baited our hook. Rhodes's British South Africa

Company was expanding, in the wake of the Fort Salisbury success. He was on the lookout for young men of the right sort. We presented him with one: good-looking lad, public school, cricketer; just twenty-three years old. He was the bait. The mole. The Judas.'

And the bait had been taken, of course. The arrangements having been keyed so nicely to the man's nature, a nature able to be studied from the vantage point of several decades on, it could hardly have failed. That the trick seemed so fragile, even foolish, something itself out of *The Boy's Own Paper* or a story by Henley, only increased the likelihood of its striking just the right note here: the coloured fanatic, Rhodes leaving his hotel after luncheon to return to Parliament, the thug stepping out of the black noon shadows with a knife just as Rhodes mounts his carriage steps – then the young man, handily by with a stout walking stick (a gift of his father upon his departure for Africa) – the knife deflected, the would-be assassin slinking off, the great man's gratitude. You must have some reward. Not a bit, sir, anyone would have done the same; just lucky I was nearby. Come to dinner at any rate – my house on the hill – anyone can direct you. Allow me to introduce myself; my name is . . .

No need, sir, everyone knows Cecil Rhodes.

And your name is . . .

The clean hand put frankly forward, the tanned, open, boyish face smiling. My name is Denys Winterset.

'So then you see,' the President *pro tem* said, 'the road was open. The road up to Groote Schuur. The road that branches, in effect, to lead here: to us here now speaking of it.'

'And how many times since then,' the Magus said, 'has the world branched? How many times has it been bent double, and broken? A thousand times, ten thousand? Each time growing smaller, having to be packed into lesser space, curling into itself like a snail's shell; growing ever weaker as the changes multiply, and more liable to failure of its fabric: how many times?'

The President *pro tem* answered nothing.

'You understand, then,' the Magus said to him, 'what you will be asked: to find the crossroads that leads this way and to turn the world from it.'

'Yes.'

'And how will you reply?'

The President *pro tem* had no better answer for this question, and he gave none. He had begun to feel at once heavy as lead and disembodied. He arose from his armchair, with some effort, and crossed the worn Turkish carpet to the tall window.

'You must leave my house now,' the Magus said, rising from his chair. 'There is much for me to do this night, if this world is to pass out of existence.'

'Where shall I go?'

'They will find you. I think in not too long a time.' Without looking back he left the room.

The President *pro tem* pushed aside the heavy drape the draconic had drawn. *Where shall I go?* He looked out the window into the square outside, deserted at this late and rainy hour. It was an irregular square, the intersection of three streets, filled with rain-wet cobbles as though with shiny eggs. It was old; it had been the view out these windows for two centuries at the least; there was nothing about it to suggest that it had not been the intersection of three streets for a good many more centuries than that.

And yet it had not been there at all only a few decades earlier, when the President *pro tem* had last walked the city outside the Orient Aid Society. Then the city had been London; it was no more. These three streets, these cobbles, had not been there in 1983; nor in 1893 either. Yet there they were, somewhere early in the twenty-first century; there they had been, too, for time out of mind, familiar no doubt to any dweller in this part of town, familiar for that matter to the President *pro tem* who looked out at them. In each of two lamp-lit cafés on two corners of the square, a man in a soft cap held a glass and looked out into the night, unsurprised, at home.

Someone had broken the rules: there simply was no other explanation.

There had been, of course, no way for anyone, not Deng Fa-shen, not Davenant, not the President *pro tem* himself, to guess what the President *pro tem* might come upon on this, the first expedition the Otherhood was making into the future: not only did the future not exist

(Deng Fa-shen was quite clear about that), but, as Davenant reminded him, the Otherhood itself, supposing the continued existence of the Otherhood, would no doubt go busily on changing things in the past far and near – shifting the ground therefore of the future the President *pro tem* was headed for. Deng Fa-shen was satisfied that that future, the ultimate future, sum of all intermediate revisions, was the only one that could be plumbed, if any could; and that was the only one the Otherhood would want to glimpse: to learn how they would do, or would come to have done; to find out, as George V whispered on his death-bed, 'How is the Empire?'

('Only that isn't what he said,' Davenant was fond of telling. 'That's what he was, understandably, reported to have said, and what the Queen and the nurses convinced themselves they heard. But he was a bit dazed there at the end, poor good old man. What he said was not "How is the Empire?" but "What's at the Empire?" a popular cinema. I happened,' he always added gravely, 'to have been with him.')

The first question had been how far 'forward' the Otherhood should press; those members who thought the whole scheme insane, as Platt did, voted for next Wednesday, and bring back the Derby winners please. Deng Fa-shen was not certain the thrust could be entirely calculated: the imaginary futures of imaginary pasts were not, he thought, likely to be under the control of even the most penetrating orthogonal engineering. Sometime in the first decades of the next century was at length agreed upon, a time just beyond the voyager's own mortal span – for the house rule seemed, no one could say quite why, to apply in both directions – and for as brief a stay as was consistent with learning what was up.

The second question – who was to be the voyager? – the President *pro tem* had answered by fiat, assuming an executive privilege he just at that moment claimed to exist, and cutting off further debate. (Why exactly did he insist? I'm not certain why, except that it was not out of a sense of adventure, or of fun or curiosity: whatever of those qualities he may once have had had been much worn away in his rise to the Presidency *pro tem* of the Otherhood. A sense of duty may have been part of it. It may have been to forestall the others, out of a funny sort of premonition. Duty, and premonition: of what, though? Of what?)

'It'll be quite different from any of our imaginings, you know,' Davenant said, who for some reason had not vigorously contested the President's decision. 'The future of all possible pasts. I envy you, I do. I should rather like to see it for myself.'

Quite different from any of our imaginings: very well. The President *pro tem* had braced himself for strangeness. What he had not expected was familiarity. Familiarity – cosy as an old shoe – was certainly different from his imaginings.

And yet what was it he was familiar with? He had stepped out of his club in London and found himself to be, not in the empty corridors of the Orient Aid Society that he knew well, but in private quarters of some kind that he had never seen before. It reminded him, piercingly, of a place he did know, but what place he could not have said: some don's rich but musty rooms, some wealthy and learned bachelor's digs. How had it come to be?

And how had it come to be lit by gas?

One of the pleasant side effects (most of the members thought it pleasant) of the Otherhood's endless efforts in the world had been a general retardation in the rate of material progress: so much of that progress had been, on the one hand, the product of the disastrous wars that it was the Otherhood's chief study to prevent, and on the other hand, American. The British Empire moved more slowly, a great beast without predators, and naturally conservative; it clung to proven techniques and could impose them on the rest of the world by its weight. The telephone, the motor car, the flying boat, the wireless, all were slow to take root in the Empire that the Otherhood shaped. And yet surely, the President *pro tem* thought, electricity was in general use in London in 1893, before which date no member could alter the course of things. And gas lamps lit this place.

Pondering this, the President *pro tem* had entered the somber and apparently little-used dining room and seen the draconic standing in the little butler's pantry: silent as a statue (asleep, the President *pro tem* would later deduce, with lidless eyes only seeming to be open); a polishing-cloth in his claw, and the silver before him; his heavy jaws partly open, and his weight balanced on the thick stub of tail. He wore a baize apron and black sleeve garters to protect his clothes.

Quite different from our imaginings: and yet no conceivable amount of tinkering with the twentieth century, just beyond which the President *pro tem* theoretically stood, could have brought forth this butler, in wing collar and green apron, the soft gaslight ashine on his bald brown head.

So someone had broken the rules. Someone had dared to regress beyond 1893 and meddle in the farther past. That was not, in itself, impossible; Caspar Last had done it on his first and only excursion. It had only been thought impossible for the Otherhood to do it, because it would have taken them 'back' before the Otherhood's putative existence, and therefore before the Otherhood could have wrested the techniques of such travel from Last's jealous grip, a power they acquired by already having it – that was what the President *pro tem* had firmly believed.

But it was not, apparently, so. Somewhen in that stretch of years that fell between his entrance into the telephone box of the Club and his exit from it into this familiar and impossible world, someone – many someones, or someone many times – had gone 'back' far before Rhodes's death: had gone back far enough to initiate this house, this city, these races who were not men.

A million years? It couldn't have been less. It didn't seem possible it could be less.

And who, then? Deng Fa-shen, the delicate, brilliant Chinaman, who had thoughts and purposes he kept to himself; the only one of them who might have been able to overcome the theoretical limits? Or Platt, who was never satisfied with what was possible within what he called 'the damned parameters'?

Or Davenant. Davenant, who was forever quoting Khayyám: *Ah, Love, couldst thou and I with Him conspire/To take this sorry scheme of things entire;/Would we not smash it into pieces, then/Remould it nearer to the heart's desire . . .*

'There is,' said the Magus behind him, 'one other you have not thought of.'

The President *pro tem* let fall the drape and turned from the window. The Magus stood in the doorway, a great ledger in his arms. His eyes did not meet the President *pro tem*'s, and yet seemed to regard him anyway, like the blind eyes of a statue.

One other . . . Yes, the President *pro tem* saw, there *was* one other who might have done this. One other, not so good at the work perhaps as others, as Davenant for example, but who nonetheless would have been, or would come to have been, in a position to take such steps. The President *pro tem* would not have credited himself with the skill, or the nerve, or the dreadnought power. But how else to account for the familiarity, the bottomless *suitability* to him of this world he had never before seen?

'Between the time of your people's decision to plumb our world,' said the Magus, 'and the time of your standing here within it, you must yourself have brought it into being. I see no likelier explanation.'

The President *pro tem* stood still with wonder at the efforts he was apparently to prove capable of making. A million years at least: a million years. How had he known where to begin? Where had he found, would he find, the time?

'Shall I ring,' the Magus said, 'or will you let yourself out?'

Deng Fa-shen had always said it, and anyone who travelled in them knew it to be so: the imaginary futures and imaginary pasts of orthogony are imaginary only in the sense that imaginary numbers (which they very much resemble) are imaginary. To a man walking within one, it alone is real, no matter how strange; it is all the others, standing at angles to it, which exist only in imagination. Night-long the President *pro tem* walked the city, with a measured and unhurried step, but with a constant tremor winding round his rib cage, waiting for what would become of him, and observing the world he had made.

Of course it could not continue to exist. It should not ever have come into existence in the first place; his own sin (if it had been his) had summoned it out of nonbeing, and his repentance must expunge it. The Magus who had taken his confession (which the President *pro tem* had been unable to withhold from him) had drawn that conclusion: it must be put out, like a light. And yet how deeply the President *pro tem* wanted it to last forever; how deeply he believed it *ought* to last forever.

The numinous and inhuman angels, about whom nothing could be said, beings with no ascertainable business among the lesser races and yet beings without whom, the President *pro tem* was sure, this world could not go on functioning. They lived (endless?) lives unimaginable to men, and perhaps to Magi, too, who yet sought continually for knowledge of them: Magi, highest of the hominids, gentle and wise yet inflexible of purpose, living in simplicity and solitude (Were there females? Where? Doing what?) and yet from their shabby studies influencing, perhaps directing, the lives of mere men. The men, such as himself, clever and busy, with their inventions and their politics and their affairs. The lesser hominids, strong, sweet-natured, comic, like placid trolls. The draconics.

It was not simply a world inhabited by intelligent races of different kinds: it was a harder thing to grasp than that. The lives of the races constituted different universes of meaning, different constructions of reality; it was as though four or five different novels, novels of different kinds by different and differently limited writers, were to become interpenetrated and conflated: inside a gigantic Russian thing a stark and violent *policier*, and inside that something Dickensian, full of plot, humours, and eccentricity. Such an interlacing of mutually exclusive universes might be comical, like a sketch in *Punch*; it might be tragic, too. And it might be neither: it might simply be what is, the given against which all airy imaginings must finally be measured: reality.

Near dawn the President *pro tem* stood leaning on a parapet of worked stone that overlooked a tram roundabout. A tram had just ended its journey there, and the conductor and the motorman descended, squat hominids in great-coats and peaked caps. With their long strong arms they began to swing the tram around for its return journey. The President *pro tem* gazed down at this commonplace sight; his nose seemed to know the smell of that tram's interior, his bottom to know the feel of its polished seats. But he knew also that yesterday there had not been trams in this city. Today they had been here for decades.

No, it was no good, the President *pro tem* knew: the fabric of this world he had made – if it had been he – was fatally weakened with irreality. It was a botched job: as though he were that god of the Gnostics who made the material world, a minor god unversed in putting time together with space. He had not worked well. And how could he have supposed it would be otherwise? What had got into him, that he had dared?

'No,' said the angel who stood beside him. 'You should not think that it was you.'

'If not me,' said the President *pro tem*, 'then who?'

'Come,' said the angel. She (I shall say 'she') slipped a small cool hand within his hand. 'Let's go over the tracks, and into the trees beyond that gate.'

A hard and painful stone had formed in the throat of the President *pro tem*. The angel beside him led him like a daughter, like the daughter of old blind Oedipus. Within the precincts of the park – which apparently had its entrance or its entrances where the angels needed them to be – he was led down an avenue of yew and dim towers of poplar towards the piled and sounding waters of a fountain. They sat together on the fountain's marble lip.

'The Magus told me,' the President *pro tem* began, 'that you can feel the alterations that we make, back then. Is that true?'

'It's like the snap of a whip infinitely long,' the angel said. 'The whole length of time snapped and laid out differently: not only the length of time backwards to the time of the change, but the length of the future forwards. We felt ourselves, come into being, oldest of the Old Races (though the last your changes brought into existence); we saw in that moment the aeons of our past, and we guessed our future, too.'

The President *pro tem* took out his pocket handkerchief and pressed it to his face. He must weep, yet no tears came.

'We love this world – this only world – just as you do,' she said. 'We love it, and we cannot bear to feel it sicken and fail. Better that it not have been than that it die.'

'I shall do all I can,' said the President *pro tem*. 'I shall find who has done this – I suppose I know who it was, if it wasn't me – and dissuade him. Teach him, teach him what I've learned, make him see . . .'

'You don't yet understand,' the angel said with careful kindness but at the same time glancing at her wristwatch. 'There is no one to tell. There is no one who went beyond the rules.'

'There must have been,' said the President *pro tem*. 'You, your time, it just isn't that far along from ours, from mine! To make this world, this city, these races . . .'

'Not far along in time,' said the angel, 'but many times removed. You know it to be so: whenever you, your Otherhood, set out across the timelines, your passage generated random variation in the worlds you arrived in. Perhaps you didn't understand how those variations accumulate, here at the sum end of your journeyings.'

'But the changes were so minute!' said the President *pro tem*. 'Deng Fa-shen explained it. A molecule here and there, no more; the position of a distant star; some trivial thing, the name of a flower or a village. Too few, too small even to notice.'

'They increase exponentially with every alteration – and your Otherhood has been busy since you last presided over them. Through the days random changes accumulate, tiny errors silting up like the blown sand that fills the streets of a desert city, that buries it at last.'

'But why these changes?' asked the President *pro tem* desperately. 'It can't have been chance that a world like this was the sum of those histories, it can't be. A world like *this* . . .'

'Chance, perhaps. Or it may be that as time grows softer the world grows more malleable by wishes. There is no reason to believe this, yet that is what we believe. You – all of you – could not have known that you were bringing this world into being; and yet this is the world you wanted.'

She reached out to let the tossed foam of the fountain fall into her hand. The President *pro tem* thought of the bridge over the Zambezi, far away; the tossed foam of the Falls. It was true: this is what they had striven for: a world of perfect hierarchies, of no change forever. God, how they must have longed for it! The loneliness of continual change – no outback, no *bundas* so lonely. He had heard how men can be unsettled for days, for weeks, who have lived through earthquakes and felt the earth to be uncertain: what of his Fellows, who had felt time and space picked apart, never to be rewoven that way again, and not once but a hundred times? What of himself?

'I shall tell you what I see at the end of all your wishings,' said the angel softly. 'At the far end of the last changed world, after there is nothing left that can change. There is then only a forest, growing in the sea. I say "forest" and I say "sea," though whether they are of the kind I know, or some other sort of thing, I cannot say. The sea is still and the forest is thick; it grows upward from the black bottom, and its topmost branches reach into the sunlight, which penetrates a little into the warm upper waters. That's all. There is nothing else anywhere forever. Your wishes have come true: the Empire is quiet. There is not, nor will there be, change anymore; never will one thing be confused again with another; higher for lower, better for lesser, master for servant. Perpetual Peace.'

The President *pro tem* was weeping now, painful sobs drawn up from an interior he had long kept shut and bolted. Tears ran down his cheeks, into the corners of his mouth, under his hard collar. He knew what he must do, but not how to do it.

'The Otherhood cannot be dissuaded from this,' the angel said, putting a hand on the wrist of the President *pro tem*. 'For all of it, including our sitting here now, all of it – and the forest in the sea – is implicit in the very creation of the Otherhood itself.'

'But then . . .'

'Then the Otherhood must be uncreated.'

'I can't do that.'

'You must.'

'No, no, I can't.' He had withdrawn from her pellucid gaze, horrified. 'I mean it isn't because . . . if it must be done, it must be. But not by me.'

'Why?'

'It would be against the rules given me. I don't know what the result would be. I can't imagine. I don't *want* to imagine.'

'Rules?'

'The Otherhood came into being,' said the President *pro tem*, 'when a British adventurer, Cecil Rhodes, was shot and killed by a young man called Denys Winterset.'

'Then you must return and stop that killing.'

'But you don't see!' said the President *pro tem* in great distress. 'The rules given the Otherhood forbid a Fellow from returning to a time and place that he formerly altered by his presence . . .'

'And . . .'

'And I am myself that same Denys Winterset.'

The angel regarded the President *pro tem* – the Honourable Denys Winterset, fourteenth President *pro tem* of the Otherhood – and her translucent face registered a sweet surprise, as though the learning of something she had not known gave her pleasure. She laughed, and her laughter was not different from the plashing of the fountain by which they sat. She laughed and laughed, as the old man in his black coat and hat sat silent beside her, bewildered and afraid.

VI: THE BOY DAVID OF HYDE PARK CORNER

There are days when I seem genuinely to remember, and days when I do not remember at all: days when I remember only that sometimes I remember. There are days on which I think I recognize another like myself: someone walking smartly along the Strand or Bond Street, holding *The Times* under one arm and walking a furled umbrella with the other – a sort of military bearing, moustaches white (older than when I seem to have known him, but then so am I, of course), and cheeks permanently tanned by some faraway sun. I do not catch his eye, nor he mine, though I am tempted to stop him, to ask him . . . Later on I wonder – if I can remember to wonder – whether he, too, is making a chronicle, in his evenings, writing up the story: a story that can be told in any direction, starting from anywhen, leading on to a forest in the sea.

I won't look any longer into this chronicle I've compiled. I shall only complete it.

My name is Denys Winterset. I was born in London in 1933; I was the only son of a Harley Street physician, and my earliest memory is of coming upon my father in tears in his surgery: he had just heard the news that the R101 dirigible had crashed on its maiden flight, killing all those aboard.

We lived then above my father's offices, in a little building whose nursery I remember distinctly, though I was taken to the country with the other children of London when I was only six, and that building was knocked down by a bomb in 1940. A falling wall killed my mother; my father was on ambulance duty in the East End and was spared.

He didn't know quite what to do with me, nor I with myself; I have been torn all my life between the drive to discover what others whom I love and admire expect of me, and my discovery that then I don't want to do it, really. After coming down from the University I decided, out of a certain perversity which my father could not sympathize with, to join the Colonial Service. He could not fathom why I would want to fasten myself to an enterprise that everyone save a few antediluvian colonels and letter writers to *The Times* could see was a dead animal. And I couldn't explain. Psychoanalysis later suggested that it was quite simply because no one wanted me to do it. The explanation has since come to seem insufficient to me.

That was a strange late blooming of Empire in the decade after the war, when the Colonial Office took on factitious new life, and thousands of us went out to the Colonies. The Service became larger than it had been in years, swollen with ex-officers too accustomed to military life to do anything else, and with the innocent and the confused, like myself. I ended up a junior member of a transition team in a Central African country I shall not name, helping see to it that as much was given to the new native government as they could be persuaded to accept, in the way of a parliament, a well-disciplined army, a foreign service, a judiciary.

It was not after all very much. Those institutions that the British are sure no civilized nation can do without were, in the minds of many Africans who spoke freely to me, very like those exquisite japanned toffee-boxes from Fortnum & Mason that you used often to come across in native kraals, because the chieftains and shamans loved them so, to keep their juju in. Almost as soon as I arrived, it became evident that the commander in chief of the armed forces was impatient with the pace of things, and felt the need of no special transition to African, i.e., his own, control of the state. The most our Commission were likely to accomplish was to get the British population out without a bloodbath.

Even that would not be easy. We – we young men – were saddled with the duty of explaining to aged planters that there was no one left to defend their estates against confiscation, and that under the new constitution they hadn't a leg to stand on, and that despite how dearly their overseers and house people loved them, they ought to begin seeing what they could pack into a few small trunks. On the other hand, we were to calm the fears of merchants and diamond factors, and tell them that if they all simply dashed for it, they could easily precipitate a closing of the frontiers, with incalculable results.

There came a night when, more than usually certain that not a single Brit under my care would leave the country alive, nor deserved to either, I stood at the bar of the Planters' (just renamed the Republic) Club, drinking gin and Italian (tonic hadn't been reordered in weeks) and listening to the clacking of the fans. A fellow I knew slightly as a regular here saluted me; I nodded and returned to my thoughts. A moment later I found him next to me.

'I wonder,' he said, 'if I might have your ear for a moment.'

The expression, in his mouth, was richly comic, or perhaps it was my exhaustion. He waited for my laughter to subside before speaking. He was called Rossie, and he'd spent a good many years in Africa, doing whatever came to hand. He was one of those Englishmen whom the sun turns not brown but only grey and greasy; his eyes were always watery, the cups of his lids red and painful to look at.

'I am,' he said at last, 'doing a favour for a chap who would like your help.'

'I'll do what I can,' I said.

'This is a chap,' he said, 'who has been too long in this country, and would like to leave it.'

'There are many in his situation.'

'Not quite.'

'What is his name?' I said, taking out a memorandum book. 'I'll pass it on to the Commission.'

'Just the point,' Rossie said. He drew closer to me. At the other end of the bar loud laughter arose from a group consisting of a newly commissioned field marshal – an immense, glossy, nearly blue-black man – and his two colonels, both British, both small and lean. They laughed when the field marshal laughed, though their laugh was not so loud, nor their teeth so large and white.

'He'll want to tell you his name himself,' Rossie said. 'I've only brought the message. He wants to see you, to talk to you. I said I'd tell you. That's all.'

'To tell us . . .'

'Not you, all of you. *You*: you.'

I drank. The warm, scented liquor was thick in my throat. 'Me?'

'What he asked me to ask you,' Rossie said, growing impatient, 'was would you come out to his place, and see him. It isn't far. He wanted you, no one else. He said I was to insist. He said you were to come alone. He'll send a boy of his. He said tell no one.'

There were many reasons why a man might want to do business with the Commission privately. I could think of none why it should be done with me alone. I agreed, with a shrug. Rossie seemed immediately to put the matter out of his mind, mopped his red face, and ordered drinks for both of us. By the time they were brought we were already discussing the Imperial groundnut scheme, which was to have kept this young republic self-sufficient, but which, it was now evident, would do no such thing.

I too put what had been asked of me out of my mind, with enough success that when on a windless and baking afternoon a native boy shook me awake from a nap, I could not imagine why.

'Who are you? What are you doing in my bungalow?'

He only stared down at me, as though it were he who could not think why I should be there before him. Questions in his own language got no response either. At length he backed out the door, clearly wanting me to follow; and so I did, with the dread one feels on remembering an unpleasant task one has contrived to neglect. I found him outside, standing beside my Land-Rover, ready to get aboard.

'All right,' I said. 'Very well.' I got into the driver's seat. 'Point the way.'

It was a small spread of tobacco and a few dusty cattle an hour's drive from town, a low bungalow looking beaten in the ochre heat. He gave no greeting as I alighted from the Land-Rover but stood in the shadows of the porch unmoving: as though he had stood so a long time. He went back into the house as I approached, and when I went in, he was standing against the netting of the window, the light behind him. That seemed a conscious choice. He was smiling, I could tell: a strange and eager smile.

'I've waited a long time for you,' he said. 'I don't mind saying.'

'I came as quickly as I could,' I said.

'There was no way for me to know, you see,' he said, 'whether you'd come at all.'

'Your boy was quite insistent,' I said. 'And Mr Rossie –'

'I meant: to Africa.' His voice was light, soft, and dry. 'There being so much less reason for it, now. I've wondered often. In fact I don't think a day has passed this year when I haven't wondered.' Keeping his back to the sunward windows, he moved to sit on the edge of a creaking wicker sofa. 'You'll want a drink,' he said.

'No.' The place was filled with the detritus of an African bachelor farmer's digs: empty paraffin tins, bottles, tools, hanks of rope and motor parts. He put a hand behind him without looking and put it on the bottle he was no doubt accustomed to find there. 'I tried to think reasonably about it,' he said, pouring a drink. 'As time went on, and things began to sour here, I came to be more and more certain that no lad with any pluck would throw himself away down here. And yet I couldn't know. Whether there might not be some impulse, I don't know, travelling to you from – elsewhere. . . . I even thought of writing to you. Though whether to convince you to come or to dissuade you I'd no idea.'

I sat, too. A cool sweat had gathered on my neck and the backs of my hands.

'Then,' he said, 'when I heard you'd come – well, I was afraid, frankly. I didn't know what to think.' He dusted a fly from the rim of his glass, which he had not tasted. 'You see,' he said, 'this was against the rules given me. That I – that I and – that you and I should meet.'

Perhaps he's mad, I thought, and even as I thought it I felt intensely the experience called *déjà vu*, an experience I have always hated, hated like the nightmare. I steeled myself to respond coolly and took out my memorandum book and pencil. 'I'm afraid you've rather lost me,' I said – briskly I hoped. 'Perhaps we'd better start with your name.'

'Oh,' he said, smiling again his mirthless smile, 'not the hardest question first, please.'

Without having, so far as I knew, the slightest reason for it, I began to feel intensely sorry for this odd dried jerky of a man, whose eyes alone seemed quick and shy. 'All right,' I said, 'nationality, then. You are a British subject.'

'Well, yes.'

'Proof?' He answered nothing. 'Passport?' No. 'Army card? Birth certificate? Papers of any kind?' No. 'Any connections in Britain? Relatives? Someone who could vouch for you, take you in?'

'No,' he said. 'None who could. None but you. It will have to be you.'

'Now hold hard,' I said.

'I don't know why I must,' he said, rising suddenly and turning away to the window. 'But I must. I must go back. I imagine dying here, being buried here, and my whole soul retreats in horror. I must go back. Even though I fear that, too.'

He turned from the window, and in the sharp side light of the late afternoon his face was clearly the face of someone I knew. 'Tell me,' he said. 'Mother and father. Your mother and father. They're alive?'

'No,' I said. 'Both dead.'

'Very well,' he said, 'very well'; but it did not seem to be very well with him. 'I'll tell you my story, then.'

'I think you'd best do that.'

'It's a long one.'

'No matter.' I had begun to feel myself transported, like a Sinbad, into somewhere that it were best I listen, and keep my counsel: and yet the first words of this spectre's tale made that impossible.

'My name,' he said, 'is Denys Winterest.'

I have come to believe, having had many years in which to think about it; that it must be as he said, that an impulse from somewhere else (he meant: some previous present, some earlier version of these circumstances) must press upon such a life as mine. That I chose the Colonial Service, that I came to Africa – and not just to Africa, but to that country: well, *if anything is chance, that was not* – as I understand Sir Geoffrey Davenant to have once said.

In that long afternoon, there where I perhaps could not have helped arriving eventually, I sat and perspired, listening – though it was for a long time very nearly impossible to hear what was said to me: an appointment in Khartoum some months from now, and some decades past; a club, outside all frames of reference; the Last equipment. It was quite like listening to the unfollowable logic of a madman, as meaningless as the roar of the insects outside. I only began to hear when this aged man, older than my grandfather, told me of something that he – that I – that he and I – had once done in boyhood, something secret, trivial really and yet so shameful that even now I will not write it down; something that only Denys Winterset could know.

'There now,' he said, eyes cast down. 'There now, you must believe me. You *will* listen. The world has not been as you thought it to be, any more than it was as I thought it to be, when I was as you are now. I shall tell you why: and we will hope that mine is the last story that need be told.'

And so it was that I heard how he had gone up the road to Groote Schuur, that evening in 1893 (a young man then of course, only twenty-three), with the Webley revolver in his breast pocket as heavy as his heart, nearly sick with wonder and apprehension. The tropical suit he had been made to wear was monstrously hot, complete with full waistcoat and hard collar; the topee they insisted he use was as weighty as a crown. As he came in sight of the house, he could hear the awesome cries from the lion house, where the cats were evidently being given their dinner.

The big house appeared raw and unfinished to him, the trees yet ungrown and the great masses of scentless flowers – hydrangea, bougainvillaea, canna – that had smothered the place when last he had seen it, some decades later, just beginning to spread.

'Rhodes himself met me at the door – actually he happened to be going out for his afternoon ride – and welcomed me,' he said. 'I think the most striking thing about Cecil Rhodes, and it hasn't been noticed much, was his utter lack of airs. He was the least self-conscious man I have ever known; he did many things for effect, but he was himself entirely single: as whole as an egg, as the old French used to say.

'"The house is yours," he said to me. "Use it as you like. We don't dress for dinner, as a rule; too many of the guests would be taken short, you see. Now some of the fellows are playing croquet in the Great Hall. Pay them no mind."

'I remember little of that evening. I wandered the house; the great skins of animals, the heavy beams of teak, the brass chandeliers. I looked into the library, full of the specially transcribed and bound classics that

Rhodes had ordered by the yard from Hatchard's: all the authorities that Gibbon had consulted in writing the *Decline and Fall*. All of them: that had been Rhodes's order.

'Dinner was a long and casual affair, entirely male – Rhodes had not even any female servants in the house. There was much toasting and hilarity about the successful march into Matabeleland, and the foundation of a fort, which news had only come that week; but Rhodes seemed quiet at the table's head, even melancholy: many of his closest comrades were gone with the expeditionary column, and he seemed to miss them. I do remember that at one point the conversation turned to America. Rhodes contended – no one disputed him – that if we (he meant the Empire, of course) had not lost America, the peace of the world could have been secured forever. "Forever," he said. "Perpetual Peace." And his pale opaque eyes were moist.

'How I comported myself at table – how I joined the talk, how I kept up conversations on topics quite unfamiliar to me – none of that do I recall. It helped that I was supposed to have been only recently arrived in Africa: though one of Rhodes's band of merry men looked suspiciously at my sun-browned hands when I said so.

'As soon as I could after dinner, I escaped from the fearsome horseplay that began to develop among those left awake. I pleaded a touch of sun and was shown to my room. I took off the hateful collar and tie (not without difficulty) and lay on the bed otherwise fully clothed, alert and horribly alone. Perhaps you can imagine my thoughts.'

'No,' I said. 'I don't think I can.'

'No. Well. No matter. I must have slept at last; it seemed to be after midnight when I opened my eyes and saw Rhodes standing in the doorway, a candlestick in his hand.

'"Asleep?" he asked softly.

'"No," I answered. "Awake."

'"Can't sleep either," he said. "Never do, much." He ventured another step into the room. "You ought to come out, see the sky," he said. "Quite spectacular. As long as you're up."

'I rose and followed him. He was without his coat and collar; I noticed he wore carpet slippers. One button of his wide braces was undone; I had the urge to button it for him. Pale starlight fell in blocks across the black and white tiles of the hall, and the huge heads of beasts were mobile in the candlelight as we passed. I murmured something about the grandness of his house.

'"I told my architect," Rhodes answered. "I said I wanted the big and simple – the barbaric, if you like." The candle flame danced before him. "Simple. The truth is always simple."

'The chessboard tiles of the hall continued out through the wide doors onto the veranda – the *stoep* as the old Dutch called it. At the frontier of the *stoep* great pillars divided the night into panels filled with clustered stars, thick and near as vine blossoms. From far off came a long cry as of pain: a lion, awake.

'Rhodes leaned on the parapet, looking into the mystery of the sloping lawns beyond the *stoep*. "That's good news, about the chaps up in Matabeleland," he said a little wistfully.

'"Yes."

'"Pray God they'll all be safe."

'"Yes."

'"*Zambesia*," he said after a moment. "What d'you think of that?"

'"I beg your pardon?"

'"As a name. For this country we'll be building. *Beyond the Zambesi*, you see."

'"It's a fine name."

'He fell silent for a time. A pale, powdery light filled the sky: false dawn. "They shall say, in London," he said, "'Rhodes has taken for the Empire a country larger than Europe, at not a sixpence of cost to us, and we shall have that, and Rhodes shall have six feet by four feet.'"

'He said this without bitterness, and turned from the parapet to face me. The Webley was pointed towards him. I had rested my (trembling) right hand on my left forearm, held up before me.

'"Why, what on earth," he said.

'"Look," I said.

'Drawing his look slowly away from me, he turned again. Out in the lawn, seeming in that illusory light to be but a long leap away, a male lion stood unmoving.

'"The pistol won't stop him," I said, "but it will deflect him. If you will go calmly through the door behind me, I'll follow."

'Rhodes backed away from the rail, and without haste or panic turned and walked past me into the house. The lion, ochre in the blue night, regarded him with a lion's expression, at once aloof and concerned, and returned his look to me. I thought I smelled him. Then I saw movement in the young trees beyond. I thought for a moment that my lion must be an illusion, or a dream, for he took no notice of these sounds – the crush of a twig, a soft voice – but at length he did turn his eyes from me to them. I could see the dim figure of a gamekeeper in a wide-awake hat, carrying a rifle, and Negroes with nets and poles: they were closing in carefully on the escapee. I stood for a moment longer, still poised to shoot, and then beat my own retreat into the house.

'Lights were being lit down the halls, voices calling: a lion does not appear on the lawn every night. Rhodes stood looking, not out of the window, but at me. With deep embarrassment I clumsily pocketed the Webley (*I* knew what it had been given to me for, after all, even if he did not), and only then did I meet Rhodes's eyes.

'I shall never forget their expression, those pale eyes: a kind of exalted wonder, almost a species of adoration.

'"That's twice now in one day," he said, "that you have kept me from harm. You must have been sent, that's all. I really believe you have been sent."

'I stood before him staring, with a horror dawning in my heart such as, God willing, I shall never feel again. I knew, you see, what it meant that I had let slip the moment: that now I could not go back the way I had come. The world had opened for an instant, and I and my companions had gone down through it to this time and place; and now it had closed over me again, a seamless whole. I had no one and nothing; no Last equipment awaited me at the Mount Nelson Hotel: the Otherhood could not rescue me, for I had cancelled it. I was entirely alone.

'Rhodes, of course, knew nothing of this. He crossed the hall to where I stood, with slow steps, almost reverently. He embraced me, a sudden great bear hug. And do you know what he did then?'

'What did he do?'

'He took me by the shoulders and held me at arm's length, and he insisted that I stay there with him. In effect, he offered me a job. For life, if I wanted it.'

'What did you do?'

'I took it.' He had finished his drink, and poured more. 'I took it. You see, I simply had no place else to go.'

Afternoon was late in the bungalow where we sat together, day hurried away with this tale. 'I think,' I said, 'I shall have that drink now, if it's no trouble.'

He rose and found a glass; he wiped the husk of a bug from it and filled it from his bottle. 'It has always astonished me,' he said, 'how the mind, you know, can construct with lightning speed a reasonable, if quite mistaken, story to account for an essentially unreasonable event: I have had more than one occasion to observe this process.

'I was sure, instantly sure, that a lion which had escaped from Rhodes's lion house had appeared on the lawn at Groote Schuur just at the moment when I tried, but could not bring myself, to murder Cecil Rhodes. I can still see that cat in the pale light of predawn. And yet I cannot know if that is what happened, or if it is only what my mind has substituted for what did happen, which cannot be thought about.

'I am satisfied in my own mind – having had a lifetime to ponder it – that it cannot be possible for one to meet oneself on a trip into the past or future: that is a lie, invented by the Otherhood to forestall its own extinction, which was, however, inevitable.

'But I dream, sometimes, that I am lying on the bed at Groote Schuur, and a man enters – it is not Rhodes, but a man in a black coat and a bowler hat, into whose face I look as into a rotted mirror, who tells me impossible things.

'And I know that in fact there was no lion house at Groote Schuur. Rhodes wanted one, and it was planned, but it was never built.'

In the summer of that year Rhodes – alive, alive-oh – went on expedition up into Pondoland, seeking concessions from an intransigent chief named Sicgau. Denys Winterset – this one, telling me the tale – went with him.

'Rhodes took Sicgau out into a field of mealies where he had had us set up a Maxim gun. Rhodes and the chief stood in the sun for a moment, and then Rhodes gave a signal; we fired the Maxim for a few seconds and mowed down much of the field. The chief stood unmoving for a long moment after the silence returned. Rhodes said to him softly: "You see, this is what will happen to you and all your warriors if you give us any further trouble."

'As a stratagem, that seemed to me both sporting and thrifty. It worked, too. But we were later to use the Maxims against men and not mealies. Rhodes knew that the Matabele had finally to be suppressed, or the work of building a white state north of the Zambezi would be hopeless. A way was found to intervene in a quarrel the Matabele were having with the Mashona, and in not too long we were at war with the Matabele. They were terribly, terribly brave; they were, after all, the first eleven in those parts, and they believed with reason that no one could withstand their leaf-bladed spears. I remember how they would come against the Maxims, and be mown down like the mealies, and fall back, and muster for another attack. Your heart sank; you prayed they would go away, but they would not. They came on again, to be cut down again. These puzzled, bewildered faces: I cannot forget them.

'And Christ, such drivel was written in the papers then, about the heroic stand of a few beleaguered South African police against so many battle-crazed natives! The only one who saw the truth was the author of that silly poem – Belloc, was it? You know – "Whatever happens, we have got/The Maxim gun, and they have not." It was as simple as that. The truth, Rhodes said, is always simple.'

He took out a large pocket-handkerchief and mopped his face and his eyes; no doubt it was hot, but it seemed to me that he wept. Tears, idle tears.

'I met Dr Jameson during the Matabele campaign,' he continued. 'Leander Starr Jameson. I think I have never met a man – and I have met many wicked and twisted ones – whom I have loathed so completely and so instantly. I had hardly heard of him, of course; he was already dead and unknown in this year as it had occurred in my former past, the only version of these events I knew. Jameson was a great lover of the Maxim; he took several along on the raid he made into the Transvaal in 1896, the raid that would eventually lead to war with the Boers, destroy Rhodes's credit, and begin the end of Empire: so I have come to see it. The fool.

'I took no part in that war, thank God. I went north to help put the railway through: Cape-to-Cairo.' He smiled, seemed almost about to laugh, but did not; only mopped his face again. It was as though I were interrogating him, and he were telling me all this under the threat of the rubber truncheon or the rack. I wanted him to stop, frankly; only I dared say nothing.

'I made up for a lack of engineering expertise by my very uncertain knowledge of where and how, one day, the road would run. The telegraph had already reached Uganda; next stop was Wadi Halfa. The rails would not go through so easily. I became a sort of scout, leading the advance parties, dealing with the chieftains. The Maxim went with me, of course. I learned the weapon well.'

Here there came another silence, another inward struggle to continue. I was left to picture what he did not say: *That which I did I should not have done; that which I should have done I did not do*.

'Rhodes gave five thousand pounds to the Liberal party to persuade them not to abandon Egypt: for there his railway must be hooked to the sea. But then of course came the end of the whole scheme in German Tanganyika: no Cape-to-Cairo road. Germany was growing great in the world; the Germans wanted to have an Empire of their own. It finished Rhodes.

'By that time I was a railway expert. The nonexistent Uganda Railway was happy to acquire my services: I had a reputation, among the blacks, you see . . . I think there was a death for every mile of that road as it went through the jungle to the coast: rinderpest, fever, Nanda raids. We would now and then hang a captured Nanda warrior from the telegraph poles, to discourage the others. By the time the rails reached Mombasa, I was an old man; and Cecil Rhodes was dead.'

He died of his old heart condition, the condition that had brought him out to Africa in the first place. He couldn't breathe in the awful heat of that summer of 1902, the worst anyone could remember; he wandered from room to room at Groote Schuur, trying to catch his breath. He lay in the darkened drawing room and could not breathe. They took him down to his cottage by the sea, and put ice between the ceiling and the iron roof to cool it; all afternoon the punkahs spooned the air, Then, suddenly, he decided to go to England. April was there: April showers. A cold spring: it seemed that could heal him. So a cabin was fitted out for him aboard a P&O liner, with electric fans and refrigerating pipes and oxygen tanks.

He died on the day he was to sail. He was buried at that place on the Matopos, the place he had chosen himself; buried facing north.

'He wanted the heroes of the Matabele campaign to be buried there with him. I could be one, if I chose; only I think my name would not be found among the register of those who fought. I think my name does not appear at all in history: not in the books of the Uganda Railway, not in the register of the Mount Nelson Hotel for 1893. I have never had the courage to look.'

I could not understand this, though it sent a cold shudder between my shoulder blades. The Original Situation, he explained, could not be returned to; but it could be restored, as those events that the Otherhood brought about were one by one come upon in time, and then not brought about. And as the Original Situation was second by second restored, the whole of his adventure in the past was continually worn away into nonbeing, and a new future replaced his old past ahead of him.

'You must imagine how it has been for me,' he said, his voice now a whisper from exertion and grief. 'To everyone else it seemed only that time went on – history – the march of events. But to me it has been otherwise. It has been the reverse of the nightmare from which you wake in a sweat of relief to find that the awful disaster has not occurred, the fatal step was not taken: for I have seen the real world gradually replaced by this other, nightmare world, which everyone else assumes is real, until nothing in past or present is as I knew it to be; until I am like the servant in Job: *I only am escaped to tell thee.*'

March 8, 1983

I awoke again this morning from the dream of the forest in the sea: a dream without people or events in it, or anything whatever except the gigantic dendrites, vast masses of pale leaves, and the tideless waters, light and sunshot towards the surface, darkening to impenetrability down below. It seemed there were schools of fish, or flocks of birds, in the leaves, something that faintly disturbed them, now and then; otherwise, stillness.

No matter that orthogonal logic refutes it. I cannot help believing that my present succeeds in time the other presents and futures that have gone into making it. I believe that as I grow older I come to incorporate the experiences I have had as an older man in pasts (and futures) now obsolete: as though in absolute time I continually catch up with myself in the imaginary times that fluoresce from it, gathering dreamlike memories of the lives I have lived therein. Somewhere God (I have come to believe in God; there was simply no existing otherwise) is keeping these universes in a row, and sees to it that they happen in succession, the most recently generated one last – and so felt to be last, no matter where along it I stand.

I remember, being now well past the age that he was then, the Uganda Railway, the Nanda arrows, all the death.

I remember the shabby library and the coal fire, the encyclopaedia in another orthography; the servant at the double doors.

I think that in the end, should I live long enough, I shall remember nothing but the forest in the sea. That is the terminus: complete strangeness that is at the same time utterly changeless; what cannot be becoming all that has ever been.

I took him out myself, in the end, abandoning my commission to do so, for there was no way that he could have crossed the border by himself, without papers, a nonexistent man. And it was just at that moment, as we motored up through the Sudan past Wadi Halfa, that the Anglo-French expeditionary force took Port Said. The Suez incident, that last hopeless spasm of Empire, was taking its inevitable course. Inevitable: I have not used the word before.

When we reached the Canal, the Israelis had already occupied the east bank. The airport at Ismailia was a shambles, the greater part of the Egyptian Air Force shot up, planes scattered in twisted attitudes like dead birds after a storm. We could find no plane to take us. *He* had gone desperately broody, wide-eyed and speechless, useless for anything. I felt as though in a dream where one is somehow saddled with an idiot brother one had not had before.

And yet it was only the confusion and mess that made my task possible at all, I suppose. There were so many semiofficial and unofficial

British scurrying or loafing around Port Said when we entered the city that our passage was unremarked. We went through the smoke and dust of that famously squalid port like two ghosts – two ghosts progressing through a ghost city at the retreating edge of a ghost of empire. And the crunch of broken glass continually underfoot.

We went out on an old oiler attached to the retreating invasion fleet, which had been ordered home having accomplished nothing except, I suppose, the end of the British Empire in Africa. He stood on the oiler's boat deck and watched the city grow smaller and said nothing. But once he laughed, his dry, light laugh: it made me think of the noise that Homer says the dead make. I asked the reason.

'I was remembering the last time I went out of Africa,' he said. 'On a day much like this. Very much like this. This calm weather; this sea. Nothing else the same, though. Nothing else.' He turned to me smiling, and toasted me with an imaginary glass. 'The end of an era,' he said.

March 10

My chronicle seems to be degenerating into a diary.

I note in *The Times* this morning the sale of the single known example of the 1856 magenta British Guiana, for a sum far smaller than was supposed to be its worth. Neither the names of the consortium that sold it nor the names of the buyers were made public. I see in my mind's eye a small, momentary fire.

I see now that there is no reason why this story should come last, no matter my feeling, no matter that in Africa he hoped it would. Indeed there is no reason why it should even fall last in this chronicling, nor why the world, the sad world in which it occurs, should be described as succeeding all others – it does not, any more than it precedes them. For the sake of a narrative only, perhaps; perhaps, like God, we cannot live without narrative.

I used to see him, infrequently, in the years after we both came back from Africa: he didn't die as quickly as we both supposed he would. He used to seek me out, in part to borrow a little money – he was living on the dole and on what he brought out of Africa, which was little enough. I stood him tea now and then and listened to his stories. He'd appear at our appointed place in a napless British Warm, ill-fitting, as his eyeglasses and National Health false teeth were also. I imagine he was terribly lonely. I know he was.

I remember the last time we met, at a Lyons teashop near Marble Arch. I'd left the Colonial Service, of course, under a cloud, and taken a position teaching at a crammer's in Holborn until something better came along (nothing ever did; I recently inherited the headmaster's chair at the same school; little has changed there over the decades but the general coloration of the students).

'This curious fancy haunts me,' he said to me on that occasion. 'I picture the Fellows, all seated around the great table in the executive committee's dining room; only it is rather like Miss Havisham's, you know, in Dickens: the roast beef has long since gone foul, and the silver tarnished, and the draperies rotten; and the Fellows dead in their chairs, or mad, dust on their evening clothes, the port dried up in their glasses. Huntington. Davenant. The President *pro tem*.'

He stirred sugar in his tea (he liked it horribly sweet; so, of course, do I). 'It's not true, you know, that the Club stood somehow at a nexus of possibilities, amid multiplying realities. If that were so, then what the Fellows did would be trivial or monstrous or both: generating endless new universes just to see if they could get one to their liking. No: it is we, out here, who live in but one of innumerable possible worlds. In there, they were like a man standing at the north pole, whose only view, wherever he looks, is south: they looked out upon a single encompassing reality, which it was their opportunity – no, their duty, as they saw it – to make as happy as possible, as free from the calamities they knew of as they could make it.

'Well, they were limited people, more limited than their means to work good or evil. That which they did they should not have done. And yet what they hoped for us was not despicable. The calamities they saw were real. Anyone who could would try to save us from them: as a mother would pull her child, her foolish child, from the fire. They ought to be forgiven; they ought.'

I walked with him up towards Hyde Park Corner. He walked now with agonizing slowness, as I will, too, one day; it was a rainy autumn Sunday, and his pains were severe. At Hyde Park Corner he stopped entirely, and I thought perhaps he could go no farther: but then I saw that he was studying the monument that stands there. He went closer to it, to read what was written on it.

I have myself more than once stopped before this neglected monument. It is a statue of the boy David, a memorial to the Machine Gun Corps, and was put up after the First World War. Some little thought must have gone into deciding how to memorialize that arm which had changed war forever; it seemed to require a religious sentiment, a quote from the Bible, and one was found. Beneath the naked boy are written words from Kings:

> Saul has slain his thousands
> But David his tens of thousands.

He stood in the rain, in his vast coat, looking down at these words, as though reading them over and over; and the faint rain that clung to his cheeks mingled with his tears:

> Saul has slain his thousands
> But David his tens of thousands.

I never saw him again after that day, and I did not seek for him: I think it unlikely he could have been found.

Acknowledgements

I am indebted to many other editors, in particular my old friend David Hartwell, and I have had welcome assistance and advice (not always accepted, alas) from Bernard Goodman, Darrell Schweitzer and Graham Sleight. Gratitude goes also to Adam Freudenheim at Penguin, who knows well the complex evolution of this volume.

mission of the author and *Astounding Science Fact Fiction* (now *Analog Science Fact–Science Fiction*).

Katherine MacLean, THE SNOWBALL EFFECT, copyright 1952 by Galaxy Publishing Corporation. Reprinted by permission of the author and *Galaxy Science Fiction*.

Bruce Sterling, SWARM, copyright 1982 by Mercury Press.

Greg Bear, BLOOD MUSIC, copyright 1983 by *Analog Science Fact–Science Fiction*.

Fredric Brown, ANSWER, copyright 1964. Reprinted by permission of the author's executors.

William Tenn, THE LIBERATION OF EARTH, copyright 1953 by Columbia Publications, Inc., for *Future Science Fiction*. Reprinted by permission of Philip Klass.

Harry Harrison, AN ALIEN AGONY, copyright 1962 by Nova Publications Ltd. Reprinted by permission of the author and his literary agent, E. J. Carnell, from *New Worlds Science Fiction* (original title 'The Streets of Ashkelon').

J. G. Ballard, TRACK 12, copyright 1958 by Nova Publications Ltd. Reprinted by permission of the author and *New Worlds Science Fiction*.

Kim Stanley Robinson, SEXUAL DIMORPHISM, copyright 1999 by *Year's Best SF 5* (ed. David Hartwell).

Frederik Pohl, THE TUNNEL UNDER THE WORLD, copyright 1954 by Galaxy Publishing Corporation. Reprinted by permission of the author and his literary agent, E. J. Carnell, from *Galaxy Science Fiction*.

Eliza Blair, FRIENDS IN NEED, copyright 2006 by *Bug-Eyed Magazine*.

Robert Sheckley, THE STORE OF THE WORLDS, copyright 1959 by H. M. H. Publishing Co. Inc. First published in *Playboy* as 'World of Heart's Desire'.

Isaac Asimov, JOKESTER, copyright 1956 by Royal Publications, Inc. Reprinted by permission of the author from *Infinity Science Fiction*.

John Steinbeck, THE SHORT-SHORT STORY OF MANKIND, copyright 1958 by H. M. H. Publishing Co. Inc. Reprinted by permission of the author's agents, McIntosh and Otis. Originally appeared in *Playboy*.

James Inglis, NIGHT WATCH, copyright 1964. Reprinted by permission of the Maggie Noach Agency.

Ted Chiang, STORY OF YOUR LIFE, copyright 1998 by *Starlight 2*.

H. B. Fyfe, PROTECTED SPECIES, copyright 1951 by Street & Smith Publications, Inc., for *Astounding Science Fiction* (now *Analog Science Fact–Science Fiction*). Reprinted by permission of the author.

Arthur Porges, THE RESCUER, copyright 1962 by Condé-Nast Publications, Inc. Reprinted by permission of the author and the author's agents, Scott Meredith Literary Agency, Inc.

Walter M. Miller, Jr., I MADE YOU, copyright 1954 by Street & Smith Publications, Inc., for *Astounding Science Fiction* (now *Analog Science Fact–Science Fiction*). Reprinted by permission of the author's agent, A. D. Peters.

Damon Knight, THE COUNTRY OF THE KIND, copyright 1956 by Mercury Press.

Bertram Chandler, THE CAGE, copyright 1957. Reprinted by permission of *The Magazine of Fantasy and Science Fiction* and the author.

A. E. van Vogt, FULFILMENT, copyright 1952. Reprinted by permission of Laurence Pollinger.

James Blish, COMMON TIME, copyright 1960 by Faber & Faber, in *Galactic Cluster*. Reprinted by permission of Laurence Pollinger.

Garry Kilworth, ALIEN EMBASSY, copyright 2006 by Humdrumming.

John Crowley, GREAT WORK OF TIME, copyright 1989. Reprinted by permission.

Every effort has been made to trace copyright holders. The editor and publisher will nevertheless be happy to correct any error of omission or commission at the earliest opportunity.